THE GYRE MISSION:

JOURNEY TO THE *SSHOLE OF THE WORLD

WRITTEN BY:

EDGAR SWAMP

ISBN: 0615655165
ISBN 13: 9780615655161
Library of Congress Control Number: 2012941881
CreateSpace, North Charleston, SC

DEDICATED TO LILY SWAMP
1999-2011

The author would like to thank Tom Kelliher for reading an early draft of the novel and offering valuable insights as to it's shortcomings and ridiculous plot holes. I'd also like to thank him for pointing out that such an eyesore as a ginormous island of trash surely wouldn't go unnoticed in today's modern world, as I'd indicated in that early, crappy draft, why, I don't know. Maybe I thought it would be more mysterious, or somehow point an accusatory finger at how negligent we, the human race, are, being overly concerned about bigger, better and faster technology but indifferent to it's nasty byproduct.

This novel is based upon the 'great Pacific garbage patch', an area of densely collected debris in the north Pacific roughly a thousand miles off the California coast that has been described as being 'twice the size of Texas'. I read an article about it in the San Diego Union Tribune in late 2009 and thought it would be an interesting setting for an offbeat survival story. The majority of what I wrote pertained to info I found from then up until 2011. I've since learned there are three garbage patches in the Pacific: the eastern garbage patch, which is between San Francisco and Hawaii, the western garbage patch, located off of Japan and, finally, the one in which I wrote about, the north Pacific garbage patch, located north of the Hawaiian archipelagos in what is known as the northern subtropical convergence zone. I also recently learned that they are in constant motion with the ocean's currents, making the job of pinpointing their exact location quite difficult. The book was finished when I found out this information, so I am sharing this with you now because I don't want to appear to be a total idiot (see rider below). Millions of tons of waste (mostly plastic particles) have accrued because of the slow moving currents of the ocean's subtropical gyre (an enormous water vortex) and, as of this writing, are steadily increasing in size with no sign of stopping. What I describe herein is merely a speculation on what 'could' happen if one of these patches was allowed to continue to keep growing without any intervention.

I would like to offer here a disclaimer: the science in this novel is wonky at best and is in no way meant to be misconstrued as 'serious' or 'probable'. I've manipulated everything to suit my needs, the bulk of my information coming from (most likely) outdated Wikipedia pages (see explanation above in which I profess to not being a brain-dead, drooling nincompoop). No professionals were consulted concerning anything (told myself I was going to do that but due to my raging ADD and deplorable laziness found it was simply easier to make everything up) so there is no one to blame but me regarding any glaring errors and I can only hope that anyone who reads this won't find them absolutely unforgivable. So…enjoy!

Edgar Swamp, September 20 2009-June 2nd 2012

Special thanks to Michael and Sandra Waldman for lending me hundreds of wonderful books and not getting angry at the terrible condition I return them in. Thanks guys!

PROLOGUE

The large sailboat pitched up and down over the choppy Pacific waters, fine sprays of mist catching the sun and creating stunning mini-rainbows. The captain and sole passenger squinted into the dying sun, relishing the dazzling hues of purple and crimson-orange. His face was seamed with wrinkles but his whitish blond hair insinuated a certain timelessness, and it was only when you saw his hands could you tell by their gnarled appearance that arthritis was slowly creeping in. It was nothing but a minor matter to him though, as he had been born to sail and that's what he would do until his legs could no longer hold him or his hands failed to work at all. For the time being he was content, traveling the world's oceans at his leisure, catching fish for sustenance and selling the surplus in order to make necessary repairs or to purchase supplies.

In the recent past he'd been known to take on light cargo for a modest freight charge, but during the last few months he'd been apt to decline, as it was more of a hassle than a real moneymaking venture, requiring he occasionally make port in places that took him out of the way of his intended destinations. It wasn't that backtracking particularly inconvenienced him; his true concern regarded the passage of time, which went by at a rate that was nothing short of astounding. Mornings melted into evenings, days into weeks. At his age he felt that squandering such a precious commodity was imprudent.

Over the years he'd also been approached countless times to transport illegal drugs (given that he looked like the last person who would embark upon such illicit endeavors and would hence thwart any investigation) yet every time he refused since that was a young man's game and criminal pursuits were of no interest to him, no matter how much they paid. As it was he no longer cared about money, not really. He'd worked hard his whole life and had a sizeable amount in a savings account, mostly sitting there and gathering interest. Every now and then he needed a few bucks for this or that, but he mostly took what he required from the sea and turned it into spending money. What's more, the thought of whiling away his remaining days incarcerated was not a pleasant one. No, he lived on the open water and he wanted to die on the open water.

Currently he was traveling east, heading for California, having left the Philippines roughly two weeks ago. He'd never sailed this far north, generally preferring the southern route because it passed through familiar territory, but this was of no consequence to him. There would be new things to see, possibly a fresh challenge to arise to, and that thought alone was invigorating, something novel for his old soul. On his journey west he'd encountered waves large enough to capsize a boat twice this size, and overturn she did, leaving him to the sea and his wits. Luck had been with him in the form of a fishing vessel a few miles off the coast of the Solomon Islands, and he'd spent a considerable amount of time there mending before carrying on with the rest of his voyage.

Many of his peers thought he was reckless, somewhat a fool. While they employed the latest in GPS navigating and Doppler equipment he chose to sail without the aid of any of these new-fangled devices, preferring instead to get by on his common sense and guile alone. It was in their opinion that when you were traveling the vast expanse of the Pacific by yourself (or any other large body of water for that matter) you had to be fastidious about your preparations so you'd know what to expect. His thoughts, however, were quite to the contrary. He enjoyed the unexpected, for it was in this environment he thrived.

Yes, he'd be lying if he said he hadn't thought the sea was going to claim he and his sailboat on the first leg of this trek, yet she'd stayed afloat while he clung to the bottom side, and for three days he drifted as dehydration almost overcame him, his strength weakening with each passing hour. It was in the late afternoon of the third day the fishermen stumbled upon him, croaking and delirious in the heat of a scorching August sun. After he'd been taken aboard and given the chance to dry out the men went about righting his sloop, making jokes about the old girl that he chose to ignore. She was an aged vessel but she was still seaworthy, a wooden relic of another time, and the two of them got along just fine without any of those modern gizmo's contemporary sailors so relied upon. To chart his course he used an archaic tool called a sextant, employing a method known as celestial navigating. Calling this technique antiquated was certainly being kind; radar and radio navigating had long replaced it before satellite technology was pioneered. But it was a hobby of his, something he'd always wanted to do since he was a young man. And what the hell, he was retired. He had the time. Also, he was of the opinion that the use of the radar or satellite-based tracking devices took away much of the thrill, for the constant threat of death was what kept him alive. It was for this reason that he seldom monitored the radio for weather forecasts as well. Worse sailor's than he had done without in centuries past and survived, why couldn't he?

This leg of the trip the weather had been mostly uneventful, bearing calm, sunny skies up until this afternoon when a sharp wind blew in from the south and the waves began pounding against the hull with an intensity he hadn't seen in over a months time. But it would be preposterous to even suggest he was frightened, no, a good sailor only felt panic when confronted by the very worst. For him this was simply the prelude, and what it was building up to he could only patiently wait and find out.

As the last of the sun slipped below the horizon he filled a pipe with stale tobacco and held his Zippo to it until he puffed up plumes of white smoke. It was time to put on the running lights, lower the main sail and make sure all the ropes were tightly fastened. Get her all battened down for the night. As a man who spent more time on the water than on land he had no fear of sleeping, even in a tumultuous sea, because he had faith in his abilities and his keen sixth sense to know when to awaken. Most solo sailors slept in intervals of twenty or thirty minutes but he was bolder than that; he'd never sleep through weather that could potentially cause trouble, but he could certainly doze and enjoy a brief respite from the day.

Whistling a song that had been popular over thirty years ago, he did his rounds, making sure his old sloop was snug for the night. After dropping his sea anchor (an apparatus that resembled a parachute; it wouldn't hold him in place but would produce enough drag to ensure he didn't drift too far off course) he went below and stretched out on his bunk, settling in for a little rest.

The clouds were obscuring the stars, a thick drizzle coming down in sheets blown erratically by hearty gusts of wind, so when he peeked out he had no idea what time it was. A quick look at his pocket watch informed him it was just past two. He'd felt the boat strike something, jarring him from his slumber, and he got up quickly to take a look. His immediate thought was that it was a bit of flotsam, just random debris drifting along, but it felt far too big, much too solid. It could be a whale perhaps, one that had gotten confused in the storm. If so he could only hope that they'd mutually sustained very little damage.

Stepping topside and into the inky blackness he could taste the raw sea salt on the air, thick, almost pungent. The wind tousled his hair, the rain peppering him like tiny shards of ice. Locating an industrial-sized flashlight, he shone it into the darkness but there was nothing to see but the foamy waves that lapped against the side of the boat, nothing to hear but the squall of the wind and the spatter of raindrops. He then shone the light across the deck until he located his raincoat, taking the old yellow slicker and shaking it out before draping it over his shoulders. Cocking his head to one side, he listened patiently to the symphony of the elements, and gradually it sounded to him as if the storm was dying down. For this he was glad. There would come a day when he'd have to admit he was getting too old to travel alone, that he would either have to take on a partner or give up on sailing altogether. Of course he knew the latter wasn't an option, but it was what he often used to threaten himself with, something to make him appreciate his travels more. Yes, one day in the near future he would have to take more precautions, would have to safeguard himself against the old age that was steadily sneaking up on him. But, thankfully, it wasn't today.

Continuing his vigil, he shined the light back and forth across the water but could see nothing but shadows outlined by creeping fog. Whatever it was, he supposed, was no longer a threat to he or his ship.

"Well, I'm up goddamnit. Might as well do the rounds, make sure everything is tip-top," he said, his breath steaming in the chilly night air. Being alone as often as he was, talking to himself was a habit he'd picked up unconsciously, a trait he took little notice of. "Least it's not raining anymore."

He walked aft and checked the old, battered compass that had come with the ship when he'd bought it (an ancient, out-dated gadget that looked like it would be more at home in a nautical museum rather than being put to any actual use), and noted with only the slightest unease that the storm had turned him about, had him pointed due north instead of east. It wasn't anything to be overly worried about; he certainly couldn't have been blown too far off course, not with the sea anchor deployed. Moreover, there was no need to do anything about it tonight. He could deal with it in the morning.

He returned to mid-ship, setting the light down and taking a seat in one of the deck chairs, feeling the weary muscles in his legs sing out in relief. He slapped his pocket for his pipe but discovered it wasn't there so, too tired to get up and find it, he decided he didn't need a smoke that badly anyway. Leaning back he felt his eyes growing heavy, a drowsy warmth creeping over him stealthy as a fox, and he could hear the sounds of angels singing, or maybe it was the sirens of the sea. Often before he drifted off his mind created voices, either singsong or speaking, and this was how he knew he was falling asleep. He'd let these gentle voices usher him into dreamland, where the images would explode behind his closed lids, memories of seas traversed, old thoughts of all the places, reminisces of all the faces…

At once the boat pitched sharply and his eyes flew open as he heard a rending crunch in the hull near the bow.

"Dear God!" he cried, bolting to his feet, hoping the sound he'd heard wasn't as severe as it at first seemed. He picked up the flashlight and walked slowly along the starboard side, searching the hull at the waterline but seeing nothing. What did he hit? Squinting furiously into the gloom he couldn't make out anything, and as he turned around and around it was clear to him that whatever it'd been it was going to remain a mystery to him for the remainder of this eerie, fog-choked night. His floodlights could barely pierce the skin of the dark; indeed the impenetrable murk seemed almost to swallow the light, as if he were on the rim of a black hole.

Next he went below deck, and once his feet left the ladder he felt the frigid kiss of the sea just over the top of his boots. It took only a moment before he became deadly certain the ship was sinking. How did he know? Well, some things are simply a given when they are second nature to a man who has sailed the oceans nearly the entirety of his life. He didn't need to see the hole in the bow to know the water was pouring in, all that was necessary was to feel the back and forth motion of the boat and straight away he knew she was listing to the port side.

He moved quickly to the hatch that led to the bilge, forgoing the ladder and jumping the meager three feet, and here it was no surprise the water was almost to his waist. Whatever he'd hit had ripped a large hole in the hull and the water was streaming in fast, so fast he feared escape was going to be impossible. His bilge pump plainly couldn't keep up.

A cold reserve shot through him, an almost impractical calm. This was no time for alarm. If this were to be his last night on earth than he would take it like a man. No need to worry or fret. If he were about to meet his maker he would do it with a distinguished flourish.

He climbed back up the ladder, returning to the upper deck. For the hell of it he decided to send out a distress call, in case there was anybody within range who could come to his rescue, even though he knew in his heart it was fanciful thinking at best. These waters were seldom navigated, and the chance of there being another ship nearby was slim to none. But he knew he should at least try for Christ's sake; he couldn't go down without a fight. He considered for a moment the life preserver he kept handy and then dismissed it. It would only prolong the inevitable. To drown would be better than to float with no protection, as it was a good way to attract unwanted attention. In his youth he'd thought it a heroic death to be ripped apart by sharks, but now it didn't appeal to him so much. He flicked a switch on the radio and picked up the transmitter.

"This is the Sea Wolf," he said evenly into his handset, glancing at the coordinates on his navigational chart and guessing his approximate position. "I'm located at latitude 140 west, longitude 38 north. Mayday, mayday, mayday! My hull has been breached and my ship is sinking. I don't think she'll stay afloat longer than an hour, possibly two at best. Mayday, mayday, mayday!"

He repeated his message for several minutes but there was no reply from the squawk box, only the hiss of static. He glanced down and saw that the lower deck was completely engulfed in water now. His estimation was exceedingly optimistic to be sure. He probably had no more than fifteen, twenty minutes tops before it reached where he stood. Taking a deep breath he gazed skyward, fixing his eyes on a bright constellation of stars that shone miraculously through the dense cloud cover.

I hope that's where I'm going, he thought, when at once the boat tilted sharply downward, flinging him headlong into the wheel, and then he knew no more.

He gradually became aware of a pounding in his head, and his mouth felt as if it had been stuffed with cotton. He tried to breath through his nose but found it impossible. Probing it tentatively with his fingertips, he felt his nostrils crusted with dried blood. For a moment he had no idea where he was or the nature of his circumstances, all he knew was that his joints seemed to be clogged with pieces of broken glass. Nearby he heard the screeching, shrieking sounds of. . .birds? Was that what it was? He opened his eyes but when the sunlight hit his dilated pupils he closed them again quickly, pain shooting through his head like a bolt of lightening. At once everything came back to him and in a moment of unadulterated glory he realized he wasn't dead, the sea hadn't become his grave. He took stock of himself, opening and closing his hands, wiggling his toes. He turned his head and slowly, very slowly, opened his eyes, allowing them to adjust to the light. He was lying on his side, his back pressed against the column of the helm. He was alive, apparently still in one piece, but what was it that had stopped the boat from sinking?

Taking his time, knowing that at a moment like this there was certainly no hurry, he found his way to his knees, eventually his feet. The light was so dazzling that for several minutes he was unable to see anything other than a vague outline, and his eyes streamed tears as he squinted savagely into the glaring luminosity, his curiosity overcoming his discomfort. And still he could hear those shrieking, squawking sounds, growing louder around him. If they were birds they were like none he'd ever heard.

Little by little his eyes began to filter out the brightness and images took shape before him. As they did his heart at once sank, for it was with a dreaded conviction that this was a fantasy, an illusion, and he had indeed perished at sea.

Scrubbing his face nervously, his index finger brushed against one of his tender nostrils, and when he dislodged a clump of dried blood the smell hit him in thick, rolling, overpowering waves. His stomach clenched painfully and his bile curdled, almost doubling him over as he gasped for air. This was not a dream, definitely not a mirage. What he was seeing before him was all too real.

"Wha…what the fuck is this?" he wheezed, taking in the desolate landscape before him, his senses finding it almost too overwhelming to believe.

Abruptly the squawking sounds doubled in volume and he realized he was no longer alone. He could hear something scraping the wooden deck directly behind him, could almost taste the fetid stench that floated around it like a dank, putrid cloud.

With measured precision he turned his head, hearing the tendons in his neck creak like rusty door hinges. What he saw made his mouth open wide in a delirious, nameless fear, and as the urine soaked through his denim pants he thought fleetingly that perhaps drowning would have been the easy way out after all…

PART ONE

THE PASSENGERS

ONE

'It is better to inflict pain than to receive it.'
Madam Coventry

Crack! The whip flashes through the air, striking the target with a precision that is only a hair less than deadly. The man winces, biting down on the red ball-gag wedged tightly in his mouth. He utters a groan that betrays his pain and in an instant knows he will get it much worse the next time.

"Quiet slave!" the dominatrix snarls, and the whip descends with an increased fervor, a flurry of blows that almost makes the man piss himself. If he could piss through a hard-on that is, which at this point he probably can, he is in so much agony. His pale, hairy, acne covered back is a mass of red welts, but he doesn't know this, can't know this. Not without a mirror. What he does know is that it hurts like hell.

The dominatrix pauses momentarily and reaches for a bottle of Jack Daniels sitting on a shelf behind her. She takes a large slug then puts it back, wiping her mouth daintily. She normally wears a leather mask with zippers over the eyes and mouth but today she has forgone it because she simply doesn't care. Her dirty, black hair hangs limply upon her shoulders, a dull look clouding her emerald green eyes.

Crack! The man flinches but this time does his best not to utter a peep. He is getting close to shrieking the safeword-which is 'peaches'-but is unsure if this will enrage the dominatrix even more. He is also uncertain whether or not he'd be understood with the gag in his mouth. And, furthermore, he wonders if this is supposed to hurt so much. He can feel thin wisps of blood feathering down his back and is hoping this experience isn't going to leave him scarred. It is his first time, after all, and he isn't all too keen on the specifics.

The dominatrix, Madam Coventry, is barely paying attention. If she was she would notice that she is whipping the man much too hard and that, yes, the marks are going to leave scars. She is generally painstakingly adroit at her trade but today she is being far less than professional. The rules of her vocation state that she must always wear the mask, be careful with the whip, and never, *ever* drink while she is working. She couldn't care less about any of this, however, because she is so pissed off right now she actually wants to kill this guy.

Not that he did anything to her, no, he is some stranger whose ad she saw on Greg's List, but right now she hates the world and it's crummy inhabitants so much it's making her sick and she just wants to get some aggression out. For the most part she is oblivious to what she is doing; her mind is a million miles away and it's all because of that prick Tyler, that skuzzy low-life she let into her home and her life and all he did was drain her, suck her dry. His smile was so full of promises when they met but over the course of seven months he proved what a self-centered, arrogant piece of shit he really was.

For starters, Tyler never got a job. He told her when they met that he was a 'business consultant' (whatever the hell that was; he hadn't bothered to give her any details and she'd never asked) and he was presently going through a slow period. He blamed the lousy economy.

("I could find a job flippin' patties at Mick and D's in the meanwhile but it would make me feel like a jerk," he'd said to her once with a casual grin and she'd laughed it off.)

She paid his way for the entire seven months, and as each month went by she became increasingly resentful, so much so that the thought of his unemployed, sleazy hands touching her made her ill. Not that it stopped her from having sex with him (for sex was essential to her well-being) but she found herself filled with disgust after she'd achieved her orgasm, and post-coital she simply wanted to be left alone, which was just fine for him because he could roll over and fall asleep.

And for seconds he was so full of self-adoration she was certain if the mirror had a hole he could stick his dick into (or he had a clone) he would much rather fuck himself than her. Not to mention he spent so much time chatting with other women on Facebook that she was beginning to feel like the odd man out at an orgy. The person in the corner with their clothes on while everyone else was naked and squirming, fucking and sucking.

It all came to a head this morning, when she'd finally asked him when he was going to resume 'consulting some businesses' and he laughed, actually laughed and told her he didn't really feel like it.

"Don't really feel like it babe," he said as he languished at the kitchen table, intermittently reading an old issue of Maxim Magazine and grooming himself.

"I'm the one who's been making all the money," she said through clenched teeth, "and I'm getting damn sick of it. You think you could do something to put a little food on the table?"

"You know my ebay scam has been shut down because of complaints. What the hell am I supposed to do?"

Ah yes, his ebay scam. What started as a lark had blossomed into quite the little money-maker for a while there, and it was sort of clever. What he did was buy useless crap off of ebay (cheap guitars, band posters, movie posters, cymbals, drum sticks, guitar pedals etc.) and then forged dead musician's signatures on them. Layne Staley, Jim Morrison, Michael Jackson, Amy Winehouse, Janis Joplin, Paul Gray, Jimi Hendrix, G.G. Allen. That sort of thing. He would find photos of their signatures on the net and then practice until he could recreate them almost flawlessly. In the instances where he couldn't he'd print them and then trace over them. Although painful, she acknowledged that he actually did a pretty good job, even if she was hard pressed to admit he did anything well except be a sponging asshole.

His ebay 'persona' was that of an elderly woman whose husband was the actual collector of the autographed merchandise who was tragically dying of cancer. Colon cancer. She needed to sell off his collection so they could pay for his chemo treatments, as it were. And people bought it hook line and sinker. His ebay feedback was fantastic, which led to more sales. This was all fine and dandy, but the thing was he took the money and spent it on more merchandise or on clothes for himself, and not a dime on her. He was a handsome man who liked to look good, and he felt his chiseled face should be equipped with authentic Ray bans, his sculpted torso with tight, silk Calvin Klein shirts, his well-built legs with $300 pairs of the latest designer jeans. It was hard to deny that the clothing vastly enhanced his sex appeal, but she wished he would spend some of it (any of it) on her.

What brought his whole scam to a screeching halt was when he sold a guitar pedal with Kurt Cobain's signature on it and it was determined by the buyer that the pedal was manufactured several years after Cobain's demise. The purchaser was livid and reported his shenanigans to ebay, who promptly investigated him and then suspended his page. Just like that, he was out of a 'job'.

"Have you ever thought about getting a real job?" she said to him this morning as he trimmed his nose hairs at the table with a small scissors and a hand held mirror.

"I hate jobs," he said dismissively, as if to imply the subject was closed, and at once she was furious.

"You think I like getting up every morning and going to work?" she said, slamming the pan she'd been holding into the sink, eggs flying every which way. "How do you think I feel?"

"Babe, you beat people up for a living," he replied, not even looking away from the mirror. "What you do isn't considered 'work'."

It was that casual remark that prompted her to kick his ass out into the street where he belonged. Going to the bedroom, she emptied out the drawers of his clothes and, bringing them into the dining room, began throwing them at him.

"Hey, hey!" he said, getting up from his chair. "Those are my new shirts. Easy!"

She cussed him out with every swear word she could think of (probably even making a few of them up) and when she ran out of clothes from the dresser she raided the closet. He ran around the apartment in his boxers, picking up the clothing as if the garments were fragile, near-extinct animals on the endangered species list.

"If that's the way you want to be about it than I might as well get the fuck out of here," he said, cradling his precious shirts and pants and expensive socks that required garters. "But you'll come calling once you see what it's like to be on your own."

At this seemingly casual (yet wholly contrived) statement her left eye twitched, and inside she felt a gnawing, hollow sensation. Truth be told, she hated being alone; even though she projected a tough, independent exterior, deep inside she was vulnerable to loneliness, and he knew it all too well, in fact had used this threat many times before. Whenever she'd gotten on his case about getting a job, or complained that he never did anything around the condo like taking out the trash or washing the dishes, he'd utter the magic words and it worked like a charm every time. She'd simply clam up, assuring herself she'd deal with it another day. And this silence began to fester within her over time, an annoyance that built steadily with each refusal, growing concurrently with his increased irresponsibility.

Yet the thing was, despite his faults (and he had a lot of them), he wasn't all bad. Sure, he was lazy and he didn't bring any money in but he was a good listener and exceedingly charming when he wanted to be. Yes, he was narcissistic to a degree that was sometimes ludicrous (see the aforementioned comment regarding a clone) but he was kind to her, tender when she needed it, rough when she didn't. Through the months, despite her irritation over supporting him, she felt she'd actually grown to love him, warts and all...until today, and not only was it the comment about not feeling like working but was also the repeated threat of leaving her alone; no one threatened her, goddamnit, no one. He'd done it in the past but no more. Today was the day she was going to throw it right back in his gorgeous face.

"There's the door," she replied, skipping the age-old adage 'don't let it hit you on the ass on the way out', choosing instead to remain as civilized as possible.

He froze for a second, unable to believe his warning was being rebuffed, but incapable (or unwilling) to take it back.

"Fine, I'm out of here!" he bellowed, dramatically collecting all of his things from the apartment as if they were priceless treasures: His Sid Vicious action figure (complete with bass guitar and syringe), his British metal band posters, his rag tag collection of trading cards that featured girls from his favorite skin mags, the last of the music gear from the ebay scam, and a number of t-shirts he'd bought at exorbitant rates that were of no value whatsoever except for their kitsch aesthetic. All of this crap he loaded into a couple of cardboard boxes and piled by the door, looking at her forlornly.

What made this whole display so pathetic was that it was a total farce. She knew he had nowhere to go. He was trying too hard to make it look like he didn't care, but she was his meal ticket; he probably didn't have a dime to his name.

"Is this what you want?" he cried, desperately wanting her to see that she was hurting herself more than he. "Is this what you really, really want?"

"Get out," she said, calling his bluff, and his face fell so comically she almost had to suppress a laugh. And on the heels of her joy she felt an instant surge of relief: his power over her was diminishing. Maybe three weeks ago she would have bought this little tirade and asked him to stay, but not now. Not after she'd finally come to her senses and realized what a self-centered waste of sperm he really was.

"Fine," he said. "Have a nice life." And he stalked dejectedly out the door, the battered boxes tucked under his arms, his head down. She'd watched him walk away, waiting for him to turn around one last time and beseech her with his eyes, but he never did. When he reached the end of the corridor he took a right toward the bank of elevators and simply disappeared. One minute here, the next gone.

She'd slammed the door (hoping he'd hear it) and stood with her back to it for several minutes before she realized she was crying. The tears felt hot and feverish, raw in their immediacy, yet cleansing, pure. That jackass couldn't control her any longer, couldn't take from her anymore than he already had.

And that's why she's so mad presently: despite everything he'd put her through she actually misses the son of a bitch. She doesn't regret kicking him out, but she knows the transition from the life she knew over the last seven months to this newfound solitude is going to be difficult, tougher than anything she's endured in quite some time. The worst thing isn't what Tyler took from her home, it's what he took from her heart.

She swings the whip again, harder, the 'crack' resonating off the walls like a gun shot and the man before her screams (tries to scream actually; the ball gag really does a good job of restraining it) and the sound of his pain infuriates her.

"I said quiet slave!" she cries, grabbing the whisky bottle and taking another hefty swig. She gasps as the liquid fire momentarily takes her breath away, then gulps some more for good measure. Setting the bottle down, she resumes her torture, attacking him with a fury that is animalistic yet machine-like in it's precision. He is grunting and groaning (and if she didn't know better she'd swear he was trying to say something) and this makes her beat him even harder. She swings the whip until her arm grows tired and, only after she feels her stomach take a nauseous turn from the booze, does she stop. She belches loudly and tastes the acidic tang of her bile coming back up.

"Whoa." She takes a step back, setting the whip down, and then notices the marks on the guys back, sees the blood dripping off of him like errant raindrops. He is sagging in the straps, his knees buckled. He isn't moving. For a moment she isn't even sure if he is breathing.

She shakes her head.

"Fucking amateur," she mutters, wondering why, if he was in so much pain, he didn't say the safeword?

Madam Coventry's given name was Melissa Grant, and how she wound up in the pain for pleasure business was purely by chance, let's call it blind luck or fate. Although she had been drawn to small acts of self-mutilation (she was a 'cutter' in high school, in that she liked to make small cuts on her thighs because it gave her an endorphin rush) she wasn't entirely abnormal. Her first forays into sex didn't require that she be slapped or handled roughly, but she found the experiences weren't entirely satisfying until her late teens when she found a guy who liked to play 'rape' with her. He started out innocently enough by simply ripping her clothes off and holding her down, but gradually progressed to spankings and light facial slapping. Of course that eventually led to being bound to the bed, which in turn opened the door to sex toys, ultimately bringing her around to whips, nipple clamps and other nasty tools of the S&M trade. It began slowly but snowballed rather quickly.

It is entirely possible that her home life had something to do with these tendencies, as her parents divorced when she was only five and her mother then adopted what could be best described as a revolving door policy on boyfriends. Sometimes these guys would stick around for a couple months, sometimes a couple days. They're faces were blurred in Melissa's mind, most of them leaving little to no lasting impression whatsoever. After two and a half years of this her mother found a man she judged to be a keeper and they married quietly and quickly at a chapel in Vegas. No one but the blushing bride and the eager husband were in attendance.

Her real father had been granted visitation rights but after the first year he stopped coming around, had all but vanished into the North American landscape. When he *had* visited he always looked disheveled and smelled of something her mom called 'wino wine'. The divorce had been very bad for him, had left his pride injured and his dignity at an all time low. He brought her cheap gifts (probably purchased at the Quicki-Mart just down the block where he got his wine) and always took her someplace close by (his driver's license had been revoked because of multiple DUI's), such as the city park, where he would sip from a bottle tucked in a brown paper bag and watch while she swung on the swings and hung from the monkey bars. His eyes always looked tired and bloodshot, his clothes rumpled and dirty. Even as young as she was she knew that her father was hurting inside but she had no idea what to do about it, how to help him. When he finally disappeared she felt ashamed of herself because her predominant emotion was one of relief.

Her mother changed drastically with the addition of the new man in their household. The once sweet and carefree woman was now a tireless nag, constantly harassing Melissa to pick up her toys, shushing her whenever she asked questions while mommy was watching television, and rarely did anything special for her besides the obligatory cake and present at her birthday.

Melissa blamed the step-father for this, mainly because he was such an unsympathetic asshole who didn't want to have anything to do with his new step-daughter, that is, until she got a little older, but her memories of those times were murky, hazy, muddled…in other words *repressed*.

So her family life had been reduced to nothing more than a necessary duty, an obligation that grew progressively more tiresome. As she got older her mother paid less and less attention to her, except to ridicule her increasingly bizarre clothing (Melissa had become a 'Goth Chick') and her choice in boyfriends. Like the boy she played 'rape' with, the majority of the guys she brought home had pierced noses and eyebrows and black hair and wore ripped black jeans and t-shirts emblazoned with metal band logos, names written in such exaggerated Goth lettering they were impossible to decipher.

Her mother and her stepfather hated these boys, of course, and that's just what she wanted. She loved to watch them squirm. Eventually they found out about her peculiar habits (cutting, tying string tightly around her finger to cut off the blood flow, self-asphyxiation) and were suitably appalled. They didn't know the extent of it until just after her eighteenth birthday when they discovered bondage and S&M porn on her computer during one of their regular snooping sessions. Shortly thereafter she moved out of the house, her commitment to them now relegated to Thanksgiving and Christmas, and those visits were strained at best, awkward and volatile at worst.

She escaped by going to a state college and there she studied business, having no clue as to what she wanted to be. She worked as a waitress at a bar and grill in the evening (she'd applied for and received financial aid but it wasn't enough to pay for everything) and it was there that she met a woman who would alter her life forever. Her name was Monica and she was in the process of starting up a phone sex business and needed women to work the phones. She promised Melissa more money than she was currently making so with little fanfare she decided to give it a try.

As the job progressed (and she showed a very adept skill at it) Monica asked her if she would be interested in writing the weekly S&M and Bondage blog that was posted on their website. Melissa didn't know if she was qualified but figured what the hell, she'd give it a whack. She excelled at it, naturally, and her pay increased and she became invaluable to the company. And it was only a matter of time before the things she wrote about became activities she enthusiastically engaged in for pay, as Monica desired to expand, wanted to open up a studio where people's sexual fantasy's could come true.

For that was the best part about the bondage and S&M game. Melissa didn't have to have sex with the clients so it was (for the most part) legal. Sure, the clientele were allowed to jerk-off when it was over, but she never touched their privates with her hands, only her whip and other assorted torture devices. That was how Monica was able to get a business license and offer other services like piercing, tattooing and massages-sans happy ending (as far as the Board of Business Ethics knew).

Against Monica's advice Melissa dropped out of college. She didn't think she needed it, and she knew she certainly didn't want to be tens of thousands of dollars in debt from the student loans. After all, she'd found her true calling. She loved dressing the part as a dominatrix, simply adored wielding the whip, and cherished the feeling of power she held over the submissive's as she pounded them into oblivion. And she never once felt that her clients were sick bastards (well, not most of them anyway) because she enjoyed the lash of the whip as well, taking great pleasure in hanging in the straps while another S&M professional gave her the business.

She even had a brief affair with Monica, the two liberally exploring their lesbian desires. It was intense but short lived, as the two of them discovered in themselves a jealous streak that simply had no place in a working environment. When they decided to call it quits they were better friends for it and were ready to channel those feelings into the business. Besides, Melissa preferred the company of men to that of women because she liked being manhandled, wanted to be treated rough. Sex with Monica had been so gentle, even with all the toys and strap-on dildos; it was vanilla to the chocolate she preferred.

And the years flew by, the business growing steadily, Melissa becoming ever more proficient at the fine art of taking people to the thresholds of their tolerance for pain, and she couldn't be happier. There was nothing else that she would rather be doing with her life, no other job that gave her so much satisfaction. The best thing was there was never any lack of clients; it might be a fetish that's mostly hush-hush out in the real world but the planet was literally crawling with people who wanted to be abused, thanks to their lousy parents, society, whatever.

Melissa kept an ongoing ad on the Internet so she could keep as busy as she wanted, as well as perusing it for ads when necessary. The studio provided her plenty of work but certain months of the year were slow. Over time she'd made enough money that she was able to convert one of the rooms in her condo into a dungeon. She pre-screened potential clients by requiring a driver's license and conducted thorough background checks on them before she gave out her address. That way no true sicko's ever got through the lobby doors.

So it was she thrived. By keeping to a strict business ethic (a code of conduct for the S&M Professional) she never lacked customers and made more money than she ever would have dreamed.

That is, until today she kept to the conduct code. But today, as she was to find, was going to usher in the next phase of her life.

The man hangs limply in the straps. He's not moving, hasn't moved in the last half hour. Melissa has been holding her breath, afraid to get near him, terrified of confirming what she thinks to be true.

I killed the stupid bastard, she thinks as she sips at the whiskey bottle. *I fucking killed the guy.*

She sees her life flashing before her eyes, knows her career as a dominatrix is over. She feels paralyzed, helpless.

Stepping closer, she carefully removes the ball-gag and his tongue lolls out hideously, a thin smear of blood crusted under his bottom lip. Jesus this guy is ugly. She can't even imagine being a prostitute, can't stomach the thought of actually having to touch him. His pale belly is ridiculously bloated, his shoulders just as hairy as his back. This guy, he wanted to be beaten in his whitey tighties. Some guys want to wear the leather costume, some don't. This guy wanted it all to hang out.

She stares at him, trying to determine if he is breathing or not but she can't tell. He is just too damn fat. She leans in closer, listening for the telltale sign of air wheezing in and out but can't bring herself to actually place her ear against his sweaty, pasty chest.

She wonders what she is going to do if he is dead, wonders whom she is going to call. Maybe it isn't her fault and he had a heart attack. Hell, that certainly is possible. The guy looks like a cholesterol overload just waiting to happen.

But she can't be sure, no, this could very well be all her doing. She'd been pretty rough with him.

Once again her wrath turns toward Tyler, and she's convinced this is all his fault. If he hadn't made her so mad she wouldn't have been drinking and gotten careless. She also knows that if he wasn't such a mooching prick he would still be in her life and she could count on him to help her work this out. She certainly doesn't want to call Monica, no matter how good of friends they are, because Monica always believes the customer is right and will ban her from the studio, will put the word around town that Melissa is an unhinged maniac. Madam Coventry is reckless and bad for business.

She shudders, sets the bottle down and wraps her arms around herself. The only good thing she can think of right now is that this happened at her place and not at the studio. At least she has time to think, has time to plan what she is going to say.

But she knows that if he *is* dead than all the time that's passing makes her look guilty, makes this look somewhat premeditated. She has to think, damnit, has to figure out what the fuck she is going to do-

Suddenly the guy draws in a loud, gasping breath, followed by almost a full minute of coughing/retching. He barfs (mostly undigested food, maybe a little bit of blood) and raises his head weakly, looking around dazedly.

"I-i-is it…over?" he asks weakly and for a moment all Melissa can do is gawk, her mouth agape, eyes wide. She's been given a reprieve, her fantasies of cops and prison receding, savoring for a moment the exquisite pleasure that her life is back within her control.

"Quiet Slave!" she barks and the guy flinches, probably expecting to be hit. His shoulders hunch and he ducks his head dramatically.

"Okay," Madam Coventry says after a lengthy pause. "I think that will be enough for today." She stalks behind him and grabs her mask and whip from the shelf where she keeps the whiskey. Strapping the leather mask on, she strolls back in front of him and extends her arm, placing the end of the whip against his chest. She stares at him fiercely for a moment before she says:

"Before I untie you I need to know: will this be cash or charge?"

TWO

'If it is waste you seek, simply examine my life'.
Dante Kellerman

The smell is the first thing that hits him when he opens the door. Well, open is a rather nice word. Kicked in would be more appropriate.

"Holy shit!" he gasps. "Ma! Ma! You in here?" he calls, but the squawking of the birds drowns out his voice. *"Ma!"*

There is bird shit all over everything. It coats the cheap linoleum floor, is caked and dried in clumps on the thin, wood paneled walls. Hell, it's even on the ceiling, hanging down like dung stalactites. How that is even possible he doesn't want to know.

He'd been trying to call her for two days but she wasn't answering her phone so, as soon as he could, he came out to see if she was all right.

"Ma!" he yells. "Ma!"

He feels a flutter of panic rise within him, and for a moment curses the fact that he couldn't get here sooner, but knows it was impossible because he would have forfeited the money from the pharmaceutical study if he had, and that simply wasn't an option. If you don't finish the study in it's entirety, you don't get paid.

Just this morning he'd completed a drug trial for an experimental heart medication that was given to him (and six other human guinea pigs) in large doses with a radioactive tracer. It was so they could examine more clearly how the drug exited the body through their shit, piss, blood and saliva. Every urination, every dump, was collected in plastic containers and handed off to a nurse ('Poop Station Girls' the guinea pigs jokingly referred to them as) who labeled it and then put it in a large refrigerator for later testing. Because of the radioactive material and the amount of time they had to stay until it cleared their systems (almost five weeks) the study paid $7000. No one knew what the potential side effects might be in the future but fuck if he cared, hell he hardly even read the waiver he'd been required to sign. The future was a big question mark on the horizon to him and each day he survived was a bonus. But that sort of changed when he'd met Leeann. Before her all he had was his drug studies and his mother. Ah yes, his mother...

Dante grew up in Indio, California, the son of a meth-head and a crazy woman. His speed freak father deserted them by the time Dante was seven years old, just up and disappeared one night after dinner, saying he was going out to get a six-pack and some Backwoods Smokes. His mother took it pretty hard. She reported his absence to the police as if he'd been kidnapped or abducted by aliens and soon enough her over-the-top hysterics had the cops on *his* side. The 'search' lasted all of three days. By that time they figured (judging by her irrational behavior) that he was smart to get the hell out while he could. The woman was freakin' nuts. As would be expected, during the seven years time he'd been around he'd managed to knock her up three times so, besides Dante, there were two other mouths to feed. After his father's hasty departure his mother (who had always been slightly unbalanced) went even further off the deep end and so it was up to Dante to help raise his younger brother and sister while dear old mom tried to keep food on the table and a roof over their heads. The four of them struggled through some very hard times, but there weren't four of them for long.

Dante never told anybody this, (God, who would?) but he was almost certain his mother intentionally killed his little sister when she was an infant. Not 'intentionally' like she held a gun to her head, but in the sense that she knew she was dying and did nothing to save her. 'Depraved Indifference' he believed it was called. The poor girl was emaciated from malnourishment, her lungs waterlogged from a cold that progressed to pneumonia, crying relentlessly while unattended in her crib as their mother roamed the streets, looking for some guy to replace the man who'd left her. Young Dante was starving and sick as well and had no idea what he could do to help the poor child. His other sibling, his five-year-old brother, was of no assistance either, and the two of them watched as their ailing sister choked on her phlegm, her little face turning blue, hands clenched into tight fists. It was only after she'd stopped crying for good that Dante and Ricky began to cry. Oh, and they got it good when their mother got home, boy did they ever.

She blamed them in the police report she filed, claiming they'd choked her to death because they wanted her share of food, but the Indio Police Department was already well aware of her lunacy and so, after a speedy trial (she was defended by a court appointed lawyer who did little to aid her, in fact helped the prosecutors make their case), Adel Kellerman was locked up in a state prison and Dante and Ricky were taken into state custody. They were fortunate enough to be relocated in foster homes relatively close to one another (they were lucky to find foster homes *period*, as opposed to remaining wards of the state), but by the time they were teenagers Ricky detested Dante and they seldom spoke. The reason for this was that Dante persisted in defending their mother. Ricky had written her off as deranged and dangerous while Dante still pined for her, wishing they could be together as a family. After Ricky graduated from high school he joined the army and was stationed in North Carolina for basic training until getting shipped overseas. Dante never heard from him again. For all he knew his brother was dead, killed in one of America's many 'conflicts', possibly Iraq or Afghanistan.

Adel was released from prison when Dante was nineteen, having served twelve years of a fifteen-year sentence and, renouncing his affiliation with the foster family who took care of him for over a decade (they'd never cemented a loving relationship, in fact had only taken Dante in to receive money from the state), he moved her and her meager belongings into his place and commenced taking care of her. Well, tried to take care of her anyway, as much as he could or as much as she would let him. She was still a very difficult woman, was still crazy as a fucking bedbug.

But that was familial love for you: unconditional.

He worked hard, even went to school to be a paramedic but never finished his degree because he couldn't find the time in between his manual labor shit jobs and taking care of her to concentrate on his studies. He'd dropped out numerous times only to enroll again and again, to no avail.

For ten years they shared a small room in a boardinghouse in a crappy neighborhood, and employing the word 'small' is beyond a doubt generous. Tiny was more like it. To make better use of the space he'd put in bunk beds. Keeping the place clean was supposed to be his mother's job, so the room was continuously filthy. Other tenants complained about the smell and the overpopulation of cockroaches that their trash invited, but somehow Dante always managed to clean it up enough not to get evicted.

And they lived like this, this squalid existence, for over ten years until Dante stumbled upon the pharmaceutical company. He saw the ad in the Indio Sunday paper. It listed the drugs they were testing, the type of people they were looking for (by age, weight, and health) and what they paid. Dante was immediately intrigued. The pay was extravagant compared to what he was getting washing dishes and delivering pizzas. Apparently they paid thousands of dollars for only a few weeks of your time, a month tops. So he traveled to San Diego and screened for his first study, was accepted, and thus began his education as to how the whole operation worked.

The pharmaceutical company was called Pharmacoastalcal Incorporated, and what they did was test medications that were close to being introduced on the market. These chemicals had already been tested several times (possibly on convicts or animals), but this phase was intended to get the approval of the FDA and to work out any kinks in the product. It was insinuated that the drugs were 'safe' although there was a great deal of paperwork for the participants to fill out, waivers releasing Pharmacoastalcal of any liability should someone become seriously ill or incapacitated. This happened occasionally and these patients had to be pulled from the trials, receiving a small stipend for their involvement.

Some of the studies conducted were inpatient (these paid more) while others were outpatient. The outpatient studies tended to take longer (could sometimes extend over several months time, thus delaying payment until their conclusion) so Dante preferred doing inpatient studies. Besides, living as far away as he did, the inpatient drug trials were really his only choice, until he at last decided to relocate. Thereafter he could do either one. It wasn't easy to get his mother to leave Indio, but threatening to desert her quickly did the job, and after a year and a half of profitable drug trials he realized he was making enough money to get her her own place. It was painful for both of them to cut the umbilical cord, but eventually he persuaded her to move into a trailer he rented for her in a quiet little trailer park in Chula Vista while he took up residence in a rooming house in downtown San Diego to be closer to the pharmaceutical facility. Spanish speaking Mexicans and poor whites populated the park, these destitute folks living six or seven to a two-bedroom trailer and raising chickens in their yards, yet Adel was reasonably satisfied. But little did he know their livestock tending ways would soon influence her in a manner he never would have guessed.

Before Dante met Leeann he was in denial as to how utterly unhappy he was, not realizing that if he didn't change things he would probably go nuts and slit his own throat. After they met, all Dante wanted was to live a 'normal' life, one that held promise instead of misery. He felt he'd made great strides in that direction by getting his mother her own place. Step one had been completed.

Of all places he met Leeann at Pharmacoastalcal, the only setting in which he probably ever could meet a woman one would suppose, given that he spent so much time there. By the time he made her acquaintance he'd become the poster child for drug trials; he had a system worked out so he could live on it indefinitely, and what the hell? The staff got to know him well and they liked him. After a while they began to give him preferential treatment, even called him when they knew there was a really high paying study coming up. And so he'd found his calling. Between studies (there was a drug wash out time one had to adhere to, you couldn't simply end one drug trial and jump right into another) he would deliver pizzas and tend to his mother.

He met Leeann in one of the many TV lounges one day after having given blood for the eighth time in six hours and was feeling woozy enough to summon up the guts to talk to her. He learned that she was in a study testing out a new heartburn medication and was only doing it because a friend of hers at UCSD had recommended it so they could make extra money to take a trip to South Padre Island for spring break. Leann was in her last year of college, getting ready to graduate with a BA in marine biology, minoring in oceanography. She didn't much like the study protocol, having to get up at all hours of the night to have her vitals checked, and liked even less having to give so much blood, but the money promised was good and she felt she deserved a break after so diligently working her way through school in just over three years time.

He also learned she was from Corpus Christi in east Texas, and had grown up in a loving family of modest means. She was slender and freckled and pretty and the second Dante laid eyes on her he fell in love. What she saw in him was anybody's best guess. Maybe it was her love of biology, the science of the organic, sometimes odd and unusual. Who knows? Whatever the case, Dante's affections weren't entirely rebuffed.

Other study members and some of the staff, as it were, often referred to Dante, as 'the missing link', although never to his face. He was tall (six foot five) and wore a bushy beard that rose high up on his rotund cheeks. His long, curly black hair was an unruly mop and the centerpiece of his face was a pair of Buddy Holly glasses so thick they made his eyes look like giant hard-boiled eggs. He was personable and reasonably intelligent but he had the demeanor of a comic book fan boy (which he was), or a hardcore 'Trekkie' (which he also was). In other words, a geek.

Had he not been so completely out to lunch from blood loss he probably never would have approached her, and even then it took quite a bit of hemming and hawing for him to manage 'hello' and introduce himself. Leeann had been keeping mostly to herself throughout the duration of the study, not because she was conceited but because she didn't like the majority of the people she met. For the most part they were slackers and lowlifes who were simply avoiding the real world, hiding out in these studies so they didn't have to do any real work. She would have hated Dante for this, given the chance, but after several conversations she realized this was his profession, and he attacked it with a zeal that was almost admirable.

It took over a week to reach that point however, as Dante didn't often make very good first impressions, but his persistence finally won her over. By the last day of her study he'd been able to get her phone number so he could call her when he got out.

"You sure it's all right?" he'd asked.

"What's all right?"

"That I can call you."

"I wouldn't have given you my number otherwise," she'd said with a sly smile and Dante felt the heat rising in his cheeks. Thanks to the beard she had no idea he was blushing.

"I suppose if we should lose touch we'll always have the 'boner guys'," he added, laughing nervously, and to this she guffawed.

"Yes," she replied. "We'll always have the 'boner guys'."

Something that aided their bonding was their shared hilarity of the pitiable old men in the boner drug trial. What with the advances made by Viagra, Ciallis and so on the pharmaceutical companies were always looking for a better drug for erectile dysfunction, and the old guys in that particular study were constantly stiff and randy as all living hell, making a general nuisance of themselves. Women and men alike were the victims of their affections, study participants and staff included. Leeann and Dante made a game of avoiding them, as they'd pop out from seemingly nowhere with a particular gleam in their eyes and a bulge in their pants, desiring satisfaction. Dante had fended off two of them in the shared bathroom while attempting to shower, and Leeann had had an encounter with one particularly lecherous old man while she was waiting on line in the cafeteria. She'd been lucky there were other people around. Dante had been lucky he was bigger and stronger than them.

So it was that the old guys and their hard dicks were the ongoing joke they shared, and eventually Dante-the-missing-link sort of grew on her. Even though there were plenty of activities offered for the patients to do while they participated in the drug trials (TV, Internet, Blue Ray's, video games, books, magazines, pool tables, board games, sleep etc.) the hours sometimes stretched on and on. This left plenty of time to talk with one another.

It goes without saying that Dante never went into much detail about his own life (his mother to be exact), but managed to be a wonderful listener while Leeann talked about college and her aspirations as a marine biologist and her up coming trip to South Padre Island. He studied her rapturously as she talked, watched the dance of her tongue, noted the cadence of her speech, loved the way her freckles seemed to glimmer beneath the fluorescent lights. He adored her southern accent; it aroused him, both spiritually and sexually.

Holding the piece of paper her number was written on like it was a treasured artifact, he watched her from the window as she exited the building into the bright morning sunshine the day she checked out. Shortly after he finished his study she'd be back from her vacation. He hoped she would still want to see him when that time came.

But, presently, those thoughts are displaced by his rabid fear for his mother's safety. Where the hell is she, and what are all these peacocks doing in her trailer? The place is a veritable zoo for Christ's sake; peacocks large and small are taking up every inch of space, tearing the cheap furniture apart and shitting on everything. The last time he was here she'd had a couple of them out in the backyard. Now they've multiplied and are living inside.

"Ma!" he hollers again before he trips on something and falls head first into a pile of bird crap. Wiping at his face, struggling to keep from vomiting, he gets back on his feet and staggers to the door. Shambling out into the hot, bright, morning, he just barely makes it down the steps before losing his breakfast on the dry, brown lawn. He retches helplessly for several minutes before he can control himself, and only after he's scrubbed the last of the puke from his mouth and beard does he notice he is making a spectacle of himself in front of her neighbors. Several Mexican women are standing in front of their trailers, watching the large man with the shaggy beard toss his cookies, and they are scowling and making the sign of the cross.

"Hey!" he calls to them, waving hands that drip the half-digested remnants of bacon and eggs. "Have you seen my mother?"

None of them reply, instead they take two steps back for every one he advances. Maybe it's because they don't speak English, or maybe it's because they are afraid of him-whatever the case, as he gets within a few feet they flee quickly into their trailers. He can hear them squealing amongst themselves through the thin walls, their language as unintelligible to him as his is to theirs.

"Well son of a bitch," he mutters, feeling momentarily like something the cat dragged in, but dismissing it swiftly in his anxiety to find his mother.

He returns to the door of the trailer, steeling himself to do a more thorough search. Holding his breath he darts back in and, when he reaches the bedroom at the end of the hall, he doesn't know if he should feel guilty, sad or liberated.

THREE

The President of The United States enters the Oval Office accompanied by two bodyguards, followed by the vice president and a group of political advisers. Among them are military, economic, agricultural, social and environmental consultants. Many of them are talking at once and, seating himself behind his desk, he leans back in his chair and scowls.

"Quiet!" he orders, his deep, baritone voice resonating loudly above the din. "Have some damn respect!"

The chatter of the elite group of upper echelon advisors dies down, their eyes and ears tuned in to the man their country has recently selected to lead them. They regard him carefully as they seat themselves, observing his solemn expression. This meeting was called on short notice and many of them are uncertain as to what it pertains. Nervous glances dart back and forth as the president picks up a sheaf of papers and briefly sorts through them before tossing the pile in his 'out' basket.

"Okay people, thank you for joining us today. For those of you who don't know why we're here I've brought in Dr. Corey Taylor, head of Oceanic and Scientific Studies to share with you his research on a situation that was swept under the rug by previous administrations but at long last requires action. I want you all to give him your undivided attention." He waves his hand and a man with a harried expression steps forward. His clothes are rumpled, his thinning hair tousled and he's wearing reading glasses perched askew on his nose.

"Good morning Mr. President," he says in a quiet yet sure voice.

"Good morning Dr. Taylor. Please be so kind as to bring my esteemed colleagues up to speed."

"Yes sir. As the president said I'm Dr. Corey Taylor, the White House's head of Oceanic and Scientific Studies, and I've prepared a presentation for you today."

The group assembled looks at him blandly, observing his disheveled appearance with open scorn.

"We are here to talk about the North Pacific Gyre, located between latitude 135 degrees to 155 degrees west, longitude 35 degrees to 42 degrees north."

The president fiddles with his tie, then motions to one of the guards that he needs a beverage. The guard on his right hand side speaks into his headset in hushed tones and at once a door opens and an aide rushes in with a cup of coffee. "Anybody else want anything?" He glances around the room but no one says a word, their faces betraying their annoyance at what surely is a waste of their time. "Okay, don't say I didn't ask." He nods to Dr. Taylor. "Please continue."

"Well sir, it seems the problem has escalated to the extent that extreme measures may now be deemed necessary."

"I think it would be best," the president says, sipping from his cup, "if you would be more specific."

"What I'm talking about," Dr. Taylor continues, "is a large garbage heap that's occupying a vast portion of the Pacific north of Hawaii, roughly a thousand miles off the California coast-"

"Garbage heap?" the economic advisor blurts. "We're here because of that damn garbage heap?"

"It was first predicted by the National Oceanic and Atmospheric Administration in 1988, regarding the study of neustonic plastics," Dr. Taylor presses, unruffled by the interruption. "The prediction was based on scientific research conducted between 1985 to 1988, detailing that a high concentration of marine debris could accumulate in accordance with favorable conditions, such as in a relatively stable body of water-"

"The ocean isn't a stable body of water doctor," the vice president counters, and the other nods.

"No sir, it isn't, but there are relatively stationary regions where the conditions become most favorable for this debris to form a solid mass. These areas of the ocean are called 'gyres', or vortexes if you will. The currents move in a circular pattern, clockwise in this case, so the debris collects in the center. In fact, there are five of them around the world. One in the Pacific, another in the Atlantic, and-"

"We all know what gyres are Dr. Taylor," the environmental advisor states flatly. "Get to the point."

"I'm sorry ma'am," Dr. Taylor replies curtly. "I certainly didn't mean to insult your intelligence."

"What does this have to do with the war effort?" the military advisor asks, raising his eyebrows. "Surely we have more important matters to discuss."

"Will you people shut up and let him talk?" the president admonishes, stirring sugar in his coffee. "Go on, please."

"Thank you sir," Dr. Taylor says, abandoning his notes. After all, he knows all of this by heart. "The trash heap began with mostly plastic particles, very small pieces actually." He pauses, looking around the room. "It was originally determined that 80% came from land based sources and 20% from ships at sea. Well, that's how it started anyway."

The room is finally silent, everyone's attention on the doctor.

"What was hypothesized in 1988 wasn't actually discovered until 1995 when a sailboat traveling from the Philippines to California ran into it. The way it was initially, you couldn't see it until you were physically in it."

"This is old news. We all know about the floating trash heap," the agricultural advisor says and the president shoots him a dirty look. Dr. Taylor, however, continues on unabated.

"The plastic particles were so small that it wasn't visible to the naked eye from the air, either by low flying plane, helicopter or satellite photos. Without someone sailing through it and actually discovering it, we had no idea it was there.

"So my department conducted a study, sending a research group out to measure the particles, to examine and determine what kind of impact it had on the environment, and we found that the marine life was feeding on and around it, the pollutants killing everything from albatrosses to jellyfish to filter feeders but, shockingly, we also discovered that a very small percentage of marine life was actually *adapting* to it." The doctor coughs into his hand, clearing his throat. "And not only adapting to it, they were thriving. We quickly realized the impact on the food chain could be potentially severe if the problem was left unattended. We also calculated that, in accordance to the conditions, the trash would only accumulate thicker and thicker as time went by."

"We've all seen the photos," the agricultural advisor says, leaning back and crossing his legs. "What are you getting at?"

"Okay, I can see you are all well aware of the background of the trash heap," Dr. Taylor says. "I think it would be best if I presented my slide show now Mr. President."

"By all means. Fire it up."

The doctor flips open his laptop and one of the aides dims the lights. When he does a white screen unfurls on the wall. At once an image appears before them.

"These are photos taken from the study conducted in 1995, shortly after it's discovery."

On the screen appears a picture of densely packed opaque plastic pieces covered in seaweed, floating on top of the water. Entwined within it are larger items: plastic water and soda bottles mostly, as well as aluminum cans, six-pack holders, plastic shopping bags, food wrappers, cigarette packs and various other items of detritus. He flips to the next photo, one taken under water. It shows the swirling mass of junk descending far below the surface, enmeshed with more seaweed and other organic life. A diver is in the photo to give the viewer a sense of its size, the accrued mass dwarfing him. He flips through several more, showing the accretion from other angles.

"As you can see in these photos there are several species of aquatic life feeding in and around it-"

"Mr. President I must object!" the economic advisor exclaims. "We've all seen these photos in magazines and on the web. Why are we wasting our time on this?"

"We're wasting our time on this now," Dr. Taylor retorts, "because the government didn't consider it important enough to pursue *then!*"

"I don't think I like your tone sir. You'd best be respectful of your superiors."

"You better skip ahead Dr. Taylor," the president advises and the other nods, advancing the photos until the desired one pops up.

"This is a photo taken from the 2005 expedition," he says. What they are seeing is vastly different from the previous photos. It now appears to be a solid mass, grown several yards above the water line.

"These photos were taken both from the water and from various altitudes above sea level."

The pictures show the 'island' in its entirety, then descend closer to reveal what it's comprised of. Close-ups disclose how the trash is fusing together, forming solid clumps.

The group continues to look upon the images with disinterest, their irritation evident by their surly demeanor.

"I hate to sound flippant," the vice president says, "but we've all seen these photos, the whole world has. Environmental protection agencies held telethons, bleeding heart sons a bitches screamed bloody murder and the liberal media made a big hoop-to-do about the damn thing a decade ago."

"That's correct," Dr. Taylor agrees. "But the reason we are here today is because nothing, and I repeat, *nothing* was ever done about it. The telethon sponsors and the media lost interest when the next big environmental problem came along, and like every great cause it was forgotten. The general public has always had a very short attention span and since this problem wasn't 'in their back yard' so to speak, it was easy to dismiss. Even Sea Green abandoned their clean-up efforts to go after the new generation of whale poachers who popped up along the Alaskan coast in 2006. And after the expedition in 2005 our funding was cut and we had to discontinue our research, unless we wanted to pursue it on our own time, at our own expense."

"Did you?" the vice president asks.

"What do you think?"

The vice president's face reddens slightly. "Well you don't have to be snippy about it."

"Surely there must have been independent researchers investigating it," the environmental advisor says.

"Of course, but none of the groups had enough funding to take on such a monstrosity as this, and why should they? Certainly they couldn't be expected to spend their own money on something their government ought to be responsible for."

"Always after the federal money, hmm? I suppose the taxpayers expect us to take care of everything. "

"These," Dr. Taylor says, ignoring her comment and advancing the slide show, "are the most recent photos taken of the trash heap. I think you'll notice quite a difference."

The images that appear on the wall are enough to hammer home the severity of the problem that lies before them, and Dr. Taylor notes with satisfaction the expressions of disbelief on their faces.

"Holy shit," the environmental adviser marvels. "It looks enormous."

"It is enormous," Dr. Taylor confirms. "In 2005 we predicted it would grow exponentially larger." He looks around, pleased to see these arrogant bastards are finally paying attention. "Our estimations, it would seem, were grossly optimistic."

"How big is it?" the economic advisor asks.

"It was three hundred thousand square miles when it was first discovered, over six hundred thousand square miles when we studied it in 2005."

"How big is the fucking thing *now?*" the military advisor asks impatiently and Dr. Taylor looks at him over the bridge of his glasses.

"As of these photos," he says calmly, "three times the size of Texas."

There is a moment of shocked silence before the room erupts, everyone talking at once. Dr. Taylor looks about him helplessly as the president tries to restore order.

"Quiet!" he hollers. "Everybody settle down!"

Gradually the clamor dies down, but the group is clearly agitated. Many of them are staring critically at the president and Dr. Taylor.

"How could this happen?" the environmental advisor asks incredulously. Her voice is soft, yet her eyes betray her anger. "How could we sit idly by and let this thing get so big?"

"Don't ask me honey. I was just sworn in last December thanks to the previous president's untimely impeachment, remember? Before this gig I was merely his right-hand man." He grimaces. "More like his boy Friday."

"How did this happen doctor, um, Taylor was it?"

"Like I already said, the two previous administrations weren't taking our research seriously. It was in their opinion that our funding could be put to better use breaking up Unions, supplying weapons to third world countries, advancing our military strongholds throughout the globe and subsidizing anti-Democratic propaganda ad campaigns…that sort of thing. The administration in power between 2004 and 2008 actually thought nature would sort itself out over time, but the problem had already grown into an inexorable mess. You see, the expedition that went out in 2005 discovered that the garbage in the eye of the gyre contained more than just the plastic flotsam and jetsam we originally found in '95. It appeared it had become an illegal dumping zone, utilized by anyone with a ship to transport the trash out there. As a result of the slow moving currents of the gyre most sailors and fishermen avoid the area because of slack winds and the lack of large sea life. So, with no one around to blow the whistle on these 'entrepreneurs', the trash heap grew at an astounding ratio, exceeding all expectations. I should know, I was along on that voyage. We found it was amassing at an alarming rate and predicted that if it were to continue to develop unchecked it would be strong enough to support the weight of a grown man within a few years, give or take."

"How come this hasn't become a media circus?" the social advisor says. "I'm surprised there isn't a reality TV show based on it, you know, like 'Survival of the Fittest' or something. This seems right up their alley."

"Satellite imagery of the area became limited to government use after the war with North Korea broke out. Subsequently the overall public hasn't seen any recent photos of it. I later found out the United States Navy requisitioned the garbage patch for use as a covert military strong point in case dire measures were required, a place the North Koreans would never suspect was occupied. The idea was later abandoned because it wasn't deemed necessary, in fact the Navy never actually went out there. If they had I'm sure this meeting would have taken place years ago. "

"Couldn't the Koreans see it from space?" the environmental advisor asks.

"Not after we destroyed all of their satellites. The only reason they have cell phone coverage and TV is because their allies allow them to use theirs."

"So how come their allies can't see it?"

"We've jammed their signals to only allow the barest necessities be broadcast. In times of war one must take any advantage they can get."

"How come I never heard about that?" the military advisor inquires, irritated. "I think I'd know about any and all covert military ops."

"Because it never went further than the planning stages at the very top," Dr. Taylor says. "I only found out recently and was sworn to secrecy-oops, guess I just let the cat out of the bag. Sorry."

"So you can't find photos of the garbage heap on Google Maps?"

"Nothing after 2005, when the new Patriot Act was drafted and ratified. You can find photos like some of these I've shown you, but all of them are over ten years old."

"I remember all the hubbub surrounding it back then," the environmental advisor recalls, "but like the doctor said it was forgotten when the next environmental disaster came along."

"That's right!" the economic advisor says. "It was all those volcano's erupting in Yosemite Park, right?"

"Yellowstone."

"Whatever."

"So why is this our problem?" the agricultural advisor butts in. "How come some other country doesn't step up and do something about it?"

"The entire world is at war," the president replies, his voice betraying his increasing annoyance, "and you think we'll just call on our allies to join us for garbage picking detail?"

"What are we doing about this?" the environmental advisor asks, having to raise her voice to be heard over the others. "Shouldn't we send a team of scientists out there to figure out our best options?"

"That's the thing," Dr. Taylor says, eyeing her carefully. "Thanks to our newly appointed president our funding was reinstated and we recently sent a crew on a clean-up slash survey mission from the Scripts Institute of San Diego, its intention being to evaluate the problem and do whatever necessary to eradicate it. We sent out important people, brilliant minds, top scientists in their field."

"And?"

"They disappeared without a trace."

The room becomes so silent the audible hum of the air conditioning can be heard, along with the occasional output of air from the doctor's laptop.

"They…what?" the economic advisor asks at length.

"We lost radio communication with them shortly after they arrived. We searched for them via satellite and air surveys but there was no trace of them. None."

"What, you mean the crew?"

"The ship, the crew…everything vanished into thin air."

"I thought those satellite photos could take a picture of a couple a cockroaches screwin' if they wanted 'em to," the military advisor harrumphs.

"You know they can, but we've turned up nothing." The doctor shrugs. "Well, no people anyway. We've seen evidence of wildlife living on the trash heap, birds, lizards, that sort of thing, but we haven't spent any time investigating them-"

"So what happened? The ship ran into trouble and sank?"

"Not according to the time lapse satellite photos nor the crew's last transmission, sent shortly after they arrived. As far as we know they made their destination and were preparing to board the heap for a closer look."

"What about a North Korean Destroyer? Maybe they mistook them for a military vessel…"

"That's something we'd definitely see on the satellite photos and there is no sign of any outside interference. Theirs was the only ship in those waters at the time, well, at those coordinates anyway."

"What does that mean?" the vice president asks.

"Well," Dr. Taylor clarifies, "There were a couple of ships heading away from the heap, probably having just unloaded a cargo of trash."

Again no one speaks for several ticks of the clock, all those present looking from one face to another.

"So what do you suggest we do?" the environmental advisor asks.

"I say we nuke the fucker into outer space," the military advisor proposes but is ignored.

The president drains his coffee and sets the mug on his desk, scrubbing his clean-shaven face with a well-manicured hand. He glances at his watch and picks a piece of lint invisible to the others from his shirt before advancing his initiative:

"We lost a number of important people from our governmental scientific community, key people who have been an asset to this country over the years. In all honesty the war effort needs them, *we* need them. The doctor and I have discussed the situation at length and feel it is in our best interest to fund another mission to try and rescue them, as well as to determine what we can do about this staggering dilemma. We've agreed we can't make the same mistake of sending people who are vital to our nation, people whose lives are essential to our future if we are to remain the leaders of the free world. What we propose to do is send out another ship and crew, only this time staff it with expendable volunteers." The president's gaze sweeps across the room, looking each and every one of them in the eyes. "*Talented* expendable volunteers. The purpose of today's meeting is to make sure all of you are on board with this idea."

"Sir, I think we should send in some Navy personnel to check it out first before we knowingly send civilians in again-" the military advisor begins but is cut short.

"We have more important uses for our military at this time," the president snaps heatedly. "The wars in Afghanistan, Iraq, Iran, Somalia, Kenya, China and North Korea are our main focus at this time. We don't have the resources to send any soldiers out there. If we relent on our crusade for worldwide Democracy the communists and terrorist groups'll eat us alive. Is that what you want, a world controlled by radical extremists? This is 2018, not 2001 when some turban wearing fuckstick with a homemade bomb could invade our country and cause billions of dollars worth of damage and kill thousands of people. Ladies and gentlemen, we have *evolved*." He glares around the room, his eyes icy, determined. "No, what the doctor and I are recommending, and what I'm hoping you'll all agree to today, is that we staff another ship with a disposable crew and this time keep track of them every step of the way to ensure the mistakes made on the previous voyage are not repeated. Even though we sent out the best and brightest I'm not convinced that someone didn't royally screw it up."

"But you don't know for sure," the environmental advisor accuses, her brilliant blue eyes sparkling with contempt.

"No," the president replies, shaking his head. "At this point we don't know anything except for what I've told you."

"With all due respect sir," the military advisor says, raising his hand tentatively, "I really think we should send some military personnel to at least offer protection-"

"Fine!" the president says angrily. His head is starting to hurt and he wants to finish this matter and move on to other things. "We'll send along some military fuck-ups. I'm sure we can find ourselves a few of those, can't we?"

"Yes sir."

"Okay, here's what we're suggesting: get the governor of California on the horn and make this his problem. California is the closest state to the garbage heap so they'll be in charge of procuring the ship and crew." He looks around. "Is someone writing this down?"

One of his personal aides scrambles for a pen and paper while the others stare blankly, absorbing what they've been told. The president chews on the end of a pen, eyeing the others speculatively, and then whirls his large leather chair around so he is now facing the American flag. Taking a deep breath, he wonders what his Daddy would have made of this, but the thought is futile because he never really understood his father and, besides, the old crank is dead. He's certain he's making the right choice in sending another ship staffed with a crew of people unessential to the war effort, hell, no use in sending out anyone they might need in the future. There certainly could be a chance the previous crew is still alive and, if so, those folks would come in mighty handy if China should decide to invade, and at this point it seems pretty damn likely. Not to mention it's in their best interest to find out what they are dealing with before they just up and blast it back to the stone age with a nuclear bomb like the military advisor suggested, right? Having finalized his decision, he spins back around and faces the room once more.

"All right then. Unless anyone disagrees I suggest we move on to more important matters. Okay?"

A chorus of mumbling voices concur and the president nods.

"Good enough. Thank you very much for your time Dr. Taylor," he says dismissively. "Now what else do we have on the agenda for today?"

FOUR

'The world needs liberals like the U.S. needs equal rights for all—it doesn't'
California Governor Ted Hallsly Jr.

Why anyone would want to be a Democrat is far beyond the reasonable line of thinking for Governor Theodore Hallsly Jr. Everyone knows that Democrats are baby-killing pacifists who would sell out their own mother just to have a bill passed to socialize health care. The governor knows in his heart that not all people deserve to *have* health care, thus the privatization of the health insurance industry. If simply anyone were allowed to get the treatment they needed for their bowel, breast or lung cancer (especially the poor people, particularly the Negroes, Mexicans, slant-eyes and Indians) than the United States would go down the tubes like those other liberal, bleeding heart countries… like France.

He shudders. *Fucking France.* He can imagine those beret wearing dickwads at their crummy wine tasting parties, eating stinky cheese and laughing like imbeciles over jokes that aren't even funny. Anti-American pieces of pussy trash…Gimmie a single malt scotch, a burger and the good ole red, white and blue any day…

His intercom buzzes and the voice of his secretary (a hot number with c-cups and a pretty mouth) informs him his ten o'clock appointment is here.

Shit, he thinks disparagingly, dreading this meeting. Overall, his job is to mollify the residents of California that they're desires are being seriously considered while allowing the business people of California free reign on resources, land, tax breaks etc. and the federal government stays out of it. Today's engagement sets him on edge because it is someone from the White House. He can't help but think that something is wrong, more so that *he* has done something wrong (wouldn't be the first time, it would just mean he got caught) and it's for this reason he's feeling a little anxious.

"Send him in," he says with a note of weariness in his voice, hoping his secretary will get the hint and perhaps tell his visitor he isn't feeling well today, maybe they should come back tomorrow.

"Right away sir," she says pertly, ignoring his tone, and for the third time in less than an hour he wonders why he keeps her on. She isn't very good at understanding his needs, in fact seems to take pleasure in his misery. Like first thing this morning when he gleefully showed her the headline of the paper, stating that the president's popularity was down in the polls, and she shrugged and said simply: "Well, tomorrow is another day."

And then when he asked her to outline his day for him she almost gloated when informing him he had a meeting with someone from Washington D.C., *sent* by the fucking president.

"What the hell do they want?" he'd groaned and his secretary flashed a wide grin.

"Didn't say," she answered sagaciously. "Just said it was extremely important."

"Can't we cancel it?"

"Nope," she said, like she held all the cards and he was merely a figurehead required to do his duty. When she acted like that he wanted to bend her over his desk and take her forcefully from behind, hike up her dress so it covered her head, muffling her screams. And when he was finished he would pull out and squirt his juice all over her big, round ass, then slap it (hard) for good measure.

He sighs deeply, smiling an insidious smile. Yes, these are the thoughts that get him through the day.

Governor Hallsly owed his political success to being born into the right family, much like other politicians before him. His father became a Texas oil baron at the age of forty-one when he'd been lucky enough to find vast reserves of fossil fuel on the farm he'd inherited from his father and the rest, as they say, was history. Almost overnight Theodore Hallsly Sr. went from dumb-ass hick to man-about-town. But it could be honestly said that wealth didn't change him: once a dumb-ass hick, always a dumb-ass hick. The only difference was that now he could buy and do whatever he wanted, and what he wanted was political control. Being what he considered the archetypal 'True American' (white, power hungry, ignorant) he hated anything that was different from him. Niggers, spicks, wops, Jews, savages, chinks, commies...he hated them all. Only amongst his true friends (his redneck drinking buddies and those he could buy off) did he express his real opinions, one of them being that he thought Hitler had been doing a mighty fine job until America had to stick their nose into his business and another that the Civil War era Northern Union was a bunch of nigger-loving pantywaists. To others he concealed his prejudices, well, at the very least made light of them.

So he went about buying local police forces and city officials, then state senators and, finally, the governor of Texas. Once he had all these people 'in his pocket' he proceeded to use up the land without hesitation, never once considering what the future may hold for the barren fields he left in his wake. The only idea he may have had was that, when the land was no longer worth anything, it could be used to house faggots and commies and pinkos after being evicted from all the 'civilized' cities. That was if they decided not to simply eradicate them via forced labor/death camps.

Ted Hallsly Jr. grew up with these beliefs firmly planted in his thick head, and he went to private schools and mingled with other rich kids who espoused the same ideals. They were so superior, these privileged children of wealthy lineage, and only their ignorance exceeded their rampant feelings of entitlement. Oh, what a fine bunch they were.

Ted just barely made it through high school with grades so bad it took donations from Hallsly Sr. to eliminate his son's need to repeat several grades. And when it came time for college, well, good old dad took care of that too. What university didn't need a new library, or a statue of some historical figure, preferably white, if at all possible Southern?

Ted attended the University of Texas in Austin, majoring in keg stands and cocaine 101. By his fourth year he didn't have nearly enough credits to graduate (having failed so many classes) so his daddy put him to work in the family business, giving him a job on an oilrig.

Hard work just wasn't in Ted's genes, and he goofed off every chance he got until one day he 'got the call' and decided he should go into politics. His father had enough money to fund his campaign, so he ran first for city council, then for state senator, then governor.

Well, Texas wasn't foolish enough to elect him governor of their fine state (not after all the racist, anti-Semitic rhetoric his father had expounded) but, eventually, California was. And his dear old dad only had to come up with three hundred and eighty million dollars to make it possible, outbidding the other candidate hopefuls by roughly seventy million. And so it was that he took up his new position, and the intelligent citizens of the sun soaked state made t-shirts that showed an image of him snorting coke off of an American flag, proclaiming 'He's Not My Governor' while the idiots who elected him into office sat back and watched the destruction commence...

(Author's note: Yes, this seems like a rather short summary of Ted Hallsly's undoubtedly illustrious life but the fact is that he is a dick and we don't really give a crap about him. The more you read, I'm sure, you'll feel the same. If not, there is a special place in Hell reserved for you. Thank you.)

There is a knock at the door and before he can holler 'come in' it opens and a somber looking woman enters the room and approaches his desk.

"Good morning Governor Hallsly," she says, holding out her hand. She is dressed in casual business attire, a pants suit with a matching scarf. He can tell the suit is tailor made and not something off the rack from Macy's. "I'm Jessica Holdsworth."

Mentally whipping himself into shape, the noble governor forces what he hopes to be a credible smile and stands up, reaching out to take her hand. He may be an insufferable prick but he'll be damned if this lady is going to figure it out. At least, not right away.

"Very pleased to meet you as well Mrs.-"

"Ms."

"Uh, Ms. Holdsworth," he corrects himself, shaking her hand, and then resumes sitting, indicating that she do the same. Reaching for the button on his intercom he asks if she would like something to drink, coffee, tea… *Bourbon* he thinks, trying to keep an evil grin and a lecherous wink from muddying his ruddy face.

"No thank you," Ms. Holdsworth replies and at once he feels his facial muscles tighten. He knows her type; forceful, man-hating, thinks the world owes her because she's been oppressed all of her life by brutes like he. She has short hair (he hates that on a woman, awfully dykey) and wears little or no make-up. Nonetheless he has to admit she is very pretty but the only way he would fuck her would be short, hard, violent thrusts with her head turned away from him. He knows he couldn't stomach looking her in the eyes.

"Okay," he says pleasantly, hoping the phony smile he offers appears authentic. "What can I do for you today?"

"The President of the United States has sent me here to talk to you."

Who did you think I thought you were talking about? The President of Bumfuck Egypt? But he skillfully keeps his poker face in place.

"Yes?" At once he wonders if someone saw him at the strip club by the airport, possibly witnessed him getting blown by a blonde named Honey who tickled his asshole as he came. He does his best to keep his expression open and honest, trying very hard not to appear guilty, but a few beads of sweat gather on his forehead.

"We've come across some information the president wishes for me to discuss with you today-"

"I don't solicit strip clubs," he blurts, unable to contain himself. "People concoct rumors like that to make me out to be a pervert, but I assure you it isn't true!"

There is a moment of silence as she stares at him, mouth agape, and after twenty extremely long seconds he forces a coarse laugh.

"Kidding! Just kidding!" he says, running a shaky hand through his thinning, silver hair. "Just thought I'd infuse this meeting with a little humor…"

"Your private life has nothing to do with my visit this morning Governor Hallsly." Ms. Holdsworth's voice is curt, her eyes solemn. "I'm sure the president nor I could care less how you spend your free time when you aren't doing meet and greets with wealthy land owners and industrialists, making 'brilliant' decisions as to how to get the state of California back on track economically."

"Uh, okay…" he says, caught off guard. That's a relief. "So what is it you want?"

"We have a bigger problem, one that needs to be addressed immediately before it becomes too big to handle at all."

"I'm listening."

"A Scripts Oceanic Exploration Team disappeared a thousand miles off the coast of California while conducting research on the enormous garbage heap located in the Pacific gyre-"

"Say what now?" When in doubt, ignorance is the best policy.

"You heard me, Governor Hallsly." Her tone is icy, as cold as her grayish blue eyes. "Surely you haven't been hiding under a rock for the last decade and you know about the floating landfill."

The governor stares back at her, incensed. Of course he's heard about the island of garbage (who hasn't?) but what does it have to do with the price of whores in Bangkok? And who the hell cares about the Scripts Oceanic Exploration Team? What have they ever done for him?

"Excuse my candor, but what does this have to do with me?" he says at length. He's trying to figure out her angle but he'll be damned if he knows what it is.

"With all due respect sir," Ms. Holdsworth says, and the governor assumes she means 'with no discernable amount of respect', "this has everything to do with you. The president has chosen you to spearhead our next operation."

"Really? What are you proposing?"

"We intend to send another scientific team out there to hopefully locate and rescue the first, as well as determine how we can best eliminate the problem while doing as little harm to the environment as possible."

"And why is this California's responsibility?" He feels a wave of anger surge through him. This is the last thing he needs, this early in the morning. A good hit of scotch might make it better, but that will have to wait until lunch, brunch if he can get away early.

"Because the president says it is," she replies tartly and this silences him for a moment. He looks at her closely, trying to determine if this is a joke. That heap's been there forever. Why is this important *now?* Unless...

"Did my Daddy put you up to this?" he asks, his wet jowls gleaming under the bright fluorescent lights. This would be just like the old man, to send him a stripper disguised as someone from the White House.

"I assure you your father has nothing to do with this," she replies, extracting a card from her purse and holding it out to him. "If you doubt my credentials I suggest you call the number on here at once. I should warn you though, the president won't be very happy with you wasting my time like this."

The governor looks at the card but makes no move to take it from her outstretched hand. Her demeanor is stern and uncompromising...if she was a stripper he's pretty sure she would have given up her ruse by now.

"So let me get this straight," he says at last, tapping his fingers on his desk nervously. "The president wants me to spend California's money on an expedition to that floating trash heap because some scientists don't know how to use a GPS tracking unit?"

"Not exactly Governor Hallsly." Ms. Holdsworth's eyes meet his with an authority that is almost disturbing. "They are going to bankroll this enterprise but we need the state of California to provide the ship and research crew. You have been selected to oversee this project."

"Well, don't I feel special," Hallsly laments but the woman is silent. The two stare at one another wordlessly, a war of wills Hallsly eventually loses.

"And what does California get out of this?" he demands at last.

"What do you mean?"

"You heard me. For helping. What does California get out of this?"

"I don't think you understand the gravity of the situation governor. This isn't a request, it's an order. Besides the fact that we've potentially lost over a dozen lives-important members of the scientific community mind you-the implications of this problem are worldwide. It could do irreparable damage to the oceanic eco-system if it hasn't already, could affect our food resources for years to come, maybe even forever. If we don't do something about it now the trash heap could double in size, maybe triple..."

"For God's sake," Governor Hallsly sighs, fiddling with a pen. "You want the state of California to spring for the ship and the crew?"

"The federal government not only expects the state of California to provide the ship but also to recruit a suitable crew of disposable members of the scientific, civilian and military community."

"What?" The governor isn't sure if he heard her right. "Disposable?"

"If this second mission should encounter problems we don't want to lose anyone important," she explains, but the governor still isn't quite sure if he is on the same page.

"So who am I going to find for this, uh, 'mission' as you so eloquently put it?"

"We don't care, as long as you find people who are adequately competent. My best suggestion would be to place ads at universities looking for unpaid interns and to recruit qualified candidates from in-state military bases."

"Are you freakin' kidding me?"

"Not at all Governor Hallsly. These orders come from the president himself, I am merely the vessel for which they are being conveyed to you."

The governor leans back in his chair, mystified. What she is saying is quite clear, he just can't believe it.

"And when does this need to be done by?"

"Yesterday," she replies, standing up. "You'll be hearing from me soon governor."

"Yes Ma'am," he says. After all, he knows when he is licked. "I'll get right on it."

FIVE

'*Sponging off of someone is better than working a real job any day*'
Tyler McNellis

Tyler stands outside of the apartment building holding two battered cardboard boxes, the whole of his existence carried within. Only five minutes ago he had a roof over his head and now he has nothing but what's in the boxes and the clothes on his back. An odd feeling of ennui fills him; he's been down this road before. He survived in the past and he'll survive now, of this he is sure, he just didn't expect her to kick his ass out so soon but, what do ya know? The bitch grew a pair overnight so here he is.

He is too suave to feel anger, too self-assured to feel pathetic. The jig is up and it's time to move on, end of story. The only thing that gets him is that he didn't have time to grab any of her shit on the way out, nothing. All those wonderful kitchen appliances: the blender he so loved making his fruit smoothies in, the toaster oven that baked all his pizzas, the set of knives that chopped, sliced and diced the veggies he tossed into his salads-they are all going to sit and gather dust now that he is gone.

And today of all days. He'd wanted to watch mixed martial arts on cable this afternoon.

He sighs, turning his head into a cool oncoming breeze, smelling the air and considering his options. He can give Wes a call, see if he can flop on his couch for a couple of days while he sorts things out. Good ole Wes-the-wet-blanket, always willing to lend a helping hand.

Tyler starts down the street, adjusting the boxes every so often, hoping they are still strong enough to hold his things without bursting at the seams. These boxes have seen many moves, have been many places. Before Melissa he lived with a waitress in Portland who'd been self-conscience about her weight and had relatively low self-esteem. That had lasted eleven months, until she caught him having a three-way in the community pool with the bi-sexual chicks who lived in the apartment below them. Before her was a lawyer with cankles and bad teeth who had a nice place in Seattle. She'd been bullheaded but loved having a boy toy around. She finally kicked him out when she walked in on him screwing her Holly Maid. And before her was a woman who'd owned a clothing store in Boise. She'd been trusting and kind and generous until the day she found out he was slowly draining her bank account, spending the money on escort chicks, booze and cocaine.

And on and on. He'd been around the country at least twice, had eventually wound up in Sacramento because that was where the wind blew him. That was what he liked most about being a mooch: you never knew where it was going to take you next.

He walks until he finds a pay phone (not an easy task in this day and age) stops, sets the boxes down and takes the receiver off the cradle. Digging several lint-covered quarters from his pocket, he plugs them into the slot, feeling like a relic from another time. He's never owned a cell phone, has always used his girlfriend's phones. He's 'old school' and he likes it that way. Besides, who needs it? Tyler does his best work face to face, mono y mono.

As he listens to the phone ring he wonders briefly if Wes will take him in, deciding he probably will. Over the last seven months Tyler has played the role of 'good friend', that is, someone Wes can chum around with when the rest of the world doesn't want him. Fortunately for Tyler, Wes doesn't have any other friends, doesn't have anybody who gives a flying fuck. And that's how he likes it.

He gets Wes' machine (that dill hole must be jerkin' it to some internet porn) and leaves a message that is cool, debonair, charming. He is homeless but he can always make his situation sound romantic, daring. He has a way of making the most trivial things in life seem like complex, thrilling adventures. Tyler can make a simple trip to the super market sound like a stroll through paradise. And he knows Wes will buy it because his life is boring, useless. *People like him need people like me.* He returns the phone to its cradle and picks up the boxes. He figures he'll head over to his apartment building and loiter around outside until someone enters or exits and he can get in. After all, he is starting to get hungry and he'll need something to eat. It's getting about time for Wes to take him out to lunch, or maybe to the closest bar to grab a couple brews.

And Wes will be happy to do it, will always and forever be glad he is in the company of someone of Tyler's caliber because Wes is a loser and he needs someone like Tyler to make him feel better about himself. And all Tyler has to do is pretend he gives a crap about him and his insignificant life, his inconsequential being.

Because that is how the con works, on either sex. Make people feel good about themselves and they won't mind spending all of their dough on you, no matter how much you ask for.

But know this: All good things must come to end, so always have a back-up plan.

Tyler was a natural born hustler but he didn't really discover his 'gift' until his mid-twenties. Prior to cultivating this talent he'd attempted a life of crime and, later, worked various menial labor jobs. He'd even been married for a short period of time, long enough to sire a child, a son.

Before he'd developed his craft into a full-fledged money making enterprise he'd worked at it only half-seriously, using his abilities to lie and steal to attain things he wanted that he couldn't afford, but it was all in fun, just a way to pass the time.

He dropped out of school when he was sixteen and ran away from a substandard home, leaving behind a family he never truly felt a part of. His father was a construction worker who disdained hard labor with a passion (preferring to sit on a bar stool and talk with his cronies about the 'good old days') and his mother a tireless wench who loved to beat Jesus into her ungrateful kids. He had two siblings, a brother and a sister who seemed destined to grow up and amount to nothing and, for all he knew, that's exactly what became of them.

He took up life on the streets of Chicago and soon found himself chumming around with a much older man, a guy in his thirties by the name of Don Givardi. Don taught him the upscale trade of breaking and entering, and for a while the two were inseparable partners in crime. Don, unfortunately, suffered from a chronic addiction to painkillers and so the money they made fencing their stolen goods went mostly to drugs and alcohol, but Tyler didn't care. He loved the excitement of it all and didn't mind living on the streets, nor the feast and famine that came with their robberies, spending sprees and subsequent poverty. Moreover, he wasn't one to rest on his laurels; he loved the adrenalin rush of breaking into someone's home (be it day or night) and taking whatever they could fit into large burlap sacks. Sometimes the owners were home and they'd have to tie them up, maybe crack them on the noggin a few times to subdue them first. Other times there were dogs, and once Don cut one in half with a sword that'd been decoratively placed over an ornate mantelpiece. Tyler would never forget the sound the large mutt made when it collapsed onto the shag rug, looking at it's top half separated from its bottom before it's eyes rolled up into the whites.

Their partnership ended when at last they got caught, well, Don got caught anyway. Tyler had been quick enough to outrun the police but fat old Don never stood a chance. When the cops hauled him off Tyler watched the proceedings from a safe vantage point, and that was the last he ever saw of him. He later heard rumors that Don died in jail; he developed emphysema and wheezed himself to death in the infirmary.

After that Tyler resorted to selling drugs, but by the time he was twenty he got busted in an undercover police sting and did two and half years in prison for dealing methamphetamine. Fortunately he got caught with less than an ounce or he would have gone away for a lot longer.

When he was released he decided to sober up and make something of himself. He got a job in a foundry and met a pretty young woman at a tavern he solicited nightly. They commenced an awkward courting ritual, skipping to the chase eight months later and getting married by a Justice of the Peace because he couldn't convince her to get an abortion. They became man and wife and a month later gave birth to a son with Down Syndrome. He wanted to be angry, wanted to rub it in her face that terminating the pregnancy would have been a mercy killing in this case, but he wasn't that cold hearted. After all he loved her (what passed for love to Tyler, that is) and he guessed he loved his son. He wasn't sure.

So life went on by and he supposed he was somewhat happy, but in the back of his mind he knew something was missing: danger, excitement, the rush of living only one moment ahead in time. Gradually he became aware that the trappings of marriage and fatherhood weren't for him. The stability was mind numbingly boring. In his increasing angst he realized he had to make a change or else he was going to lose it, was going to do something he might later regret. Having limited options, he decided to start a house painting business, figuring that being his own boss would improve his frame of mind, allowing him more time away from his family to blow off steam. Besides, what idiot couldn't slap on a few coats of paint? It sounded like a breeze. And maybe that way, he rationalized, his home life wouldn't seem so tedious. He printed up business cards and flyers and after a few successful jobs it grew quickly, the demand for his services unexpected in what could best be described as a slack economy. Soon he was working more hours than he'd been when he was at the foundry and he again became frustrated, having too little time for himself. But the money was rolling in so, instead of hiring more help, he chose to take it all on himself, over-charging for deliberately slapdash work and getting a kick out of acting like an asshole in the meantime. And for a while this scratched his itch, this unscrupulousness, as well as bringing in a nice haul to boot, but it didn't last long.

In less than a year several clients were suing him for windows that were calked shut and paint jobs that were peeling after only one winter season. The court costs alone were killing him (not to mention the steady flow of doctor bills the kid piled on them, being sickly and all) and suddenly Tyler's bank account was empty, his business in ruin, at the end of his patience. In a flash of inspired brilliance he decided to simply take off, to disappear. He hated doing that to his wife, leaving her saddled with raising the 'tard and having to face all those debt collectors, but he was more in tune with his own sense of self-satisfaction than hers so he simply broke loose. As far as he knew his wife never discovered what happened to him. One night they went to bed together and the next morning she awoke and he was gone. He'd stashed some money away (not much, only a few thousand dollars), but he decided it was enough to start a new life so he'd left everything behind, his clothes, possessions, everything. It was easier that way and he wanted to start with a clean slate. He figured his belongings would remind him of her and the life they'd had together, and when all was said and done it was a period of time he wanted to forget. Fuck her, fuck the retard. For all she knew maybe he'd been kidnapped by a Mexican drug cartel or abducted by aliens…who knew? Who cared? Not him. Once he cleared the threshold they were no longer a part of his thinking process, no longer took up any space in his tiny, scheming brain.

The last thought he entertained on their behalf was his supposition that the government would take care of them, offer them food stamps and shit, making sure they had a roof over their heads and what have you. I mean, they wouldn't just let her become homeless would they? Not in America. Sure, they'd struggle a bit, like the health care might not be so great and the boy might suffer but what the hell, it wasn't like he was going to live very long anyway, the doctor's said so themselves. Soon enough he would no longer be her problem, and after that she'd be free to do whatever she wanted. So it wasn't entirely bad, this decision of his and, anyway, they'd never find him. For all practical purposes he vanished right into thin air, slipping completely off the grid.

Thus began his mooching ways. His first con he pulled on a woman in her late forties who'd inherited a large sum of money from her parents. He met her in a bar in Tomahawk, Wisconsin. How he got there was a long story, suffice it to say that it involved some questionable characters he'd met in Rockford, Illinois and a bank job that didn't go quite as planned.

He wined and dined the older woman becoming, essentially, her sex slave, and was invited to move in with her, all expenses paid. This lasted about six months, until she caught him trying to have sex with her teenage daughter, who wasn't exactly saying 'no'.

And so forth commenced a long list of women who supported his lazy ass, and to his ever-lasting pride he'd avoided the work world for many years running, fading anonymously into the outer fringes of society. Because he didn't work he didn't need his social security number, and he changed his name often, only using his real moniker when he had to flash his ID card for some reason or another. With each new 'relationship' he became someone else, inventing a past that suited each situation, tailor made for each lady. And what the hell, he never knew how long any of the affairs would last, never had any idea what it was that would ultimately break them up (although he could make an educated guess), but he knew their ending was as eventual as the tides and every new day was very possibly his last.

This was the case all the way up until today, when the latest in a long line of gullible chicks tossed him out onto the street. And, once again, here he was.

But one thing he'd be hard pressed to admit, a fact that was very slowly growing within him subconsciously (for he wasn't entirely aware of it at first, thinking her to be just like all the others) was that he actually *missed* Melissa. Never before had he felt this way. Never. Not even for his wife and child, and he'd fucked them over worse than anyone.

You see, that was the game for the true hustler, the ultimate conman. To know when you were bested and to walk away. He never groveled, never begged. When something was over it was over and he moved on to the next game, the next rube.

Yet there was something in him (again, very dim, so far undiscovered) that missed the dominatrix and wanted her back. A weakness inside of him that was willing to eat crow, to beg, to offer apologies. And this was simply not in his nature, unless it was the beginning of another ruse, one in which he intended to get as much as he could before he cut and run. Maybe it was that of all the women she had been the youngest, the most beautiful. Finding a good-looking woman to support you (even though he was quite handsome) was a daunting task. He'd mostly exploited older, fatter, uglier broads. Hell, he'd even told Melissa his real name, something he'd *never* done previously.

These thoughts, unclear, undefined, were flitting about in his brain under the radar, and he would only become aware of them by and by. ,

"She's a fucking bitch," Wes is saying as he stuffs a handful of peanuts in his mouth. "Just forget about her."

"Aren't you listening?" Tyler drains the last of his beer and refills the mug from the pitcher. "I have forgotten about her. She's nothing to me."

Wes shrugs, taking a sip of his beer. He hates to contradict his friend but all he's been talking about for the last hour is Melissa. Everything is 'Melissa this' and 'Melissa that'. He is getting totally sick of hearing about her. He figures if he says what Tyler wants to hear maybe he will move on to another topic.

Not that he doesn't feel his buddy's pain, hell, the chick was one hot tamale. Wes knows he can never score a babe like that, money or not. Her long black hair tickling his stomach as her plump, red lips encase his member has long been a masturbatory fantasy of his, and he can't help but think what an idiot Tyler is for not at least pretending to comply with some of her demands. But Tyler thinks he is 'God's gift', so the idea of meeting her terms simply wasn't an option.

Tyler empties the pitcher into his glass, shaking it to get every last drop.

"Looks like we need some more beer dude," he says and feels a certain satisfaction as Wes merely nods, extracting his wallet from his back pocket and waving for their server. She arrives a few minutes later, her long blonde bangs hanging in her face, her make-up barely concealing the problem acne that torments her.

"Another of the same?" she asks and Tyler nods.

"And a couple menu's. I need some food in me if I'm going to keep drinking." He says this to Wes, who bobs his head in agreement.

"Sure," Wes concurs, but he is starting to wonder why he puts up with this shit.

Thing is, Wes is a generous guy to a fault, but Tyler has never offered to pay for anything, like, ever. It's like he sincerely believes Wes has to pay a toll to hang out with him, and this is really starting to bother him. It's not like he doesn't have any other friend's...okay, maybe that's not true. He doesn't have any other friends. But it's not because he is totally unlikable, it's just that he doesn't try. He really doesn't have the time, being as busy as he is between his job and his hobbies. His hobbies, of course, are of no importance to anyone but him, but that doesn't make them any less of an achievement as far as he is concerned. To some people the building and collecting of model airplanes and ships is a very significant and rewarding endeavor. Tyler has never asked him about his collection but that shouldn't come as any surprise because all Tyler cares about is himself. And Tyler doesn't have any hobbies; he simply exists to mooch and lie around, tending to his good looks.

The beer and the menu's arrive and Tyler drains his glass again.

"I'll take a double cheeseburger extra onions hold the tomatoes," he says without even glancing at the menu. The waitress rolls her eyes. Why the hell would he bother to ask for a menu if he already knows what he wants? "What do you want buddy?" Tyler asks Wes, as if he is the one who is paying for it and not the other way around, and Wes suppresses the urge to roll his eyes as well. Sometimes Tyler can be such a *douche.*

But instead he says: "I'll take the same please. Hold the onions."

SIX

'Life can best be described as a happy accident, so make the most of it.'
Leeann Vanhorn

Floating on her back on top of a rented boogie board, Leeann looks up at the dazzling sapphire sky and wonders how she'll ever be able to leave this paradise and summon the motivation to finish the semester after all of this unadulterated fun. Last night she bungee jumped for the first time in her life and, if that wasn't enough stimulation, she also rode a mechanical bull. She doesn't normally drink very much but over the course of this vacation she has become quite the lush, enjoying tequila shots, Jello shooters and Mexican beer as if they're going out of style. Not that she is very concerned; she knows she isn't going to become, like, an alcoholic or something.

The warm salt water of the gulf helps her hangover, helps restore clarity to her booze-addled mind. Next to her floats her friend Stacy, the one whose idea this trip had been, also the one who'd suggested they get the money for it by doing a pharmaceutical study.

"Aren't you glad you listened to me?" Stacy asks, spitting water into the air and closing her eyes as it splashes down on her face.

"Yup," Leeann says, giggling at her friend's antics.

"So are you really going to go out with that guy? The one you met in Pharmacoastalcal?"

"I don't know," Leeann says thoughtfully. "Maybe."

"He's kind of a goon."

"I guess."

"I mean, what the hell do you see in him?"

Good question. Leeann calls up Dante's image in her mind, his hulking form, his bushy beard and hard-boiled egg eyes. She guesses that the thing she likes about him is, when he wasn't being serious, he made her laugh a lot. She likes someone who can make her smile, and his oddball sense of humor made her day more than once. Besides, looks aren't everything, right? Personality is always a big plus.

"I asked you a question," Stacy says, splashing water at her.

"And I was thinking of an answer," Leeann laughs, splashing her back.

"Took you long enough." Stacy rolls off of her boogie board and submerges herself in the temperate water. "So what is it?"

"He's funny."

"I'll say. Funniest looking guy I've ever seen."

"I don't mean that you goof!" Leeann splashes water at Stacy again but her friend ducks under the surface just in time. When she comes up Leeann decides to clarify:

"He makes me laugh," she confides. "He has a very interesting way of looking at the world."

"If I looked like that I suppose I would too."

"That's not very nice."

"Who said I was nice?" Stacy says haughtily, climbing back onto her board. "We should probably head back in, I'm getting hungry."

"Me too," Leeann agrees and they paddle toward shore.

Growing up practically on the border of Louisiana, it was hard for Leeann to feel like a true Texan; mostly she felt like a product of the south in general. But her parent's choice of name guaranteed she would always be associated with the Lone Star State, for better or worse, not to mention her family tree included an abundance of cowboys, ranch hands, gunslingers and deserters of the Confederate army. Yet she felt more like a kindred spirit to the Louisiana swampland than to the dust-swept plains, preferring to immerse herself in the wetlands and their unique life forms.

Unlike Dante, her childhood had been a happy, sheltered one. Her parents were middle class, hard working, decent folks who aspired to give their children the very best they could. She had two siblings, a brother and sister. Her brother (true to his Texas heritage) wore tight Wranglers and cowboy boots and went line dancing every Friday night at a local honky tonk. By day he was a used car salesman and had never lived outside of Corpus Christi. Her sister had been too good for their Podunk town and had escaped to New York as soon as she graduated high school, having enrolled and been accepted at NYU. She was studying film and dating a guy with a goatee and beret who made (according to her) 'experimental art films'. Leeann knew what that meant, having taken a film course to satisfy an art requirement: grainy, black and white 8MM films that had no discernable plot with characters who brooded and smoked a lot of cigarettes.

Leeann knew she could never be a city girl, could never find true contentment living in a carbon monoxide world of concrete like her sister. And her sister, as she quickly found out, couldn't stand the dreariness and boredom of living in what she called 'the sticks'. Different strokes for different folks, so it goes.

Leeann's interests were more in tune with the earth, or, more so, the creatures that inhabited it. As far back as she remembered her favorite thing to do had been to spend her time down by a small pond about a half-mile from their house, watching the frogs, insects, birds, snakes and squirrels go about their business. In the late spring the frogs would spawn their tadpoles, and Leeann would look on in amazement at the thick clumps of squirming life, reaching in to feel them wriggle between her fingers. She was always very careful though, as she didn't want to disturb them, she merely wanted to feel the life that pulsed within them.

Sitting next to that pond, the sky enormous overhead, watching wisps of clouds floating by and creating shapes she made out to be horses and piglets and bunnies, she was happier than any other time she could recall. This was her special place, and she loved the solitude and the quiet, with only the sounds of the wildlife around her.

Her brother would sometimes join her down by the pond, but he would infuriate her because all he wanted to do was throw rocks at the frogs and catch them, maybe poke their guts out with a stick. She would forever be chastising him, running after the little boy as he kept just a few feet ahead of her, laughing as he plundered the wilderness for his own pleasure.

And sometimes she would cry, looking at the broken bodies of the frogs, the crushed bird's nests and the broken eggs. She would sit there and cry because it was all so beautiful and her brutish brother just wanted to destroy it, wanted to kill everything in sight so as to feel superior. She loved her sibling but she hated him for this, hated that he could so willingly kill things that were smaller and (supposedly) less important than he was. It made Leeann appreciate her sister's indifference.

Because of these traits Leeann wasn't the most popular girl in school, that and because she was somewhat a tomboy. While the other girls wanted to wear make-up and get their ears pierced she was busy worrying about the creatures in the pond, animals on the extinction list, the melting polar caps, and the poor besieged whales off the Alaskan coast. While her peers were playing with Barbie's she was off in her own fantasyland where she lived in a log cabin and ate food from her garden and planted flowers in the spring and weaved baskets to hold the flowers. Unfortunately, poor Leeann didn't have many friends.

As soon as her parents were ready to accept her decision and provide the required sustenance, she became a vegetarian. She simply couldn't stand the thought of eating anything that had walked (or crawled or swam or slithered or flew) on this planet, enjoying as best it could it's own existence. This was another life choice that made her unpopular with the kids her age.

By high school she was openly scorned and laughed at by the trendy kids because of her lackadaisical notions of fashion (or simply her complete disregard thereof). While they were all busy trying to look, act and talk like one another Leeann was consumed by the all burning passion to simply live life as best she could, to be the best person Mother Nature could expect her to be. She was unconcerned by her peers taunts, undaunted by the fact that she missed a lot of birthday parties, wasn't invited out to movies or to go bowling. She figured they were just another strange life form (a rather arrogant and stupid life form) that would eventually evolve.

The boys liked her though, that is, they were attracted to her ample bosom, her curly, silky, red hair and the adorable spattering of freckles that covered her cheeks, although not many were brave enough to really get to know her unless they wanted to be ridiculed as well. There were many who pined for her at a distance, although they made fun of her openly to their friends.

And just like that, high school passed and Leeann enrolled and was accepted at the University of California at San Diego. Her parents had wanted her to stay in state, urging her to attend the University of Texas in Austin, but San Diego had a better biology program, and she wanted to minor in oceanography. What better place than one residing by the sea?

So it was in San Diego that she truly came into her own, and was where she found out her intelligence and sensitivity toward the planet was a good thing and not something others would harass her for. In college she made many friends, girls and guys who were like her with a love of science and the environment. Sure, there were plenty of girls like the ones in high school, shallow beauty queens with unrealistic and exaggerated opinions of themselves. The sorority houses were full of them. Leeann looked down on them just as much as they no doubt looked down on her, these mindless, conformist drones who segued from the high school clique and into the college clique with hardly any interruption, with barely a ripple on the surface of the pond, so to speak. And the frat houses were full of guys who wanted to date these high and mighty trust fund princesses, and that was just fine with Leeann.

After two semesters she decided to switch her major from general biology to marine biology; living along the Pacific gave her a new admiration for the mysteries of the deep and the creatures that lived within. Also, she'd come to love San Diego and could easily see it as her permanent home. While she'd been happy in East Texas, it was nothing compared to the beauty and splendor of this seaside city, with mild temperatures year round and flowers and fauna so stunning they made her weep with joy. This decision made, she excelled; the only subjects that had given her any trouble were some of the required courses, the math and art classes, and for these she'd gotten help from some of her friends so she could make passing grades. Otherwise her science courses had been a breeze, with the exception of a biology course in which she'd been required to dissect animals. She hadn't wanted to but, in order to pass, she was required to do so. The only solace was that the creatures were already dead.

And now, only a few months away from graduation, she'd maintained an excellent GPA and was excited at the prospect of finding work in her field. She had no idea what the future would bring but was simply glad she had the training to do what she loved, that she had persevered and now life was whatever she wanted to make of it.

"These are, like, the best road kill tacos I've ever had," Stacy says, swallowing a bite and chasing it with a swig of Corona.

Leeann makes a face at her friend's terminology but has to agree with her: the food is really good.

They are sitting on stools at a roadside taco stand while a warm breeze blows over them, the sun high in the sky promising another gorgeous day. It hasn't rained once in the duration of their trip (hasn't even been more than a spattering of clouds on any given day) and again Leeann feels a sort of magical wonder, the kind of sensation one gets when they are on a trip 'away from it all' and your real life seems so far removed as to be nothing but a vague memory, something that will only become tangible once you are back in it, bustling through the everyday grind.

Yet, Leeann's life isn't truly a grind; it's just that she needed a break, a change of pace. She supposes the brief inpatient stay at Pharmacoastalcal could be considered a diversion, but it was nothing like this.

"So what are you guys going to do when you go out?"

"What?" she asks, for a moment having no idea what Stay is talking about.

"You and that sasquatch from Pharmacoastalcal. What are you two going to do when he asks you out?"

"I have no idea."

"So you are going to go out with him?"

"Why the hell is this so important to you?" Leeann demands, maybe with a little more force than she means to. She eats the last of her taco and swallows the last of her beer.

"Whoa, someone sure is defensive," Stacy says, but her voice is light, her eyes smiling. "I just think you can do better than him is all."

"What, and go out with some skateboarder or punk rock guy like you?" Leeann retorts, smiling back. Stacy, as she has found over the years, likes 'bad boys' who listen to noisy music and drink Old Milwaukee straight from the can. These guys usually have green Mohawks and don't own cars, preferring to travel around on skateboards or motorcycles.

"Is there something wrong with my choice of guys?" Stacy asks, finishing her beer and standing up.

"Nope," Leeann says, getting up as well. "As long as there is nothing wrong with the guys I choose."

"He's just, well, I think…you can find someone, uh, better looking, ya know?"

For the zillionth time Leeann does think about it, pictures Dante in her mind, the bushy beard, the long, wavy, unruly hair.

"Not to sound conceited or anything," Leeann concurs, fishing a couple bucks out of her purse and throwing them on the counter. "But I think you're right. I think I could find a better looking guy."

"Than why don't you?"

"Maybe I really don't care that much. Maybe I'm not shallow and superficial like you are."

"Dating a guy with a pierced septum and a tattoo of a dragon on his face is being 'superficial'?"

"You might have me there," Leeann laughs as they stroll back toward the hotel where the thought of an afternoon nap seems very appealing. It's going to be another long night and who knows what new wonders San Padre Island is going to dish up. They've been to most of the watering holes on the strip; tonight might be the night for a cookout on the beach, maybe a late night swim.

"Let's not talk about it anymore," Leeann suggests, looping her arm through her friend's. "Let's just enjoy our vacation and not think about our real lives, huh?"

"Deal," Stacy says as the two of them negotiate the traffic and cross the street toward their hotel.

SEVEN

'Crushing skulls has always been a favorite pastime of mine'
Kenny Howard

Slouching on his barstool, Kenny downs a double Jack and Coke and waves to the barkeep for another. It's his fifth drink but he hardly feels it; weighing in at over two hundred and eighty pounds it takes a lot of liquor to get him buzzed. And, besides, he had a large breakfast this morning, which was about thirty minutes ago.

"Another double?" the bartender asks and Kenny nods. "Man, you can really put 'em away," he comments and the ex-pro football defensive end scowls. If he wanted the other's opinion he'd beat it out of him.

"Just pour," he says, "and don't go bein' stingy on me."

This is just another day in the life for Kenny. He'd like to say he is drowning his sorrows but he isn't that kind of guy, you know, touchy feely. He prides himself in being pretty damn even-keel. He rarely expresses any other emotions than anger, rage, hostility or dull insincerity. He once knew what it was like to feel happiness, but those days are long gone.

The door of the darkly lit pub opens and for a moment a beam of light brightens the dim interior. Kenny reaches up to shield his eyes but seconds later the door closes and it passes. Instead he uses the hand to reach for the drink the bartender wisely poured and presented quickly, keeping his stupid yap shut lest the big brute gets angry...well, angrier. Draining most of it in a swallow he sighs, wipes his mouth and slumps further into himself.

"Hey big guy, can I buy you a drink?" someone says and for one crazy moment Kenny thinks some homo is coming on to him. He swivels around, ready to pop this fairy in the mouth when he sees it's his buddy Hank, a hard drinking, crazy son of a bitch who can never say no to a good time.

"Why shit, Hank, sure," Kenny says, managing a taut smile. "I'm ready for another one any-time."

Hank takes a seat next to him, extracting a fat wad of bills from his front pocket and tossing it on the bar. Hank made his money the old-fashioned, all-American way: he faked severe injuries when involved in a minor fender-bender and extorted the other driver (who was driving a Mercedes) for over three hundred thousand dollars. Fraud had always been a specialty of his.

"Two of whatever he's having," he says and the bartender nods.

"You got it."

Moments later Kenny has a fresh drink and his buddy has his and they toast to the new day.

"Here's to never drawing another sober breath again," Hank says.

"Here, here," Kenny replies, taking a long pull and setting the glass down. "So what ya up to?"

"Woke up with some crazy broad passed out on top of me, pushed her off so I could blow chunks and then I wound up here. You?"

"Somethin' like that," Kenny lies and Hank grins.

Truth is, Kenny hasn't been with a 'real' woman in so long he almost can't remember what it feels like. Sure, he's had a few prostitutes, but he doesn't trust their 'hygiene' standards enough to fuck them, just lets them blow him (if their mouth appears free of cold sores) or give him a hand job (if not) and he never, *ever* takes them home. It's been a long time since he's had a woman over at his place, and it's a damn good thing too because if any decent lady saw the hell hole he called home they'd probably run screaming, after they puked their guts out, of course. Kenny isn't what you'd call a real homemaker.

The two sit in silence, drinking their drinks, watching the TV. Dr. Phillip is discussing teen pregnancy with two young girls with pierced tongues and garish make-up, both looking ready drop their cargo any second.

"We should have some music," Hank says at last, getting off his barstool and walking over to the juke. "What do you want to hear Ken? Some of that jungle music you black dudes dig so much?"

Kenny smiles at the racist remark because with Hank it isn't meant to be malicious. It's a term of endearment.

"Surprise me."

Hank feeds the machine a couple dollars and soon the twangy strains of Cletus Black fill the room.

"You couldn't a picked somethin' classic like Dr. Dresden, maybe 30 Cent?" Kenny grins and his drinking buddy smiles back.

"Can't stand that jungle shit this early in the morning. After a few drinks maybe."

"Then lets get us another round. Barkeep! Another two doubles!"

Kenny used to be somebody, and it's for this reason he lives everyday like it's his last. Hell, he wishes it would be his last.

He used to play football for the Green Bay Packers, but that was before he shattered his left knee, ending his career during a playoff game that should have taken Green Bay to the Superbowl. Instead they lost to the fucking Chicago Bears while Kenny was carted off to the hospital. Lying in the hospital bed, he knew without being told that his contract would be terminated. Hell, a team of surgeons from the best hospital in the Midwest, the Mayo Clinic (flown in from

Minneapolis), told him he would be lucky not to walk with a limp for the rest of his life, much less play football. It was in that bed, watching Wheel of Fortune on the overhead TV, that something in Kenny died, just simply shriveled up and disappeared. A strong, capable, content man entered the hospital, and an angry, depressed, bitter man walked (with the aid of crutches) out. Maybe it would have been a little easier if he had a wife and children, but he'd never married, just kept an endless string of girlfriends who never lasted longer than a few months. Besides his football career, he had nothing.

Kenny grew up in a small town outside of Green Bay, Wisconsin called Crivitz. And to call it small was surely being kind; it was an unincorporated burg with a main street running down the middle lined by a bank, a store, a gas station, a saloon and a church. It made Green Bay look like a thriving metropolis.

He was born big, the biggest baby ever on record at St. Vincent Hospital on Webster Ave., and his mama was awful proud. She loved all her children dearly but to her Kenny was special, destined to do great things. The young boy basked in the glow of her affection, soaking up her love like a sponge, which she smothered him with from day one.

Kenny never got a chance to get to know his father very well because his old man practically worked day and night, and then he was killed when Kenny was only eight years old, in an accident at the paper mill he'd given some of the best years of his life to. It was with great sorrow that they laid Reginald Howard to rest in Crivitz's lone cemetery, on an atypically sunny Sunday in late autumn. All his friends came (owing to the Packer's having a very poor season that year) and Imogene greeted them all with open arms.

Eventually the company paid out a generous sum to the Howard's because the accident was the fault of defective machinery, so Imogene was able to keep them all in food and diapers without having to take a second job. Times was still hard, but at least the bank wasn't going to take the damn house.

What Kenny remembered of his Daddy was that he was always trying to make everybody laugh, even though his life surely wasn't no picnic. He busted his ass to make sure they had food on the table and a roof over their heads and yet he constantly had a smile flitting on his lips, a joke at the ready. He'd tell his jokes at the dinner table and goose Kenny in the ribs with his thumb, trying to get him to laugh along with him, but Kenny took after his mother in that he took things maybe a little bit too seriously. Reginald would get him laughing eventually though, even if it meant tickling him under the armpits or on the soles of his feet. Yep, his Pops had been a good man, honest and cheerful even though they were always on the verge of poverty. That's what he'd always remember about him.

Back in the day, the term 'minority' still applied to African American families living in the Green Bay area. While Milwaukee to the south was without a doubt a racially mixed urban center, Green Bay (Crivitz especially) wasn't a very ethnically diverse city in the early 1990's, the majority of the populace being white, of French and Dutch origin, mostly Catholic. They did, however, have a growing Asian population (much to the chagrin of the hardcore white supremacists) and plenty of Native American residents who populated the many nearby reservations.

Be that as it may, Imogene Howard's parents had lived in the area for over seventy years, having relocated from Chicago in 1946, shortly before she was born. Her father loved football (yet for some reason detested the Bears) so she was raised to be a rabid Green Bay Packer fan. They'd make the pilgrimage to Lambeau Field at least three or four times yearly to watch their beloved team, even though they were so poor they had to watch from outside the fence. Reginald worked as a groundskeeper at Lambeau and that's how he and Imogene met, sneaking glances at one another that eventually became kisses.

When Kenny was born Imogene knew in her heart that her son would grow up to be a pro football player because of his size, in fact, wanted it for him more than anything in the world. She was such a zealous fan that, given a choice, she'd rather give birth in the bleachers of Lambeau field rather than go to the hospital if the Packers were in the playoffs. Hell, she'd chew through the umbilical cord with her teeth and wash the taste out of her mouth with a cold beer if that's what it took. Luckily that wasn't the case when Kenny came into the world, for obvious reasons regarding sanitation and what not.

Kenny was bigger than the other kids his age so he never worried about the usual stuff while growing up, like bullies and racial prejudice. When he was in third grade he was larger than most sixth graders. Even the high school kids didn't pick on him.

Imogene liked to boast proudly that she didn't raise no morons but, truth be told, she most certainly had. She had six other kids, four girls and two boys, and of the four girls there wasn't a one of them who hadn't been knocked up by the time they were seventeen. All four dropped out of school and married the respective fathers; farmer's kids all. Fortunately none of her daughters were worldly enough to desire travel or education, so they weren't entirely unhappy. And Imogene was just glad they were out of the house and out of her hair. Money was tight enough as it was.

Kenny's two brothers were large boys as well, but he towered and lorded over them. Kenny inherited the brains of the bunch (which wasn't saying much as his brothers were such dumb-asses) and so he knew how to play them against each other. One of his favorite pastimes was watching his younger brothers fight, usually over something that Kenny rumored one of them to have said about the other. Boy could those two scrap. Between the two of them they had their share of broken bones, much to Imogene's vexation, as she barely had the means to pay for it. In fact, unbeknownst to her children, she traded sexual favors for medical treatment when she could (there were several doctors in town who were bachelors or unhappily married) and one thing about Imogene: she was strikingly beautiful and could give a mean blowjob when she took her dentures out.

Sometimes Kenny would take on both his brothers at once, when he was in the mood, but he never hurt them too bad. He left that for them to do to each other.

And they loved him, the two numbskulls, loved him fiercely.

Kenny wasn't much for learnin', and not because of a mental deficiency but because it held no interest to him. History, science, math...none of it concerned him in the slightest but he stuck with it anyhow, preferring it to hard labor. By the time he was in eighth grade his football coach (and his mother) had thoroughly drilled it in his head that all he had to do was coast through school and he could go to any college he wanted, as long as they had a decent football team.

Kenny'd picked up the sport in fifth grade and, because he was bigger and stronger than everybody else, loved it immensely. There was nothing quite like the feel of shoving someone out of your way and knocking them to the ground all in the name of fair play.

He made the varsity squad in high school and because of his status as a star athlete he had his pick of cheerleaders. He wasn't exactly handsome but he wasn't unattractive, hadn't been smacked with the ugly stick that'd so unkindly swatted his brothers, so the sports affiliation definitely helped him get dates. A part of it too was that he was one of very few black kids in his school. He was looked upon as a novelty. He lost his virginity when he was sixteen to a white girl he virtually dwarfed. She was four foot seven to his six foot six, proving that opposites really *do* attract.

He received a sports scholarship to the University of Nebraska and played with the Cornhuskers all four years. Lucky for him the coach hired a tutor to help him with his homework or he would have been on academic suspension from the get go. After four years of collegiate excellence on the field he was fortunate enough to be drafted by the Green Bay Packers in 2013. His mama was so proud she cried like a schoolgirl at the ceremony.

And life was great. For three years he had it all: fast cars, girls, money, fame...nothing could spoil what he'd achieved.

Well, almost nothing. Since the beginning of his professional career he'd been plagued by injuries. Nothing really serious, but he never played a whole season all the way through. His first year it was a groin pull in the eighth game, his second a hamstring injury that benched him right before the playoffs. It was in his third season (one in which he'd really made a name for himself because of his excellent ability at stripping the ball from opposing players) that he sustained the injury that would take him out of the game forever. During a Divisional Playoff game against archrival The Chicago Bears, while trying desperately to get at the quarterback, the ball got loose and he dove for it, scooping it up and hoping to make a game saving play that would take them to the Superbowl. He made it about five yards before a Bears offensive lineman threw himself at his legs with surprising force, his helmet crashing dead center into Kenny's left knee. A jarring bolt of pain shot through him with a nauseating crunch and his leg bent backward at an impossible angle. He crumpled to the ground, still clutching the ball tightly in both hands, when the weight of nearly a dozen bodies crashed down on him like Dorothy and Toto's house, and as he lay there on the field, feeling like he'd been hit by a freight train, he knew it was serious this time. The crowd noise had dimmed; all he could hear was the blood rushing through his body, the beating of his heart. His memory of being put on the cart and taken off the field was vague, a gray area. The next thing he knew he was lying in a hospital bed, staring up at a TV on the wall, eating tasteless pudding and shitting into a bedpan.

His mood became so sour he hardly acknowledged the visitors who came to pay their respects, just waved them away. The only visit he paid any attention to was from his coach, and he'd known from the look on the man's face that it wasn't merely a social call, no, this was strictly business.

"From what the doctor's say," his coach had said, avoiding looking him in the eyes, his gaze somewhere over his left shoulder, "you'll never play again."

"What the fuck do they know?" Kenny'd growled, feeling a bottomless anger well up inside him.

"Yeah, well, management doesn't want to take that chance."

"What are you saying?"

And that was when the coach finally did look him in the eyes.

"We're going to terminate your contract."

"Just like that," Kenny said flatly, looking away, his face flush with rage.

"This decision wasn't made overnight Kenny," the coach argued. "We think it's in the team's best interest."

"I'm sure you do."

"I'm sorry." And the coach got up and that was the last visit he ever paid. Many well-wishers came to see him, his teammates, girlfriends, his family, but Kenny was sullen, withdrawn. He rarely talked and, when he did, it was with vehemence that he spewed forth his opinions of the General Manager, the owner and his coach. After a while people stopped coming to see him, except his mama and his siblings, and even they didn't stay very long.

When he got out of the hospital and returned to his home on the outskirts of Green Bay he became a hermit, allowing very few people into his world. He hired a couple of personal trainers (ex-Marines for Christ's sake) with the idea of getting back into shape and showing the Packers he could make a comeback, that he could overcome his injuries and play again, but the damage he'd suffered was too severe. He soon found the doctors had been right. He couldn't move like he used to, and his walking was hampered by a limp. When the weather was cold or damp, which was often in Wisconsin, his knee ached excruciatingly and he had to use a cane.

So he'd put his house on the market and moved to California, figuring the climate to be more suitable to his recovery, and he settled in San Diego because of its consistently temperate climate. But the damage he'd sustained was too great, and even though he could eventually walk unassisted by a cane it became clear that he was never going to play football again, like it or not. It was with this realization that he suddenly wanted nothing more than to just disappear, his shame was so great. He got angry and frustrated whenever someone recognized him and asked for an autograph, and occasionally violent altercations ensued, eliciting unwanted publicity and more than a few lawsuits. And it wasn't long after his move that he discovered his funds were dwindling, owing to his frivolous spending during his short career. Inevitably he was going to have to look for a job. This was met with deep depression, for he had no idea what he was going to do. During his college years he hadn't paid attention to anything other than football and girls; he couldn't even recall what he majored in.

When at last it came time to enter the working world again, he found employment as a body-guard. One of his old teammates helped out by recommending him to an LA based firm who handled upscale clients in Los Angeles and San Diego. So for about six months he did security for various celebrities and rock stars, traveling with them in their limo's and accompanying them to clubs, social functions, Grammy Award shows, concerts, movie sets and the like, but his demeanor was so icy he never made friends with anyone, not even Jonathon Deep, who'd tried to get to know him because he was a football fan. It made no difference to him. And time, as it was wont to do, passed by, yet he was still unhappy. The money was good but after a while he got sick of the job because he was still publicly visible, occasionally getting caught on camera while accompanying the various celebrities. He needed to work but he didn't want something so high profile. So he talked with his supervisor and, because of his excellent work record and conduct (as well as pass-ing an extensive background check that proved he was squeaky clean and not in any way a threat to those in political office) was given a job doing security for the governor of California, which included not only Cali's Main Man but other key staff members as well. Taking this position required that he move to Sacramento, which he did without complaint. And it went well for a while, as there was very little public pressure put on him, at least none that mattered. People didn't hound politicians (at least, not in a good way) like they did movie and music personalities. In fact, eventually, people were beginning to forget about him, which suited him fine.

It was during this time that he started slipping. What no one knew, not even his family, was that since his injury he'd become addicted to pain killers. On top of that, he was also a heavy drinker. Eventually the opiates, in combination with the booze, gave him away and shoddy work performance forced his employer to let him go. Fired again, his disposition sunk even lower.

Good thing for him the security positions had paid exceptionally well and he'd been smart enough to sock a lot of it away, enough to live on for a while if he was frugal about it. And that was where he was at, his football career long behind him, his personal life nonexistent (except for his friendship with Hank), growing increasingly alienated and lonely, spending his days in dive bars getting trashed. Oh how the mighty can fall.

"You gonna eat that?" Hanks asks him and Kenny looks at the congealed remains of a Philly cheese steak sandwich for a moment before shaking his head. Hank scoops it up and devours it in a matter of seconds.

"Jesus Christ, it's like feedin' time at the zoo," Kenny says and his friend smiles through a mouthful of food.

"Almost," he replies, barely articulate through the bread, meat and cheese, "except the animals have better manners than I do."

"Damn straight," Kenny agrees, pushing his plate away from him and looking out the window at the overcast day.

When Hank is done chewing he takes a drink of his water, wipes his mouth and looks at his friend speculatively.

"Ya know, we've only been friends for about a couple months, but even I can tell you look gloomier than usual," Hank observes, unafraid to say whatever is on his mind. Thing is, Kenny has always needed someone in his life who can tell him how it is-how it *really* is. When he was a celebrity he was surrounded by 'yes men' who told him exactly what he wanted to hear, and he liked that. But he always had a friend (at one point it was his mother) who cut through the bullshit and fed it to him straight. Kenny felt it helped his perspective, helped to keep him from looking at the world entirely through rose-colored glasses. So he allowed Hank to be that person. Hell, at this point, Hank was his only friend.

"Sometimes everythin' just seems so fuckin' hopeless Hank," Kenny says, fidgeting with his napkin. "Some days I wish I could just forget about everythin' I had. When I think about all I lost I…I, shit man, I don't know. It just don't seem fair."

"Life ain't fair," Hank says, looking at him earnestly. "You gotta keep that in mind at all times."

"Yer damn tootin'." He pauses, sighing grandiosely. "Ya ever feel like ya just wanna get the hell outta Dodge, just up and split?"

"Of course, who doesn't?"

"Yeah?"

"Yeah."

The two are silent for a moment, Kenny studying his fingernails for accumulated grime, the other picking at the remnants of bread crust.

"So where would you go if you could go anyplace in the world?" Hank asks at last, feeling his pockets for a smoke, even though he knows he can't smoke in the restaurant. "And what would you do once you got there?"

Kenny thinks about it, *really* gives it some thought, and it is no surprise to him that his mind is blank.

"I got no idea man," he says, attempting a half-smile. "I got abso-fuckin'-lutely no idea."

"Sounds great," Hank says, tucking a cigarette between his lips. "Can I come too?"

EIGHT

'Some people look for trouble, but somehow it always finds me'
Dave Zimmerman

"Can't this thing go any faster?" Travis bellows over the wind blasting in his face and when the driver smiles back at him (a look just this side of certifiable) he almost regrets he said anything. Maybe he should have been happy with the 120 MPH they were currently holding.

Dave pushes down on the gas pedal and the Porsche Carrera convertible's speedometer jumps to 140 without hesitation. G-forces glue the two of them to their respective seats.

"Holy crap!" Travis says but the wind takes his words and whisks them quickly away.

"This ain't shit dude!" Dave hollers. "The speedometer goes ta 220!"

Thirty minutes ago the two of them were drinking at a tourist bar in Ocean Beach, the place decorated with palm trees and gaudy paintings of sunsets over the ocean. They were arguing about something that neither of them could remember now if a gun was held to their heads. The bartender told them to take it outside so they did, but while they were out in the parking lot circling one another some rich asshole in a Hawaiian shirt came tearing into the parking lot in the Porsche and, after parking askew in a handicap spot, he sort of oozed out from behind the wheel and staggered into the bar.

The two of them stopped what they were doing and walked over to the car, admiring the way the sun glinted off the chrome and the deep crimson hues of the surreal looking paint job.

"I'm gonna get me one a these some day," Travis said, eyeballing the interior acquisitively. It was probably only a concentrated effort that kept him from drooling all over the seat.

"Not on yer crappy salary ya ain't," Dave sneered, looking into the opposite side, brazenly resting his palms against the glass.

"I ain't gonna be in the Navy my whole life dude," Travis informed his friend. "I got bigger plans in mind."

"Yeah, what are ya gonna do? Wash cars?" Dave replied when at once he spotted something that made his heart skip a few beats before resuming, albeit faster.

"Fuck off man, I ain't a derelict like you-" he stopped short as he watched his buddy open the driver side door. "What the hell ya doin'?"

"I don't know bout you," Dave said, smiling recklessly, "but I think I'm gonna take this biotch for a little joy ride."

"Yer gonna hot wire the car? Man, yer freakin' nuts!"

Dave slid behind the wheel and fired up the engine.

"Don't have to, the guy left the keys in it."

So now here they are, blazing down the Strand in the stolen Porsche, drunk off their asses, braying laughter, slapping one another on the back, messing with the car stereo…when the sound of a police siren suddenly cuts short their revelry.

Dave looks in the rear view mirror, sees the cop gaining on them.

"Oh shit!" Travis groans. "If we get busted for drunk driving we'll end up in jail fer sure!"

"Drunk driving?" Dave laughs sourly. "That's the least of our problems dude!"

Travis thinks about it for a second before reality dawns on him.

"Oh man," he says, sinking down in his seat. "We're screwed."

Dave joined the Navy for the same reason some guys get married: he had to pick a lesser of two evils. He hadn't wanted to, but because of certain decisions he'd made during his short life it was his only choice, which was a shame because he was a very intelligent fellow and could have done anything if only he'd applied himself. The cause of this predicament was his predilection for getting into trouble, the basis for which could have been hereditary but no one really knew for sure, they could only speculate.

Dave never knew his real mother and father; the only information he had was their names and the address of the shelter for battered women where he'd been born. According to his stepparents, his birth mother had taken care of him for about six months before disappearing one day, leaving him in the care of the gentle souls who ran the facility. Every year on his birthday his adopted parents told him the story of how they chose him over countless other children because he seemed like such an outgoing, happy little fellow, every year, that is, until he got a little older and didn't want to hear it anymore. By then the 'happy little fellow' had become quite the little hell raiser.

By the time he was seventeen curiosity got the better of him and he looked up the address and drove from his home in Milwaukee to the shelter in Prairie Du Chen to see if he could learn more about his birth parents, but the place had long burned down and no one in the neighborhood could offer him any further information. His roots, it would seem, went up in smoke along with the building.

As it was already postulated, maybe it was because of this questionable lineage that he was such a troublemaker. From the time he could talk he offered nothing but sass to anyone who told him 'no' or got in his way. This went for teachers, his parents, his siblings, neighbors, friends… anyone. And if someone persisted in giving him a hard time he was quick with his fists, which often backfired on him because he was small and skinny. He spent his childhood getting his ass kicked.

His stepfather was of the opinion that a few sound thrashings would help the boy to come around, but it only made him ornerier and he would fight that much harder, even if his nose was bleeding or he'd had a tooth knocked out. His stepparents talked it over and they finally decided to bring Dave to a shrink who, following a thorough evaluation, prescribed Ritalin. Once the medication kicked in Dave became a shadow of his former self, quiet, reserved, no more insolent backtalk or destructive behavior. His parents, of course, welcomed this change because his grades improved and he even met some friends they didn't mind having at the house.

Then Dave hit puberty and everything went to hell in a hand basket again. He began listening to heavy metal and running with a crowd known to commit petty larceny and use drugs. Truth be told, Dave was the one who pressured these new friends to filch prescription medications from their parents medicine cabinets and shoplift useless crap from local retail chains, but every parent always wants to think it's some other kid than their own who is the negative influence. It's hard to accept that your own little darling is actually the bad seed.

With the clashing of his hormones came another endowment that would further help to enhance his wicked ways: nature bestowed upon him a growth spurt which took the diminutive five foot three kid and turned him into a six foot two thug. His arms became long and ropy with muscle, his legs strong as pistons from all the running he did (mostly from the cops). The once skinny little boy was now a deep-chested, towering hulk who no longer had to take shit from anybody, his stepfather included. Dave's last spanking occurred when he was fifteen and, when the belt failed to make an impression on the growing boy, his dear old stepdad decided it was time to use his fists. But Dave made a stand, countering with a left hook to the chops that had the bewildered senior drinking his meals through a straw for the next three weeks.

Yet despite his surliness and unremitting insubordination there was a smart kid trapped in there; in his sophomore year of high school Dave scored extremely high on an IQ test. The school guidance counselor almost went into shock when she reviewed the results; his IQ, unbelievably, was much higher than her own. She decided to make it a personal goal to get him on track, to persuade him to take school more seriously so he could get into a good (hell, any) college.

His response to this unwanted concern was to cause even more trouble. He torched a school bulletin board (which was inside the main office), got into a fistfight with his gym teacher (trouncing the lecherous bastard in front of the girl's volleyball team) and smoked a cigarette in his fifth period English class, blowing smoke in the beleaguered teacher's face when the man implored Dave to put it out.

Regardless of these sociopathic transgressions he also showed promise as a young entrepreneur. He sold weed and mushrooms out of the trunk of a beat up old Plymouth Charger he'd bought for a couple hundred bucks and funneled the money back into the car, fixing it up so it was suitable to take girls out on dates. Other ventures involved sponsoring parties, offering to buy the kegs if someone would put up their house and, charging five bucks a head at the door, would make his money back and then some. No one could say that Dave wasn't an enterprising young man.

Time passed, and soon the glory years of high school were behind him, having easily earned enough credits to graduate-surprisingly-with honors, although it seemed as if he'd slept through all his classes. But he had no plans for college; he didn't have any idea what he wanted to be.

Things changed drastically when he turned eighteen, however. Because he was no longer a minor the criminal charges he'd racked up as a kid now held ramifications he wasn't prepared to deal with. Stealing was now a serious misdemeanor, if not a felony, and the drug charges could put him in prison for a long time, what with mandatory minimums for possession and sale of schedule one and two narcotics.

So it was that Dave found himself at the crossroads of life. After several arrests for disorderly conduct, assault and battery and psilocybin possession he was looking at doing some serious time, but his stepfather intervened, speaking on his behalf to the authorities and working out a plea bargain that offered him a choice: go to prison or join the armed forces. His stepfather didn't care if it was the Army, Navy, Airforce or Marines, Dave just had to pick one and get his shit straightened out. It was either that or the cops were going to haul him off to the state pen for three to five years where he would use a roll of toilet paper as a pillow and the term 'sausage party' would take on a whole new meaning.

Dave opted for the armed forces, choosing the Navy. He was then swiftly shipped off to San Diego where he would begin his new life. And that was all well and good but the thing is, you can put on a uniform and learn some new moves, but you are always going to be the same person inside. They could shave his head and dress him up and tear his ego to shreds with cruelty and brutality but in the end trouble is trouble, like, it or not.

"Can ya outrun him?" Travis yells, looking nervously in the passenger side mirror as the cop steadily gains ground.

"What the fuck ya think I'm tryin' to do?" Dave says, his grin gone, replaced by a look of bleak resolve. He knows that if he gets caught the jig is up; do not pass Go, do not collect two hundred dollars. Part of his agreement with the police was that he had to stay out of trouble, and this is most assuredly *not* sticking to the agreement. For him this not only means he'll have to face charges for grand theft auto and drunken driving, but he will also have to face the charges his stepfather helped to get him out of. He'll be dishonorably discharged from the Navy and his next address will be the slammer…watch your back, don't drop the soap, don't ask don't tell (oh wait, that's the Navy) and all that happy crap. Jesus, that's all he needs.

Pushing the pedal to the floor, he gets the stolen Porsche up to 180, holding the wheel with both hands as the front end starts shaking.

"Stupid thing needs a wheel alignment!" Dave shouts as the wind buffets the car, but he sees they are gaining distance from the cop, who is progressively shrinking in the rearview mirror.

"Go go go!" Travis urges, reaching for his seat belt as an after thought.

The Porsche comes up on a slow moving Toyota and Dave veers around it, leaving the other driver to wonder what the hell just passed him at the speed of light. They are nearing the end of the long, narrow strip of land and will soon be back in regular traffic. Dave figures if they lose the cop they can ditch the car and hide out in one of the Naval base's appointed housing units along the Strand. Either that or across the way at the beach or the RV campground.

"I think we're gonna to make it!" he cries triumphantly as the cruiser becomes nothing but a speck behind them, when at once he sees the roadblock set up a hundred yards or so down the road, the cop cars parked across both lanes, and it is at this exact moment he realizes nothing in this world comes easy.

Dave is sitting at the far end of the bullpen, legs drawn up to his knees, staring vacantly at the floor. Travis is at the front of the cell, hands on the bars, watching the guards take the other detainees through processing.

"When we gonna get our phone call?" Travis asks a guard as he passes by and is ignored. "Thanks!" he calls after him. "I preciate yer attention to this matter!"

"Shut the fuck up in there!" an officer behind a desk shouts, his face beet red from either anger or alcoholic burst capillaries. "I told you, you guys don't get a phone call; the Navy is going to handle this themselves."

"I know ya said that," Travis scoffs, "but what the hell? *Everyone* gets a phone call."

"Not you two," the officer replies curtly, turning away. "Now sit down and shut the hell up. You're botherin' me."

"Shit!" Travis turns away and walks to the back of the cell, taking a seat on the bench next to Dave. The other has been silent throughout the whole thing, during their arrest, the drive over, since they've been in lock-up…he's never seen Dave so subdued before. Not that Travis blames him; hell, he's scared shitless. This is the most trouble he's ever been in before. Grand theft auto, evading capture, resisting arrest…

He knew he should have just given himself up when they were finally forced to the side of the road, but his fight or flight instincts kicked in and once he was clear of the car he made an all out dash for the RV park. Little did he know there were cops all over the place, expecting just that. He was caught in less than two minutes, tackled by a guy twice his size, forced to eat sand while the fat bastard cuffed him and rudely jerked him into an upright position before dragging him to the cruiser and unceremoniously tossing him in.

Dave had been another story all together. When he got out of the car he simply put his hands over his head and waited to be cuffed. He'd been manhandled, but not too roughly. The arresting officer even had the presence of mind to politely put his hand on Dave's head so he wouldn't bump it when he got in the back of the cop car. Travis was surprised the guy who caught him hadn't deliberately slammed *his* head into the car.

They rode to the jail in silence, well, silence on their part. They received an unsolicited lecture from one of the arresting officer's, the one who'd tackled Travis:

"You know, I can't believe you boys would be that stupid. Here you are, serving your country, getting ready to ship out to Afghanistan or Iraq or North Korea at any time and you two have the audacity to commit a felony like that. Are you guys just too chickenshit to fight for your country? Is that it? Is this your way out?"

Neither of them answered because no, that wasn't it at all. In fact, they really didn't care where they ended up, as long as they could serve their time and get on with their lives. The truth be told, they were drunk as hell and there was little to no thought behind it. No bizarre puzzle: the car was there, the keys were inside and they took it. End of story. A to fucking B. You didn't need a rocket scientist with four or five degrees to piece this one together. Take two dumb asses and mix with equal parts alcohol, shake, and see what happens.

"Man, we're screwed," Travis says and Dave nods.

"Ya got that right." He feels a massive headache building behind his eyeballs and in his temples. What the hell had he been thinking? Now he was really up shit creek. He'd been sent to the Navy as recourse from going to prison and in one fell swoop he was now heading there anyway. At the moment he felt like he probably belonged behind bars.

"Whatta ya think the Navy is gonna do ta us?"

"How the hell would I know?"

"This is yer fault. It was yer idea ta take the damn car."

"I don't recall hearin' any objections from you," Dave says and Travis shakes his head.

"How could I? I was too goddamn drunk."

"Ditto."

They quit talking, staring blankly ahead. The bullpen is mostly empty so early in the day, only a few other drunks and a couple of robbery suspects occupying space on the metal benches. The others keep to themselves, no one saying much of anything. Occasionally someone gets up and uses the toilet, having to drop troue and squat in front of everyone because of the absence of a latrine door.

Hours pass, and one by one the other's names are called and they are taken out for processing, but not Dave and Travis. Day turns into evening and soon it's standing room only as the pen fills up with new offenders. They are served a meal of baloney sandwiches on stale white bread accompanied by lukewarm, tasteless coffee. After five, they are told, no one gets processed until the next morning.

"That's just great! They expect us ta sleep in here?"

"What?" Dave smiles, but there's no humor in it. "Ya never spent a night in jail before?"

"I been in jail," Travis growls. "But, naw, I never had ta stay the night. My Dad always bailed me out."

"Well, get used to the accommodations, cuz this is it." Dave turns away from him, lying on his side. "If we're lucky we might be able ta keep our spots on the bench. If it gets too full we might hafta sleep on the floor."

"The hell with that. Who's gonna take my spot?"

As if in answer to his question the cell door opens and four large, heavily tattooed gangbangers are ushered in. They take a look around the cell, sizing everyone up before deciding to head to the back.

"Ya hadda ask," Dave says, getting up and moving away. "You just hadda go an ask..."

The next morning creeps upon them like a slow moving fog. Since there are no windows it's impossible to tell what time of day it is, except that from the hours of eleven to five most of the lights are turned off. Travis and Dave are huddled on the cold concrete floor, shivering. The guards hadn't found it in their hearts to hand out blankets.

During the night the cell has filled beyond capacity, and when the lights come back on the men are practically lying on top of one another. The predominant ethnic group in the bullpen is Mexican, the majority of them non-English speaking. Most of them were probably picked up for expired or nonexistent green cards, while others look like they are either affiliated with a street gang or drug cartel. Travis and Dave do their best to keep to themselves and avoid eye contact.

It's during breakfast that their status as the lone white boys becomes an issue. Standing in line to receive their complimentary oatmeal and orange drink, they find they're only in possession of the food for mere seconds before being stripped of their trays by dark, work calloused hands. Silencing their protests are glares as black as shark's eyes with grimaces to match.

"Hey..." Travis begins before Dave can shush him.

"You got a problem with that gringo?" a stocky Mexican asks him, one with all the telltale signs of gang affiliation for life. He has cobweb tattoos between the thumb and forefinger of each hand, and several teardrop tattoos beneath each eye. His evil grin flashes gold and at the casual wave of a hand his posse appears.

"No sir," Dave says quickly, "no problem. Y'all enjoy yer breakfast."

"You tryin' to tell me what to do gringo?" The gangbanger licks his lips, massaging a fist with his other hand. His gang steps forward, closing the distance between them.

"No sir, not at all," Dave says, his eyes betraying his trepidation. At once Travis realizes they are in serious trouble. "Was just wishing ya a good mornin' is all."

"Yeah? Well I don't need no good wishes from a gringo, not when I can break his face and ass fuck him."

Abruptly everyone in the vicinity clears out, leaving Dave, Travis and their new 'friends' plenty of room to play.

"Look, we don't want any trouble," Dave says but in response the gangbanger steps even closer.

"I don't think you got any say in the matter." His face is barely two inches from Dave's, so close he can smell the other's breath. From the scent of it, this guy hasn't brushed in a while. "You got a choice," he continues, "you can either fight or you can get yer butts kicked into next week." He turns, smiling at his compadres before returning his attention to Dave. "So what's it going to be?"

Silence so thick it can be cut with a knife (or shiv, or shank) envelops the cell. Dave can sense the others almost drooling with anticipation, can feel sweat trickling down his brow. He doesn't know how long they're going to be locked up in here, but he knows that right now is a pivotal moment, one that can't be changed once a decision has been made. He takes a deep breath, holds it for a second before he shakes his head, looks the other in the eyes... and delivers a swift right-handed uppercut to the other's jaw, following it with a head-butt and a knee to the groin.

The gangbanger is caught by surprise, doubling over, and before he hits the ground Travis dives in, his fists a flurry of motion as he takes on one of the others.

At once an explosion of shouting voices obliterates the silence, and everyone in the cell turns on Dave and Travis.

"Come on ya fuckers!" Dave roars. "I'll take on alla ya spick bastards!" His legs and fists are flying furiously, connecting with anything that gets in front of him. "La Chinga tu Madre!" he shouts deliriously before the crush of bodies overtake he and Travis, cornering them against the far wall and finally driving them to the stone floor, where the Mexican's commence to do the Macarena all over their sorry assess.

"Good goin' back there," Travis mutters between clenched teeth. "I think my jaw is busted."

"No matter what we did they was gonna fight us." Dave is holding a wad of wet toilet paper to his head, soaking up some of the blood. "At least we was men about it."

"Yer diplomatic skills suck."

"Hey, at least we're in solitary now. We got plenty a room ta stretch out."

"Let me guess, yer one a those 'glass is half full' kinda guys?"

"You got it."

Lucky for the two of them the guards intervened before they were seriously hurt. Clubbing their way through the thick horde, the guards were able to extract them before any of their bones were broken. At least that they are currently aware of.

"Man, how long we been in here?"

"About a day an a half I think." Dave leans back on the bench, putting his feet up. He notices he has a hole in his sock.

"Ya think the Navy forgot bout us?"

"You wish," Dave says wistfully. "I think we're safer in here."

"How can ya say that?" Travis groans, sitting up. "Once they process us an put us in the general population we're either gonna be tossing salads like this is the Julia Child's show or be the center of every pillow party planned for the next year, give or take a few years."

Dave heaves a sigh. Travis is right. They won't last very long in this population. Unfortunately they got busted close to the Mexican border so they are in the minority. They are either going to have to submit or fight until some kind of truce is made, but Dave doubts that will ever be a possibility. Not after what happened in the holding cell.

"Hey," he says suddenly, a thought occurring to him.

"Yeah?"

"That's the thing: we ain't been processed yet."

"How long does somethin' like that take?"

"Well, the last time I was busted it was within twenty-four hours. It's been more than that by now."

"Ya been busted a lot?"

"More'n I care to admit."

"So ya have this whole 'jail etiquette' routine down pat by now, is that it?"

"Look man, stealin' the car was a stupid idea, I admit it. In fact, you should be lucky ya ain't sittin' in my shoes because, like it or not, I'm the one who was drivin'. Technically I'm the one who stole it and yer merely a accessory-"

"Yeah, merely."

"I also got a rap sheet a mile long. Ya ever been in trouble before? Serious trouble?"

Travis rubs his aching jaw and looks at his friend curiously.

"No," he concedes. "Why?"

"Without a string a priors ya really got nothin' ta worry bout." Dave eyes the other resolutely. "I'm the one that's gonna fry, specially cuz I'm gonna tell 'em this was all my fault."

"What?" Travis stares at the other in disbelief.

"There's no use in both of us goin' down for this," Dave says. "I'm trouble, I've always been trouble and chances are pretty good I'll always be trouble. There's somethin' I never told ya: I didn't choose to be in the Navy, it got chosen for me. It was either this or go to prison. I chose this."

"What the hell did ya do?"

"Don't matter," Dave scowls, "trouble is trouble. I didn't kill no one and I ain't a perv; it wasn't like I was goin' away for life, but I hadda choice, and I thought the Navy could help straighten me out." He pauses, studies his feet for a moment. "I guess I was wrong."

"Look man, we're in this together-"

"Shut-up and listen to me!" Dave interrupts with unexpected vehemence. "This was all my fault. I'm sure they'll be happy if one a us goes down for this and you probably got a better chance a makin' somethin' of your life. When they finally do talk ta us just let me handle it. I'll take the rap. You didn't know I was gonna take the car, ya wanted to get out but I wouldn't let ya."

"I can't let ya do it man, I can't hang ya out ta dry-"

"Ya can and ya will."

"I won't!"

"Yes, ya will-"

Suddenly the cell door clangs open and before them stands their commander. He is a tall man with a stout build and unfathomable slate gray eyes and, judging by the fact that he has come to retrieve them, they are in some serious shit.

"Attention!" he hollers and the two jump to their feet and salute.

"If you two are finished blowing each other than I think it's time you come with me," he orders and the two nod, figuring their troubles have just begun.

NINE

Peacocks, Dante is thinking as the priest drones on and on. *Fucking peacocks.*

The service is attended by only a handful of people, a group, for the most part, that Dante has never met in his life. He doesn't know who they are, doesn't care. All he knows is that he doesn't have to worry about his mother anymore; she is no longer the noose around his neck. A part of him is relieved while another, larger part, questions what the hell he is going to do. Even though she was such a pain in the ass she gave him something to live for, something to do. Now he has no one.

Well, maybe not no one. He wonders where Leeann is right now, what she is doing. He wishes he could call her and tell her what happened, maybe cry on her shoulder, but he knows it isn't possible. She isn't due back in town for a couple of days and, even if she were here, is that how he wants to start things off with her? By using her as someone to unload his misery upon? He isn't even sure if she is going to follow through with their plans, honestly doesn't blame her if she doesn't. He knows she is too good for him, knows she could do better. After all, he's seen it happen before with other women he's met in Pharmacoastalcal studies. She isn't the first girl he's asked out that he's met in there, and none of them (absolutely zero) has ever worked out. It's like meeting someone at summer camp; the relationship ends once everyone goes home.

But he's going to call her, is going to pursue her even if it means rejection. What the hell, you gotta try, right? Can't win if you don't play.

The service ends and the attendees approach him, offering their condolences. He nods, smiles, points them in the direction of the food and drink, the consolation prize for coming. It isn't first class fare but it cost him enough; the whole kit and caboodle exhausted most of the money he just earned from the last drug trial. But who else was going to pay for it? His mother's estranged sister in Albuquerque who hasn't spoken to her in over ten years? She didn't even show up for the funeral although he'd called and left a message on her machine to let her know Adel had passed. The bitch never replied, possibly finding it beneath her to take time out of her 'busy' schedule to call him back.

Dante follows the crowd to where the food is laid out on folding tables. He takes a paper plate, fills it with fruit, coldcuts and cheese. The priest approaches him while he is stuffing a melon rind in his mouth, offers a thin, wan smile.

"I'm so sorry for your loss son, I really am. A boy needs his mother."

Dante nods. *Does this guy know I'm thirty-two years old?* he thinks but doesn't have the energy to say anything. How could he know that for the last fourteen years Dante has been taking care of her and not the other way around?

"Are you going to be all right?" the priest asks. "Do you need someone to talk to?"

"No thank you Father, I'll be all right," Dante replies, but actually he wouldn't mind bending someone's ear, just not this decrepit relic in a robe. He'd love to talk to Leeann but, since that isn't an option, he guesses he'll settle for nothing.

The drive home is miserable, the traffic on the 8 gridlocked. The funeral was held at a church in Chula Vista, and the traffic around down town San Diego is congested as usual. What Dante desires most right now is a hot shower and a nap. After that he doesn't know what he's going to do. The pizza place gave him a couple days off so he could grieve, but he doubts he needs it. What he wants is something to do to keep his mind off of things but he can't think of anything appealing.

Walking down the hallway to his room he sees a couple leaning against the next door, making out. They are really going at it, issuing loud, wet, slurping noises that sound vaguely disgusting. Doing his best to ignore them, he fishes the keys out of his pocket and unlocks the door.

"Get a room," he mutters, but not loud enough so they hear him. He enters and closes the door, the small confines of his living space enveloping him.

With the money he makes from Pharmacoastalcal he could get a bigger, better place but, since he spends most of his time at the drug facility, there's no reason. All he needs is a room for his few possessions and a bed to sleep in.

He takes off his suit coat and tosses it on the back of a chair, his only chair. Doesn't matter if it gets wrinkled, he won't need it until the next funeral he attends. For one chilling moment he hopes the next funeral will be his own, but then does his best to rid himself of the thought.

He lies down on his bed, kicks off his shoes. He's decided against the shower because he doesn't feel like walking to the shared bathroom down the hall. He'd have to pass the couple again and he's certain he couldn't stomach it.

Closing his eyes he thinks of Leeann: her warm smile, her freckled face, her sunny laugh. More than anything he really needs her right now, needs *somebody*. He wonders if that somebody will ever be there for him, or if he is going to go through life just as he has all these years: awkward, ineffectual…alone. He doesn't think he can continue on like this, can't imagine such a cold, dreary existence.

Suddenly an image of his mother's corpse appears behind his closed eyelids, her body laid out in the coffin looking better than she'd looked in years. In his mind's eye she sits up, glaring at him accusingly.

"Thanks a lot for not being there when I needed you Dante," she says, *her painted lips turned downward in a nasty sneer, the lipstick staining her yellow teeth. "I always knew I couldn't count on you."*

"Mom, no, it's not like that…" he murmurs, bitter sorrow overcoming him, his chest heaving mightily as a sob escapes him. "I promise you it's not like that…"

"Oh, I know how it is all right. It was that girl that distracted you, some bimbo who promised she'd suck on your thing, your tiny little thing…"

"God mom, no! It was nothing like that! I love you, I've always loved you!" Tears run down his face as he clutches his pillow, his head rolling from side to side.

"You didn't love me enough," she says with grim finality and the vision dissipates, leaving Dante alone to cry himself into a light, troubled sleep.

TEN

Melissa can't shake the feeling that she is being followed, has had the creeping sensation for the last several minutes as she makes her way up and down the aisles of the sex shop, past the butt beads and edible underwear, moving toward the S&M gear. She looks around and sees no one but the lecherous guy manning the cash register, and it can't be him because he's perusing the latest issue of 'Barely Legal', his right hand out of sight beneath the counter. Any second now and they'll need a clean up in aisle five.

She passes the blow-up dolls and the rubber vaginas, pausing briefly to regard a large double-headed dildo. *Maybe this would be a suitable replacement for Tyler*. She fingers the plastic packaging, running a lacquered nail along one huge, protruding vein. *He fucking wishes he was packing this kind of heat.* Smirking, she continues her browsing.

She's shopping here today because she ruined the whip on her last client (she can't get the dried blood out of the tassels no matter how hard she tries) and figures she'll pick up a new bondage suit while she's at it. Since she broke it off with Tyler she's gained a few pounds. She's up to a size seven from a five, and the leather suit feels too tight. She doesn't normally overeat when she's depressed but this time has been the exception. That and the drinking. She's up to a fifth of whisky a day, sometimes adding beer or wine to the mix. Right now her head is pounding and her mouth tastes like something curled up in it and died but she knows she has to buy new gear and get back to work before she gets too far behind on the bills. What's more it will do her some good, help get her mind off of things.

Reaching the end of one aisle and turning into the next she sees someone dart out of sight as she approaches and her suspicions are at once confirmed.

"All right you scumbag, I know you're there. Either state your piece or I'm gonna call the cops." She says this loudly so that the other patrons in the store can hear, but they mostly ignore her (especially the guy behind the counter; his arm is moving at a rapid pace now, his eyes nearly squinted shut). No one wants to get involved in a place like this (at least not in that manner) yet her threat does the trick of flushing out her spy.

"Sorry," a guy says sheepishly, stepping out from behind a rack of brightly colored g-strings. "I didn't mean to scare you, I just didn't know what to say."

"Than don't say it," Melissa says, eyeing him judiciously, deeming him 'undoable' and waving him away. "Whatever you have to say I don't want to hear it. Just get the hell out of here." She swivels on one heel and starts walking away when he says:

"I didn't want to do this but Tyler put me up to it."

She stops and turns back, looking at him warily.

"And you are...?"

"I'm Wes, Tyler's best friend." His voice carries a touch of pride.

"Somehow I doubt that," she says and his smile fades. "Tyler is his own best friend."

He stares at her silently for a moment and then nods solemnly.

"Your right," he agrees. "He just uses people to get what he wants. I should have known you'd be well aware of that." He spins around quickly, looks as if he is about to scurry away when she calls to him:

"Hey! Not so fast!" and he stops in his tracks, glancing at her over his shoulder. "So what do you want? And don't tell me you're here buying your good buddy a new blow-up doll. I don't think they have John Holmes in stock."

He shrugs desperately, not knowing what to say, when at once her features soften.

"I'm kidding, all right?" She smiles, and it is the careless beauty of her grin that disarms him. "So what did he send you here for? You're not leaving without telling me that much."

Wes sighs audibly and relaxes, returning the smile and taking a tentative step forward.

"He wanted me to talk to you, wanted me to tell you he's sorry."

"Why doesn't he tell me himself? And how the hell did you know to find me here, unless... have you been following me?"

"He told me where you lived and...well..."

"And you followed me here? Nice. Real classy."

"I'm sorry. I'm just doing what he asked me to."

"Do you always do that?"

"What?"

"Carry out the crazy shit he tells you to do? I could call the cops, tell them that you're stalking me."

"Listen, this was a bad idea and I'm sorry, really I am." Wes backs away. "I'll just be going-"

"Wait a minute," Melissa says, her anger slowly receding. This guy looks harmless and she knows how persuasive Tyler can be. Especially with a wet blanket like this shmoe. If his appearance tells her anything it's that anyone can walk and talk all over his wretched little ass. "How sorry is he?"

"He's really, really sorry."

"Sorry enough to get a job and pay me back-rent for the last seven months?"

"Uh, I don't know about that..."

"He's horny and he needs to get some, right? That's probably what he really said."

"No," Wes says, shaking his head. "I think he really, truly misses you-"

"Misses me paying the rent and feeding him."

"No, I've never seen him like this. At first he was all 'she can go to hell!' but after a few days he looked pretty despondent, and all he could do was talk about how much he missed you, how much you meant to him."

Melissa frowns.

"He said I could go to hell?"

"Only at first, then all he could do was piss and moan-"

"Sounds like typical Tyler," she says, deciding she's heard enough. "If he feels that strongly he should talk to me himself instead of having his little butt buddy do it."

"His what?"

"You heard me." Suddenly she's bored with the conversation. "Look, truth be told, I'm done with him, caput. But if he actually has something to say than it's in his best interest to say it himself. Got it?"

"Sure, sure," Wes says, getting the idea he is being excused. He takes a step back, then another, wanting to get the hell out of here before she changes her mind about calling the cops.

"Hey!" she hollers after him and he stops.

"Yeah?"

"Let me give you my card," she says, an evil grin lighting up her face, "just in case you feel naughty and need to be punished like a man."

"No thanks!" he chirps, exiting the store so fast he doesn't hear her laughing in his wake.

ELEVEN

After the vacation Leeann's classes plod along for a few days before she gets back into the swing of things. Her only courses left before graduation are all pertaining to her major (hence interesting) yet she can't get the cerulean skies and the feel of the warm gulf water out of her head.

I freakin' bungee jumped, she reflects fondly as her Advanced Biology professor expounds the virtue of a prompt arrival upon a tardy student. *And I rode a mechanical bull.* This brings a smile to her face and it suddenly occurs to her that she's become tired of academic life and what she really wants is to finish all this and get out into the real world. Do some fieldwork. Apply her knowledge and see what life outside of school is like. After eighteen years in the same town and then three point five years at the university she realizes she hasn't seen much of the world other than Texas and San Diego. Not that there isn't quite a bit to do here, as it really is a very lovely city, but she's hardly been anywhere outside of the United States. Sure, she's been to Mexico; who could grow up in Texas and not visit at least once? But it was Nuevo Laredo, a dirty, crummy border town where it seemed the majority of the inhabitants wanted to be on the other side of the river. Not that she could fault them; she sure as hell wouldn't want to live there.

What she wants, she decides, is an adventure. Her first job should take her outside of the states, some place where she can see and do new things. She needs excitement.

Her cell phone vibrates in her purse and, looking to see if anybody notices, she removes it and takes a peek at the number. Not recognizing it, she fears it might be Dante and mixed feelings course through her, none of them exhilaration she notes coolly. Mostly it's guilt, because after six days of Stacy's incessant badgering she eventually wore her down, bringing to light all of Dante's flaws. By the end of the trip Leeann decided that going out with Dante would be a bad idea. It isn't that he's not sweet and funny in a weird kind of way, but they really don't have much in common, and the age difference has begun to bother her. She is only twenty-one (on the verge of twenty-two) and he is over thirty. He's practically a senior citizen! What the hell was she thinking, giving this guy her phone number? She should have simply taken his and promised she'd call, giving her the option to let it go quietly. After all, he'd never find her. San Diego is large enough. Of course, he could look her up in the school directory, maybe show up at one of the lecture halls in search of her. She wonders if he would do something like that and, calling up his face in her mind, decides he would.

She hits the 'ignore call' button and turns it off. She knows she can't simply disregard him, that she opened this can of worms and it's up to her to own up to it and tell him, but what a drag! What was that stupid phrase everyone used to use that was so trendy a decade ago? 'Man-up'? Well, that was what she needed to do. Yes, she could just avoid his phone calls but, then, he might turn up on campus like a bad penny. The thing to do is talk to him, bite the bullet and do it face to face. She could meet him in a coffee shop and tell him she is sorry but this isn't the best time for her, so close to graduation and all. She'll explain how she wants to do some traveling and that she's not prepared for a long distance relationship. He'll understand, won't he?

She stuffs the phone deep in her purse and tries to concentrate on the lecture. Finals will be starting in a few weeks and she needs to keep up her GPA.

And if no isn't good enough for him than that will inspire me all the more to get out of dodge.

She smiles to herself, almost laughs at the idea that in order to avoid some guy she has to leave town. This is a first for her. Hell, surprising it hasn't happened before. But, then again, it probably has…to Dante.

She takes her purse and sets it on the ground next to her feet.

Soon this will be all over and I can move on. Soon.

TWELVE

Ducking into the nearest doorway to get out of the rain, Tyler sees it's a book store/coffee house and decides it's as appropriate a place as any to take five. He's been walking around all morning, trying to get Melissa out of his head but he can't. He even went so far as to apply for a job at a photocopy shop for Christ's sake. He must be fucking delirious!

"Hey," he says to the young girl at the counter, "can I get a large black coffee?"

"Six dollars," she says, looking bored and tired, like she stayed up all night at a rave party and the last place in the world she wants to be is right here, right now. She has blue hair and a pierced eyebrow and is almost cute in a Goth sort of way but she is way too heavy for Tyler. Unless she's ready to throw him some serious coin there's no way he could stick his dick in her.

"You gotta be kidding me! Six bucks for a cup of coffee?" Tyler feels the scant roll of bills in his front pocket, jingles the spare change. If he buys the coffee he'll have to go without lunch unless he tracks down Wes at his minimum wage shit job, selling camera equipment to the elderly and the mentally challenged at the mall…Ah, what the hell. He guesses he wouldn't mind some nachos from the food court, maybe a corndog.

"Take it or leave it," the girl says, snapping her gum.

"That better be one huge fucking cup of coffee." He tosses the money on the counter and the girl scoops it up, puts it in the register.

"One large black coffee!" she calls to a short guy with wire-rim glasses and the beginnings of a patchy beard. "Extra special."

"Hey," Tyler warns, dismissing the girl and addressing the guy. "I know what you're up to. You spit in that and I'll be waiting for you outside with a rusty razor and a can of shaving cream." He tilts his head back, glaring through slitted eyes. "And it ain't that 'beard' I'm gonna trim either."

The coffee slinger looks Tyler up and down, decides a goober isn't worth an ass kicking, and just pours the coffee.

"Sorry," he mutters to the counter girl as he passes it over to her.

"One black coffee." Her voice harbors blatant contempt, eyes hard, cold pinpoints, and Tyler takes the cup a little too aggressively, spilling some all over his hand and the counter.

"Shit!" he fumes, reaching for the napkin dispenser. "Enjoy your crummy lives you pricks." When he turns away he notices that the few customers strewn about the shop are staring at him, trendy little poseurs living off of mommy and daddy's money no doubt, dressing themselves to look like the models in an Abercrombie and Fitch catalogue. They think they are witty, sophisti-cated. Six bucks for a cup of coffee means nothing to them. They probably wipe their asses with twenties.

"The hell are you pussy's looking at?" he barks and they quickly turn away. "That's what I thought."

He takes a seat at a table by the front window and looks out at the dismal, rainy day. It's been almost a week now and he can't get Melissa out of his mind. He's been absolutely down, and that's unusual for him. Normally he doesn't get emotionally attached but something about this chick is different. Maybe (and this is climbing wayyy out on a limb) he really likes her. Dare he even say love? He doesn't think it's possible, as he's never loved anyone in his life (his self excluded, of course). He's certain he never loved his wife; the only reason he'd married her was because she was knocked up and he was trying to start a new life. When he walked out on her and the 'tard *(the boy, for Christ's sake, the damn boy)* he felt nothing...nothing at all. He's not even sure he knows what love is supposed to feel like.

Maybe this *is what it feels like,* he considers, sipping the bitter coffee and grimacing. *Maybe this is what all those ridiculous, weepy songs are about...and all those stupid 'chick-flicks' that I hate so much. Could it be that this is what they are getting at?*

Is it possible that somewhere deep down inside he actually has stronger feelings than his standard sexual needs and monetary issues? Is that what's really on the table here? This is all so new, so, so...unexpected.

He recalls the report Wes gave him after his little field trip. According to his indispensible food source, uh, *resource,* she said he should talk to her himself, but what's that all about? Maybe a chance for her to get back at him? And what about the comment regarding back-rent? Does she truly expect him to pay her if he wants to be a part of her life?

And here is where it gets weird, ladies and gentlemen, but Tyler almost feels like he would do these things for her, that he'd get a job and for once bring something else to the relationship other than his cock and a devious grin. Crazy, yes. Entirely impossible, no.

She's beautiful, and she was so good to me.

It's amazing to think that a woman like her (a pain dealer) could be so loving and gentle. She'd tried to get him interested in a little light bondage and S&M but that was never his style. For Tyler sex was about pleasure, not pain. Pain sucks. How the hell anyone could get off while being beaten is beyond him. And she was all right with that, didn't force the issue. There were times she'd asked him (and he complied, to a certain degree) to slap her when she was about to come, mostly on the ass but sometimes in the face, but that was the extent of it. He refused to cut her, or use a whip on her and she didn't complain.

I think she really loved me. Abruptly another sentiment overtakes him that he rarely experiences, one of regret. *I really miss that bitch. I really, truly do.*

For the moment he isn't quite sure if he loves her but he understands that, if anything, he must be damn close. No one has ever made him feel this shitty...no one.

Taking another sip of the rancid coffee, he decides that maybe he should talk to her after all. He has no idea what he's going to say or how he's going to approach her, but he knows if he doesn't he's going to be sorry, maybe not today, maybe not tomorrow, but sometime down the road when the ship has sailed off into the sunset without him onboard.

He turns and eyeballs the two numbskulls behind the counter.

"Hey, dingle wad!" he yells and the kid with the patchy beard looks up.

"Made ya look!" Tyler exclaims, laughing, and at once he realizes he's feeling a little better.

THIRTEEN

"Sir?" Governor Hallsly's secretary's grating voice warbles through the intercom. "There's a call for you on line one."

"Take a message, I'm busy."

"She says it's important."

"Take a message!" he fires back, angry at being interrupted. What with his many obligations as governor and his family life to contend with he needs every spare second he can get to pursue his hobby, which is going through the sex pages in the back of the local independent paper. Not only does his hobby consist of reading the lurid text, but also finding a candidate worthy of his attention. Thing is, there are never enough choices for what he really needs, which right now is a good, sound spanking, maybe a little light bondage and torture.

Now, the governor is what you would call 'happily married', which in political terms means he never has sex with his wife but keeps her around to satisfy his constituents. A single governor is trouble, one that won't get re-elected. He and his wife have a mutual agreement in which she can entertain her Latino boy-toys and he can visit prostitutes and the occasional dominatrix or two. The plan works well for them and as long as they get tested twice yearly for HIV it's win/win all the way around, but the catch is they can't get caught; should this happen they are ready with a scripted public apology and a song and dance about renewing their marital vows and going into couple's therapy.

When he doesn't turn up anything in the paper he decides to turn to the Internet, the horny man's almanac for all things pornographic. You'd think the only reason it was created was for reasons of a sexual nature and, what the hell, that's probably right on the money. Thank God for the World Wide Web.

He scrolls around for several minutes then, on a whim, decides to try Greg's List. He's had luck with it before.

His intercom buzzes again.

"Sir, you really need to take this call, it's extremely important."

"For Christ's sake! I'm trying to get some work done in here!"

"I can't put them off any longer sir, it's a call from the White House."

"THE White House?"

"Is there any other?"

"Fine, put me through," he groans, wondering why he hired her in the first place. All she ever does is bother him to take business calls, go to meetings and review budgets. Doesn't she know he has better things to do?

"Very good."

He picks up the phone, clears his throat, then punches line one.

"This is Governor Hallsly speaking."

"Hello governor, this is Ms. Holdsworth. We spoke the other day."

"Yes Ms. Holdsworth, what can I do for you?"

"I'm calling to check on your progress."

"Progress?" What the hell is she talking about?

"Yes governor, your progress. Are you getting everything in order for the trip to the garbage heap?"

"Oh! That progress!" Governor Hallsly replies, suddenly alert. He forgot all about that. "Everything's fine."

"So you have a ship and crew lined up for the mission?"

"Uh, not yet, no, but I *am* in the process of working on it…" he stalls, wondering how he could have dropped the ball like this after the bitch practically sliced off his nuts with a rusty razor and then offered to feed them to him the other day.

"Are you having trouble getting Scripts to comply?"

"Uh, no ma'am, not at all. They, uh, told me that, um…they just have to do a few repairs on the boat and, uh, yes I believe that's it, uh…and when they're, um, done they'll get back to me…"

"You haven't done anything yet, have you governor?"

"No…"

"Is there anything in particular you're waiting for?"

"Uh…"

"My guess is you forgot. Am I right?"

"I wouldn't say forgot so much as I've had a lot of other things I've been taking care of-"

"Like perusing the local papers for prostitutes?"

"Certainly not! Where would you even get an idea like *that*?"

"Trust me governor, we know a lot more about you than you think." Ms. Holdsworth's voice is cold, her tone ruthlessly unsympathetic, and at once the governor knows he's made a big mistake misjudging her. "Do you think this is a joke? Wasting our time like this?"

"I'm sorry Ms. Holdsworth, really, something came up and-"

"What came up? Your penis?"

"Huh?" Governor Hallsly is almost taken aback by her candor, but for him 'almost' is quite a stretch. Actually, he feels somewhat aroused.

"The president wants the mission to commence by the end of the month which is in, let me see here, one week." She lets this sink in. "Do you want me to tell the president that this operation is going to be delayed because you've been too busy getting your dick wet?"

"Um, no, no, certainly not…"

"Than I suggest you get a move on. Surely you have people who take care of these things for you?"

"Of course Ms. Holdsworth, I most assuredly do. I'm sorry about the holdup. I'm sure I'll have all the details worked out by then."

"I'll leave my number with your secretary. Please contact me as soon as the arrangements are made."

"Of course," the governor says and hangs up. Shit, how could he have forgotten about his meeting with her? She'd made him feel like a schoolboy about to get his ass smacked with a yardstick. Right now there is only one thing to do and that's to get this handled pronto.

"Candice," he says over the intercom, trying to keep his voice calm.

"Yes sir?"

"Listen, we have a situation here and I need you to find someone who can make it happen fast."

"Sir?"

"Just shut-up and listen."

After a long lunch and a trip to a masseuse (happy ending, of course, the old rub and tug), the governor is lounging in his limo, contemplating what to do with the rest of the afternoon. The woman from the White House put the fear of God in him and what he needs to do now is relax. Suddenly he remembers an ad he saw on Greg's List and, grabbing his Video Phone, looks it up.

Are you a naughty boy who needs serious discipline? Call Madam Coventry for all your bondage and S&M needs. Discretion guaranteed. # 555-6667.

"Ah, just what the doctor ordered," he cackles and the driver looks over his shoulder at him.

"Sir?" he asks.

"Nothing, nothing. I have to make a phone call and then we're going to make one more stop before we go back to the office."

"Where to sir?"

"Give me a second and I'll tell you," the governor replies lasciviously, dialing the phone.

FOURTEEN

Rolling over on his sheetless, stained mattress, Kenny wonders what the point is. Why should he get out of bed when the world is just going to kick him in the face anyway? He belches, tasting sour bile with notes of bourbon and suddenly his stomach does a nauseating flip-flop. He gets up quickly, his head pounding, heart booming, the room spinning, and realizes he isn't merely hung over, he's still completely smashed.

"Fuck," he mutters, his fears confirmed as he feels a rumble from down under. "Fuck!"

Running to the bathroom, he makes it just in time to unload in the sink, his head shrieking in agony as he coughs and gags miserably. When the last of the spasms taper off and he looks up, he notices flecks of orange colored puke speckling the mirror like a deranged connect-the-dots puzzle in the Sunday funnies, and when he catches a glimpse of his face what he sees scares him. His eyes are red-rimmed with large bags beneath them and his pupils are dilated, his iris's dull. There is gray in his beard that is splotchy and uneven and his skin looks waxy and pale. Pale for a black man, so he looks sort of ashen gray, like his beard. He sticks out his tongue and cringes at the thick yellow coat covering it.

"Ya don't look so hot buddy," he tells himself, running water to wash his face. "Damn, it oughta be against the law ta feel this shitty..."

He knows there is nothing that can save him from a hangover like this but to have a drink. It's either that or be sick, he has a choice. Opening the medicine cabinet he fishes out his toothbrush, finding a crushed, almost empty tube of toothpaste. He can't even remember the last time he brushed his teeth, but now seems like a good time.

"Shit, I'm livin' like a animal," he grumbles as he scrubs the grunge off of his pearly whites (in this case murky yellows). Of course, animals aren't as self-destructive as he is, unless there is something seriously wrong with them.

"Jesus, help me," he says, but he knows the 'Son of God' can do nothing for him. He'd have more luck if he called Jesus Manuel, ex-kicker from the University of Nebraska, and asked him for advice. But that Catholic bastard would probably tell him to go to church or something. Pray for forgiveness. What a crock.

I don't need forgiveness, I just need a purpose. Kenny spits out a glob of toothpaste and rinses his mouth with tepid water from the tap that tastes like lead and chlorine. A thought occurs to him and he laughs out loud. *I could kill mysef by drinkin' enough a this tap water, I bet.* He turns both faucets on all the way, watching the water gush out. "Don't try an stop me! I'm gonna do it!" he cries into the mirror, a look of unhinged mirth on his face and, at once, he feels better. He's never had a keenly attuned sense of humor (taking after his ma) but occasionally he surprises himself.

He laughs for a couple of minutes and it clears his head, cleanses him. He can almost feel the tension slackening, some of the pent-up emotions of the last couple years slipping away. All due to laughing. Maybe he should try it more often. Hell, drinking never made him feel this good, nor did the goddamn pills. All they ever did was put him in a murky place where reality became blurred like a dream, hazy, soft, incomprehensible. It was for this reason he finally kicked the painkillers, just up and went cold turkey one day. It wasn't easy (in fact he shit his pants more than once and had waking nightmares so bad he was glad he didn't own a gun or he might have popped himself) but he did it. After a week in hell he came out the other side a changed man, if you could call a suicidal alcoholic 'changed'. At least he didn't need drugs anymore, and that was something.

Maybe I've turned a corner. He regards his visage more closely in the mirror, pulling down one eyelid to peer within its muddy depths. *Maybe things can get better if I help ta make 'em better.* A wistful thought comes to him, one that makes his heart thud in his chest, makes his already dry mouth even drier.

Maybe I can go without drinkin' today. He feels tendrils of fear unfurling in his stomach at the thought. Whoa, his crutch, his reason for getting out of bed in the morning…is it possible?

He runs a tongue over lips so dry they make a crackling, scraping sound.

"Yeah," he whispers, eyeing himself thoughtfully. "You can do it man, you can do it. Today can be the first day a the rest a yer life…"

And then the phone rings, startling him, and his ruminations fade.

"You'll never believe what I was thinkin' bout today," Kenny says, tipping back his sixth triple whisky sour.

"Don't tell me suicide cuz I don't want to hear it." Hank guzzles the last of a boilermaker and signals the bartender for another.

"Shit Hank, I think a suicide ever day, that ain't nothin' new."

"Than what, playing football again?"

"No man, I was thinkin' bout quittin' drinkin'."

"What?" Hank chokes; he coughs and sputters for several minutes while Kenny pats him on the back. "You're joking right?" he finally manages when he sees something else that startles him: Kenny is smiling. That's one thing he has to confess he doesn't see a lot of.

"I guess so, cuz here I am."

"But you were really thinking about it?"

"I was really thinkin' bout it," Kenny admits, nodding, and his drinking buddy shudders.

"Don't talk like that man, you're scaring me."

"It *is* a scary thought."

"Maybe you just need a woman. Some good sex will clear out your head."

"I was thinkin' maybe a job."

Hank has another coughing spasm.

"Jesus Christ what the hell has gotten into you? Are you fucking kidding me?" Hank looks around the room wildly. "Hey, anyone, can you tell me where my buddy went? Big black guy, ex football player?"

"Don't have a freakin' fit Hank, I just need somethin' more, I don't know...somethin' else. My life used ta be so busy; I guess I can't stand all a this free time. I think too much."

"Obviously, because the thoughts you're having are whacked!"

"I need ta do somethin' I can be proud of."

"You can drink me under the table," Hank notes with a wry smile. "If I was you I'd be damn proud of that."

"Better than that," Kenny prods and Hank shrugs.

"Suit yourself. I just think it's a mistake."

"Guess I'll hafta give it a try and see."

"Yeah, I suppose you will," Hank nods. "Well, I'm not going to stand in your way. If there's anything I can do to help just let me know."

"Nothin' I can think of 'cept be my friend. You can do that, right?"

"I can do that Kenny, I swear." Hank picks up his fresh drink, takes a sip. "So when is this 'change of life' going to commence?"

"You can bet yer ass it ain't gonna be today," Kenny says and they share a laugh. "Now how bout some music?"

FIFTEEN

"Look, I need to be assured that my visit will be completely confidential. I can't have anyone finding out that I sought out your services."

"You read the ad pal, you know what I have to offer."

"Yes, I know, it says 'discretion guaranteed'."

"Well than what more do you need to know?"

"I'm, well, um, what you might call famous. I need to be sure this isn't going to make the tabloids."

"Famous, huh? You some big shot actor?"

"No…"

"Rock star?"

"No…"

"Super model?"

"Hah! No."

"Well what the hell are you, and what makes you think you're so damn important?"

"I'm in politics."

"And you consider that famous? What planet are you from?"

"Look, is this going to be on the down low or what?"

"Totally. You can count on it."

"Will you sign a waiver confirming that?"

"Sure, whatever, so do you want to make an appointment or not?"

"Would sometime this afternoon work?"

"Let me check my schedule."

The governor waits, hears the sound of pages rustling.

Melissa holds the phone away from her and shakes a newspaper in front of the receiver. After a minute she throws it on the floor. It's two-thirty now. What the hell, might as well get this over with.

"How about three?" In her despondency she doesn't even care about doing a background check. Maybe she'll get lucky and this client will be the psycho she's been preparing herself for after all these years.

"Just tell me where."

She gives him the address, hangs up the phone.

The governor does an address search using his Video Phone. He then plugs the phone into a portable printer, scooping up the pages as they're ejected from the machine. He hands them to the driver.

"This is where we're going. I'll probably be about an hour."

"Yes sir."

"I know I don't have to tell you this trip never happened."

"No sir."

"If anyone call's I'm at the gym."

"Of course sir."

"Okay, drive."

The door opens and before the governor can say a word a hand reaches out and grabs him rudely by the lapels, dragging him across the threshold.

"You've been a very naughty boy and you need to be punished!" barks a woman in a full body bondage suit complete with zippered mask, and for a second he doesn't know if he is going to get a boner or pee his pants.

"Holy shit!" he says, smiling. "You really do take charge."

"Silence! Come with me!"

She leads him through her condo to the torture chamber, closes the door behind them.

"Take off your clothes and put these on." She tosses him a pair of leather underwear outfitted with oversized chains.

"Um, before we go any further I have a form for you to sign-"

"Call me ma'am! And don't look at me when you speak. Address the floor!"

"Yes ma'am," he says, loosening his tie. "I have a waiver for you to sign-"

"Put it over there, along with your payment."

"How much?"

"Depends on how long our session is, slave!" Taking him entirely by surprise, she slaps him across the face. "I told you to call me ma'am!"

"Hey, not the face, alright? I don't want to have to explain any marks to my constituents."

She raises her hand. "What did I say?"

"Uh, I mean please don't hit me in the face ma'am! I'll be a good boy!"

"How much do you think you can take?"

"About an hour, uh, ma'am?"

"That'll be three hundred dollars. You can put it right over there." She points to a small table, which is littered with the tools of her trade. He spies a cat o' nine tails, nipple clamps and a dildo with spikes protruding from it. He tosses the form down (a standard contract he's carried for years to keep him from getting extorted by professional sex workers) as well as his wallet. He then continues to get undressed.

Madam Coventry walks over to the table, looks briefly at the form then opens the wallet, takes out three Benjamin's and a twenty.

"Hey, I thought it was only three hundred!"

"And I thought I told you to shut the fuck up!" she snarls. "Get those goddamn clothes off now before I get mad!"

"Yes ma'am!" The governor is getting aroused, the kind of arousal that only being abused can bring about. He takes off his pants, tosses them over a nearby chair.

"Alright then, we'll start you in the stocks and then move you to the wheel of pain." She chooses a tool to begin with, pointing him over to the torture device. "Not one more word out of you unless I address you first, got it?"

He nods eagerly.

"The safety word is 'bananas'. Can you remember that?"

"Yes ma'am!"

"Alright you dirty, rotten, nasty little bastard, time to take your punishment."

If any of his staff were present they would think, judging by her appraisal, she already knew him…

"I'm not bleeding anywhere, am I?"

"I already told you, no!" Melissa says, taking off the mask. She really worked up a sweat pounding on this guy and can't take it a minute more.

"Feels like I am."

"Look, I'm a professional, okay? You're going to have some marks for a few days but otherwise you're fine." She shakes her head, swipes damp hair from her forehead. "Jesus, I thought you've been through this before."

The governor puts his shirt on slowly, being careful of the tender skin.

"Yeah…" Truth be told it's been a while since he's gone this route, but after this session he knows he'll be back. He just wants to be sure he can trust her.

"Did you sign the waiver?"

Melissa barely glanced at it, much less signed it.

"Look, who the hell are you? Am I supposed to know, because I don't have a clue."

"You don't watch the news much, huh?" he chuckles and she scowls.

"Maybe not," she says, sitting down, crossing her legs. "So…who?"

"You don't recognize the governor when you meet him?" he says and instead of acting surprised, maybe gushing that it's nice to meet him she merely nods.

"Ah," she says. "The governor. Whoop de doo."

"Maybe you'd be more impressed if I was Justin Beeper?"

"Not impressed, no, but I would definitely think it's funny, seeing as he converted to Hinduism."

He appears forlorn for a second but it passes. His personality is like that of a Labrador retriever; depressed for an instant after being rebuked but moments later wagging his tail again.

"So, can we do this again?"

"Why not? It's your money." Melissa doesn't normally fraternize with the clients when she's done but her professionalism has been slipping lately, ever since she threw Tyler out. She's relieved she hasn't heard from the last client, was actually on pins and needles for a few days, waiting for his lawyer to call.

"Great, great. Maybe we can do Monday's and Wednesday's? I'll call you and let you know. Same time?"

"If you want to book in advance that's fine," she sighs. She can't help but feel slightly awkward (perhaps even a little perverse) after dealing with a sick puppy like this guy. The things he cried out while she was whipping him will haunt her dreams for some time (*no mommy, I wasn't wearing your panties, I swear!*). She used to really love her profession (she actually took a bit of enjoyment in chastising this freaking bozo) but she's starting to wonder if there isn't something better she could be doing with her time. She could always return to cocktail waitressing again; maybe it would rekindle her desire to dish out punishment. Sure, a few weeks taking orders from arrogant pricks in suits (getting her ass pinched and listening to stupid, demeaning pick-up lines) and she'd be ready to flog these bastards until blood is running out of their ears.

"Well, I should get going." The governor is tying his tie, smoothing out his shirt. "That was very nice."

"Wow, that's the first time I ever heard anyone say what I do is 'nice'. I must not have done my job."

"Oh, you did alright. I came harder than I have in a long time," he says with a grin and Melissa suppresses the urge to gag.

"Glad to hear it." She offers a dour smile, leading him out.

"Okay, great, well I'll call you."

"You have my number." And she ushers him out and shuts the door before he can say another word.

SIXTEEN

Leeann's phone rings for the third time in less than an hour as she is diligently trying to study for one of her finals, prompting her to finally pick it up. Glancing at the caller ID she sees that it's Dante-again. She labeled his number so she didn't accidentally answer it.

Oh man, this guy isn't going to give up. Just take the damn call.

Reluctantly, she hits the 'answer' button.

"Hello?"

"Hey Leeann, how are you? It's Dante. I've been trying to call you for days."

"Have you?" she says, a whirlwind of excuses swirling through her brain. One thing she hates is lying, and another jerking someone around, but a biggie for her is confrontation. She really hates that. "I just got it back. I left it at my girlfriend's apartment and I thought I lost it." She feels shitty about the lie but decides it's better than telling him that she's been dodging his calls.

"I knew there was a good reason!" he exclaims, the relief in his voice unmistakable. And here he'd thought she'd been avoiding him. "What are you up to?"

"I've been really busy," she answers truthfully. "I'm getting ready for finals and I've been study-ing my tail off."

"And a beautiful tail it is," he says, making her wince. "So what are you doing tomorrow night? I was thinking we could check out the new Robert Rodrigo movie, maybe get a bite to eat after."

"Yeah, I don't know Dante, I have a lot of work to do."

"But it's a Friday night," he wheedles, a note of disappointment in his voice. "You don't have classes on Saturday do you?"

"No, it's just that..." her voice trails off because she can't think of anything offhand and she isn't a very adept liar. She's surprised she actually came up with the 'lost the cell phone' bit already. She really should have given this more thought before she answered the phone.

"It's just that you don't want to see me, I know." His tone reeks of dejection, yet he doesn't seem very surprised. "I'm used to that." He waits a beat then adds: "My Mom just died. While you were in South Padre I found her dead in her trailer."

"Oh my God! What happened?" Leeann can't help it; she is at heart a very caring girl and the thought of someone suffering (even if she doesn't want to go out with him) evokes her sympathy.

"Well, right after the study I went to see her and I found her, um, not moving…lying on the bedroom floor in her trailer. She, uh, well, I guess it turns out she had a sever allergic reaction to peacock dung…"

"What?"

"It's a long story," he says, not really wanting to go into it in depth. "But I guess she was in there for a few days before I found her. No one in her neighborhood noticed she was missing."

"Oh, your poor mother!" Leeann commiserates, unable to imagine how horrible that would be, for anyone. "I am so very, very sorry."

"Thanks, I appreciate it."

There is a long pause, the silence drawing out until finally Leeann says:

"This might be a stupid question but, um, how did she come in contact with peacock dung?"

"Like I said, long story babe," he exhales noisily. "Long, long story."

Leeann is torn. She wants to tell him he isn't right for her or, even better, she isn't right for him but, at this juncture, would feel as if she is being unfair. She knows her friend Stacy wouldn't have a problem telling a guy she didn't want to see him, but the fact is she and Stacy aren't very alike at all. Leeann has a certain weakness in her that can't cast people aside so easily.

"Dante," she says at last, "I am truly sorry for your loss, I am, but I am very busy right now. Maybe when I'm done with school-"

"Just tell me straight Leeann," he interrupts, but there's no anger in his voice. He sounds like a man who has been down this road many, many times and just wants to know if he can take his heart off of his sleeve and put it back in his chest where it belongs. This makes her feel worse than hearing about his dead mother. "Just tell me you don't want to see me."

Here it is. Here is your chance to end this whole thing now. Get it over with.

She opens her mouth to speak, to tell him yes; not seeing one another would be for the best. They had a good time in Pharmacoastalcal but that was then and this is now and she really must get on with her life. She wants to wish him well in his endeavors, say how sorry she is about his mother one more time and hang up the phone, disconnect him from her life for good but she suddenly finds she can't do it. Her compassion for others is too strong, her disposition too sweet to be so callous. She knows he isn't the man she wants to be with (she's pretty sure) but she simply can't kick him while he's down. And she did say that when he got out of his drug trial and she got back from her trip they would go out. She didn't promise anything beyond that, so maybe she should honor her commitment and then she can move on with her life. She sighs, shrugs to herself, makes up her mind.

"Okay," she says.

"Okay?"

"The answer is yes. What time do you want to pick me up tomorrow?"

SEVENTEEN

Tyler hasn't slept in three days, has hardly eaten, hasn't showered or shaved. Wes is starting to get concerned, but there is nothing he can say because Tyler doesn't listen to him. Never has before anyway.

He sits at Wes's kitchen table, a cup of coffee before him, patchy fuzz covering his sunken cheeks. He stares out the window with a vacant expression that is somewhat unsettling. His eyes are out of focus and his mouth is slack. It's almost as if he's asleep with his eyes open, or possibly in a trance. Wes decides he can't take it anymore.

"Tyler, hey buddy," he says softly, waving a hand in front of the other's face. "Earth to Tyler…come in Tyler."

Tyler doesn't move, doesn't blink. Shit. Wes has never seen him like this before, especially over a woman.

"Tyler!" he shouts, but there is only a subtle movement, a twitch in his left cheek. This is downright crazy. The time for action has come.

Wes takes a deep breath, psyching himself up, then slaps Tyler across the face, hard.

"Hey! What the hell are you doing man?" Tyler demands, rubbing his cheek. "That hurt!"

"I'm worried about you," Wes explains. "It's like you can't even hear me."

"Of course I can hear you; I was just ignoring you." Tyler looks at him crossly, his irritation at the other giving him a new focal point. "How would you like it if I hit you?"

"Dude you're sitting there like a zombie; you're off in outer space and you got drool running down your chin! What the hell was I supposed to think?"

"That I'm deep in thought? Duh!"

Wes rolls his eyes. 'Deep in thought' is a misnomer for good old Tyler. What he really means is 'deep in calculating/planning/scamming mode. Tyler doesn't think so much as he plots.

"Well, since I have your attention, is there anything I can do to help?"

Now it's Tyler's turn to roll his eyes.

"You already blew that days ago, dude. I think I can do without your help."

Wes has always been subservient to his friend, has always played the fool and acted like second best. He can't help it, he has low self-esteem. Throughout his entire life he's always put his friend's needs before his own because he was happy just to have them around. Maybe he's never felt worthy of an equal, someone who could look up to him, maybe listen to and trust his opinions for a change.

And it is for this reason that he finally snaps, at long last realizing there's no way he's going to just sit here and play second fiddle to someone who consistently treats him like shit. The hell with it. Why bother?

"Yeah?" he says, standing up quickly, knocking his chair over. "Well you're the pussy who couldn't go and talk to her yourself!"

"What?" Tyler says, surprised. "What did you say to me?"

"You heard me, you leeching bastard!" Wes fumes, picking up steam. "Since you're too big of a wuss to talk to her yourself she's going to slip away! Is that what you want? And what the hell did I do but try and help? You've been acting like a dick for days!" Spittle flies from his lips, and at once he's aware of a strange sensation, one he isn't accustomed to. It's like a weight has been lifted off of his shoulders. So this is what it's like to just let go.

"Did you just call me a 'leech'?"

"Don't act stupid! You are a 'taker' Tyler, that's all you've ever been. You used that poor woman until she couldn't stand it anymore and now that's what you're doing to me, hell what you've done to me since I've known you!"

"Hey man, that's not true-"

"Isn't it? Tell me when you've ever paid for anything, huh? Tell me when you actually spent any money on me, bought my beer, my sandwich. Go ahead, tell me!"

"Well, I...I..." Tyler stammers and Wes nods vigorously.

"That's right, you don't know, do you? Hard to remember something you've never done."

"Dude, I really don't need this right now-"

"I don't think you are in any position to tell me what you're in the mood for or not. This may surprise you Tyler but you know what? I OWN you! Got that? Where are you going to go if I kick you out of here, huh? Where?"

"Hey man, please...you wouldn't do that to me would you?" Tyler implores, dropping his angry façade and beseeching the other with eyes that take on a Bambi-esque quality, his voice tremulous with sudden emotion. "I thought we were friends man..."

"We're only friends because you need someone to look after you, to pay for your food and give you a place to stay. If she hadn't thrown you out I would only see you whenever there was a football game on and you wanted someone to supply the beer and pizza."

"You can't really believe that." Tyler's face remains calm but inside his guts are roiling. *The little bastard is totally on to me. I wonder how long this has been building up?*

"Tyler," Wes says, as if reading his thoughts. "I've been on to you since the day I met you and bought you your first beer. Shit, I'd be an idiot if I wasn't. I've been playing this game my whole freaking life." This last part is said with resignation, and Wes picks up the chair and plops down, slumping forward. For a second it seems as if the fight has gone out of him. Tyler watches him warily for a couple of minutes when at once a feeling rises within him, something he doesn't recognize. Could it be pity? This is new for him, much like his feelings for Melissa.

"Well if you knew than why did you let me, you know, take advantage?" he asks earnestly, but he knows the answer, they both do.

"Because I look up to you and I don't have any other friends," Wes replies dejectedly. "I figured it wasn't so bad, renting friends. At least I'd have some company and someone to pretend my jokes are funny."

"Hey man, don't get down on yourself. I really enjoy hanging out with you, really."

"You wouldn't say that if I cut you off and kicked you out of here," Wes retorts. "You're just trying to get back on my good side so you can continue your work free life, can continue mooching off of me."

"You know, you're probably right," Tyler agrees, surprising Wes as well as himself.

"Say what?"

Tyler shakes his head. He doesn't know what the hell is happening to him but for once in his rotten existence he actually experiences empathy for the people he uses and abuses. The feeling is terrifying, as it is entirely new. It's also somewhat exhilarating, like doing anything for the first time.

"I know what I'm doing is wrong but I just can't help myself, never could."

"You…you're accepting responsibility?" Wes's face registers shock. He never, ever would have seen this coming. Unless it's some kind of trick…

"It's my nature to take, I'm simply powerless to stop. It's been like this my whole life."

Wes stands up again, figuring this is Tyler's new ruse: culpability coupled with bogus self-loathing. He'll be damned if he's going to let it work on him.

"You're an even bigger asshole than I thought!" he declares.

"What? I'm trying to open up to you man-"

"The hell you are! This is just a new kind of scam. You're worse off than I thought you were *man*. I would have accepted it if you'd gotten angry but this self-deprecating bit doesn't fool me for a second." Wes glares at him venomously. "It's time for you to get out of here Tyler."

"What-"

"Just get your shit and go." His decision is final, his mind more than made up. "You heard me! Get up, get your shit and get the hell out of here!"

Tyler jumps to his feet. His surprise is so complete that there's nothing he can do but what is asked.

"Okay man but-"

"I don't want to hear it! Just get your things and go!"

Tyler scuttles out of the room, gathers a few of his possessions and stuffs them in his mangled backpack. Maybe if he leaves his boxes of junk he can use them as an excuse to come back later, but Wes follows him into the next room.

"Get all of your things Tyler."

"Fine." Tyler grabs his crummy boxes, which he hasn't even bothered to unpack.

"When you get a clue maybe we can talk but until that day you can just wallow in your own crapulence for all I care!"

"But I have gotten a clue," Tyler tries to explain. "I realize what I've been doing is wrong-"

"Quit playing me for a fool! I didn't fall off the banana boat yesterday! Just get out of here before I call the cops!"

How many times has Tyler heard that one before? Too many to count. He knows when his number's up.

He shuffles to the door, head down, ragged backpack slung over one shoulder, crappy boxes tucked under his arms.

"Wes..."

"Out!"

"All right then." He steps out the door and Wes slams it behind him.

What now genius? He feels like an idiot for expressing his new outlook. If it wasn't for this sudden change of heart he probably wouldn't be standing here right now, in his tattered bathrobe with his few belongings crammed helter skelter into a backpack that saw better days years ago, old cardboard boxes bursting at the seams holding items that possess little earthly value. He has no idea what he is going to do, where he's going to go.

And then a thought hits him. He knows someone who might appreciate his new views, someone who might listen to him when he says he has changed. He'd meant to talk to her several days ago but for some reason he put it off, afraid to confront her after what she'd said about back-rent. Well, homelessness has forced his hand once again. It's time to have the conversation he'd been planning on having with her since the day in the coffee shop.

Straightening up, feeling better than he has in quite some time, Tyler puts one foot in front of the other and marches purposefully down the hall.

EIGHTEEN

"Yes dear, I know, I know, the curtains look simply *atrocious*. You're right as always. What? Sure, whatever color you want. I just want you to be happy." Governor Hallsly sighs, slouches in his chair and stares out at the beautiful late spring day. Winter was a cool one for Sacramento and it's good to see the plants and flowers in full bloom again. Not that he has an eye for earthly beauty (in plant form) but it does give him something to look at while the old battle axe bores him to tears with her pissing and moaning. They've been in the governor's mansion for over three years and NOW she's hot and bothered about redecorating the whole place. Does she think it will sway the voters to elect him for another term? "No, I don't care what anybody else thinks about this but you, trust me. What? Of course you can trust me. Would I lie to you?" He grimaces. "Okay, would I lie to you about *that*? See, I didn't think so."

His intercom buzzes and the voice of his secretary announces he has a call on line two.

"Look honey I have to go. Business calls." He reaches to push the button for the other line but stops short. "No dear, nothing is more important than you but if I don't take this we might have to find some place else to live. You want those new curtains or not? I thought so. I love you too." He pushes the button. "Governor Hallsly here."

"Hello sir, this is Ben Bradly and I wanted you to know we're just about set to go."

"Excuse me?" Hallsly says, wondering if this is in regards to his lunch or his meeting with the economic committee this afternoon.

"It's all being arranged sir," the other explains patiently. "Everything's coming together beautifully."

"Why that's excellent, uh, Bradly is it?" Hallsly says, slightly irritated. "But would you mind telling me what you're talking about?"

"Uh, the ship sir."

"The ship, right, the ship...what fucking ship?"

"For the expedition to the giant trash heap sir," Bradly replies, fighting the urge to add 'you stupid asshole'. He's been working around the clock making arrangements for a ship and crew, scrambling to assemble a scientific team while trying to keep the budget as small as possible. To save money he's posted ads at a few select colleges for unpaid scientific interns and put out his feelers as far south as San Diego to find adequate and competent security for all these 'people of import'. And he has done all of this on the behest of one Governor Hallsly.

"Oh, right, that ship! Good work young man, good work!"

"I'm only five years younger than you are sir," Bradly says a touch peevishly, but Hallsly doesn't notice.

"So everything is coming along then, huh?"

"That's what I've been telling you."

"Wonderful, just wonderful. Well, keep up the good work." Hallsly is about to hang up the phone when the other says:

"So will you be ready to set sail in three days sir?"

"Uh, what?"

"According to my information you'll be going along as a political liaison, a representative of the California people."

"I will be?"

"Yes sir."

"Oh, um, well, let's not get too hasty about this. I'll have to make a few calls and get back to you."

"Okay, let me give you this number-" he's saying when the phone goes dead.

Meanwhile Hallsly gets his secretary on the intercom.

"Do you know anything about me accompanying the ship out to the trash heap?" he snarls, wondering if she had something to do with it.

"Yes sir, that's part of the arrangement."

"Really? Than how come I don't know about it?"

"Well you should, the woman from Washington specified when she talked to me that you'd be going as well-"

"Get that bitch on the phone!"

"Excuse me, sir?"

"I said 'get that bitch on the phone'! I want to hear it from her."

"Very good."

Hallsly takes his finger off the intercom and leans back in his chair. Why do they need him to chaperone a bunch of sailors and scientists? Like, how boring would that be? The hell with that noise. *When I talk to that cunt from Washington I'm going to tell her to stuff it up her ass. Screw that shit.*

"Sir?" his secretary says. "She's waiting for you on line one."

"Thanks." He punches a button. "Hello?"

He can't believe he actually has to go, in fact is feeling rather sorry for himself right now. It isn't fair. Just because the damn trash heap is off the California coast doesn't make it his responsibility. Fucking hell. He wishes it were further north so it would be the governor of Oregon's problem, but no such luck. Bastards.

(*Think of all the respect you'll get from your peers,*' the bitch from Washington said. '*No one needs to know you were required to attend, you can say you volunteered, just so you could see for yourself what type of environmental hazard it posits.*'

'*But I couldn't care less about the environment!*'

'*Look, the thing is, we need to put a good spin on this thing. The idea is that we nip this in the butt; we take care of it once and for all. Don't you want to be on the forefront of a brand new future, a day when we can say we've made a mess but we've cleaned it up because that is the American way?*'

'*No!*'

'*I don't care you're going anyway. The president was adamant about that.*'

'*That's because he wants to see my nuts on the chopping block,*' Hallsly moaned and the other snorted derisive laughter.

'*Probably so, yeah. But don't worry, you only have to go out there and put in a political appearance. After a couple days we'll have the coast guard pick you up. You don't have to stay out there for the entire mission.*' She issued another burst of contemptuous laughter. '*I'm sure you have all kinds of important things you need to be doing there, hmm?*'

'*Are you implying I'm not doing my job?*'

'*If the shoe fits, have sex with it.*'

'*What about my constituents? What will they think if I disappear for a few days?*'

'*I'm certain they won't even know you're gone,*' she'd said and that was the end of it.)

He shakes his head miserably, thinking about what a waste of time it will be. Stuck on some ship in the middle of the ocean, nothing to do but stare at miles and miles of endless water. What is he going to do for fun? Surely they don't expect him to go several days without blowing off a little steam. Being the governor is a stressful job, lots of responsibility and all that. And what about his need for chastising? Who is going to administer a sound spanking whenever he needs one?

And then it hits him, an answer to all his woes. A smile suddenly spreads across his ruddy face. He pushes the button on his intercom for his secretary.

"Hey babe, cancel all my appointments today will ya? I have to be out of the office."

"I don't think that's going to fly sir," she explains patiently. "You're expecting a big wig from L.A. at two and the economic committee wants to discuss the state budget at three thirty-"

"Look, I need to make preparations for my trip out to the trash heap, okay? It takes precedence, trust me."

"But sir-"

"No buts'!" he proclaims, but he can think of one he wants on board that ship with him...

NINETEEN

Studying a cantaloupe, trying to decide if it is too ripe (or not ripe enough) Kenny finally tosses it in his cart. *Gotta start eatin' healthy.* Fruit's probably a step in the right direction. Maybe from there he can gradually ease himself into vegetables. No more meals consisting entirely of foods either fried or chicken fried.

"Holy God in Heaven!" someone exclaims, startling him. "What are you doing in the fruit aisle? Is the world as I know it going to hell or what?"

Kenny turns and sees Hank's smiling, greasy face. Even from several feet away he can smell the booze oozing from the other's pores, can see the sweat stains spreading around his armpits. *So this is what he looks like in 'normal' light. Do I look that bad?* This is the first time he's ever seen his buddy while sober, and he has to admit it ain't pretty. Hank has rosy cheeks cobwebbed with broken blood vessels and a nose as bulbous as it is shiny. His rumpled clothing looks like it saw better days a decade ago, and even then they weren't exactly in the height of fashion. But it's good to see a friendly face; Kenny's been holed up in his crummy room for the last four days, trying to kick the sauce and get his life back on track.

"Hank ya ole dog," he says, unable to suppress a grin. "What the hell ya doin' here? Ya gonna buy some oranges and make toilet wine?"

"Maybe I will." Hank rubs the scruff on his face with a dirty hand while his eyes wander around the brightly lit store. "Maybe I will." Hank looks at him for a moment, actually studies him. "You look good," he decides. "Healthy."

"I only been on the wagon four days Hank."

"Yeah, and it shows."

"Thanks." As pleasant as it is to see his friend, he feels a flicker of apprehension erupt in his stomach, a vague uneasiness. Surely Hank knows how hard it is to be around other drinkers when one is trying to quit. It's not that he doesn't want to see him but he barely has a grasp on this just yet. Every day has been a fight for survival, a battle not to just give in and buy a bottle of Old Granddad and drink until everything gets soft and fuzzy around the edges. Sobriety is terrifying. Just leaving his crappy apartment makes his heart pound fiercely, makes him sweat like its 100 degrees outside.

"How you holding up?" Hank asks and Kenny shrugs.

"Shitty."

"Yeah, I guess that's how it goes." Hank examines the melons as he talks. "I couldn't interest you in having a drink with me, could I?" he says suddenly, eyes boring into him inquisitively.

Kenny feels heat suffusing his cheeks and for a second can't place if it is anger or embarrassment. He opens his mouth to speak but has no idea what it is he is going to say, as if his body and brain have become disconnected. He sputters feebly, a string of words that are completely unintelligible, and all the while Hank watches him, a smirk sitting askew on his face.

"I'm just testin' your resolve man," he says at last. "You passed with flyin' colors."

"I was tryin' ta work up the nerve to say 'no' when I was dyin' ta say 'yes'," Kenny confesses, blowing out a shaky breath and the other reaches out and puts a hand on his shoulder.

"Shit, I wouldn't do that to you partner, I was just seeing how serious you were." He gives Kenny's shoulder a squeeze and lets go. "I been looking for you so I could tell you the good news."

"What?" Kenny looks at Hank curiously. At this point what could possibly be considered 'good news'?

"You got a call at the bar yesterday."

"Yeah?" he says, confused. If someone wanted to talk to him, why the hell didn't they just call his room? Course, they might not have been able to find his number, as it's unlisted. It seems the only time the phone rings is when it's a wrong number or a telemarketer randomly dialing. Occasionally it's his ma, but not so much anymore because he hardly ever answers, just lets it ring and ring. For all he knows, whoever called the bar tried his room first.

"It was somebody from the governor's office. Said they wanted you to give them a call."

Kenny's heart misses a beat. Did he do something wrong? What the hell would anyone possibly want with him?

"What'd they say?"

"Gave the bartender a phone number, and he gave it to me to give to you."

Kenny shakes his head. "No, no, did they say what it was about?"

Hank's face splits in a grin. "Said it was about a job offer, if you were interested."

"Really?" Kenny says skeptically. "Why the hell would they go and do that?"

Hank shrugs. "Don't know, but that's what they said."

"So how tha hell did ya find me here?"

"Saw your car in the parking lot."

"Oh," he nods. "Right."

"So are you gonna call them or what?"

Kenny considers the question, picking up a cantaloupe and tossing it back and forth between his hands. He's not sure if he is ready for the 'real' world; it's entirely possible the stress of working would awaken the terror in him, the fear of confronting and embracing reality. These last few days have been agonizing, unadulterated hell, but hiding in his room it wasn't as bad as it would be out in public, dealing with people and their problems, situations that are beyond his control. In hiding all you have is yourself and your misery, and you can make of it whatever you want. But outside the safety of those walls, well, anything can happen. Is he prepared to hop out of the skillet and into the fire so soon?

"Well? Inquiring minds want to know."

"Maybe…" he stammers.

"Maybe hell. You call them." Hank fixes him with a frigid stare. "Ya know, I wouldn't push but the fact is I like you. I think you actually have a shot to beat this. I don't say this often but here goes: you can do better."

"Why Hank, I'm touched," Kenny jokes, but in his guts he detects a stirring of mawkish sentiment, a poignant reminder that he's still human and not the detached, cynical man he embodies with every word, every gesture. He's been so neglectful of his family and anyone he used to call a friend that Hank is the only person he really has left. This old wino sod has become much more to him than a drinking buddy, it's like he's become his freaking lifeline.

"I got the number in my pocket," Hank says. "Let's go find a payphone."

"I could take it…call 'em from my place," Kenny says hesitantly, and something in his tone causes Hank's eyes to narrow distrustfully.

"Nah, I want to be there when you call, and I ain't goin' anywhere near your place."

"Then where? Ain't no phone here."

"Let's go to the bar."

"You know I can't do that Hank." Kenny's eyes beseech the other for leniency, for mercy, and Hank can see the fear shining brightly within them like a lighthouse's beacon. Beads of sweat pop up on the large man's brow.

"All right," Hank says quietly. "We'll make the call from your place."

"What's this 'we' shit?" Kenny says roughly, but there is a smile forming around the words.

"Thought you might have trouble dialing…" Hank plays along amicably.

"Gimmie that phone number ya bastard before I shake ya down for it."

"That's not very nice."

"Ain't ya noticed? I'm *not* very nice."

"Nah," Hank waves a hand dismissively. "I never noticed."

TWENTY

A sea of faceless bodies rush past Leeann as she makes her way through the commons to her last class of the day, hordes of anonymous strangers whose only function, it would seem, is to impede her progress. She jostles her way through impatiently, caring very little if her elbows 'accidentally' jab anyone in the ribs, ignoring any grunts or complaints in her wake. The late afternoon sun is shining brightly through the floor to ceiling windows and right now she simply wishes she were outside basking in it's warm rays and far away from this institution that's been her world every waking hour (well, almost) for the last three years. Every year the freshmen look younger and younger and the magic of the campus and its time-honored traditions becomes more tedious. She is so over it. She just wants to move on.

Her cell phone rings and for a second she's tempted to ignore it, fearing it may be Dante again. What more could he want that she hasn't already told him?

Digging the phone out of her bag, she looks at the name and sees it's Stacy.

"Hello?"

"Hey girlfriend, where you at?" Stacy says with an overabundance of enthusiasm and at once Leann is suspicious.

"I'm in the commons," she replies warily. "What's up?"

"Perfect place for you to be. Meet me by the job board."

"What for? I have to get to class."

"Pardon me, but fuck that. There is something you really need to see."

"Look, I don't have time for this. I really have to get going-"

"Didn't you hear me? I said, and I quote: 'fuck that'. This takes precedence over your stupid class."

"It won't seem so stupid when you find out I need it to graduate," Leann counters, starting to get pissed off, but Stacy's laughter on the other end is playful, girlish.

"Would you believe me if I told you that you don't need it to graduate?"

"What are you talking about?"

"Look, just get your ass over to the job board. See ya." And then there's nothing but dead air.

"What the hell?" Leann muses, and against her better instincts decides to investigate.

Leann has read and re-read the ad at least five times while Stacy stands beside her, beaming.

"Can you believe it? This is just what you are looking for."

"Yeah..." Leann says uncertainly, for the moment not quite able to accept it as true. It's like someone read her mind. The ad says:

'Job of a lifetime for a few select candidates. All Science majors welcome but those in marine biology and oceanic studies preferred. Only third and fourth year students may apply, and if selected your involvement will count as your final examinations. Volunteers needed for scientific investigation of neustonic particles off the coast of California. Position entails data collection that will be used to potentially eliminate future pollution problems in the world's oceans. This is your chance to do something positive, to make a difference. Please call (916) 555-5721 for more details.'

"You just spotted this today?" Leeann asks and Stacy nods.

"Yeah, like ten minutes ago. I was looking to see if there were any 'tutors wanted' ads so I could make some extra money and this stood out like a sore thumb."

"When do you think it was posted?"

"Looks pretty new, I mean, there isn't anything covering it up yet. Give it a call."

"Right now?"

Stacy grins. "What the hell are you waiting for, Christmas? Give it a call before they reach capacity."

"Do you think they will?"

"Of course they will you dummy! Some research trip that will count as your finals? What the hell do you think?"

"Alright," Leann says, removing her phone from her bag. "Here goes nothing."

Leann never made it to her last class of the day, not after she spoke with someone representing the ad. There simply seemed to be no need. With a speed that was positively spooky she found herself being interviewed over the phone, and was then instructed to forward her academic credentials and special studies information to their official website. She'd raced to her apartment like a woman possessed, sending them what they requested and, after only thirty short minutes, received an email reply that instructed her to call a local number immediately. When she called, the person on the other end set up an interview with her for the following day.

"When does the trip start?" she'd asked and to her surprise was told 'In a few days.'

A few days? That sure didn't leave much time for any extensive planning. This seemed like a seat of your pants, toss some things in a bag and get the hell out of dodge assignment if she ever heard one…and it was right up her alley. She'd asked a few other questions, regarding the ship, length of the trip etc. and she'd be lying if she said she wasn't aware that the other was being deliberately vague about the details. She felt she owed it to herself to ask, as these were important queries, but something inside nagged her that it really didn't matter. All her life she'd always been the safe one, the one who never did anything unless she knew all the facts, always looking before she leapt. She'd be damned if anyone was going to get anything over on her. But suddenly she just doesn't care. Maybe it was all those years staying on the side of caution; maybe it was all the time spent in controlled environments. For once she wanted to step out and take a chance (at least, a controlled chance) and this sounded like a great opportunity for her to leave the classroom and get out into the world and see what she's really made of.

She'd also be lying if she said that this decision didn't have to do with the evasion of a certain individual, one who's expecting her company tomorrow evening. When she tells him she can't see him because she's been selected for a research trip what can he do? Beg her not to go? Surely he'd realize how selfish that was, asking her to put her career on hold so they can explore a 'relationship'.

No, Dante isn't going to like this, not one bit, and she finds it bothers her not at all. Her parents, on the other hand, are going to be thrilled…

TWENTY-ONE

"All right," Madam Coventry says apathetically, releasing the man hanging before her. "You can jerk yourself off if you want to."

"Thank you Ma'am," the muscled, shaved monkey gushes, reaching for his painfully erect penis and tugging at it for all he's worth.

As he gasps and moans she places a hand to her lips to stifle a gag. Some days this job really is *work*...

At last he comes and she hands him a towel, tells him to clean up. He does as instructed, and after he's dressed she sends him on his way.

"That's it," she mutters gratefully, taking off her mask and walking into the living room where she settles into a large, overstuffed chair. "Last customer of the day."

And then her phone rings, and for a second she's tempted to take the damn thing and throw it at the wall. But business is business and if she wants to make sure the bills get paid she has to line up clients to fill in her schedule for the week...

Things just haven't been the same since the day she'd gotten careless with that client; she's been avoiding Monica's 'spa', afraid she might do something similar and disgrace herself publicly, and because she hasn't been coming around they've stopped calling her. It's up to her to dredge up her own business now.

"Madam Coventry's Dungeon."

"Hey baby, have I got a job opportunity for you!" someone says and Melissa has to restrain herself from simply saying 'fuck off' and hanging up the phone.

"Who is this?" she demands instead.

"It's me!"

"You're going to have to be a little more specific than that." She crosses her legs and slouches further into her chair.

"I, uh, don't want to say my name over the phone you know, it's a matter of, um, public security…"

She groans softly, closing her eyes and massaging her forehead with her free hand. Of course. Governor what's his face.

"And what can I do for you today your majesty?"

"Can I come and see you?"

"Right now?"

"I can't think of a better time."

"I can, and that time is tomorrow. The shop is closed, I'm done for the day."

"This can't wait."

"I guess it's going to have to," she says and is about to hang up when he says:

"The job I'm offering pays a thousand bucks a day plus expenses."

This gives her a reason to pause. "Come again?"

"You heard me. Are you interested?"

"Who do I have to kill?" she asks, sighing.

"No one…at least, not yet," he replies, chuckling.

"Are you messing with me?" These political assholes always think they can get whatever they want by throwing cash around, as if they are immune from the rest of the world.

"No babe I'm dead serious! I have the job of a lifetime for you-"

"If this is some kind of stupid joke…"

"No joke, I swear. Just let me come over and I'll tell you everything."

"I want to see some money upfront or no deal."

"You got it, no problem," he says, waiting a couple of beats before adding: "So I'll see you in about thirty minutes?"

"You know where to find me." And she hangs up the phone.

"Make yourself comfortable," she says when the governor comes blustering in, tossing his jacket over a chair and making an immediate beeline for her liquor bottles.

"Sorry babe, I just need to unwind a little. I've had a rough day." He pours himself a stiff shot of whiskey into a dirty plastic cup and tops it with a little tap water. He stirs it with his pinky and looks at her with his beady rat's eyes. He then has the audacity to toss her an insidious wink and for the second time in less than an hour she feels as if she is going to throw-up.

"Well? Are you going to spill it or do I have to beat it out of you?"

"I told you, I have a job offer for you." He knocks back half of the drink and frowns. "Damn, you should get one of those water filter things. This tap water tastes like shit."

"There's bottled water in the fridge ya dumb-ass," Melissa says. "Take a seat, huh?"

"Sure, sure." He drops into the overstuffed chair she'd recently been occupying. Sipping his drink, he looks around at her condo as if he is seeing it for the first time. "I love the color scheme you got going in here. It really has 'dungeon' written all over it."

"So what's this job you're talking about?" she prompts, her tone implying he should get to the point quick before someone (namely he) gets hurt.

"It's a little trip actually, a boat trip-"

"A boat trip?" she huffs, shaking her head. "What, a cruise? Like on a cruise ship?"

"No, this is totally work related, honest. Just give me five minutes and I'll explain the whole thing."

"The clock is ticking."

"So I'm supposed to be, what? Your secretary? Is that what you have in mind?"

"You got it babe. Personal assistant is what I'll be calling you officially, but it doesn't really matter, it's basically just a title to throw everyone off."

"And this boat trip is for what, science?"

"Yup. I've been ordered to go by the President of the United States himself and I figure as long as my participation is mandatory I might as well make a party out of it, if you know what I mean."

"Are you saying I'm the party?"

"Well, you and dozen bottles of whiskey…"

"And you're going to pay me a thousand bucks a day?"

"Plus expenses."

"What sort of expenses does one incur on a ship out in the middle of the ocean?"

"I don't know, clothes? Whips? Whatever floats yer boat babe."

"No pun intended I'm sure."

"None, naturally." He guzzles the remainder of his drink and gets up to make another.

"I'll have to think about this," she says, caressing her chin thoughtfully. "I have regular customers who need their daily sessions, and I have friends who will want to know where I'm going." This last statement she says as a matter of principle only. This merry fucking asshole has no idea she doesn't currently have any close friends, but she's seen enough movies to know politicians can't be trusted. Like all those fucking Kennedy's. Any woman who hopped in a car or a plane with one of those bastards was simply out of her mind.

She studies him with narrowed eyes, watches as he pours a double-make that triple-shot into the plastic cup, forgoing the water. What a numbskull. You can never trust politicians because they are all lying scumbags purposely crafting their agenda to cater to their fragile egos. Hell, issues have nothing to do with anything, she's sure. It's all just a bunch of posturing and self-serving crap dreamed up by men and women who were chased around the playground as kids.

Twisted little bastards who've been dreaming of revenge since the last time they got sand kicked in their face or mud shoveled into their underpants. Melissa knows enough not to trust herself in the care of someone who uses the phrase 'blah blah blah my constituents...' but the money sure sounds good. She really needs it, but is there some way she can safeguard herself? Have her cake and live long enough to eat it too?

And then, as if in answer to her silent question, the doorbell rings.

TWENTY-TWO

Shambling down the street like a man heading to meet his destiny, Tyler goes over and over in his head what he is going to say to Melissa, hoping desperately that this pre-planning will serve him well.

'You see honey,' he half says/thinks, mouthing the words as imperceptibly as he can, not wanting to make a scene on a city sidewalk, 'I know I've been a dickhead, I know I've been totally selfish, and with your help I can change. Please, help me to help myself.'

He shakes his head. No, that's not it, but he's getting close.

'I am a taker Melissa, always have been and, up until this point, I was sure I always would be. But that time is over, and I want you to know I've changed or, more so, I've accepted I *can* change...'

Okay, that's better, but how can he best describe how he's suddenly feeling? This newfound mindset that prompted Wes to toss him out on his ass, thinking it was just another one of his tricks? How can he convey it and have her understand?

'In this world we all get one chance at greatness, and I see that greatness in you, Melissa. You can help me to be a better person; can help me to realize my full potential. Please, help me to become the man I know I can be...'

"Who the hell are you talking to?" someone asks, startling him. He glances around but there is no one on the sidewalk. "Over here man."

He turns and sees its Wes, sitting behind the wheel of his crappy car, pulled over in a No Parking Zone.

"Hey Wes," Tyler says lamely. "What's up?"

"Look, I might have over reacted a bit back there..."

Tyler looks at him silently, his humility forgotten for a moment, his scheming brain taking over. Wes is apologizing? Oh man, what a sucker, what a fuckin' rube...I really could use a beer and a sandwich, maybe a game of pool at that strip club across town…But instead he closes his eyes, takes a deep breath and holds it, letting it out slowly. No, not like this. Not if he wants to get Melissa back.

"You weren't wrong," he says quietly.

"What?" Wes asks, unable to believe Tyler is continuing to take this stance. Maybe he's serious after all. It hardly seems possible but, hell, stranger things have happened.

After kicking Tyler out he'd paced the length of his apartment, wondering what he was going to do now that he no longer had any friends, had severed his only connection to the rest of the hostile world, and he'd finally come to the realization that if it wasn't Tyler using him than it would be someone else. Shit, it might as well be Tyler because he already knows him so well. And it isn't like he hates the guy, he just wants things to be a little more evenly balanced…but, if that isn't possible, than he just wants his friend back, no matter how debasing.

"I said, 'you weren't wrong dude'," Tyler repeats, looking at the other with an expression that mimics worldliness. "I'm glad you finally came out and said it. You deserve a better friend than me."

"No I don't!" Wes blurts, unable to help himself. "I'm a loser!"

"Jesus dude, don't ever say that!" Tyler scolds, continuing to walk. "You're just a pushover, and that's how come I took advantage of you."

Wes follows Tyler slowly up the street, not caring that other pedestrians are taking notice. "Come on man, get in the car and we'll go and get a beer, like old times."

"You've shown me the error of my ways," Tyler says sagely, as if he has aged many years in the last sixty minutes. "I can't take your money anymore."

"Come on, I'm offering as a friend-oh shit!" Wes hasn't been paying attention to where he's going and he looks up just in time to see he's about to rear end a parked car. He swerves to avoid it and then pulls back alongside the curb.

"Get a room!" some joker yells from somewhere unseen and onlookers laugh, but Tyler pays no mind.

"You aren't helping me by doing this Wes. You did the right thing by cutting me loose."

"Well, at least let me give you a ride," Wes suggests. "Where are you going?"

"I'm going to talk to Melissa. I think maybe I'm ready to be what she wants me to be."

"Isn't that a line from a cheesy 80's song?" Wes says, crinkling his face in distaste and Tyler shrugs. "Look dude, don't make a scene, just get in the car."

Tyler stops, looks closely at the guy he's bilked for cash over the last several months.

"I just want you to know you don't have to feel obligated Wes," he says. "I am a big boy and I can take care of myself."

"I know man, I know," Wes agrees. "But if you want I'll give you a lift. No obligations, nothing…" Incredibly, his voice breaks and he actually swipes a tear out of one eye. "I'm sorry I was so hard on you man."

"Jesus Christ," Tyler mutters, the fagot quotient finally getting to him. If it will shut him up…"Okay man, I'll take a ride." He walks over to the passenger door, hops in.

"You hungry?" Wes asks.

"Well now that you mention it…"

"So that's your idea? You're going to march in there and tell her you've changed?"

"I *have* changed," Tyler insists, gulping from a mug of beer and stuffing the last bite of a sandwich in his mouth. "I just need to make her see it..."

And believe it. Yet Wes sighs, happy to be back with his friend.

"Okay, you've changed. But what does it mean?"

"It means what you think it means. I'm going to get a job."

Wes chokes on his beer. "You gotta be shitting me!"

Tyler gives him the evil eye.

"Not very supportive," he says, wiping his mouth, and Wes falls all over himself to apologize.

"All right man, I believe in you. I know you can do it." He frowns thoughtfully. "You think she'll believe it?"

Tyler shrugs. "Good question." He looks at the other's half eaten sandwich. "Are you going to eat that?"

"No, go for it," Wes says and Tyler dives in. They sit there for several minutes in silence, well, relative silence save for the loud chewing noises Tyler is making. When he's finished he looks at the other speculatively, as if seeing Wes for the first time.

"You know, you aren't helping me by doing this."

"Hey, you gotta eat."

"I would be better off if you left me to fend for myself."

Now you say it, after you've eaten your food and mine. But again he lets it slide.

"I know man, but let a guy do you a favor, huh?"

"You've done me enough favors."

"Well, let me do one more for you."

"What's that?" Tyler looks at the other suspiciously, hoping like hell Wes isn't going to offer to blow him. He really can't see it coming to that...not if things go well with Melissa...

"Let me give you a ride over to Melissa's place. It's the least I can do."

Tyler picks up his napkin and wipes his hands. He shrugs and then nods.

"Okay, cool."

TWENTY-THREE

Kenny drives along in the hazy sunshine, enjoying the mellow feel of the day. For the first time in years he feels like he has a purpose, and it helps baby, it really helps. It makes it seem as if his recent quest towards sobriety is worth it. Hank sits next to him, his window rolled down, arm hanging out.

"I'm kinda nervous bout this, but I feel kinda excited too," Kenny says and Hank nods, turning away for a second and pulling a flask out of the inside pocket of his jacket. He twists off the cap and takes a quick pull, sighing audibly, and tucks it away as quickly as it appeared. Kenny smiles, shakes his head. *Fuckin' old wino sod...*

"You got nothing to be nervous about Kenny. They wouldn't be calling if they didn't need you."

"Maybe that's what I'm worried bout."

But that isn't all. Since he's last seen anyone from the governor's mansion he's undergone some changes that aren't too appealing. For one thing he looks pasty and bloated, his once rock hard physique gone to pot from all the booze and sitting on his ass in dark barrooms, hiding from the outside world. Those festering, dank holes where the smell of piss, vomit and whiskey linger in the air like the specter of a fallen comrade, where 'tomorrow' everything will be all right, as long as there is always another drink in front of you today...

"Where are you going to stop?"

"I don't wanna go by my place, I'm tired a lookin' at them walls." Kenny fidgets with the car lighter, adjusts the rearview mirror. "I figger I should test my resolve a little, like ya said, see if I'm really up for this."

"You're going to Jack's Saloon? Don't you think it's a little too soon?" Hank says. "There's a lot of temptation at Jack's."

"Nothin' I can't handle," Kenny affirms and Hank shrugs.

"Okay," he relents, wanting to add 'it's your funeral' but resists. Kenny turns a corner and parks the car.

"Alright good buddy," Kenny says, putting the car in park and killing the engine. "Let's see what they got to say."

Hank bellies up to the bar and Kenny heads for the payphone in the far corner, near the restrooms. The place is drawing more flies than people as usual, and the bartender is watching a soap opera on the overhead TV. He looks at them briefly as they enter, nodding his head in their direction before returning his attention to the show. Hank waits a full two minutes (until the commercial break) before he is served but it's okay with him; he has his flask to tide him over. Until then he watches Kenny dump four quarters in the slot and study the number on the paper before him. Even from this distance Hank can see Kenny's dialing hand is shaking, and his other he uses to rub his bald head in a continuous circular motion, like he's polishing a bowling ball. Is it the age-old smell of the ghosts of liquor past or is it the prospect of working? Perhaps a little bit of both, Hank decides.

Kenny punches the numbers and waits, the phone ringing in his ear. He wonders if this is a good idea, is also curious why, after firing him, that the governor's office would consider taking him back. It doesn't make sense but, at this point, who is he to question? And he did say (to himself and to his friend, but most importantly to himself) that he wanted to get back to work. Well, this may be his opportunity.

Someone answers and Kenny identifies himself, tells them he's returning a call. He's immediately put on hold while they transfer him. He looks over at Hank, sees him sipping what can only be a whiskey sour and watching 'Weeks of Our Lives' or some shit on the tube. Kenny's tongue creeps out of his mouth, licking lips that feel too dry. Hank's drink looks awfully good and here he is, so damn parched he can't even work up enough spit to successfully moisten a postage stamp. Maybe he should have just one to wet his whistle, you know, to take the edge off. One little drink couldn't hurt, could it? Because he could stop after that, sure he could, no problem. Just sit there and sip the one drink and watch television with Hank for a while. Nothing much else to do anyway...

"Thank you for holding," someone says abruptly. "This is Kenny Howard?"

"Uh, yeah," Kenny replies, fighting hard to dispel the image of a chilled glass beaded with drops of condensation, the amber liquid inside smelling faintly of wood smoke and caramel. "I'm returnin' someone's phone call."

"My phone call," the other informs him. "I called you."

"Great, great, Mr., um..."

"Bradly. Mr. Bradly. How are you today Mr. Howard?"

"Okay." Kenny stares at the payphone and swallows, hearing a dry clicking sound in his throat. "What can I do for ya?"

"I have a job offer for you Mr. Howard, that is, if you aren't currently employed."

Employed? Oh yeah, sure. I bust my ass ever day gettin' so drunk I can barely stand and then I crawl home an lay in my filthy bed, prayin' ta God I don't fuckin' die but hopin' like hell I do...

"No," he replies. "I ain't workin' right now."

"Splendid," Bradly says crisply. "The governor is in need of security personnel for an up coming trip and your name came to mind as we were looking for qualified candidates."

"Really?" Suddenly, for no apparent reason, a reeling sensation of suspicion steals over him, freezing little fingers that squeeze and tighten, squeeze and tighten. "Is that so?"

"Yes Mr. Howard, that is so."

"I don't unnerstand, I mean, you guys canned me for bein' a, uh, for tha fact that I was, uh..." He can't say it. For God's sake he's simply unable to spit the word out of his mouth.

"For being an alcoholic Mr. Howard, yes, I'm aware." The man's voice is cool, detached. "In fact, I know you are calling me from a pub right now."

Kenny pauses a second, looking around. "How do ya know that?"

"Caller ID Mr. Howard."

"Oh, yeah, sure," he says, slightly embarrassed. "So how come ya didn't call me at home?"

"We tried several times. There was no answer."

"I ain't there much-"

"Are you still an alcoholic Mr. Howard?" Bradly interrupts and Kenny's heart thuds in his chest like a Chinese gong, reverberating for what seems to be a very long time.

Oh no sir, I just woke up one morning and discovered I wasn't, praise Jesus! Just like that tha good Lord took me on high and proclaimed me to be free a my demons! Hallelujah!

"I'll always be a alcoholic, sir," Kenny mutters thickly, closing his eyes. He can just picture this prick sitting in his little office, probably with a skyline view of the city, pictures of his wife and kids on his neatly arranged desk, his feet clad in three hundred dollar calf-skin shoes and his brilliant smile positively blinding from the thousands of dollars of dental work he's had over the years.

"But are you drinking, um, presently?" Bradly says, a hint of condescension in his voice. "The fact that we tracked you down at a pub is rather telling."

"So it would seem but, no sir," he answers truthfully, "I quit."

"And you *are* looking for work?"

Am I? Is this what I really want?

"Mr. Howard? Are you there?"

"Yes sir, I'm here."

"Well? Would you like a second chance?"

Come on Kenny, time to shit or get off the pot. You wanna continue the way you been livin' or do you wanna make some major changes? This could be exactly what you need. The guy said it involves a trip; sounds like you can get outta town for a while, get away from this crummy lifestyle. This can be a chance ta get yer life turned around once and for all.

"Tell me what ya got in mind," Kenny finally says.

"Hey Kenny, haven't see you in a while," the bartender says. "The usual?"

"Gimmie a lemon lime soda."

The bartender looks at him dumbly, opens his mouth to say something when Hank says: "Get him a fucking Pepsi Rick."

"Okay," the bartender sulks. "You don't gotta be a dick about it."

"So what's up?" Hank asks, sipping his drink.

Kenny fiddles with a bar napkin, twisting and tearing it. His hands are shaking badly now, Hank notices with no surprise.

"Christ I wanna drink so bad."

"Bad news?"

"I guess not. He wants me ta meet him at the capital buildin' tomorrow for a interview." He shreds the napkin in seconds and starts in on another one. The bartender sets the soda in front of him and quickly moves away, returning to the comfort of his soap opera.

"Really?"

"Yeah, pertty early in tha mornin'. I gotta make sure I get my beauty sleep."

"Sounds like they're going to hire you."

"Maybe, but I wonder if I should question their motives."

"What the hell do you mean?"

"It's just, I don't know, it's for some trip the governor is takin' and, and…"

("Why tha hell would you guys take me back? I thought I was a disgrace to your organization."

"Yes, well, Mr. Howard, we here at the state capital believe in second chances." The other said this in a brusque manner, his voice oddly hollow but not entirely insincere. "Certainly you believe yourself worthy of that, don't you?"

And here Kenny had paused, listening to the swirling sound of light static funneling through the other end of the phone, his eyes closed tightly, trying like hell to get this to make sense to him.

"Don't you Mr. Howard?" The voice persisted. "Surely you owe it to yourself to give this some serious consideration."

"Why?"

"Why?" the other repeated.

"Yeah, why. Why would ya give me a second chance? Is there a reason that I deserve it?"

Silence on the other end except for the sound of breathing, or maybe he was smoking a cigarette, Kenny couldn't tell. At last he spoke, slowly at first, but as the words unfolded he gained momentum.

"Kenny," he said, "you knew what it was like to be important, to be treated well, to be better than other, average people. And this suited you, truly it did, for you were wonderfully talented, gifted if I may be so bold to say. When tragedy struck and you were no longer able to share your gift with the world I imagine things became pretty damn bleak, hell, anyone would feel that way. But you turned it around, showed you were able to put that aside and do some good for your community by aiding the state government, and you did a damn fine job too, had an impeccable record. But when we found out that you were 'misrepresenting' us, shall we say, we felt it was in everybody's best interest to allow you the time to battle these issues, to lay them to rest once and for all. And now here we are, and we need you Kenny, need you to come back to work for us, for the governor. And it sounds like you're ready, hmm? So what do you say? Would you like to do it?"

"Yeah," he'd whispered faintly, feeling emotion growing within him, a sense that he was important, was actually needed for something.

"What Mr. Howard? I can't hear you."

"Yeah," he'd said with more force, opening his eyes and confronting his image in the finger-smudged chrome of the pay phone. "You bet your ass I do."

"Then let me fill you in on the details.")

Hank regards the other. "You don't look too happy about it."

Kenny doesn't say anything, just takes a sip of his soda and stares in the mirror across from him. He feels like he looks old, well, older than he should look for a man who is only in his late twenties. And that's in bar lighting. He can only imagine how he must look in broad daylight.

"I don't know how I feel Hank," he says at last, casting the other a quick, nervous glance. "Maybe I'm jumpin' inta this a little too soon."

"Hey man, trial by fire. Sometimes it's the only way."

"Sure Hank, sure."

"Well," Hank says, choosing his words carefully. "Change doesn't happen all at once. If you want to kick-start your crappy life than this might be a good way of going about it. One step at a time, you know?"

"That's easy for you ta say."

"Yeah, it might be. I'm just an old drunk who'll probably while away the rest of my days in shitholes like this, but at least I'm not some crazy nigger who decided to give up on life just because his high-paying football career went down the crapper."

Kenny looks at his buddy in surprise, anger rising swiftly within him, but it passes just as quickly when he appraises the look in the other's eyes, realizing he means no harm, he's simply making a point.

"Ya know," he says softly, almost marveling, "There was a time when nobody could talk ta me like that. I mean it. *Nobody*. Not my coach, my friends, my women, no one. I woulda popped 'em in the fuckin' mouth."

Hank smiles wide, showing off a mouth that's missing several teeth.

"You don't get a grill like this from censoring yourself," he says. "You want to pop me you go ahead and do it. I know you, and I'm just telling you how it is."

Kenny startles him by putting his arm around his shoulder, growling, and slapping him into a headlock. For a second Hank thinks he might have gone too far because the other's thick bicep is cutting off his air…and then just as quickly he's released and Kenny is clutching him in an awkward hug.

"And I love ya for it man, I do. You say whatever tha hell you wanna say. I can take it."

"Jesus Kenny, don't go fag on me now. I don't think I can handle it," Hank complains, squirming, but he's grinning. He raises an arm and pats the other's shoulder.

"Well, I certainly owe you somethin' for pushin' me to make the call," Kenny says humbly, feeling a catch in the back of his throat. Goddamn if he doesn't feel the sting of tears in his eyes.

"Hey, it's all right big guy, really. It's the least I can do for a friend."

"All right." Kenny swipes at his eyes, snuffles back a load of snot. "Let me buy you a drink."

"I won't turn you down."

"Ya better not." Kenny looks at Hank closely, smiles the most sincere smile that's graced his mug in a long time. "And hey, thanks."

"For what?"

"For what? What do ya think? For believin' in me."

"Any time buddy, any time."

TWENTY-FOUR

"You sure you want to do this? You don't have to you know."

"No," says Tyler, "I have to. It's the only way I'll ever know if I have another shot with her or not."

"And what if she laughs in your face? Then what?"

"Then I walk away and feel good that I tried, that's what."

Wes nods. He wants his friend to be happy, would like him to follow what he believes to be right, but quite frankly he wishes that things could be like they were before, even if it means Tyler is sleeping on his couch until noon, eating all of his food and putting his less than clean shoes on the coffee table where he takes an occasional meal.

"You know," Tyler says, eyeing Wes carefully, "since we're being honest and all… you really are a wet blanket. You can't let people walk all over you like this."

"Shit man, I've been doing it my whole life. I'm too old to change," Wes replies with a shrug and for a second Tyler feels like clocking him a good one.

"The hell you are! You need to be a man and tell people what you really think. You have to stand up for yourself!"

"And what if I don't want to, huh? Did you ever think of that?"

"Jesus dude, than what was that little hissy fit all about, huh? What were you trying to prove if you're going to turn around and take back everything you said?"

"I don't know," Wes says, a blank look on his face. "Maybe I'm complex?"

"Yeah, about as complex as a super model."

"Whoa, now that's an insult," Wes grumbles and Tyler looks at him gravely.

"Damn right it is. Get with it dude." Tyler rolls down his window so he can open the door from the outside because the handle on the inside is broken. "Look man, here's the deal: no one should put up with the crap you do. No one. Today is the last day you put yourself down like this, alright? Tell you what. If Melissa laughs in my face and sends my ass packing than I am going to ask you politely if I can maybe sleep on your couch for a few more days until I get a job and can take care of myself. Sound fair? I'm not going to let you take any more shit, not from me, not from any one. You gotta treat yourself how you treat others. Understand?"

"Sure," Wes agrees hesitantly and Tyler shakes his head.

"No you don't man, no you don't. But I'm gonna make sure you do. That's my new goal, after I go and beg for my girlfriend back."

"Okay. Good luck."

"I'm gonna need a lot more than that."

Tyler only has to wait a minute or so before someone exits the building and he can get in the door. He doesn't want Melissa to have the option of not letting him in; he wants to see her face to face. He takes the elevator up, thinking about all the things he wants to say, trying to get them straight in his head, but is having a hard time. He decides he'll just have to wing it.

At her door he rings the bell and almost instantly hears footsteps on the other side. Is she expecting someone? Is she already seeing somebody else? That two-timing bitch...

The door swings open and there she is, wearing her leather bondage suit minus the hood. And damned if her eyes don't light up when she sees him, a smile on her lips to match.

"Well if it isn't my good friend and body guard Tyler!" she says enthusiastically, taking him completely by surprise. "Come on in, make yourself at home!" She takes him by the hand and leads him inside and at once he realizes what's going on: she wants to use him to scare off some other guy. Oh yeah, he's familiar with this routine. What guy isn't? The telltale signs are:

Suddenly treating you nice when the last time they saw you they pretty much wanted you dead.

The word 'friend' being used to describe you when the last time you were either referred to as 'asshole' or 'dickhead'. And, last but not least:

You are allowed back into their home without the aid of an armed guard or police escort.

"So how's it going baby?" Tyler asks, playing his role, when he catches a glimpse of the guy in question, the reason for this charade no doubt. Must be some nut case who was getting rough with her and he just happened along at the right time.

"Who's this jerk? He giving you trouble?" Tyler nods toward the old guy in the suit holding a pink plastic cup. The other regards him suspiciously as well, a look that all men are used to exchanging when in the presence of a woman both are vying for. "This prick need a lesson in manners?"

"Who the hell is this ruffian?" Governor Hallsly groans, his good spirits dissipating rapidly. What kind of crap is this broad trying to pull?

Melissa hastily steps between them, looking from one to the other.

"Tyler, this is Governor Hallsly-"

"Shit! Don't use my name!"

"Governor, this is Tyler."

"Wow, are you, like, a governor?"

"One would be tempted to think so," Hallsly says, a note of distaste in his voice. One look at this uncouth young man and his opinion of Madam Coventry almost takes a serious nosedive but, then again, maybe he need not be so rash. "And who are you supposed to be?"

"I'm Tyler."

Okay, maybe I'm not being rash enough.

"Tyler works for me," Melissa explains quickly. "He's my body guard."

"This pathetic pretty-boy? He doesn't look like he can punch his way out of a paper bag!"

"Can to!" Tyler offers as a witty rejoinder and for a moment Melissa wonders what she is doing. First of all, is she really giving serious thought to taking this seedy politician up on his offer? And, secondly, is she really thinking about taking Tyler along for protection? The third (and maybe most important) question is: Has she lost her freakin' mind? Let's take a good look at why she would consider such a dubious venture:

1. She really, really, really needs the money.
2. She wouldn't mind getting out of town for a while, and:
3. Maybe she still has feelings for the 'pathetic pretty-boy' after all, and if he is willing to make amends, perhaps prove he can change...ah fuck it...she really needs the money...

"Look governor, this whole thing has come as such a surprise. You can't really expect me to take off with you on a moment's notice without some kind of insurance policy."

"You can trust me," Hallsly exclaims, "I'm a politician!"

"Where is he taking you?" Tyler demands, a hint of jealousy in his voice. "Are you leaving town?" His eyes narrow to slits. "Were you going to leave without telling me?"

"Look, quiet you two. Why don't we all just sit down and talk this through, shall we?" Melissa leads them over to her sparsely furnished living area. "In fact, governor, why don't you make yourself another drink while I talk to my partner in private."

Tyler stirs at the word 'partner'. Oh boy, this oughta be good...Melissa must be feeding this sucker some line of bullshit and he's falling for it hook, line and sinker.

"Fine." Hallsly stalks into the kitchen and grabs the bottle of Jack. "But you better make it quick or I might rescind my offer."

"Certainly, no problem," Melissa replies, knowing he'll do no such thing. She takes Tyler by the arm and drags him into the dungeon, shutting the door.

"Why are you here?" she hisses at him once she believes they are out of earshot.

"I came here to see you, to, to, say I'm sorry," he says, a little too loudly, and she shushes him. "I want to say I'm sorry!" He tries again in an overly loud whisper.

"Well I don't accept it! You'll have to earn it!"

"How can I do that?"

"I have a job for you, and you can't screw this up, you hear me?"

"Yeah, yeah, sure! I want to work, that's what I was going to tell you, that I'm going to get a job and be responsible and everything-"

"Shut the hell up and listen! This guy wants to pay me an enormous amount of money to go on a boat with him for a few days, maybe a week, and I want you to come along and act as my chaperone...my bodyguard if you will."

Tyler laughs, and the relief in it is unmistakable.

"Is that all? Sure, sure, no problem." Man, the way the bitch was building it up, you would have thought he was going to have to do something difficult. "Anything to be with you babe-"

"Quiet! I haven't forgiven you, so don't get the stupid idea that I want to take you back."

"Oh," Tyler looks crestfallen. "Okay..."

"Look," Melissa relents. "I'm not saying it's out of the question but I'm going to need some really hard work on your part, you got that?"

"Yeah baby, sure-"

"And I won't stand for any of your crap. You're doing this job for room and board, is that clear?"

"Whatever you want-"

"And if I tell you to shit or go crazy you'll do it without any back talk, am I right?"

"Absolutely-"

"Now we're going to go out there and take his job offer and I want you to keep your yap shut! Not a peep out of you, got it?"

"Yes Ma'am-"

"Good. Let's go."

The two walk back into the living room and Melissa gives the governor a cheery smile.

"Okay governor, we're in."

Hallsly stares at her like she's lost her mind.

"I can't take the two of you! It's either you or nothing."

"Take it or leave it pal. I don't go anywhere without security." She looks at him with a measured degree of engineered, calculated coolness. Would he call her bluff?

Governor Hallsly looks as if he's just taken a boot to the nuts. He paces back and forth, wondering how he is going to explain this nimrod to the people in charge. And then it hits him: he is the person in charge.

"Alright, fine. But he doesn't stay in the same room as us."

"We're sharing a room?" Melissa balks, the thought filling her with dread.

"Hey, I don't know how big the ship is. All I can assume is that we are."

"I don't know if I like the idea of you two sharing a room," Tyler refutes but is shut down by a withering gaze from Melissa. He sighs, flops down in a nearby chair.

"Don't get too comfy big boy, it's almost time for you two to leave."

"But it's only five o' clock! Besides I thought we could..." Again she fixes him with a look that silences him. He stands. "Maybe I ought to get going."

"Excellent," she says, and then turns to the governor, raising an eyebrow.

"What? Oh, I see. Guess I'm dismissed too, huh? Well, I suppose there are government things that need tending to."

"I'm sure there are," Melissa concurs, walking to the door and opening it. "Have a wonderful evening gentlemen."

Tyler straggles over, shuffling his feet. He and the governor look at one another for a second, then Tyler concedes. "After you."

"That's all right son, after you."

Tyler shrugs. "See ya," he hollers to Melissa. "Call me."

"You know I will dumbass."

"Y'all be ready to leave in two days, got it?"

"Sure," Melissa says. Tyler nods.

The two ride the elevator down in silence, observing one another warily. At the bottom Tyler allows the governor to exit first, then follows him to the door.

"So, where ya headed?" Hallsly asks when they step outside. "Need a ride?"

Tyler sees the waiting limo. He smiles, forgetting all about Wes who's parked three cars behind it.

"Sure…"

TWENTY-FIVE

Dave and Travis' last couple of weeks could have been worse spent in the county jail, this much is true, but the brig is really no picnic either. Although they don't have to fend off angry, racist Mexican gang members they still have to contend with being locked up, and to add to their misery they still have no idea what is to become of them. In short, they were tossed in with little fanfare and since have been cooling their heels in relative seclusion; with the exception of the guards who bring their meals and the few others incarcerated in nearby cells (a motley group of rejects who've come and gone as their brief sentences were fulfilled) they've had no other human contact. No one has told them how long they have to stay imprisoned, nor what they're status will be once their time is over. This has taken a toll on Travis, ruining his appetite and giving him insomnia, while Dave takes it in stride, greeting each new day as it comes, just thankful he doesn't have to fight someone to keep possession of his meal tray. Communication with anyone on the outside has been denied, however, and Dave is slightly apprehensive about what his stepdad will think once he finds out, how he'll react to his ungrateful son winding up in prison anyway, after all he did for him. In fact, Dave feels sort of bad for the old guy, actually feels worse for him than he does for himself.

"I can't take the fuckin' suspense!" Travis complained after the first week.

"Beats stayin' in the city jail," Dave mumbled, finishing the last of his Salisbury steak and mashed potatoes.

"But what're they gonna do with us? Nobody's told us nothin'!"

"Be glad."

"I just can't figure it out and it's drivin' me crazy."

"They'll tell us somethin' eventually, trust me," Dave said, spooning cold, lumpy potatoes in his mouth. "Commander Sparks has a real hard-on for justice; you seen the way he treated us when he brung us in. When the time comes he'll probably tell us himself."

When the commander retrieved them from the county jail he'd silently accompanied them through processing, watching dourly as they had their mug shots taken, were fingerprinted, informed of their charges, and finally given their meager possessions back. He then led them to a waiting vehicle, instructed them to get in the back, and got behind the wheel.

"I don't want to hear a word out of you two," he'd said and that's what he got. The trip back to the base was a tense affair; save for the glares they received from their escort, a man with little (no) sense of humor and enough testosterone to fuel a fleet of warships, there was no verbal communication. His suit was pressed and starched, his demeanor nothing short of menacing. Compared to his rumpled charges he presented a sturdy image of the Naval elite.

Upon their arrival to the base he'd taken them to the Naval Police Headquarters, leading them past the main desk and into the back of the facility to the jail cells. One quick call and the guard on duty opened the door to the last cell on the block.

"Get in," he'd said and they complied. He then took his leave and that was the last they saw of him, which was nine days ago.

"You should eat somethin'," Dave says presently, looking at Travis' untouched breakfast. "It ain't healthy to starve."

"Hell with it. I ain't hungry."

"Don't mind if I do." Dave takes the others tray and commences to wolf down the oatmeal. "This stuff really ain't that bad. Kinda tastes like Elmo's glue but otherwise it's good eatin'."

"Oh yeah," Travis frowns. "Be my guest."

Suddenly they hear the clanking of the main gate and the two look up expectantly. That sound means either a new detainee is being admitted or someone is coming to talk to them. Human curiosity being what it is, when you're locked up with little to no stimulation, anything out of the ordinary becomes interesting.

The two watch the hall eagerly, waiting. There is no sound except for the slap of hard soles on the cement floor. When the visitor approaches their cage he has one word to say:

"Attention!"

The two hop up like automatons, their backs rigid, saluting. It's Commander Sparks, looking stern as ever. His eyes flicker back and forth between them for a moment, disgust evident in his gaze.

"At ease."

They relax, but not too much.

"I trust you gentlemen have been enjoying your stay?" he asks, but it isn't really a question.

"Yes sir, very much sir," Dave says anyway and the man's scowl deepens.

"Glad you find the accommodations so pleasing," he says sharply, noting the look of playful boyishness on Dave's face, the tense anxiety on the other's. "It would seem you two have caught a lucky break."

"They ain't gonna press charges?" Travis says hopefully and Commander Sparks smiles, shakes his head.

And then the door opens, smooth and quiet on well-oiled hinges.

"Come with me."

The commander leads them into the Naval Police Station holding room, stops before a small metal bench and tells them to have a seat.

"Keep your traps shut and wait here."

They nod and he spins around on one heel and disappears.

When he is out of their sight and, hopefully, earshot, Travis whispers to Dave:

"Whattaya think is goin' on?"

"How would I know?" Dave hisses back, but there is a cocky grin on his face. "Enjoy it, at least we're outta the cage."

They wait for an hour, a stretch of time that passes as slowly as time is allowed. Around them the Navy police and assorted staff bustles about their business, some of them shooting quick glances in their direction, but no one speaks to them, and this increases Travis' unease.

"We're screwed," he decides gloomily and Dave shrugs.

"Maybe."

And then a petty officer third class approaches, calls them to attention. They stand and salute. "Follow me," he orders tersely and the two fall in step behind him. They pass through a maze of corridors until reaching the end of a long hallway. Before them is a thick metal door.

"In there," he instructs after opening it. "Someone will be in presently."

Wordlessly they obey, passing over the threshold. Once inside the door is closed and they hear the unmistakable sound of the lock engaging.

The room is ten by twelve square feet with a table and three chairs. Two chairs are against the wall, facing a large mirror, which can only be two-way glass.

Travis eyes it ominously, taking no more than a step or two into the room while Dave, no doubt used to such treatment, takes a seat in one of the chairs and puts his elbows on the table, leaning his face in his hands.

"Their gonna interrogate us man!" Travis moans. "That's two-way glass!"

"Ya watch too many movies," Dave says, leaning back in his chair and staring at the ceiling. "Next you'll think they're gonna ship us off to Guantanamo Bay where they'll torture us for alleged hate crimes against an innocent Porsche."

"Ya think so?"

"Sit the hell down dude," Dave says and his friend complies, although reluctantly.

So they sit there, Travis impatiently drumming his fingers on the table when, finally, they hear a key hit the lock and the door swings open. The commander returns and they are surprised to see he's holding a cardboard carrier holding three cups of coffee and a bag of Scrumptious Donuts.

"Hungry for something other than jail food boys?" he asks and they smile enthusiastically. He sets the food and drinks on the table. "Help yourself."

Showing little restraint, they dig in greedily. After the jail's barely adequate cuisine the dumpster behind a fast food joint would probably be appealing. Travis' appetite seems to have returned, Dave notices.

The commander watches as they make pigs of themselves and after a few minutes he chuckles.

"Jesus, you'd think you boys were locked up for a month." He leans back in his chair, sipping at one of the cups of coffee. He sets it down and removes his cap, taking care to brush off a speck of dust or lint neither of them can see.

The two eye him carefully, wiping donut crumbs from their faces, trying their best to refrain from slurping the coffee.

"You guys feel a little better?" he asks and they nod vigorously. "Betcha wonder what the hell is going on, don't ya?" He looks back and forth between them but neither replies, the uncertainty clear in their eyes. "It's all right, I'm asking. You can speak, can't you?" he prods, and at last Dave runs the back of his hand over his mouth and clears his throat.

"Yes sir," he says. "This is unusual sir."

"You boys know how stupid that was, stealing a car, right?"

"Yes sir," Travis says quickly. "It was a mighty dumb thing to do-"

"He didn't have nothin' to do with it sir," Dave interrupts. "It was all my idea. I made him come along with me."

"Is that right?" The commander says, scrutinizing them thoughtfully. "It wasn't a joint decision?"

"No sir." Dave shakes his head. "I take full responsibility for what happened. We were drinkin' and I saw the keys in the ignition and I just kinda lost it. Travis didn't know what I was doin' when I got in, didn't know I was gonna take it."

"Is this true seaman apprentice Merkle?" Commander Sparks addresses Travis. "You didn't have any idea what was going on?"

Travis drops his eyes to the table and fidgets with his coffee cup.

"Well sir, ah, well, no, that ain't exactly right..."

Dave shoots a sharp look at Travis, who shrugs.

"Then what *is* right?" the commander prompts and Travis licks his lips slowly, shaking his head, finally raising his eyes to meet the others.

"I knew them keys was in there. Dave is just tryin' to protect me, cuz he was drivin' and all." He swallows, drawing a circle on the table in some spilt coffee. "I knew what was goin' on the whole time. I'm just as much ta blame as he is."

"I see," the commander nods, flashing an odd looking smile. "And why do you think your cohort is trying to protect you?"

Travis looks at Dave, expecting corroboration but gets none, and he shrugs again.

"I guess cuz he figgers there ain't no sense in the both of us gettin' discharged for this."

"Is that what you think is going to happen? That you are going to get discharged?"

Dave looks up quickly. "It is, ain't it? I mean, this ain't the first time I been in trouble..."

"It certainly isn't," the commander says dryly, "but I'm proud to see you've upped the ante from stealing beer and breaking curfew."

Heat rises in Dave's cheeks and he has to look away. He should know that nothing he does will ever get by this man. He may have been able to pull stunts with his parents and his teachers but the navy is a different beast all together. Not to mention the San Diego Police.

"So what's gonna happen?" Dave asks after a few minutes of seemingly endless silence in which the ticking of the commander's watch echoes loudly in the confines of the small chamber. Apparently Commander Sparks enjoys watching them squirm, sitting there with a half grin on his face, drawing the tension out. He takes a sip of his coffee then sets the cup down, looking from one to the other.

"Normally I would've let you sit in jail until the Mexicans beat you silly before sending some-one to collect your sorry asses. Then, after you were formally dishonorably discharged, I would hand the two of you back over to the police, upon which time they could either continue to hold you until your arraignment or arrange for bail." He glares at them through fiery eyes. "I would simply wash my hands of you."

This admission stuns them, especially after his peace offering of donuts and coffee. Neither of them knows how to respond.

"But this isn't 'normally'," he continues, "and you two sorry jerk-offs, like I already said, are catching a lucky break." He takes another sip of his coffee and Dave lifts his eyes to meet the commander's.

"To what do we owe the honor?" he asks, unable to hide the slight note of sarcasm in his voice.

"You two have a chance to serve your country in a way that is, well, a little unorthodox."

"Ya gonna force us to be suicide bombers?" Travis asks fearfully, his voice breaking, sounding like a rusted bicycle chain.

Commander Sparks laughs, a hearty, full-bellied laugh.

"Now that's funny!" he howls, slapping the table with one hand. "That's a fucking hoot!"

Dave and Travis look at one another, confused.

"Are ya sendin' us to North Korea?" Dave queries and the commander, still laughing, shakes his head.

"No fellahs. No." He wipes tears from his eyes and looks at them soberly for a full minute or more before he says: "I'm going to send you dumb-asses someplace much worse."

"That's some shit, ain't it?" Travis says as the two of them walk back to their barracks to pack their things.

"I don't know," Dave muses. "It don't sound too bad to me."

"But he didn't say how long we was gonna be there, and what was gonna happen when it was over…"

"You think too much," Dave says, turning to the other. "Can't ya accept a break when ya get one?" He stares at the other crossly. "I don't know what yer thinkin', but they usually lock car thieves up in this country."

"Yeah, but sendin' us out in the Pacific on some trash hunt? Sounds like Russia's version a bein' sent to Siberia."

"Sounds like we lucked out," Dave says glibly and Travis can tell the other is through talking about it.

"We never shoulda took that car," he says and Dave issues a disgusted grunt.

"Woulda coulda shoulda man." They reach their barracks and Dave turns to look the other in the eye. "It's all water over the dam now."

"I'm gonna quit drinkin'," Travis vows solemnly. "Don't do nothin' but get me in trouble."

"Ya picked a good time to quit," Dave says, smiling, opening the door. "After you 'semen apprentice Merkle'."

"Ah, fuck you."

TWENTY-SIX

When the doorbell rings Leeann looks at the clock on her laptop and nods. Right on time. She should have expected that.

"Coming!" she calls, shutting down the computer and crossing the room to the door. She feels thrills of excitement course through her, but it has nothing to do with her suitor in waiting, not by a longshot. In fact, part of her dreads having to tell him, and another part (maybe a deeper, more threatening side of her that she rarely acknowledges) is looking forward to it. What a way to get rid of someone! And to think it takes leaving town.

She peaks through the peephole and isn't quite sure what she is seeing at first until she realizes it's Dante's flannel shirt. He is so tall that his head and shoulders are out of sight, towering above the range of the eyehole. She sighs and opens the door.

"Hi Leeann!" he greets her excitedly and she can't help but catch the contagion of his vigor.

"Hey Dante," she says, not unkindly, a smile forming easily on her lips. "You want to come in for a minute? I have to put on my sandals and grab my bag."

"Sure." He wipes his feet on the mat even though it hasn't rained in weeks. "Nice place," he says, glancing around, appraising her small studio apartment, noting the petite desk and narrow futon.

"Yeah," she says over her shoulder as she throws some things into her purse. "It ain't much but I call it home." *Well, for the next two days anyway*, the thought making her feel giddy.

"I brought something for you." Dante presents a hand he was hiding behind his back and proffers a small gift.

"What is it?" she asks, turning toward him, tucking her purse under one arm and stepping into a sandal.

"Take it," he insists, a smile flitting on the corners of his mouth.

"Okay." She puts on the other sandal and steps within reach. "Thanks."

Taking it from him, she at once feels a trifle guilty for the news she is going to share with him this evening. Here he is all gussied up, his face scrubbed and shiny (well, what she can see, what the beard doesn't cover), looking like a little boy on Christmas morning, shifting from one foot to the other as if he has to pee. His mouth is in constant motion, his lips pursing and smiling, pursing and smiling...

She unwraps the little bow, which is somewhat sloppy (indicating, no doubt, that he tied it himself) setting it aside on her coffee table. She then tears the paper carefully, trying to find a crease. She looks at him again as she gets to the box beneath and can't help but feel a tiny trickle of amusement at his grizzled countenance: that shaggy head of curly hair, the thick glasses magnifying his eyes, his Amish looking beard. For a moment she almost feels a small thread of endearment for him, and has to bite her lip to contain a giggle when she mentally likens him to that caveman guy on the Gietco Insurance commercials. 'Just let me be me...' Warbles the singer over the still of the guy's hairy face. 'I just want to be me...'

She drops the wrapping paper to the floor and opens the box. Looking inside, she stares mutely at the item, confused.

"Oh Dante," she starts, words failing her. "You shouldn't have."

"Hey, it's nothing," he says awkwardly, but he feels his heart pound in his chest, can feel radiant warmth creeping over him. In his mind's eye he can see her setting the box down and stepping into his arms. She presses tightly against him, her lips meeting his, and they are soft and warm and taste like honey. He clutches her hair, twisting the fine, silken strands between his fingers, marveling at how smooth and shiny it is. He can feel the heat of her crotch next to his, wriggling and grinding against his rigid member...

"What is it?" she asks, jerking Dante from his fantasy and depositing him back in the real world.

"Huh?" he says, resisting the urge to shift his pants because of the wood he is suddenly sporting inspired by his improbable daydream.

"I...I'm not sure what this is..."

He offers her a dazzling smile, shifting gears easily. "It's a little keepsake from the study at Pharmacoastalcal. I used my wristband to make a bracelet. I found the stone centerpiece at Moonlight Beach." He arches an eyebrow. "You like it?"

"It is very...unique..." Her smile is at once detached, her vacillation genuine. The wristband is rumpled and sweat-stained. The stone is a simple piece of sand rock that looks dull under her 100-watt eco-friendly light bulbs. "Thank you," she continues, feeling as if she has just received a present from a Kindergarten-aged child. "I'll treasure it always." She sets it down and looks at her watch. "Shall we get going?"

But he stands there, looking at her expectantly. He has an eager look on his face that reminds her of a dog standing by the door with a leash in its mouth.

"Well?" he says and her grin falters.

"Well what?"

"Aren't you going to put it on?"

She looks at it again, the thought of putting that thing on her wrist akin to wearing someone else's underwear. With great effort she stifles the urge to shudder.

"I don't think it will go with my outfit..." she says, and with this casual remark the light drains from Dante's eyes, a frown forming on his robust lips. *An omen of things to come.* Shit.

She reaches for the box, takes the 'bracelet' out and holds it in her hand. It feels tawdry and nasty in her grasp, but she takes a deep breath, blows it out, and slips it on her wrist. The skin beneath it squirms, as if she's just put on a piece of jewelry made of live worms, but she takes another, deeper, calming breath and manages to smile. He is now beaming back at her, the threatening storm clouds long gone, as if they had never been there in the first place.

"What do you think?" he asks and for a second she has to grit her teeth, has to hold back what she really wants to say: *"It is the ugliest thing I've ever seen! Did you make this in pre-school?"* But instead she sputters: "It's very nice Dante. Thank you."

"My pleasure," he grins, still shifting from one foot to the other. "Shall we go?"

The new Robert Rodrigo movie is ridiculously violent, going far beyond what Leeann considers to be in good taste. It's like a cartoon, the dialogue, the action, everything. She stares uncomfortably at the screen while Dante sits beside her enraptured. Despite his desperate infatuation with her the movie has kept his attention from the first scene. He laughs whenever some bad guy gets his comeuppance and cheers on the hero as he hacks the villains to bits with a circular saw. This type of lowbrow entertainment has never been a favorite of Leann's, preferring romantic classics like 'Restless in Tacoma' or 'Dine, Worship, Adore'. *Why do guys love this kind of shit?* she wonders, not for the first time in her twenty-one years of life.

She steels herself for another 60 minutes of this crap, anticipating their conversation over dinner. She knows that no matter what she says, whatever positive spin she puts on it, he will no doubt be upset, but those are the breaks. This is her life, after all. No one tells Leann what she can and can't do. Especially some ape she just met in a drug trial study.

"This is awesome!" Dante guffaws, putting his face much too close to hers, his mouth full of popcorn, his breath rank with its smell. "You like it?"

Leann offers what she hopes to be a sincere smile.

"Oh sure, you bet," she says, trying not to breathe through her nose. She can take the smell of popcorn breath from someone she likes, but coming from Dante it is absolutely repulsive. "Good choice."

Stealthily glancing at her watch, Leann simply waits for the movie to finish so this evening can run its eventual course.

"I can't believe you've never been here," Dante gushes as they stand in a cafeteria-style line. "This place is the best!"

Leann looks around the Homestyle Buffet's large dining room, sees people who look like perfect candidates for 'Hollywood Fat Camp' at just about every table. One woman, who gets up slowly from her chair because of the enormous bulk she carries, looks as if gravity and her weight combined may make her knees buckle. She can't help but feel a little sorry for her.

"Don't be fooled by the décor, the food is awesome," Dante persists and she simply smiles. If you can't say something nice…"Did I mention it's all you can eat?"

Only about eight times, ya big lug.

When they finally get to the serving line she sees the restaurant actually has a number of vegetarian items and is glad she kept her comments to herself. She figured this place would be like all the other buffet joints and the main course would be meat served with a side of meat. For desert there would be meat, to drink, a glass of liquid meat. She is relieved to see she is wrong.

"Get anything you want," Dante says, "it's all included in the price."

"Okay." She picks out several veggie items as Dante loads up on chicken, ribs, roast beef, shredded pork, bacon wrapped shrimp and several types of potatoes, including mashed, fried and baked.

When their trays are full they wander into the dining area and find a table. Setting his food down, Dante sees that the condiments on the table aren't suitable so he goes off in search of more A-1 and cocktail sauce.

Leann watches him go, suddenly filled with anxiety. This guy, in all his blustery weirdness, is going to be, like, totally crushed. She thanks God (not that she believes in God as she *is* a science major) that her excuse is based on her career and she isn't merely giving him the brush off; in all actuality she has a very good reason. She's sure it's happened to him many times in his life but, at this juncture, she's hoping this isn't the occasion that sends him off the deep end.

When he returns he seasons everything to taste and commences getting his grub on. Leann tries to ignore the sound of his mammoth lips smacking, and the grotesque ripping and tearing that is meat being stripped from the bones of various animals that were slaughtered so he and all the other carnivores can fill their bellies, not to mention the slurping noises as he licks his fingers clean of grease and BBQ sauce. If it hadn't been for her upbringing this spectacle would make her physically ill, but fortunately she grew up around this kind of dietary arrangement. She'd become a vegetarian in her teens, had, indeed, eaten her share of meat.

When Dante's plate is empty he notices that Leann has barely touched her creamed spinach, asparagus tips and boiled baby carrots, much less the garden salad with low fat vinaigrette and walnuts.

"Aren't you hungry?" he asks, sounding disappointed, and for a second his sulky tone annoys her. What the hell does he have to mope about? Is it because he likes a girl with a healthy appetite, or is it that he paid $9.99 for her to simply pick at her food? As far as she's concerned he can just shut up and deal with it.

"I guess my eyes are bigger than my stomach," she replies weakly and Dante nods, the look on his face doubtful, but he says nothing.

"I'm going back for seconds," he announces, standing up. "Can I get you anything?"

"No. I'm fine."

"How about some corn bread? They make a mean corn bread." He smiles, revealing a chunk of pork stuck between his front teeth.

"Okay," she smiles in return, struggling not to gag. "I'll have some cornbread."

"Excellent choice ma'am," he says grandly and is off.

Ah shit, this is really going to suck. She decides that when he returns she is going to tell him, like it or not. She can't hold out any more. The tension is killing her.

When he comes back she sees he has again filled his tray with just about every animal that represents the core basis of a farmyard, with the exception of maybe lamb, she can't tell.

"They just put out some mutton," he says, handing her two warm slices of cornbread on a napkin. "I have to find some mint jelly." He gets up to add to their already condiment heavy table and she sighs yet again. Fortunately he doesn't hear her.

When he arrives back at the table from his latest task, she decides it is now or never.

"So, Dante," she eases in, wanting to be as gentle as possible. "There's something I want to tell you."

He pauses mid-feeding, the color draining from his face. Well, from the part of his face she can see.

"You don't want to see me anymore," he says with mournful conviction. "I could tell while we were at the movies. You wouldn't eat from my box of popcorn."

"No, no, you've got it all wrong!" she blurts, desperately not wanting to crush him like so many have before her. The last thing this guy needs is another high-heeled kick to the groin. "It's not that at all."

"Than what is it? Because I can tell that whatever it is you're going to say it isn't good news."

"I'll be honest," she nods, "you are right to a certain extent that it isn't good news, well, good news for *us*..."

He does a double take at her emphasizing the word 'us'.

"So it's good news for you, bad news for me." He drops his fork (which she is actually surprised he was using at all) next to his plate and removes the napkin that's tucked in his shirt collar, wiping his lips with it. He smiles at her cruelly. "It's always bad news for me: 'Dante, I don't want to see you anymore', 'Dante, your breath is awful', 'Dante there's no room in the car so you'll have to ride in the trunk,'" he whines, his voice high, petulant. "'Dante, your mother is dead'", he goes on, "'Dante, stand over there your B.O. is suffocating me', 'Dante, why would you wear that hideous shirt with those pants?'"

For a moment her heart goes out to him, it truly does. She does agree, however, that his choice of slacks combined with the check-patterned shirt is a little too much and his pits smell a little less than fresh, but she'll let it slide.

"Let me explain-"

"You don't have to, I already know what it is," he retorts, but his voice is soft, his manner resigned. "I've been through this many, many times."

"Dante, please, just hear me out."

"Why? So I can hear a new version of the song that's been playing for me since I hit puberty? If it's all the same, you can just skip it."

"Dante, it's my career, it has nothing to do with you," she declares, quieting him for a moment as he gazes at her silently. "I've been given an opportunity I'd be crazy not to take, and it's going to involve some travel."

"You... you have a job offer?" he says slowly, his eyes shifting down to his plate, color returning to his cheeks (just the top, the part of his face she can see).

"Well, it's more like an internship but I think it will be a wonderful opportunity for me, something that will give me a leg up once I'm on the job market."

"An internship? For what?"

"Well, this is going to sound a little weird, but I've been chosen to join an ecological team on a mission out to the North Pacific Gyre." This she says with no small amount of pride. Her blue eyes sparkle, the light dancing in them for the first time this evening. "I have a chance to do something fantastic, something that can help the entire world!"

His demeanor changes; she can see the anger and sorrow slipping away, can see he is genuinely curious.

"So...this has nothing to do with me?" he asks finally, picking up his fork and twirling pasta around it.

"Not at all!" She grabs an as of yet unused utensil and stabs a broccoli spear. "I just found out about this position yesterday. I applied on line and received confirmation that I was accepted this morning. I've been trying to think of a tactful way to tell you."

His fork stops midway between his plate and his mouth and Leann knows instantly that she screwed up.

"Than why did you wait for now?" His eyes narrow suspiciously. "Why didn't you tell me when I came to pick you up?"

"I knew you would be happy for me but you would also be sad," she answers truthfully, the sincerity evident in her words. "I have no idea how long I'll be gone, how long the voyage is going to last."

"No idea at all?" He shovels the pasta into his waiting maw.

"The only specifics I have is when the ship leaves and from where." She sets the fork on her plate, the broccoli untouched. "We leave in two days."

"Two days!"

"Yes, it's all moving so quickly."

"I...I guess I thought I meant something to you...really...meant something to you," he mutters, his voice breaking, and for one nerve wracking second Leann is afraid he is actually going to break down and cry. God, she hopes it doesn't come to that. The last thing she wants to see is this behemoth crying like a little girl with a mouthful of pasta.

But he doesn't so much as whimper; he simply looks shell-shocked. The wind has been taken out of his sails.

"You do mean something to me Dante, you do." Leann reaches out and puts one of her hands over his. "And we can get together when I get back, we can do something then." She knows she shouldn't say this because she doesn't mean it, but she figures a little white lie won't hurt. She doesn't want him to beat himself up, to feel as if he has blown it again. He and his missing link, Cro-Magnon looks.

"Really? Do you mean it?" His eyes meet hers and for one terrifying instant she swears she sees tears in them.

Oh shit, here come the water works...

A lone tear streaks down his face, getting lost in his incredible tangle of beard.

"So...if you were staying here...would you go out with me again?"

"Of course I would Dante, you know that," she says, hoping she isn't going too far. It's one thing not wanting to hurt the guy's feelings but another entirely to lead him on. At once she decides that when the trip is over she can't return to San Diego…ever. She'll simply have to live somewhere else. Maybe she can go to grad school in Austin, Texas. She's heard such nice things about the university there.

"Okay," he nods, smiling, issuing a shaky laugh (like someone would make if they just survived a car crash or a shark attack). "I'm relieved to hear that." He reaches out with his other hand (the giant paw greasy with congealed animal fat) and caresses her cheek, softly, slowly.

"You are so very beautiful you know," he whispers gently, and at once she thinks of the heartfelt scene from the movie 'Gorilla's in the Fog' and is afraid she is going to laugh out loud. She bites the inside of her cheek to keep a straight face and mentally chastises herself for being so cruel. Poor Dante. Hopefully someday he will find someone who will love him back, love him just as much he loves her. She truly, dearly, desperately hopes this for him, more than anything.

She just knows in her heart that it will never be her. Never. Ever…*ever.*

TWENTY-SEVEN

"She what?" Wes gasps, not believing what he is hearing. Never in a million years would he have thought Melissa would give Tyler another chance. Not in a billion years.

"You heard me: I'm going on a boat cruise with Melissa and the governor of California," Tyler says, knocking back a beer and refilling his glass from the pitcher. "I knew she was still into me, and this is her way of proving it."

"Holy crap," Wes mutters, and damned if it doesn't bother him. "How long will you be gone?"

"No idea." Tyler gulps half the beer before setting it down and helping himself to a chicken wing from Wes' plate. "All I know is that the boat leaves the day after tomorrow. I have to pack my things."

Wes stifles the compulsion to laugh. Pack his things. Yeah, that's a good one. Tyler's 'things' consist of two pairs of designer underwear, some ripped $300 jeans and a couple of porno magazines.

"Tell me all of it from the top again," Wes urges, intrigued, deciding he must have missed something.

So Tyler goes through it again, how the governor is an S&M freak and he has to take a trip in which he hired Melissa as his 'personal assistant', and Melissa in turn recruited Tyler as her 'body guard'.

"I can understand why she doesn't want to be left alone with that guy," Tyler finishes, draining the last of his beer. "He's kind of a creep."

The pot calling the kettle black, Wes muses, but has to push the thought aside because in truth, when all is said and done, he realizes he's actually jealous. After all he's done for this sponging son of a bitch and here he is running off with Melissa and the freaking governor of California on some excursion to the middle of nowhere…what are the odds? How can this shit for brains continue to be so lucky when it comes to finding people to take care of him? How? Wes decides that life is beyond a doubt completely unfair. In a world that will let this bastard slide after all of his transgressions it is obvious the random order of things is definitely stacked against him, the hard working 'everyman'.

"You don't look too happy about it," Tyler comments, observing the long look on Wes' face. "I thought you'd be glad to have me out of your hair."

"Sure," Wes shrugs. "I guess so. It's just that…" He trails off, not quite knowing exactly what he is going to say.

Oh man, here it comes. This little pansy has been after me all along. I fucking knew it!

But Wes just shakes his head, pours himself another beer.

"You'd think I'd be happy to have you off of my couch," Wes begins, tilting his mug to his lips. "But the thing is, I'll probably miss you." He winces. "Don't take that as it sounds," he adds quickly but Tyler is way ahead of him.

"Hey man, you've been there for me for everything," he says with what he hopes sounds like sincerity. "I would have been on the street if it weren't for you. I owe you big time pal."

"How long is the trip?" Wes asks after a few minutes of silence while Tyler stares vacantly at a TV in the far corner of the bar.

"No idea man, didn't ask."

"And you'll be doing what? Protecting Melissa from the crazed governor?"

"I guess so. Pretty wild huh?"

"Yeah," Wes nods, "pretty wild."

Tyler regards Wes as the other stares at the table, one hand around the handle of his mug, the other scratching his head slowly. Tyler knows he has been unkind, overbearing and a total mooch since they first met but he can't help it if people want to give him things, can't help it if people get sucked in by his charm and charisma. That's their fault, not his. He's just using what God gave him (and using it well as far as he is concerned). His earlier epiphany now seems distant, far removed from what he currently perceives. The events that transpired little over an hour ago have convinced him of a few things, some things he was sure of a long time ago and now realizes he'll never question again: he is impervious to the human condition, there is no such thing as 'karma' and if you got it, flaunt it. Let's face it friends, there will always be someone waiting in the wings to bail out the Tyler's of this world. The odds are incredibly in his favor. As long as there are lonely, self-deprecating people there will forever be someone to pick up the pieces for him when the chips are down. Guaranteed. No, guaran-fucking-teed. It's for this reason, he decides, that there is no need for him to change, to try and be something he's not. Maybe he truly does harbor strong feelings for Melissa, then again, maybe he doesn't. Now he isn't sure, seeing how easy it was to get her back. He's always been a sucker for the chase, but after the catch swiftly comes the release. It's generally how it goes. He supposes he'll come to some sort of conclusion of their status by and by, possibly after nailing her a couple times. And this little twerp sitting across from him, this amazingly stupid loser (yes, let's face it, the little puke is a fucking LOSER) doesn't deserve any more than Tyler has already given him, despite what his inspirational speech in the car may have suggested. It's obvious by the dillhole's downtrodden demeanor that should the need arise Tyler can undoubtedly count on him to help out, again and again and again. Of that he is certain.

"Hey, come on dude, we still have today," Tyler says encouragingly. "Let's get shitfaced and go harass some homeless people."

"If it wasn't for me you'd be one of those homeless people," Wes replies, but he says it quietly, without any real conviction, and for a second (well, maybe not a whole second) Tyler actually feels sorry for him. This guy is so pathetic; he doesn't have any friends (not even work friends, and *everybody* has work friends) and chicks won't give him the time of day. If that were Tyler's life, well, bad as it sounds, he would kill himself. Seriously. Just put a shotgun in his mouth and pull the trigger. What else is there to live for if not pussy and the freedom of never having to work? Think about it. What else is there? This little faggot lives a life of quiet desperation and when he dies no one, fucking *no one* is going to give a rat's ass. Won't be anybody at his funeral unless Tyler decides to show up and bring a few friends along. . .

"You're right," Tyler relents, deciding it's time to cheer Wes up. "I owe it all to you man, seriously." He lifts his beer, notices the glass is empty and pours the remainder of the pitcher in it and hefts it again. "Here's to Wes, uh, to Wes. . .say, what the hell is your last name?"

"Stancowitz," Wes offers, the trace of a smile on his lips. "Wes Stancowitz."

"Here's to Wes Stancowitz," Tyler begins again, loud enough for the whole bar to hear. No one looks up. No one cares. "The best friend a leeching son of a bitch like me could ever have!"

Wes breaks into a grin and lifts his half-full mug, clinks it against the others.

"Cheers," he says.

Tyler drains his glass, slams it on the table and calls to the bartender:

"Another pitcher of swill Charlie! Wes is buying!"

TWENTY-EIGHT

The conference room door is locked to anyone who isn't already present and the people are restless, fingering their ties and fidgeting in their seats. The President of the United States sits at the head of the table, studying a memo he's been given by one of his aides. He reads in silence for a minute or so and then glances up, sees that all eyes are on him.

"So," he says at length. "It seems the arrangements have been adequately set into motion."

"Yes sir," the economic advisor confirms. "It appears to be coming together nicely but..."

"What is it? Spit it out."

"Some of us are curious why Theodore Hallsly is accompanying the crew."

The vice president looks up from the paperwork he's studying. "Is that the governor of California?"

"Yes sir."

"We needed a political liaison and I thought he'd be the best candidate," the president says impatiently. "Is this a problem?"

"Well, no sir, it's just, well, isn't there someone else who might be a bit more, um, qualified?"

The president tosses the paper onto the desk and chuckles, a rumbling sound emanating from his belly. "Ah yes, the illustrious Theodore Hallsly, a fine, upstanding man if ever there was one."

"Sir?" the advisor asks tentatively.

"Jesus Christ," the president sighs, picking up his cup of coffee and blowing on the tepid liquid. "I know he's a fool, Jack, I wasn't born yesterday."

"Then...why?"

"Hasn't any of this been made clear to you people or do I have to spell it out for you again? This crew-from the interns to the security to the sailors-is expendable. If anything should happen at least we won't lose any one of importance. Besides," he says, sipping from the cup. "I'm sure his constituents won't miss him anyway."

"Mr. President," one of his aides says, "you have to meet the Prime Minister of France at two."

"Then we better proceed, I guess, unless there are any more questions regarding Governor Hallsly?" He glances around the room and, when no one further broaches the subject, he nods. "Very good. Then I'd like to introduce Dr. Taylor. Why don't you bring us up to speed on the trip's developments."

"Certainly sir." He stands and produces a piece of paper from his jacket pocket. "I've a list here of the candidates we've chosen for the trip. You all have an identical one before you."

"Who are these people?" the president asks, studying the photocopied sheet.

"We located the interns through ads placed in California universities, the security personnel through various other sources statewide."

"These are the most competent applicants?"

"Yes sir."

"Excellent," the president nods. "So all is going according to plan."

"So it would seem. Scripts is prepared with a ship and crew, a vessel that should meet all our needs."

"What about a captain?"

"A retired Naval commander volunteered for the job, a war hero."

"I don't like the sound of that," the president scowls. "We need men like him."

"He's old sir, past his prime. Besides, it was either him or a man who was dangerously inept."

"We didn't get many volunteers for that particular position, I take it?"

"No sir, indeed we didn't."

"All right then, fine." He sets down the sheet of paper and glances at his watch. "So has someone been sent out to take a look at the ship?"

"I'll do it myself, Dr. Taylor says diffidently, his eyes on the table. "I've decided I'm going with them."

The president, who is lifting his coffee cup to his lips, pauses, looking at the doctor over the rim.

"Do you think that's a wise decision?"

"I'm certain it is sir," Dr. Taylor replies, meeting his gaze. "I don't feel comfortable sending these people out there without the proper supervision. Without my aid they'll surely be lost."

"You're well aware of the dangerous nature of this operation. Are you sure you want to put yourself through it? You have no idea what you are up against."

"Yes sir, I know."

"You said yourself it could be any number of reasons why the ship disappeared."

"Yes sir, I did. But amongst these candidates there is no one experienced enough to oversee the research, and without leadership they won't be of any use to us."

"As long as you are conscious of the inherent dangers than I have no reason to stop you. As it stands, your participation isn't essential to our overseas war efforts."

"No sir."

The president looks around the room, taking in the blank stares of the others, sighs, and returns his gaze to the doctor. "Is there anything else you would like to discuss?"

"No sir. You've seen all the information we have. All that's left is to carry on with the mission."

"Very well then," the president says. "Ladies and gentlemen, that will be all for today."

PART TWO

THE JOURNEY

ONE

Kenny's interview was merely a formality; he met with one of the governor's aides, filled out some paperwork and they sent him on his way.

"Be ready to leave for the Scripts' facility tomorrow morning at three a.m. A car will be sent to take you to the airport," the aide informed him after glancing briefly at the forms Kenny filled out.

Kenny spent a mostly sleepless night wondering if he was doing the right thing; he'd never spent much time on the water, in fact was uncertain if he would get seasick or not. Sometime around midnight his mind finally shut down and he got a couple hours of sleep, but it was fitful, plagued by dreams. His alarm clock woke him up around two-forty, and it took no more than ten minutes to pack his things and brush his teeth. At two-fifty nine a car met him outside his building, the driver instructing him to toss his bag in the trunk, and they were off to the airport. The flight was uneventful, and it was only a matter of hours before he was deposited at the Scripts Oceanic Institute. After inquiring with a receptionist at the front desk he was sent to the dock where the ship's crew was awaiting the passenger's arrival.

And now he stands in the gray early morning light, feeling nervous and tired. As he mulls over his decision, the sight of the ship reminds him of a nightmare he had during his brief period of sleep. He can't remember much, but it had something to do with garbage, piles and piles of rotting garbage that stretched as far as the eye could see. In his dream he'd been desperately clawing his way through it, certain that something was tracking him like a bloodhound, following his bumbling progress through the waste. And that's all he can remember, but even now the hair bristles on his arms as he thinks about it.

While he waits he regards the Navy seamen guarding the ship. They look like a pretty green bunch of bananas all right, and he hopes his overall safety isn't riding on their shoulders. Hell, two of them appear to be asleep on their feet whereas another can't seem to take his eyes off the craft, craning his neck ridiculously as if he's trying to do an impression of the little girl from 'The Exorcist'. Yep, all in all a pretty sad lookin' group...

Hearing footsteps, he turns and sees someone approaching, a man with long, unruly black hair and a bushy beard a lumberjack would be proud of. He's wearing an Army fatigue jacket and carrying a duffle bag.

"Mornin'," Kenny greets, trying on a smile that feels too tight for his face. "Ya part a tha scientific crew or ya security, like me?"

The man starts, eyeing him with a cagy, apprehensive expression, and damned if there isn't a furtive look that comes over his face, his eyes darting back and forth as if he's been caught jerking off in the ladies room. And then, just as fast, the guy's face smoothes over and he offers a smile in return.

"Part of the security team," he says, holding out his hand. "I'm, uh, Derrick."

"Nice ta meet ya Uh Derrick, I'm Kenny." The two shake hands, Kenny sizing the other up. The guy is damn big, about as tall as himself, and exceptionally hairy. Reminds him of a gorilla, or that mythical monster Big Foot that's always showcased in blurry photos by people with fewer teeth than they have brains, which isn't saying a whole hell of a lot. The fellow has a firm grip though, and Kenny likes that in a man. It shows he has character.

"So what's the drill?" he asks, and Kenny shrugs.

"Don't know, just got here myself." Kenny looks back at the Scripts building, sees a group of people advancing toward them. "Maybe one a them can fill us in."

The guy looks toward the oncoming assemblage and once again his face undergoes a transformation, as if he's seen a ghost. Turning his back to them, he gets down on one knee and fiddles with the laces of his boots. Kenny watches him bemusedly, shaking his head. This bozo is a character all right. If he didn't know better (which he doesn't, not really) he'd think this guy had something to hide.

As they get closer Kenny tips his head, offers a salutation. They nod in return, but only a couple of them meet his eye.

"Y'all members a the scientific community I presume?" he asks a pretty young woman with red hair and freckles and she smiles. "It will be my honor ta serve ya ma'am." As she passes, Kenny swears he can smell her shampoo, and it is sweet. Delectably sweet.

"Holy man is that a hot number right there," Kenny notes, although not too lecherously. "Be nice if she needed a little extra security, huh?"

Derrick gets up slowly, keeping his back turned to the group. He looks at Kenny briefly, then peaks over his shoulder surreptitiously at the retreating group before turning back to face him.

"I don't think getting involved with the crew is a part of our job description," Derrick says and the smile falters on Kenny's lips. *Asshole with a capital 'a'…*

"Yeah, I spose not," he agrees, and the guy flashes a grin.

"Though I have to admit she is really pretty."

"There ya go. I was kinda worried about ya for a second."

"No need to be," the other replies before his face retains its stoic expression, hidden behind his massive beard and Buddy Holly glasses.

Kenny grunts and returns his gaze to the ship, observing that it looks pretty sound, like she'll hold if the weather goes sour. Not knowing what else to do, he figures he'll wait right here until other members of the security team arrive or someone from the ship tells him what to do. As it turns out, he doesn't have to wait long.

Dave stands on the dock contemplating the ship. It's an impressively large vessel (bigger than he thought it would be) and he guesses it can hold twenty-five, maybe thirty people comfortably. There are two other Navy seamen besides he and Travis. One is a seaman apprentice like them and the other is a lieutenant junior grade. They are under strict orders not to talk amongst themselves, but he knows they are here for the same reason as he and Travis: it was this or the clink. They form a line between the ship and the entrance to the dock, allowing only authorized personnel to pass. Though why anyone other than a confirmed passenger would want to board this ship is a complete mystery to him. It's not like they're sailing to the Bahamas for a week of fun in the sun, but these are the orders they've been given.

As of seven-thirty Pacific Time he and his fellow Naval brethren have allowed three members of the local governmental staff to pass (the governor of California and two aides), a scientist sent from Washington D.C. (a rather serious looking man who barely acknowledged their presence), four college interns (one of them a hot young babe with red hair and freckles who gave Dave an instant chub), and four private security officers (one of them an ex-football player and another a large mongoloid who looked like a cross between Charles Manson and Sasquatch). When asked for his papers the Sasquatch impersonator merely scowled, showing his teeth. Because of his impressive size the Navy seamen left him alone, allowing him to pass. Even the lieutenant junior grade had nothing to say to him. Again, who would want to stowaway aboard this ship? They'd have to be crazy.

Dave figures it probably takes ten or twelve crew members to run this ship efficiently, so that puts the total passengers at twenty-four people, give or take. In order for Dave (and the other Navy seamen) to be excused their transgressions they have been ordered to make sure that all of these people find their way back to the states safely. *"You fuck this up and you'll be swabbing toilets with your tongues for the rest of your miserable lives,"* Commander Sparks told them in no uncertain terms and Dave believed him.

He has no opinion either way as to the importance of this mission, but he figures (because of his recruitment) there is a chance it might get ugly. He understands he is here for no other reason than the Navy has no use for him, and if one thought about it long enough the obvious conclusion would be: 'that ain't good'. He can only hope that whatever the government expects, it doesn't happen. Or, if it *does* happen, he is able to rise to the occasion and prove himself worthy of another chance. Sink or swim baby, sink or swim...

TWO

The ship bobs gently up and down on the calm waters of the San Diego Bay as the crew scurries about, preparing for their departure. The captain, Oswald Harvey, watches from the fore deck as the passengers' board. The governor and his entourage (an exotic looking broad and an unkempt pretty-boy) are allowed onboard first, followed by the civilian scientists (led by a man sent from Washington), then the security personnel. The Naval escorts stand patiently on the dock, waiting to board shortly before they depart.

Captain Harvey spent his entire adult life at sea as a career Naval man, rising swiftly within the organization to eventually attain the status of NATO rank code OF-5 captain. He is more at home on water than land, a fact verified by his bandy sea legs. This will be his inaugural voyage as captain for the Scripts Oceanic Institute, his first post at the helm of a non-military craft, but after a thorough inspection he's found it to be to his liking. The accommodations are quite spacious compared to what he is used to, and exceptionally contemporary, the only drawback being that she doesn't possess the most up-to-date technological devices as a military ship in regards to stealth radar and infrared night-vision hardware, yet he feels it will do for the purposes intended. More importantly, his personal quarters are the finest the ship has to offer, so he imagines he'll be quite comfortable throughout the journey.

He'd heard about the position through an old war buddy at the Point Loma Naval Base and, having nothing better to do, volunteered. The committee in charge of putting together the operation voted him in unanimously because he was the most qualified candidate interested in the job. The only other applicant was a Naval reject who made a living smuggling cocaine for various Columbian drug cartels, a brash, irrational braggart who probably would have landed the job had Captain Harvey not turned up.

When asked by the selection committee, Captain Harvey was impetuously straightforward in his opinion that the problems concerning the first research vessel were most likely due to the inadequacy of the captain and crew (which didn't make the Script's members very happy as they'd been, after all, the most experienced people under their employ), and that if it had been he overseeing the previous voyage it would have gone off without a hitch. Not that he was personally familiar with the previous captain, his men or their work ethic but, he'd stated immodestly, in opposition of the former crew he was a man who made very few mistakes, a captain who could be trusted to make decisions at lightening-fast speed even when everything was going to hell around him. He assured them he wasn't inept enough to lose a ship and crew, not with all the fail-safe equipment onboard such a modern craft, and laughed at the mere idea that the others were missing 'without a trace'.

"In this day and age that is simply impossible," he'd chortled, his seamed face crinkling comically. "Obviously the work of numbskulls who couldn't find their own peckers without a GPS unit, a tweezers and a search party."

This comment was met with dour silence, of course, given the level of skill the preceding group possessed, but they kept their views to themselves, if only to placate him.

His beliefs regarding the sparse documentation of the earlier journey (which he studied carefully), were that inclement weather wasn't a factor concerning safe passage, nor was there any seismic shifts that would have caused unexpected rough waters or high seas. The only explanation that could be seriously considered was outside interference, and pirates weren't known to travel those coordinates, preferring areas closer to land, and heavier trafficked. If it *was* a rogue ship of scallywags than possibly it was one of the many trash-dumping vessels, but that was also highly unlikely because there was little to no motive. No, Captain Harvey opined, it had to be chalked up to good old-fashioned incompetence.

At that time the committee made it known that the second ship wouldn't be staffed with crewmen as experienced and proficient as the prior voyage and did, in fact, pale in comparison to the former vessel, which they claimed to have been twice as modern if not twice as sound, outfitted with far superior navigational equipment, worthy of Naval battle crafts.

"That is of no matter," he'd told them confidently. "As long as they know their way around the ship and can be counted upon to take direction than we'll be fine, trust me." And then he added: "A captain as accomplished as I is worth ten men, and that's all you need to know."

And apparently, as they had no more questions, it was…

He scowls as he watches the passengers climb the ramp, sizing up the riff-raff. It's a veritable parade of fucking amateurs: unpaid college interns, Naval misfits, security personnel who probably couldn't get a job guarding the parking lot at a mini-mall…it all amounts to a load of crap as far as he is concerned but they'll have to do, take it or leave it. He and his less-than-stellar crew will have their work cut out for them, making sure these wingnuts get back safe, but he's up for the task.

He spits over the side of the ship, a thin stream of tobacco juice, and wipes his mouth with the back of one hand. He surveys the sky and is happy to see the marine layer is starting to lift. The weather forecast for the next week will entail a bit of rain, potentially some rough seas and a thunderstorm or two but, because of the time sensitive nature of this trip, he sees no need to postpone. Moreover, he's traveled through squalls so hairy it would make a man's shit turn white; he's handled it before, he can handle it now. The committee had questioned his judgment concerning the matter but he insisted it was of little consequence; as long as everyone did their job and the passengers stayed out of the way it would be fine, he'd see to it. It was mutually agreed, however, that the crew would be kept in the dark as to the potential threat until the voyage was well underway, in order to avoid any last minute personnel changes. At this point they had to take anyone they could get; there was no sense in scaring anybody off.

By his best calculations they should arrive at their appointed destination in about two and a half days. Their orders are to search for the missing vessel and to allow the scientific crew to survey the trash heap, take samples, and make the president proud that America The Beautiful is doing it's part to keep the world's oceans clean.

"You're needed on the bridge captain," his first mate, a dumbass named Jake Anderson, says from behind him. "Our course is routed but we'd like you to double check the coordinates."

Without turning around the captain nods. "Aye."

"Shall I have the Naval seamen board?"

"Just do your damn job and leave me alone."

"Very good sir."

Oswald Harvey was born into a long family bloodline of men who felt it to be their patriotic duty to serve in the armed forces, so it was virtually predestined that he would also join one of its various branches and with any luck have the honor of fighting for his country. Although his grandfather and his father had been Marines (his father served in World War Two, miraculously surviving against all odds to return home and impregnate his newlywed wife), it was because of Oswald's love of the sea that he chose the Navy. His father had been infuriated, of course, because it had always been his opinion that Navy men were a bunch of flaming faggots, but he couldn't stop his son from doing what he wanted. Besides, when Oswald knocked up his high school sweetheart it became pretty obvious he wasn't playing for the other team.

It is interesting in hindsight that his mother and father chose to name him Oswald Harvey, but in 1948 (the year he was born) JFK was merely a young congressman in Massachusetts, having dutifully served his country during World War Two with the Navy, and no one could possibly foresee his fate in 1963 at the hands of alleged gunman Lee Harvey Oswald in Dallas, Texas. And, after the fact, no one was ever stupid (or suicidal) enough to make tasteless jokes regarding the name correlation, as Oswald stood six foot four with a build like a tank on steroids and had a demeanor akin to that of a cornered rat: all teeth and claws. Moreover, growing up on a turkey farm in Ramona, California (an unincorporated burg in the foothills of the Laguna Mountains that had been known as the 'turkey capitol of the world' until the industry suffered a sharp decline after WW two and ended completely in 1959, then turning to chicken egg production), it wasn't exactly the intellectual epicenter of southern California. Many of Oswald's peers had very little insight regarding politics, much less deranged gunmen, even though the repercussions of JFK's assassination were felt in the most remote corners of the continental United States. Suffice it to say it was a non-issue. People were more concerned with tending to their chicken farms, the Harvey's being no exception.

So, having nothing to do with his sympathies for the deceased president and everything to do with his love of the sea and his desire to further pursue his ancestral heritage, Oswald expressed his aspiration to join the Navy when he was seventeen. His father wasn't happy about his decision, in fact tried to persuade him otherwise, and subsequently Oswald did what any good son would do: he challenged him to fight. Now, his dear old dad was a crazy son of a bitch with a record number of kills in World War Two, but he wasn't so far gone that he'd take on the beast he and Martha called their 'boy'. No sir. When push came to shove he let the kid do what he wanted, figuring he'd dig his own grave. If his boy wanted to go to Vietnam with the pussies in the Navy instead of the real men in the Marines than so be it. His only hope was that he stayed safe and returned unharmed to the farm when his tour was done.

But what his father didn't realize was that the Navy was more than just an intermediary point in his son's young life, a way to make the transition from 'boy' to 'man', he wanted to make a career of it. Oswald had absolutely no interest in chicken farming, in fact couldn't see any other life for himself if he returned to Ramona after the service as his forays in formal learning had been informal at best. Growing up as poor as they were, an education wasn't important; they needed all the healthy, able bodies they could get to work the farm from sunup to sundown, learnin' be damned. So he focused all his attention on his boot camp training and once 'in country' rose through the ranks quickly, proving himself worthy of continuous rank reassessment during five tours of duty in Vietnam, leading his men to feats of heroics that most thought insane. He was decorated three times, receiving a Medal of Honor, a Legion of Merit and a Purple Heart.

After Vietnam he took part in several other military coups, some of them 'Top Secret Eyes Only' ops the public never knew about, and throughout he always made the U.S. proud. He was a man the United States Government could always count on to get the job done, no matter how bad the odds. He'd fearlessly go where rational men wouldn't and always found a way to come out ahead. Within the Navy, his notoriety grew.

On his sixtieth birthday, at the behest of his wife, (his high school sweetheart whom he'd impregnated shortly before leaving for boot camp) he retired but quickly found himself bored and restless. He owned and sailed a fifty-foot sloop, which he manned in some of the worst weather his generation had ever seen yet always managed to come out alive, but it still wasn't enough for him. He wanted to continue helping his fellow man (so he claimed) but his old Navy buddies speculated he was happiest if there were others around to witness his courageous deeds. If anything, he thrived off the recognition he received for his daring exploits.

When he caught wind of the job opening for the Scripts Oceanic Institute he was instantly enthralled. With his service record it sounded like a job tailor made for him. After a brief interview he was hired, but after hearing the details he was dubious whether it would offer him the thrills he was looking for. If anything maybe it would serve to pass the time until something more interesting came along.

The one man who actually appears as if he knows his asshole from a hole in the ground is Dr. Corey Taylor, the scientist sent by the federal government. Captain Harvey has had the pleasure of speaking with him briefly and is glad he is onboard. The other 'scientists' are college interns who have never been in the field professionally (some of them never at sea!) and he's afraid it is this fuck-up contingent that is going to get them in trouble.

And then there's the governor of California. This guy looks like a sex scandal just waiting to happen. Captain Harvey isn't sure, but he suspects his 'personal assistant' is going to be handling a lot more than his scheduling and travel arrangements. And what about the doufus accompanying them? What the hell is his role in all of this? The captain has seen some messed up shit in his day and he doesn't even want to speculate what kind of nonsense is afoot. He is certainly going to have to keep an eye on them.

The governor's security personnel will need supervision as well, of this he is sure, and amongst their ranks is a surprise celebrity guest, ex-football great Kenneth Howard. This job assignment would look great on a 'Where Are They Now' TV biopic, but hell, besides a vague limp the man seems to be all right.

And then there's the Naval recruits, who appear to be a little wet behind the ears, and the captain figures this is because the government didn't want to send anyone better suited to be shredded in the Afghan, Korean, African, Iranian, Chinese or Iraqi meat grinders. They all look like a bunch of imbeciles who would have been dishonorably discharged had they not been needed for a suicide mission or something equally ridiculous, such as, say, this operation.

Captain Harvey's assessment of the passengers having been made, he decides that now is as good a time as any to get underway. He can poke and prod at this cast of losers over the next few days, see what makes them tick, see which of them will be the weak links in the chain.

He coughs into his fist, a deep rumbling sound, and wipes spittle from his lips, examining it quickly before he rubs it on his pant leg. Spitting over the side once more, he heads to the wheelhouse to get the show on the road.

THREE

Dr. Taylor greets the interns who comprise the scientific team on the deck at the stern of the ship. He is dressed casually (wrinkled khaki pants and an oxford shirt that's seen better days), carrying several folders that he hands out to everyone as they assemble. There is a slight breeze ruffling his light brown hair, and behind him stretches the vast expanse of San Diego Bay. Gulls flutter overhead, crying out to one another as they sail through the air, the fragrant aroma of salt and brine strong in everyone's nostrils. The sun is just over the horizon, slowly driving away the marine layer, and the intermittent rays feel warm and inviting as they splash across the deck.

Besides Leann there is a young Asian woman from UCLA, rather studious in appearance, who merely nods when Leann says hello and won't (or can't) respond to small talk. She stands apart from the other interns, her eyes trained on Dr. Taylor.

To Leeann's left is a guy from Berkley who looks as if he slept in his clothes (he probably did) and hasn't seen the working side of a bar of soap in as many years as it's been since Lady Googoo had a hit record (2015). He swipes at his nose every so often, making loud snorting noises as he tries to turn his snot into the more workable form of phlegm. He looks tired but, then again, almost everyone does. Leann wonders if anyone got a very good night of sleep last night, due to excitement (which is the case for her) or anxiety.

To her right is a guy from UCSD (like herself) wearing a shirt that says 'I'm with stupid' and there is an arrow pointing at his crotch. He has longish hair, an earring in his left ear and a smirk plastered on his face like a stain, one that has been there since she met him just under an hour ago. He is moderately good looking and he knows it. He also thinks he is smarter than everyone else, Leeann can tell, but she expects she'll prove that to be untrue by and by.

"Good morning. I'm Dr. Corey Taylor and I will be overseeing the scientific portion of this mission. I work for the United States Oceanography Department and have been examining the effects of the trash heap in the North Pacific Gyre since the late 1980's, when the first studies were conducted regarding neustonic particles. I will be leading you in gathering our research." He looks around, making sure he has everyone's attention. The sooner they get through this the sooner they can get on to other things.

"The reason we are making this trip is that the trash heap has shown it has the ability to grow exponentially in a short amount of time, due to both the currents of the gyre and illegal dumping. I'm sure all of you have a cursory knowledge of the garbage heap, based upon what you've seen on television and the Internet, or possibly learned about in school. We'll be going into it's evolution and subsequent unchecked growth with the idea of understanding it's main components and discerning what these toxins are doing to the environment and surrounding wildlife. This investigation is intended to collect new data so that we can hopefully eradicate it permanently. If you will all open up your folders please, I will go through some of the information contained within."

There is a rustling of paper as the interns open their folders and turn to the required pages. He waits patiently, brushing his bangs over his forehead even though they flop back into the same position. He seems not to notice.

"As you can see, my original studies focused on the effects the trash heap had on the marine life surrounding it. My first and last trip was in 2005, at which time my colleagues and I noted the severe changes that had been made to their biological habitat. Many species were being rapidly wiped out, succumbing to starvation when they mistook the debris as food or, in other cases, choking to death, but it was also ascertained that various life forms were successfully feeding on and around it, somehow thriving even though they were inadvertently ingesting minute pieces of plastic, the neustonic particles if you will-"

"This problem is so out of hand there's no way of safely getting rid of it," the smirking guy from UCSD says. "The idea that we can remove the trash heap completely is insane, and will no doubt cause irreparable harm, negatively effecting the environment and sea life for decades to come."

Dr. Taylor eyes him warily, but nods.

"I agree it is going to be a very daunting task," he says, "but it's our job to figure out what we can do to effectively eliminate the problem as well as preserve the environment."

"It's going to be impossible," the smirking guy retorts. "We either get rid of it and kill off the marine life or we say 'fuck it' and call it a day."

Dr. Taylor sighs. "What is your name, son?"

"Perry," the smirking guy answers. "Perry Marshall."

"Well Perry, I'm sure your vast knowledge of this subject eclipse's my own, but presently I'm the one who is leading the group." He looks around at the others, but there is no mistake he is speaking solely to Perry: "I welcome each and every one of your personal observations and suggestions and will later open the floor to a Q&A session but, for now, please just listen and let me finish. We have a lot to cover before we arrive at our destination and I want to make the most of our time."

Perry appears as if he has something to add but decides against it. Instead he nods, keeping his mouth shut.

"Okay, we can continue that discussion later. Right now you are probably wondering about the presence of the Navy. If you've all read the information given to you when you signed on than you know we are embarking on this trip because a crew traveled to the trash heap roughly a month ago for the same purpose as ours but never returned. We lost radio contact with them shortly after they arrived and satellite photos and flyovers have been unable to locate their ship at the appointed coordinates. At this time we aren't going to speculate as to what happened to them-"

"Maybe pirates got them," Perry interjects. " Hell, anything's possible."

Leeann turns a jaundiced eye on him, lets out an exasperated breath. She knows his type only too well; he is one of those fabulously arrogant geeks who thinks his every thought should be broadcast to others. He probably just loves arguing so he can hear the sound of his own voice and has no idea how irritating he really is.

"Hey, dickwad," she says, "will you shut the hell up?"

"No one asked you."

"As far as I can tell, no one asked you either."

"Look, will you both just shut up?" someone says, and heads swivel around to see it's the girl from UCLA. "Some of us want to get this over with and use the bathroom, okay?"

Leeann regards her briefly, slightly embarrassed, but says nothing. Perry scowls at her and rolls his eyes.

"Eat me," he mutters and the Asian girl flips him the bird.

Dr. Taylor watches this interplay, ready for an argument to ensue, but is glad to see the obnoxious bastard turn away, silenced. He knew that bringing aboard college interns would result in juvenile hyjinks as such but unfortunately he had little say in the matter of who was hired. When it came down to the eventual selection he could only base his decisions on their academic records, not their quirky personality traits. Besides, he has to piss like a racehorse himself so he just wants to get this over with.

"Okay," he says, "if that bit of business is through let's move on, shall we?"

The others nod. Perry, however, just stands dumbly with a sullen expression on his face. Dr. Taylor could care less. As long as the kid keeps it zipped than they don't have a problem.

"Okay, flip to the second page and we'll continue." He looks around. "Unless someone else has something to say?" He raises an eyebrow questioningly and waits. No one in the group makes a peep. "Very good. Without any interruptions we should be through with this in about fifteen minutes."

As it turns out, they get through it in ten.

What most people see when they look at Dr. Taylor is a serious man, one well suited for his position. He appears at ease in his tatty Valumart sky blue and burnt sienna oxford shirts (plastic pocket guard in place to keep the ink of cheap pens from staining these well-worn artifacts from a previous decade) and his trousers, also from Valumart, look threadbare, as if he's surviving on the most meager of salaries. It is a fact that his income is far from generous (his research is occasionally subsidized by charitable donations from wealthy philanthropists) but the truth is he makes enough money to buy better clothes yet he simply doesn't care to. The stylistic accoutrements the politicians so readily employ are of no interest to him as they have no place in the scientific world, have no bearing on his work. Also, he very seldom has to deal with the public.

Upon meeting him it is often noted that his manner is brusque, frequently distracted, but when he speaks there is a gleam in his eyes that bespeaks his intelligence, as well as a cold disregard for other members of the human race. This indifference is often mistaken for aloofness or arrogance, sometimes disrespect, but none of these are true. The fact is that he no longer wants (or needs) what other humans have to offer; their petty emotions, their insufferable boorishness, their lazy, unrepentant brashness pertaining to matters they are oft ignorant of-what he appreciates most is simply being left alone. When he does have to wallow in the mire of human company he does so with great disdain, only hoping that it will be over quickly.

But he wasn't always like this, this somber, quiet, bespectacled man with thinning hair and aging, unraveling clothes. Although this is the face he wears now, beneath it lies the ghost of a man it is most likely no one will ever know, the man who was a boy for only the briefest period before the world proved to him what a foul place it could be.

Corey was born into a large Catholic family, one of four boys and five girls, residing within the confines of a three-bedroom one-bath house on the south side of Detroit. To say he came from modest means is being generous, as the teeming Taylor brood was always at their wits end to keep the ship afloat. Because he was the youngest child it is safe to say that the burden of monetary expectation did not weigh upon him too heavily, yet by his seventh year he was pitching in and doing his part, if only to stave off his own cold and hunger. In the summer he mowed lawns and in the harsh winters shoveled snow, using the money to help put food on the table or pay one of their many delinquent bills.

His father wasn't itinerant, but he did find it hard to stay at one job for any length of time for varying reasons, most arising with each singular occasion, the grounds for which were never twice the same. Corey's mother, who couldn't work because she was perpetually pregnant, met this with great disparagement, as it meant an interruption in the food gathering and utility paying process. She wanted to work, but no sooner had she popped out another child than the mister would come home drunk, unemployed again, a raging rocket in his pocket that desired satisfaction. And because of their religious belief's it went unspoken that there would be no attempts at birth control.

"If the good Lord wants you fat with child than that's what it shall be," he was fond of saying, mostly after he'd finished his business and was tying his shoes, getting ready to head down to Grady's for a nightcap while she lay twisted in the bed sheets, their commingled sweat drying upon her, the urge to cry always at the back of her throat.

And so, obviously, with he and his siblings vying for a position at the supper table (hoping for firsts much less seconds) it was understood that if these needs were to be met it was in their best interest to help things along. Corey's eldest brother had dropped out of school when he was fourteen to take a job in an auto factory (one that had once employed the senior before a drinking binge and subsequent fist-fight with his line supervisor gave them enough reason to hand him his walking papers) and the next oldest had plans to join the army when he turned seventeen with the idea of sending his checks home until the youngest were out of school. Although honorable,

Corey instinctively knew from a very young age that forsaking education was a mistake, definitely not one he'd make himself, but he appreciated his brother's sacrifice.

Naturally smart beyond his years, Corey had no trouble taking on odd jobs after school because he coasted through his classes so easily. Homework that may have been taxing for others was a breeze for him, most often completed at school so there was no need to bring his studies home. He had a natural aptitude for math and science, but excelled at history and English as well. The only class he was openly contemptuous of was gym, one he found to be loutish and trivial. What did it prove? he often wondered, and where would this land him in the work world when the time came? Not that he was puny and weak, but sports were rather awkward for him, not having developed the coordination required to throw or catch a ball, much less make such trifling pursuits interesting to him in any way.

Although he was an excellent pupil and very dedicated to helping his family, what made him stand apart from his peers was his playfulness, not to mention a wild streak that baffled his teachers expectations of him. He had a well-rounded sense of humor, but one that could occasionally be described as delinquent. Sometimes his pranks were in good fun (mimicking teachers behind their backs for his fellow student's amusement) and other times they were almost criminal (using chemicals from the chemistry lab to build a toilet exploding bomb, which he placed in the faculty lounge). No one was ever hurt from these practical jokes but feathers were ruffled and punishment swift. The only problem the after school detentions wrought (certainly no reprisal from his parents as they had enough on their plate to deal with) was his tardiness for his after school jobs, but he managed.

It was in his junior year of high school that these crazy shenanigans would come to a screeching, grinding halt for two very good reasons: one was that he would never get a full scholarship to an accredited school if he kept up with the tomfoolery and two was a curvaceous brunette named Heidi Clotzke. She'd lived just down the street from the Taylor's since the age of seven but Corey had never made her acquaintance until one day when he noticed her in his third period calculus class. It was there, seated one desk ahead of him on his right side, that he first became aware of her budding breasts and ardent sexuality, not to mention her charming personality and brimming intellect. After a bit of hemming and hawing, he managed to ask her to the Junior Ball and she accepted.

Soon the two became inseparable and, much to his teacher's relief, his pranks tapered off as he spent more and more time with her, studying, cuddling, and necking. Near the end of their senior year the two began making plans to go to the same college, both so gifted academically they were mutually rewarded with a full scholarship to the college of their choice. It was really no great decision; an East Coast Ivy League school seemed to be the best option, and thus they applied for and were accepted at Yale.

Corey had never been so happy in his life as when he was with Heidi, her smile the sun in the sky, her charisma the galaxy in which all orbiting bodies revolved. He would do anything for her, absolutely anything. In their freshman year of college they became engaged, agreeing they would wed upon their graduation, because there really was no hurry was there? They had the rest of their lives to be together and that way their education didn't have to suffer an ill-timed childbirth. For they did want children, lots and lots of children they could spoil and mold in their own image.

Heidi had come from a large household as well, was in fact one of the eldest in her family. She was used to changing diapers and performing midnight feedings. All these duties would be second nature to her and wouldn't interfere with her career, which she intended to be in the political sciences. And she was smart as a whip, this fiery midwestern girl; surely with her inspired acumen she could eventually do whatever she wanted.

Corey was simply head over heels for her, had found in Heidi the one true companion he'd been looking for all his life. She was the Jane to his Tarzan, the Bonnie to his Clyde, the Courtney to his Kurt. In her was all he ever wanted from life, and she motivated him to a greatness he never knew he possessed. With her he felt he could do anything, could become whatever he wanted so they could have the very best life offered. And she loved him back fiercely; he knew this with all his heart.

During the second semester of their senior year (a year that had been spent making important future plans) she started suffering from headaches and dizzy spells. At first they seemed like nothing, maybe just the stress of studying so hard, trying to keep a perfect GPA. But by the end of the semester she was missing classes, and by summer she was hospitalized.

The doctor's ran extensive tests (EEG's, MRI's, CAT scans) and eventually determined it was a large, inoperable brain tumor. There was nothing they could do but give her medication to ease the pain. The best oncologist they could afford predicted she had five months to live.

And like an aging photograph seeped of color she faded away, weight dropping from her already thin frame until she was all bones and ribs and stretched skin. But Corey did his best to remain strong, to keep the face of optimism as her candle grew shorter and shorter until, at last, was snuffed out all together.

Four months after the diagnosis she was buried in Mt. Vernon Cemetery near her old home, her family and his in attendance, not a dry eye in the house. It was there, proceeding the open-casket wake and subsequent burial that he hardened his heart, shunning his Catholic leanings and turning to science for comfort. As for the human race, well, he was through. After all the pretentious doctors he'd dealt with, all the phony sympathy from 'well-wishers', he'd simply had enough. No one was her equal, no one. If he couldn't have her, he didn't want anyone at all.

He finished his degree in Oceanic sciences and continued on to get his Masters, then his Doctorate. After many years working for a private company an old classmate, one who held a prestigious position with the federal government, sought him out. What he wanted to know, of course, was would he come and work for them? The pay was crappy and the hours were terrible but he would be doing his country a favor in offering up such a brilliant mind as his own. After a weekend of deliberation he accepted.

And that's where he's been ever since, working long hours, living a solitary life, getting by on the sparsest amount of human contact as possible. Yet he wasn't completely adrift; he did have colleagues he looked up to, those he enjoyed the occasional snifter of brandy with, but for the most part he relished being alone with his books and studies. He still visited his family occasionally, on the odd holiday every year or so, but by and large he'd become estranged from them and their simple ways. None of them possessed half the intellect as he, their lives a trivial parade of child rearing and meaningless job promotions so they could buy 3D televisions and new cars, gossiping with neighbors about suspected infidelities and whose children may or may not be getting engaged. In the end their interests simply did not coincide with his own and they became strangers.

As for his decision to join this trip, well, he may not enjoy being surrounded by amateurs and others of their ilk, but he took the position on the ship because somebody had to, somebody as capable as he. He felt it was his duty as a patriotic, responsible American. Because, when it comes down to it, he and the captain of the ship are apparently the only ones with any practical experience. God help them all...

FOUR

The governor and his two aides are shown to their quarters, the crewman leading them down a ladder to the lower deck and then through a narrow passageway into the belly of the ship.

"Wait a minute," the governor says after Melissa is deposited at her room and they are about to proceed down the corridor to their appointed cabin. "Who decided upon these arrangements?"

"The captain, of course," their escort replies. "Is there a problem?"

"Well, it's just that, um, well, I thought that...um..." Hallsly sputters, withering under the intense gaze of the young man before him. Here he is, an accomplished public speaker and important statewide figure and somehow he can't find the words to explain that he needs to be shacked up with the chick because, *duh*, she's his hired sex slave...

"You thought...what?" the crewman prompts, resisting the urge to break out in a wild, reckless grin. The captain had taken him aside and told him that under no circumstances was the woman to share a room with either of the men, especially not the governor.

(*"Aide my ass, I'll bet he's banging that chick," the captain had said. "You put the governor in a cabin with that weasely looking guy and the woman by herself. If he has a problem with it you let me know. I'm not going to encourage that sleazeball's sex life on my watch."*)

"It's just that my other aide and I have a lot of work to do and it would be easier if we were in the same room," Hallsly says lamely, not quite meeting the other's eyes. Why the hell should he have to explain himself? He's the governor of California for Christ's sake. He didn't even want to come along on this stupid trip; he shouldn't have to put up with sharing a room with this, this *weirdo*.

"Sorry, you'll have to take that up with the captain," the crewman says, not unkindly. "Those are his orders."

"I guess I'll just have to talk to him myself then."

"Certainly. Right this way." They continue down the corridor and, arriving at their room, he opens the door and they wordlessly follow him inside. He looks at Tyler, and then the governor. "Will there be anything else?"

"Yeah," Tyler says, sitting down on the lower bed of the bunk beds. "Where is the bar? I could sure use a stiff one about now."

The crewman looks at him in amazement. "The bar?"

"Yeah man, the lounge, or, uh, the gallery or whatever. Or maybe you could just send me a bottle to the room? Whiskey would be good."

"For crying out loud it's only nine in the morning!" the governor scolds, his face reddening slightly. "We have work to do!"

"I guess beer would work, maybe a twelver of something imported." He smiles at the crewman. "I'm on my break."

"Melissa will be joining us shortly, at which time we shall be going over my agenda for the day," the governor says tersely, looking at Tyler and then shifting his eyes to the crewman and back. "We have a lot of work to do."

"I thought I was just here to-"

"These quarters will do just fine," Hallsly interjects abruptly, stepping forward and putting his arm around the crewman. He stuffs a twenty-dollar bill in his pocket as he leads him to the door. "Thank you very much for all of your help. If we need anything we'll give a holler."

"But I, that is, um-"

"We'll call," the governor persists, shoving him out the door. "Ciao."

"And send me a bottle of whiskey!" Tyler calls after him. "Early Times or Crown!"

The door closes and the crewman stands there a moment, the grin he'd been restraining spreading wide across his face. He's glad he didn't vote for that asshole, and whatever rock he found that doofus under must have been near the Pacific Beach Pier. He doesn't know if they are aware of it or not (apparently not) but he doesn't work for them, he works for the captain, and in turn the Script's organization. The passenger's needs aren't a concern to him, only they're safety, and what it all boils down to is the governor has no real power over any of them once they reach international waters. At that point the captain's word is law. He doesn't know why someone as useless as Hallsly is aboard (public relations probably) but obviously the man doesn't realize he is merely a figurehead. He guesses they will understand in due time though and, whistling, he carries on with his duties.

Meanwhile, back in the cabin:

"What the hell are you doing?" Hallsly is saying to Tyler. "This isn't the fucking Love Boat you moron! There is no lounge! This is a research vessel!"

"You mean I can't get something to drink?" Tyler balks, a genuine look of dumbfounded concern on his face.

"Nope," Hallsly replies with some satisfaction. "Is that going to be a problem?"

"You bet your ass it is! I didn't sign up for a trip aboard the AA Enterprise!"

The governor fixes him with a glare that could take paint off a wall. He's been mulling Tyler's presence aboard the ship since Melissa first suggested it, and now that he has to share a cabin with him his anger is boiling over.

"Just why the hell are you really here?" he demands, rolling up his sleeves as if he is ready for a rousing turn at fisticuffs. "Explain it to me because I, for one, am really confused."

"I'm here as her bodyguard," Tyler says. "You know that."

"Protecting her from who? Me? I'm the governor of California!"

"Exactly!" Tyler agrees. "She thinks you're kind of a scumbag."

"See I told you-" the governor stops, the words sinking in. "She...what?"

"Doesn't trust you to save her freakin' life," Tyler clarifies. "She's got this thing against guys who wear suits ever since she saw the movie 'American Psychotic'."

"She...she thinks *I'm* a scumbag?" He looks Tyler up and down, notes the long hair, the ripped jeans, the tattoos on his forearms. "And what does that make you?"

"What the hell do you think dude, I'm a *stud*."

"So you're her pimp?"

"Something like that."

"Either you are or you aren't. Which is it?"

"I am."

"Somehow I don't believe that."

"Whatever dude," Tyler says. He lies back, stretching out on the bed.

"I think you're her boyfriend, that's what I think."

Tyler turns his head, looks at the governor with a distrustful glare. Hallsly stares right back, his beady eyes holding the others. He may be an arrogant, overinflated jerk but he knows a lie when he hears it. Hell, he's a professional liar. Takes one to know one.

"Can I tell you something?" Tyler says at last, sitting up.

"Be my guest."

"You gotta keep this between us, you can't tell Melissa."

"Sure, sure. Why would I tell her?" Hallsly looks around the room, spots a chair and takes a seat.

"I used to be her boyfriend, before she figured me out."

"Figured you out?" Hallsly's interest is suddenly piqued.

"Yeah," Tyler nods. "I was scamming her, living off of her so I didn't have to work."

"Ah, so you *are* a pimp."

"No man, no. She takes care of the business herself. I just lived off her, letting her pay the rent, buy the food, that sort of thing."

"And she was okay with that arrangement?"

"For a while, but then it started pissing her off and she threw me out."

"So you aren't dating anymore?"

"Nope."

"So...when you came over to her place the other day, she didn't call you?"

"She hasn't called me in weeks," Tyler says peevishly. "I went there to beg her to take me back." He's silent a moment, wondering how much he should share with this guy, then continues, not really caring either way. "I had this, like, epiphanamy while we were apart. You know what an epiphanamy is?"

"Sure," the governor replies, searching his inner thesaurus and drawing a blank. He decides it doesn't really matter anyway.

"I felt like I was mistreating her, that she deserved better, and that I was willing to change for her, you know, to be a better person."

"How long were, um, how long were the two of you, uh..."

"Fucking?" Tyler asks. "About seven months." A lascivious look comes over his face. "She's a great lay," he confides. "I don't go for that whips and bondage stuff, I just like it a little rough, you know, maybe we play 'rapist' every now and then but otherwise pretty normal. Man, she jumps all over your dick, like she has a virus and your jizz is the cure. She's put my back out more than once..."

Hallsly raises his eyebrows, aroused. "So the sex was good?"

"The sex was great! But that's not why I was missing her. I felt like I was actually, you know, in *love* with her." Tyler says this last sentence like a guilty admission, as if he's baring his soul. "You know what I mean?"

"I have a wife."

Tyler blows a loud raspberry and repeats: "You know what I mean?"

The governor shakes his head. "No."

"Yeah," Tyler says. "I don't think I do either."

The two fall silent, each man thinking their own thoughts. Tyler is wondering what he is going to do without alcohol while the governor is pondering what he's been told.

"So she's finished with you but she brought you here as protection from me?" Hallsly says at last. "Why'd she do that?"

"Sorry if it sounds harsh dude, but she doesn't think she can trust you."

"That's not what I meant-"

"I mean, *can* she trust you?" Tyler asks and Hallsly is about to answer 'Yes, of course!' but then he is given to pause as he remembers a hooker he solicited in Vegas in 2015, right after he became governor. She was drop dead gorgeous with a set of cans that would have made Dolly Pardon jealous, but when she told him he couldn't titty fuck her, well, he just sort of *lost* it. He'd beaten her so badly that he had to pay for her facial reconstruction surgery plus a whopping sum just to keep her mouth shut. And somehow the press hadn't found out about it, surprisingly.

"I...I'm a nice guy," he says unconvincingly and Tyler rolls his eyes.

"She's smart as hell dude, believe me," he says, observing the governor closely. "She got some kind of vibe off of you. In her business it's in her best interest to trust her instincts, and something about you didn't add up."

"And what, she didn't have anyone else but you to come along as protection?" Hallsly says, turning the subject back toward the other, his feelings intact despite the negative allegations regarding his character.

"Apparently not, otherwise I wouldn't be here."

"So," the governor begins, piecing things together, "you don't think she'll take you back, like you were hoping?"

"I don't know dude and, personally, I really don't care."

"So why are you here?"

"Sounded like fun I guess," he says, smiling. "Thought maybe I'd get a chance to nail her again."

"But what about your, um, *epiphanamy*?" the governor says accusingly. "So you aren't going to change?"

"I'll never change," Tyler confesses. "I may want to, but I'm never gonna. Never. It ain't gonna happen."

"So…are you in love with her?"

Tyler considers this a moment, his fingers fiddling with the covers on the bed. He lifts his eyes to the sky momentarily as if he is weighing something in his mind, then rolls them back to meet the governors own.

"I'm in love with the idea of her, yeah," he admits casually. "And I like the thought of being in love but…"

"But?"

"But…I don't think I'm capable of real love. I've never been before; I don't know how that's going to change now."

"That's…pretty heavy."

"Yeah."

The two regard one another awkwardly for a moment before Tyler stands up and stretches, eyeing the other soberly.

"Like I said, this is between us. If I find out that you shared any of this with Melissa I'm gonna tell her you have genital herpes. Agreed?"

A sly grin spreads over Hallsly's face. This guy sort of reminds him of himself. He extends his hand.

"Mums the word," he says as they shake. "Mum's the word."

"Cool."

"And I have just the thing for us to seal the deal." Hallsly reaches into one of his bags, produces a bottle of Glenlivet. "Care for an eye opener?"

"Oh hells yeah!" Tyler beams approvingly. "Break that puppy open!"

Finding some water glasses, the governor pours and the two of them toast to each other's continued good health. Little does either of them know that the other is being insincere. Go figure.

FIVE

The cabin is rather tiny and cramped but Melissa doesn't care; she has money on her mind. What she'll clear from this will make her month and then some. She'll have to put up with the lecherous governor on a daily basis, of course, but she knew that coming in. No doubt she'll survive; she's certainly dealt with his sort before. Besides, how long can this trip take? A few days, maybe a week? The longer it is the more she makes and that's enough incentive for her.

Setting her suitcase on the bed, she opens it and removes a few items of clothing she doesn't want to get wrinkled. The cabin comes equipped with a miniature chest of drawers, the perfect place for her 'unmentionables'. Might as well make herself at home.

In all honesty she isn't much for boats, in fact doesn't have a whole lot of experience traveling on them, but she decides it's a small matter. A minor detail she needn't worry about. What's the big deal? The governor assured her their stay at the trash heap would be short, that the Coast Guard would pick them up a few days after their arrival if the mission wasn't complete. Sounds like a breeze.

As she neatly folds her clothes into the drawers, she ponders if it was a mistake to bring Tyler along. The guy has done enough damage in her life; there is really no sense in allowing him to do any more. But, and here is where she is desperately torn, she still has feelings for the bastard. She'd been sort of crushed that he hadn't come to her sooner, like after she caught his weirdo little butt-buddy spying on her in the sex shop. She'd assumed that after her discussion with the annoying little pillow biter Tyler would have appeared at her door hours later, but that wasn't the case. He'd waited several days. Could it be he hadn't been too sure of it himself?

Well, hindsight is twenty/twenty as they always say, so if this venture goes belly up she can at least console herself with the fact that she got paid.

Finishing loading the drawers, she moves the suitcase over and sits down on the bed, leaning back and gazing absently at the ceiling. She giggles as she recollects the stares they received from the crew when they boarded the ship, especially the expression of indignation on the captain's face. Man he looked pissed. She wonders what the governor told them, what he could have possibly said to explain hers and Tyler's presence. Whatever it was they'd seen right through it.

She gets up, digs around in her suitcase again and extracts some of the tools of her trade, uncoiling the cat o' nine tails. Good thing she brought the little one along as well; the one she normally uses is longer than the length of the cabin. Is this where the governor thinks they are going to be risking their escapades? Her cabin isn't nearly large enough to accommodate such activities. And the noise it would make? There is no way they are going to get around that. Obviously the governor knew next to nothing about their allotted space. Probably thought he was going to get a cabin the size of a freakin' penthouse. What a dipshit.

And speaking of dipshits, we go back to the subject of Tyler. What exactly does he hope to get out of this? Does he really want to be with her or is this just a lark, something to pass the time? Maybe he just wants to see if he can seduce her again, and at once the idea makes her feel sad because she realizes she doesn't know him as well as she thinks, which isn't very well at all. To make herself feel better, she starts ticking off things in her head she *does* know about him and, after only a few seconds, the list comes to an abrupt end. She runs out after his star sign (Virgo) and his favorite food (Chinese). Well, she also knows he loves sex, hates commitment and isn't into bondage and S&M but, then again, that could be almost anybody. He adores nice things but doesn't enjoy paying for them himself. He's lazy, self-centered, egotistical and thinks he owns the world.

Shit, and I was trying to keep it positive. . . .

She gets up from the bed again and looks out the porthole, which is almost too opaque to see through. She can barely make out the San Diego Bay and not much else. Maybe the window was made that way or it just needed to be cleaned, who knew? Does she really care? No, she finds, she doesn't. Store that in the file with her examinations of Tyler's motives. Chalk it up to plain old 'just-don't-give-a-rip' and leave it at that.

Not knowing what else to do (not knowing if there is anything she is supposed to do) she decides to lay down and try and take a nap. She didn't get much sleep last night and there is no TV and she forgot to bring along something to read. The governor will come and find her when he needs to, him or Tyler.

And what if it's Tyler? Will she let him in? After all, she isn't sure if he truly wants to redeem himself or if he's still up to his old tricks. At the very least, she supposes, he's a buffer between the governor and she, should the man turn out to be more than she can handle. That's something anyway.

Resting her head down on the pillow, she closes her eyes and listens to the shrieking of the gulls, and they gently lull her into a peaceful sleep.

SIX

The ship sets out at 9:33 a.m. Pacific Time, Captain Harvey and the crew smoothly navigating the vessel out of San Diego Bay into the infinite expanse of the Pacific. The passengers have all been shown to their quarters with the exception of the Naval personnel, who are stationed fore and aft, firearms slung casually over their shoulders, arms at their sides.

Kenny and the other security guards are stationed below deck, in a cabin near the governor and his aides, and currently they are talking amongst themselves as they get settled. Only one of them isn't saying much, and that's Sasquatch; he looms near a porthole, silent and brooding.

"Easy money," a Mexican man with hardly a trace of an accent says, taking a deck of cards out of his shirt pocket. "Any a you cholos up for a game of poker?"

The other guards fall in except for Sasquatch, who stares out the window with a look in his eyes that nobody can decipher.

"I've gone over the passenger list, captain, and I've found a discrepancy," one of the crewmen says as the sun shifts into the western portion of the afternoon sky. They are five hours into their trip when the crewman brings this to the captain's attention.

"What's the problem?" Captain Harvey asks, directing the first mate to take the wheel while he studies the navigational equipment.

"It seems we may have an extra person aboard."

Captain Harvey cocks a weary eye at him. "Seems to be or is it a fact?"

"Well, according to this list of names there's a person on board who isn't accounted for."

"So it's a fact then."

"Yes sir."

"Who is it, a member of the scientific team?" A sudden look of bemusement creases his face. "Or is it that broad the governor brought with him, claiming to be his 'aide'?"

"No, sir."

"So who is it?"

"It's a member of the security personnel," the crewman answers, looking at the roster. "According to the passenger itinerary there are only supposed to be three of them but there are four."

"Are you sure about that?"

"I counted heads when everybody came aboard," he confirms. "The list specifies three security guards for the governor."

"Why didn't this come to your attention while we were still at the dock?"

The crewman blushes, his pale cheeks suddenly a fiery red.

"I wasn't consulting the list while they were boarding sir," he replies sheepishly. "I was just counting heads."

"Hmmm, this in direct disregard of ship policy," Captain Harvey notes. "Isn't it general procedure to consult the list while the passengers are boarding? Or have the rules changed and I haven't been made aware of it yet?"

"I made a mistake sir," he acknowledges humbly. "I'm very sorry."

"It's a simple job really, not much to it."

"I don't know what I was thinking sir," he says but, in fact, he knows very well. His mind had been a million miles away, thinking about the girl he'd met at Harry's Bar and Grill last night, a hot little number with perky breasts and a tush so small he'd bet that when you put your hands around it your fingertips would touch. She'd laughed at all his jokes and responded positively to his sexual overtures, overlooking his blatant attempts at peering down her shirt. They flirted shamelessly all night, their table littered with empty beer bottles and shot glasses but, at closing time, he'd been unable to seal the deal. After some rather inspired cajoling he talked her into giving him her phone number, promising her he'd call when he got back. He, for one, already can't wait for this trip to be over.

"Shall we agree that you weren't thinking…about your job anyway?"

"Yes sir."

"Okay," Captain Harvey says, looking away. "I suppose it isn't entirely your fault. The Navy rejects were supposed to check everybody's papers. Regardless, you have to deal with it. Go down to the security guard's quarters and bring this guy to me. I want to know why he stowed away aboard my ship."

"Very good sir," the crewman replies, executing a sharp salute before exiting the bridge.

"Gotta be one every time," the captain mutters. "It's the nature of the way things work."

"A stowaway?" one of the others asks and Captain Harvey shakes his head.

"No, an idiot."

When the crewman appears at their door, a querulous expression on his face and a sheet of paper in hand, Sasquatch looks away from him uneasily.

"Kenny Howard?" the man asks and Kenny raises a hand.

"Here," he says.

"Didn't you used to play football for the Packers?"

"Yep."

"Did you retire?" he asks, and for a moment the room is deathly quiet. All eyes are on Kenny, who is leaning back in a wooden chair, holding his cards just below the level of the table. The ex-football player studies the crewman carefully, wondering if he's being a smart ass but, when he sees nothing on his face but mute expectation, he shrugs his massive shoulders.

"You could say that, I guess."

"Man, you were awesome!"

"Thanks, I 'preciate it."

"Sure." He consults his list again: "Cole Hernandez?"

The Mexican man raises a hand. "Here."

"Okay, and Robert Levine?"

The third man at the table raises a hand, leaving only the large, hairy fellow who's standing by the porthole.

Figures it would be that guy. The crewman doesn't like the looks of this. Could be trouble. He clears his throat. "Um, you there, yes, you." He clears his throat again, hoping this isn't going to get ugly. The guy is a full foot taller than he is and twice as broad across the shoulders. "I don't have your name on my list."

The man turns and stares at him mutely before his head drops and he sighs.

"Yeah," he says. "I'm not on the list." He offers a guilty smile. "I 'm sort of tagging along."

"I'm going to need you to come with me."

"Of course."

"What the hell?" Kenny laughs. "Why on God's green earth would ya wanna stowaway on this ship?"

"I've got my reasons," the man mutters and suddenly Kenny remembers how strangely he acted when the scientific crew walked by, and his acerbic remark when Kenny mentioned the redheaded girl. He nods.

"I'm sure ya do brother," Kenny concedes. "I'm sure ya do."

SEVEN

"Who are you?" the captain asks and the man shifts his feet uneasily. Unable to meet his eyes, he looks around the room instead, taking in the lavishness of the captain's quarters. There is an impressive bookshelf stocked with everything from navigational charts to 'The Old Man and the Sea', oak paneled walls that are practically hidden behind world maps (some of them appearing to date back to the previous century), large, gilded plaques hailing the captain's legendary achievements, and nautical knick-knacks such as anchors and coiled ropes decorating every inch of available space. Captain Harvey is seated behind an expansive mahogany desk, twirling a globe that's resting near his left hand.

At last the man's gaze rests on the captain, his expression one of uncertainty. He wonders if he should lie, ponders what the consequences would be, then decides to tell the truth.

"Dante Kellerman, sir."

The captain shakes his head.

"Your name doesn't mean squat to me son," he says. "Let me rephrase the question: What the hell are you doing here?"

Dante opens his mouth to speak but falters. How will it sound if he tells him he stowed away aboard his ship so he can be near the woman he loves...at least, thinks he loves. Hell, he knows how it will sound: improbable if not outright ridiculous. Unless of course the captain is a romantic at heart, which he doesn't appear to be. In all actuality the captain looks like a hardass who will most likely have him walk the plank (if indeed there is a plank to be walked; maybe he has watched too many pirate movies).

"I...uh...I just wanted to part of the crew," he says hesitantly, and the answer sounds false, even to him.

Captain Harvey regards him coldly, spinning the globe faster and faster. This guy looks like a throwback from Neanderthal times, but it's possible that it's a disguise. Could he be an eco-terrorist sent to infiltrate the ship and get crucial information about the mission? If so, to what end?

"Sounds like a load of shit to me," Captain Harvey states flatly and Dante lowers his head. The captain possesses a gaze so penetrating and intense it's hard to look him in the eyes for very long.

"All right," Dante confesses, "that isn't the truth." He shuffles his feet, addressing the floor. "The truth is, well, a little stupid..."

"I'll be the judge of what is and what isn't stupid son, and if I don't get an answer from you that makes sense you're going to be in a world of hurt. You understand me?" Captain Harvey's voice is stern, but inwardly he is perplexed. *This guy doesn't appear smart enough to be an eco-terrorist; he looks like a sorry ass son of a bitch who's a long way from home.*

"It's kind of a long story sir."

The captain runs a hand over his white flattop and sighs. "Give me the abridged version then."

"Okay," Dante nods, swallowing several times. "I did it for love."

Captain Harvey's lips peel back in a smirk. "Come again?"

"I did it because I love her, and I thought if she went on this trip without me she would forget I existed...I figured she would find someone else..."

"You're in love with a passenger on board the ship? Who is it?"

"Her name is Leeann. She's part of the scientific team."

"Let me guess: the redhead."

"That's her."

"You better not be lying to me," Captain Harvey warns. "You're only digging yourself in deeper." He suddenly turns his head, coughing with incredible force into his fist. He opens his hand and glances inside before extracting a handkerchief from his pocket, cleaning his palm, and then stowing it in a drawer. "Not that you aren't in a lot of trouble already. You do know it's against the law to stowaway on a scientific vessel carrying out a federally sponsored assignment, don't you? You're looking at some serious charges."

"I'm not lying," Dante insists, "and I know what I did was stupid, but I had to be near her! I couldn't let her go without me!"

The captain nods, continues spinning the globe. *The guy appears to be telling the truth; his body language emanates a certain pathos that verifies his claim.*

"So this is a love story then, I take it. I'm supposed to be sympathetic because you got a hard-on for some dame?"

"Well, no sir..."

"And if I bring this woman in here-"

"Leeann," Dante interrupts and the captain shrugs.

"If I bring Leeann in here, she'll confirm that you are who you say you are?"

"She will..." Dante says tentatively, "but she might be a little upset, seeing as she's so excited about this job and all."

Oh boy, the captain thinks tiredly. *One of those kinds of love stories.*

So Dante tells the captain (in as few words as possible which, given the nature of the tale, isn't all that condensed) about how he met Leeann and the circumstances regarding their 'relationship'.

The captain listens, spinning the globe, his face an expressionless mask that seems to invite Dante to plunge deeper and deeper into the story.

He tells him how he and Leeann met in a clinical drug trial and how they bonded over long conversations and their mutual amusement regarding the horny old men in an erectile dysfunction study. He pontificates on the loss of his mother (going into detail about her untimely demise), expressing how he desperately needs a female in his life and how badly he wishes it could be Leeann. He tells him about their date, and how she told him of this trip, which leads him to how he found out where she was going by calling the number from the ad posted on the student bulletin board.

"How the hell did you think you were going to get on the ship?"

"I didn't. I thought I'd intercept her before she boarded, maybe tell her I loved her, possibly give her something to think of me while she was away…"

"And?"

"I was waiting on the dock and I started talking with one of the security guards, and when he assumed I was with security too I just went with it. I figured I'd try and get aboard, to hell with the consequences." He doesn't bother to add that he packed a bag, just in case he could find a way to stow aboard. He figures (probably correctly) that this little tidbit of info may anger the captain further.

So ends Dante's account and the captain chews it over. In his opinion a pretty little number like Leeann would have to be crazy to want a serious relationship with this brute. There's just no way in hell it's going to happen. He'd be better off shacking up with a gorilla, if she'd have him. He'd probably have to shave off that beard first…

So what is he going to do with him? For his numbskullery he has half a mind to lock him up and feed him bread and water, maybe waterboard him for good measure, just to make sure there isn't anything he's not telling him. Decisions, decisions…

"So this girl, Leeann, she doesn't feel the same way about you?" he asks at length.

"I really don't know if she does now, but if she got to know me I think she would in time."

"In other words: no," the captain says and Dante winces. "What is she going to do when she sees you?"

"Do, sir?"

"Yes, what is she going to do? Is she going to get angry, hysterical, horny…what? I don't need a member of the scientific crew getting too upset to do her job."

"I don't think she hates me sir," Dante answers honestly. "I'm just not sure if she is in love with me."

"And so you stowed away on my ship just to see if you could make this woman love you, is that what I'm getting?"

"You make it sound so arbitrary but, yes, I guess that's it."

Captain Harvey stares hard at the other, his face unreadable. To Dante it looks as if he is making up his mind about something, but what it is he can't even guess. The captain takes a tin of chaw out of his pocket and places a pinch in his cheek, spitting a thin stream of juice into the wastebasket.

"You know anything about ships?" he says at last.

"Nothing, sir."

"Are you a fast learner?"

"You bet!" Dante exclaims, jumping to his feet. He is so tall his head bumps the ceiling. "If I put my mind to it I'm sure I could learn anything, trust me!"

"Okay, okay, easy big fellah," the captain says, indicating that Dante should sit back down. He does, albeit with a goofy grin on his face. "Here's what I'm thinking: I'll hire you on a trial basis doing some of the shit work my crew doesn't want to do. You do what you're told and don't complain and maybe I won't lock your sorry ass in the brig."

"I'd really appreciate that sir!" Dante cries, bounding up again, clasping his hands before him like a little girl enraptured by her first viewing of 'The Tiny Mermaid'.

"Whoa whoa whoa!" the captain says, holding out his hands like he is pushing a rather enthusiastic dog off of him. "I got some rules, and if you break 'em you're toast, you hear me?"

"Loud and clear, sir!"

"First of all, if that chick freaks out and doesn't want you near her, you stay the hell away. I can't have her working conditions compromised because of you, comprende?"

"Yes sir."

"Second, you're working for room and board. You're just lucky I'm letting you wander amongst the general population."

"Yes, of course-"

"And I don't want to hear that you're giving anyone any trouble, got it? I'm willing to pretend I hired you, that you're supposed to be on my ship, but only on the condition that you keep your nose clean and do what you are told."

"Alright."

"Do you understand you're going to be swabbing decks and spit shining toilets until they're so clean I can eat lunch out of them?"

"Certainly, sir," Dante replies, and the captain actually believes the big idiot is sincere.

"My crew and I will be assessing your work. You fuck up and I'll lock you up and throw away the key."

"Thank you sir, thank you so much!"

"Don't thank me until you see where you're going to be staying, and then you just might reconsider the whole thing and ask me to have you cast off in an inflatable dinghy with nothing but a canteen of seawater and an empty bottle of sunscreen."

"Anything is fine sir, trust me," Dante says gratefully, tears stinging his eyes. Why this man has taken pity on him is a mystery, but he will do everything in his power not to betray his trust.

"And I can't have you wearing those clothes. I don't know if we have a uniform that will fit you but we'll have to find something," the captain concludes, and then thinks of something else: "So she hasn't seen you onboard yet? She doesn't know you're here?"

"No sir, I've been very careful to avoid her."

"Good, that way you can start with a fresh slate." The captain looks at him earnestly. "You better make up a good story and stick to it. But believe me, if she doesn't want you around her you stay away, got me? You don't and that dinghy has your name written all over it. If you're lucky you might get eaten by sharks before you succumb to sunstroke."

"I will sir, I promise," Dante says, then dares ask a question: "Why are you helping me out like this?"

The captain shrugs and leans back in his chair again.

"Either I'm getting old and soft or I'm out of my damn mind," he replies, smiling a crooked smile that seems genuine. "Or maybe I just feel sorry for you, what with the story you just told me about the peacocks and your mother and all...I really don't know. But if I find out you lied to me, or if it comes to my attention you're making scurrilous allegations about your little honey simply because she doesn't want you around, I'll put you out of your misery in a heartbeat. Are we clear on this?"

"We are, sir. I won't let you down."

"It's in your best interest that you don't," the captain says dismissively. "Now report to the first mate. He's on the bridge. Tell him to have someone find you a uniform and a mop."

"Yes sir!"

"Now get out of here before I change my mind."

Dante doesn't waste a second. He gets up and exits as fast as he can.

The captain sits at his desk a while longer after Dante is gone, his hand resting on the globe but no longer twirling it. Another coughing spasm overtakes him and he retrieves his hanky in time to catch anything that might threaten to stain the exquisite surface of the mahogany desk. Tucking it into one of his pockets, he looks out his window, gazing at the endless stretch of sea.

The throwback might come in handy in the long run, given his size and stupidity. He's as eager as a puppy to please and all he has to do is dangle that chick in front of him like a carrot on a stick and he'll do anything he's ordered. And if he doesn't he can always be persuaded, one way or the other. Most likely 'the other'.

Captain Harvey smiles and spits into the trash can again, peering down to see what he's dredged up besides tobacco juice. Changes are coming, he can feel it, and with them there will be questions unless he begins phase two of his plan, and damn soon at that. If luck is with him the storm will keep everybody out of his way, if indeed he can count on a good squall to insure these assholes are kept off-balance, confused and scared.

He takes a hand mirror out of his desk and glances at himself, notes that the circles under his eyes are growing darker, and in bright light his skin is taking on an ashen gray complexion.

Have to do something about that, he decides, putting the mirror away. But it won't be long and they'll be at their destination. After that his appearance won't matter anymore, not in the slightest. When that time comes nothing will matter but his own iron-clad will, a force that none of these jerk-off's will get in the way of, not if they know what's good for them.

Oh, they won't all right. Not when they see what I got lined up for 'em.

At this thought he chuckles, a deep, penetrating resonance that reverberates off the wood paneled walls.

Just wait until they get a load of me...

EIGHT

Leeann is sharing a cabin with the Asian girl from UCLA (her name is Kim Leung and she is Chinese), and for all practical purposes this shouldn't be a problem except that Kim is, apparently, an uptight bitch. It began with a terse discussion over who would sleep on the top bunk; Leeann compromised and took it. That segued into a debate over how many drawers each of them would get to use in the chest of drawers. The problem? There were five drawers. Who would get the extra one? Leeann had suggested they could split it but Kim was reluctant to have her clothes mixed in with Leeann's. Again, she conceded and let the other have it. She could have been stubborn and claimed it for herself, but Leeann was certain this would surely start a war of wills that would only intensify as the trip progressed. The only problem with her caving in, of course, was that she didn't want to look like a pushover but, she decided, she would save herself for that which truly mattered: their data collection. If this sniveling little c-u-n-t gets in her way while they are trying to do their job, God help her.

Leeann climbs up on her bunk and lies down, closing her eyes. She thinks of how lucky she is to have gotten a break like this; this will really look good on her resume for both grad school and her future job(s). She also marvels at the convenience of the timing, being able to split town before Dante became any more of a problem. Not that she dislikes him, no, it's just that she can't see herself growing very fond of him. He's got a good sense of humor but he's challenged in the looks department. And, for what it's worth, he's the epitome of damaged goods. The few things he'd told her about his family just about made her sick, and she wonders why he even shared them at all. Was he trying to scare her away?

Well, that's behind her. When this trip is over she'll think about what's next on the old agenda, but she's in no hurry. Getting her Masters degree would be a good idea but at this point Leeann is tired of school; what she wants is to jump into the job market, see what's in store for her there. Maybe this trip will clarify her position on that. Should she hide in the easy world (for her) of academia or should she launch herself into the 'real' world? Hard to say and, fortunately, not a decision she needs to make any time soon. At the moment she's bound for the research trip of lifetime, and right now that's enough for her to think about. She can't wait until they reach the trash heap and she can put to use some of the things she's learned during her whirlwind college career. And after that, let the accolades commence.

Travis and Dave are positioned at the bow of the ship. Their job: give the impression that all is secure. Not that there is anything *to* secure; in fact they feel as if they are just taking up space. Around them the crew scuttles about tending to the ship and, funny enough, the inbred looking Sasquatch guy is now wearing a sailor's uniform and mopping the deck. He'd come aboard claiming to be part of the security crew and now, half a day later, he's changed job titles.

"I wish I could switch jobs," Dave says. "I wanna switch from Navy seaman apprentice to porn star. I'll start by filmin' my first stag movie with that hot chick the governor's bangin'."

"In yer dreams man," Travis laughs. "That lady probably only does it with serious, political types. She wouldn't bonk a Navy seaman; yer outa her league."

"She don't know what she's missin'."

"Sure she don't-"

"Attention!" a bullying voice commands and at once they cut the chatter and stand rigid, executing a professional salute. "At ease."

It's the lieutenant junior grade, and the look on his face promises he's more than just a little pissed off. In Dave's humble opinion this guy is a first-class dickweed but, unfortunately, he is the man the Navy put in charge.

"I suppose a part of your job description is to make lewd comments about the female passengers aboard the ship. Is that correct?" He leans into Dave's personal space, his face inches away, and Dave can plainly see the craterous acne scars that speckle his cheeks and neck like nasty reminders of a hard fought battle with puberty.

"No, sir."

"What did you say?"

"No sir!"

"That's more like it! Now drop and give me fifty!"

Dave looks at him blandly. "Really? Ya think that's gonna change anythin'?"

The lieutenant's face grows red, a vein bulging on his forehead.

"Do you remember what Commander Sparks told y'all back at the base, about how you conduct yourself on this trip is going to determine what happens to you when it's over? Do you recall?"

Dave recalls all right, and he's going to do his damnedest to make sure he shines above the others, but he doesn't like the idea of being pushed around by this shit for brains, who in all likelihood is in as much hot water as he and Travis. He's not sure of the specifics, but he thinks he can probably fill in the blanks. Maybe this dill hole got caught nailing an Admiral's wife. What the hell, it's happened before. Some fat old hag who wasn't getting any dick at home, eager for a young stud (someone young anyway) to plow her back forty while the old man was out to sea. Or possibly he got busted blowing another sailor, ya know, don't ask, don't tell, over the teeth, past the gums, look out tummy here it comes…the facts really don't matter. What does is that he's a screw-up just like them, and having to listen to him (and obey him) is almost more insulting than anything else the Navy has done.

"Yeah, I remember."

"Then what are you waiting for? I said give me fifty!"

"Look man," Dave says, his voice low, his eyes a flicker with a mischievous light. "I'll give ya twenty and yer gonna be happy with that."

"You have the audacity to try and negotiate-"

Dave reaches out and takes the other by the throat, tightening his hand until the lieutenant's eyes bulge from their sockets. Dave is shorter but stockier, and in an actual fight he could kick the crap out of this chump any day.

"I'm gonna do twenty push-ups *lieutenant*, and yer gonna be happy with that," he hisses. "Either that or I'll take ya below deck and kick yer sorry ass from one side a the ship to the other."

"H…h…how…duh…duh…dare…you," the lieutenant wheezes and Dave squeezes harder.

"You ain't in charge a me dude, this is all for show. Hell, I'll let ya pretend ya are, within reason, but if ya get in my face again I swear I'm gonna throw yer ass over the side a the boat. Are we clear?"

The lieutenant snarls at this outrage, but then sees (out of the corner of one eye through rapidly blurring vision) one of the ship's crewmen approaching. He can't let him witness this, not if he wants respect.

"Okay!" he chokes. "Fuh-fuh-fine! Just let me go!"

Dave slowly relaxes his hand and removes it just as the crewman is abreast of them. He is no more than a few feet away when Dave gets down on the tips of his toes and the palms of his hands and counts out twenty quick push-ups, complete with a handclap between each one. He then climbs back to his feet, salutes the lieutenant and stands 'at ease'.

"Very good," the lieutenant junior grade says weakly. "Carry on."

Now that the governor has a buzz on he's feeling a little, shall we say, *randy*. He's been a naughty boy and needs discipline, in fact requires it very badly. His cabin mate is passed out on his bunk, just like the governor wants. That ought to keep him out of the way. It took most of the bottle of Glenlivet to do the trick but eventually it prevailed. Stupid asshole thought he could go toe to toe with him in a drinking contest, did he? Hallsy proved he knows his way around a bottle of scotch, that's for damn sure.

Slipping silently out the door, he makes his way toward Melissa's cabin, keeping an eye open for anyone who might make things difficult for him, like the pesky captain or one of his crew. As far as the governor is concerned they should mind their own damn business and let him mind his, but he is aware (because of their assigned quarters) that they aren't about to let sleeping dogs lie. Okay, fine. Whatever. It's nothing he can't get around.

He knocks on her door, softly at first and, when he gets no response, a little harder.

"Who is it?" a sleepy voice asks and, in a loud theatrical whisper he says: "It's me!"

"Me who?"

"Your boss! Now open the damn door!"

Almost a full minute later (the governor waiting in suspense for one of the crew to walk by) the door opens, but only a few inches.

"What do you want?" Melissa asks, yawning.

"I've been a very bad boy and I need a spanking." He's wearing a shit-eating grin on his leathery face, an eyebrow arched lasciviously. "Maybe even something a little more severe than that."

"Can't you come back later? I was taking a nap."

"You can sleep on your own time. I hired you for this trip so you would be available to me whenever I needed you."

She sighs. "Fine." The door opens wider and she lets him in. He steps inside quickly, taking off his sport coat and loosening his tie.

"Aren't you supposed to be, like, doing shit? You know, stuff that a governor does?" She reaches into a drawer and extracts her mini cat o' nine tails and a pair of handcuffs.

"I don't know what that entails," he answers truthfully. In fact, no one has told him anything. He figures he'll go up to the bridge later and make an appearance but, after that, he has no clue. The president (nor anyone else from the White House) gave him any idea what it is he's supposed to do while aboard the ship. He guesses his presence is all for show, and that's just fine with him. Real work sucks donkey balls.

"Must be a rough life." She surveys the room, wondering not for the first time how they're going to go about this in such a small amount of space. "Sounds like a tricky job description."

"Being the governor of California is a very difficult post with many meaningful tasks I'll have you know." He takes off his shirt, throws it onto her bunk. "I have important decisions to make every day."

"Regarding what? How many singles you should have in your wallet at any given time to tip strippers?"

"More important than that, trust me." He looks around, frowning. "Not a lot of space to work with..."

"Just noticed, huh? This isn't exactly a Carnival cruise ship." She eyes him glumly, wondering if this was such a good idea. The money he offered is fantastic, but she has the distinct feeling that something unsavory will happen to make her regret this.

"Well, we'll have to make do," he says, unbuckling his pants.

"Where's Tyler?" she asks, watching him strip to his underpants. She wouldn't put it past this jerk-off to try and make a move on her, judging by the bulge he's sporting. Not a big bulge, but a bulge just the same.

"He's sleeping," the governor replies, noticing her sudden apprehension. "And don't worry, I'm not going against my word. All I want is a good, sound thrashing."

"Okay then," she says, smacking the whip against her palm. "Turn around."

"Um, aren't you, uh, going to, you know, put the suit on?"

"What?"

"You know, the bondage suit? I like it better that way."

Melissa groans. "Is it really necessary?"

"Oh my, yes."

"For Christ's sake, fine." She opens a drawer and removes the suit. "But you're going to have to turn around while I put it on."

"Really? I don't get to have a peek?"

She gives him a look so frosty he swears he can feel the hairs on the back of his neck stand up. "You can either turn around or you can step outside. It's your choice."

"All right, all right, I'll turn around. Geez, don't get your panties in a bunch."

"Oh, you'll know if my panties are in a bunch all right," she says, a hint of menace in her voice. Not much, but it's there. She wants him to know that just because he's a politician doesn't mean she's going to take any of his crap, even if he is paying her a thousand bucks a day. "Now do it before I decide to kick you out of here."

"Oh! I love how you take charge!" The governor turns around, facing the door. After all, he is good at taking orders, that is, when they're coming from someone higher up than he is or a sexy woman in a bondage suit holding a whip. "Let the good times roll…"

NINE

Kenny and Cole Hernandez stand near the bow of the ship, leaning on the railing and watching as the water splashes up in silvery rainbows. They are smoking cigarettes and talking, well, Cole is talking and Kenny is listening. Once the guy gets going it's hard to shut him up, but Kenny doesn't mind. He doesn't really have much to say anyway.

The governor is locked inside his cabin (presumably taking a nap) so it's not like there's much for them to do. And since no one on the ship appears to expect anything of them they are left to their own devices. Two of the Navy seamen are stationed nearby, standing idly as well. The two young men stare at the horizon as the boat slices effortlessly through the water, talking quietly amongst themselves.

As Cole drones on (telling Kenny about his family; sounds like this guy has a *lot* of relatives) Kenny wonders if this is what's going to comprise the majority of their time, standing around, shooting the bull. Not that he minds; can't complain about not having to do anything strenuous, but the time isn't exactly going to fly by. The problem is, with the downtime, having little to distract him, every so often he feels a nervous pang within him, a tugging (no, wrenching) sensation that a drink would certainly hit the spot right about now, and he finds himself occasionally cursing the fact that it's no longer an option. He chose this position so he has to own up to it, and he's cool with that, but the decision sure came at a price. He isn't suffering full-scale D.T.'s, but he can't seem to shake the image in his mind of a lowball glass filled to the brim with whiskey, expensive, rotgut…it's all the same to him. Whatever gets the job done baby.

Cole switches topics, starts talking about their job, and Kenny tunes back in. He bitches about this, that and the other but Kenny feels impartial. The only thing he finds questionable about this assignment is that they haven't been issued firearms; all they've been given are Billy clubs. He mentions it to Cole, and the other fixes him with a squirrelly grin.

"Yeah, what kind of security can we offer if we ain't got guns?" he says, then leans in close. "*I* got a gun," he whispers. "In fact, I got more than one, man."

"Yeah?" Kenny says, looking around to see if anyone can hear them. "Ya got one fer me?"

"I can take care of you, don't worry," Cole confides. "If the shit hits the fan our asses are covered."

"Cool." Kenny takes a last drag of his smoke, pitching it over the side. "I never thought bout bringin' one. I thought they'd have it taken care of."

"I had a weird feeling about this job, if you know what I mean," Cole says and Kenny looks at him curiously.

"No, I don't know what ya mean."

"You didn't think it was funny that *we* were hired? I mean, I got a criminal record longer than the Dead Sea Scrolls and they picked me? What the hell is that about?" Cole laughs. "And I know about you. You got a bum knee you been medicating with pills and booze. Not exactly championship thoroughbred material."

"I quit takin' the pills a long time ago and I ain't drinkin' no more," Kenny says defensively, but he does have to admit (only to himself) that it *is* odd. When he was being interviewed they didn't even ask him to piss in a cup. You'd think they'd want to know if he was stoned to the eyeballs on opiates or not. "But I guess I thought, well, I spose I figgered it din't really matter." He studies the other inquisitively. "What do'ya got a record for?"

"Shit man, you name it. Breaking and entering, arson, assault and battery, fraud...the list goes on and on, but I never killed nobody, I'll tell ya that. Only reason I applied for this job was to satisfy the conditions of my parole, didn't think I'd get it and what do you know? Here I am."

"But that don't make no sense," Kenny frowns. "Why the hell would they hire an ex-con to guard the governor? Unless..." Kenny reflects on it all, considering the goofy politician and his suspicious looking 'aides', the apparently inexperienced scientific team-hell, they're all *kids* for Christ sake, not counting the guy from Washington.

"Go on, you can do it," Cole says. "I know you can put it together. I did in the first freakin' hour aboard."

Kenny stares at the other, startled, a sudden insight hitting him like a ton of bricks. He shoots a look over at the Navy seamen; they look even younger than the college kids. When it comes to experience he's sure between the two of them they don't have enough to adequately fill out a job application to work at a gas station. Who the hell does anyone think they are fooling?

"Is this," he starts, lowering his voice so that Cole can barely hear him, "is this a suicide mission?" He feels shivers running up and down him in alternating waves, cold prickles of fear tickling his belly.

"If it ain't," Cole replies, "it sure ought to be."

Tyler awakens from a drunken stupor, wondering where he is. This sure doesn't look like Wes' place, and the way the room is moving he figures he must have one hell of a case of the spins.

But then he sees the light pouring through the porthole, sees the nautical paintings on the walls and at once comprehension dawns on him. Smacking his lips (tasting the musky tang of whiskey) he swings his legs over the side of the bunk and before he becomes conscious of the bed's height he falls five feet to the floor beneath him.

"Shit!" he moans. He forgot he was on the top bunk.

He rolls over, not wanting to get up for a moment, content to lie there and feel the pounding in his head move in tandem with the motion of the ship. *How the hell did I get so fucking drunk?* And then he remembers the governor generously pouring the booze, insisting he drink his fill. Why that dirty son of a bitch would bestow such kindness upon him makes no sense, unless he had an ulterior motive…

He sits up, oblivious to the skull-crushing headache that greets him, knowing immediately where that scumbag is and why he was so liberal with his precious stash.

Lurching to his feet he stumbles to the door, fumbling it open and staggering out into the narrow passageway. The movement of the ship acts as a counter balance to his already impaired equilibrium and he sways back and forth, groping along the wall, finding his way toward Melissa's cabin.

When he arrives he pounds on the door.

"Hey!" he roars. "Open up in there!"

He swears he can hear giggling coming from inside. Is she screwing that bastard? Does she need money that badly? But, more importantly, did governor Sleaze Bucket let her in on his little secret? That mother humper is *so* dead.

He pounds on the door again, this time with more force. If these doors weren't reinforced steel he might try and break in, but he knows that all he'll succeed in doing is hurting himself.

"Melissa! Open this door right now!" He grabs the handle, jiggles it urgently but it seems to be locked. Either that or he's too drunk to operate the damn thing. "Open the goddamn door right now you stupid bitch!" he screams at the top of his lungs, the ferocity in his voice almost on the edge of madness. "Whatever he told you, it isn't true!" In his hung-over/half drunk state the thought of the governor sharing his secret with her has him in a near frenzy.

Then he feels hands gripping his shoulders and he spins around quickly, fists up, ready to punch first and ask questions later.

But it's one of the crewmen, and he's looking at Tyler as if he's just lost his mind, which, in all actuality, he probably (momentarily) has.

"Can I help you sir?" the crewman asks, studying the other with a fixed, calculated reserve. He smells the sour stench of stale whiskey emanating from the other's pores like a homeless man's cologne, notes the large beads of sweat trickling down his feverish looking forehead.

"Oh, hey, man." Tyler unclenches and lowers his fists. "Sorry." He stands unsteadily, listing back and forth, his eyes mere slits, unfocused and bloodshot. "What do you want?"

"I came down here looking for you," the crewman explains calmly. "We're having a meeting on the top deck and everyone is present except you."

"Okay." Tyler tries his best to stand still, to present a better image of himself, even if it's only for this butt-munch's benefit. "Sure."

"May I ask what you are doing?" the crewman inquires and Tyler shakes his head.

"No, you may not."

"Okay then." He shrugs. "We should go."

"No problem, after you."

The captain is standing at the stern of the ship, his back against the rail, a light breeze blowing pleasantly against his back. The late afternoon air is humid, the sun scorching, unrelenting, but by tomorrow that should change, and soon enough the crew will know, possibly question his judgment and motives. Well, he'll deal with that when the time comes.

He looks around at the people assembled before him, taking in the calm, bored looks on their faces. If they knew even a fraction of the things he did they wouldn't be standing there like a bunch of idiots, would they? He thinks not.

"I'm sure you are all wondering why I gathered you here," he begins, nodding imperceptibly to one of his crewmen, who in turn nods and disappears below deck. While the captain keeps the passengers otherwise occupied his men will search their cabins, seeking and confiscating contraband such as weapons, drugs, alcohol and, if possible, obtain evidence linking any of the passengers to an eco-terrorist group. If anyone aboard intends to sabotage this mission he wants to know posthaste, before any damage is done.

The passengers murmur amongst themselves, and he let's them get it out of their system before he continues:

"I wanted to personally welcome you all aboard and allow you to ask any questions if you have them. Then Dr. Taylor is going to introduce himself to those of you who haven't made his acquaintance and answer anything I can't. When he is finished, my chef has prepared a sumptuous feast for our dining pleasure." He chuckles. "And don't believe what you've heard. The food aboard a research vessel is actually quite good."

Cheers welcome this last part; most of them have subsisted on only snack foods since they last ate breakfast many hours ago.

"I certainly hope none of you has any dietary restrictions that will render our good will incompetent, as we will be serving fresh fish and vegetables."

"What do you have to drink?" the governor, ever the most obnoxious of the bunch, asks and the captain smiles at him beneficently.

"We have your choice of apple juice, water, coffee, tea, clear soda or brown soda," he replies and several among the group loudly voice their complaints.

"We ain't little kids," Cole says. "I'm sure some of us can handle a beer or two."

"I'm sure *you* can handle a beer or two," the captain says mildly. "In your case I'm sure you could drink a beer or six." There is general laughter at this. "But, and I know I don't have to remind you, this is a business trip and you, sir, are currently 'on the clock'. There will be no consumption of alcoholic beverages during our voyage. It's for the safety of everyone involved. And to make this demand easy to enforce we didn't so much as stock cooking sherry. So, really, you have no choice."

He doesn't know about my supply, the governor thinks smugly, suppressing a grin. *Good thing too, because I don't have enough to go around.*

"Now, besides any questions involving the refreshments, does anyone have any serious queries they'd like addressed?"

Again there is a general mumbling amongst the crowd, and then a hand goes up.

"Yes ma'am, what's on your mind?" Captain Harvey points to the young woman with the red hair whom the stowaway cum deck swabber is interested in.

"Yes, hello captain," she says politely and at once he is moved by her earthy beauty. He can see why the big guy is attracted to her. *Hah. Good luck with that partner.*

"How can I help you dear?"

"I was wondering how long it's going to take us to get to the trash heap."

"Ah, thank you for reminding me, I was going to expound upon that before we adjourned." He offers a broad smile. "Judging by the latest meteorological report we may have a bit of a headwind tomorrow, possibly some rain, but that notwithstanding we should arrive at the trash heap by late morning of the third day."

There is general excitement over this, for different reasons. For the scientific crew he's certain it's because they are anxious to arrive and proceed with their tests. For the governor and his 'aides' he's sure they just want to get this over with as soon as possible. Ditto for the security personnel, ditto for the Navy seamen.

"Any more questions?"

"I got one," Cole says, waving his arm around like a third grader.

"Yes, uh, Mr. Hernandez is it?"

"Wow, yeah," Cole smiles. "Can't believe you know my name."

"I try and get familiar with all the people I am transporting. Know that I will do my best with all of you."

"Great, great," Cole says impatiently. "What I want to know is how we're equipped for firearms."

"Excuse me?"

"You heard me, how are we sitting in the weaponry department? Because I for one don't feel very comfortable with all the guns being in the hands of those little kids over there." He points toward the Navy seamen, who stare back at him contemptuously.

"Am I to take it you are unarmed?"

"We, that is to say myself and the other security personnel, were issued Billy clubs. I don't know if you're aware of that or not, governor."

Governor Hallsly looks up when he hears his title mentioned, but he hasn't been paying attention. He was thinking about the beating he just received from Melissa and is presently looking forward to the next one.

"I'm sorry?" Hallsly says, and Cole misunderstands him.

"Yeah buddy, I'm sorry too. Sorry I won't be able to do nothing but club anyone who tries fuckin' with ya."

"If you could please watch your language Mr. Hernandez," Captain Harvey protests. "There are ladies present."

"Oh, in that case I want to apologize to your crew," Cole says and this gets a small laugh.

"Ah, yes, good one," Captain Harvey says without cracking a smile. Of course he knows the security team has no firearms, that is all part of the plan. It will make things easier by and by. "And, to answer your question, we do have a small cache of weapons but they are intended to be used by the crew, and only in the event of an emergency." He fixes Cole with an icy glare that would make a flower wilt. "A *life or death* emergency."

"Is there any other kind?" Cole jokes, but this time no one laughs. The thought of a life or death emergency hits home with most of the passengers, and it isn't something they care to make light of.

"If that answers your question-"

"Not quite," Cole says. "What if there *is* an emergency and we need to get them guns? Where you keepin' 'em?"

"Surely that is none of your business Mr. Hernandez. If such a situation should arise you can trust that the crew and I will see to it that everyone's safety is our number one priority. Is that clear?"

"Oh, crystal, I'm sure."

"Are there any other questions?" the captain asks, and this time no one raises their hand. "Very good, than I would like to turn this meeting over to our next speaker. Dr. Taylor? If you would, please." And without further adieu the captain steps aside, allowing the other to take the floor. The doctor looks distracted, and he clears his throat unnecessarily a few times.

"Yes, well, I really don't have much to say, I just wanted to introduce myself and thank you all for accompanying my scientific crew and I."

Here good-natured cheering and catcalls interrupt him, and to this he responds humbly but pleasantly, waving his hands, trying to quiet everyone down.

"I don't want this to take very long because I know everyone's hungry and wants to eat-" This prompts more whistling and clapping. When they finally simmer down he continues:

"The nature of our task is very simple: my scientific team and I are to take samples of the trash heap and the surrounding water to examine the extent of it's impact on the aquatic life and extrapolate to what degree the pollutants have altered the food chain. We hope to acquire knowledge that will help us learn how to break down it's basic components and figure out how we can best eradicate it without doing further environmental damage." He glances around at the group, making sure no one has any questions, then proceeds: "We are also looking for the scientific vessel that went missing a month ago. While my team and I perform our research I assume the rest of you will be conducting a search and rescue mission." Here he turns to the captain. "The government has been so kind as to supply us with a number of Hazmat suits. I assume you probably have several onboard as well for use by your crew?"

"Certainly..." the captain answers vaguely but the doctor doesn't appear to notice.

"Are there any other questions?"

If there were crickets aboard the ship they would be chirping. There is no sound except for the hiss of the bow as it carves through the water.

"Alright," Dr. Taylor says. "Let's eat!"

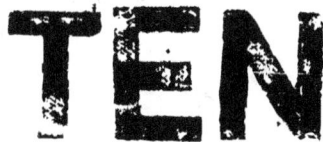

TEN

Captain Harvey politely excuses himself from the group and makes his way to the bridge where he will be waiting for a full report from the crewmen assigned the task of searching the cabins. When he arrives he relieves the man at the helm, taking the wheel and looking over his navigational charts.

"Radio down to the men and let them know the meeting is over and dinner has begun," he tells his first mate, who nods and removes his walkie-talkie from his belt.

"This is first mate Anderson," he says into the device, "advising you to finish up with what you are doing and report to the bridge."

Given that Leeann is a vegetarian she forgoes the fish and helps herself to a generous portion of what appears to be steamed vegetables. On further examination it's obvious the green beans, carrots, broccoli and cauliflower were microwaved, but this doesn't bother her. Did she really expect a gourmet meal? Taking her plate and a plastic cup of apple juice (from concentrate; not exactly first rate but, again, not at all unexpected), she finds her way over to the railing on the port side and eats while watching the sun descend over the water. The brilliant hues of magenta and orangish/purple are so beautiful they are breathtaking, and not for the first time does she experience a giddy thrill about where she is and what she is undertaking. She holds her head back and breathes deeply of the salty air, savoring the aftertaste that sticks in the back of her throat. She exhales and breathes deeply again, emitting a contented sigh, when suddenly she becomes aware of someone standing just to her right. Turning her head, a dazed smile lingering upon her lips, she gasps, believing she is either hallucinating or seeing a ghost.

"Hey Leeann, how are you doing?"

Her mouth is open but she finds she's unable to speak, and it can't be a very pretty sight because it's full of half-chewed carrots.

"What the hell?" she manages, barely, when the ghostly vision steps closer.

He is wearing a sailor's uniform (one that fits rather poorly because of his height and girth) and is holding a mop in his meaty paws.

"Are you enjoying your dinner?"

"Dante?" she asks, even though she knows there could be no other person on the face of the earth who resembles him this closely, unless he has a twin brother.

"Yeah," he confesses, "it's me. I didn't want to startle you, but I thought I'd let you know I'm working on the ship too."

The confusion on her face is almost laughably comic, but Dante isn't in a humorous mood. He's been planning this meeting in his head for the last several hours and he wants to get it right. And hey, no better time than the present.

"I...I...don't get it," she says, involuntarily retreating a step. "How did you get a position on this ship? You didn't know about this trip until I told you!"

"Yeah, that's true," he starts, wanting desperately to give her a satisfactory reason but finds he's momentarily unsure how to continue. Normally he'd stick with the truth but he knows how creepy it would sound: *'Hey Leeann, I followed you here because I simply couldn't let you go.'* And how would that make her feel? *Like she is being stalked*, a dark voice inside his head answers, and he can't help but shudder as a chill passes through him. "I thought it sounded like fun, you know, so I looked for the ad and called to see if there were any more job openings..."

Her face clouds with anger. "Are you following me?"

"No, no, it isn't like that, I-" he begins but stops short because he knows she's right. He *is* following her, that's the bitch of the whole thing. He is following her because he didn't want her to disappear from his life like all the others have. Because even though he has only known her for a brief period of time he's certain he is in love with her, and until she makes it undeniably clear that she doesn't love him in return he won't give up. He wants to say this, wants to tell her his most heartfelt feelings but she is positively fuming, and she lets him have it between the eyes with both barrels:

"You son of a bitch! I should have known you'd pull some crazy, dumbass stunt like this!" Her voice is high, shrill, her coarse language shocking to all of those within earshot. She supposes they don't expect such vulgarities coming from someone who appears to be an 'innocent' little girl. Well screw 'em.

Dante stares at her, stunned. He knew she would be surprised, maybe thrown off guard, but he didn't expect her to be *angry* about it.

"You can't get the hint, can you?" she snarls as he stands there dumbly, the mop hanging loosely and forgotten in one large hand. Even though he towers over her he can't help but feel like he is three feet tall, just a little child being chastised by his mother or stepmother or one in a long line of teachers and social workers who were of the opinion he couldn't do anything right, no matter how hard he tried. "You are *so* fucking dense, you know that? Can't you tell when someone is trying to get rid of you?"

He blinks and fat tears roll down his cheeks, disappearing into his beard, his lower lip quivering. "I...I...didn't realize..."

"You didn't realize because you didn't want to!" she spits, unable to control herself. "You are lost in some silly fantasy world you demented moron!" She doesn't know why, but the sight of him here simply enrages her, as if his true goal all along is to interfere with her chance at tackling the world on her own, at getting some much needed job experience. In her mind his presence is plainly meant to make her look like an idiot in front of her peers. Even the tears in his eyes irritate her; she doesn't (not even remotely) feel sorry for his stupid ass. "What were you thinking, that I'd be happy to see you? I signed up for this trip to get away from you, you big ape!"

Dante retreats several paces, unable to believe there can be this much hostility stored in such a petite package. Her eyes blaze rabidly as her mouth hurls obscenities, and for a crazy second he almost wants to launch himself over the side of the boat just to get away from the look of disgust that distorts her beautiful face, utter revulsion manifest in her furrowed brow, her pursed lips.

"I…I didn't want to make you upset…" he tries to say but she bats his words aside like so much wasted breath.

"The hell you didn't! You probably weren't even thinking about that! All you were concerned with was how you would feel!" She glares malevolently. "How *does* it feel? Is our little reunion going as you expected?"

By this time her voice has long attracted the attention of the crew, and before Dante can reply hands are grabbing his arms, pulling him backward. He doesn't resist, doesn't dare to. There is nothing he can say, nothing he can offer to Leeann that will make her change her mind. She is right, after all. What did he think, that she would take him in her arms, kiss him and tell him this was just what she was hoping he'd do? Was that what he really expected? If he did than he is a bigger fool than his mother or any of his teachers ever accused him of being. He is a bigger idiot than any of the other study rats at Pharmacoastalcal, those unsung heroes who have chosen the path of least resistance, hiding from the world and a stable career by bouncing from one drug trial to the next, hoping it never ends.

"Nice sailor suit, by the way!" she calls after him. "I'm surprised they had your size!" Unexpectedly she realizes she is shaking, the veggies tumbling off the paper plate she's clutching in a death grip. "You can bet your ass I'm going to lodge a personal complaint with the captain!"

Oh yeah, Dante thinks as he's dragged away, *I'm certainly expecting that.*

The captain surveys the smuggled goods strewn on the table before him, marveling at the nature of a few of the found items. Some of them he expected, others he did not. There are several bottles of liquor (taken from both the governor's cabin and the security guard's cabin) a small arsenal (found in Cole Hernandez's suitcase) that includes three handguns (a snub nose .38, a .357 Magnum and a Glock .9 MM), not to mention an AK-47 assault rifle that has seen better days and several flash bombs. There is also a baggie of marijuana (stashed in a 'secret' compartment in one of the intern's suitcases) that looks to be high-grade stuff. These things he anticipated. What he did not expect are what appear to be tools of the trade for a dominatrix: two cat 'o nine tails (one large, one small), a pair of handcuffs, a leather bondage outfit complete with zippered mask, a red ball gag, a set of nipple clamps and a large, black dildo with tiny bumps protruding from it like warts. Not surprisingly, these items were taken from the governor's female aide.

Besides these items there are a wide assortment of porno magazines (which the captain intends to give back) found in almost all the cabins (the only rooms that were porn free were the apparent dominatrix, the two female interns and Dr. Taylor), and several pill bottles containing Percocet's and Vicodin. The Perc's were discovered with the dominatrix's belongings, the Vicodin in the female intern's cabin.

"Is this everything?" he asks first mate Anderson and the other nods.

"Yes sir."

"I want you to bring me the woman who owns these 'toys'. I think I'll start with her."

"Very good sir," the first mate says, turning toward the door, when another member of the crew pokes his head inside.

"Sorry to bother you captain, but we have a situation."

"I'm busy."

"It's pretty important sir."

"What is it?"

"You know that stowaway who joined the crew? Well apparently that chick he followed here isn't too happy about it."

"Son of a...." Captain Harvey shakes his head. "Bring him here."

"I got him with me right now sir." He opens the door further and Captain Harvey sees Dante standing in the hall, his shaggy head hanging in shame, his glasses perched at the end of his bulbous nose.

"Okay, very good," he says, returning his attention to Anderson. "Bring the woman to my office. I'll join her presently."

"Yes sir."

"Get in here," he orders and Dante steps inside, a hangdog look on his hairy face. "And close that door."

Dante closes the door and takes a couple of steps inside.

"Relax," the captain says. "Have a seat."

Dante drops his large frame onto a metal chair. It creaks under his weight.

"Didn't I tell you to stay away from her?"

"Yes sir," Dante says dismally, unable to meet the other's eyes.

"You know this means I'll have to relocate you to the boiler room now, don't you?"

"The boiler room?"

"Think of it as a promotion. It's harder work but you'll feel like you're making a difference."

"O-okay."

"This will ensure that you don't upset her, understand?"

"Yeah," Dante sighs. "I found out what I needed to know anyway."

"Women can be tricky son," Captain Harvey says, coughing into his fist and flicking his hand over the garbage can by his feet. Dante hears something splat solidly against the side, making a flat, pinging sound. "We're never quite sure how they tick, all we know is we're willing to give them whatever they want until we find out."

"Yes sir." Dante finally looks up, catches the captain's eye. "Thank you."

"Think nothing of it," Captain Harvey says glibly. "You'll find the boiler room on the lowest deck. Tell the men down there I sent you. They'll put you to work."

"Okay." Dante gets up, straggles over to the door.

"Oh, and sailor?"

"Yes sir?"

"Any more trouble from you and it's no more mister nice guy. Is that clear?"

"Yes sir," Dante says sincerely and the captain waves him out.

ELEVEN

Melissa is just finishing her dinner when she is approached by one of the crew.

"Excuse me, ma'am?" he says. "The captain would like to see you in his quarters."

She freezes, fork enroute to her mouth. She'd like to imagine this isn't about what she thinks it is, but what else could it be? She'd told that bastard Hallsly to keep his voice down while she administered the whip, but he kept making loud grunting sounds, every now and then punctuating them with a thunderous "Yahoo!" She knew that was what would get them busted.

"Yeah?" she says casually. "What does he want?" She looks over at the governor, who is standing next to Dr. Taylor (talking about God knows what, seeing as he has no skills of any kind other than bullshitting people and paying woman for sex) and when he looks over and sees her in the company of the crewman, the man taking her by the arm and escorting her away, he shoots her a look that says it all:

'*Don't you dare tell him about the arrangement we have,*' his look says. '*You say a word and you forfeit the money.*'

"Sorry ma'am, I'm not at liberty to say," he replies curtly. "Now if you'll just come with me."

"Certainly." She returns the governor's look with a vacant expression as she is lead away.

"I trust the dinner was to your liking?" Captain Harvey asks after Melissa has been shown to a chair.

"I've had better," she remarks dryly and at this he smiles.

"We aim to please." He takes a cigar out of a wooden box on his desk and rolls it under his nose. "You mind if I smoke?"

"Do whatever you want," she says, not looking at him, appraising the room instead. "You're the captain."

"Yes, indeed I am," he agrees, snipping off the end of the cigar and producing a Zippo. He holds the flame to the tip of the cigar and, when it is going to his satisfaction, he replaces the lighter in one of the many desk drawers. He takes a deep drag, blowing the smoke to one side so as not to blow it in her face. He takes another and then sets it in an ashtray shaped like an anchor. "I suppose you're wondering why you are here." This is a statement, not a question. He is too shrewd a man to play games. He knows it won't take long to get what he wants out of her. It is only a matter of time.

"I have no idea." She gazes at him coldly, her green eyes sharp, penetrating.

The captain is familiar with this look, has seen it on the faces of Vietcong soldiers he interrogated during the Vietnam War. It is a look that implies it will give up nothing without first being tortured, if that's what's necessary. God how he loved it when it became necessary…

"Really? No idea at all?" he asks, smiling, trying to infuse their conversation with a bit of levity, hoping it will help her feel at ease, but her expression doesn't change. She crosses her legs and folds her arms.

"Look, if you have something to say, spit it out," she says and Captain Harvey silently approves. He likes a woman who plays hard to get.

"Okay, fine. I had some of my men conduct a search of everyone's cabin during dinner…" he starts and is disappointed when he sees her wince. He was hoping her poker face would hold strong, that she would prove to be a worthy adversary. Apparently he was wrong. "I need to ask you about some of the things I found in yours."

Oh shit. She brushes a stray lock of hair out of her eyes. *How do I explain this?*

"So… you found some of my…toys…"

"Indeed," he nods. "Am I to assume you use these, uh, toys on…yourself?"

"Maybe," she says, looking away.

"So you whip yourself?"

"Sure…"

"Self flagellation, like those religious nuts?"

"You got it."

Captain Harvey exhales loudly, deciding the pussyfooting is over.

"You aren't really an aide for the governor are you? He hired you to supply him with sexual favors."

This statement raises her ire, and she glares at him insolently.

"I don't do sexual favors for anyone, got it? I'm a dominatrix, not a hooker. I administer punishment for those who need it, all at a low, low price."

He arches his eyebrows, picking up his cigar and puffing on it slowly.

"So the governor pays you to spank him whenever he needs it? Whenever he has been a bad little boy?"

"You got it," she admits. *So much for keeping it a secret.* "What are you going to do? Throw me in the brig?"

"I don't think we are quite ready for that…yet." He watches her through a haze of blue smoke, the smile lingering on his lips.

"So why are you tossing our cabins?"

Captain Harvey leans back in his chair, puffing grandly on his cigar, eyeing her contemplatively. He puts one, then two boots up on the desk, groaning when he leans over to place the cigar in the ashtray.

"I'm the captain; I have a right to know what the passengers are carrying so that I may ensure the safety of the others."

"And I might hurt someone with…a dildo?"

"I just want to know what is what." He takes his feet off the desk and leans forward. "I had a gut feeling that jerk-off Hallsly was just a figurehead. Your presence here proves it."

"Really? How so?"

"Well, for starters, you'd think he'd be needed in California…you know, doing his job."

She laughs. "I'm sure most of the taxpayers aren't quite sure what that is."

He laughs as well, a hearty boom of belly laughter that turns into a cough. He quickly covers his mouth, but not before Melissa sees something white and slender pop out between his lips. It's there for only a fraction of a second before the captain sucks it back in like a strand of spaghetti.

"Yes, yes, I'm sure they don't." He wipes his lips with the back of one hand. "So you aren't a regular employee of his?"

"Not in so many words. He used my service a couple times back in Sacramento and then hired me to accompany him on this trip."

"And that other man? Is he really one of Hallsly's aides?"

"Hell no. That dumbass is my ex-boyfriend. I asked him to come along just in case Hallsly got too grabby with me."

"I see. Anything I need to know about him?"

"Nothing you wouldn't figure out yourself; he's a selfish asshole who thinks the world owes him a living. He only cares about one thing: himself."

"Do I detect a note of resentment in your voice?"

"No…maybe…yeah…I guess."

"Well, which is it?"

"Look, you got what you wanted from me. No more spankings for the governor, I got it." She folds her arms over her chest. "I don't want to talk about Tyler."

The captain nods, smiling slightly. He's always been particularly efficient in this regard, determining what bothers people the most and then badgering them until they squirm. In this case he decides he'll let it go. He leans forward to extinguish his cigar and she looks away, studying the plaques on the wall.

This old coot has been around the block a few times, that's for sure. It seems he's a got a medal or a commemorative plate for just about everything. Bravery, valor, honor, going above and beyond the call of duty…if ya can't brag about it why bother, huh?.

When she finishes her examination and turns toward him once more he is leaning back in his chair, hands folded behind his head. His expression is unreadable.

"So…is that it?"

"One more thing," he says, eyeing her frankly. "The pills I found in your room…are they prescription?"

She colors slightly. "I'm not a pill freak, if that's what you're getting at. Yeah, they were prescribed to me just over a year ago for my wrist. Repetitive motion injury." She grins, imitating cracking a whip.

"Ah." His smile returns. "Sort of like Carpal Tunnel Syndrome."

"Yeah, exactly. I brought them along in case I needed them."

"Alright. As long as they are prescription."

"So, do I get my things back or are you going to keep them as 'evidence'?"

"This may not make you very happy, but I'm going to keep your bondage gear for the remainder of the trip."

"Not going to let the governor have his fun?"

"This trip isn't intended to be fun, let's get that clear." The captain is serious again, all playfulness gone.

We are clear baby, make no mistake about that.

"So…what are you going to do?"

"About the governor?" A strange expression comes over the captain's face, it's onset quicker than the blink of an eye. One moment his was the façade of the amiable host and the next it becomes that of a hostile predator. In the space of a few seconds she swears she is looking at someone else entirely. She does a double take, her eyes blinking rapidly, but whatever she thought she saw is gone. Maybe it was never there in the first place. The captain is just the captain, hunched over, fiddling with the butt of his cigar.

"Why, I guess I'll just have to have a little talk with him, now won't I?" he's saying, his eyes trained on the cigar.

"Yes, I, I suppose so," she says, feeling slightly muddled.

"Are you all right missy?" he asks, glancing up and smiling graciously "You don't look so hot."

"I think my, um, stomach is upset." She waves a hand in front of her face, fanning herself. "I felt nauseous for a second there."

"That will happen to you landlubbers."

"I suppose." She smiles weakly.

"Okay, we're done here." He gestures toward the door, indicating she can go. "Enjoy the rest of the trip."

"Thank you." She gets quickly to her feet, stumbling a little. "I will."

"And you let me know if the governor gives you any problems, all right? As of now he no longer receives any of your services."

"Yes sir, I will, and he won't."

"Very good," the captain says. "Thank you for your time."

Captain Harvey toys with the butt of the cigar, the tips of his fingers black with ash. The woman was most useful; she confirmed his thoughts about the illustrious governor. He knew his presence here was a sham, something to get him out of the way while the real politicians in California actually got some work done.

And this is a good thing, a very good thing indeed. When all is said and done no one will miss him, should something bad happen.

He laughs, a thick (almost chunky) spittle wetting his robust lips. The governor's attendance shan't be a hindrance on this trip, won't affect them negatively in the least. Should any harm befall the governor the captain doubts anyone will bother to come to his rescue. And that's just the way (uh-huh uh-huh) he likes it.

TWELVE

Leeann storms from the deck to her cabin, discarding her paper plate absently along the way. She can't believe that Dante would do this to her, would have the nerve to follow her here. How utterly pathetic is that? If she could have foreseen such an event she never would have told him the truth in the first place, would have fabricated some story involving missionary work in the Congo. And at the moment she feels like a fool because she'd actually felt sorry for him; he's proved he is nothing more than a stalker, plain and simple.

Letting herself in, she's relieved to see the room is empty. She approaches the table and picks up the folder of information Dr. Taylor put together, holding it loosely in one hand as she stares out the porthole, eyes looking but not seeing as she reflects on what just happened.

Thought I'd given that chump the slip back in San Diego but what do you know? Here he is, all two hundred and sixty pounds of him, give or take a metric ton...

She shakes her head disgustedly and climbs up onto her bunk, lying down. She opens the folder and flips through the pages, and it's only after she reads the same sentence three times that she realizes she can't concentrate. Trying to distract herself isn't working.

She sits up and tosses the folder aside, her mind awhirl with misgivings. How did *he* get a job aboard the ship? This is the principal question that bounces around in her head like an out of control pinball. Don't these people have any standards? Does it mean that *anyone* could have gotten a position on this crew, anyone willing to carry out this asinine assignment? The idea makes her feel contemptibly insignificant, as if she is no more important than the lowliest deck swabber, which in this case is Dante. And to think she'd felt exceptional at receiving the offer to accompany this ship on what seemed to be an important mission, one in which the fate of the world (ecologically speaking) rested. What a joke...

An even bigger question though, of course, is what is she going to do about it? Is she just going to let it go and pretend it doesn't bother her, that it simply doesn't matter?

No way. She jumps down from the bed and heads to the door. *I'm lodging a formal complaint. Maybe that will at least ensure he doesn't come near me.*

Exiting the cabin, she marches down the hall in search of the captain.

After eating Tyler is feeling a little better, not so dizzy anymore. Now that his stomach is settled he's thinking another drink would really hit the spot. And why not? He knows where the governor keeps his stash and, if that dirty old bastard wants to keep him out of the way so he can enjoy playtime with Melissa than he shouldn't mind if he helps himself.

Speaking of Melissa, where is she? He glances briefly around the deck. He caught a glimpse of her when he came topside but lightheadedness forced him to sit down while the meet and greet was taking place and he lost sight of her. And when they announced dinner he forgot about everything except the hollow gnawing in his stomach.

Hallsly must be going for round two. He chuckles, picturing that numbnuts with a ball-gag crammed in his mouth, tight leather underwear bunching up his belly fat in grotesque folds…

But no, that's not the case. Across the deck he sees the governor chatting it up with one of the college interns. She's a slender Asian girl and Tyler can't help but admire her darkly pretty face and thin (but curvaceous) body. He has always had a thing for Asian chicks but they've consistently proved to be elusive prey, far too intelligent to fall for his ruse. Now, if he could just meet a *stupid* one, then he'd be in business…

So if the governor is up here, where is Melissa? Taking a catnap? If so, maybe she's in the mood for a little rendezvous, hot beef injection style. Hell, he's an able bodied, strapping male; he's always 'up' for a little action.

Tossing his paper plate over the side of the ship, he exits the deck and heads for Melissa's cabin.

"Do you think your team can find a way to get rid of the problem?" Governor Hallsly asks Kim Leung, unabashedly leering at her, oblivious to the fact that he's compulsively licking his jowly chops. The governor considers himself a connoisseur of all women but when it comes to Asians he can't get enough. He certainly wouldn't mind whetting his appetite with this little number.

"We hope so," Kim says, indiscreetly leaning away. His sweat smells acrid, like stale booze, and he has a large piece of spinach stuck between two of his teeth. She is trying not to look at it because it is grossing her out, but for that reason her gaze continues to focus on it. She glances around, hoping for a distraction so that she might slip away, but none is immediately forthcoming.

"Well, if anyone can solve it, I'm sure you can." He leans toward her and the stench of his breath blows warmly (rancidly) in her face. "You Asians are so damn smart there's nothing you can't do," he says, then shakes his head, reconsidering. "Well, except play rock and roll. You guys really suck at that."

"You are so kind to say," she replies absently, literally squirming. If she could just figure out how to get away from this disgusting man while retaining her cool...

"I really love Korean movies. I'm a big fan." Leaning closer, closer.

"I'm Chinese-American," Kim says, her will breaking. The hell with being polite. "Well, nice talking to you," she says, turning away. "Bye."

"Wait!" he calls after her but she slips quickly into the crowd, disappearing. Hallsly is left standing near the guy from UCSD, who smirks at him as he forks beans into his mouth.

"Nice try old dude," the kid sneers, "but you'd probably have to be born sometime during this century to tap that ass."

Hallsly regards the other as if he is a particularly nasty crap he's just taken.

"That's 'governor' to you, assmunch," he remarks dryly. "And I'm sure the ladies aren't exactly lining up around the block to smoke your pole."

The intern stares at him with a mouthful of baked beans, trying to wrap his head around the fact that he's just been dissed by an old fart with a spray-on tan when a member of the crew steps between them.

"Governor Hallsly?" the crewman says. "The captain would like to see you in his quarters."

Hallsly nods, smiling. "Ah, I was wondering when he was going to request my help." Returning his gaze to the kid, he grins maliciously. "After all, I didn't come along on this trip to baby-sit college interns with shit for brains."

Following the crewman the governor exits, leaving the intern gaping in his wake.

"Hello, governor," Captain Harvey says wearily. "Please sit down."

"Certainly," Hallsly chirps, seating himself, but he can't help but notice a hint of aversion in the captain's voice. Who pissed in his coffee? And doesn't he realize he is addressing someone who is higher up the food chain than he is? "What's on your mind?"

"I'm not going to dance around this governor, I'm going to give it to you straight-"

"As well you should," Hallsly butts in. "After all, time is money."

"Ah, quite," the captain agrees. "No one knows that better than you."

"Excuse me?"

"I had my men conduct a search of the cabins for contraband; weapons, alcohol, controlled substances, that sort of thing." He pauses, waiting for the governor to protest this intrusion of his privacy but the other is silent. "I made an interesting discovery in your female aide's cabin. Do you know what I found?"

"Surely I have no idea," Hallsly says brashly, but at once his mouth is dry. "Why don't you tell me?"

"Don't be coy with me governor. Certainly you don't think I'm an idiot, do you?"

"I can't say, I hardly know you." Hallsly looks at him in a quizzical/authoritative manner, a calculatingly choreographed facial expression that won over the white, conservative, wealthy, republican, male, over forty-five voters. "*Are* you an idiot?"

The captain leans back in his chair, his lips twisting into an insidious grin. He picks the butt of a half-smoked stogie out of an ashtray and fires it up, blowing smoke in Hallsly's direction.

"You think you are so damn smart," Harvey says, rolling the cigar between his fingers. "When I look at you one word comes to mind. Know what it is? No? *Smarmy*. That's what comes to mind."

"I beg your pardon-"

The captain blows smoke in the governor's face. "Unctuous also comes to mind, and creepy, but they all mean the same thing."

"What the hell are you babbling about?" Hallsly cries, coughing. "I won't take this kind of insubordination-"

"I'm afraid that's where you have it wrong, you fucking windbag," Captain Harvey overrides, cutting him off. "On this ship my crew and I are the law, and what I say goes. You are merely, shall we say, window dressing. A measly figurehead."

Hallsly stands abruptly. "One call to the White House should clear this matter up in a jiffy, don't you think? We'll see who the 'figurehead' is now won't we?"

"Sit your ass back down and shut up. I'm not finished."

"Who's going to make me?"

The captain sighs. "Jesus Christ…" He leans forward and presses a button on his intercom. Straight away two of his crewmen enter the room, their large hands encircling Hallsly's biceps, grasping him tightly.

"What is this?"

"Do I need to use restraints on you governor? Is that what you're asking me to do?"

"You must be out of your mind…" he wheezes, struggling feebly. The two crewmen force him back down in the chair and let him go, but they remain on each side. "What gives you the right?"

"Hmm, what could possibly give me the right to treat you like a common man on my ship?" the captain muses, scratching his chin. "Could it be you gave up your leadership rights when you smuggled alcohol aboard, clearly disregarding the ship's substance abuse policy? Could that be it? Or maybe it's those sketchy aide's of yours. I'll bet they don't really work for the California government, do they?" Harvey winks at him. "Go on, you can be honest with me."

The governor's face turns beet red. He opens his mouth to deny these fanciful accusations but nothing comes out but garbled, sputtering sounds.

"That's what I thought. Maybe I should put you in the brig; that will give you a little time to come up with a feasible explanation, hmm?"

Hallsly feels as if every nerve in his body is wired with explosives, ready to blow sky high. He hasn't been treated this rudely since…well, since he can't remember. Who does this man think he is? Does he actually believe he is going to get away with this?

"I'm sure the president will be very interested to hear that the governor he has duly appointed to chaperone this operation has been put in the brig," Hallsly says at last, trying to keep his tone measured and strong, even though his guts are churning. "And no doubt he'll question the authority of those who did."

"Would he?" Captain Harvey smiles. "I'm not so sure about that. What will he think when he hears that the same elected official has brought a hired sex worker aboard my ship, along with some derelict who's been doing nothing but getting piss drunk since he arrived?"

"What did that bitch tell you?" Hallsly thunders. "Is she the one who filled your head with these lies?" *That whore gave me up to save her own ass I bet. She'll be very sorry she crossed me, mark my words. . .*

"She didn't tell me anything I couldn't have gathered all by myself," the captain says. "In fact, I intend to prove it right now, unless you object that is." His grin stretches broadly, like that of the Cheshire cat, and there is something in it that hints at danger.

"What. . .what do you plan to do?" Unexpectedly the governor feels a sharp stab of panic; he doesn't know why but for some reason he fears that the man sitting across from him is insane. It's the hideous expression that takes over his face, a crazy gleam glowing in the other's eyes. Gone is the civilized, rational looking man, replaced by something that reminds him of a Halloween mask.

"Gentlemen," the captain says, "help the governor up and have him remove his suit coat and shirt for us."

"Wait, no!" the governor protests but the crewmen haul him to his feet, one stripping him of his coat as the other proceeds to rip the buttons off his shirt.

"Okay, turn him around for me boys."

They spin Hallsly around and the captain lets out a low whistle.

"My my, doesn't that look nasty." He takes a long pull on his cigar and places it in the ashtray. "You can let him go now."

Hallsly scrabbles for the torn remnants of his shirt, avoiding the other's eyes.

"Are you going to try and tell me you did that to yourself? Call me crazy, but those marks on your back look like something, I don't know, maybe a whip would make? What do you guys think?"

His men nod, grinning.

"Alright, you got me. Happy?" Hallsly croaks, covering his pale, distended stomach with the tattered shirt. He sinks back down in the chair, sighing expansively. He now understands all to well what he saw in the captain's eyes, in fact has seen it in his own on a few occasions. The man is a sadist, and this stunt was performed for one reason only: to prove who the alpha-dog is.

You won this battle Harvey, but I'll be damned if you'll win the war.

The captain fixes him with a steely gaze. "Not happy enough."

"And what do you expect *me* to do about it?"

"Act like a man," Captain Harvey says disgustedly. "For Christ sake." He grinds out the butt of his cigar in the ashtray violently, sparks flying. "This meeting is over," he declares. "Get this jack-ass out of my sight."

Rough hands pull Hallsly to his feet and show him, most unceremoniously, to the door.

THIRTEEN

"I can't believe ya talked ta him like that," Travis says in between mouthfuls of shrimp. "I thought that son of a bitch was gonna blow a fuckin' gasket or somthin'."

"He's in the same boat as we are," Dave says, forking a bite of seafood salad into his mouth and washing it down with a drink of lukewarm water. "No pun intended." He swallows, takes another bite. "If he wasn't in trouble he wouldn't be here, so I don't give a good goddamn what that idiot thinks."

"Yeah, but somebody's gotta be in charge. They chose him."

"None a this is really how it seems," Dave says, shaking his head grimly. "Ya been watchin' what's goin' on? The crewmen been takin' people below deck over the last hour. That hot chick, the Sasquatch guy...even the governor. Look who they're takin' now."

Travis looks to where Dave is pointing, sees that two of the men hired as security, the Mexican and the black guy, are being ushered away.

"Shit man, ya think we're next?"

"Maybe. I guess we'll find out soon enough." He looks at his friend. "Why, ya got somethin' ta hide?"

"Naw, it's just that, well...I don't do too hot when I'm confronted by authority figures."

"Then ya need ta find a new occupation," Dave says, laughing, and after a moment of perplexed silence his partner joins in. When their mirth has run its course the two resume eating, keeping a close watch on the others while silently pondering what, exactly, is going on.

Kenny feels his old friend dread returning for a visit as he and Cole are led below deck. He doesn't know why, but something is nagging at him, some unknown fear. What bothers him is he can't place it; there is no reason he should feel this way. As they are passing through the corridor to the captain's chambers a snippet from his dream returns to him, the mazes and heaps of garbage that reached to the sky, blotting out the sun. And then they arrive and just as quickly as it came it disperses like a cloud of smoke.

"Come in!" the captain calls when the crewman announces himself, and when the door is opened it is no surprise to see the captain seated behind a large desk, his feet up, looking expectantly at them. "Come on in gentlemen," he says, and Kenny and Cole cross the threshold.

"What do you make of that?" Cole asks Kenny when they've returned to the top deck, standing at the railing where they had a completely different discussion only a few hours ago.

"I don't know, but I gotta hand it to that captain; he ain't as dumb as he looks."

"It's like he read our fucking *minds* man," Cole says, his tone one of disbelief. "Now we got nothing to protect ourselves with."

"The question is: protect ourselves from what?"

"I'm not sure I really want to know." Cole leans against the rail and stares at the sea. "What, ya think we're gonna find somethin' out at the trash heap?" Kenny fishes a cigarette out of his pack and slaps his front pants pocket for his lighter. Cole takes a Bic from his shirt pocket and passes it to the other, shrugging.

"I don't know. Maybe."

Kenny lights his smoke and hands it back. "Whattaya think is out there?"

"I don't know man, but I told you, something about this whole thing don't seem right." Cole fires up a cigarette as well. "I was paranoid before, ya know, when we had weapons..." He takes a long, jittery drag. "Now that we ain't got nothing how do you think I feel?"

Kenny stares at the other silently, puffing on his smoke. He'd like to pretend he doesn't know what Cole is talking about but it's no use, he understands full well what's going on in the other's head. When you get right down to it this assignment has a bad feel to it, from the sketchy circumstances regarding their employment to the inexperience of the rest of the crew (not to mention an unexpected shakedown by el Capitan and his loyal henchmen), it just don't add up. And, now that they've been stripped of their firearms, let's just say Kenny would feel a whole lot better if he was back in Sacramento hanging out with his old buddy Hank. But that's not the face he's going to put on for Cole, no sir-ee bob. This guy needs some encouragement in a bad way so, instead, he says:

"Relax man, I won't let nothin' happen to ya."

"Yeah? You gonna put that in writing?"

"Not a chance."

"Pinky swear?" Cole asks with a grin, holding out his little finger.

"Get the hell outta here."

Dr. Taylor has been watching the proceedings with vague interest. As he eats he observes as individual passengers are marched below deck, and he anticipates his turn will come in due time. He isn't sure why these interrogations are taking place (if that is indeed what they are) but he isn't concerned. He has nothing to worry about should he be called in. He is, after all, a representative of the United States Government, approved for this mission by the president himself. Moreover, he's done nothing wrong; these sorry asswipes should simply be glad he's along for the ride.

Working his mouth around a melon rind, he ponders how the interns will fair, and can only hope that the adolescent conduct he'd witnessed this afternoon will be kept to a minimum. He knows they're just kids (and let's face it, given the nature of the world they live in today, the youth sustain a sort of arrested development because of all the TV and video games and rap music-more so than his generation anyway) yet he expects to see a little maturity on their part. He needs them to think and act like adults and forget their petty squabbling or they are going to have nothing but trouble. Christ, he wishes he could have at least one seasoned veteran here with him, someone who has been in the trenches like he has, but he knows that would be a mistake, a waste of valuable resources.

If they keep it up I'll have to take away their videophones. . .no more 'Irate Canary's' or whatever that shit is.

He spits out the melon rind and wonders, not for the first time, if the search for the missing ship and crew will be successful, if it will find them alive and well, awaiting rescue. If so, the data they've already collected will be most helpful, will pave the way for further studies. If, that is, they've had time to gather information. For all he knows they've had their hands full simply trying to survive in an environment not meant for human inhabitation.

Finishing the last of his meal, he leaves the deck to seek the solace of his cabin. If anyone is looking for him, that is where they will find him.

Tyler arrives at Melissa's cabin door for the second time that day, but on this occasion the knock he administers is civil, almost a caress.

"Melissa?" he says softly. "Are you in there?"

He hears footsteps approaching the door, and quickly blows into his cupped hand to see if his breath is bad. As usual he smells nothing. He takes this to be a good sign.

The door opens and Melissa peers out at him.

"What do you want?" she groans. Since her meeting with the captain she doesn't want to have anything to do with the two men in her life who appear to do nothing but complicate things. In fact, now that this trip is no longer a moneymaking venture, she just wants to go home.

"I just wanted to see you babe, maybe talk to you for a little bit." He smiles what he hopes to be his most sincere smile. "We haven't really talked since, well...since you know..."

"Since what Tyler? Since I realized you're a parasite? That you live only to satisfy yourself and don't give a crap about anyone else around you?"

"Whoa, hold on there!" he pleads. "Hear me out, huh?"

"Let me guess: you're jealous of the governor, is that it?" She looks at him with a pitying look. "Well worry no more, the captain has put a halt to those activities."

He shakes his head, reaches out and puts a hand on the door. "Look," he says, his eyes searching hers, "I don't care about that, okay?"

"Than what do you want?"

"Why did you ask me to come along on this trip, huh?" His voice is no more than a whisper, almost pouting, and she suspects he is faking it. "Because, if I remember right, it was you who asked me along." He reaches out to put a hand on her shoulder but she shrugs it off. "You wanted me here, didn't you?" he implores and she looks away.

"I'm not sure what I want," she says, glancing at him briefly and experiencing a twinge of pleasure when she sees him flinch. "I just needed someone as a buffer between his Highness and me."

"Is that really it? If it is, fine, I'll go back to my cabin and leave you alone, no problem. But," he reaches out again and, this time (although she doesn't know why) she allows him to keep his hand on her shoulder. "If there's something more to it than let me in and let's talk about it, okay? What can it hurt? We've got nothing but time before we get wherever the hell it is we're going."

Melissa looks at his hand threateningly, as if she's considering biting it off. She wants to pull away, wants to slam the door in his lying face…but there is something about him (damned if she wants to admit it) she still clings to, some idea of him that far outweighs reality. She knows in her heart he is a scumbag who will lie to her face, but her confliction lies in her heart where a part of her (a larger part than she wants to acknowledge) still yearns for him and wants to believe there could be something between them. She looks up from his hand and into his eyes, not entirely sure what she sees there, but a spark of amorous electricity passes between them and the next thing she knows she is letting him in.

After a visit to his cabin to get a fresh shirt, the governor stalks back to the main deck, breathing deep of the sea air to clear his head. He's desperately trying to make sense of what happened in the captain's quarters. Being a man of privileged lineage he isn't used to being treated in a manner that is, frankly put, *servile*. No one treats a Hallsly like that, no one. Many men have met terrible fates simply because they chose to mess with his family, important people too. In fact, the American landscape is simply littered with the corpses of men who thought they could get away with making fools of the Hallsly's, their bodies ground into a fine dust and mixed into cement that later became the foundations for buildings and bridges and tunnels. You fuck with the Hallsly's and they fuck you back.

The captain knew what he was doing all right, knew where his breaking point was and exploited it. The nerve of that pompous asshole. Well, alls fair in politics and war. Once this trip is over he's going to make sure that Captain Harvey sees the error of his ways, oh yes, and we'll see who's laughing then.

But, presently, he has a bone to pick with a certain dominatrix. The bitch gave him up and he wants her to know he is on to her, in fact wants to rub her face in it. He is certain she turned on him when caught with her 'toys', and not only is he furious, he's downright homicidal. She could have said they were for her own enjoyment, maybe even something she used for fun on Tyler, but no, she had to go and drag him into this. He, for one, wants to make it right.

When he'd left the captain's quarters he'd felt dirty and abused. Raped, if you will. He isn't used to feeling like that and damned if it doesn't leave a nasty taste in his mouth.

Maybe it's time to give that bitch a dose of her own medicine, see how she likes it. What the hell, it wouldn't be the first time he knocked a woman around, and it certainly won't be the last.

Heading for the passenger cabins, the governor rolls up his sleeves, needing more than anything to feel like a man of power again.

FOURTEEN

After thirty minutes spent searching the ship in vain for Captain Harvey, Leeann eventually finds him on the bridge. She probably could have saved herself some time and looked there first, but it just shows how jumbled her thinking is, she is so distraught. The first mate tries to stop her from entering, but the captain waves a hand, allowing her to come in.

"What can I do for you ma'am?" he asks, looking up briefly from his charts. He knows what she wants, and as far as he's concerned the matter's been handled.

"I need to talk to you," she says and he nods, straightening up and meeting her gaze.

"What's on your mind?"

"What is *he* doing here?" Her heart tells her that this is all wrong; Dante is supposed to be in San Diego, hundreds of miles away moping about his lost girl and his dead mother. He isn't supposed to be on this ship, making this journey seem to her like a frivolous charade.

"Who, Jake?" the captain asks, playing dumb. "He's my first mate. He ain't much to look at but we keep him around just the same."

But Leeann ignores him, lost in her own misery. "How could you hire someone like him? Don't you have any standards, or is this entire ship staffed with imbeciles?"

Scowling, the captain fixes her with a stern look.

"I don't like your tone miss," he says. "I think you'd better explain yourself."

Leeann wants to yell, to scream, but there is something menacing in his eyes, roiling storm clouds that suggests he is capable of even greater fury. Her fists clench and unclench, and she feels the blood pounding dangerously in her head. She knows she has to control herself, that this isn't the way to get anything solved.

"Dante," she breathes, the word a thin hiss of air.

"Excuse me?"

And then her anger turns to sorrow, a profound sadness wrought from her stricken feeling of betrayal.

"Wha...wha...what were you thinking hiring Dante?" she sobs, unable to help herself, and at once she feels Jake's hands on her shoulders, offering a soothing touch, but instinctively she flinches and he lets her go, backing away. She turns to him, her face a contorted mess of tears, and she grabs him by the shirt, clutching double handfuls of fabric. "He isn't supposed to be here," she cries, shaking him. "I'm supposed to do this on my own!" A thin trickle of snot runs down her nose but she pays it no mind. "I left him there and I am doing this for me! For me!"

"Okay, okay, calm down miss," the captain insists. "Why don't you take a seat and we'll talk about this-"

"There's nothing to talk about!" She releases Jake and turns back toward him, swiping viciously at her nose. "I'm supposed to do this alone! I don't want him anywhere near me!"

The captain exhales loudly, rubs a hand over his jaw. Looking into this girl's red-rimmed eyes, listening to her whiny, sniveling tone is starting to give him a headache.

"Look, I couldn't just kick him off the ship, could I? The only sensible thing to do was put him to work."

"What?" Leeann asks, confused. "What do you mean?"

"He didn't tell you?" The captain studies her carefully.

"Tell me what?"

"He stowed away onboard. We didn't discover him until we were too far to turn back. The only thing I could think to do was give him a job."

"He…what? Are you, are you saying you didn't hire him?"

"Not in so many words. Didn't have much choice in the matter. It was either put him to work or lock him up and I figured we could use all the help we could get."

Relief and a renewed sense of purpose fills her, realizing that Dante didn't simply apply for and get a position aboard the ship. It dashes her feelings of worthlessness, makes her again believe in the importance of her role here. But, still, she shouldn't have to pay for Dante's stupidity. "Than he should be locked up for what he did! He shouldn't be able to just wander around like he owns the damn place!"

The girl is irrational, this much goes without saying. The only thing the captain can do is try and talk some sense into her, and God knows how long that will take.

"Please," he says softly. "Take a seat."

"Fine." She sits down, wiping away the last of her tears. "But I want you to know I won't change my mind. I don't want him near me."

"Okay, just relax and I'll tell you what I've already done to remedy the situation. I've thought of something that should make everyone happy."

"I'm listening."

So the captain tells her about Dante's new position, out of sight from the rest of the passengers, below deck, and after a few minutes he's able to dredge a smile out of her, even make her laugh. Jake watches in awe, witnessing the master in action.

That's why he's the captain; he's one part boss, two parts shrink. Grinning, he backs out the door and carries on with his duties.

Without any preconceived notions (surely not on her part; she doesn't know if she can say the same for Tyler) they find themselves on her bed. When she allowed him to enter her cabin the conversation was slow to start, neither of them able to think of much to say. In fits and starts the words came, their progression from the door to the bed happening gradually, almost naturally, at least, that's how it seems to Melissa. Just like that, here they are. She is looking into his hazel eyes, alternately watching the dance his lips and tongue make as he speaks. After a while she tunes out his words, is only aware of his manly presence beside her, the acidic odor of his sweat mingled with shower gel and stale booze. If asked later she'd have no idea how it came to pass; it was just one of those animal/electrical/biological things and before she knew it, it was happening. And she wanted it to happen, God yes she did. That much she can admit afterward, even if she's angry that she let her guard down.

His lips meet hers, soft, gentle, yielding, and she finds she has no power over herself; she kisses him back. What starts tentatively rapidly becomes more forceful, increasingly passionate, and she pushes him against the headboard, her fingers clawing at his shirt, yanking it over his head.

Tyler wants to warn her to be careful with the shirt; it cost him (her) $175.00 but he knows enough to keep his mouth shut. He doesn't want to ruin the moment by saying something (anything), because chances are good she'll get pissed off all over again. Instead, he reaches up and slides her shirt over her head, unhurriedly, tenderly, and she exhales warmly, her breath the scent of desire commingled with Juicy Fruit. She is wearing a black lace bra that stands out against the backdrop of her porcelain white skin and suddenly he feels his manhood stirring, his pants growing uncomfortably tight.

She falls against him and their kissing becomes frantic, surging with an urgent ardor that betrays their mutual sexual deprivation. Gasping for air, they writhe together in a frenzied manner that resembles two horny teenagers in the back seat of a battered Camero, fumbling with each other's clothing.

"You son of a bitch…" she whispers, leaning back, reaching for the button on his pants. As she undoes it and gropes for his zipper his fingers simultaneously find hers, and he can't help but savor the musical sound of both of them unzipping in tandem. Tugging his pants to his knees, she jerks his boxer briefs down and his penis springs out like a jack-in-the-box clown, red nose and all. She takes it in her right hand, stroking and squeezing it lightly, teasingly.

Tyler's breathing quickens, and with shaking hands he reaches around her waist and wrenches her pants down, cupping the warm mound of her crotch through her panties. The warmth (combined with wetness) is the most pleasant thing he has encountered in a long time, and it is at this precise moment he silently thanks the powers that be that he's right here, right now. Nothing is better than this. Nothing. Well, maybe two chicks, but that's a given…

He slips a hand inside her panties, caressing the lips of her vagina, rubbing slowly, steadily applying more pressure. She grinds against him, allowing him to slide one finger inside, then two, her vaginal walls contracting and pulsing. With escalating speed he moves them back and forth, in and out, listening as her breathing becomes more pronounced, producing a high-pitched squeal in the back of her throat that brings his arousal to a near fever pitch. Extracting his hand (looking her in the eyes as he licks his fingertips), he slides her panties down and cups her cheeks, the smooth feel of her skin exhilarating, heady. Her ass is so perfect, so round.

He rolls her over on her back and with one deft motion unhooks her bra, discarding it carelessly. Taking one of her nipples between his lips, he probes it lightly with his tongue, biting down just hard enough that she's squirming beneath him. He moves from one nipple to the other, tracing a line of saliva between them as he kisses his way down, the taste of her pale, silky skin enticing, delightful.

His breath is hot against her skin as he gets to her belly button, his licking and teasing stimulating her in a manner that's making her lose control. Her legs feel weak, her breathing protracted. And when his mouth finally descends upon her, his tongue hesitant at first before plunging in, a shiver runs through her that makes her whole body tremble. Using both hands, she presses his face tightly against her, pumping her hips as his jaws work furiously. After a glorious, rollicking orgasm, she takes him by the ears and pulls him up toward her.

"Fuck me you bastard," she begs and Tyler is more than happy to comply. Slipping in bit by bit, he feels the skin on his scrotum crawl pleasantly, the hairs standing on end. Issuing a pleasant groan, he stops when he reaches the base of his shaft and then gradually backs out, deliberately working up speed. She clenches his buttocks in both hands, digging her nails into his skin.

"Holy shit!" he gasps, gaining momentum. Their pelvises slap together, making flat smacking sounds that reverberate off the cabin walls, punctuated by the din of their tortured panting as they clutch one another like drowning victims, only stopping when their act reaches its inevitable conclusion.

"The only reason I let you in is because I'm a nymphomaniac," Melissa jokes, her head resting on Tyler's chest. She's snuggled tightly against him, a finger tracing figure eight's between his hairless nipples. "If you hadn't come along I probably would have had sex with one of the crewmen."

Tyler lies there breathing in her smell, an enticing musk that attracts him like nothing else in the world, and for a moment he ponders how he could have treated her so callously, ignoring her needs in favor of his own.

Because she has money and I don't want to work, he reminds himself. *Duh.*

"That's okay," he whispers, his lips beside her ear, his tongue circling her earlobe. "I probably would have too."

This makes her laugh and he joins in, feeling for the moment like things are back to the way they were, the two of them together.

"You crazy bastard," she says, still giggling. "That was really good. I needed that."

"Hey," he says, smiling generously, "you're welcome."

At once her fingers stop their aimless meandering and she freezes mid-snigger. In a space of seconds as quick as a heartbeat all of her playfulness is gone. She sits up abruptly, her fingernails grazing his skin painfully as she retracts her arm.

"What is *that* supposed to mean?" she demands, sliding away from him. "'You're welcome'? What kind of bullshit is that?"

"Huh?" he says, not understanding. "Didn't you come?"

Melissa gets off of the bed and rummages around the room for her clothing.

"Jesus Tyler, you're a jack-ass all right, I've got to hand you that." She finds her panties on the chest of drawers, puts them on.

"Melissa, wait-"

"How do you get off thinking you can say something like that to me, huh? You are such a self-centered prick!" She finds her brassiere on the floor and snaps it back on.

"Come on baby, don't be mad," he says. "I just thought I did you a favor is all…"

"Did *me* a favor?!" She looks at him as if he has just lost his mind. "Of course, his majesty the King Stud has been so kind to bequeath me with a royal shagging! Aren't I lucky!" Her hands are shaking as she locates her jeans, and she almost falls down trying to put them on, she is so angry.

"Hey baby, come on-"

"You are an asshole Tyler, you know that? I don't know what I was thinking, getting involved with you again! I must be out of my mind!" She finds her shirt, tugs it over her head and realizes it's on backward. She takes it off and tries again.

"Listen Melissa, I'm sorry," he back-peddles, trying to get her to calm down. "I don't know why I said that. I didn't mean to piss you off-"

"It's a little too late for that you cocksucker! Get your clothes on and get out of here before I really get mad."

"I don't know why you are so upset. I wasn't trying to be a dick, honest!"

"The thing is Tyler," she says coldly, her voice low, dejected, "you don't have to try."

Tyler climbs off the bed, feeling the onset of a savage, fathomless rage growing within him. He wasn't trying to be cruel; he just said the first thing that came to his mind. He can't help it if he's fantastic in the sack, it's, like, a gift he has, his one true talent. Well piss on her. At least he got laid.

"Alright, alright," he says, reaching for his boxer briefs. "Let me get dressed and I'll go."

But before he can so much as get one leg in, the door suddenly crashes open.

"Oh shit," Tyler mutters, and then all hell breaks loose…

FIFTEEN

Tiny dust mites float lazily on a brilliant shaft of light that shines through the window of the captain's quarters. In another hour the sun will be near the horizon, the late afternoon giving way to twilight, evening giving way to night. Smoothly, almost silently the ship splits the water and, without anyone noticing, dolphins swim alongside, splashing and playing in the ship's wake, chirping and babbling to one another in their foreign tongue. Soon the running lights will come on automatically, illuminating the sea as the miles disappear behind them, taking the passengers and crew ever closer to their destination...

Captain Harvey enters the room, closing the door and taking a seat behind his desk. Retrieving the butt of a cigar from his ashtray, he tucks it into the corner of his mouth as he thinks about the conversation he just had with Leeann. She's a fiery little bitch, he reflects idly as he reaches into a drawer for his Zippo. She was pleased as all get out to hear that Dante is now working below deck, as far away from her as the ship's space will allow. She's now free to roam about and not worry about running into him, and as long as it keeps her out of his hair than he's done his job. Ditto for Dante. There are so many final preparations that have to be made, the last thing he needs is to be playing ship psychologist.

He spins the dial on the lighter and puts the flame to the butt, inhaling deeply and expelling a large plume of smoke over his head. He feels something stir within his chest and he uses his free hand to absentmindedly rub a small spot around his heart. Another day and they'll be at the fringe of the North Pacific Gyre. Half a day later and they'll be at the trash heap, if all goes as planned. And meanwhile he's charged with the duty of baby-sitting these idiots, from the college interns on up.

Unexpectedly there's a knock at his door, and for a second he wants nothing more than for whomever it is to go away, to leave him to his thoughts. Can't he get a moment's peace around here? Instead, he calls out:

"Come in!"

One of his crewmen enters, face ashen, his shaking hands tightly clutching a piece of paper.

"What can I do for you Corbin?"

Kurt Corbin is the ship's official 'meteorologist'. He's been tasked with keeping tabs on their weather conditions via the onboard Doppler equipment as well as by radio transmissions coming from as far west (or east, depending on how you look at it) as the Philippines and China. What he doesn't know (fooling him was almost too easy; since the crew Script's provided is the 'b' team he isn't exactly trained in meteorology) is that he was given a false weather report shortly before they set out, supposedly issued from the United States Weather Bureau (they'd used their authorized letterhead, producing an extremely authentic looking replica). The phony report predicted mostly sun, slight winds and mild rain showers over the coming week. This he accepted at face value, unsuspecting of any deceit. The real trick was keeping him occupied once he was aboard so he didn't have time to check the equipment until they were well underway. Based upon his abrupt intrusion, he's now had time to do so.

"Captain, it appears that the initial weather report was *way* off," he says, obviously still unaware that he's been had. "In fact, by the looks of the latest statement, we'll be running into a full force tropical gale. It's been moving steadily east over the last couple of days, originating just off the coast of the Philippines. They've reported high seas, exceptionally strong winds, lightening, thunder storms-"

"I know, Corbin."

"You...what?" His face registers confusion, and he runs a hand over his sweat-slick forehead.

"I said, 'I know'. We gave you a bogus weather report."

"'We'?"

"Yes, the Script's organization and myself, at my request."

"But...but why?"

"Because I didn't want to hear any whining, suggesting that we postpone the trip until all was clear. We have a time sensitive mission on our hands and I didn't need you Union-lead cowards slowing down our progress."

"I don't know if you realize it or not sir," Corbin says, trying his best to keep his tone civil, "but this isn't just some rain we're heading into, it's a full on shitstorm."

Captain Harvey regards the other slyly, a slight smile creasing the corners of his mouth. When all is said and done he has to admit he genuinely admires the cohones on this guy.

"Yes Corbin, it's going to be quite a ride, of that I have no doubt." He holds out his hand for the report and after a long moment the other passes it to him. The captain glances at it, his face neutral. "How many of the other's know about this?"

"Sir?"

"You heard me: how many of the other's know about this? Did you make it a point to tell everyone on board before coming to me with this?"

"No sir, I came to you first."

"Very good then." Captain Harvey tears the sheet of paper in two. "Let's keep it that way." He deposits it in the trashcan next to his desk.

"Sir," Corbin says, a touch uneasily, "since you were involved with issuing the falsified information, surely you know the storm will be hitting us within the next twenty-four hours, give or take."

"Yes Corbin, I'm aware."

"Wouldn't it be a good idea if we alerted the crew so that we might prepare ourselves?"

Captain Harvey glances at his pocket watch, then turns to look out the window. His man does have a point. As it is they are far enough out that turning back would be foolish; it might be good form to warn his sailors to batten down the hatches...

You never know how some of these pussy sons a bitches will react; they just might insist we turn the ship around no matter how much distance we've gained. And, in the end, I can't stop them if their fear inspires mutiny. I am, after all, only one man, even if I stand head and shoulders above the rest of them. Fuck it, we ride it out.

"No," he says at last.

"No?"

"You'll inform them of the imminent storm in the morning, after we've gained sufficient ground so as to make turning around impossible."

"But the danger we're sailing into...don't you realize you're jeopardizing the passengers as well?"

At the mention of the passengers the captain's anger is at last engaged. He rises to his feet quickly, leaning over the desk and grabbing the other by the lapels.

"I've been sailing ships since long before you were pissing in your pampers son. If I say that I can get us through a rough patch of weather you damn well better believe it."

"Maybe *you* can," Corbin persists, "but what about the ship?"

Captain Harvey grips the other's shirt even tighter, the urge to smack Corbin in the kisser so strong he has to physically will himself to let go and back off.

"The ship will be just fine," he says, releasing a pent-up breath. "With me at the helm you nor anyone else has anything to worry about." He sits down, puts his feet up on the desk. "Got it?"

Corbin looks at him warily, sensing blood in the water. When the captain stood he had the distinct feeling that he was going to strike him, just haul off and backhand him one...and what the hell? If he can forge phony weather documents than no doubt he can knock his crew around as well. Apparently Script's has given him cart blanche.

"Yes sir," he says quietly, looking away.

"Good," the captain approves, "very good. Just until tomorrow morning, mind you. After that you can tell anybody anything you want about the damn weather."

"You mean I can do my job?" Corbin ventures, wondering if he's going too far, but the captain ignores him, ashing his cigar (which has gone out) and fishing around in his desk for a lighter.

"Yeah, sure, whatever." the captain says, putting the flame to the tip. "Dismissed."

Corbin knows not to wear out his welcome and beats a hasty retreat, shutting the door gently behind him.

When the other is gone he sets the stogie in the ashtray, swiveling his chair and gazing out the window at the dying rays of the sun as it streaks toward the horizon, turning the blue sky into a patchwork quilt of crimson, jade, purple and orange. Looking at the gorgeous sunset you'd never guess that tomorrow their world may very well be a tempest of wailing wind and raging water, but that's most likely what they'll get. Oh well, nothing they can do but adapt.

He leans as far back as his chair will allow, his boots up on the desk, puffing his cigar grandly. For all intents and purposes he feels good, damn good. And it is in this fine state of repose he sits when the next problem comes down the pipe.

"So here you are!" Hallsly cries, storming through the door. Tyler's head spins toward the voice, startled, but he makes no attempt to cover himself.

"Jesus Christ!" he complains. "Don't you know how to fuckin' knock?"

Melissa's heart jumps into her throat; for one crazy moment she thought it might be the captain or one of the crew and here she is, figuratively caught with her pants down. Unlike Tyler, who is literally caught with his pants...off.

The governor gapes at Tyler's naked body, his eyes coming to rest on the other's impressive member, truly his finest attribute. Tyler follows his gaze downward and smirks.

" Pretty nice, huh? And it's all natural, no enhancements or anything."

"I could care less you moron! I'm here to see Melissa."

Judging by his tone, Melissa notes, he's probably just had a conversation with the captain and is, shall we say, less than pleased.

"I need to have a word with you honey."

"What's up?" she asks guardedly. His jaw is set and his eyes are blazing, not to mention his nostrils are flaring like an enraged rhino's.

"You," he says to Tyler, "get out of here."

"I think I'd rather stay," Tyler says, crossing his arms over his chest.

"Yeah, whatever you have to say to me you can say in front of him," Melissa concurs but Hallsly ignores her, focusing on Tyler instead.

"It wasn't a request shithead. I told you to get out and I meant it!" The governor takes a step forward, raising one hand. "Unless you have a hankerin' for a knuckle sandwich I suggest you scram!"

"I ain't hungry," Tyler says, also stepping forward. In the small confines of the cabin they are only a foot apart.

"I don't think you want a piece of this," Hallsly threatens. "I have business to tend to with the whore."

"I'm not a whore!"

The governor looks at her coldly, his eyes mere slits. "If the bondage suit fits, wear it."

"You better back off man," Tyler says, bringing his hands up and clenching them into fists.

"Or what? You think you can take me?"

"I *know* I can take you, old man."

They both move closer and are now standing almost chest-to-chest, glaring at one another, fists at the ready. They stand this way for what feels like an eternity to Melissa, their eyes locked, muscles tensed, when Tyler leans his head closer and whispers: "Boo!"

The governor issues an ominous sounding growl and takes a shot, but Tyler jumps out of the way just in time and the momentum of the swing pivots Hallsly around and he slams into the chest of drawers before falling down on one knee.

"Too slow, governor," Tyler says, dancing on the balls of his feet, keeping his hands up and in motion, just like he's seen in all those boxing movies, feinting a jab here, another jab there. "I think you better give it a rest before you have a coronary."

But the governor is up in a flash, and now he really looks mad.

"You're going to wish you stayed out of the way dumbass," he says forebodingly, his voice a Clint Eastwood-esque paper-thin whisper, and at once Tyler feels a nervous pang of regret at his rash behavior. The governor may be old but right now he looks kind of scary. Maybe it's the way he's breathing: rapid gasps of air that puffs out his cheeks like a toad's, or maybe it's his eyes, which appear to be flashing fire. Tyler may be taller and broader across the shoulders but this guy looks like a pit bull off his leash, ready to sink his teeth into the nearest flesh sandwich.

"Look dude, take it down a notch, huh? Let's talk about this."

"I don't think so," the governor says, a small, murderous grin spreading across his face. "We're done talking."

"What's that supposed to mean?" Suddenly Tyler doesn't feel so tough anymore. After all, he's a lover not a fighter. He might be in over his head...

"AAAAHHHHHH!!" Hallsly rushes forward and, acting on instinct alone, Tyler does the only thing he can think of: he dashes out the door and runs like the wind, the governor right on his heels.

Several members of the crew, as well as several passengers including but not limited to Dave, Travis, Kenny, Cole, Robert, Kim Leung, Steven and Perry are startled when a naked man streaks past them, followed closely by Governor Hallsly.

"I'll kill you, you son of a bitch!" Hallsly bellows, waving his fists, face red with exertion.

"Get away from me dude!" Tyler cries over his shoulder, feet pumping furiously. He can't believe the old guy has this much energy, nor can he believe he is currently running for his life after having recently evacuated his seminal fluids in such a pleasant manner.

They race around the top deck, from stern to aft and, after the initial surprise wears off, the witnesses burst into relieved laughter.

"Naked man running!" hollers Cole. "Naked man running!"

Tyler does his best to shake him but the governor is fueled by sheer psychotic rage, keeping right on his bare-assed tail.

"Jesus, someone help me here, huh?!" Tyler begs, dodging left and right, his pecker bouncing up and down like an obscene party balloon. His legs are aching and his feet sore from slapping the hard deck.

"Anybody gets in my way and they're next!" Hallsly informs the onlookers, and anyone who actually thought of jumping in falters for a moment, reconsidering.

"Stop it!" Melissa shrieks, emerging from below deck, hair hanging in her face, eyes wild. "Leave him alone!"

"Ah, the plot thickens," Travis mutters and Dave laughs.

The governor corners Tyler at the stern, trapping him against the rail before several members of the crew finally advance upon them.

"All right governor, just calm down," pleads one of the deck hands. "We can all talk this out like civilized human beings-"

"The hell we can! I'm gonna beat this creep to a pulp!"

"Easy now big guy," Tyler says, holding his hands up, palms outward. "Let's be reasonable..."

Governor Hallsly is nearly hyperventilating, the running finally taking its toll. His gray hair is mussed, his comb over revealing the bald spot he tries so hard to conceal.

"You disgust me," he wheezes, his voice failing him momentarily as he tries to catch his breath.

Other passengers are now appearing on deck, drawn by the sound of the commotion. They stand and watch, mouths agape. Kim Leung's eyes are especially drawn to Tyler's penis, which is larger than any she has ever seen in real life. In fact, she thought penis's of that size were a myth, you know, like the flash of green light at sunset or a good looking man who offers to take out the garbage.

"Just let it go governor," one of the crewmen says, stepping toward him, hands outstretched. "Whatever is going on I'm sure we can discuss it rationally."

"He...he shouldn't have gotten in my way," he mutters weakly, running a hand through his hair.

"You got something to say to me than say it," Melissa says, stepping forward. "Quit carrying on."

"It's none of his business."

"You're making it everyone's business." She gestures at all those gathered. "Are you upset that the captain found us out? No more mid-day beatings?"

"Oh yeah," Dave says to Travis. "Now it's really getting good."

"This is hardly the place-"

"You should have thought of that before you chased Tyler all around the ship like a lunatic!"

"That's right girl!" Tyler cheers. "You tell him!"

"And you shut up! Get out of here and put some damn pants on!"

"Hey baby-"

"Don't you 'hey baby' me! I've heard enough of your crap for one day!"

"Listen sugar-" Hallsly starts and she turns her wrath on him.

"Likewise to you dillhole!"

There is a moment of awkward silence as everyone stares at one another, no one knowing what to say. Melissa glares at Hallsly, then at Tyler, then at the deck.

"You guys are both a couple of idiots," she says quietly, shaking her head. She turns, glancing at all of the people gathered, embarrassed that she is caught in the middle of this. "I want you both to stay away from me for the rest of the trip, understand?" She looks each of them in the eye individually. "Got it? Stay as far away from me as you can." She spins around and exits the deck quickly, avoiding the eyes that follow her.

"You heard the lady," Hallsly says after she is gone. "Why don't you go put some pants on?"

"Why don't you bite me?" Tyler sneers, apparently forgetting that only minutes ago he was running for his life in fear of the other.

"You want to watch that tone with me boy or I'll smack that expression right off your face."

"Yeah? You and what army?"

Suddenly the governor finds a renewed burst of energy and, howling at the top of his lungs like a man possessed, he bum-rushes Tyler and they both topple over the railing into the cold water of the Pacific.

"Man overboard!" one of the crewmen calls out as others come running. "Man overboard!"

 SIXTEEN

"I should have let you two assholes drown," Captain Harvey says as Hallsly and Tyler stand shivering before him. Both are draped in thick, itchy wool blankets, teeth chattering in unison. Dante stands by the window, regarding the two of them with idle distaste. He, for one, finds it preposterous that he should have to be in their company.

"The passengers and crew have spoken and it has been determined that you two are to be banished from their sight for the remainder of this journey." He turns to Dante, gives the large man a reproachful look. "I'm sorry to do this to you Dante, but since it isn't working out for you in the boiler room I have to put you in with these guys. We simply don't have enough space on the ship to accommodate you otherwise." He returns his attention to the other two. "You are going to be placed in a holding area and it is there you will remain until this mission is complete."

"You can't do this to me!" Governor Hallsley balks, but it is hard to make out what he is saying because of his uncontrollable shaking. "Th-th-th-the Wh-wh-wh-white H-hu-hu-hu-house su-su-su-sent mu-mu-mu-me to-to-to-to overs-su-su-su-see th-th-th-th-this o-o-o-o-o-operation!"

"The only thing you've been overseeing is the bottom of a bottle and your own twisted sex games." The captain shakes his head disgustedly. *I was right, they were having a three-way.*

"I don't see why I have to be locked up with them," Dante complains, speaking for the first time since entering the room. "I haven't done anything wrong."

"I hate to break this to you son, but you stowed away aboard my ship. I'd call that 'doing something wrong'."

Dante shrugs, looking away. How was he to know his attempts at helping out in the boiler room were going to be so poorly received? Those guys acted like he was an idiot for Christ's sake, like he couldn't even handle the simplest of tasks. In an effort to prove he could be useful he took it upon himself to polish some of the equipment and he accidentally put his elbow through a glass-plated temperature gauge, inadvertently causing a piece of machinery to overheat. The apparatus was salvaged, but it took a considerable amount of effort on the crewmen's part, more than they'd wanted to expend, it would seem. So, here he is.

"It's not my fault captain," Tyler interjects. "He's the one who came after me!"

"Yes, we could sit here and play the blame game, but the thing is you aren't even supposed to be here. Hallsly doesn't have the authority to allow a prostitute and her pimp aboard my ship, even if they are disguised as 'aides'."

"She isn't a prostitute!"

"Call her whatever you want, but anybody who's hired to trade sexual favors for money is a whore, plain and simple."

"It wasn't sexual favors," Hallsly implores. "It was S&M-"

"I don't want to hear it," Captain Harvey interrupts and, truthfully, he doesn't. He's made an irreversible decision and right now what he wants more than anything is these two out of his sight. "Rest assured Melissa isn't exactly in my good graces either. She's to be removed from the general populace as well." This part is a lie; he's ordered no such thing.

"Dude!" Tyler exclaims happily. "Can she stay with us?"

The captain glares at the longhaired, tattooed man for a long moment, wondering how much brain activity actually goes on in his head. He pictures one lone brain cell, creeping around in that vast expanse of empty space, looking for others but finding he is all alone.

He reaches for the intercom, paging a member of his crew. A few minutes later three men arrive at the door.

"Ready whenever you are boys," he says, and they take Tyler and Governor Hallsly into their custody. "You two be good," he warns. "I don't want to hear that you can't play nice or I just might decide not to feed you."

"What about him sir?" one of his men asks, indicating Dante.

"You can come back for him later. For now take these two and then check on the rest of the passengers. Hopefully no one was traumatized by all the hubbub."

"Yes sir."

"Care for a drink?" Captain Harvey asks, taking a bottle of Cutty Sark and two tumblers from one of the desk drawers. "And take a seat, you're making me nervous."

Dante looks sullenly at the captain but complies. He sits across from him, crossing his long legs.

"Well?"

"Sure," Dante says. He isn't much of a drinker but he could use something right now. Inside his guts are twisting tumultuously. It occurs to him that he is very far from home, and the thought depresses him. What had he been thinking, following her? Obviously he hadn't been thinking at all.

The captain pours two drinks and nudges one of them toward Dante.

"Why do you have to put me in the same room as them?" Dante asks, picking up the tumbler and sipping the whiskey carefully. It burns as it hits his belly but it feels good, helps him to relax.

He tips the rest of it back and holds out the glass. Captain Harvey pours him another. "Are the guys in the boiler room really that mad at me?"

"The piece of equipment you almost wrecked is necessary to keep the engine running. I know you're not familiar with ships but it's important, trust me."

"Look, it was a mistake, honest, I certainly didn't mean to-"

"Shut the hell up," the captain says flatly and Dante looks at him in surprise. His demeanor has suddenly changed, and his eyes…his eyes don't seem like they belong to the same person. They are dark, almost black, and even though the overhead lights adequately illuminate the room it appears as if a shadow passes threateningly over the captain's face.

Captain Harvey coughs, a thick, hacking sound, and his cheeks bulge, his mouth filling with fluid. Gagging, he leans over a metal garbage can and expels a mouthful of something that makes a sickening plop as it hits the bottom. He swipes at his lips with one hand, rubbing his chest with the other. Dante watches silently, overcome with perplexed apprehension, and all the while the captain's eyes have never left his own. At last he speaks:

"Do you even know where this ship is going?"

Dante swallows and hears a clicking noise in his throat. For some reason he has this bizarre idea that he's dealing with someone else, that Captain Harvey has left the room and in his wake his evil doppelganger remains. He knows it's irrational, but he finds the notion hard to dispel. "All I know is we're heading out to the middle of the Pacific, sir. That we are going to research a floating pile of garbage." He keeps his tone even, trying not to divulge his increasing discomfort.

"There's more to it than that," Harvey says, firing up a stogie.

"Yeah?" Dante takes another sip of his drink, trying to keep his hands from trembling.

"Yeah. We lost a ship out there, a research vessel. It disappeared about a month ago, just dropped right off the grid."

Dante nods, saying nothing. He was present at the meeting; this information isn't new to him. He watches the captain's eyes, which seem to indicate a homicidal rage is lurking just below the surface.

"What do you think of that?" Captain Harvey prompts and Dante clears his throat nervously.

"Do you mean it sunk?" he asks tentatively and the other shrugs.

"Don't know. All of these ships are equipped with GPS units, navigational gear. It means we can track the location of the ship from anywhere in the world. *Anywhere.*"

"Yeah?"

"Yeah." The captain takes a deep drag on his cigar. "Problem is, we can't find a signal."

"So it probably sank?"

"Could have, but we'd still get a signal from the GPS, unless the tracking system was destroyed." Dante takes another sip of his drink. "You think it was sabotaged?"

Captain Harvey chuckles. "Sure, sabotaged, or maybe unintentionally destroyed if the ship caught fire somehow."

"Hmm," Dante says, setting his glass down. "So what do you think, they were attacked?"

"Oh, there are many things that come to mind," Captain Harvey says ominously, his eyes narrowing, and at once goose bumps break out on Dante's arms. He doesn't know why, but the captain is giving him a first class case of the creeps. "Like maybe they got what was coming to them, meddling where they don't belong."

"Excuse me?"

"Excuse me? Excuse me? What did you do, fart?" the captain mocks in a high falsetto, his head rocking back on his colossal shoulders, the muscles in his arms bunching up and tightening. The two are almost evenly matched size-wise, but the captain is all lean muscle whereas Dante's bulk consists more of fat. "You heard me."

"Yes sir." Dante wishes he could flee the room this very instant, just up and run out the damn door. This man obviously has some issues he's been concealing all too well. "I did."

"There are some places that people aren't meant to go, places that are best left undiscovered." The stogie burns unnoticed in the captain's hand, the ash growing longer and longer. "But if people insist on going anyway, they shouldn't be surprised at what they find, should they?"

Dante licks his lips anxiously, his eyes shifting from the captain's face to his hands and back. He can smell violence in the air like a rotten piece of meat, can feel the tension mounting like a teakettle on the verge of boiling.

"I asked you a question!" he roars and Dante jumps, his hand knocking over his tumbler of whiskey. It falls off the table and shatters on the floor, but the captain pays no mind. "Answer me sailor!"

"No sir!" Dante cries, the hairs on the back of his neck fully erect.

"What?!"

"No they shouldn't!"

The captain cackles, at least, that's what Dante thinks it's supposed to be, but it's a strange, grating noise that's nothing like the conveyance of mirth. His lips twist with the cadence of it, looking like two earthworms writhing under a hot, noonday sun. He then leans his head forward and his eyes metamorphous, growing malevolently dark, ensconced in a shimmering cloak of velvety blackness, two murky pools like tar pits drawing Dante in, suffocating him. He takes a ragged breath, then another, and suddenly it's as if the captain is inside his head, his work-calloused hands digging into the soft meat of his brain, whispering cryptic nonsense that swirls around and around like wind-swept fog. An image flares brightly in the recesses of his mind, exploding vividly, an image that takes him unwillingly by the hand, leading him...

to a place where demons walk amongst animals of no discernable species, ugly, brutish things that make sounds unimaginably horrible even in the light of day...come with me and we shall rule this land together, shall watch as the others become walking skeletons, their bodies nothing but dried flesh that holds together a network of brittle bones...your pain will no longer exist, and in this land of glorious waste we are gods Dante, immortal, unstoppable...

Dante stares into these eyes, open-mouthed, feeling a scream building in the back of his throat that's trying to claw it's way out, and at once he wants nothing more than to get to his feet and run for the safety of...*anywhere*...anywhere but here. Broken shards of glass crunch beneath the soles of his shoes and his mouth opens and closes silently as the captain's face twists and wriggles around the appalling sound he's making. And then, like the climax of a dreadful night plagued by terrible dreams, he sees past the captain's lips and down the yawning expanse of his throat, and there appears a tidal wave of greenish/whitish fluid just at the back of his tongue, crowding his epiglottis, and swimming in it are worms like strands of spaghetti, whipping wildly about, slapping against the insides of the captain's cheeks. Dante's eyes are wide as saucers, his heart trip-hammering in his chest, his hands clenching the armrests of his chair as he stares into this gaping, inconceivable horror...

"-I know how it might sound to you, but when something of this nature happens to a perfectly responsible crew and a sound sea faring vessel, there has to be some explanation. Am I right or am I right?"

"What?" Sweat is pouring down Dante's brow; his armpits and his chest feel slick with it. The captain is looking at him oddly, leaning back in his chair and puffing grandiosely on his cigar.

"Are you okay son? You look a little green around the gills."

"I...I guess I..." he mumbles, at a loss for words. Could it be the whiskey got to his head, made him see something that wasn't there? The captain is looking at him benignly, a fatherly smile on his seamed, weathered face. "I...I don't drink very often," he finishes lamely.

"Happens to the best of us," Captain Harvey says jovially, exhaling a large plume of smoke. "Do me a favor and pick up the larger pieces of that glass will you? I'll have one of my crewmen sweep up the rest."

"Of course," Dante says, getting out of his chair and kneeling on the floor. He collects them carefully, not wanting to cut himself, reaching under the desk for a few that strayed farther than the rest. As he picks up the shards he shoots a glance over at the wastebasket, noticing a small pile of white goo next to it.

The pile of goo is pulsating, wriggling as if it is alive.

Dante gets up quickly, pieces of glass cutting into his hands.

"Put 'em in the trash son," the captain instructs and Dante nods, experiencing a vertigo-like feeling as the world seems to fall away beneath his feet. He steps forward until he is an arms length from the wastebasket and, avoiding looking at whatever it is on the floor, he drops the pieces in. His heart is clamoring at train wreck speed, pounding and thumping madly. He feels dizziness creep over him, and he wonders vaguely if he is going to pass out.

"You sure you're all right?" he hears the captain ask faintly, and then everything fades to gray.

SEVENTEEN

Morning breaks gray and cold, a hard, steady rain pouring down.

So much for the initial weather report, Jake Anderson muses as he mans the helm, sipping from a cold cup of coffee.

Waves smack forcefully against the side of the ship, the sea much choppier than the previous day, and Jake strains against the wheel, every so often taking a peek at the Doppler equipment and navigational readouts. They are still making good time so, if all goes as planned, they should arrive at the fringe of the North Pacific Gyre late tonight, the trash heap by the following day. Unless the weather gets worse, in which case they might be slightly delayed.

"Hey," someone says from behind him just as he is in mid-sip, and he spills coffee down the front of his shirt. "Sorry, didn't mean to startle you."

Jake turns to see Corbin standing by the Doppler radar unit and, frowning, he brushes at the spreading stain.

"Just the man I wanted to see," he says. "I thought we weren't expecting anything more than some light rain."

"Yeah, about that..." Corbin starts, undecided whether or not he wants to let the cat out of the bag regarding the captain's indiscretion. Does it really matter what the truth is? It may only make the rest of crew wary of his other decisions, and right now they need a unified front, if only to keep order. As it stands they already have the governor and the two freaks in holding; there's no sense in riling up the crew when the passengers are already on edge.

"Yeah?"

"Sudden change," Corbin says shortly, plucking the readout from the printer. "We got a storm blowing in."

"A storm? You telling me that gizmo and the weather reports from the east didn't know a squall was coming?"

"Apparently not."

"Jesus Christ, that's all we need." Jake takes another sips of the bitter coffee and sets the mug down. "Better alert the rest of the crew, let 'em know they should look sharp. Does the captain know?"

"Oh yeah," says Corbin. "He knows."

"Okay then." He looks over his shoulder at the other. "You might want to think about finding a new source for your weather information. If it gets ugly we could be in for one hell of a ride."

"Yeah," Corbin sighs expansively. "That's what I'm afraid of."

The passengers are holed up in their cabins, waiting out the rain, and as a courtesy that is seldom (if ever) bestowed, the captain has their breakfast delivered. It isn't exactly room service at the Ritz Carlton, but it's a nice gesture any way.

The only passengers who are indifferent to their in-cabin service are the three locked up in what passes as the 'brig', which is actually a converted storage room in steerage. The ship doesn't have a 'brig' per say, being that it is a civilian vessel.

Governor Hallsly mumbles something the crewman can't make out when he's handed his tray, and Dante takes his food without a word, feeling disjointed, out of touch. He still isn't quite sure what he saw yesterday; all he knows is something scared him badly, he passed out, and he woke up here.

As for Tyler, he's still sleeping so it's debatable whether or not he is going to get breakfast, judging by the way the other two are eyeing it up...

Leeann and Kim are silent as they eat, the very basest of civility all that either of them can muster. Leeann shoots the other a glance every so often, wanting to say something to break the tension but unable to bring herself to do it. She feels she is a reasonable person and Kim is acting like a diva. If the other can't find it in her to be decent, far be it that she is going to try.

Kim, on the other hand, is insulted that she has to share a room with someone who is so beneath her, and small talk is something she considers, trivial, useless. She eats her breakfast and looks out the porthole at the sheets of rain coming down, wishing she were somewhere else...

Dr. Taylor is reading over his notes when breakfast arrives, and he smiles vaguely, appraising the sensible offering of toast, oatmeal and juice.

"Please set it on the table, if you don't mind," he requests and the crewman nods and does so, exiting without a word. Dr. Taylor nibbles at the toast as he continues to review his materials, every so often glancing at his watch. He knows he has it easy compared to the crew, but if the rain keeps up it's going to be a very long day...

Melissa starts when she hears the knock on her door, and only after determining who it is does she open it and take the proffered meal.

"Thanks," she says, closing the door quickly. After the stunt Hallsly and Tyler pulled yesterday she's too embarrassed to speak to anyone. She just can't take their recriminating stares, real or imagined. The one weak ray of sunshine in this otherwise gloomy scenario is that the captain has gotten them out of her hair; at least she won't have to worry about running into those clowns should she venture topside. That she fell for Tyler's typical bullshit angers her, but what's done is done, can't take that back. Now she just has to wait it out until she can get off this ship and return to Sacramento. And she fully expects to be compensated for her time, no matter how things have turned out. It's not her fault the governor is an incompetent boob...

Kenny, Cole and Robert are given their food and told to be ready in case their services are needed.

"What do you mean?" Cole asks, staring at the crewman as if he's crazy. Their charge is currently cooling his heels in lock down. As it stands there is no longer anything for them to do.

"If the rain gets worse we may need you guys to help out."

"Doing what?" Kenny says.

"You'll know when the time comes," he answers and the three stare at him silently as he shows himself out...

Perry is in the middle of an angry tirade when their food arrives, and it is only this intervention that puts his complaints on hold momentarily, much to Steven's relief. He has long grown tired of the other and doesn't think he has the wherewithal to put up with much more. He's hoping breakfast will offer him a brief respite from Perry's ramblings, but he continues on unabated, talking with his mouth full.

"I can't believe they took my weed!" he whines. "It's my medicine dude, I need it!"

"Well don't look at me, it isn't my fault. You heard what the captain said."

"Yeah, I heard him all right but he's wrong! I brought it for therapeutic purposes!"

Sure you did, Steven thinks but says nothing, shoveling a spoonful of oatmeal in his mouth.

"It's legal, I have a prescription and everything!"

"You're a tool," Steven mutters, taking a sip of his juice.

"What?"

"Just be cool. You'll be all right."

"Yeah…"

As the passengers are receiving their deluxe, four-star treatment, Travis, Dave and the other two sailors are standing out in the cold downpour, standard issue rain gear doing little to keep them dry, shivering as water pools at their feet.

"This blows dude," Travis says.

"Yep, nothin' but the best for us seamen."

"At least that numb nuts lieutenant is out here too. I'd be pissed if I knew he was inside, warm and dry."

"Yeah, there's that anyway. But I bet he'd rather be kissin' the captain's ass."

"Shit, more like rimmin' it," Travis says and this cracks them up.

"Thanks dude, I'll never get that image out a my head."

"Sorry."

Just this morning they watched with ensuing hilarity as the lieutenant attempted to buddy up to the captain, buttering up the veteran sailor with words of praise that he all but ignored. It pleased them to no end to witness the captain rebuff the lieutenant's efforts, dismissing him quickly. The man is no fool: he knows a suck-up when he sees one. Travis and Dave may be young and inexperienced but the one thing they have going for them is they know their place and are content (resigned) with it. The lieutenant, however, seems to be ignorant of the fact that this job is his punishment, and he continues to strive for privileges he doesn't deserve. More than anything this denotes what a knucklehead he is, in their humble opinions.

Also, since their brief altercation yesterday, he hasn't said more than two words to either of them, which suits them just fine.

"Gonna get a lot wetter before it gets dry," Travis observes, looking at the sky.

"Yeah, I think so…"

The captain stands at the bow, watching as the cloud cover turns from gray to black. He's been up since long before dawn, (as the years advance he sleeps less and less and usually doesn't get more than three or four hours a night when he is on duty) keeping tabs on the imminent squall.

"Let's see what you got," Captain Harvey addresses the sky. "Impress me." Although it isn't in his best interest, he can't help but challenge the rain gods because, when all is said and done, he enjoys a good storm. It's a test of his mettle.

As if in answer a brilliant flash of lightening explodes a few hundred yards off the stern, followed several seconds later by a crashing boom of thunder. The storm is close, only a few miles away and closing. And by the looks of it she's going to be a doozy.

Little do the passengers know, but they've all received a dose of Dramamine, the pills crushed into their oatmeal. It's a first on his part, definitely not something that adheres to standard protocol, but he thought it might aid the more inexperienced at sea, maybe help hold their fear in check if their stomachs aren't upset. He hopes like hell they've all eaten, or else his crew is going to be swimming in puke. There's nothing quite like the queasiness of being seasick; it's relentless. Even though he has a strong stomach he's experienced it a few times, once during his second tour of Vietnam. He was adrift for three days in a life raft after his ship sank, the only member of the crew who got out alive after she'd been hit by torpedoes. He'd had nothing in his belly but bile yet his gag reflex felt like it was working overtime. He'd been lucky a low flying plane spotted him because the nausea and resulting dizziness had left him unable to save himself. He'd spent most of the time in a state of delirium, his raft hosting an endless stream of hallucinations, the men he'd killed coming back from the grave to exact their revenge.

Captain Harvey looks up into the light rain as it becomes stronger, steadier. If it gets heavy he has no doubt they'll be fine, given his abilities, but it will most likely churn the sea into a rabid froth of huge waves and deep troughs, throwing them off course and costing them valuable time, and this bothers him more than anything.

As the fat drops fall onto his face he feels mounting tension, a sudden panicked urge to get to the trash heap as soon as they can. For he feels, as surely as he knows how to handle himself at sea, that this voyage is purgatory and at the other end therein awaits nirvana...

EIGHTEEN

"The rain is really coming down," Tyler comments bleakly, looking out the small porthole and scratching his belly. "And I'm hungry. I wonder when they're going to serve breakfast."

Dante and Governor Hallsly exchange a guilty look; they've stashed the breakfast trays under the bottom bunk after deciding to split Tyler's.

"Just shut up," Hallsly scowls.

"Whatever, ya old windbag." He looks over at Dante. "You don't talk much, do you?"

Dante grunts disgustedly and turns away, taking a seat on one of the two chairs the room provides and putting his head in his hands. It's going to be a long trip from here on out, that's for sure, and as far as he's concerned this voyage can't be over soon enough. He's well over his surprise at Leeann saying all those horrible things; he's certainly heard worse in his thirty-odd years. But it would have been nice if she hadn't led him on, acting like there was a chance for a relationship when in reality she didn't want anything to do with him. Let's face it, she's just like all the rest of them, all the women who've done nothing but make him feel unwanted, unlovable. He's angry, but finds he doesn't have it in him to condemn her. There's really no point, and right now he has bigger problems to deal with, most notably the two bozo's he's currently locked up with. The governor reminds him of a spoiled, faded Hollywood actor, a coddled man past his prime but still reveling in his early year heyday, what with his spray on tan, silver, balding hair and his obvious attachment to yearly nip/tucks. And Tyler isn't any better; this guy clearly sees himself as a worldly chick magnet and all Dante sees is a selfish kid who never grew up.

And then there's the captain…can he let it go, try and believe what he saw was a hallucination, possibly brought on by lack of sleep, stress and liquor? When it comes right down to it, what did he *really* see? His memories of yesterday are hazy, indistinct. Like a bad dream that dissipates seconds after awakening he has no clear recollection of the events that transpired, only that something frightened him badly. In the light of day the whole thing seems positively silly when he gives it any serious thought. All he's truly sure of is that he doesn't want to be alone in the same room with the captain if he can help it.

Hallsly walks over to the bed and reclines on the bottom bunk. He wishes he had his cell phone, that way he could call someone with the power to supersede the captain's authority and get him the hell out of here. The gall of that asshole locking him up with a porno movie reject and an escaped mental patient. He wonders if Dante is what you would call an 'idiot savant', heavy on the 'idiot', light on the 'savant'. He's tried to get his story but the animal isn't talking. All the governor knows about him is that he stowed away aboard the ship, and how fucking stupid is that? Who in their right mind would come along on this trip willingly? Well, without getting paid. Tyler did it for an obvious reason, and her name is Melissa. And speaking of the illustrious dominatrix, he's curious what she's doing right now, if the captain is turning a blind eye while she doles out punishment to willing crewmen with a few extra bucks on their hands. Wouldn't that be just like a bitch? If she thinks she's getting one red cent from him, she can think again.

Tyler leaves his vigil at the window and wanders over to the other chair, straddling it backward and slumping forward. He isn't one for heavy thinking but currently he's pondering what he got himself into. Melissa is so pissed off that he doesn't know if she'll ever see the end of her rage to give him another chance in the sack. He should have known that saying 'you're welcome' was a bad idea, but he isn't one for foresight. Just not in his genetic encoding. The furthest he can see into the future is his next meal or lay, which generally occurs within the same day, considering. And he's long forgotten about Wes, given that he doesn't have any use for him. He will certainly remember him when this trip is over, when he needs money for a ride home, and then a home. When that time comes he'll have to get out and mingle in the single bars, find some aging woman with low self-esteem and a generous income and convince her she needs a guy like him around to make her life worth living. They're out there, and he'll sniff one out. He's like a bloodhound that way.

However he will miss Melissa, that much is true. More so, he'll miss having sex with her because, *goddamn* she's fine. When all is said and done she really is a sexual dynamo, and he regrets having to see her fine ass go shimmying off into the sunset. Of course there is always the possibility of regaining her good graces, he's just not sure how to go about it. Maybe he can use this time to come up with a plan, something so scheming, so clever, so foolproof-

Ah, who is he kidding? It's freakin' over...

Melissa listens to the rain as it splashes against the window, increasingly aware of the ship's pronounced motion, tilting sharply forward and back. If it keeps up she's afraid she might get sick, and she hates puking, simply despises it.

"This is just what I need," she sighs, running her hands through her hair nervously.

At present she just wants off this ship; the thought of being at sea any longer is driving her crazy. What was she thinking? She's never liked boats, or the water for that matter. How could she jump into this so blindly, with so little regard for what it may entail? Did she really need the money that badly?

Feeling restless, she decides to get dressed and wander topside to see if anything is going on. Anything will be better than just sitting here, even if she has to face the recriminating eyes of the other passengers. The captain recommended she lay low after the incident, but it wasn't an order. She's certain he doesn't care either way what she does.

Picking out some clothing, she hums the melody to a popular song as she gets dressed.

"The rain is getting heavier, sir," Jake Anderson says, his eyes betraying his growing trepidation.

"Tell me something I don't know, Jake," Captain Harvey says, surveying the purplish, bruised looking sky, watching as it grows darker and darker, lightening flashing at regular intervals that are too close for his liking. "Just hold 'er steady." He bends his knees as the ship pitches steeply to one side, holding on to the navigational gear to keep from toppling over. "And radio the deck crewmen. Tell them to keep the passengers inside."

"Aye aye sir."

Leaving her cabin, Melissa gropes her way along one of the walls as the lights flicker and disappear momentarily. The ship is rocking back and forth in a manner that is starting to worry her, but she continues to tell herself she has nothing to fear. This is a big vessel, manned by professionals who work for the Script's Institute. Surely if anyone knows what they are doing these guys do, right?

Just as she reaches the ladder at the end of the corridor and takes one of the rungs in her hand she hears someone approaching from behind her, their footsteps echoing loudly in the narrow corridor.

"Excuse me ma'am, hold up," somebody calls to her and she swivels her head to see it's one of the crewmen, a good looking guy who appears to be in his early twenties.

"Yes?"

"No one is to go topside, captain's orders," the man says apologetically. "Pretty rough up there this morning."

"Apparently," she replies, the rung of the ladder still gripped tightly in her hand. "Is it supposed to get worse? "

"I can't say." He flashes her a wan smile. "Well, I'm not supposed to say."

"Not supposed to?" A flutter of fear streaks through her. "Is it that bad?"

"Best thing to do is to go back to your cabin," he says, the trace of a smile now gone. "When it clears up we'll let you know."

"Jesus, you're scaring me. Are we alright?"

"We're fine," the crewman says quickly. "Just stay in your cabin until further notice."

"Until the rain subsides?"

"You'll know when it's safe to come out," he says, reaching out a hand to take hers. "Now let's get you back safely, okay?"

Reluctantly she releases the ladder rung and lets herself be led down the hall to her cabin.

"Jesus Christ, it's really comin' down out there," Kenny says, squinting through the porthole.

Cole is pacing back and forth, muttering to himself.

"I knew I never should have taken this job, never should have, nope. Knew I would wind up regretting it…"

"What's the matter?" Kenny says, turning toward him. "Fraid of a little rain?"

"It isn't the rain I'm worried about, man. It's the wind. Those waves can get pretty fierce and they'll toss this ship around like a soda pop bottle."

"I'm sure we're in good hands. The crew knows how ta handle this," Kenny says, but he's not sure if he's reassuring Cole or himself. He's had the same nagging suspicion but has yet to admit it, even to himself. He wants to trust them, but because he has little to no experience with this kind of thing he's finding it difficult. And underlying his fear is a compulsion that gnaws at him like tiny, razor sharp teeth, making him tense and jittery. What he wants right now, *really* wants, is a goddamn drink. A little something to take the edge off.

"You think so, huh? And what, exactly, do you base your opinion on?"

"I dunno," he replies harshly, not in the mood to talk anymore. "But it sure beats worryin' mysef to death."

"I ain't worrying myself to death, I'm just sayin'."

"The hell ya ain't! Put a cork in it, will ya?"

"I don't feel so good," Robert murmurs weakly, and the two abandon their argument momentarily, regarding him curiously. He is sitting on his bunk holding his stomach, and damned if he isn't white as a sheet.

"Good thing ya din't eat much a your breakfast," Kenny says. "That way ya won't have much ta lose."

"I ate the toast, but I hate oatmeal."

"Goddamnit I feel trapped in here!" Cole complains. "I need to get out of this cabin!"

"Jus shut up man, everythin' is gonna be fine!"

"What if we run into a hurricane?"

Kenny wants to cruelly debunk his theory just to silence the little twerp, but since he knows next to nothing about anything except football and drinking all he can do is shrug.

Great. The sum bitchs's gave me one more thing ta worry bout.

"Dude, the waves are hitting our window!" Perry says, and Steven looks up from his reading to glance out into the meager light.

"Yeah, so?"

"Aren't you concerned? I don't think this is normal."

"I'm sure everything is going to be fine," he says dismissively, but with each passing minute he has to admit it feels as if the ship is pitching more and more to each side.

"I hate the water," Perry confesses, glancing at the other with a frightened expression that casts a shadow across his tanned face. "I don't know why I signed up for this."

Steven ignores him, focusing on his reading. Jesus, can't he just shut-up? And why on earth did he study marine biology if he hates the water? What an idiot.

"How can you just sit there and read man? Look at this shit!"

Steven sets the report down with a sigh. "Look Perry, I'm sure it seems a lot worse than it really is. If we were in any kind of danger they'd have to tell us-"

Abruptly a small speaker above the cabin door emits a burst of static. Since neither of them is aware of it's presence, it takes them by surprise. In every cabin this scenario is playing itself out, everyone jumping at the sound of the squawking box.

"Ladies and gentlemen this is the captain. I want to thank you all for your patience and for staying in your cabins this morning."

"It's about time!" Perry says and Steven shushes him.

"As you are all well aware we are experiencing some weather we hadn't anticipated, but rest assured that everything is completely under control. The ship has been built to withstand a lot worse than this, and the crew and I are old hands at traversing rough seas. I want you to know your safety is one of our top priorities so please, just bear with us. Members of the crew will be stopping by your cabins momentarily with water and Dramamine if anyone needs it. Any other requests may be made at this time, however keep in mind we are very busy and if it can wait, all the better. I appreciate your patience and will keep you updated as the storm progresses. Thank you."

NINETEEN

The president sits behind his desk in the Oval Office, listening to his aides describe the progress being made on the 'Gyre Mission', as they've taken to calling it. This news isn't exactly at the top of his list of things that needs his attention, so as he receives this information he's also glancing at a report from his military analyst detailing the developments in North Korea and eating a sandwich.

"They've run into the storm, sir," one of his aides is saying as he thumbs through the thick report.

"Uh-huh," he says distractedly, mentally cursing the administration that got them into this skirmish, wishing he could tear them all new assholes. Not that a conflict with North Korea could be avoided, he just thinks they could have gone about it with a little more tact instead of threatening a trade embargo and then bombing a city comprised mostly of civilians. "How are they holding up?"

"I'm afraid it isn't good, sir" an aide says. "By the looks of it, it's worse than the captain anticipated."

"That son of a bitch!" The president tosses the report aside and pops the last of the sandwich in his mouth. "If that gung-ho moron gets them all killed simply because he couldn't wait a few days for it to pass we've just wasted a lot of time and money." He's silent a moment, considering. "And lives, I guess. Well, Dr. Taylor's at any rate."

"Yes, quite. And there's more: the captain has also taken security measures into his own hands. He currently has the governor under ship arrest."

The president grins. "Really? What did he do?"

"Apparently the two assistants he brought aboard were hired sex workers."

"He brought a couple of hookers onboard with him?" He shakes his head ruefully, gazing at his aides with a wistful smile. "That douchebag never fails to amaze me."

"Yes sir."

"Did you receive this message from the captain himself?"

"No sir. The Naval base at Pearl Harbor is maintaining contact with the ship, requesting they radio in a report every few hours."

"Good ole Hallsly. I should have expected he'd pull a stunt like this and make a mockery of the whole thing."

"Yes sir."

"I'll bet he's fairly livid at being incarcerated," the president chuckles. "Has he asked to be removed from the ship?"

"He has, but at this time it's impossible. There's nothing they can do until the storm passes. It would be suicide to send anyone out in that."

"Good." Like it or not, Hallsly is going to be with the mission until the bitter end. And maybe, if they are lucky, someone from the Navy will leak the info about the governor's reprehensible behavior to the press. They'd have a bona fide field day with that. Stupid prick; he's the virtual poster child of a plutocracy in action. It's no wonder other countries despise America so much; most of the politicians are nothing but billionaires with very little knowledge of politics, just deep enough pockets to buy their way in. The majority of funds raised for his own candidacy were paid for by pharmaceutical companies and venture capitalists however, unlike Hallsly, he actually knows something about the machinations of affairs of state, such as foreign policy and not getting caught in the sack with a chamber maid.

"Alright then," the president says, returning to his report. "Keep me posted as anything new develops."

"Very good sir."

TWENTY

"ARRGGG!"

"Jesus Christ!" Hallsly rasps, fighting urgently with his rising gorge, his face tucked into his armpit. "If that fucker pukes any more I swear I'm going to be next!"

Tyler has spent the last thirty minutes emptying the contents of his stomach into the cabin's toilet. Unfortunately for the other two, the cabin is small and the bathroom doesn't have an exhaust fan. The stench of his vomit permeates the room, the odor lingering like a malevolent spirit.

"Get me the hell out of here!" Hallsly yells, pounding on the cabin door, but there is no one to heed his impassioned cries. The crew is hard at work maintaining the ship and the speaker system is one-way. Messages can come in, but they can't go out.

Dante is standing as far away as he can (which isn't all that far) holding his nose and battling the urge to blow chunks as well. He's always prided himself on having a strong stomach but this is too much even for him.

Hallsly ultimately gives in, tasting rancid oatmeal coming back up.

"Oh shit!" he moans, running for the bathroom, and he lets loose into the sink.

This finally does it for Dante. Hands over his mouth he dashes for the toilet, pushing Tyler out of the way.

"What are you doing-" Tyler burbles before he is sent ass over nuts into the wall, the larger man taking his spot at the throne.

Dante chokes piteously as he loses his breakfast, his beard half-submerged in the polluted toilet water, cursing again his asinine decision to stow away aboard the ship. Of all the things he could be doing right now (delivering pizza's, mourning his mother, watching TV while in a drug trial) he has to be on his knees before a filthy toilet, getting barf in his beard while his stomach lurches nauseatingly.

"AAAAGGGG!" he ralph's miserably, feeling as if his stomach and small intestines are soon to follow.

Hallsly hangs onto the sink as the ship rocks precipitously back and forth. It's taking all his strength to stay planted where he is, and if he lets go he will crash into Dante, who will in turn crash into Tyler.

"Man," Hallsly says weakly, regurgitated oatmeal dribbling off his chin, "this really sucks."

On the bridge, the captain is growing concerned. Not for the passengers, mind you, but for the fact that they might get thrown markedly off-course, delaying their arrival at the trash heap. Colossal waves crash over the side of the ship, submerging the main deck, and half of the crew is out there with pumps and buckets, bailing water and securing anything of importance they don't want swept over the side.

Down below, crewmen are working frantically to keep the engine room from flooding. As the ship rises with the swell of the waves and then drops into the cavernous troughs, water surges over the sides, finding its way into the deepest recesses. The men curse and flail about as the water rises from their ankles to their knees.

With the storms increasing fury it's all the captain can do to keep his sea legs about him. With each dip he staggers back and forth, clutching the wheel to stay upright. And to make matters worse the navigational equipment has begun sputtering in and out, beeping weakly, and there's nothing to be seen outside except for a heavy sheet of pouring rain and flecks of sea-churned white foam. Light is scarce, barely penetrating the thick clouds and fog, the day almost as dark as night.

His first mate returns from his inspection, soaked from the waist down.

"We're taking on too much water captain," Jake Anderson says. "What should we do?"

Captain Harvey grits his teeth, gripping the wheel with both hands. He's been through more storms than he can remember but this one, it would seem, has got them securely by the balls. If they are driven drastically off course and the navigational system fails they will be flying blind, and little does any of the crew know that sending out an S.O.S. is not an option.

"Keep yer chin up," he grunts. "How bad is it?"

"Pretty bad," Anderson acknowledges, grimacing. "So far we're able to keep the engine room from flooding completely, but if this continues the pumps won't be able to keep up."

Suddenly an enormous wave looms into sight before them, massive, bigger than the sky itself it seems. It rears above them like a sentinel guarding the gates of Hell, it's ferocity unfolding as it breaks, a million tons of water on a seek and destroy mission.

"Hold on!" he hollers as it crashes over the bow and at once their field of vision is gone, nothing but roiling water lashing against the glass. Captain Harvey hangs tightly to the wheel, trying to keep it steady, but the force of the wave knocks him down and he is sent sprawling across the floor, Jake tumbling after him. They come to rest against the far wall and the two of them scramble to their feet, racing toward the helm. Captain Harvey gets there first, and as he seizes it, it spins in his hands. Using every ounce of his strength he is at last able to hold it still, but it fights him like some living, breathing thing.

"Should I send out an S.O.S. to the Coast Guard sir?" Anderson shouts over the din of the rain and the sea, and for a brief moment Harvey closes his eyes, anger coursing through him, his nerves like twisted wires spitting out bolts of electricity. He has an insane urge to grab the first mate by his shirt and throw him through the plate glass window. Nothing is going to keep them from making their destination, *nothing*. If the sea decides to take them for it's own than so be it, but the last thing he's going to do is call for help and abort the mission.

"We're going to be just fine," he says, a tense grin on his face. "I've been through worse than this."

Jake looks at the captain incredulously, unable to conceal his rising terror.

"But captain–"

"But nothing!" Harvey roars, his voice thunderous in the confines of the room. "Now get down on the main deck and help the rest of the crew! Everything's under control up here!"

Eyes wide, Jake's Adam's apple bobs up and down as he swallows compulsively.

"But–"

"Go!"

Jake exits the bridge hastily, not sparing another glance behind him.

Leeann and Kim have come to a truce of sorts; they've suspended their mutual contempt for one another and are now huddled close together as the ship tosses steeply to and fro. They are perched on the lower bunk, holding each other and the railing of the bed to keep from toppling to the floor. Neither one of them says anything, they don't have to. At this point words are useless, just wasted hot air. Nothing either of them says will change anything, like it or not.

Kenny and Robert are doing their best to keep their wits about them but Cole has lost the battle.

"I hate ships man!" he protests bitterly. "I fucking hate them!"

"Than why did you sign on for this?" Robert asks, trying to keep from landing on his ass as another wave hits, causing the ship to dip sharply toward the stern.

"I didn't expect to get the job!" the Mexican says. "They weren't supposed to hire me!"

Steven has decided to set aside his dislike of the other, not wanting to suffer alone. Nothing can bring people together like disaster.

"This shit is getting worse man!" Perry cries as the lights flicker and go out briefly before coming back on, dimmer than before.

"Fuckin' a!" Steven agrees, wishing with all his heart he was still at school, taking one of the exams he got out of because he volunteered for this. Any exam, it didn't matter which one. Anything was better than this.

Melissa is fighting back panic so strong she is having trouble breathing. Being all alone in her cabin, she has no one to compare notes with. She is clinging to the railing of the bed and silently praying. She doesn't believe in God per say, so much as she believes in overwhelming powers that are out of her control. If there is a God, she supposes it is the force of nature, so this is what she prays to.

"Please don't let the ship sink," she mutters over and over. "Please don't let the ship sink."

Her faith in the captain and his crew is unshaken, but all the experience in the world can't save you if the storm has you outmatched. Through her porthole the world is nothing but an obscure world of water, a murky landscape that promises no escape. So far the score is: the sea=1, the ship=0.

"Please!" she implores the forces of nature. "Please don't let the ship sink!"

Topside, Travis, Dave and the other two Navy recruits are getting the ride of their lives. Because of their status they've been offered no respite from the storm. The crew, in order to keep the deck clear of the ever-rising water, has enlisted their aid. At the moment they are scrambling back and forth madly, receiving and carrying out orders from various crewmen. In the melee there is no time for thought or personal reflection; survival is foremost in everyone's mind, limbs simply acting in response to the stimulus the storm provides. Time becomes intangible, surreal, yet every second creeps by at a snail's pace. As the crewmen holler over nature's clamor, the Navy seamen do their damnedest to keep up.

Dave is in the midst of corralling equipment from being washed overboard when he hears (dimly) a man screaming for help. He squints through the wall of water, trying to determine where it came from, and he catches a glimpse of the lieutenant, his body draped over the rail on the starboard side, a monstrous wave crashing down on him.

When the water clears, the lieutenant is gone.

The lights flicker, on, off, on, off, on...and then they go out. The entire ship is plunged into blackness. Abruptly the door to the bridge crashes open, lumbering footsteps treading unsteadily over the threshold.

"We've lost power to the generator sir!" Jake Anderson cries, bumping into the other in the dark. "We musta been hit by lightening!"

"No kidding," the captain says, pushing him away. "Don't just sit there and play with yourself, do something about it before we get blown entirely off course and get lost in this shit!" When the other doesn't reply he adds: "Move it! Flash lights are in the cabinet by the door!"

"Yes sir!"

Seconds later a bright beam of light cuts through the gloom.

"Give me one of those, quick! And grab as many as you can carry and give them to the crewmen."

Anderson hands him a light and the captain shines it on his navigational equipment. For the time being everything is out. They need to get the power on, fast.

"Go to the engine room and see what's going on down there, in fact, make that your top priority. Get Charlie working on the generator if he isn't already. Tell him we need it up and running stat."

"What about the flashlights?"

"Give one to anybody you run into on the way. Now go! We don't have much time!"

"Yes sir," Anderson replies, although weakly. Apprehension has got him in a stranglehold; he can feel it in his stomach, a pit of fear that rises like a lump in his throat.

Captain Harvey shines the light on him and sees that all the color has drained from his face.

"Don't you go soft on me now Anderson!" he bellows. "I need you to focus! Our lives depend on it!" For the second time in less than twenty minutes the captain wants very badly to seriously hurt his gutless first mate but, unfortunately, that would be a frivolous gesture at this point. His words apparently cut through though and, what the hell, that's something.

"Right," Anderson says, coming around. "You can count on me."

"I hope so," Harvey says, setting his jaw and gripping the wheel tighter. "Now get out of here."

TWENTY-ONE

"Let me out of here now!" Hallsly is beyond panicked; right now it is safe to say he is more than just in need of a change of underwear. "Let me out now or I swear I'm going to sue every damn one of you until you have nothing left but the smiles on your faces!"

Dante and Tyler are crouched on the floor, trying to ignore the governor's inane raving but it's impossible, given the diminutive size of their quarters. His voice reverberates loudly throughout the tiny room, aggravating their already dismal situation. It's bad enough that their stomachs are twisted inside out and the room reeks of undigested regurge while the ship continues to dip and pitch precariously, but it's another that the lights have gone out, leaving them in total darkness.

"This is like a bad acid trip," Tyler mutters, his hands groping at the walls to try and steady himself, to keep from rolling away like a loose dice. "It just keeps getting more and more intense…"

"I swear to God someone is going to pay dearly for this!" Hallsly hollers frantically, clutching the door handle to keep from falling over. The thing that has him the most frightened isn't the rain, isn't the crazy tilting of the ship or even the darkness. It's being locked inside a room he can't escape. It's this feeling of vulnerability he hates and fears more than anything else in this world (well, with the exception of Democrats). His whole life he's been immune to any obstacle that's reared its ugly head, thanks to the wealth and power wielded by his family. He's used to being well insulated from the problems of the common man, the great unwashed masses who spend the better part of their lives worrying about money and disease and misfortune, all the while breeding like cockroaches, the stupid bastards. Their bloodlines are sullied with ignorance, Busch Beer and Nascar, unlike his own bloodlines, which run true with arrogance, aged single malt scotch and polo.

You see, being rich means you never have to say you are sorry, or that you give a shit…about anything. You are impenetrable, protected from everything the gods choose to toss your way. And that's the way he likes it.

"You let me out of here or I'm going to make sure none of you works for the state of California ever again!"

Don't they realize whom they are toying with? Don't they understand that by holding him here they are only making things worse for themselves in the long run? Oh they'll pay all right, they'll pay dearly...

Tyler shivers uncontrollably, wishing like hell he had a blanket but lacking the balls to crawl over to the bed and grab one. He doesn't want to lose his balance and crash into something in the darkness, doesn't want to risk messing up his pretty face on the off chance they do survive, which seems pretty slim at this point. He never would've guessed it'd end like this though, never in a million years.

What he figures, in his own crackpot/idealistic way, is that everyone conceptualizes the manner in which they are going to die. Everyone. If you are into extreme sports, maybe you think your parachute won't open someday. If you are a professional musician, possibly you have the notion you'll overdose on drugs or die in a plane or bus crash at some point during your career. If you are a politician or some other despised public persona, perhaps you assume you'll be assassinated after the trusting public finds out what a thieving fraud you are. After all, these things happen.

For Tyler, being a professional hustler, he's certain that eventually one of the broads he screws over will kill him, probably while he's naked, definitely while he's in her bed. Seriously. It just seems like the only way, and totally fitting to boot. It doesn't worry him, this thought, because at least he'll die doing what he loves.

Now this, this is completely unexpected, yet all things considered he's currently in this position *because* of a woman, so his death premonition is partially right. It's just that he thought his death would be caused directly by a scorned woman, not indirectly by some other cause...

Dante backs into a corner, placing each hand on an opposing wall to keep himself in place. He is thinking of Leeann, wondering how she's holding up. Even though she rejected him his heart goes out to her, hoping not only that she is okay, but also if escape becomes necessary she has every chance to do so, more so than himself even. Ultimately, the world needs people like her more than they need losers like him.

But if the ship is truly in danger of sinking he presumes the majority of the passengers will have a chance to get away, as there are two lifeboats onboard; he saw them yesterday while he was swabbing the deck. Actually, if push comes to shove, he thinks there is enough room for all of them if they squeeze together, but there certainly wouldn't be enough for all the members of the crew. So maybe the crew would 'forget' about the three troublemakers they locked away; it just might 'slip their mind'. That would certainly allow them extra space for other, more important people. Not that the governor of California isn't important...okay, let's stop playing around... it's clear that he isn't.

"I saw the movie Titanic!" Hallsly bawls. "You can't just let us die like those goddamn Irish bastards in steerage! No fucking way!"

Dave can't believe his eyes. One second the lieutenant was there, the next he's gone, washed away. He calls out to the others but his voice barely penetrates the screaming of the wind and the smacking of the rain. As he looks on in horror another enormous wave crashes over the starboard side and sweeps all those in it's path clear across the deck, the unfortunate men hanging on to the railing for their very lives, trying their damnedest to save themselves from being plunged into the churning sea.

He looks around for Travis, trying in vain to make him out in the compromised visibility, but can't recognize him from the others. The men taken by the wave are yelling for help as they cling desperately to the rail, but he doesn't dare attempt to cross the deck to aid them for fear that another wave is out there waiting. 'Try it Dave, see what happens,' the ocean whispers ominously. 'This one might have your number on it.'

And maybe he deserves to die, more so than any of the others. He is, after all, a pretty lousy person. The only reason he is here is because he didn't want to stay in jail. The only reason he is in the Navy is because he didn't want to go to jail in the first place. For Dave, all roads lead to incarceration.

A bright flash of lightening arcs across the sky, striking the highest point of the ship, and a shower of sparks cascades down. It is followed immediately by a burst of thunder so deafening it seems to detonate in his head, and this snaps him out of his fear-clouded reverie. He has never been one to give up or give in. Never. That's not the way he is designed. He knows that as long as his heart is beating and there is air in his lungs than he will fight with everything he has to keep it that way. Never give in, never surrender.

Crouching low to keep a stable center of balance, he begins to make his way over to the other side to assist anyone in need.

Across the deck, Travis is among the men submerged by the wave. He is clutching the railing in a death grip, hoping he can regain his footing before the next one crashes down. As the water subsides he gets to his feet, and when he feels it is safe to do so he bolts for the door leading to the lower deck. His heart is beating in his chest like a jackhammer, his breathing ragged, his lungs feeling like two wet, crumpled tissues yet his head is clear and that's all that counts. But in this state of heightened clarity dread rises within him, a cold certainty that he isn't going to make it out of this, none of them are, and with it he feels an overwhelming tedium. *Shit, whatever. Either kill me or let me go home. Just get it over with.*

Another wave crashes over the side with the force of a freight train, hitting him from behind. His feet go out from under him and the water scoops him up, jerking him backward. He is amazed at how quickly it happens, and has no clear notion of the direction in which it's taking him. He flails his arms wildly trying to catch hold of something secure but the water is twirling him like a sheet in a washing machine. He can't even reach the deck below him, and his lungs are starting to ache from the lack of air.

This is it. Over the side and into the drink.

But then he feels something tugging at his leg, halting his process momentarily, giving way... slipping...then suddenly bringing him to a stop. Hands reach for him and yank him above the water and the first breath he takes tastes better than his first kiss at the age of thirteen, given to him by a sweet little blonde haired girl named Danica. He hauls in another lungful of air before the water rushes over him again and he feels the hands holding him loosen and let go. He struggles, thrashing hard against the current, and is able to get his head above the water again.

"You've got to get over here!" he hears someone (Dave?) yelling. He hones in on the sound of the voice, turning in its direction, but it's no use. The current is too strong and he's tired, so damn tired...the last of his strength is ebbing, his motions futile against a force so overwhelmingly powerful he's nothing but a piece of flotsam compared. He might as well accept the fact that the whole of his existence has all come down to this...

And, just when he thinks all is lost, that the storm and the sea are going to claim him as their own, his life is given a reprieve when another wave counters the momentum of the first, bringing him back toward his savior. This time the hands grip him tight and pull him onto the upper deck where he collapses, lying on his back quivering, looking up at his rescuer.

"Holy shit," he gasps, trying to get his wind back. "You su-saved my fu-fu-fucking life dude!" Every muscle in his body is sore, stretched beyond their normal capacity, and his lungs feel torched from the inside out. A rush of dizziness flows through him but fortunately passes quickly, and he blinks several times, flushing the sea salt from his burning eyes.

"What are friends for?" Dave says, clutching the other. "But even without me you would have been fine. Remember, we're the fucking *Navy*."

"That's right," Travis smiles weakly. "Here we come to the rescue."

TWENTY-TWO

When her cabin is plunged into darkness, Melissa utters an involuntary shriek. She'd resigned herself to riding out the storm alone, convincing herself it was no big deal, when out of the blue scary just got scarier. She blinks rapidly, her eyes adjusting to the gloom, the room dimly illuminated (barely) by the weak light that filters through the porthole.

She's balanced on the lower bunk, her sweating hands slippery on the bed frame. So much for the captain and crew having everything under control. This, it would seem, is the complete opposite of that.

But, although it seems bad, she isn't going to give up hope entirely and throw in the towel just yet; if there is one thing about her that attests to her stoic nature it's her refusal to lose her cool. She does, however, recognize that her prayers to the powers that be have gone unheeded, but this is no big surprise. Have they ever been answered... ever?

Don't think so, she accepts sadly, and this makes her feel even more justified in her belief that they are indeed truly alone in the universe, no matter what the Christians, Jews, Buddhists, Muslims and the Church of Latter Day Saints have to say.

Her eyes half-closed, she envisions the church she and her mother used to attend when she was a little girl, a big, gothic structure with a statue of the Virgin Mary and a ravaged, emaciated Christ on the cross who was rumored to cry tears of blood when little kids sassed their parents. Did her stepfather ever go with them? she wonders, recalling only herself and her mother walking through the enormous double doors and into the vestibule containing the fountain of holy water in which they dipped their fingers to bless themselves. She sifts through the data banks in her mind (file folders with 'for your eyes only' written on the front in heavy, black ink) thinking back to her childhood, picturing her mother in her Sunday dress, a long, powder blue affair with ruffled fringes around the collar. She can remember her own dress, a knee-length plaid number she'd been so proud of and, in the darkness of the ship's cabin, recollections of her childhood begin to tumble forth, unbidden and startling. The images are jumbled at first; she remembers the stuffed bear she couldn't live without, and the saddest day of her life when 'Ms. Penelope' had to be thrown out because the poor thing was mangled and worn from years of being clutched desperately during nightmares and her myriad illnesses. The pitiable Ms. Penelope had soaked up so many of her tears she'd begun to smell like an old gym sock, her seams unraveling and bleeding stuffing, the button eyes becoming loose before falling off all together...

She remembers a big German Sheppard that lived next store, and how she was sweet and gentle and loved to be petted. She recalls her neighborhood friends, especially a little boy named Jimmy who chased her and tried to kiss her. His breath smelled like peanut butter but he was cute and his parents were always sitting on the porch with glasses in their hands, clinking the ice cubes and handing out candy to the children...

And suddenly, with an unexpected ferocity that makes her breath catch, Terry's haggard visage comes to mind, and with it a barrage of reminiscences, a hodgepodge mash-up of images that swirl like lurid phantoms beneath her closed eyelids. Some of them are rather benign, nothing but stock footage in the montage of her life, but the internal home movie at once comes to rest upon one that is truly shocking, something she'd tucked away in the furthest corner of her brain, possibly hoping it would never see the light of day:

She was nine years old and she'd awakened in the middle of the night and smelled the sweat, smoke, booze and cheap cologne that were to her the familiar scents of her stepfather. She'd opened her eyes just a little, saw him seated on the end of her bed, staring at her. That first time she'd caught him she hadn't been afraid, for Terry had seemed to her to be a good man, a decent replacement for the negligent drunkard her mother had divorced. By this time her real daddy had been reduced to a faded snap shot in a family album, someone she dimly remembered as the years passed by.

'Hi daddy Terry,' she'd addressed him that first time, thinking he was there to calm her from the nightmares and terrors she suffered almost nightly. She remembered that she'd startled him from some personal reverie, heard liquid slosh around in a glass as his head snapped up, his eyes wide.

'This is just a dream,' he'd told her, setting the drink down and reaching under the covers, under her nightgown.

'A dream?' she'd asked innocently.

'That's right. Now you go back to sleep honey,' he'd whispered in a husky voice as his fingers probed in places that were oddly pleasant at first, then deeply terrifying.

(A single teardrop runs down her cheek, followed by another, and then another. Her mouth twists into a snarl of anger and involuntarily she bites her bottom lip so hard she draws blood.)

After that first encounter, whenever she awoke and found him there she'd begin a silent litany of prayers to the God she'd learned about in Sunday school, the man with the long white beard (like Santa Claus) who wore a robe and sandals. Supposedly he was the God who helped all those in need, but he never helped her, never stepped in and made her pain go away. Step daddy Terry still appeared in the middle of the night despite those prayers, his hands probing under the covers unwanted, and her potty place (sometimes her pooping place) always ached afterward. And all the while he did this he held himself in his hand, his arm jerking back and forth with a brutal intensity as his eyes glazed over and his mouth curled into a grimace of pleasure...

Up until the age of twelve this was a regular occurrence, when at last she couldn't take it anymore. The guilt and shame wrought great heartbreak within her, and she detested that she felt like a freak, an abhorrent monster that even Jesus in his infinite compassion would be unable to love. For she felt as if this was all her fault, that somehow she'd brought this upon herself, so when the prayers didn't work she determined that it was up to her to end it, by any means necessary.

On what would be the last night he ever came calling (the kitchen clock tolling midnight, the witching hour) she sat and waited, the largest, sharpest kitchen knife they owned clutched tightly in her sweating hand, her heart beating in tandem with the shrill chimes, her breathing ragged, feverish.

Terry came to her, the scent of drunkenness and corruption exuding from his pores like beads of sweat, and his hands felt for her, the blackness pierced by the diffuse glow of her Raggedy Ann nightlight. His calloused, oil stained hands reached for her as he'd done so many times before, seeking the soft, innocent flesh, but what he found instead was sharp, the object warm and moist from her clammy hands.

'You touch me and I'll kill you,' she'd told him, finding within her a strength she'd never known she'd possessed. At that moment she felt as if she could do anything, could at least save herself from the nightly terrors this man had visited upon her for the last four years. By God she could take back control of her life, a life that had become almost unbearable.

'We're all friends here,' he'd said, but he pulled his hands back, watching her carefully. 'Why don't you give that to me before you hurt yourself?'

'I'll give it to you all right,' she'd threatened, wielding it like she'd seen the serial killers do in all those horror movies she wasn't supposed to watch. 'I'll plant this so deep in your heart it'll stop beating, and you'll wish you'd never hurt me!'

'I never meant to hurt you darling,' he'd said, his eyes flicking back and forth, possibly looking for a weapon of his own. 'I love you. That's what this is all about.'

'You can take your love and shove it up your ass!' she'd cried and he'd winced, his eyes darting toward the door.

'You be quiet now!' he'd whispered ominously, his greasy, acne-scarred face looking pale and scared in the wan light. 'You shush now and give me that knife before I get mad and do something you'll regret!'

'You just try and take it from me,' she'd whispered back, feeling something click within her like a switch being flipped. At once she knew she had him, knew that she could take control if she wanted, could end this all and come out on the other side untouched.

He reached out then, his hands clumsy, slow, and she lashed out with the knife in a crosswise, slashing motion, and at that moment time stood still as he uttered a pained shriek that broke the stillness of the night like a water glass shattering on concrete, and as fat drops of blood dripped onto her bedspread, lights went on in the house.

Terry had backed away from her, his eyes wide, his hands in front of him, warding her off, the blood now dripping thickly on the carpet. When he stepped into the hallway she heard her mother's voice, her accusations, and she thought yes, please mother, please keep him away from me! but his voice rose to meet hers, and between the two there commenced a great clamor. She listened from her room until one of them reached out and slammed her door shut, and after that their words were muted, indistinct. She'd laid there in the dark, tears running down her cheeks, clutching the knife in both hands until long after the sun came up the next morning.

But with the new day there came no justice, no appeals from Terry beseeching that she forgive him, and no compassion from her mother because of the cruelty she'd suffered at his hands. Instead there was only a cold silence from the two of them, an unspoken assurance that this had all been *her* fault.

And there would be no investigation, no police, no social workers in rumpled cardigans holding stuffed dolls asking her to point to the places where her step-daddy had touched her. Nothing save for icy, recriminating glances stolen while she sat at the table doing her homework, their lips pursed in disgust as she sat down for the evening meal. Her own *mother* for Christ's sake, even she blamed her, the stupid fucking bitch. She'd never once accepted any responsibility, nor did she place any on Terry. After a while maybe Melissa began to think she *was* to blame, that poor Terry was the victim of her wily sexual charms. Hell, anything is possible, and the human brain capable of so much self-deception.

So after a while what happened drifted into her subconscious, simply wandered off one day and never came back. She locked it away with all the other terrible memories, things that no little girl should ever have to deal with and, eventually, the key got lost in the turbulent storm of her rapidly dawning adolescence. Time passed, as it has a way of doing, and she moved on, grew-up as it were. And somehow she forgot, just simply…forgot…

"Lousy fucking God," she says now in the dimness, her face wet with tears, the memory so vibrant in her mind it feels as if it happened yesterday. That she'd had the ability to repress something so horrible stuns her, and now, in the gloom of a ship's cabin that very well may become her tomb, she begins to question how much her life would be different had those events never taken place. Who would she be, *where* would she be? Definitely not here, doomed to drown in the middle of the Pacific on an excursion to a goddamn floating trash heap.

"Ahhhh!" she cries out in anguish, her hatred bubbling to the surface, intermingled with a deep sorrow for her lost innocence, gone at such a tender age. "You rotten bastards!"

Gradually her sobs subside and she listens to the screaming of the wind and the spattering of the rain against the porthole. "You were never there for me then God, why should I think you'll be here for me now?"

And she clutches the bed railing even tighter as the ship continues to heave to and fro, the storm pounding and battering it around like some useless piece of trash in the infinite sea.

Prayers are being uttered in many of the cabins, some aloud, some internally. Steven and Perry are now united in a monotone chant of the 'Our Father', their voices growing tremulous whenever the ship takes an extremely sharp dip. One thing they have in common (besides being marine biology majors, besides being stuck on this ship) is that they both grew up Catholic. Perry abandoned his faith when he was fourteen, believing in the god of science and shunning the Catholic's outdated modus operandis while Steven has continued to attend Sunday services, taking comfort in the conviction that there could be something out there, something larger than all of this. It is this belief that has got him   through some tough times in his life, some instances rather minor in the grand scheme of things (like praying to God to help him pass a test), but also some serious tests of faith and strength, occurrences in which he truly felt the Big Guy actually came through for him. And this is why he believes, will always believe.

"Our Father who art in Heaven, hallowed be thy name," they chant in unison as the ship dips and dives, the murk almost total.

Perry, he does this because he figures what the fuck, can't hurt. *Like, ya know, if you aren't busy saving starving kids in Africa maybe you could do something about this storm? Thanks, I appreciate it.*

For Steven, this is what a good Catholic does in the face of an insurmountable situation: they petition their God for any more time He will possibly allow, any at all.

Shortly after being cast into darkness, the security guard's door is flung open and a light disperses the shadows.

"We need you fellows," a crewman says, shining the light into the squinting eyes of Kenny, Cole and Robert. "Follow me."

"Got any flashlights for us?" Kenny asks gruffly, glad to get out of the cabin, glad to be doing something. Sitting in there had become maddening, and listening to Cole whimper and babble like a little girl had brought forth in him a homicidal anger that made his hands itch, made him yearn for a drink to quell this insuperable hostility.

"Gonna just have to see by the light of mine."

"Alright."

Cole, however, doesn't move from where he is crouched, his eyes wide, sniveling.

"I ain't going nowhere," he declares defiantly. "I'm a bad swimmer, and I didn't sign up for this shit!"

"Look, we don't have time for your crap, we need everyone to pitch in."

"What do you need us to do?" Robert asks, ignoring Cole's evident misery, stepping forward on knees that are shaking like leaves in a cold, autumn wind.

"We need you in the engine room. The pumps can't get the water out fast enough so we're forming a chain to bail it out with buckets."

"Shit," Kenny says, realizing the full scope of their problem immediately. "What the fuck're we jawin' for? Let's go!" He turns to Cole. "Get yer sorry ass up an come on. Cryin' like a little pussy ain't gonna help us any."

"Shit man, I didn't want to be here in the first place!"

"Yeah, well ya are so deal with it." He reaches out a hand to the other and, reluctantly, Cole takes it, allowing himself to be hauled to his feet.

"This way," the crewman says and they follow him into the blackness.

Kim's body feels soft and reassuring against her own, and Leeann marvels at how they've gone from being enemies to gal-pals in the space of an hour. Not that this would have happened without the storm, and not that she forgives the other for her obstreperousness, but she certainly is glad she doesn't have to go through this alone, even if it is with the egotistical Asian girl. And who knows, maybe they've turned a corner and this will help them to work together when the time comes (*because we will get out of this, yes, of that I'm certain*) yet she has no illusions that when it's over the two of them are going to be friends. She feels Kim's breath blowing warmly on her cheek, is aware of the slight press of her modest bosom against her own.

"It's okay," she whispers. "It's going to be all right."

"Sure," Kim says, shivering slightly. "We'll be fine."

When the lights went out the two had already been holding hands, despite their shared derision for one another, and this display easily segued into the grasp they are currently engaged in, their fear overcoming them.

I'll be fine, Kim reflects hollowly, bitterly. *I couldn't care less about you.*

What Leeann doesn't know (how could she? they just met) is that Kim is possessed of a singular trait, one she shares with other human oddities (serial killers, sociopaths), and that is her lack of empathy. It is this inability that shapes who she is: a cold, calculating bitch who's every motive, every decision has her own best interests in mind. It hasn't been a burden, this failure, it has actually been a boon, keeping at bay the human element that time and time again wants to slow her down, simply getting in her way with all their problems and melodrama. But that said she does have feelings, well, *yearnings* that tempt her from time to time, and right now she experiences a stirring within herself, an insistence she can't (doesn't want to) ignore.

This hayseed may have all the intellectual clout of a common housefly but she does enjoy the sensation of Leeann's hands stroking her back, and she pulls the other closer, burying her face in the nape of her neck, feeling the soft, downy hairs with her cheeks and chin. She becomes increasingly aware of Leeann's smell, an aroma that reminds her of jasmine and lilac, a sweet, flowery scent that surely must be the girl's shampoo, and its bouquet is intoxicating, arousing a strong desire within her she can't suppress. At once warmth spreads through her, accompanied by a sudden craving to brush her lips against the other, to see how she tastes. She pulls her head back slowly, feeling the others supple skin against her own, then leans in and nuzzles softly on Leeann's neck. The girl tastes sweet, inviting.

"What...what are you doing?" Leeann asks, trying her best to sound aggrieved, but she knows full well what's going on, has, in fact, had similar encounters before. No more than a couple of times, mind you, and no one ever (to the best of her knowledge) found out, but since the start of her illustrious college career she has experimented with a few different things, and this is one of them. But she's not a lesbian, thank you very much. The long periods between episodes (as she likes to consider them) adequately prove it. "I think you should stop."

"Do you really want me to?" Kim says, moving her hands from Leeann's back down to her jean clad rump, caressing her gently. "I don't think you do."

Leeann struggles against her, trying half-heartedly to pull herself away, but the allure of the other's touch is appealing, the prospect of a discreet liaison with this Asian girl at once thrilling, arousing her. Her breath catches in her throat, coming out in short pants as she succumbs to the other's touch, making inquisitive advances of her own.

Time and thought stop as their heads part, then in the dimness their lips find each other's. The kiss is tentative at first, gradually growing in intensity. Their tongues dance together, tasting one another. To Leeann the other's flavor is exotic, smoky. To Kim, Leeann tastes sweet, like vine-ripened fruit.

Kim eases Leeann back on the bed, oblivious to the furious rocking of the ship, her hands finding the buttons of her shirt. Fingers trembling, she touches the warm skin, leaning over and trailing her tongue down from her breasts to the waist of her jeans. Leeann utters a sigh, reaching up blindly and pulling Kim's shirt over her head, tossing it away. She unclasps her bra and reaches up with her mouth, taking one of Kim's small breasts between her lips, her excitement growing as she tongues the other's rock hard nipple, suckling it tenderly.

Kim unzips Leeann's pants and slides her hand in, underneath her panties, and finds a warm, moist, mostly hairless treasure waiting there. She strokes her gently, sticks an experimental finger inside, then removes her hand and puts the finger in her own mouth, then in Leeann's. Leeann tastes herself and then returns to Kim's breast, her hands seeking the other's pants button. Struggling against one another, Kim unfastens the button herself and slips them off, kicking them to the floor. She then tugs Leeann's pants off, removing her panties, and the two young women feel their nakedness pressing warmly against each other. They writhe together, grinding their pelvises, savoring the musky scent of their commingled aroma's as they kiss deeply.

Kim breaks the kiss and trails her lips down Leeann's body, from her breasts to her belly button and beyond, settling between the other's legs, kissing the insides of her thighs gently before moving in toward the center. Her lips probe this delicate flower, her tongue tracing circles around the clitoris.

Leeann releases a low, lustful moan, clutching Kim's head and combing through her short dark hair with her fingers. She pulls her head closer, feeling a spreading heat that blocks out everything, even though the ship is still rocking at crazy angles and the sound of the wind and the rain are reaching a fever point.

It is this milieu that sets the stage for their lovemaking, this din that becomes the crescendo. Kim spins around and Leeann tugs the other's panties down, placing her mouth against the warm succulence, caressing it with her lips and tongue.

They continue on in this fashion until they are both breathing hard, squirming together in an act that takes them both far away from the terror that once consumed them. Sex, the ultimate opiate, the one act that can distance one from fear, pain, certain death…

And then, abruptly, shockingly, unwanted, the lights come back on.

TWENTY-
THREE

Hands groping blindly through the dark, Dr. Taylor steadies himself against the desk as the ship tilts to one side. He'd already been having trouble concentrating on his work when the lights went out, and with its unexpected absence all thoughts of the trash heap were abandoned as his survival became paramount over anything else.

Dr. Taylor spent most of his life as an academic, a scholar. He saw the world through books, articles and research papers. He hadn't spent a lot of time working 'in the field'. His explorations were mostly done in the safety of his office over the Internet and, before that, as a student, in the library. While his peers spent summers digging through archeological ruins in Egypt or collecting raw data from either the depths of the sea or in brutally hot or cold climates, he eschewed such expeditions to ruminate over the studies done by others, creating hypotheses based entirely upon conjecture and other's findings.

Because, truth be told, he didn't necessarily like to travel, what with all of the inherent risks and discomforts. He preferred to sleep in his own bed at night, ideally working within the safety of his beloved institutions. He didn't consider himself a coward so much as a man who hated to be bothered.

That isn't to say he never traveled anywhere for research development, it's just that such trips were seldom. His choice to travel to the trash heap over a decade ago hadn't been made overnight; it was only through careful thought and planning that he eventually deemed it necessary to make a pilgrimage, if only to see it for himself. And, quite frankly, the trip had been a pain in the ass.

Dr. Taylor knew when he volunteered for this expedition he would be inconveniencing himself to an extent that would ultimately make him miserable, but he figured it was a risk he had to take, in the name of science and for the betterment of Humankind. Besides, without him these incompetent nincompoops would be dead in the water (no pun intended surely). Without his tutelage they would be completely lost. But, lo and behold, it's been just over a day and already he's become frustrated with the interns, as well as some of the others aboard the ship. He doesn't like the close quarters or the fact that his privacy is disrupted so often but what's done is done. He simply has to make the best of it.

And now, sitting here in the shadows as the ship rocks and rolls in the crazy swells of an ocean gone haywire, he finds himself regretting the decision. He wishes he was sitting behind his desk in his office, casually reading the Smithsonian Journal of Scientific Findings or, better yet, writing an article for their fine publication as the Washington D.C. sun shone through his window, birds singing innocently in the trees as politicians scurried about like carpenter ants, making a mockery of bipartisan Democracy as we know it.

But there is no time for such nonsense, no call for petty whining. No amount of wishing can undo the choice he's made.

So he holds on for dear life, hoping against hope that the storm will pass or, at the very least, the captain and crew can take back control of the ship.

It is with these last thoughts that, finally, the lights come back on with a flicker and a hum. Heaving a sigh, he wipes away a thin sheen of sweat that's collected on his brow and upper lip and searches the floor for the papers he discarded when everything went belly-up not more than forty minutes ago.

A cheer rings out in the engine room when the lights come back on and damned if Cole's voice isn't one of the loudest of the bunch. Kenny smiles at him, relief as palpable as a slap in the face overcoming him, a release of tension in his shoulders that makes his large frame feel lighter, buoyant. Jesus H. but that had been hairy. For a moment there he can honestly say he joined the Mexican in his certainty that this was the end, that they would surely perish while passing buckets of ice-cold water from hand to hand in the dim recesses of a ship soon to become their grave.

The men halt what they are doing to give each other high-fives, and when Kenny holds out his hand Cole ignores it and embraces him in a sloppy hug, kissing him quickly on the cheek.

"Christ almighty, did the storm turn ya gay?" Kenny complains, but his grin remains in place. And when Robert raises his hand to high-five, Kenny gives him a hug instead, forgoing the kiss on the cheek, of course.

Captain Harvey's struggles with the wheel are finally rewarded when the power comes back on and steering becomes manageable again. Without the power the rudder had been a curmudgeonly beast to manipulate.

"Holy hell," he mutters, swiping an arm across his forehead. Taking a peek at his watch, he observes that barely thirty-five minutes have passed since the power went out. Even for someone as experienced as he, it felt like a goddamn day.

He looks at his navigational equipment and sees that somehow he kept them mostly on course, despite the storms best efforts to derail them. Not entirely, but not as bad as it could have been. And he owes it all to sheer guts and determination because the manual handling of the tiller was hard work, requiring every bit of strength he had.

It's a good thing I had it in me, he reflects, blowing out a shaky breath. *I don't think I can wait much longer.*

He reaches up, flips the switch on the ship's intercom and decides to give the passengers and crew some good news.

'Looks like we made it through the worst of it," the captain's voice crackles through the cabin's tiny speaker and Steven and Perry slap palms. Steven won't say this aloud (not to Perry) but he is convinced that God has once again come through for him in a pinch. He looks to the heavens and silently expresses his gratitude while Perry mentally thanks the skill of the crew and the eventual slackening of the storm.

"The rain is still coming down pretty hard but I think we've passed through the roughest patch of sea we can expect at this time. The Doppler tells me we'll be sailing into clearer skies by late afternoon, so as soon as the water calms down y'all can feel free to exit your cabins and stretch your legs on the main deck. I'll let you know. In the meantime, as soon as I no longer need the cook helping out below deck, I'll have him back in the kitchen and working on some lunch-if any of you are hungry, that is." The captain utters a low chortle.

Hallsly, Tyler and Dante are scowling at the speaker, knowing full well this message doesn't pertain to them. Even after the storm passes they are still stuck where they are, like it or not.

"That rotten son of a bitch can go to hell," Hallsly mutters and for once Tyler agrees with something the governor says.

"Here here," he says, casting an eye toward the bathroom and the mess that has become of it. "Here fucking here."

TWENTY-FOUR

The afternoon brings a welcome respite from the storm and the passengers are finally allowed out of their cabins. The sun shines weakly through the dense clouds, the rain reduced to a fine mist. To the south Dave sees a rainbow, and it is in this moment that he feels an aching, heartfelt joy to be alive. The wind is still gusting, billowing the bottom flap of his jacket, and his muscles are sore from his strenuous contributions to the ship and passenger's safety, but he is wearing dry clothes so at least he is comfortable.

He points out the rainbow to Travis and the other gazes at it silently, in awe. He has never seen such a beautiful thing in all his life, he decides, and he looks to the sky, giving silent thanks to whatever or whoever must have surely been looking out for him. He's never been a spiritual person but at this moment he truly feels the weight of the universe around him, that special relationship human's have communing with nature.

Melissa approaches, fixing her eyes upon the natural wonder created by an optical illusion of light and, gently, she sighs.

"Pretty, ain't it?" Travis says and she nods.

"I guess it's our reward for what we just went through," she replies, smiling a naked, honest smile. "It isn't much but I guess it will have to do, huh?"

Travis smiles back. "Yes ma'am."

"I'm sure you boys saw the worst of it first hand."

"Closer than we woulda liked to."

"Well, good job." She looks wistfully at the roiling water. "At least some of us are earning our keep."

"I'm sorry?" Travis asks but she shakes her head, glancing at him briefly before turning away.

"Nothing."

The two watch her go, and when she is out of sight Dave mumbles:

"Now that the governor's outta the way I probably got a shot at nailin' her."

241

"Yeah," Travis snorts, "in yer fuckin' dreams."

Leeann is standing at the stern, watching the wake as it churns behind the ship. She stares idly at the water, emotions running through her she simply doesn't want to confront, mixed feelings that demand answers she doesn't have. Gripping the rail tightly, she closes her eyes and lets the motion of the ship take her away for a moment, outside of her head and into the gray/blue strata. Her face tilted up into the light mist, she hears footsteps approaching, then the touch of a hand on her shoulder. She tries not to flinch but does anyway, an almost imperceptible shudder. Turning her head slowly, she sees it's who she expected it would be.

"Hey, it's me," Kim says, and Leeann feels a wave of guilt ripple through her. After what they did in the cabin she is at a loss for words. When the lights came on she'd frozen in place, Kim's privates nestled snuggly against her lips, the heady scent of her juices dripping from her chin. Under the harsh fluorescents what they were doing seemed wrong, seemed so *dirty*. Under the cover of darkness it had been okay, and maybe it was because she was afraid they were going to die, that the touch of another person, even a member of the same sex, was comforting to her. But once the crisis was over, well, it was time to let it go, to act as if it never happened. That's how Leeann had dealt with it in the past: she'd basically pretended it hadn't taken place. As much as she was a willing participant she simply couldn't live with herself after the fact, no matter who the other girl was or what the circumstances had been. The two girls she'd experimented with in college happened as a result of alcohol overindulgence, and the aftermath had been ugly, to say the least. She'd spent weeks screening her calls and scurrying to and from classes, one eye always looking over her shoulder. Eventually they left her alone, but one girl, the second, had cornered her at a party three months later, glaring at her balefully.

'I thought we shared something special,' she'd accused.

'Excuse me?'

'So it's like that, huh?'

'Like what?'

'You used me.'

'I don't know what you are talking about.'

And she'd fled, the girl, the conversation, the party, everything. And she swore it would never happen again, never. And she thought that was true. Until now.

She looks at Kim silently, wishing she would leave her alone. When the ship had suddenly come back to life she'd pushed her away and quickly put on her clothes, keeping her back turned. She couldn't stand to look at the other's naked body as it all but screamed out her guilt. And Kim said nothing, her silence all the recrimination she needed to compound her shame. How did she feel about it? Leeann had wondered, but didn't want to pursue a conversation to find out. As soon as they were allowed to leave the cabin she hurried out without a word.

"You keep your mouth shut about what we did," Kim says. "And stay in your own bunk for the rest of the trip, got it? No more playing footsy."

"You stay in your bunk," Leeann hisses through clenched teeth. "I'm not a lesbian."

"Neither am I."

The Asian girl's denial stirs something within her, a feeling of anger derived from the perceived insinuation that this is her fault. Kim appears cool, detached, and in her manner Leeann can't help but feel an accusation is being made concerning her character. She'll be damned if the guilt is going to rest solely on her shoulders. "Than what was that?"

Kim shrugs. "I don't know and I really don't care. Just don't expect it to happen again, honey. And like I said, keep it to yourself. I don't need something like this getting around."

"*You* don't need something like this…" Leeann sputters, incensed. "*You* took advantage of me!"

"What?" Kim gapes disbelievingly. Even though she has the ability to walk away from this as if it never occurred, to forget all about this mousy little hick and the intimacy they shared during the storm, the simple idea that she seduced the other and took her against her will is infuriating. "I didn't hear you saying 'no' you little slut!"

"I didn't have to. You should have been able to tell by my body language."

"According to your body language," Kim leers, "You were saying 'eat my wet pussy Kim', at least, that's what I heard."

"I think you need to leave."

"I don't see a sign with your name on it. Why don't you leave?"

"Please, just go."

"I think I'll stay right here. I like the view."

"Get away from me you bitch!" Leeann bawls unexpectedly, swiveling around and shoving the other with both hands. Kim cries out in surprise, stumbling and falling onto the slick deck. A moment of thick silence ensues before she looks up in astonishment, an expression of anger clouding her face.

"You stupid whore! You didn't have to push me!"

Leeann glances about her quickly, hoping no one saw what just happened. Looking across the deck and upward she sees two members of the crew watching from the balcony of the bridge (*are those two assholes smiling?*), and it is because of this that she fails to see Kim get to her feet, wiping her mouth with the back of one hand.

"You never should have messed with me, honey," Kim says, lunging toward her, tackling Leeann around the waist and slamming her onto the steel deck. A constellation of stars explodes behind Leeann's closed eyelids on impact and her breath whooshes out from her. Kim quickly straddles her chest, pinning her arms with her legs.

"Say you're sorry."

"Get off of me!"

Kim slaps her across the face, hard.

"Ow! That hurt! What the hell are you doing?"

"Say you're sorry that you accused me of seducing you," Kim says calmly. She isn't even breathing hard. "Admit you're a lezzy and you love munching rug."

"Get off of me!" Leeann wails and Kim slaps her again.

"Now this," Kim says with a smile, "is taking advantage of you."

"What the hell is going on down there?" Captain Harvey says, hearing the cries coming from the deck. Two of his men are standing on the balcony, gawking like a couple of kids on the playground.

"It looks like we got ourselves a good old-fashioned cat fight sir," one of them says and the captain glowers.

"Well don't just stand there with your peckers in your hands, do something about it before someone gets hurt!"

"Yes sir!"

The men scramble from the bridge, the captain watching them retreat with a weary expression of irritation.

"If it isn't one goddamn thing it's another," he mutters, returning his attention to the sea.

Dave and Travis are the first on the scene. Approaching on either side of her, they grab Kim under her arms and tug her off of Leeann. Kim allows herself to be removed, offering no resistance.

Leeann rubs her cheeks and gets slowly to her feet.

"What's goin' on here?" Travis asks but the two women are silent. The white girl glares at the Asian girl, who says nothing, just sneers. Then Kim raises a hand, all of her fingers tucked in except for one, the universal sign of peace and love.

"Sit and spin bitch," she says before turning and walking away.

The two members of the crew finally arrive, looking on ineffectually. Leeann straightens her shirt and darts quickly the other way.

"What was that all about?" one of them asks and Dave shrugs.

"I think we just witnessed a lover's spat."

"Oh man," one of the crewmen says, smiling lasciviously. "How hot is that?"

Leeann's face is flushed, the hot sting of tears doubling her vision. She dashes to the other side of the ship, knowing full well the cabin is now 'no man's land' as far as she is concerned. She has no idea where she can go, to whom she can turn, but at the moment all she wants to do is hide. The humiliation she feels at what Kim just did to her is almost worse than the shame she's suffering because of their sex act. She chastises herself mentally, scolds the weakness inside her that commanded her to commit such an atrocious deed.

You are so stupid! Stupid! How could you have allowed that to happen? And we have the entire trip before us! This will be hanging over your head the whole time!

She stumbles over by the life rafts, two moderately sized boats covered with large, silver tarps, and leans heavily against one of them, sobbing. Her chest heaves and she feels feverish, her whole world shattered by one foolish, impetuous act when suddenly, unwittingly, Dante's image comes to mind, his bewhiskered face, thick glasses, massive belly and robust, overly moist lips. In her mind's eye he is smiling, his mouth pursing slightly as if he is nervous, and damned if she doesn't feel a mild sense of relief that she actually knows somebody onboard. Yet this thought offers her only the slightest reprieve, and she swipes angrily at her face with her fists, shaking her head from side to side.

I don't really know *him. It's just that I know him better than anyone here.*

But that's something, isn't it? In the grand expanse of human existence and human kindness isn't it better to know someone (albeit only vaguely) than to not know anyone at all? Everyone aboard this ship is a stranger and she hasn't really connected with any of them. Dante is the only one here that she's actually spent a significant amount of time with.

Her girlfriend Stacy's smiling face comes to mind, and at once she strongly desires the company of a trusted companion, someone she can *really* talk to. Somebody she can confide in, who will make her feel better about herself, about what she has done. But, then again, could she tell Stacy about a sexual encounter with another girl or would Stacy maybe shun her for such a transgression? Possibly be afraid that Leeann is indeed a lesbian and their friendship has been a lie, a sham, and at some point Leeann will want her for the same purpose? She desperately wants to believe her friend wouldn't be so shallow, but inside she honestly doesn't know. She'd never shared with her the other experiences for just that reason.

Scrubbing tears from her eyes with the heels of her hands, she realizes that only a man can look upon such an act in an unbiased manner, can view it from a distance and possibly yield sympathy. Dante could be that man, if she wanted, that lame-brain son of a bitch…

She giggles, the outburst taking her by surprise. And she reacted so horribly to his presence, treated him as if he were a contagion that needed to be quarantined. The look on his face when she told him to get away from her was almost comical in its sorrow, and at the time it had made her even madder. How cruel is that? Is she really so insensitive that she can treat another person unfairly merely because they harbor deep feelings for her? Well, apparently so.

At this she feels remorse for poor Dante, all alone just like her. He followed her here, risking his ass sneaking onboard, and she acted as if he was a misbehaving puppy who got out of the gate and followed her to school, making a mess of everything. He didn't deserve that, the big goofball; his heart was certainly in the right place. A tidal swell of compassion arises within her, and it makes her feel better, relieves her of some of the humiliation she's presently wallowing in. She should really talk to him as soon as she can, let him know she isn't mad anymore.

Yet, still, she doesn't want to give him the wrong impression, that she is attracted to him sexually, because it wouldn't be fair to him. But they could be friends, couldn't they? She's certain it would please Dante to at least have a confidant aboard the ship, someone he can talk to as well. And if not, it's a place to start, to possibly get their selves back on track and, also, to maybe get Dante out of any trouble he is in. Even if he didn't want to be friends she is sure he'd be glad to get out of the doghouse she'd advertently placed him in. And there is only one person who can make this happen. Wiping her hands clean on the lifeboat's tarp, she decides it's high time she went and spoke with the captain once again.

TWENTY-FIVE

"Are you telling me that you believe in the existence of a God simply because you prayed and the storm broke?" Perry asks Steven skeptically as they stand by the ship's rail, watching the sun sink on the horizon.

"It's not that cut and dried but, yeah, I guess so."

Perry shrugs. "Whatever floats your boat..."

"No pun intended?"

"None."

The two share a laugh as the heavens above turn a bright crimson/orangish color, the hues startlingly beautiful against the pale blue sky, littered with only the faintest traces of clouds that merely an hour ago were an ugly, bruised black.

"And what about this?" Steven gestures toward the sunset. "Surely this is also ample proof of the existence of some divine maker, an otherworldly presence who's seen fit to gift us with something so stunning."

"Dude," Perry says, waving his index finger at the other. "I believe in the god of science. You can't pass off reflected light as a 'miracle' to me."

"Thought I'd give it a try."

"Hello boys," someone says, and they turn and see it is Dr. Taylor. "Enjoy the storm?"

"Just glad it's over," Perry says, and Dr. Taylor notes a distinct lack of sarcasm in the boys voice, notices he is carrying himself much differently than he was during the meeting yesterday. Could it be the storm was just what he needed to put his ego in check? If so, score one for the storm.

"How about you," he asks Steven. "You all right?"

"I might have crapped my pants a little, but otherwise I'm fine."

Dr. Taylor laughs. "Yeah, you're not the only one." He looks to the sky, appraising the dying sun as it nears the water. Looking at it, you'd never guess they just sailed through a veritable typhoon.

"We have a lot of work to do tomorrow," he continues after a moment, "and the more focused we are on carrying it out, the more efficient we'll be."

"Yes sir," the two say in harmony.

"Have either of you seen Kim or Leeann? We need to go over some information so I can assign duties."

Steven and Perry glance at one another briefly, exchanging a look that puzzles the doctor.

"What's the matter?"

"Well," Steven starts, "I think the two are going to have a little trouble working together."

"What gives you that idea?"

"Something happened during the storm," Perry explains. "I don't know what it was, but they're totally pissed off at each other. They got in a fight."

"A shouting match?" Dr. Taylor has been in his cabin. He hasn't heard a thing.

"No," Steven says. "A *fight* fight. Two of the Navy guys had to pull Kim off of Leeann."

"You've got to be kidding me."

"That's what we saw."

"Great. Any idea where they are now?"

"Leeann stalked off toward the front of the ship and Kim disappeared below deck."

"Fuck," Dr. Taylor says, his course language surprising the two young men. "That's the last thing we need right now." He runs a hand over his face, looking troubled. "We need to find them. You," he addresses Perry, "check below deck. And you," he nods at Steven, "check around up here. When you find them please inform them we have work to do. Got it?"

"Sure," replies Steven. "Where should we all meet?"

"Right here," Dr. Taylor sighs. "I'll be waiting."

"What does she want?"

"I don't know captain, she just said she wanted to talk to you," Jake Anderson says, looking at the other expectantly.

"I'm very busy right now," Captain Harvey replies gruffly, barely glancing up from the charts he's studying.

"She says it's important."

"It always is," he says, taking off his reading glasses and tossing them on the table. "Send her in."

Leeann enters the bridge, shuffling her feet slowly, a furtive look on her pale, freckled face.

"All tuckered out from the fight, I imagine?" he jests and she scowls.

"I would say I'm sorry but Kim started it," Leeann replies and Captain Harvey shrugs his massive shoulders.

"I'm sure," he says matter-of-factly, "she would say the same thing."

"Maybe."

He looks at her keenly, waiting for her to proceed. After a minute of silence he clears his throat, puts on his glasses and resumes studying the nautical chart.

"What can I do for you?" he asks at length.

"I wanted to talk to you about something."

"As the grass said to the cow: 'no shit'."

"It's about Dante."

He looks up in exasperation. "For the love of Pete what the hell are you worried about now?" he growls and for a second Leeann is speechless. She'd already felt awkward about coming to him, but now she feels downright silly. Her cheeks rapidly suffuse with blood, but she decides she will have her say. She's come this far.

"I think I got a little carried away, you know, with all those things I said." She shoots a quick peek at him before looking away, continuing: "And in wanting him out of my sight."

Captain Harvey eyes Leeann speculatively, wondering what's gotten into her. First she can't get rid of the bastard fast enough and now she wants him out? Jesus H. Christ this bitch doesn't know if she's coming or going.

"Is that so?" he says. "I hope you understand that this teeter totter you're playing on has a lot of important things he has to do."

"Yes sir."

"Only a day ago it wouldn't do that Dante be allowed to mingle amongst the general population, for fear he would disrupt you and negatively influence your job performance."

"Yes sir, I am aware of that," she replies, gathering her courage. "That's why I decided to come here and tell you I was wrong."

Captain Harvey lets out a loud exhalation, then lifts his arm and waves her over. She looks at him questioningly.

"Come here," he says. "I want to show you something."

Something in his gaze gives her pause, a look she hasn't seen there before. His eyes are dark (*probably a trick of the light*), his pupils incredibly large. Creeping tendrils of fear unspool within her, a seemingly irrational, nameless dread that bursts within her belly and wriggles up her throat, but his manner is forceful, demanding, and she finds herself walking toward him. When she is by his side he reaches an arm around her shoulders, turning her so that she is looking at the papers spread out before him.

"Look there," he commands and she does so.

"What is it?"

"I guess you haven't been trained to read navigational charts, have you?"

"No sir," she admits.

"Well," he says, not too unkindly. "I want to show you why you are currently wasting my time." He points at some markings on the chart, moving his finger from one spot to another. "This," he indicates, "is where we are heading. See the latitudinal and longitudinal markings?"

"Yes…"

"Very good. Now this," he shows her, moving his finger lower "is where we are currently. Do you know why this is a problem?"

Her shoulders feel twitchy and uncomfortable where his arm rests. "No," she whispers.

"I didn't think so." His voice is getting louder, his grasp on her tightening. "The storm knocked us off course and we are currently playing catch up. But that's not the only problem." He turns his head toward her and now his eyes are entirely black. The whites, the corneas…gone, eclipsed by his pupils. She quickly looks away.

"Oh?" she gulps and he utters a sound she supposes might be a laugh, albeit a deranged, unearthly one.

"Oh? Oh? How eloquently put my dear!"

She squirms, trying to wiggle away from him but his fingers grip her firmly, digging into her shoulder.

"Not to give *you* a science lesson, but the current in the gyre is extremely sluggish. It is for this reason that very few people travel this way, why they go around it if they can."

She swallows thickly, her dread turning into outright terror, a warning that clangs in her head like a doomsday siren, but she nods, if only to appease him.

"O-o-okay…"

"Because the storm knocked us off course we are now approaching the trash heap from a different direction, one in which we are fighting directly against the current." He studies her carefully but she's staring at the floor, an expression of consternation marring her pretty features.

"Do you know what that means?"

"No sir," she says meekly, almost inaudibly.

"What?" he barks.

"No sir!"

"It means we have to work twice as hard to stay on schedule, and interruptions like yours are a waste of my time! I have important preparations to make and what I don't need is some whiny little bitch bothering me every five seconds! Do you understand me?"

"Yes sir," she replies, striving to keep her voice calm, steady, and against her better judgment she lifts her gaze to meet his and what she sees nearly takes her breath away. His eyes are so black, glossy, almost bottomless…as she stares into their liquid depths she catches a glimpse of her reflection there, but the image is distorted, more akin to a bad caricature or something out of an evil Grimm fairytale. As she focuses on it, it metamorphoses, and the figure that stares back at her is horrendously emaciated, cheeks sunken in, arms as skinny as broomsticks. And there are things crawling in her thinning hair; large, spiny, many-legged creatures awash in slime, bloated as blood-gorged ticks, and when she opens her mouth in shock she sees her teeth are black and rotten, what's left of them that is, and writhing and squirming amongst these derelict porcelains are plump little maggots, swimming greedily in her rancid saliva…

"All right then," he says at last, letting her go, and the spell is broken. She takes a staggering step away from him, then another. He looks normal again; his eyes are a watery slate gray, the pupil's mere pinpoints dotting the center. "Anderson!"

"Yes sir!" his first mate calls.

"Go down below and let Dante out of the pokey." He turns back to Leeann, gives her a lecherous look. "And tell him his girlfriend wants to talk to him."

"I...I'm not his girlfriend..."

"Oh, so sorry." He smiles but there is very little humor in it, and again he changes before her eyes, so quickly the transformation is imperceptible. "She's *not* his girlfriend." His voice is suddenly deeper, and in his words she can hear the flap of leathery wings, the creaking of rusty hinges, the screaming of small animals crying out in pain as brutal hands crush the life out of them: "Tell him his cum dumpster is waiting for him."

When the handle of the door rattles, Governor Hallsly is up like a shot.

"It's about damn time!" he says, moving quickly to the door. "You guys are going to be very sorry for treating me like this, mark my words!"

Jake Anderson pokes his head inside the door.

"Sorry governor, I'm not here for you." He looks around, spots Dante standing by the porthole, looking out into the darkening sky. Stars are coming out, pale against the midnight blue. "I'm here for Dante Kellerman."

Dante's head swivels around on his huge neck, an expression of fright plastered on his ugly mug.

"What is it?" he asks, his eyes darting back and forth between the first mate and the governor.

"I've come to release you," Jake says, smiling.

"What?"

"Come with me, there is someone who wants to talk to you." Jake gestures with his hand, waving him forward.

"The captain?" he queries uncertainly, wondering what kind of trouble he is in now.

"No," Jake answers, "somebody much prettier than the captain."

"Who?"

"Just get out here, huh? I don't like the way the governor is looking at me."

"I swear to God I am going to have your ass for breakfast," the governor promises as Dante creeps past him, toward the open door.

"You betcha," Jake nods as Dante slips out. "And you can have that with a side of balls too, if you like." He offers the governor a tight salute. "Goodnight, sir," he says curtly before closing and locking the door.

"You fucking asshole!" Hallsly roars, awakening Tyler, who was asleep on the top bunk.

"Is the storm over?" he asks, yawning expansively, and Hallsly frowns at him.

"Not for us it isn't buddy, trust me." He stares hard at the locked door. "Not...for...us."

TWENTY-SIX

"Man, I thought we were goners there for a while," Cole says, stuffing a whole muffin into his mouth and chewing noisily.

"Like I din't notice," Kenny replies, watching the other with a disgusted expression on his face. "Chew with yer mouth closed for Christ's sake."

"I'm hungry man, I can't help it."

The two are sitting in the mess hall, enjoying a light dinner they've unquestionably earned after helping the crew bail out the engine room. They've also changed into dry clothes. Cole is wearing a t-shirt bearing the San Diego Chargers logo accompanied by a ridiculous pair of Bermuda shorts and sandals. Kenny gave him flack about it but Cole was unfazed:

"I only brought along one 'formal' outfit, man. This is all I have."

"Ya call Dockers an a flannel shirt 'formal'?" Kenny had said, amused. "Besides, whatcha saving the 'formal' wear for, the big dance?"

"We're havin' a dance?" Cole had asked, bug-eyed.

Kenny is wearing a set of clothes eerily similar to those he wore previously. The way he sees it, it keeps things simple. Same colored shirts, same colored pants. That way you don't have to pick out your clothes each day; you just wear the next thing in the closet or, in this case, the suitcase. He learned this trick from the scientist in the old remake of 'The Fly', who in turn claimed he learned it from Albert Einstein. Great minds think alike, he supposes.

"Ya act as if yer starvin' ta death."

"All that worrying gave me an appetite." Cole blows on his coffee. "What about you? All you're doing is picking at your sandwich."

"I guess I ain't very hungry."

Kenny figures he could explain that after what they've just been through his nerves are shot, and what he really needs is a whiskey and water, but what's the point? Wouldn't help anything, and it would bring his problem to light. Cole would probably want to talk about it, maybe offer him some advice, and what he doesn't need is Cole's input.

"These muffins are awesome man, but I guess anything would taste great right now, huh? After having been so close to the end and all. My mom used to make these totally bitchin' muffins when I was a kid. Blueberry, raspberry, apple, raisin…all these really choice muffins man, it was so cool- "

"Can't ya keep it zipped for two fuckin' minutes? Jesus, yer worse than a chick!" Kenny snaps, and instantly feels bad about it. It isn't the other's fault that he's greatly in need of something to dull the pain.

"Sorry for livin' dude!" Cole says, hurt, and Kenny offers an apologetic smile.

"Hey, my bad. I guess the storm shook me up more'an I'm willin' ta admit."

Cole nods eagerly, his reaction as automatic as a dog's wagging tail.

"It's okay man, I'll chill out."

"Ya don't hafta," Kenny sighs. "So, those muffins… pertty good huh?"

"The best!" Cole stuffs another one in his mouth. "Not as good as my mom's but, ya know…"

"I can't believe they let that bastard go!" the governor fumes. He's sitting on the bottom bunk, rubbing his hands on his pants, which are getting grimy from his sweaty palms. First they take his booze, then they take away his entertainment, and to add insult to injury they lock him up to boot.

Of course, the ultimate slap in the face is letting Sasquatch go. That fuckstick isn't even supposed to be aboard the ship!

"I'm the governor of California for Christ's sake!" he exclaims, smacking the bed frame above him. "How do you like them apples?"

But Tyler doesn't reply; he went back to sleep after he found out there was nothing of interest going on. Not that it matters. The dumb ass wouldn't have anything intelligent to add anyway. As stupid as that guy is, he probably can't wipe his own ass without two hands, a flashlight and an engraved invitation.

He puts his face in his hands and moans softly. Could this get any more screwed up? How is it going to look when the president finds out, if he hasn't already?

He gets up and looks out the porthole, but he can't see anything save for the ship's lights because of the inky darkness outside. Tomorrow they are supposed to arrive at the trash heap, so maybe they'll let him out of this cabin. It would be the very least they could do.

Hallsley's stomach rumbles and he realizes he hasn't had anything to eat since breakfast. What the hell is going on here? They trying to starve him?

"Man, I could really go for a Twinkie right about now," he mumbles, but his words go unanswered, his request unheeded. "That and a bottle of aged scotch."

Dante breathes deep of the cool, briny night air. After being locked in that cabin all day he would probably welcome the scent of dead, rotting fish...anything but the latrine stench of vomit and shit. Eventually he'd adjusted to the smell of the puke, and that was when that dipshit Tyler decided to empty his bowels, proving that some odors are definitely worse than others.

Clutching the railing, he looks out at the dark sea, reflecting on all he has been through in the last couple of days. According to what the first mate said he'd half expected Leeann to be waiting for him when they let him out, maybe to say she's sorry, but she was nowhere to be seen. Figures.

He has an out of body experience for a moment, one in which he is looking at himself from high above, watching as he goes through the motions of his life. He can't believe he is here, that he actually went above and beyond his normal routine, stepping outside his comfort zone for the first time in as long as he can remember. The first thing he'd done when he made this decision was to call his pizza delivery job, informing them he needed to take some time off for himself. Given that he was their most reliable (and long-term) employee they said yes without asking any questions. He then packed a small bag and went down to the Script's dock, not quite sure what he was going to do until he actually did it. Definitely not his usual fare. His typical life consisted of nothing but tried and true activities that led him to their standard conclusions, but this time he went against the grain and climbed out on a limb, all in the name of Love.

But is it really love? Or is it an obsession with Leeann that he refuses to let go of? Since he's been in love so seldom in his life he has no idea, no basis for comparison. Maybe he never *has* been in love; perhaps he's simply been stalking all of the women who've eluded him the whole of his teen and adult life.

Lifting his face into the gentle breeze, he inhales deeply and holds it for a count of thirty seconds before letting it go, feeling cleansed, renewed. He ponders how the rest of the human race does it, how they manage to battle the odds and find someone right for them, a person who will love them unconditionally. It seems to him that his every crush, his every romantic notion has always been greeted with indifference, as if he is somehow unlovable. He pictures the faces of all the women he's met throughout his life, envisions the frightened look they always got in their eyes when he broached the subject, watching the friendship he'd built with them slowly (or quickly) dissolve in a torrential rain of embittered acrimony.

And it makes him angry, this less than stellar response to his own intimate yearnings, and he finds that he momentarily hates the opposite sex, hates them for how miserable they've constantly made him feel. Like he is less than a person, unworthy of their affection. Because he'll be damned if he thinks that of himself, hell no. In fact it is in his opinion he would do right by any woman he chose. She would never have to worry about his love growing cold after a few years. Of him being unfaithful. He is like a dog: loyal to a fault. Why can't anyone see that?

"Dante?" a soft voice says, startling him. He turns quickly, sees it's Leeann.

"Hey," he says simply, turning back to the water.

"What are you doing?" she asks and a long moment passes before he shrugs apathetically. He isn't going to let her off the hook that easily, he decides.

"Collecting my thoughts," he says at last, his voice barely above a whisper. "And getting the smell of that stifling cabin out of my nose."

She steps up beside him at the rail, taking hold of the cold steel and gazing out at an ocean she can hear better than she can see.

"You want some company?" Her voice is reticent, her manner self-effacing.

"You think you can stand to be around me? I don't want to make you uncomfortable."

She sighs, closing her eyes and lifting her face into the oncoming wind. She knows she has mistreated Dante, has acted as if he were less than a man, but she wants him to know why, in fact really hopes he will hear her out.

"I feel really bad about getting you in trouble," she says, not looking at him. His hard-boiled egg eyes are a distraction, so she addresses the sea.

"I'm just lucky the captain didn't decide to set me adrift," he retorts, but he doesn't sound cross. In fact he sounds resigned. "He threatened to do that to me, you know."

"You shouldn't have followed me here," she says, getting it out. With that said she turns to face him, and as she expected his expression is somber.

"I know I shouldn't have, but I couldn't help it," he starts, wanting to spill it all, to tell her of the compulsion that came over him when he saw the ad, but something inside stops him short. She doesn't care, how could she? To her he is nothing but a problem that has to be dealt with so she can get on with her life. Maybe this is her way of relieving herself of some guilt.

"It's kind of touching, actually," she says and this takes him by surprise. He studies her eyes, searching them guardedly.

"Touching how?"

Touching in a creepy sort of way, she thinks, but then amends the thought quickly: *No, his behavior isn't stalkerish, it is more like a love sick little child who simply can't take 'no' for an answer.*

"I guess because of what you went through to get here, to be on this ship."

"I really hate water," he confesses and the two of them share a laugh.

"Well," she says, "That must have taken a lot of guts to overcome."

"Oh, and I got 'em." He rubs his generous belly and again they laugh. When it subsides he examines her closely, wonders how candid he can be. He'd hate to ruin this 'moment', but it would make him feel a whole lot better if he could just share his feelings, to try and make her understand him a little more.

"I'm not trying to frighten you or put you off," he ventures, looking away, his eyes wandering along the surface of the dark water. "I knew I was taking a huge chance sneaking on this boat. I didn't really expect you to be overjoyed about it."

"I was that obvious?"

"Look, I told you before and I meant it: you aren't the first girl I've ever scared off, trust me. After a while I became all too familiar with the signs. With you I got the idea it wasn't going to happen when you didn't return my calls, but there was no way I wasn't at least going to give it a shot." His big eyes are moist, earnest. "I wanted to know beyond a shadow of a doubt that you weren't interested in me and then, and only then was I going to let it go. When you told me you were leaving you made it sound as if we had a chance together." He looks away again, embarrassed. "I came here because I wanted to know if that was true. If I realized you were using this trip as an excuse to get away from me than I was simply going to give up, was going to crawl back to San Diego and carry on with my life."

"Did you come out here planning to stow away on the ship?"

"Hell no!" he exclaims, and then laughs nervously. "I just wanted to see you before you left, but when I saw you on the dock I lost my nerve because you were in a group with the other interns. I didn't want to make a spectacle of myself in front of a bunch of strangers."

"But didn't that happen anyway?" she asks, smiling, and he grins as well.

"I suppose I didn't think the whole thing through too carefully."

"Maybe not," she agrees and the two of them lapse into silence. They can hear voices coming from the bridge, the captain and his first mate probably. The breeze is acting as a sound conductor, taking people's words and ushering them from one side of the ship to the other, but they are garbled, indistinct. Not that Leeann cares about what is being said; following her interaction with the captain she never wants to be alone with him again. She isn't certain what happened, all she knows is that the man is totally unhinged, probably dangerous. In fact, the incident leaves her desiring Dante's company even more so.

A few minutes slip by as they stand together in silence, listening to the water sloshing against the side of the ship. Dante has so much more he wants to say but he feels tongue-tied, hopeless. He wishes she could appreciate how truly awful his life has been thus far, how her radiant smile is like a dazzling beacon, driving away the darkness. In a world bleached of all color, a sepia-toned monotony where a silver lining looks gray at best, she's the one person who makes him want to crawl back from the edge, even when his mind is telling him to jump. But, unable to express himself, he stands there mutely, fidgeting, struggling to articulate a feeling he simply can't put into words.

"I hope you don't hate me," he finally says, the best he can manage, and that's okay because it works for her.

"Dante, I don't hate you, I never did," she replies, and she sounds sincere.

"Well, I didn't come here to be a burden."

"I understand now why you came here, and you are not a burden, trust me." She surprises him by reaching out and placing her hand over his on the railing. "Don't get the wrong idea," she says quickly, "but I would like to be your friend."

"I'd like to be your friend too," he gushes, his words rushing over themselves, tumbling out. "You don't have to worry about me trying to mack on you, I am very much a gentleman-"

"I know." She tightens her grip on his hand. "The one thing I did know about you right away was that you knew how to treat a lady."

"Even if I have little to no experience?" he quips and she chuckles.

"Even so," she concurs. "But I doubt that you lack the experience. I am sure you have been a very polite man all of your life." She catches his gaze and holds it. "And I am sure that someday you will find a woman who will appreciate you for who you are. I really do. I am a firm believer that there is someone for everyone out there, they just have to find them."

"So are you saying it can never be you?" he asks but she sees he is making light of it, he isn't putting her on the spot.

"Never is an awfully final word," she says, her voice airy, a smile dancing upon her lips. "I'd like to shy away from the word 'never', but for now I could really use a friend, a good friend and nothing more."

She'd probably feel different if I was better looking, he considers bitterly, but then tosses the thought aside. Fuck it. *I am who I am, and there is nothing I can do about it. Take it or leave it. Looks aren't everything.*

"I could really use a good friend too," he says and the two of them share a smile that takes them beyond words. Their hands still linked together, they stare off into the night, listening to the hum of the ship as the gentle wind ruffles their hair, simply enjoying a quiet moment as the boat cuts through the cold, deep water, taking them ever closer to their destiny.

TWENTY-SEVEN

Captain Harvey leans back in his chair, a strong magnetism growing within him the closer they get to their destination. He notices stirrings inside his body, nerve endings that lay dormant awakening and crying out for release, for sustenance. And feed himself he shall, oh yes. All will be right once they arrive at the trash heap, and that which is alive in him shall be liberated, set free to claim what by all rights is his. Nothing can get in his way now, nothing.

He pours himself an inch of scotch and sips it slowly, his eyes glazing over as he stares blankly, letting his mind wander. He rubs his chest and coughs powerfully into his fist, wiping what he expectorates on his pants. Flicking a switch on the intercom, he picks up the microphone.

"This is the captain," he says, waiting for his first mate's reply.

"Aye aye cap," Jake replies. "What can I do ya for?"

"Are we holding steady?"

"Steady as she goes, sir."

"Have you made contact with the proper authorities?"

"Yes sir. I've given them a full report."

"Very good." He takes another sip of his drink. "Is there any news?"

"No sir."

"Good," Captain Harvey says, setting the glass down. "Let the men know they did an excellent job today."

"Aye aye sir."

He flicks another switch on the intercom, activating the speakers on the main deck, the mess hall and the cabins. Best to address the passengers before they get any closer, before the changes in him become more advanced. No sense in letting the cat out of the bag when they are this close to achieving all that must be done. It is for their own good.

"This is the captain," he says evenly, choosing his words carefully. "Our mission is still on track, despite the storm. Our Doppler shows clear skies, but rest assured the crew and I shall remain vigilant should foul weather return and we run into any unexpected rough water. So, with that in mind, try and get some rest. We'll arrive at the trash heap tomorrow as planned, only a few hours after we'd initially anticipated." He puts a hand to his mouth, suppressing a cough, swallowing hard several times. "We lost a member of the Navy today, a young lieutenant who valiantly gave his life to ensure our safety. We honor his sacrifice and offer a sailor's blessing upon his soul." The captain grimaces, rubbing his chest with increased agitation. "I want to thank all of you for your cooperation so far and wish you a restful night's sleep. That will be all. Good night."

He switches off the intercom and finishes his drink, letting the liquor roll around in his mouth before swallowing. It hits his gut hot and fiery, just the way he likes it, and it dulls the cough that is growing more pronounced the closer they get. He pours another, knowing it will take several drinks for him to get any rest tonight, but that isn't important, as he has work to do. Tomorrow is the beginning of a new life, for him as well as the others, and he needs to make certain that his crew is onboard with the operation. They may not like it at first, but they will learn to love it, just as he has. Oh, it was a struggle in the beginning, the hardship was almost unbearable, but he endured it and survived. Not all of them will…survive, that is, but those who do will be grateful in the end, of that he is quite sure.

Tomorrow is the first day of the rest of your lives. Sleep well, while you can.

TWENTY-EIGHT

The stench is unbelievable, hardly bearable. It rolls across the deck of the ship, permeating every corner, nook and cranny. It is like a living thing, this foul odor. It's as if the very bowels of the earth have opened and millions of year's worth of well-preserved excrement has surfaced, saturating everything with its fetid presence.

The passengers are gasping, gagging, hands over their noses and mouths, wiping tears from their eyes.

Dr. Taylor has his interns assembled despite his failed attempts at finding the Hazmat suits. He's searched everywhere and made inquiries of the crew but there is no trace of them. As they stand on the deck their notes and instructions are forgotten in the wake of this assault on their nasal passages. Through blurry vision they can hardly see the trash heap, can barely make out anything except for a vague outline. But what they can see is horrendous, terrifying.

Down below, Governor Hallsly blames Tyler for shitting the bed, only to realize the stink is more concentrated than one human being could possibly produce. He looks out the porthole and what he sees defies his imagination, defies all reasoning.

In a cabin nearby, Melissa throws up into her cupped hands, and then stares at the puke with an odd sense of fascination.

Did I just do that? she wonders absently, contemplating what she is going to do with it.

Back up top, Dave and Travis have their jackets pulled over their noses, doing their best to stand guard without doubling over, struggling to hold on to the breakfast they ate only a few hours ago. Like the interns, their vision is compromised because of their tear-distorted eyes. Dave swallows and damned if he can't taste the smell; it is the single worst taste he has ever encountered in his life. Nothing he's ever put in his mouth even comes close to matching the utterly atrocious nature of this foul flavored effluvium.

On the bridge, several crewmen gape at the sight before them, truly aware for the first time what they've signed on for. The heap is sprawling, colossal, absolutely astonishing. It towers before them, shimmering in the heat of the day, it's presence an affront to man and beast, to the very planet itself. It is a testament to mankind's existence, verification that they truly don't know what they're doing and how badly they are fucking everything up.

Captain Harvey is seated at his desk in his quarters. He has smelled their approach to Garbage Island for the past three hours, but the aroma doesn't bother him, no, to him it is the scent of coming home.

"Holy freakin' hell!" Perry moans, trying not to breath through his nose. "We can't stay out here without the Hazmat suits! The stench is going to kill us!"

Dr. Taylor has no choice but to agree. "Everybody below deck at once!" he orders and they scurry from the main deck, crashing into one another in their haste to get through the door. Tumbling over one another they half climb, half fall down the ladder, but no one complains. No one wants to open their mouth to do so.

Kim leads the way deeper into the ship, where at the very least they are spared the wind blowing the smell in their faces. The odor is still strong but at least down here it's diluted. Coughing, gagging, they pile into the mess hall, stumbling around, tripping over the chairs.

Kenny, Cole and Robert are gathered, hands over their noses, eyes betraying their collective dread.

"You tellin' me this is the enda the line?" Kenny says to Dr. Taylor but he gets no reply; the doctor merely sits down, drawing deep, ragged breaths through his mouth.

Cole shifts his gaze from Kenny to the doctor, his eyes wide, fearful.

"Answer him," he prods the doctor, who finally glances in their direction.

"Pardon me?" he wheezes, as if seeing them for the first time.

"Tell me this ain't what I think it is," Kenny says, his words muffled by his hand. "This is our destination?"

"We are an astute one, aren't we?" Dr. Taylor mutters and Kenny cocks his head to one side, looking at the other closely.

"Tell me ya din't just call me a idiot," Kenny glowers threateningly. "Please tell me ya din't just call me a fuckin' idiot!"

Dr. Taylor realizes immediately that this is neither the time nor place to make this giant man's shit list. Managing a benign smile, he puts his hands out in front of him in a placating gesture.

"Sorry, very sorry," he says. "I'm obviously not thinking properly right now..."

"That's what I thought," Kenny harrumphs. He'll let it slide for the time being, but anyone gives him any lip and he's going to punch first and ask questions later.

"Ladies and gentlemen," the captain's voice suddenly crackles through the speakers. "Welcome to The Great Pacific Trash Heap!"

According to the smell and what Dr. Taylor saw through tear slit eyes, the problem is far more advanced than he expected, to say the very least. Thanks to the recent satellite photos he knew they'd be confronting a veritable monstrosity, but what the photos couldn't convey was the odor. It is so strong he can almost see it hanging in the air before him like an opaque shower curtain. He simply can't imagine going out there and walking on the surface to collect data without the Hazmat suits. In fact, without them this operation has come to a screeching halt.

Why the hell did I volunteer to come? I must be out of my mind.

God only knows how it can be eradicated. Clean up crews would be out here for years, fuck that, *decades* trying to pick this crap up, and the U.S. doesn't have the money or the manpower to spare, not to mention they wouldn't opt to take full responsibility; this is the world's problem, after all. Trying to get a planet this divided to work together clearly isn't feasible. The fact is, there is no straightforward solution, and they can't take the 'easy' way out (as suggested by the military advisor) and nuke it back to the stone ages because such a desperate act would screw up the ecosystem beyond their wildest imaginings. Not only would the aquatic life be irreparably harmed for centuries to come but the ocean itself. It simply isn't an option, never has been in his opinion.

Returning to the smell, it goes far beyond the stench of your average waste products; only raw sewage combined with thousands upon thousands of decomposing bodies could give off a stink this foul. It would seem the chemicals from the melted plastic have mixed with other noxious chemicals, creating a squalid cesspool of indeterminate composition. Only extensive testing can give him an answer as to its core ingredients, and he guesses that, given the nature of its formation, there will be elements he doesn't recognize, a plethora of bizarre new substances the likes no one has ever seen. And, on top of that (if that isn't bad enough), he can only imagine what new strains of bacteria have developed because of this festering mess.

Take the E. coli bacteria for example. Mankind had never before seen anything like it until the need for mass food production brought it into existence. By feeding cattle a steady diet of corn instead of grass they inadvertently created a new type of bacteria that quickly found it's way into the food chain thanks to the unsanitary conditions of the slaughterhouses, as well as the negligence of the underpaid, uneducated workers. Fuck with nature and it fucks you back.

"Son of a bitch," Dr. Taylor mumbles, looking around the mess hall at the others and noticing they are all watching him. He removes his glasses and swipes at his eyes, wiping the moisture on his pants. They will have to send for replacement Hazmat suits in order to carry on with their tests. There is plainly no other option. "We have a serious conundrum here," he states sourly.

"Conun-what?" Kenny balks, his hands clenched into fists. "Speak English man."

As much as Dr. Taylor doesn't want to be on this man's bad side, he is somewhat put out by having to explain words a sixth grader should know.

"A serious problem," he says with more force than he intends. "We have a serious goddamn problem on our hands!"

"Shit Doc," Kenny says with a slight smile, "tell us somethin' we don't know."

They've got to let him out of here this instant! Now wouldn't be soon enough. Those bastards! How can they do this to him?

Tyler is finally up and around but the big dumb oaf is of no use. Would you believe it is the rank aroma that at last brings him to his feet?

"What did ya do," Tyler asks, scratching his nuts, "shit yer pants?"

"Believe it or not, that is what I was accusing you of only a few minutes ago," Hallsly says calmly, while inside his mind is reeling unsteadily with frantic emotion.

"Where the hell are we?"

"Ask your nose, what does it tell you?" he groans, his contempt for the other grown to the point of exhaustion. Maybe he should have smothered the dipshit with his pillow while he was sleeping.

"Smells like we're up shit crick," Tyler jokes, a thin smile spreading across his face. "Did the toilet overflow?"

"No you frickin' dummy, we're at the trash heap!"

Tyler looks at him wordlessly a moment before peering out the porthole.

"We'll I'll be damned!" he cries. "We are!" He turns to the governor. "What do you think happens now?"

"How the hell should I know?"

"Well, you're the governor, aren't you?"

"Yes…"

"Than if you don't know, who does?"

"Good Christ…" Hallsly drops into a chair and places his face in his hands. He seriously feels as if he is going to cry, just let loose and start sobbing like a little girl. This whole thing totally sucks the big one. But right now isn't the time for that, and what good would it do? Instead he decides to berate his cellmate, if only to make himself feel better.

"For someone who has taken so many blows to the head you sure are smart."

"Thanks dude!" Tyler says, a touch of pride in his voice. He knocks on his forehead. "Got a mind like a steel trap-every now and then something gets caught in there!"

"You don't say…"

Captain Harvey feels like a man who's been quarantined in a plastic bubble and is at long last allowed to be free. Inside him there are living things gnawing and surging, controlling his thoughts, moods and actions. Now that they are this close to Garbage Island he can shed his disguise, can morph into that which was promised of him if he delivered more bodies, more souls…

"Heh heh heh heh," he laughs, feeling giddy, free. "I'm home!" he cackles madly. "I'm home!"

"I can't go out there." Kim gags, her face puckered like she's taken a bite of a lemon. "You can't make me."

"I agree," Steven says, nodding his head vigorously. "No one should have to breath that shit."

"I'm going to have the crew radio for replacement Hazmat suits," Dr. Taylor assures them. "When they arrive we'll proceed with our tests."

"Screw it," Perry counters, looking around the room at the others. "I vote we nuke this thing into outer space-"

Abruptly four members of the ship's crew enter the mess hall. They are armed with M-16 automatic rifles, butts tucked tightly into their armpits, barrels aimed at the passengers heads. The first mate, Jake Anderson, leads the charge.

"Okay everyone, you heard the captain: we're here," he says, thumbing the safety off. "Now hand over your cell phones and let's head up top."

The passengers are gathered on the main deck, including the governor, Tyler and the Naval seamen, who have been relieved of their weapons. They are trying their best to be attentive but the scent of the trash heap is making it very hard. What they do understand, however, is that they are now Captain Harvey's prisoners.

The better part of the crew (all except those needed to run the ship) is armed, keeping the passengers at bay.

"What is this?" Dr. Taylor asks, his throat sore from coughing, his stomach churning explosively.

"Shut up," Jake says. "The captain will explain everything."

"It better be good," Kenny says gruffly. If any of the crewmen get close enough he's going to strip them of their rifle and start shooting. That's a promise.

Although he appears to be in control, Jake is wondering the same thing. A little over an hour before their arrival the captain called an emergency conference with the crew, in fact held the meeting down in the engine room so that all could be in attendance (except Lieutenant Michael Ronson, who stayed at the helm) without alerting the passengers. What he told them was odd; in all honesty odd doesn't even come close. It sounded more like the paranoid raving of a schizophrenic than their able leader.

"I've found out some information about the passengers that is quite disturbing," he'd told them, his eyes looking from face to face, his voice low, even. "This isn't a data collecting/ rescue operation at all, it's a sabotage mission. Many of the passengers are in fact saboteurs working for an eco-terrorist organization. It's my guess that they intend to take us and the ship hostage in order to delay our assignment."

"Eco-terrorists?" Anderson had asked skeptically. "How did you find out?"

"That isn't important," Captain Harvey had snapped. "What's imperative is that you, my loyal crew, act accordingly, as I tell you, and don't ask any more questions. There isn't time. We'll be at the trash heap in just over an hour."

"How can they take us hostage?" Skip Wagner, his second mate, asked. "We got all the weapons."

"What did I say about asking questions?" Harvey barked, turning to Jake. "If anyone so much as looks at you funny, you have my permission to open fire."

Anderson gaped at him. What the hell was going on? Since when had they become his personal army? "You mean the passengers?"

"I mean anyone," Harvey said curtly. "If any of you are thinking of disobeying my orders, think again. You will be shot. Understood?"

"You got our full support captain," one of the crewmen said, his eyes murky, his speech pattern muffled, slurred. "Right guys?"

Jake watched as several others nodded, clutching their guns tightly. Something didn't seem right about them, the muddy looks in their eyes, their slack-jawed appearance. And the captain, well, he seemed somehow...*different*.

And that was when Harvey extracted an enormous pistol from his belt and waved it before them. "I would prefer to have you men on my side but, if any of you make it difficult, I won't hesitate to start shooting. Is that clear?"

Jake and Skip nodded anxiously. It was easier for them to believe he was telling the truth than to think he was suddenly suffering from psychotic delusions.

"Okay," Jake had said, "what do you want us to do?"

And now, as they are waiting on the captain, Anderson goes around passing out small surgical style facemasks for the passengers to wear. They take them from his hands silently, their eyes aptly conveying their contempt. He keeps his best poker face in place, not wanting to betray his own doubts, but occasionally he glances over at Skip, who looks back at him guardedly, hands locked securely on his rifle. It doesn't take more than a few minutes before all the passengers have one. They snug them firmly in place.

"Looking good," Captain Harvey says, approaching from the direction of the bridge. "Let's get things underway, shall we?"

TWENTY-NINE

"For starters, you are all under arrest for conspiracy to commit acts of sabotage, a form of treason. This offence is punishable by death."

"What the hell are you talking about?" Governor Hallsly recoils, his words muffled by the surgical mask. "You've got to be out of your mind!"

The captain spins toward him and jams the muzzle of his long-barreled .45 Magnum against his forehead.

"Just give me a reason Hallsly," Harvey says coolly. "I'd love to see what's on, or rather, in your mind." He snorts laughter, a wheezing, discordant sound. "Probably a hamster running on a little wheel."

Hallsly has never had a gun held to his head before and finds the experience utterly terrifying. Even if he wanted to offer a sharp retort he doesn't believe he can; his vocal cords are frozen.

"Anyone else want to protest the charges?" he asks and silence ensues save for the sound of labored breathing. Everyone is wearing a mask except for Captain Harvey; the odor doesn't appear to be affecting him at all.

"I could simply shoot all of you right now, but I think that would be a waste of good human resources." He shakes his head, pacing before them. "No, we came here to do a job and by God we are going to do it."

"You want us to collect samples from the garbage heap without Hazmat suits?" Dr. Taylor asks and Harvey swings the gun toward his head.

"Did I tell you to speak?"

"This is ridiculous," Dr. Taylor says, pulling the mask away from his mouth so he can be heard clearly. "You would actually shoot us for a deed we haven't even committed? You must be joking."

The captain smiles, a rakish yet brutal contortion devoid of any humor, and he points the gun skyward. "Shooting you would be letting you off easy," he says. "I am not going to give you that pleasure." He scans the crowd. "Not unless you give me a reason."

"Whatta ya want us ta do?" Kenny asks, unruffled by this sudden twist. The situation hardly seems real, as if at any time the host from the show 'Duped' is going to pop out and declare they have all been the subjects of a rather unethical and cruel prank. In fact, Kenny isn't all too sure that won't happen, given the nature of 'Reality TV' in the 21st century.

"We're all going to the trash heap where the scientists can take some samples, the Naval and security personnel can search for the missing ship, and my crew and I can make ourselves comfy. Doesn't that sound wonderful?"

"Over my dead fuckin' body," Kenny says, his eyes glaring defiantly.

"Okay," Harvey says congenially. He studies his men, selecting a member of the crew only a handful of the passengers recognize as the second mate. "Shoot him Skip."

The crewman looks at the captain in disbelief. "In cold blood sir?"

"You heard him, he said, and I quote 'over my dead fuckin' body'. Please give him what he wants."

Skip stands mutely, his gun hanging at his side. He scratches his head, wondering how this situation went south so quickly. He looks at Kenny, observes the insolent look in his eyes, then switches his gaze back to the captain and isn't sure what he sees there. Rage? Insanity? What has transpired that this seemingly good-natured man is now a gun-wielding maniac? And is it really possible that these people (*all these people*) are eco-terrorists? Even the governor of California? Well, maybe that isn't such a stretch… But something has gone very wrong, and Skip knows in his gut that shooting the passengers isn't the way to get things done. *Fuck it. This just isn't right.*

"No," he says at last, removing his mask so the captain can see his face, even though the unpleasant smell makes his stomach flip-flop queasily.

"What?" Captain Harvey snarls. "What did you say?"

"None of this makes sense captain," Skip says, holstering his weapon. "I think we should put our guns away and just talk to these people. There's no way that all of them could be saboteurs-"

The sound of a gunshot rips the relative silence to pieces, and the passengers drop to their bellies onto the deck.

Skip's head explodes, pieces of his skull and brains spattering the onlookers. The expression on his face (the bottom half, the only part left) is one of confusion as his knees fold forward and he collapses.

"Anyone else want to question my authority?" Captain Harvey inquires of his crew and the men answer by keeping their rifles trained on the passengers. "I told you the price you would pay for insubordination and I meant it." He swings the barrel of his gun around until it is pointing once again at Kenny. "Still want to take one for the team?" he asks the big man, who is lying prone, gaping disbelievingly at Skip's body, his face considerably paler.

Kenny shakes his head vigorously. He's changed his mind. Maybe it won't be so bad on the trash heap after all.

"That's what I thought."

The ship is 'anchored' about two hundred yards from the trash heap, bobbing in the gentle current. At this depth the actual anchor chain isn't long enough to reach the bottom, so they employ several 'sea anchors', contraptions used to create a certain amount of drag, keeping the ship more or less in the same place while it's in idle. The ship will inevitably drift with the current but, since the water in the gyre is extremely slow moving, it's nothing small corrections of the wheel won't fix.

Where they sit is about as close as the captain will allow before the crew has a chance to check the surrounding water for clearance. He doesn't want the ship to become mired down in the accumulated debris they can't see below the surface. Getting themselves stuck is not on the agenda today. At present he's instructed two crewmen to take the canvas tarps off the lifeboats and lower them into the water.

"This is completely crazy," Perry murmurs to Steven, who nods but doesn't say a word in reply. He doesn't dare. Flecks of Skip's brain are spattered on his cheeks, drying in the sun.

Tyler moves through the crowd until he is next to Melissa. She looks at him warily, but has to admit she's comforted by his presence. Governor Hallsly squirms through the others to get next to her as well, but she merely glances at him with distaste.

Leeann and Dante are standing next to one another, and unconsciously they reach out and take each other's hand. Dante smiles at her reassuringly but the mask covers it. Instead she sees his eyes crinkle and nothing more. She in turn looks at him tersely, her eyes darting about wildly.

The thing is, Leeann has a scientific mind, which is useful as it allows her to perform amazing feats of deduction, but it doesn't permit vast surges of fanciful imagination. She simply can't understand what it is the captain wants from them, why he's doing this. That said, her last encounter with him comes to mind, and she wonders if she'd seen the precursor to this inevitable breakdown, if that is indeed what this is.

Dante, on the other hand, has an overactive imagination, and after his experience with Harvey in his quarters this does not surprise him, in fact seems like an unavoidable conclusion. The guy is slipping, losing it, and he's taking it out on everyone around him. He envisions the captain slaughtering them executioner-style once they are on the garbage heap and leaving them to decompose amongst the waste. What he can't picture is Harvey's subsequent move; what's next on the old day-planner? Build himself a house out of garbage and take up permanent residence?

Kim stands apart from the crowd, eyeing the captain and crew carefully. There is no way they are going to make her get in one of the lifeboats. Not without a fight.

Dave's mind is whirling, trying to think of a way to take control of the situation. If he can get one of the rifles and duck behind something protective maybe he can wound the captain or the first mate, and that may help to disperse the others. After all, he is a pretty damn good shot, almost sniper material. He nudges Travis, who appears to be in a state of shock, and tries to convey to him with his eyes and subtle nods of his head what he is thinking, but the other appears to have no comprehension of what he is trying to express. Dave turns and looks at the other Naval reject, but he too looks scared shitless. He is wringing his sweaty hands together, mumbling a muted prayer.

"We have to do something," Dave says quietly, and the other looks at him as if he has lost his mind.

"There's no way," he says in return. "We won't make it."

"We have to try!" Dave whispers forcefully, but the other shakes his head vehemently.

Dave looks around, counts six crewmen with guns, plus the captain and the first mate. It shouldn't be that hard. All he has to do is get the jump on one of them, get his gun and hope his aim is true. If he doesn't have a clear shot at the captain or the first mate he'll simply take out as many of the crewmen as he can. In the commotion maybe the others will be able to run, find a place to hide.

He tenses his muscles, readying himself, searching for an opportunity, when suddenly the Naval reject (Dave can't recall his name, hasn't even said more than two words to him the entire trip except for right now) shatters the calm by doing something completely unexpected: he makes a run for it and dives over the side of the ship.

"Man overboard!" the captain sings out merrily, his voice a crazy falsetto, his eyes rolling around like loose marbles in his head.

Three of the crewmen run to the railing, following his progress with their guns as he swims in the direction of the garbage heap. They are about to open fire when the captain yells "Halt!" and they stop, looking at him questioningly.

"Let's just see how far he gets," he says, and the passengers watch dismally as the man performs a jerky overhand crawl. Dave looks on with sick fascination. No matter how you slice it the guy is screwed; there's no place to go except for the garbage heap, and since that's their final destination he got wet for no reason. And, from this vantage point, he has no clear idea how he is going to gain access. The garbage towers above the water, sheer cliffs that climb nearly a hundred feet into the sky. Scaling them would be madness, suicide. Squinting his eyes against the glare of the sun, blinking away tears, he spots a flat, indented area, a cove harboring a 'beach', if you can call it that. It occurs to him that it is probably where the captain intends to take them.

The Naval reject (whose name is Timothy Greene and was assigned this position because he accidentally killed another seaman during a scuba diving drill-the details are unimportant) is about twenty-five yards away from the ship when he stops short, crying out.

"Holy fuck!" he bawls, flailing around. "AAAHHH!"

Kenny narrows his eyes, the reflected sunlight on the water making his head hurt, and thinks he sees a flicker of movement just below the surface, but he can't be sure, not with his limited visibility.

Kim gasps, a loud explosion of breath, and she points to something that pops out of the water a few yards away from Greene, a creature that looks oddly familiar with the exception of it's size.

"Look out!" she calls and the captain laughs, a thick, full-throated resonance that betrays how dangerously unhinged he's become.

"Good luck friend!" he hollers at Greene, who has stopped swimming and is treading water, his head swiveling wildly back and forth.

There is a flash of black as something cigar shaped breaks the surface, something with a segmented body and large, thick feelers on what may or may not be it's head. It comes halfway out of the water and attaches itself to Greene's face, enveloping it with thick extensions that could very well be legs. He manages a garbled scream before another one emerges on his other side, wrapping itself around his neck. He stops treading water and tries to wrench one of them off, but his legs aren't strong enough to keep him afloat and he slips beneath the waves.

"What the hell *are* those things?" Leeann whimpers, but Dante doesn't answer, just stares wordlessly as the water begins to churn. He isn't certain, but if he were allowed to hazard a guess he'd say they were giant insects. Three-foot long amphibian insects.

Greene struggles to the surface, arms thrashing erratically, but it now appears there are more of them attached to his body. He is unable to scream because one of the creature's broad thoraxes has encircled his face, and as he agitates the ocean with his exertions the area around him turns a dark shade of crimson. He goes under again, and the passengers collectively observe something that makes their skin crawl with revulsion: the sea has suddenly become choked with the creatures. Greene's struggling has brought them out by the dozens and they are now so profuse they are like one gigantic, squirming mass, trying to get a piece of the morsel that used to be a member of the United States Navy. They flop and roll against one another, fine sprays of blood droplets misting the air as they succumb to their bloodlust and begin attacking one another in an all out feeding frenzy. The ocean foams scarlet and the passengers' turn away, unable to comprehend this mind-boggling horror. Leeann sobs piteously as Dante clutches her tight against his chest, attempting to soothe her. Kim stares in amazement, her eyes wide, fearful. Kenny and Cole are silent, and Dave has momentarily forgotten his plan to try and overtake the crew. He looks at Travis and sees a single tear course down the other's face, disappearing into his mask.

Dr. Taylor's skin bristles as if he's been stung by an icy wind, and a swift realization hits him:

Those are giant sea cockroaches, he marvels, his bowels feeling loose, his stomach twisting sickeningly. *Giant carnivorous sea cockroaches.* He wishes he had his camera, but then dispels the notion quickly, appalled. Yet it is apparent the evolutionary cycle here has taken a definite turn for the worse. If the ocean surrounding the trash heap contains creatures like that…than what the hell is living *on* it? His body is instantly covered in a thick film of sweat that has nothing to do with the insane captain or his armed men. *Welcome ladies and gentlemen, we have just officially stepped off the grid.*

"Alright!" Captain Harvey roars with madcap glee. "Anyone else want to go swimming?"

PART THREE

GARBAGE ISLAND

ONE.

Without a word of complaint the passengers climb into the lifeboats, except for Kim who backs slowly away, trying to distance herself from the others.

"Get back here missy," the captain warns when abruptly she makes a break for it, dashing across the deck toward the ladder to the wheelhouse. Pivoting deftly on one heel, the captain fires several shots in her direction and she stops, raising her hands over her head.

"Alright!" she cries. "Don't shoot!"

"Come on back here now honey. We're not leaving without you."

Slowly she returns, her eyes imploring the closest crewman but the expression on his face is blank, his eyes unfocused and faraway, as if he is drugged. Getting in the lifeboat, she searches the first mate's eyes and is astonished to read confusion there. Is it possible that he isn't exactly sure what is going on? It's as if Captain Harvey knew there was something in the water, and if he knows that, than what does he know about the trash heap? What is he leading them to?

The three crewmen appointed to chaperone the lifeboats hesitate before boarding, looking at Jake uncertainly. Kim sees clarity in their eyes and, like the first mate, an air of bewilderment that contradicts their loyalty to Harvey. Jake shakes his head, shrugging almost imperceptibly.

"Is there a problem gentlemen?" the captain inquires, showing them the barrel of his gun.

A long moment draws out as the men fidget, looking from Jake to the trash heap to the captain and back.

"No sir," one of them mutters at last and they climb into their respective boats.

When everyone has boarded, Captain Harvey gets in last, making sure to keep a good distance from the passengers. The crewmen remaining on deck lower the boats into the water.

He gestures with his gun to the oars, nodding at Tyler and Cole.

"Start rowing."

The masks do very little to hinder the scent, and as they get closer the overpowering odor permeates them easily. Their purpose is purely perfunctory.

"Don't worry, you'll get used to it," the captain assures them, breathing deep of the tainted air. "Soon you won't need them at all."

As they get closer strange sounds become discernable, carried on the fetid breeze, sounds that can hardly be described as animal or human—loud shrieking noises that seem ethereal, disjointed from reality. As they grow louder, more distinct, the passengers eye the ever-looming shore, seeking their source.

"What could it be, I wonder?" Captain Harvey says, his voice obscenely cheerful. "What do *you* think it is honey?" he asks Leeann and she cringes. Dante quickly places a comforting arm around her, lowering her head to his shoulder. "That's right boy. Whatever it takes to get in her panties, huh? 'Cept she might not cotton to your kind, what with the sausage you're swingin'. No, this girl, she's got herself a taste for something else."

"Leave her alone," Dante musters the courage to say but the captain simply laughs, amused.

"You'll find out, oh yes, in time." And he turns his gaze back to the water, cocking his ear to listen to the growing din. The others in the lifeboat try not to look at him, focusing instead on the other boat in front of them, observing how low in the water it rides.

There are seven passengers to a boat, with two crewmen guarding them. Although the boats are moderately sized it is clear they weren't intended to hold this many people, and one look at the faces of the crewmen indicates their growing trepidation. The boats are hard to maneuver because of the excess weight and, even though they are armed, the passengers greatly outnumber them. Yet mutiny is the last thing on anyone's mind because in the melee they might end up in the water. No one wants to fall in the ocean, not after what they just witnessed.

"The sea is a cold, harsh mistress," the captain sings in an off-key baritone that sounds unhealthy in its timbre. "And she'll take you down if she gets a chance."

Dr. Taylor glances sidelong at him, sees his pallor has changed; his skin now appears jaundiced, his eyes murky, dark, ringed with black circles. He coughs occasionally, producing a thick, greenish/whitish substance that he spits over the side of the boat. When it hits the water it separates into little globules that swim away in different directions, reminding the doctor of sperm. He shudders and looks away.

As Dr. Taylor watches the garbage heap approach he figures that, like any junkyard, it contains any and every conceivable type of trash humans produce on a daily basis: various pieces of old, broken furniture, foil blister packs that contained pills, snacks or whatever, soiled diapers, food cartons, cigarette butts and empty packs, cat, dog and human food cans, plastic wrap, waxed paper, shredded tissue, used paper towels, scraps of paper from books, magazines and newspapers, used oil filters, food wrappers, fast food bags, coffee grounds, plastic wrappers and cups, tinfoil, plastic water and soda bottles, plastic grocery sacks, aluminum cans, toilet paper, gift wrapping paper, small bits of metal that might be paper clips or staples or what have you, glass bottles, electronic devices such as computers, TV's, stereo's (despite environmental recommendations to dispose of these items properly), batteries, CD's, DVD's, plastic CD cases, lawn furniture, broken pottery, doilies, old appliances, shredded clothing, food scraps, bones…the list is endless and pointless to attempt to catalogue. This vast, unimaginably enormous 'island' is simply mountains and mountains of trash. One would only have to comb through it to see it's simply what gets thrown away on any given day in any given household or business.

Of course there's also the medical refuse, not to mention industrial waste and toxic materials by the boatload (no pun intended), peppered throughout the debris like malevolent little surprises. It could be these various substances that are responsible for the nasty, nasal-searing odor, evidenced by the dark, effervescent sludge that floats atop the surface of the water surrounding the heap.

And this is where the captain is happily bringing them, singing a jaunty sea chant along the way…

Leeann cries softly while Dante does his best to offer her comfort; his efforts are well intentioned but it's merely a formality. Fear is coursing through him in sickening waves, making rational thought nearly impossible. He wants to be strong but right now he feels anything but. He shoots a glare at the two crewmen but they ignore him, focusing instead on a strident, piercing, buzzing resonance that suddenly fills the air.

"What the hell is that?" Hallsly cries, and all heads swivel furiously, looking for the source of the noise.

"Jesus Christ!" Cole screams, pointing, and Dante follows his finger, his heart leaping into his throat when he sees a massive cloud of angry, swarming insects circling the air above them. They engulf the lifeboats, descending upon them with a ferocity that is otherworldly. The swarm is so thick it blots out the sun. At once the air is choked with their large, furry bodies, and a general panic ensues amongst the passengers.

Captain Harvey grins from ear to ear, his eyes ablaze with an unearthly glow, watching the passengers swat at themselves and dance about in the small confines of the lifeboats. The insects cover his face, hands and neck and, smiling cruelly, he continues to sing as they fly in and out of his open mouth:

"Sing the song of the mighty sea, so powerful and full of grace!" he bellows at the top of his lungs. "If ye can't stand to submerge yourself than stay away from this place!"

Travis feels the boat rocking precariously, knows that at any moment it will upend, sending them all into the water where monsters from their worst nightmares await, but it becomes distant, unimportant. He smacks his arms, legs, and face in an effort to fend off the insects but they are too multitudinous. He whacks one of them from his neck (knocking his surgical mask askew so it now appears as if he is wearing an eye patch) and gets a good look at it as it writhes dying on the floor of the lifeboat. It looks like a mosquito crossed with a tarantula; it has translucent wings, a plump body with long, fur covered legs and its elongated, shiny stinger is twitching back and forth like a deranged pendulum. Milky fluid leaks from the tip of the hypodermically sharp appendage. He has only this short respite before they descend upon him twofold, the stingers sinking easily through his clothing, their bodies growing plump and feverish with his blood, and in one fleeting, panicked moment he wonders if they are injecting him with the cloudy solution that flows within them.

"Abandon the boat!" he cries and an insect flies into his mouth, one that is larger than the others, it's stinger dripping venom, and it punctures the inside of his cheek. He bites down and feels it squish between his teeth, filling his mouth with foul tasting liquid. Spitting it out, he forgets about everything else and jumps into the water.

Leeann's head is buried in Dante's chest, trying to keep the insects off of her face. As she cowers they cover her back, crawling inside her shirt, into the waistband of her pants. The pain is enormous, intense. Growing up in Texas, she'd been stung by just about anything you can think of: honey bees, wasps, hornets, deer flies, horse flies, even a dragon fly once…but nothing compares to this. It feels as if these things aren't just stinging her but taking large chunks of her flesh as well.

"We have to get in the water!" Dante hollers, flailing about wildly. Because of his efforts the rubber band holding his mask in place snaps, falling away, and the insects alight in his beard. He shakes his head briskly but they become entangled within its hairy grasp.

"No!" Leeann's blood runs cold at the thought of coming face to face with one of those, those…*things* that killed the Navy guy. "No Dante, we can't!"

"We don't have a choice!" he cries, stuffing his glasses into his pants pocket and picking her up as easily as a bag of groceries. "Hold your breath!" And without hesitating he launches them over the lip of the boat.

Shit! Tyler thinks as the boat suddenly pitches steeply to one side and he is jettisoned over the edge into the ocean. He's immediately surprised to find the water is strangely warm, almost like bath water. His first feeling is one of relief to be away from the swarm, but then he remembers the giant cockroaches and his heart thuds thickly in his chest. Tearing himself to the surface, he flounders toward the shore, not caring that he is swimming toward a giant mass of contaminated waste, only wanting to get out of the sea before he encounters something out of a B grade horror movie.

As he dog paddles clumsily to the trash heap he blindly bumps into others, shoving them carelessly out of his way. As far as he's concerned, it's every man for himself.

Dante has never been a very good swimmer; he's proved to himself time and again that his efforts are clumsy and awkward at best. But when his ass is on the line he finds he can manage just fine, if only at treading water. Leeann is clinging to him frantically, her voice shrill in his ear, when something unseen under the water tears them apart. Gasping, she's yanked below the surface, and without thinking he takes a deep breath and submerges as well, groping blindly for her. He opens his eyes and almost loses his breath when a sharp pain shoots through him with the swiftness of a dentist's drill. He closes them quickly, the searing sensation brutal, agonizing.

Jesus, it feels like acid was just thrown in my eyes!

Yet he ignores the urge to rub them and instead sweeps his arms madly back and forth, trying to find Leeann in the darkness. His lungs ache terribly, crying for air, but he disregards it, propelling himself ever deeper into the rank, disturbingly warm water. If he loses her he doesn't know what he will do, doesn't know how he'll continue on. With her by his side he feels as if he stands a chance, for she gives him something to live for. Without her, well, he might as well die. If he loses her here, in this disgusting water surrounding a pile of floating shit, he can see no other choice than to join her in the murky depths. Fuck it. This life just isn't worth living.

Unexpectedly his fingers find her by getting snarled in her long, curly hair, and he clutches it urgently. Flexing muscles that haven't seen any real exercise since God knows when, he pulls her toward him as she thrashes about wildly, fighting whatever it is that has a hold of her. Tightening his grip, his hand brushes against something that feels rubbery and yielding, and he cringes in disgust, pulling his hands away.

Gotta be strong you son of a bitch! Gotta be strong!

He reaches out again and takes hold of it, peeling it off of her like an especially large and sticky band-aid. It doesn't give way easily, writhing and squirming in his grasp like an agitated snake, but he gets a hand on each end of it and, using all his strength (strength he didn't even know he possessed) he rips it in two, releasing it and letting the water carry the pieces away. He then wraps his arms around her waist and drags her to the surface, kicking his legs powerfully against the pull of the under current. They reemerge amidst the black, bubbly sludge, the noxious fluid revoltingly thick and slimy, reminding Dante of spilled oil. Leeann is gagging and spitting out water (her mask hanging from one ear, tangled within her hair) but otherwise she seems to be all right, and he feels a triumphant burst of energy renew him.

"Are you okay?" he splutters, doing his best to keep them both afloat.

"Sh-sure," she says, her teeth rattling, her fingers gripping him so tightly as to be painful.

"Good," he replies, trying to keep his chin (and mouth) out of the black, putrescent substance, helping Leeann to do the same. "We have to get to the shore."

"O-o-o-okay."

Dante's sinuses are clogged with the rancid water and his stomach is lurching unsteadily, but he concentrates on what he is doing, on getting them both to safety. Hooking an arm around her chest, he performs a slow, one-armed stroke, moving backward toward the trash heap, toward a break in the immense cliff walls that appears to be a 'beach' of sorts. If they are going to get out of the water anywhere, that's where their only hope lies.

Kenny has never learned to swim, so when the boat tips steeply to one side and he slips from his seat (cracking his head sharply on the side and thrown upside down into the filthy brine) he has no concept of how to save himself. He drops like a rock, the air whooshing out of him in large, lazy bubbles, when at last he feels something solid he mistakes for the bottom. Trying to push off from it, his arms sink into the squishy, elastic material, and he realizes with growing horror that it isn't solid ground but submerged waste. He struggles backward, kicking his legs mightily, but he's become entangled within it; it's wrapped around his arms and torso, ensnaring him.

Thrashing his arms recklessly, he tries to release himself but becomes increasingly enmeshed in the debris. He unwittingly somersaults backwards and forwards as underwater currents wrench him to and fro, and he's growing lightheaded, the lack of air muddling his thinking, making his movements careless, sloppy. His limbs feel heavy, sodden and clumsy, and a growing apathy steals over him the more tired he becomes.

So this is what it feels like to die, to drown. . .

The thought suddenly sobers him, forces him to concentrate on the task at hand. It seems he's caught in a fishing net and, working his fingers around it methodically, he somehow manages to free himself, backing away quickly. He strips the mask from his face and claws at the water, immediately realizing he has no idea which way is up. He opens his eyes to get his bearings straight but upon doing so feels a burning pressure and closes them quickly. Panic overtakes him then, flooding his nervous system as he twirls around indecisively. If he chooses the wrong way he will run out of air and surely drown. He swivels his head back and forth, the last of his air nearly gone, and he starts to feel a growing blackness in his head, a calm numbness that tells him to relax, to just let go. . .

And then strong arms are clutching him under his armpits, tugging him upward. A moment later his head breaks the surface and he takes in a great breath that's simultaneously invigorating and excruciating. Recoiling, he slips under briefly and water pours into his open mouth. He coughs, choking on the venomous bilge. But the hands are still grasping him tightly, and it is only later that he will find out it was Cole who saved him from what could have been a very nasty death.

One by one and in pairs the passengers and crewmen wash up on the shore of the trash heap. Even though they are safe from the treacherous waters, their arrival is certainly not a pleasant experience.

As observed by Dr. Corey Taylor in his brief field notes (unfortunately never published):

Arrival at the trash heap was met with relief, having escaped the water and the mysterious creatures that lurked therein. But the experience of stepping onto an island comprised entirely of garbage was surely no reprieve as one was left to question whether or not it could sustain the weight of a full grown human being. This issue was quickly laid to rest as the survivors climbed aboard, squirming over the rancid outcroppings and collapsing onto the relative safety of the compost heap. The insects we'd encountered were no longer a concern at this point as the water acted as a natural repellent, for reasons I can only speculate (deleterious chemical compounds from the water, possibly, but I could be wrong).

The 'island' was squishy to the touch; it was almost like stepping onto a giant sponge, and everything was coated in a slimy film of moisture, with a slippery and sticky consistency. Of course the odor was beyond any description I can report here that would be thoroughly understood, but suffice it to say it was a strong mixture of excrement and rotting food, chemicals and corpses. It was the kind of smell that caused one to vomit involuntarily and incessantly.

Upon our advent to the 'island' we were prisoners of Captain Harvey as was his crew; this hapless situation was made no different by the apparent similarities of how we suffered, for as badly as we, the captives, agonized over the situation, the crew did as well. The only person who wasn't struggling with this position was Captain Harvey who, upon arriving at the 'shore', found himself a bit of decomposing carrion and had a snack.

It is in my opinion that the captain suffers from some sort of viral or bacterial madness; of what type and origin I have no idea. Well, I will posit a theory here, only because it is the only thing that possibly makes sense, given the circumstances: he somehow came into contact with material from the trash heap and the bacteria growing within or upon it made him ill, causing a neural breakdown. It probably traveled through his bloodstream (through an open wound) or intestinally (through his digestive tract) and then worked it's way to his brain. In other words, the toxic components of the trash heap contaminated his system, causing a form of insanity.

It goes without saying that the likelihood of all of us contracting this sort of 'disease' is all but inescapable; if indeed that is truly what it is. Without further testing there is no way I can really know for sure...

Sickness engulfs everyone as they crawl upon the trash heap; the passengers and crewmen alike are rendered helpless by uncontrollable bouts of diarrhea and vomiting.

"Holy Christ in a side car!" Kenny gasps, doubling over, grasping his stomach. He jettison pukes a thin, watery gruel and concurrently feels a wet, slippery warmth running down his legs. "Goddamnit!" he howls. "I just shit my pants!"

It is in this misery that they stumble about on the 'beach' of the 'island', each and all finding an appropriate place to do their nasty business. The sounds of retching and the wet splat of shitting become the symphony that highlights their arrival, accentuated by an emergent racket of mysterious origin. And Captain Harvey, the conductor of this inharmonious, chaotic disaster-piece, looks on with an expression of rapturous glee.

TWO

"Welcome to fantasy Island!" Captain Harvey hollers, raising his voice to compete with the swelling cacophony of shrieks that echo off of the surrounding walls, the sound reverberating about them maddeningly. "My name is Mr. Roarke, and this is my buddy Tattoo," he laughs riotously, gesturing to a mound of trash beside him, "and we will do our best to make sure all your wishes come true!" He screws up his face and cries with unbridled delirium: "Look boss, da plane! Da plane!"

The passengers and crewmen are scattered before him on the 'beach' of the 'cove', all of them lost in their own personal hell. He looks from one to another, giggling irreverently as they get acquainted with their new home:

Governor Hallsly is crawling around in circles, throwing up in intermittent bursts. His head is spinning and throbbing, little spots dancing before his eyes. He's so disoriented he's aware of very little except that his ass is on fire and his nostrils seem to be packed with raw sewage...

Melissa is lying on her back, dried vomit crusting her lips. She stares blankly into the blue sky, eyes half open, tears rolling down her cheeks. Her stomach roils irately, and every few minutes she blasts either liquid or air from her rectum. She wants to sit up but it involves more energy than she has, so she abandons her efforts and simply lays where she's fallen...

Jake Anderson is on his knees, retching miserably and gasping for air. He has no idea where his rifle is and he doesn't care. There is nowhere for the passengers to go anyway. And, besides, the way he sees it, he and the other crewmen are just as much captive as they are...

Steven is lying face down, having lost consciousness. Perry sits beside him, tracing his finger in a puddle of puke and humming tonelessly...

Dr. Taylor sits at the edge of the trash heap, staring into the black, bubbling ooze, heaving again and again until he brings up nothing but air and foamy spit. His eyes are bulging from their sockets, his throat expanding and contracting as his chest shudders from the effort. Despite his torment his analytical mind is whirling a thousand miles per hour:

We had no idea it could be this horrific, this out of control! Maybe that's why the crew from the first expedition hadn't sent any photos or made contact with the outside world after their arrival: they'd been physically unable to. Perhaps whatever is making this awful ruckus got to them before they could return to the ship...but what about the others onboard? What happened to them?

Running a shaky hand through his hair, he feels something crawl across his scalp. He explores tentatively, jerking his hand away in disgust. Whipping his head back and forth he watches disbelievingly as the bloated, writhing bodies of hundreds of maggots rain onto the ground around him.

"Ahhh!" He slaps at his head with both hands, feeling them pop and squish beneath his palms...

Her face a detached façade of indifference, Kim sits atop the remnants of a porcelain sink as still as a statue, her vacant eyes unblinking. Shocked so profoundly she's been rendered catatonic, she's unaware the surgical mask is still on, even though it's full of barf. Unconsciously she is slowly masticating and swallowing it...

Kenny has never (even in his worst days as an alcoholic) lost his lunch with this much painful force. He feels as if his guts are being ripped out with a wire hanger. Beside him, Cole is straining so hard that his face is crimson, tears streaming from his eyes. Nearby, Robert lies motionless, his upper body perched on the edge of the trash heap, his legs submerged in the stinking ooze. An expression of agonized horror is frozen on his face, his eyes wide, unseeing. From his mouth seeps the black fluid, staining his lips and tongue.

As his nausea briefly subsides Kenny glances about him, wiping his face with the back of one hand, summing up their situation:

Fucked, he thinks, when queasiness ripples through him yet again. *We are totally fucked...*

Travis lies prone, his breathing quick and shallow, his arms and legs jerking uncontrollably. His left cheek is red and swollen and his head bobs up and down as he seizes, striking the ground repeatedly.

Dave stands nearby, appearing not to notice his friend's suffering. He's watching the sky, waiting for whatever it is making those infernal sounds to show themselves. He looks about him for a weapon, picking up a rusted shower curtain rod out of the moldering waste. As he clutches it tightly in his sweat slick hands he is unaware that shit is slowly leaking down his legs, filling up his shoes...

Tyler lurches to his feet, pulling at the seat of his pants, the soggy fabric sticking to his legs. Against his better judgment he raises his hands to his face, sniffs, and immediately vomits again.

"Jesus," he moans, peeling the disintegrating mask out of his hair and tossing it aside. He looks to the sky, trying to locate the source of the awful, bone-jarring screeches, when he sees something sail overhead he can't quite comprehend. It's obviously some kind of bird, no mistake there, but that's where the similarities end. It appears to be part albatross and (*What the hell?*) part lizard. But the truly peculiar feature that makes his brain hurt isn't the apparent cross-species mating but it's breastplate. No fucking shit, but it resembles a plastic six-pack holder, and if he looks hard enough he realizes he can see the organs inside, the heart, the stomach, the lungs...

It squawks raucously and swoops down toward him, its open beak revealing a mouth full of serrated teeth, and he drops to his belly, covering his head in his arms.

Dante looks up just in time to see this monstrosity plunge toward Tyler, just missing him by scant inches. It lands on a tattered sofa nearby and issues a squeal so unruly that Leeann (who he is cradling in his arms) begins to cry anew.

"Shhh," he says, stroking her back. "It's going to be okay."

"This is crazy," she whimpers, her teeth chattering. "I want to go home."

"It'll be all right," Dante reassures her, rocking her back and forth, when another creature comes plummeting from the sky, balancing itself delicately next to the first one.

"Uh-oh," Dante says, watching as the two birds eye them judiciously.

They throw back their heads and in unison utter one of the most loathsome, dissonant noises Dante has ever experienced, and within seconds the sky overhead darkens, the creature's cawing now accompanied by the flapping of leathery wings.

Dante gets to his feet, dragging Leeann with him.

"We've got to hide!" he calls out to the others, hoping to roust them for their sickness-induced daze. "Come on people, on your feet! We've got to go!"

Captain Harvey barks maniacal laughter, dancing from one foot to the other.

"Unless you want to be the Rancor Bird's lunch I suggest you do as he says!" He dashes over to Jake Anderson, kicking him with a sludge-encrusted boot. "The beasties are coming mate! Best to make like a fart and blast off!"

Anderson's gaze jerks skyward, seeing their approach, the grotesque fluttering of their thick, heavily veined wings driving him to his feet. Glancing about him he spies his rifle a few yards away, and he hastens to snatch it up. Firing several shots into the air, he hollers: "Come on people, let's move!"

"Oh, look who thinks he's in charge now!" Captain Harvey says with mock disdain. "Sir yes sir and all that happy crap!"

The sudden tumult brings most of the passengers out of their torpid stupor and, slowly at first but gaining speed, they straggle to their feet. Overhead, the sinister looking birds are growing in number, their skull-penetrating shrieks drowning out all other sound.

"Grab your rifles!" Jake shouts to the remaining crewmen (one is missing), who've misplaced them in the confusion. Stumbling about, they find their weapons, checking the chambers for live rounds and shouldering them.

"Come on everyone! We have to hide!"

No one needs to be told twice. They follow Jake as he runs forward, deeper into the maze of the garbage heap.

Dizzy, faltering, Hallsly figures he'll be better off on his own. He watches them run one way, and he scuttles off in another. It's every man for themselves at this juncture, there's no point in letting anyone bring him down. Scrambling behind a dilapidated refrigerator he loses them quickly, kicking a sodden cardboard box out of his way and running on wobbly, uncertain legs. But the floor of the heap is riddled with divots and obstructions, and he slips and stumbles on something sticky and moist. Falling face first into the offending substance, he snuffles a good snort before reminding himself not to breath. Whatever it is, he can taste it deep in the back of his throat, and it reminds him of dead things, long dead and rotten. He gags piteously but somehow gets back to his feet, staggering momentarily before righting himself.

Feets don't fail me now...

He runs heedlessly, paying no attention to which way he is going, simply fleeing as fast as his under-exercised legs can carry him. An indeterminate amount of time passes, he has no idea how much, or how far he's traveled, yet he can still hear the birds squawking overhead. He scans the landscape frantically for some place he can hide; the junk heap is a quagmire of disintegrating, decaying debris, there has to be something he can crawl under...

In his haste he isn't watching where he's going, and he steps into an indentation and loses his footing. He tries to spin away, but gravity has him in its clutches and, yowling dolefully, he falls backward into the yawning chasm.

In their mad rush to escape, the passengers splinter into smaller groups. Dante, Leeann and a member of the crew (Dante is no fool; he wants to be with someone who has a gun) dart off in one direction while Tyler, Melissa and another crewman dash off in another.

Dr. Taylor runs in the same direction as Kenny and Cole, valiantly trying to keep up with them. Dave helps Travis to his feet (with the aid of the third crewman) and they reel off in the same general direction as Dante.

Perry and Steven are on their own, left behind by the others without so much as a goodbye. *Just the two of us*, Perry thinks bleakly. *We're dead.*

And to make matters worse, Steven is barely conscious; he is lying on his side, his mouth slowly opening and closing like a fish out of water, his eyelids fluttering.

I might have to leave him. It's either that or we both die.

Keeping an eye tuned to the bird's movements, Perry takes a step backward, and then another, when his eyes come to rest on Kim, seated atop a cracked porcelain sink. She is gazing up into the darkened sky as the birds' circle above her, but her eyes are dull, empty. She's still wearing her mask and Perry sees fluid leaking out on either side of her mouth.

"Kim!" he calls, trying to get her attention, but she doesn't respond, doesn't even blink. It appears as if her mind has exited her body and what's left is just a husk, merely a human form that is nothing but flesh and blood; food for the taking. Shit, as if he doesn't feel bad enough deserting Steven...

Steeling his nerve, Perry abandons his plans for retreat and takes a step forward, watching as the reptilian winged-creatures swoop lower and lower, their screeches deafening, mind-bending.

"Goddamnit," he mutters. "You two are gonna owe me big time for this."

Returning to Steven, he kneels down beside him and rolls him onto his back, then puts his hands under his head, lifting it up.

"Come on man, you gotta get up or you're done for!"

"Leave me," Steven says, his voice faint, his eyes unfocused. "Save yourself."

"Fuck that!" Perry growls, taking the other by the arms and hauling him into a sitting position. "You're coming with me dude, that's final!"

"If he doesn't want to go, he doesn't want to go!"

Perry looks up, startled. It's Captain Harvey, and he's standing with his arms spread wide like a scarecrow, an eager smile planted on his sickly looking face. "More food for the Rancor Birds!"

Perry watches as the revolting creatures descend from the sky, landing on the captain's outstretched arms and perching there, fixing him with their malicious gaze. In a matter of seconds the captain is covered with them, their wings flapping in the foul breeze, their high-pitched cries clanging and warbling like sirens in a loony bin.

Steven turns his head, bearing witness to this horrifying spectacle, and in his terror finds the strength to get to his feet.

"Kim!" Perry calls anxiously. "Come on!"

But it's as if the girl doesn't hear him, or she simply doesn't care.

"She's over the rainbow now!" Captain Harvey chortles, completely enveloped in the squirming, repugnant bodies. "She's gone where the wild things go!"

"Forget it, we have to leave her!" Perry relents, taking Steven by the arm and tugging him in the opposite direction. The other doesn't fight him; he finds his footing and they dart off into the contiguous swells of rank, teeming trash, the sound of the captain's laughter ringing in their ears, interspersed by the cawing of the nightmarish, avian atrocities.

Behind eyes that see nothing but a blank blue sky, her mind flies…up, up and away. Up here there is no sound, no pain, no scent, nothing to remind one of the earthly trappings that make life such an endless struggle, a battle of wills, a contest of man versus the elements, man versus the animals, man versus itself. It is quiet, peaceful, and she feels rested, as if she is dancing on clouds aided by angel's wings…

'What is this place?' she asks of a man who steps forth, swathed in a flowing robe of shimmering colors so vivid it's as if the garment is alive.

'You are safe now, my child,' he answers, his voice a rich baritone, husky but not guttural.

'Where am I?'

'You've left the world of the tormented humans, those whose judgment is clouded by anguish and fear, their easily-swayed minds consumed by rabid commercialism, war and greed. You are in a better place now, one in which you are free to explore at your own will.'

'I…I'm free?"

'Free of everything, yes. All of the earthly matters that once bound you are no longer an obstacle; the shackles have been taken off. You can now be anything you want, go anywhere you please.'

'What is required of me?' she inquires, certain there must be a price for such freedom.

'There is a small toll you must pay, hardly a trifle really.' He smiles benevolently, reaching out his hand, and his cloak flickers, rustling as if blown in a gentle breeze, and at once it appears there are hundreds of glittering eyes watching her. 'All you have to do is take my hand.'

'That's all?'

'That's all my child,' he whispers. 'Come.'

She takes a tentative step forward, raising her arm, her fingertips twitching ever so slightly. He grins, a toothy grin that turns into a leer, a long rope of saliva dripping from one corner of his mouth, and he stretches his long fingers toward her, the cape suddenly awakening, aflutter with motion, the peering eyes accompanied by dozens upon dozens of sharp appendages. Without warning they split open and issue the most unnerving of utterances...

Their hands touch and a spark of electricity passes between them, bonding them together, their skin melting, making them one.

'Welcome home dear,' he says, and his cloak explodes into a hundred single, living entities that rise up and swirl around her, enshrouding her within their feathery/scaly being. 'We've been expecting you.'

Abruptly she feels the sharp point of a beak poke through her left eyelid and, screaming desolately, tries to wrench it off of her face as it's serrated teeth dig in. It's squirmy, scaly body eludes her grasp, however, and with a tremendous, wrenching tear it severs her optic nerve and comes away with her eyeball in it's mouth. In one swift moment the illusory world of twisted, distorted truths slips away, and reality reveals itself before her in all its hideous glory. There is no splendor, no beauty, no; this world is excruciatingly dismal, grotesque...far, far beyond that which was promised.

Throwing her head back, she issues a penetrating, heartbreaking wail, and as the sound passes over her lips she becomes aware of barbed talons sinking into her flesh, on her arms, legs, face. The agony is like liquid fire as her skin is torn and shredded, stripped away and revealing the muscle and sinew that lies beneath.

Her vision marred by the thick, hot blood collecting under the rim of her remaining eye, she struggles to focus her gaze on the man before her, this gruesome, deceitful beast who capers enthusiastically like a fairy-tale ogre.

"Soon you'll see things my way," he decrees, his idiot grin atrocious, derelict. "Soon."

Kim utters one last petrified scream, the resonance rolling out of her mouth as fluidly as the most beautiful song, and abruptly she feels a tooth filled beak clamp down on her tongue, gripping it snuggly and ripping it savagely from her mouth.

And then darkness takes her, whisking her swiftly away.

THREE

"Sir, I've just received word from the research vessel. According to my Intel they've made their destination."

"Excellent," the president says. "Anything to report?"

"Nothing," the aide replies in a clipped voice, his manner crisp as a newly minted hundred-dollar bill. "The scientific team is preparing for their first expedition and the crew is 'holding her steady'. Their words."

"Very good," the president says dismissively, turning away and holding out his hand expectantly. His caddie places a nine iron in his palm and, when the president glares at him, he retracts it and hands him the seven. "Learn your damn job," he grumbles and the other sulks. If his wife wants him to be nice to her brother, the least he can do is study up on the game.

The aide turns to go when the president asks:

"Have they seen any sign of the other ship?"

He shakes his head. "Not yet sir."

The president sighs, hefting the club and taking a few practice swings. "Just getting anxious for some answers I guess."

"That's understandable sir."

"If we weren't so mired down with all of these goddamn wars we might actually have the resources to take on this problem with competent men, not the group of amateurs we recruited."

"Yes sir."

"Is there a satellite designated to track their progress?"

"None at this time," the aide replies. "We can't spare it."

"Yeah," the president says, "should have figured that." He glances down at his ball, wondering why in the hell his brother-in-law picked neon pink. Does that moron think he's blind? They still have at least thirty minutes of daylight. "As soon as we *do* have the availability I want someone tracking the garbage heap, got it?"

"Yes sir."

"I hope Dr. Taylor knows what he is doing."

"I am sure he will surpass your expectations, sir," the aide says with a forced smile, smoothing his tie.

"He better," the president replies, taking a swing and missing. "It's our ass on the line."

"Ya can't stop now," Kenny urges Cole, who is on his knees, breathing heavily, swiping at his grimy face with even grimier hands. "Those things'll find us."

"We're going to die here man!" Cole blubbers, his voice cracking and breaking like a prepubescent teenager. "We are so fucked!"

Dr. Taylor leans over, placing his hands on his knees, catching his breath. He looks up at the two men, opens his mouth to say something, decides better of it. Let them hash it out. He needs to get some 'air'. For the moment it appears as if they've escaped the immediate threat of the bird/lizards, so if they want to stop and take five, maybe fret and worry about it some, he can't see why that isn't all right. All they have to lose is time, the only thing they have left.

As far as his calculations go, they have about three days to escape; after that things are going to be rather difficult. He guesses that it's between eighty and ninety degrees, possibly about seventy or eighty percent humidity. In this kind of heat the longest any of them can hope to survive without water is probably five to seven days, but after three days their minds and spirits will begin to weaken, with disorientation soon to follow. He takes into account that there may be the possibility of rain, but it would be unwise to factor it in, as they have no way of knowing for sure. By all practical considerations they are without food and water, being stalked by bizarre creatures straight out of a crack-head's nightmare, on an island made completely of trash. Not the best situation to be in, in his humble opinion.

Squatting down, Dr. Taylor notes that, for the meantime, the bugs aren't a big concern; the insects presently circling their heads are substantially less vicious than the swarm over the water. What they're dealing with now appears to be a larger species of fruit fly, but they are slow, sluggish.

Probably because they have an all-you-can-eat smorgasbord at their ready disposal, making them fat and lazy. As soon as they get a taste of us I'm sure that will change.

Even though their lives have been in a near constant state of peril over the last hour or so, Dr. Taylor has managed to keep his wits about him, viewing their situation with a healthy mixture of patience and common sense. After all, it's what he's trained to do. As they've made their way through the debris-strewn landscape his scientific mind has been methodically cataloging what he sees for future reference. What this is, he can honestly admit, is nothing short of amazing. A true testament to the callous and stupid nature of human kind. One can learn so much about a person by going through their trash, so it only goes to show what this heap has to say about society at large. America has been leading the way since the earliest part of the 20th century, ushering in an era that can best be described as 'disposable'. With the need to have everything done cheaper and faster, and the end goal to cut costs and make outrageous profits, the market place has become overrun with products designed to exhaust the world's natural resources just as quickly as their dangerous by-products pack the landfills. It's gluttony at such an advanced level it boggles the mind. Most people would probably be shocked to learn that the United States alone is responsible for about 220 million tons of trash yearly, and this only accounts for 4 percent of the world's population. An estimated four to five billion tons of trash is created yearly worldwide, but this figure isn't concise; no one really knows for sure.

He examines the area immediately surrounding them, ignoring his better judgment and digging into the detritus, stopping when he feels a solid, compacted shelf. Studying it curiously, he notes that the 'ground' appears to be comprised mostly of the plastic (neustonic) particles his earliest studies revealed, but these, of course, are merely the beginning. By his best guess (which is all he can really do without research), what gives the 'island' it's stability is the accumulation of larger, more solid pieces of debris which, all added together, helped it to attain the mass that was then capable of holding even larger pieces of rubbish and so on. As this waste built up over time and the sun's rays beat down on it, it gradually melted and molded itself into this form, possibly aided by all the toxic chemicals thrown into the mix, helping to harden it.

And over, under and permeating all of this is some kind of 'natural' growth, most likely a form of mold, spawned from the accrual of all this crap. Everything Dr. Taylor touches feels slimy, and it is hard for him to tell if this is an organic slime (he almost has to laugh at the use of the term 'organic') or if it is the chemicals oozing out of the various types of garbage as they liquefy in the sun. He's not sure if he really wants to know but, what the hell, it's his job…

"-think bout that Doc?"

"What?" Dr. Taylor dismisses his reverie, turning toward the other two. Cole, it appears, has calmed down somewhat, while Kenny now has a look on his face that betrays his own fears.

"I said," Kenny repeats, "whatcha think bout that?"

"Think about what?"

"We can't keep runnin' deeper inta this shit, we'll just git lost. We should head back ta the ship."

Dr. Taylor nods. "That, it would seem, is our only recourse. However," he pauses, looking at the two men levelly, "although we've evaded those creatures for now, we have to assume they are still a threat and, once we find our way back to the cove, how are we going to get back to the ship? Did either of you notice if the lifeboats made it ashore? We certainly can't swim."

Kenny recoils at the prospect, the image of the sea cockroaches no doubt bringing back memories of the Naval seaman's untimely demise. And not only that, swimming through that black, bubbling tar simply isn't an option. His skin feels chafed, irritated, and he notices with distaste that there are red lesions on his arms, probably from the insect stings. He detects more of these on his legs and stomach, some of them itching like a motherfucker. There is no way he is going back in the water. For all they know the cockroaches are the least of their problems; they may have simply been the first of many nasty creatures to show up when the dinner bell rang. There could be a host of even more insidious ocean dwellers out there, just waiting for someone foolish enough to take a dip.

"We could make a raft if the lifeboats is sunk," Kenny says, gesturing at the debris all around them. "With shit we find."

"We'll need something a little more sturdy than shit," Dr. Taylor says, smiling, "but I think you have the right idea."

"My name is Kurt," the crewman says, holding out his hand. "Kurt Corbin."

"Pleased ta meet ya Kurt," Dave says, shaking his hand. "I'm Dave."

"Pleasure's all mine," he says sincerely, then looks at Travis, who is leaning against a rusty stove with his eyes closed. "Who's he?"

"That's Travis."

Travis, upon hearing his name, glances over, his eyes red, puffy. He nods and picks at the seat of his pants, grimacing.

"Can't wait 'til the crap dries," he says and the other two laugh, although there isn't much humor in it.

They've found a cave of sorts, an enormous indentation in the trash where they're currently hunkering down. The temperature is hot and sticky, the sky mostly clear with scattered clouds, but there is an occasional breeze blowing loose pieces of trash around like diseased tumbleweeds, making the scent of the island stronger at intervals.

Dave finds that, after a while, the smell doesn't seem so bad. Not that it's presence can be ignored, he's simply getting used to it.

"So what's with the captain?" Travis asks, brushing some indeterminate gunk off his hand onto his pants, which used to be white but are now an off-gray color.

"I'm not sure," Corbin answers, wondering how much he should divulge before quickly deciding it doesn't matter. At this stage he can probably feel free to say anything he wants. "But I'm not entirely surprised."

"Whatdaya mean?" Dave says, shifting his legs to get more comfortable. "He done somethin' like this before?"

"I don't know, this is the first time I ever worked for him," Corbin starts, looking closely at the other, sizing him up. By his best guess he'd say the Naval seaman appears to be a reasonably intelligent fellow, although he's not too sure about his partner. "From the git-go I thought there was something kind of off about him." He's silent a moment, considering. "You know that storm?"

"Yeah, what about it?"

"He knew it was coming, yet he didn't tell anyone until about an hour before it hit."

"What?" Dave says. "How do *you* know?"

"I am, well, *was* I guess, the ship's meteorologist. I'm not exactly trained in the study of weather patterns but, hey, someone had to do it. Basically it entailed keeping an eye on the Doppler radar equipment and monitoring radio transmissions of weather reports coming from the Philippines, Australia, what have you. It was a job anybody could have done. Well, before we left I was given a copy of the latest weather read-out, a document that claimed all was clear skies and smooth sailing. Turned out it was a dummied report, one to keep us all in the dark so that the mission wouldn't be postponed."

"You fuckin' kiddin' me?"

"Nope."

"It ain't no big loss, but that decision got the lieutenant junior grade killed."

Corbin nods, saying nothing.

"Wonder why he was so hot an bothered to git here?"

"Your guess is as good as mine," Corbin says, then adds: "but he doesn't seem right. Like he's sick. He's been like that since yesterday, only today it's worse."

"He's completely bonkers," Travis adds to the conversation.

"That too."

"And what the hell is this eco-terrorist nonsense about?" Dave continues. "As far as I can tell there ain't nothin' out here to sabotage; blowin' this place up would be an improvement."

"Beats me. About an hour before we got here he called us all into a meeting and told us this crazy story, told us if we disobeyed he'd shoot us…" He stops short, looking away. "And then that bastard shot Skip." He closes his eyes, clenches them shut actually, and swallows hard several times. "I've known Skip for over three years and that guy was about as harmless as they come. When he shot him, well, I knew things weren't adding up but I didn't know what to do. I figured I'd just go along with Jake."

"Jake?"

"Yeah, Anderson, the first mate. I could tell he wasn't entirely buying the whole thing either, but the captain's in charge, ya know?"

Dave nods, glancing over at Travis, who is swatting away the insects and scowling as he does so.

"Bugs ain't so bad in here," he remarks, slapping at one on his arm and exploring his face tentatively.

All of them are bitten up pretty badly from the onslaught of the swarm, but Travis looks to have gotten the worst of it. His cheek is bright red and swelling up to the size of a golf ball.

Travis notices them looking at him and he shrugs. "Fuckin' bug bit the inside of my cheek. Hurts like a bitch."

"You probably don't want to scratch that," Corbin says. "It might get infected."

"Yeah," Travis says, giving it one more scratch before reluctantly removing his hand. "Man, if I coulda grabbed some a my gear before we was forced into the boats I'da had somethin' ta put on this."

Dave considers for a moment their lack of supplies. Like Dr. Taylor, the first thing he thought of was their need for water. Without it they can't even clean their wounds, not to mention slake their thirst. His stomach rumbles mildly, but he doubts its hunger so much as lingering queasiness from all the puking.

"So ya never met the captain before this trip?" Dave asks and Corbin slowly shakes his head.

"Nope. Never laid eyes on him until two days before we left. Seemed all right then." Corbin glances around them, his eyes falling on the remnants of an old microwave covered in blackish/greenish slime. The thing looks ancient, a relic from the '80's no doubt. "I guess first impressions don't mean everything, huh?"

The three fall silent, Dave mulling over what he's just been told. The captain knew about this place, apparently, and he wanted to bring them here for…what? What could possibly be his motive for stranding them on a floating pile of trash? It just doesn't make any sense, but the longer they sit here trying to figure it out the worse things will become for them. They've only been on the trash heap for about an hour (according to Dave's watch) but it feels like a lifetime. All any of them have is the clothes on their back; no food, no water, no communication devices...if ever there was a situation that required survival skills of the highest degree, this is it.

"We gotta do somethin' and fast," Dave says at last. "There ain't no way we can survive out here."

"We have to get back to the ship," Corbin says. "That's our only hope."

"What about the other crewmen?" Travis' fingers linger over the large lump on his face. "Ya think they'll figger somethin' is wrong and call for help?"

"I don't know about that..." Corbin recalls the appearance of several others left aboard, the dull look in their eyes, their sluggish, awkward movements. "I think the captain might have drugged them or something."

"Speakin' a the captain, either a you see which way he went?"

"Wasn't paying attention," Corbin says. "But I hope those goddamn birds ate him."

"He dint seem to be afraid a them."

"I'm telling you, it's because he's sick. He isn't thinking right."

Dave agrees, but he thinks there's more to it than that. There's no doubt the man looks ill (his skin color is way off, as if he's jaundiced) but his jittery eyes gave the impression he was receiving information from another radio station altogether. One that was definitely not on the FM band.

"His antenna's pickin' up channel zero," Dave says, "and I ain't sure I wanta stick around here long enough ta see what else he's got up his sleeve."

"Well, fortunately we got half a day left, still plenty of light." Corbin nods toward the sky. "I think we should head back to the beach and see if the lifeboats made it ashore."

"What about them birds?" Travis asks, and when Dave turns to reply he sees his buddy clawing furiously at the protuberance on his face, his fingers dripping blood and dark green pus.

"Don't pick at that!" he scolds, and Travis casts his eyes away, wiping his hand on his shirt.

"Can't help it man. It's all itchy and it feels like somethin' is crawlin' around in there."

"Yer gonna get it infected dude, and we ain't got nothin' to put on it."

"Yeah, well if ya knew what this feels like you'd be doin' the same thing."

"Maybe," Dave relents. "Just knock it off, all right?"

"Yeah, whatever...fine," Travis says with no small degree of irritation. "But I asked you a question: what're we gonna do bout them damn bird things?"

"You an me need some weapons," Dave says, looking around them at the surrounding debris. "I'm sure there's somethin' in all a this crap we can use ta defend ourselves with. I had me a shower curtain rod but I lost it when we was runnin'." He eyes Corbin's rifle. "How many shots ya got left?"

"Full mag."

"Just what I wanted ta hear."

Corbin stands up, placing his hands on the small of his back and cracking it. "Okay," he says, "let's see what we can find for you guys."

FOUR

Through partially open eyes the governor looks up at the small patch of sky above him, for the moment keeping very still, forgoing any attempts to get up. The pain in his back is so intense he isn't even sure he *can* get up. He turns his head slowly to one side, seeing nothing but a wall of trash. He turns to the other side and sees the same. He'd like to know if he is completely enclosed but the slightest movement evokes a torrent of misery through his entire body; he doesn't even dare lean forward. Whatever he landed on is incredibly sharp, feels as if he's lying in a bed of broken glass. And to make matters worse there are, like, a hundred flies buzzing around him, alighting on his face and crawling over his eyelids, up his nostrils. He exhales powerfully, gingerly lifting his head and shaking it, but it does nothing to scatter them.

He attempts to raise his left arm but the motion shifts his weight to his right side, tipping him, and the pain increases. He lowers it and when his weight is once again evenly dispersed it returns to a steady throb.

"Help me!" he shouts at the top of his lungs, but his cry goes nowhere. The garbage deadens the sound of his voice like a baffle; there is no echo, no reverberation. The hole he's fallen into appears to suck the sound right into its very core.

A sob escapes him, wrought of hopeless despair and, if he knew better, he would avoid doing so because he can't afford to lose the moisture. But he doesn't know this so he carries on for a while, wallowing in a violent flood of self-pity. Maybe it would have been a good idea to stay with the group, but how could he have known? It was every one for themselves, and he didn't need anyone bringing him down, doing something stupid that would get him killed. But now he is paying for it, that's for sure. He's trapped, plain and simple, with no clear idea of how he is going to get out.

He takes a deep, shaky breath (careful not to get any bugs in his mouth though a couple sneak in anyway), noticing for the first time that he is getting used to the smell. It's still bad, stifling and pungent, but it is no longer making him sick to his stomach. Yet that's the least of his worries. If he doesn't get out of here he'll be a sitting duck for anything that comes along. This thought alone fills him with a bottomless dread.

What if those bird creatures find him, or something else even more terrifying? For all he knows there are all kinds of carnivorous critters inhabiting this shithole, just waiting for a chance to snack on the tasty morsel known to his constituents as Governor Theodore Hallsly Jr. Esquire the third.

"Help me!" he shrieks again, his voice cracking, his throat feeling raw, broken. Against his better judgment he gradually shifts his weight, ignoring the pain in his back, buttocks, arms and legs. Using his left hand to brace himself against one wall he rolls onto his right side and finally sees what he's lying in.

Jesus Christ! He stares at the back of his left arm, stunned. *You've got to be freakin' kidding me!*

Sticking out of his arm are dozens of syringes, the needles imbedded almost to the hilt. For a moment he lies still, eyeing them in a detached manner, as if this is happening to someone else.

I am lying on a bed of hypodermic syringes, he thinks serenely. *The thousands of pricks I'm feeling on every square inch of my body? Yep, that's what they are all right.*

And then his composure breaks, like an icicle that's become too heavy and breaks free from it's mooring, shattering on the ground below it.

"AAHHH!" He flails about, fighting to get into a sitting position, but with every move he makes he drives the needles deeper. He waves his arms around wildly, twisting his head back and forth, but all he manages to do is acquire more syringes, this time in his cheeks and temples. One pierces the inner wall of his left ear, causing him more agony than he's ever known, and another punctures his right nostril.

"Goddamnit! Goddamn all of you!" he bellows hoarsely. "I'll get every one of you, I promise! You can't mess with me! I'm Theodore Hallsly Junior the third!"

He screams until his voice finally quits and the pain becomes overwhelming. At last he ceases his struggles, issuing choked, strangled sobs.

"I never should have come on this mission," he snivels. "Goddamn you all…"

"Hey," a syrupy voice says, startling him into silence. "You be…*uhnnnggg*…quiet."

Governor Hallsly becomes very still, his eyes darting back and forth. He has never in his life been so happy to hear the sound of a human voice. He tries to swivel his head to look in their direction but can't move it more than a couple inches.

"Help me," he begs in a husky whisper. "I got, like, a million needles sticking in me."

"*Uhnnnggg*…pit trap," the voice says indifferently.

"What?"

"Pit trap. To…*uhnnnggg*…catch things."

"What in God's name for?"

"For…food."

His mind reeling, he suddenly makes a connection.

"Are…are you someone from the first ship?" he croaks, but the man doesn't reply. Instead he says something Hallsy doesn't understand. "What?"

Another voice (eerily similar to the first) replies, and Hallsy realizes he is addressing someone else. He hears movement above and, by the sound of it, several more people are arriving. He wonders, perhaps a touch irrationally, if he is saved or caught.

Caught? The hell you mean caught? What would they want with me?

Yet the fear persists, lingering until his self-control breaks once again.

'Answer me!" he bawls but they offer no response, continuing to confer with one another in their raspy, oddly cadenced speech above him.

"Oh Christ," he mutters, wishing for the umpteenth time that he'd never gotten on the god-damned ship.

"Look, Leeann, you've got to calm down," Dante pleads, attempting to hold her arms at her sides as she lashes out at him. The crewman with them simply watches in bewildered silence, and Dante shoots him an angry glance. "A little help?"

The guy rushes forward, taking Leeann around the waist, pressing his legs tight up against her to try and keep her still.

"Let go of me!"

"Shhh!" Dante says urgently. "Please, Leeann, for all of our sakes, just shut up!"

"I want to go home!" she cries, tossing her head around like a mad, whirling dervish, and when Dante accidentally gets too close her forehead smacks him in the nose, right on the bridge of his glasses.

"Ow!" he yelps, tears stinging his eyes, and at last he's had enough so he releases her. "What are you trying to do, break my nose?"

When he lets her go the crewman follows suit, ducking out of the way of her swinging arms. She takes several steps back, drawing rapid, panicked breaths.

"This can't be happening!" She looks from one to the other, her eyes wide, pupils dilated with fear. "This isn't real, none of this is real!"

"Leeann honey, calm down, okay? It's going to be all right, you just need to relax-"

"It's not going to be all right Dante, just look at where we are! Does this seem 'all right' to you?"

"I know it seems bad but we'll get through this, you just need to settle down-"

"The hell I will!" she howls, unleashing a calamitous cry that's nothing short of heartbreak-ing. "The! Hell! I! Will!" Abruptly her chest hitches and her eyes roll back to the whites, head lolling loosely on her neck, and she collapses to the ground in a heap.

"Leeann!" Dante yells, hurrying to her. He hunches down and turns her over on her back. Putting his ear next to her mouth, he feels warm air on his cheek. He blows out a pent up breath. "Thank God," he pants. "She just fainted."

"At least she finally shut-up," The crewman says. "'Bout damn time."

Dante looks at the other sharply, incensed, and is instantly surprised by his sudden onrush of anger. For a fleeting second he wants to bash this asshole's unsympathetic brains in but, instead, brushes a stray lock of hair out of Leeann's face and gently sets her head down before getting back to his feet.

"I'm Dante Kellerman," he says, holding out his hand. The guy is obviously scared, hell, they're all crapping their pants right now, literally and figuratively. He's rattled and he's taking it out on the only person who can't defend them self. Figures.

"Craig Kennedy." They shake, a quick, dry, three-pumper before letting go and returning their attention to the now silent girl. "She your girlfriend?"

"Uh, long story man," Dante says, shaking his head. "I don't want to get into it."

"You're the guy who stowed away aboard the ship, huh?" Kennedy asks, a small smile tickling the corners of his mouth. "For her, right? You did it for her?"

"Yeah. Another in a long list of stupid things I've ever done."

"But you don't regret it, do you?" the other wheedles, a certain knowing look in his eyes. "Even though you ended up here?"

Dante wants to say '*Of course I regret it! Why, I could be back in San Diego right now, delivering a large sausage and pepperoni to a frat house and getting stiffed on the tip, just waiting for the last remnants of the drugs to wash out of my system so I can hop into another pharmaceutical study and while away the rest of my lonely life...*' but he knows it wouldn't be true, that in all honesty he just wanted to be wherever Leeann was, even if it's here.

"No," he replies at last, looking at the crewman with a conviction that is unsettling. "My life wasn't worth living without her. I'm probably better off here."

"We're all better off here," Kennedy affirms, his grin spreading wide, and Dante doesn't like it, it's a little too 'gallows humor' for him. "Welcome to the best place on earth!"

"Yeah, right," Dante says disgustedly, looking away. "More like the asshole of the world if you ask me." It appears Leeann and he inadvertently picked the wrong guy to escape with. This dude is starting to give him a first class case of the willies. "So what do you think we should do?"

"I don't think there is any question of what we should do." Craig runs a gunk-covered hand through his short, red hair, smearing streaks of unidentifiable shit across his broad forehead. Abruptly his smile disappears, replaced by a forbidding look that, it would seem, spells their doom. "We have to turn ourselves in."

"What?" Dante gawps, aware for the first time of the sickly pallor of the other's skin. While large beads of sweat dot Dante's forehead and drip off his chin, the other's yellow-tinged face is dry, his eyes muddy, sketchy. "Are you crazy?"

Craig snarls, showing his teeth, and swings his rifle forward.

"Did you think I was just going to let you go?" he asks in a quiet, menacing tone, and Dante's gaze drifts toward the gun. "Who do you think you are?"

"Whoa, hold on now." Dante's voice is composed, his movements unhurried. "I'm not your enemy." He glances back at Leeann, can see her chest rising and falling evenly with each breath. "We have to stick together."

Craig laughs, a harsh, grating sound.

"I don't know if you noticed or not, but I work for Captain Harvey."

"You *worked* for Captain Harvey," Dante says, taking a small step forward, "and you know as well as I do that he's gone crazy. I mean, look around you! What are we doing here?"

"We've got a job to do." Craig thumbs off the safety. "And you and the others are trying to stop us. We can't let you do that."

"Stop you from doing what? From becoming like him? Is that what you want?"

"I guess it's all just a matter of perspective," Craig leers, twisting his head so he can scratch the back of his neck, and that's when Dante notices the large gash at the base of his skull, disappearing down his shirt. The laceration looks raw and inflamed, dark green pus bubbling within it. "Things look different from where I'm standing."

"I'm sure they do," Dante mumbles as the other digs at it, frowning in concentration, his middle finger slipping inside all the way to the knuckle. He watches with morbid curiosity, a sudden realization hitting him:

He's got it too, whatever it is. He's sick. . . just like the captain.

Dante moves away as Craig becomes more involved with his wound, his face contorting unpleasantly as he slips in another finger, and then another. He claws at it feverishly, his head pitched so far forward his chin rests on his chest. He closes his eyes and utters a strange, guttural purr that makes the hair stand up on Dante's arms.

"Ah, God it itches so much!" The hand that's holding the rifle goes slack, and the weapon falls from his grasp. Dante sees his chance and leaps forward, snatching it up, but the other doesn't notice. "This itches so Christ humping much!" He raises his other hand and, as Dante looks on, stunned, he peels apart the skin on both sides, ripping it wide open as thick freshets of blood and pus gush forth.

"Holy shit..." Dante whispers through frozen lips when Kennedy abruptly jerks his head up, his eyes meeting Dante's. All color is gone from them; they are now wholly black, nothing but pupil, and his flesh molts in the space of seconds, becoming the consistency of crinkled tissue paper. Thick veins stand out beneath his mottled skin, squirming and rippling across his cheeks.

"You...*uhnnnggg*...come with me to...*uhnnnggg*...captain..."

"Juh-Jesus Christ!" Dante exclaims, involuntarily retreating several steps.

Kennedy shambles forward, reeling from side to side as if he's intoxicated, but incredibly his footing is sure. His breathing is harsh, exceptionally labored, like his lungs are full of liquid.

"Stay back man!" Dante warns, lifting the gun, pointing it at the other's chest.

"We...*uhnnnggg*...go to...*uhnnnggg*...captain now..."

Dante takes yet another step back and something trips him. He sprawls backward, falling on his ass, but he somehow manages to keep hold of the gun. What he stumbled on felt soft, yielding...

"Dante..." Leeann whimpers, eyes fluttering open, consciousness returning to her just in time to witness the thing that used to be crewman Kennedy shuffling toward them, mouth stretched wide in an appalling grin, long strings of slaver dangling from his chin, swinging pendulously from side to side. She looks around and finds Dante trembling on the ground behind her, clutching the crewman's rifle in both hands. "For God's sake!" she screams, grabbing his leg and shaking it. "Shoot him!"

He looks at her uncomprehendingly, his hands shaking so badly the rifle jitters in his grasp.

"Dante!" she says again, louder, and slaps him across the face. In the process one of her nails gets tangled in his beard and pulls out a clump of curly hair.

"Shit!" he complains, rubbing his cheek, but clarity returns to him, and he raises the gun to his shoulder and looks through the sight, his finger tensed against the trigger. "Stay back or I'll shoot!"

Kennedy continues forward, oblivious, hands out before him, fingers opening and closing spasmodically, black eyes glistening like polished ebony orbs. He runs a sandpapery tongue over his swollen, discolored lips, making a sound like fingernails on a chalkboard.

"I'll shoot you, I swear!"

"Just do it!" Leeann shrieks and Dante pulls the trigger, the butt of the rifle slamming into his armpit as the muzzle flashes fire.

The left side of Kennedy's head vaporizes in a hot, sticky burst as he simultaneously falls to his knees.

"We...*uhnnnggg*...go to...*uhnnnggg*... captain..." he croaks from what remains of his mouth, crawling forward, and Dante fires again and again until all he hears is a dry clicking sound. At last Kennedy stops, crumpling face down with a sickening thud.

Leeann gets up quickly and takes the rifle from Dante. His eyes are dazed, lost, and she places a hand on his cheek and directs his gaze to hers.

"It's okay Dante," she says. "We should go now."

"Alright," he says listlessly, standing up.

Clutching the rifle in her left hand, Leeann takes hold of Dante with her right and, together, the two of them bound off through the labyrinth of the trash heap.

FIVE

"Christ, if I have to wait for you one more time you're on your own, got it?" The first mate's face is flushed with anger, spittle flying from his lips. He holds his rifle at chest level, his nerve endings attuned to any sign of preconceived danger.

"Okay, okay, I'm going as fast as I can! Give me a break!"

Tyler has Melissa draped over his shoulder and is doing his best to keep up with the other, but he keeps darting this way and that around the endless mounds of trash, and every few minutes Tyler loses sight of him and has to back track. This would be a lot easier if Melissa were conscious, but there is nothing he can do about it now.

("Run faster Melissa!" he'd urged, clutching her hand firmly. "I can't!" she cried, and as she lagged back he continued to pull her, obstinately plowing forward. A trio of Rancor Birds swooped down from the sky, the one in the lead landing on her head and getting tangled in her hair. She wriggled out of his grasp, seizing the foul thing and wrenching it free, screaming painfully when it's talons tore out a large clump of her jet-black locks. As she turned to hurl it away she wasn't watching where she was going and she collided with the rusted body of a wrecked car, her head striking the metal with amazing force, knocking her to the ground. Knowing he only had a few seconds before the other two birds descended, Tyler had scooped her up and tossed her over his shoulder, running like a man possessed to keep up with the first mate, who hadn't even bothered to slow down.)

Zigging this way and zagging that, they manage to lose the birds, but this doesn't comfort his travel companion, who continues his mad headlong dash into the unknown.

"Holy hell dude, slow down will ya? We lost 'em!"

"Can't take that chance!" Anderson yells over his shoulder, rounding a bend and disappearing from sight yet again.

Lungs heaving, his heart feeling as if it is going to explode, Tyler finally has to stop and rest. He gently places Melissa on the ground (hoping he isn't setting her into anything too disgusting) and leans over, hands on his knees. He remains like this for several minutes, trying to catch his breath, and it is in this moment he's grateful he quit smoking all those years ago. Thank God for the little things, right?

He glances at the sky, his breathing finally evening out, and sees nothing but clouds floating by. There's no trace of the birds that were following them, and this makes him feel a little better. Well, as best as can be expected, considering their circumstances:

Let's see, we're out in the middle of the freakin' ocean a zillion miles from land, stuck on a floating heap of garbage inhabited by birds that look like they were bred with lizards and then dipped in plastic. . .I'd say I've had better days.

He looks down at Melissa, wishing desperately for her to regain consciousness. Who knows how long they have before the flying lizards pick up their trail, not to mention anything else on this Godforsaken heap. Sitting still makes him feel jumpy, cagey, but what other choice does he have? He can't continue carrying her; she's just too damn heavy. If they do eventually catch up with the first mate he's going to bust him a good one in the chops for being such a prick.

"Fucking coward," he mutters, slapping at the flies circling his head. Lousy bastards are a goddamn nuisance.

Tyler squats down next to Melissa and puts his hand on her forehead. She feels slightly fever-ish, but that's not surprising. He puts a hand to his own forehead and finds he does too.

Tilting his head skyward again, he sees the sun is well past the midway point. The day is over half gone, and night should be a real hoot out here. With the exception of the white-knuckle ride they'd just been through on the ship, he's never in his life felt so certain he was going to die. The only question is when and, unfortunately, how,

Those stupid jack asses! Jake Anderson curses as he relentlessly continues onward, plunging ever deeper into the mire of trash. *They should have kept up with me!*

So caught up in his own terror, Jake had no idea Tyler was carrying the woman. His mind is filling in the gaps with it's own information, and all he remembers is the two of them rapidly falling behind, no matter how hard he tried to egg them on.

Ducking under the wing of a demolished, single engine plane, Jake stumbles into a vast area that is flat as far as the eye can see. His heart beats rapidly in his chest, his mouth suddenly very dry.

No man's land. No place to hide.

He turns, staring hard at the landscape behind him, realizing at last that he's been making turns without paying attention.

Which way back to the ship? A film of cold sweat covers him instantly. *I have to go back to the cove where we came ashore.* For that is the only escape route, correct? It's not as if he is going to find anything out here that's going to save him. An Exxon station where he can buy a cold soda and a sandwich and ask the proprietor for directions.

Fuck! Fuck fuck fuck!

He scans the sky, trying to locate the position of the sun, but a light scattering of clouds temporarily blocks it, offering him no answer.

Well, going back the way I came will work for starters.

Slower now, more deliberately, he backtracks through the network of rubbish, hoping to find a recognizable landmark that will indicate which path he should follow.

"Where the hell are we going?" Steven asks despairingly, his lungs on fire, his legs rubbery.

"Shut up and keep running!" Perry answers as he slogs frantically through the morass of rotting crap.

"We shouldn't have just left her there man! We should have done something!"

This stops Perry cold. He turns to the other, grabs him by the frayed remnants of his puke-spattered shirt.

"Yeah? What should we have done, huh? Gotten ourselves killed too? No thanks!"

"We could have helped her..." Steven says miserably, breaking into uncontrollable, wheezing sobs. "This is all just so, so...messed up!"

"Tell me something I don't know you goddamn pussy!"

"Why can't we stop and find a place to hide? I can't run anymore."

Perry searches the sky for the flying creatures, seeing nothing. Apparently they've ditched them, but that's no reason to let their guard down. Taking a deep breath, he notes idly that the only living thing they have to worry about now are clouds of a rather large and lumbering species of fly. They swarm around their heads in lazy, erratic circles, reminding him of those commercials about the starving people in Ethiopia, all those little kids with bloated bellies sitting in the dirt, eating worms as flies crawled all over their faces, too apathetic to even swat at them. And behind these wretched sons a bitches stood a grossly obese ex-sit-com star turned saint, looming over them like a god, begging the good folks of the US of A to give until it hurts, please, before it's too late and she decides to eat them herself. *Jesus.* He lets go of Steven and takes a step away from him.

"Okay," he says, looking at the other in disgust. "Let's find someplace to hole up."

"I think this will be fine." Steven falls to his knees. "We have to come up with a plan." He swipes at his face and instantly regrets it; the filth on his hands gets in his eyes, evoking a sharp, burning sensation. He winces and groans: "I feel so...*dirty.*"

"Yeah, well join the crowd." Perry squats down next to his shipmate. They say nothing for several minutes, their silence accentuating the stillness that hangs heavy in the air around them. Besides the minute buzzing of the flies there is no sound, the quiet so profound it reinforces the inestimable extent of the heap. It's like being in the middle of a National park, only this particular place would have the American Indian from that old TV commercial bawling his fucking eyes out instead of just the one lone tear that trickles down his sun weathered face.

That's right, this whole experience can be summed up by freakin'TV commercials. What a world, huh?

They sit like this for some time, each one cataloging a litany of silent complaints.

"I'm hungry," Steven says at last and Perry shoots him a dirty look.

"Good luck with that."

"What the hell is your problem dude?"

Perry feels unbridled rage rise swiftly within him, fighting the almost irresistible urge to punch the bastard in the mouth so hard he splits his lips open. Grinding his teeth like a speed freak, he glares at the other malignly.

Just do it, come on! Slug the whiny asshole, he deserves it! Bash him in the face until his eyes glaze over and he's a snack for the flies...

Perry starts at this thought; so lucid and visualized in his mind's eye yet so unwarranted. He glances away, ashamed. What the hell *is* wrong with him?

At last he looks over at the other, who is watching him expectantly. Perry shakes his head.

"I don't know man." He swallows, tasting something slimy slide down his throat. "I guess I'm just as freaked out as you are and I'm channeling it into anger. I-I'm sorry."

Steven nods eagerly, offering a wan smile.

"Its all right dude, this is, like, totally messed up." He slaps at the side of his head, trying to kill a rather persistent fly before adding: "And you're right. There was nothing we could do for her. You think she was in shock?"

"Yeah, probably. She was like a deer in headlights."

"Yeah..."

Again they lapse into silence but it's obvious the air between them is cleared, no more tension acting as a wedge to drive them apart.

"We should rest up and then hike back to the beach," Steven says at length. "I'll bet that's what everyone else is doing, unless they, you know..." He stops himself, not wanting to finish the sentence.

Unless they can't. Perry supplies silently, but simply nods. "Yeah," he agrees. "We don't want to get caught out here after dark."

"Hell no."

"So we take ten and move out. Okay by you?"

"Sure," Steven says. "Sounds fine."

The bizarre group says very little as they facilitate Hallsly's safe exit from the pit-trap, carrying out the task in a stolid, somber manner that is vaguely unnerving. Their hands are cool to the touch, and the governor is surprised at the strength they display, being as gaunt and sickly looking as they are; their faces are an unhealthy color, their eyes a dark, muddy brown/black hue that is rather disconcerting.

After assisting the governor in removing the myriad needles stuck in his hide, the man who initially discovered him indicates that he should follow them, pointing the way further into the trash heap.

"Wait a second guy, I appreciate ya'all's help and such, but I'm not going anywhere until you answer a few questions."

The man stares at him blankly, his face (especially his eyes) betraying nothing.

"Ques...tions?" he asks.

"Yeah," the governor nods. "Are you guys from the first ship? Is that where you came from?"

"The...first...*uhnnnggg*...ship?"

"For the love of God yes!" Hallsly snaps. "Is that how you're sorry asses ended up out here?"

The man studies him, his face unreadable. Hallsly waits, watching, swatting away the flies that continue to buzz around him yet for some reason leave the others alone.

"Time," the man begins, turning his head toward the sky. "Well…it doesn't…*uhnnnggg*… really exist…out…here…not…*uhnnnggg*…in the…normal…sense."

I didn't ask you about time you stammering retard. I asked you how you got here.

"It is…hard…for me…to…*uhnnnggg*…think back to…a…beginning…*uhnnnggg*…of…anything." He offers what might be a grin. "All I… know…is…that… I am…*uhnnnggg*…here… now…and…before I…..*uhnnnggg*…was my…*uhnnnggg*…life didn't…matter…much."

"You don't remember anything before being here?" Hallsly asks skeptically. This ain't exactly an island paradise.

"It isn't…important. What is…*uhnnnggg*…important…is…obeying the…Master…and… *uhnnnggg*…living to keep…our…creation…*uhnnnggg*…growing in…numbers."

"Your, um, creation?" *Or should I say 'uhnnnggg'…creation?*

"Yes," the man says. "You must…*uhnnnggg*…follow…me. I'll take…you…to the…*uhnnnggg*… village."

"The village?" A distinct feeling of alarm arises within him. You mean these leprous dick-holes live here, and they are *content* with that? That ain't right, not by a longshot.

"Yes. Come…with…us to…*uhnnnggg*…the…village."

"Oh, I don't think so." He sidles away from the other, keeping tabs on his buddies standing behind him. "I have to find the people I came here with, see if they're okay…"

"The…Master will…*uhnnnggg*…make sure…they…are…okay," the man replies firmly, stepping forward. "They…will all…*uhnnnggg*…be…at the…village."

"Great, great, but just the same-"

"You…*uhnnnggg*…have to…come…with me…*uhnnnggg*…now." The man reaches out and takes Hallsly's arm.

"Hey! Let go of me!"

"You will…*uhnnnggg*…understand…more in…time, but… for now you…*uhnnnggg*…will… come…with me."

The man's grip is like steel, employing a strength that seems impossible for his build.

"I said let me go!" Hallsly cries, trying to jerk his arm away but the other has him snuggly in his grasp.

The others approach, surrounding him. Their muddy eyes stare vacuously, gnarled hands taking hold of him.

"You will…come…with…*uhnnnggg*…us now…please," the man repeats and, as Hallsly sees it, he pretty much has no choice.

SIX

Captain Harvey stands at the water's edge, staring out into the ocean, his dark eyes unblinking although the glare that radiates off the black, sludge-encrusted surface is terrifically bright. He's bid the Rancor Birds to disperse, leaving the passengers to explore without their distraction, and now he is contacting the ship, giving them new instructions. Holding the walkie-talkie loosely in one fist, his other hand absentmindedly rubs his chest, feeling the life that grows within him. This life has been inside him a long time, but with his second coming to Garbage Island he knows it is escalating, maturing to a level that will surpass everything he's recognized so far. He has no idea what the next step in his evolution is, but he isn't afraid, nor is he impatient. When the time is right it will show him, as it always has.

A mounting anticipation gnaws at his belly like a great hunger as he thinks ahead to the upcoming days. He looks forward to sharing the secrets of the island with the passengers, can't wait to see understanding dawn on their faces when they truly begin to appreciate the tremendous importance of the roles they have to play here.

"Captain Harvey here," he addresses his next in charge. "I want you to send a message to the mainland that everything is going as planned, and then I want you to shut off the radio."

"Aye sir," the other replies.

Harvey scans the horizon, for what, he doesn't know. "Hold a radio silence until I say so. Comprende?"

"Aye sir."

"I have some new coordinates for the ship. Write these down."

Captain Harvey gives the man the location and then clicks off. Stuffing the walkie-talkie into one of his jacket pockets with one hand, he fishes around in his mouth with the other, finding a loose tooth. He takes it between two fingers and twists it until warm blood runs down his chin. He licks at it, enjoying the salty taste. Wrenching the tooth out, he examines it before putting it in another of his pockets.

He turns, studies the girl lying behind him. She is still alive; this he knows because he can see her intake of breath, but she isn't conscious, not yet. When she comes to she will indubitably have an altogether different opinion of her situation here on Garbage Island, in fact, she will find things to be to her liking. The captain is ready to help her make the needed adjustment to improve her state of mind, to show her that there is nothing for her to fear.

But have no doubt there are many things to be afraid of here, oh yes. The horrors of this little pit of hell have yet to reveal themselves entirely to the captives, but they will in due time. And then…the next phase of his plan can begin. , _

"What the hell was that?" Leeann sputters, feeling a stitch growing in her side. "Did I really just see that?"

Dante has resumed leading the way (having recovered from his brief spell of panic-induced lassitude) and Leeann is trailing along behind him, but it's still a case of the blind leading the blind. The garbage heap is such a vast network of paths, which spiral around and around (eventually leading to inevitable dead ends), that after a while he has no idea which direction they are running. Are they still traveling east, as he hopes, or have they gotten turned around, heading back the way they came? For the moment he simply isn't sure, and the sun can't help them because it's blocked from their view, the colossal piles of trash casting long shadows that envelop them like giant, skeletal fingers. He stops, catching his breath, glancing at Leeann as she eyes him expectantly.

"What?" he asks.

"You heard me," she says, a trace of irritation in her voice and, unexpectedly, it pisses him off. It's her tone; it positively reeks of disrespect, something he's been dealing with his whole life. "What *was* that?"

"How would I know?" he replies harshly, hostility and resentment combining to give her a good, old-fashioned one-two punch. "Do I look like the resident authority on weird-ass bullshit?"

She looks at him in stunned surprise, her mouth hanging open.

"Well you don't have to be an asshole about it!" Tears form in her eyes, her lower lip trembling, and at once he feels like a tool.

"Hey, hey, I'm sorry." He reaches for her but she bats his hand away.

"Don't touch me!" She turns her back to him, her waterworks a full- blown geyser now and Dante curses himself mentally. *Way to go genius, real tactful.*

"I don't know what happened back there," he says calmly, keeping his hands to himself. "Something made him sick I guess…"

She rubs her eyes, smearing the dried dirt that covers her face, and gives him a plaintive look that's nothing short of heartbreaking. Here she is just barely a woman, her teen years only recently behind her, in an unfamiliar environment that's proven to be an extremely dangerous place. She certainly doesn't need to be yelled at.

"I'm really sorry," he says earnestly, wishing he could take back the last couple of minutes and do it all over again. He doesn't know why, but for a second there he'd just snapped, seen red. And that's unusual for him; generally he's a very even-keeled person. "I didn't mean to holler at you." He waits patiently, allowing her all the time she needs to get herself together, and at last she offers a strained smile.

"I'm all right. I guess I'm a little on edge."

"We both are," he says, smiling and shrugging in a manner he hopes to be a sincere gesticulation of submission. "And I really am sorry. I shouldn't have spoken to you like that."

"This is all so…surreal…"

"You got that right."

"I feel as if I am asleep on the ship right now and this is a nightmare I can't wait to wake up from."

"God, I wish that was true," Dante says, seriously desiring nothing else more strongly in his life. He's been through some horrible shit during his stay on planet earth (like watching his baby sister choke to death and finding his mother dead in her trailer) but this surely takes the cake. You could pretty much sum it up as one hell of a bad day for Leeann, and just another fucked up scene in the life of Dante.

"What are we going to do?" She wipes away the last of her tears, taking a step toward him, and in this gesture he finds a small amount of comfort. He reaches out a hand to her and she takes it.

"For one thing we have to avoid getting bit by those birds."

"Do you think he was bit and, and it made him…"

"I think it could be possible," Dante admits.

"Where are we going?"

"I've been trying to head east, in the direction of the cove. We need to get back to the ship; there's no way we can survive out here."

"Do you think the others are all right?" she asks tentatively, and he can tell she needs reassuring right now, needs to hear something positive.

"I'm sure most of them are just like us, wandering around lost and scared. But I'll bet they're thinking the same thing, and they're trying to find their way back to the cove too. When we get there we'll all think of a way off this floating cesspool. At least we'll have power in numbers."

"Do you think anyone will find us? Like the Coast Guard, or the Navy or something?"

"Maybe, but at this point I don't know if anyone is aware we're missing. That's why we have to get back to the ship."

"He tricked us," she says with grave certainty. "Captain Harvey lead us to believe everything was all right until he could get us here."

"Yes, he did."

"I…I knew there was something wrong with him," Leeann says, looking at Dante shamefully. "I mean, before we got here, I knew he was acting strange."

"Really?" Dante asks, intrigued.

"When I went to talk to him to have you released, he…I don't know if I can put it in words because my memory of it is really hazy…but he wasn't right, and the things he said were just… horrible."

Dante nods, knowing exactly what she means although she's having a hard time articulating it. He did, after all, have an odd experience with the captain himself.

"Its as if, as if…he were a part of this somehow."

"Yes it is." He looks at her closely. "I knew there was something wrong with him too."

"You…you did?"

"Before he locked me up we had a talk in his quarters and…I don't know…same thing, I guess. One minute he seemed fine and the next it was like I was talking to a whole different person."

"That's how I felt!"

"Yeah, it was strange though, like, later I wasn't really sure if I saw it or not, like maybe I'd hallucinated the whole thing."

"Me too!" Leeann exclaims, and something about their shared experience draws them closer together. They trade a look that's almost intimate, and Dante feels a flush creeping up his cheeks. "What do you think is wrong with him?"

"I…I don't know," Dante says truthfully. "But I think he's sick. He was coughing a lot and spitting stuff in the trashcan. I saw some of it and…" Dante recalls the quivering puddle of white goo on the floor, how he had the distinct impression it was somehow…*alive.*

"And?"

"I don't know. I can't explain," he says dismissively, deciding it's probably best not to share that little tidbit with her, why, he doesn't know. Maybe because he doesn't want her to worry more than she already is.

"But if a bird bite made the crewman sick, how could the captain have it?"

"No idea. Maybe it wasn't a bird bite, maybe it was something else."

"What else could it be?"

"Maybe Dr. Taylor will have an idea," Dante says, suddenly wanting nothing more than to get moving.

"He brought us here for a reason though, I know it," Leeann says with a conviction that is startling. "I just can't figure out what it is."

"Yeah…" By all reasonable considerations one could speculate his conduct to be indicative of some ulterior purpose, but what that could possibly be is far beyond his scope of understanding. "It sure seems that way."

Dante glances at his wrist and notices his watch has stopped. Leeann utters a short laugh and holds up her hands, showing him her bare wrists.

"Didn't remember to put mine on this morning," she says. "It should be on the bedside table in my cabin." She laughs again. "Are we in a hurry?"

"I just don't want to be out here after dark, you know?"

This wipes the smile right off her face and Dante curses himself yet again.

You moron, watch what you say to her!

But Leeann surprises him and doesn't fret. Instead she shows she has the strength of mind to overcome it, to push past her fear, her once troubled eyes resolute and penetrating.

"Damn straight we don't." She takes him by the shoulders and turns him around. "Now get us out of here."

Her might is contagious, steeling his flagging fortitude. They have to be strong for each other.

"Yes ma'am."

Taking five to collectively catch their breath, Dave, Travis and Crewman Corbin stand at the edge of a vast plain of flattened waste, considering their options. Before them, as far as the eye can see, there is nothing but an endless, sprawling wasteland.

"There's no way we passed this before," Corbin says, his rifle clutched tightly in one hand, the other mopping sweat from his brow.

"Yeah, we woulda noticed this," Dave replies, glancing over at Travis, whose entire cheek has become a festering, swollen mass. "Yer not scratchin' that are ya?"

"Fuck no! I ain't no idiot!" he says hotly, but the truth is he's been picking at it every time the other's backs are turned, sometimes using the splintered tip of the axe handle he'd found. Shit, they would be too if they could feel what this is like. It's as if there's a swarm of pissed off insects inside his cheek and they desperately want out. No matter how much he scratches it doesn't feel any better, in fact it feels worse. One would think such misery would be a deterrent, but Travis isn't exactly in his right mind at this point. Its incessant itchiness is driving him to a certain degree of madness.

"It don't look too good."

"Yeah, well you don't look so great yourself."

"I'm just tryin' to help-"

"Screw your help!"

"Boys, boys, cool it," Corbin interjects, stepping between them. "We've got bigger problems right now. Somehow we got turned around. We're walking deeper into this shithole."

Dave concedes, putting his hands up (one holding a lamp minus the bulb and shade), and Travis scowls at him.

"I'm a big boy ya know. I can handle myself."

"And yer really good at it," Dave says, attempting to make a joke. "Ya know, handlin' yerself."

Travis grins. "At least *I* hafta use two hands."

"I wish mine fit in my hands," Dave sighs wistfully and the two share a laugh that harbors more anxiety than humor, but it's a laugh just the same. Corbin waits, letting them get it out of their system.

"I'll try an leave it alone dude," Travis relents, "but it itches like a mother fucker."

"Alright, and I'll quit naggin' ya. But, really, ya don't want it ta get infected." *Even though it already looks like hell.*

"Okay," Travis agrees and, for the time being, that's the end of it.

"What was it that scientist said?" Dave asks Corbin, bringing him back into the conversation. "Somethin' about this thing bein' three times the size a Texas?"

"At least that big, that's what he said."

"We could get lost for months out here if we go the wrong way."

"Try years. I used to live in Texas, and that's one big fucking state."

"Son of a bitch..." He turns and looks out across the plain. For some reason the trash hasn't piled up out here; it's uniformly level. He sees black goo (like the stuff in the water around the trash heap) bubbling up in isolated spots like tar pits, and it emits a gaseous smell that reminds him of sulfur but it's much more concentrated.

"I think we should-"

"What was that?" Corbin interrupts, cocking his head to one side.

"What?" Dave says. "I don't hear nothin'-"

Abruptly a loud, mewling noise erupts from somewhere unseen, its unearthly cry shattering the relative silence.

"Jesus Christ!" Travis raises the axe handle over his shoulder like a baseball bat and Corbin quickly puts a finger to his lips to shush him.

Dave swivels his head around, trying to extrapolate the direction from which it came, but he's noticed that sound travels very peculiarly here. It could have come from behind them, but for all he knows it might be coming from out on the plain.

The three whirl about brandishing their weapons, eyes wide, muscles tensed, when a similar cry arises from what seems to be a different location. It's simply impossible to tell where it's coming from exactly.

"I think it might be comin' from out there," Dave whispers, pointing, and the others stare into the distance, using their hands to shield their eyes from the pounding sun.

"Whatever it is, it sounds big," Corbin whispers back.

"I don't know bout you guys, but I don't wanna stick around an find out," Travis says, retreating a step, and Corbin bobs his head up and down.

"I'm with him on that one."

"Wait," Dave says. "We don't wanna go off half-cocked. We could walk right into it."

"I think it came from that way," Corbin says exasperatedly, pointing ahead.

"But sound travels funny here. We don't know that fer sure."

"Only one way to find out." Corbin turns around, starts heading back in the direction they initially came. "You guys coming?"

"Come on man, give it a minute-" Dave starts when suddenly a gigantic mound of trash explodes and heaps of rotten garbage rain down upon them. Travis darts backward, uttering a surprised yelp, and Corbin raises his hands to protect his head. He instantly disappears beneath an avalanche of waste. Now you see him, now you don't.

Dave is frozen in place, staring at the spot where Corbin once stood, and when he looks up he sees something that takes the wind right out of him, a monstrosity unlike anything he's ever imagined.

Corbin issues a muffled, anguished cry, but for the moment there is nothing Dave can do for him. Travis is motionless, mouth hanging open, his right hand on his inflamed cheek rubbing furiously.

Dave swallows thickly; the thing is so big it eclipses the sun.

"No freakin' way..." he mutters, his whole body feeling numb, paralyzed, until it starts moving toward him.

SEVEN

Tyler is staring blithely at the sky, swatting away the flies that swarm around his head when Melissa finally stirs and sits up.

"Hey, it's about time you woke up," he says, relieved. He'd been worried she was seriously hurt, had actually been contemplating what he was going to do if that was the case. He didn't want to leave her but, if push came to shove, he supposed he'd have to do whatever was necessary to save himself. For what it's worth, he's glad it didn't come to that.

"So...this isn't a dream." She touches her head carefully, probing what feels like a giant lump, and Tyler shakes his head.

"'Fraid not."

"How long have I been out?"

"I don't know, I don't wear a watch. But long enough for that dickhead to ditch us."

"The guy from the ship?"

"The one and only."

Melissa gets to her feet, her head aching terribly. The last thing she remembers is running from those foul birds, how one of them got in her hair and ripped out a clump...She shudders at the memory of the repulsive feel of the bird's squirming body in her hands.

"What did I hit?"

"An old car," Tyler says. "I think it was a Honda Civic."

"Well I'll be damned," she says wistfully. "This place has everything."

She takes stock of their surroundings, noticing that the sun has entered the western portion of the sky. There is a light breeze but it's merely pushing warm air around, as well as the ever-present stench of trash. But it doesn't seem so bad now. She must be acclimating.

"Which way did he go?" she asks.

"No idea. I was carrying you for a while, trying to keep up, but I lost sight of him pretty quickly." He looks away. "If I ever run into that asshole again-"

"Thanks for doing that," she says abruptly. "You know, for not leaving me."

He starts at her saying this, knowing how much she'd hate him if she realized how close he'd come to ditching her while she was unconscious...He gradually raises his eyes to meet hers, shrugging modestly. "Hey, you would have done the same for me." He grins and she smiles in return.

"Sure," she replies. "Sure I would."

The two stare at one another, her words hanging in the air, an assertion she very well may never have to make good on and they both know it. If it's a lie, well, than so what? They'll never know unless they're in that position again.

"So what are we going to do now?" she says. "You have a plan?"

"Been thinking that over while you were out. I have to warn you though, we don't have a lot of options."

"What are they?"

"Well," he drawls, squinting at her seriously, "we can either sit here and feel sorry for ourselves or we can try and find the others."

She shakes her head, laughing. "Jesus, you're such a dumb-ass."

He laughs as well, genuinely glad to be taking her abuse. For a while there he was afraid he was on his own, and this is no place to be alone.

"Maybe you should be the brains of the operation and I'll be the brawn," he suggests.

"Alright," she agrees, using the back of her hand to brush a stray lock of hair out of her face. "That works for me. On your feet and let's go."

Dr. Taylor inspects the pit of needles, stroking his chin thoughtfully.

"Pretty strange how all them needles happen to be sticking straight up," Cole observes with a lucidity that would be profound for a seven year old but, coming from a man his age, is just plain irritating. "'Cept the ones that are bent."

"It's a trap," the doctor sighs and the two look at him blankly.

"A trap?" Kenny asks, but then comprehension dawns in his eyes. "That would mean them people from the other ship is alive!" He looks at the doctor excitedly. "Right Doc?"

"That's what I was thinking, yes."

"How do you figure?" Cole says, confused.

"This, my friend, is a pit trap. Although it is crude in design it's purpose is quite clear. Just look at the blood on the needles."

"Something fell in there?"

"That's the basic idea of a pit trap," Kenny says and Cole shrugs.

"Okay."

"The blood looks fresh, don't it Doc? Somethin' fell in there recently."

"I think so."

"So what you're saying," Cole says slowly, putting it all together, "is that the people from the first ship are alive...and they're hunting?"

"What else do ya think it means ya moron? They gotta eat."

Cole blanches at the thought. "I don't think I'd want to eat anything from here."

"They have no other choice, do they?" Dr. Taylor says and Cole shudders.

"Damn…"

"Wouldn't eatin' these animals make 'em sick?" Kenny asks, and Dr. Taylor wipes sweat from his brow, hunkering down near the edge of the pit.

"Have a squat boys. Let's chat." He isn't so sure about Cole, but he thinks the black man has a few brains in his head. The pit trap reinforces an idea he has, a theory that might explain the captain's behavior, and this seems like a fine time to air it out, if only to hear it aloud himself. The two crouch down beside him and he begins to talk:

"Based on everything I've seen today, the ecosystem at work here is entirely unique, something I've never come across (or even imagined existed) in the whole of my professional life. We've encountered animals that, put quite frankly, appear to have taken a great leap up the evolutionary cycle, cross-species that have, to the best of my knowledge, gone undocumented thus far. You both saw the things that killed the Navy seaman; have you ever heard of giant carnivorous cockroaches? And what about the insects that attacked us in the boats? They looked like tarantulas with wings and stingers. Not to mention those fucking birds… As we can all attest to, these creatures are fantastic beyond our wildest dreams, and predatory in nature probably because we are intruders to their bionetwork." He pauses a moment, takes a deep breath, exhales, then continues:

"The research I'd done prior to this trip allowed me access to satellite photos, images taken at random coordinates because this place is so huge we couldn't possibly study every square inch, we simply didn't have the time or resources. Suffice it to say none showed clear evidence of anything other than birds, lizards and basic marine life capable of living here. I suspected that any of these animals consuming the refuse would either become poisoned and die or, very possibly, gradually become accustomed to the dietary change enough so that they could continue to exist, albeit with great difficulty. I surely didn't expect to come into contact with such radically altered life forms, and can only hypothesize that some of the wildlife have undergone transformations because of the toxins they've ingested. I mean, with everything that's being dumped out here, we have no idea what combination of chemicals these poor creatures have been exposed to, and what in turn will become of their long-term development. That said, here is my point: this trap indicates that the survivors are eating the mutated animals-"

Cole opens his mouth to interrupt (possibly to point out that the birds *are* lizards) but Kenny silence him with a glare.

"-and what we need to find out is if this is infecting them, causing them to behave in a manner that is, shall we say, erratic…"

"You mean it's making them puke and shit?" Cole says and Kenny rolls his eyes.

"I think it runs a little deeper than that," the doctor replies, frowning. "It may be possible that the contaminants have deviated their neurological faculties. In other words, the people might be dangerous. We all know that Captain Harvey appears crazy, but did you also notice the symptoms he was displaying? Bad color, dilated eyes, bronchial spasms…on the lifeboat I saw him produce mucous that swam away when it hit the water."

"No fuckin' way," Kenny says unbelievably.

"Way," the doctor answers gravely. "There has to be a reason for that, and what I am getting at is the possibility of a viral or bacterial contagion, which may be something he got from eating the animals."

"So ya think the other survivors got it too?"

"I can't say for sure, but it makes a lot of sense."

"Shit Doc, none a this makes sense," Kenny laughs and Doctor Taylor shrugs.

"Like I said, it's just a theory."

"I don't understand," Cole says, looking perplexed. "The captain just got here, like us. How could he be sick?"

"Because he's been here before," Doctor Taylor answers confidently. "I'll bet he was here before the other ship arrived, and I'll go even further and suggest he's the reason they're stuck here in the first place, just as we are. In fact, taking this even deeper down the rabbit hole, I'd guess he brought us all here for a reason."

"If you was ta make a guess," Kenny says uneasily, licking his lips. "What would it be?"

Dr. Taylor mulls this over for a moment while studying the trap.

"Well, if they are making traps to catch food it is only logical to assume they've formed a social order. With the development of a civilization come assigned tasks, such as creating shelter, hunting and gathering, food preparation and so on."

"Yeah?"

"So what else is important to a burgeoning society?"

"Cars?" Cole suggests and the other two ignore him.

"Propagating the species," Dr. Taylor supplies.

"Ta do what now?"

"Reproduction. The thing with life (all forms of life, from the most microscopic single-cell life forms to the largest mammal) is that it wants to recreate itself, over and over and over. It lives simply so that it can keep living. That's why the earth is teeming with so many different varieties of plants, animals, people...we are biologically programmed to reproduce and then to survive at all costs. In fact, for humans, it is considered to be a lapse of sanity should one not wish to engage in sexual congress. There are several reasons for this, some of them extremely superficial, but I think it's steeply rooted in the fear that it innately proves the afflicted party doesn't wish to maintain the status quo, which is successfully bringing more life into this world. Truth be told it is this weakness, this genetic trait, that causes so much trouble, from the overpopulation of urban areas, to the tens of thousands of unwanted children who starve to death yearly because there is no place for them, not to mention our intolerance of homosexual or individualistic behavior."

"So yer crazy if ya don't wanna screw...well...bitches anyway?"

Dr. Taylor smiles. "That's the gist of it."

"Wow." Kenny grins. "At least I know I ain't crazy."

"So what you're telling us," Cole says, "is that the captain brought everyone here so he could make more people...like him?"

"In so many words, yes."

"How the hell could anybody live on this thing?" Kenny asks, simultaneously mystified and disgusted.

"They've adapted to the conditions or, maybe, the conditions have adapted to *them*."

"So, in layman's terms they've all been poisoned?"

"That's another way of looking at it."

"Than if we was goin' with the supposition that they're hostile," Kenny says, looking down into the trap, "ya think they might a made this ta capture people?" He shivers, then looks back at the doctor. "Like us?"

"Yes," Dr. Taylor affirms. "I think they very well may have."

"Motherfucker," Kenny says. "As if we dint have enough to worry about."

"Run Travis!" Dave yells, but the other is frozen in place, his face a mask of fear. What he is staring at defies reason, challenges everything he's ever known. It's as if this place is a lunatic's playground of all that is bizarre and revolting.

Ya gotta be shittin' me! Is that a giant snail? Travis wonders, staring intently into its mouth, which is full of dinner plate sized serrated teeth. The goddamn thing is bigger than an elephant, its shell decorated in a blinding swirl of day-glo colors. It throws its head back and mewls again, giving Travis a whiff of halitosis that makes Chicago's sewer system seem like a breath of fresh air.

"Get the hell outta its way!" Dave watches as it moves with lightening speed, topping a mound of trash in the space of seconds. If he doesn't do something quick, he is about to witness his friend get eaten by something the French consider a delicacy.

He hears the muffled yells of crewman Corbin but, for the time being, he's better off where he is. Besides, there's really no time to think. He's reacting on pure instinct alone.

Searching the ground around him he spies the mangled remnants of a chair and he snatches it up, hurtling it at the approaching snail. It smashes against its head with the musical sound of splintering wood, a lucky shot, and it shifts its attention to him.

"That's right ya bastard! Over here!" He waves his arms around wildly as the enormous creature swings its head toward him, its great, beady eyes locking on his own. It switches directions, and Dave stares in amazement as it glides effortlessly over the trash, closing the distance between them quickly. "Oh shit!"

He turns tail and hauls ass, hoping it follows him and doesn't change its mind, deciding to hunt the easy prey. A hot breeze blows on his neck and, looking over his shoulder, sees it's right on his heels. He doesn't know if he should feel relieved or screwed (*ya owe me one Travis my man, that's a big ten-four*). Without any conscious planning he heads for the flat, open area. At least that way he can see where he is going and not get trapped in a dead end.

He stumbles into the clearing, tripping and falling over some unseen object. He lands face first, his chin taking the brunt of it, and his jaws click together with a sickening crunch. There is a flash of pain as he bites his tongue, but he ignores it and scrambles madly to his feet, swallowing blood. He dares another look over his shoulder and sees that it's within five feet and closing. It's mouth is open and it's tongue is flopping around like a banner in a high wind, a clear substance dripping off of it that spatters the back of Dave's legs.

He heads straight out into the clearing, running as fast as he can, his lungs, heart and legs screaming, when he hears another, similar cry coming from a different direction. He looks about him frantically, seeking the source of the sound, and when his eyes fall upon it his stomach drops into his shoes before bouncing back up and lodging in his throat. He stops dead in his tracks, his mind awhirl with many thoughts, but none of them an answer as to how he is going to solve this particular problem.

Before him, stretching as far as he can see, is a herd of the giant snails, looking like something out of 'Jurassic Park 6, Welcome to Garbage Island'. They vary in size, but the smallest of the bunch (by his best guess) is the one pursuing him.

"Holy shit…" he mutters as their heads pop up, their eyes as large as trash can lids, pinning him where he stands. "Holy...fuckin'…shit…",

"How do we know if we're going in the right direction?" Steven pants, wincing as he touches the back of his neck.

"We're going in the opposite direction of the sun." Perry points to the sky. "We came from the east, so we have to go back this way."

"At least the sun is good for something," he grumbles. "I feel like I got third degree burns."

"Do you have anything else to add to this situation," Perry snorts derisively, "other than pissing and moaning?"

"Sorry," Steven says, grinning. "I'm just really good at it."

"Duly noted," Perry replies, holding a hand up. "Wait," he whispers.

"What?" Steven whispers back, but the other shakes his head. A minute passes by. Then another. And then they hear it, the sound of voices close by, coming from beyond their field of sight.

"Alright!" Steven blurts excitedly. "We found somebody!"

"Shhh! Keep your voice down!"

"What the hell are you talking abou-"

"Listen!"

The voices are brusque, coarse. They speak in short staccato bursts interposed by long, gasping, watery breaths, as if they are struggling to expel every word.

"What the hell?" Steven says and Perry shoots him a black look.

"Quiet!"

The two crouch down, hiding themselves within the endless sprawl of debris, listening. It is hard to hear exactly what they are saying, but they quickly determine that the voices don't belong to anyone from their original group.

"-round them…*uhnnnggg*…all…up before…the…*uhnnnggg*…sun sets," one of them is saying.

"The...Master...*uhnnnggg*...wants them...all in...*uhnnnggg*...one...piece...if we...*uhnnnggg*...find them...that way," another adds, issuing a laugh that sounds like two pieces of rusted metal rubbing together. The other joins in and their combined jollity makes for a beastly, unsettling racket. Eventually they pass into the distance, their laughter growing fainter, until they are gone.

The two interns trade a solemn look.

"Who the fuck were they?" Steven says at last.

"I don't know." Perry's eyes are wide, scared. "But I don't like what they were talking about."

"You think they were talking about us?"

"Who do you think?" Perry stands up, clarifying: "I mean, I don't think they were talking about *us* us, but about our group from the ship."

"What do they want?"

"Damned if I know, damned if I want to find out." Perry reaches out a hand to the other, helps haul him to his feet. "Come on. We have to find some of the others and fast."

EIGHT

Several crewmen are gathered on the bridge, huddled around Lieutenant Ronson as he charts their new coordinates. Because the captain and first mate aren't present (and the second mate is no longer with them), he's now in command.

"What do you think about this?" one of the men from the engine room, Barry Slovovich, asks and Ronson peers up from the GPS tracker, looking askance at the other.

"What do I think?" he says, his voice low, steady, but there's a trace of malice lurking beneath the surface. "What's to think about? We've been given our orders and we'll carry them out."

Slovovich exchanges a troubled glance with Graham Edelstein and Ronson scowls at this hint of dissention. He straightens up, stares querulously at the two men.

"Are you questioning the decisions the captain has made?"

Barry regards the other with an air of insolence but says nothing.

"If you feel that what we are doing is wrong than you haven't been paying attention. Captain Harvey was only acting in accordance to standard protocol in dealing with a potentially hostile situation." He glares at Slovovich and Edelstein, the two men's eyes boring into him like steel drill bits. He catches and holds Slovovich's gaze, directing this next part to him specifically:

"The captain wasn't going to sit idly by, allowing the eco-terrorists to get the upper hand. He felt it best to expedite the process himself."

"But he shot Skip," Slovovich says. "There was no call for that."

"Are you saying you know what is best for this ship, that you know better than the captain?"

"No sir, I'm not but-"

"Do you realize I am authorized to act on his behalf, my instructions being to shoot anyone who doesn't do as they're told and asks too many questions?" Ronson unsnaps his holster, placing his hand on the butt of a long barreled .38 Special revolver. The men standing closest to Slovovich quickly step away, but Barry holds his ground.

"So you'd shoot me", he says, "for asking questions?"

"Would you like to find out?"

"His request for radio silence doesn't make sense," Slovovich persists. "Isn't the White House going to wonder what's going on?" He looks at the other beseechingly. "We have a right to know what all this mission entails."

Ronson sighs, removes his hand from the gun and runs it through his hair. "You know, Barry, I remember when you started working on this ship, how many years ago was it?"

"Four."

"Four years. My how time flies." He clears his throat and smiles congenially. "When you first started, why, I recall withholding most of the details of our missions from you. Do you know why that is?"

"No sir." Slovovich shakes his head." I don't."

"There was no reason to tell you," Ronson says in a hard voice, "because your opinion was irrelevant."

The crewmen shift their feet uncertainly, looking from one face to another, the accuser and the accused. One of the men utters a loutish chortle.

"How much do you think your opinion means to me now, after all these years?" Ronson's lips curl back in a sneer. His hand returns to the butt of his gun, a gun he never carried before today.

"I don't know sir," Slovovich answers quietly, but his voice doesn't waver, he keeps his composure.

"Jack shit, that's how much." He waits a beat, lets this sink in. "How do you like that?"

"I don't sir."

"Well, tough fucking titty." Ronson turns toward the men, taking a large padlock from his pocket and setting it next to the radio. He pulls down the chrome hood that houses the unit, clasping the lock in place.

"I am the only one who knows the combination to this lock, and until the captain says so no one will have access to the radio. Is that clear?"

"Yes sir," the men say, their voices calm, subdued.

"We have the new coordinates from the captain," he says, looking from one man to the next. "There will be no questions about this. You will do as you are told or you'll be removed from active duty. Is *that* clear?"

Again they mumble their assent. Ronson nods.

"Very good." A smile as tight as a drum flits about his lips. "Well what the hell are you waiting for? Get back to work!"

The men disperse quickly, all except for Slovovich and Edelstein, who linger after the others are gone. When he's sure the coast is clear, Edelstein closes the door.

"Permission to speak freely sir," Slovovich says.

"Permission granted."

"You've never acted like this before, sir," Slovovich begins earnestly. "I'd like to know what's going on."

"Acted like what?"

"You're carrying a gun for Christ's sake! Since when do you carry a gun?"

"Since I am now in charge. If you have a problem with that I suggest you take it up with the captain."

"The captain, yeah, that's a good one. Edelstein and I think there's something wrong with him, something *really* wrong. Nothing he's said has made sense since we got here."

"Is that so?"

"You bet your ass it is! Ever since we had that meeting in the engine room this has been playing out like a bad science fiction movie. Accusing the passengers of some ridiculous plot, shooting Skip, taking everyone to the trash heap without Hazmat suits…and now switching our coordinates without alerting the mainland and enforcing radio silence? This is crazy sir, crazy!"

"I'm sorry to hear you feel that way about it, but I'm afraid you have no say in this matter."

"Jesus Christ!" Slovovich swears helplessly. He looks at his companion. "Come on Edelstein, tell him what you think!"

Ronson shifts his gaze toward the other man. "Yes Edelstein, tell us all what you think…"

Edelstein advances, taking Slovovich from behind and putting him in a headlock. Slovovich struggles, but he is no match for the other man, who outweighs him by twenty odd pounds and stands several inches taller.

"What the hell are you doing?" Slovovich gasps. "I thought you were on my side!"

Ronson quickly steps forward and stuffs a wadded up handkerchief in his mouth. Slovovich tries to cry out but all he can issue are muffled grunts.

"Didn't you know? Edelstein works for the captain so, in turn, he works for me."

Slovovich struggles within the other's grasp but he is no match for him; his arms are locked solidly in place. Ronson leans forward, his face so close that Slovovich can see black tendrils filling the lieutenant's eyes like smoke and, startled, he begins to choke, trying to draw air around the obstruction in his mouth.

"Listen you little punk, and listen good," Ronson whispers in his ear. "We are a crew, therefore a team, and presently there are only a few of you left. We don't need anyone to stir up trouble before everything is complete."

Slovovich utters a cornered groan as manic thoughts reel through his feverish mind. Why would Edelstein sell him out? Just last night they'd agreed the captain was reckless, knowingly leading them into a veritable typhoon while keeping the crew in the dark. And this business with the passengers…surely the man was slipping if he truly believed there was a plot afoot. Goddamnit, Edelstein's turn around doesn't make any sense!

But what makes even less sense is the gripping unease he gets looking at Ronson's horrible countenance; it twitches and writhes with tidal waves of ticks surging just below the surface of his skin, veins pulsing darkly, his façade one of absolute depravity.

Ronson reads this in his eyes, his confusion and fear and, uttering a bitter laugh, he pulls away and says in a hideously deranged voice:

"He's one of us now Slovovich, just like you will be soon enough. Just like the rest of the men. My suggestion? Roll with it."

As the afternoon kicks into full swing it brings with it high temperatures that are nothing short of oppressive. Humidity hangs in the air like mist, a liquid cloak that enshrouds everything within its dank vapor. The heat amplifies the stink of the heap, anything that was once living rotting in the sweltering haze. The foul stench finds its way into Melissa's sinus cavities, coating her nose and throat with a substance thick enough to swallow. She gags and dry heaves, but all this manages to do is make her stomach hurt. Her eyes watering, she holds a rank hand to her face.

"I don't know how much more of this I can take."

Tyler, who isn't faring any better, nods his agreement. He has long discovered that the fusty odor of his hand is far more pleasant than the atmosphere without.

They've been walking tirelessly for the better part of an hour, heading in the opposite direction of the sun. If luck is with them they'll soon stumble upon the cove or, at the very least, the cliffs surrounding it. Of course, if luck isn't with them, they could wind up anywhere. What they've discovered as their trek continues is that it is very hard to track the sun because until it moves through the sky it's positioning is hard to pin down, very difficult to calculate. It's for this reason that they've made nonstop adjustments to their course, going in an erratic, zigzag pattern that frustrates them both.

Melissa studies the terrain for anything familiar, something she recognizes, but it all looks the same. After a while, trash looks like trash looks like trash. Is there any way to really tell? Certainly they passed something that stood out from the other detritus, something that didn't blend in with the rest of the scenery.

Unexpectedly she spots an item that jogs her memory: a ripped up mattress lying atop the miscellany of a child's box frame. The frame may have once been painted a pretty pastel pink but it's now faded to an off-white color, speckled with mold and unidentifiable crud. She's not a hundred percent sure, but she thinks she saw it on their way in, shortly before the birds swooped down on them.

"I think we're getting close," she says, kicking a deflated football that bounces off a crumbling bookshelf and lands with a muffled thud. "It's this way."

"God, I hope so."

Melissa glances upward, relieved to note there's still no sign of the birds (nor anything else for that matter, save for the flies) but decides that's no reason to abandon her vigilance. Who knows what else is lurking out here amongst the festering accrual of humankind's sloth. For all they know the birds are the least of their troubles.

Keeping attuned to the slightest noise, or even a suggestion of movement, she scours the trash strewn about them, considering how many thousands (screw that, millions) of tons it took to create something this formed, this solid. She remembers seeing a program on TV about this place over a decade ago, a special hosted by a handsome news reporter who talked as if his tongue was stapled to the roof of his mouth, the jack-ass smiling smugly at the camera like he knew something he wasn't telling. She was just a girl then, and she'd thought the whole thing was hilarious. Imagine, an island of garbage! What a gas! Who'd have thought she'd have the rather dubious honor of touring the place herself one day? Certainly not her. In fact, if her childhood self could witness this, could see what she'd become (this fantasy occurred to her sometimes, wondering what her innocent, fourteen year old self would make of her at the age of twenty-five) she'd probably be scared shitless.

I'd probably run screaming from myself, would refuse to believe that's what I'd turn out like.

This thought evokes in her a great sadness, as always feeling pity for the lost, lonely little girl who trusted her elders even as they abused her, believing in them although they always let her down.

A single tear runs down her cheek and, angrily, she swipes it away.

The hell with that, I'm *that little girl! Like it or not she is me.*

Tyler trails along carelessly behind her, inattentive to the passing landscape, shoe-gazing and feeling sorry for himself. His thoughts are essentially mundane, in that he is fixating on his discomfort:

> *Jesus H it's hot out here. I must have lost half my body weight in sweat. This place totally blows balls man, big, fat, hairy donkey balls bro. A fuckin' cold beer would really hit the spot right about now. That and a roast beef sandwich. . .*

Making their way between two mountainous ruins of engine parts, putrefying animals and various plastics, Melissa suddenly catches sight of the ocean, lazing in the near distance.

"Speed it up slowpoke!" she says. "We're almost there!"

"It's about freakin' time," Tyler pants and, a few minutes later, they stumble upon the 'beach'.

Melissa steps ahead cautiously, keenly aware that the captain could be lying in wait, hoping they'd be foolish enough to come back. She gazes furtively up and down the coastline, seeking out his hulking, ravaged form, listening for the sound of his rasping, chronic cough and, after a long, tense moment, finally concedes they are alone; there's nothing here but themselves and the desolate shore.

Tyler lingers behind her but his expression is that of a college frat boy awaiting the checkered flag to signal the beginning of the festivities. She nods to him, waving him forward.

"We made it!" he exalts, taking Melissa in his arms and swinging her around.

"Hey, take it easy," she warns, although she is smiling. "I just might barf all over you."

"Barf away my good lady," he says, letting her go. "I'll even hold your hair for you."

"My, what a gentleman. . ."

They turn toward the sea, shielding their eyes against the glare off the water, searching for the ship. What they see (or, rather, don't see) puts a direct halt to their celebration. The horizon before them is empty, no sign of the research vessel bobbing up and down placidly on the clement waves, no flash of sunlight reflecting off of polished chrome.

"We must have come out in the wrong place," Tyler says, looking desperately up and down the 'beach'. "This must be a different cove."

"I don't think so," Melissa says, pointing. "Look."

Tyler stares ahead to where she is indicating, apprehension making his stomach churn unpleasantly.

The lifeboats are lying on the shore, one upside down, the other tipped over on its side. The repugnant black water that surrounds the trash heap laps against them, varnishing the boats in its slimy filth. There is absolutely no doubt, this is where they came on all right.

"Wait!" he cries jubilantly. "The lifeboats! We have a way off of here!"

Melissa's heart jumps at the thought, but as her eyes search the immensity of the sea beyond the blackish/brownish sludge she realizes it doesn't matter, they won't do them any good. Summarily the courageousness she'd felt as they trampled through the wilds of the heap extinguishes, leaving her as quickly as it came.

"Where will we go?" she asks in a small voice. "We're thousands of miles from anywhere, and we don't even know where the hell we are."

"Any place is better than here."

"But we don't have any drinking water," she says, dropping to her knees. "We'll die out there."

Tyler squats down next to her and puts an arm around her shoulder.

"Think of all the ships that come out here to dump illegally," he says optimistically. "Maybe one of them will spot us."

Melissa shakes her head, tears spilling from her eyes, surprising her with their sudden onset. To think she'd been so strong, so determined and now, with the absence of the ship she feels her strength ebb away like the last rays of the evening sun.

"Let's face it, without the ship we're screwed."

"Someone will find us," Tyler insists. "They have to."

"No one has to do anything!" she cries, her rage and utter disappointment at the bleakness of their situation exploding from her in a tumultuous burst of animosity. How can he be so dense? She twists free of his arm, sneering at him maliciously. "This isn't a fucking movie you idiot, this is real life! In real life bad things happen and there is nothing you can do about it!"

Tyler stares at her dumbly for a moment, unable to comprehend what she's saying. Didn't he just, like, save her life? You know, when everyone else was running all helter skelter, trying to save themselves, didn't he just make sure she didn't become a feast for those birds? Why the hell is she yelling at him?

"Hey, hey, I'm just saying that-"

"You're always 'just' saying something! Do me a favor and keep it zipped for a change!" She glares at him, the fury mushrooming within her. Just looking at him makes her want to punch something. "Think you can do that? Keep your goddamn trap shut for two seconds? Jesus Christ!"

"I really think you should calm down-"

"Calm down? Calm down? And what, my poor deluded friend, would that do for me? It's hopeless Tyler, hopeless! The sooner you get that through your thick skull the sooner we can get on with more important things!"

Tyler is stunned, his cheeks turning bright scarlet, his vision blurring, expanding and contracting as anger rises swiftly within him. After all he's done for her (well, it wasn't much, but he did save her life) how can she treat him like this? What gives her the right?

And, just like that, something snaps inside. He can almost hear the sound it makes, like the roar of some unearthly monster dredged from the deep.

"Yeah?" he retorts, his nerves hackling, his indignation fully engaged. "Let me tell you a little something about 'real' life! In real life people don't do stupid shit like following sex-crazed politicians on boat trips, especially when they don't even know where they're going!"

Her head pops up, eyes blazing. "I didn't see you stopping me! In fact, you thought it was a great idea!"

"I only thought it was a great idea because I saw it as a way of not having to work!"

Melissa recoils as if struck. "I thought you wanted to be with me!"

"Not as much as I didn't want to work," he tells her honestly, rising to his feet and backing away. "There, I fucking said it."

"You son of a bitch," she says softly, marveling at her own stupidity. "I totally misjudged you." She glances at him briefly and looks away. "I should have known you had an ulterior motive."

For an instant Tyler regrets what he said; she didn't need to know that, it's just that she pushed him. But there's no reason for her to attack him, not after what he did for her…and like it or not she's the one who started it.

"I could have left you out there to die."

"I don't want to hear it." Her anger is dissipating, the hopelessness of their situation over-whelming her. "Save it for someone who cares."

"You started it," he says. "Besides, you don't understand-"

"What's to understand? You're just a self-centered, lazy bastard who didn't want to lift a fin-ger to earn his own keep so you came on this trip with me because you thought it was easy money. Probably thought you'd get a little nookie to boot. You're an asshole Tyler, a total fucking asshole. There, I fucking said it."

He stares at her wordlessly, unsure how this all went sour so quickly. One second they were celebrating their discovery of the lifeboats and the next they're at each other's throats. Well, if that's the way she feels about it, he doesn't give a damn. The bitch can fend for herself for all he cares.

"Fuck you," he says, unable to come up with anything better.

"Fuck me," she nods, agreeing. "That's what got us into this whole mess."

The enmity that had been slowly subsiding suddenly flares up again; Tyler can feel it build-ing inside him, a restless, pointless fury. She's the one who lashed out at him simply because he'd offered a solution to their situation, a way to save themselves. What it all boils down to is she is an irrational, overemotional cunt. He'd like to point this out to her, maybe start by calling her every name he can think of, segueing into a little gender classification abuse then round it all out with a thought provoking slap in the face, but in the end he feels drained, spent. And, shit, he shouldn't have told her he only came along so he didn't have to work. Bad form, baby, bad form…

"Melissa-" he starts but she lifts a hand, waving him off.

"Not now Tyler, I have a headache." She sighs, feeling all used up. She doesn't want to fight. Why expend the energy? For the moment she is through with him.

"No, really, listen-"

"Tyler," she says, her voice calm, quiet. "Just shut up and don't talk to me, huh? You've already said enough."

He opens his mouth to say something else, to further his point, but her resigned tone sud-denly defuses him. Instead he sits down and for once does what she asks. It's obvious even to him that he's shown himself for what he really is: an unrepentant prick.

However, he still thinks his idea to take the lifeboats is a good one, and after she calms down he'll bring it up to her again. At that time if she doesn't want to go he'll simply leave her, adios muchachos and all that happy crap. Just see if he doesn't.

Looking behind him, Dave calculates that the giant snail chasing him should reach him in less than thirty odd seconds, give or take. Looking ahead, he sees that the herd has sounded the charge, blatting out deafening cries that would almost be funny (if this was a Saturday morning cartoon and they were friendly monstrous snails) but instead is nothing short of underwear soiling. Their heads reared back, mouths stretched wide, they emit yowls so resonating he can feel them in his chest, competing with his heartbeat. And they move quickly. That's the part that really sucks.

Seeing a clearing, he darts forward and strategically dives out of the way of an approaching snail, tumbling into a somersault and then getting back to his feet, which are already running. He doesn't want to lose momentum by sneaking a glance behind him; he figures he'll know if they are close by feeling the heat of their breath on the back of his neck.

His breathing rapid and shallow, his heart hammering, he runs like he's never done before, with his life *truly* on the line. He jumps over a patch of melted plastic, noting (in some dim corner of his mind) that it looks like the remains of a Big Wheel interspersed with waste from a million fast-food wrappers. He lands hard on his right ankle and for a second thinks it's going to give way as a sharp burst of pain shoots up his calf, but his military training wins out and he is able to ignore it, to shove it away so that it doesn't exist. Nothing exists except for him and these enormous slugs, and they are not going to get him, not today my friends.

The good thing about the open area is that he can see everything coming at him. The bad thing about it is there's no place to hide. Not that hiding would do any good, not if they are serious about finding him.

Fuckin' man-eating snails. . . He almost wants to break into delirious laughter. *They must have gotten tired of being the entrée.*

He hears the sound of the trash heap's floor being churned up, and what it reminds him of is the tracks of a tank, how they grip the ground and propel their large, awkward metal bodies forward through all types of otherwise impassable terrain. It occurs to him that this is how they are moving, thrusting themselves relentlessly onward at a speed that is terrifying.

Chancing a quick look over his shoulder, he sees they are gaining. Unless he can outrun them or find a place to hide he is about to experience what it's like to be eaten alive by something that shouldn't even exist, something no human in his or her right mind would ever *believe* existed.

And then, at last, he feels it, the warm breath parting the hair on the back of his head. He can hear the snorts of their exertion, can feel his legs getting rubbery, the muscles weary, played out. All it would take is a Charlie horse and it would be all over for him; his short life finished before he even had a chance to do anything useful with it. Is this what everything has been leading up to? Really? To go through all this shit only to be consumed by a creature spawned in a cesspool overridden with rotting fast food cups?

He trips over a massive truck tire and this time he can't keep his balance. He pitches forward, his arms extended before him to break his fall but, really, is that necessary? What does it matter that he protect his face and head when it is going to be chewed up and shit out in about as much time as it takes to cook a turkey…

But instead of hitting the ground he falls further, into a hidden recess. At once he is immersed in brackish bilge, about the temperature of bathwater.

Those bubbling pools, he realizes as he submerges, gravity and momentum sinking him deep into the pit. *I must have fallen into one of those.*

He wants to open his eyes but remembers the burning sensation when he did so in the ocean, and this water is thicker, almost the consistency of mineral oil. It wouldn't be a good idea.

Flailing his arms he spins himself around, trying to fight his way to the surface as quickly as he can but the gelatinous water is making his every movement that much harder. Against his own best advice he opens his eyes and an intense pain sears his eyeballs. It's as if he is soaking in gasoline.

Searching frantically, his fingers brush against something solid and he snatches at it, trying to use it as leverage, but it slips from his grasp, the oily water making it too slick. He reaches for it again and his head pops above the surface, only to collide with something that sends him back under. Blue dots dance behind his eyelids, and when he tries again he resurfaces much slower. Easing his head out of the tainted brine, he finds there is no opening above him, merely a small pocket of airspace in between the water and the ceiling of the trash heap.

The current must have pulled me away from the spot where I fell in. It's like being trapped under ice except worse: I'm trapped under a floor of garbage.

Something brushes against his leg and involuntarily he cries out; he recalls vividly the giant cockroaches that made quick work of the other Naval seaman and the thought is enough to make his skin crawl. This is it. Any time now he is going to be shredded by some unseen terror, an ecological nightmare created by man's excess. He waits to feel it again, long seconds that tick by like hours, the sour smell almost choking him in the confined space, claustrophobia closing in around him like a thick blanket.

Treading water, he wonders how long he can keep this up before he tires and if, God help him, he'll be able to find a way out by then.

NINE

"Hang on!" Travis yells hoarsely, clawing through the trash, honing in on Corbin's voice. Sweat pours down his face, his cheek itching infuriatingly. He'd love to stop and scratch it but for now he does his best to ignore it, fighting valiantly to save the other because he doesn't want to be left alone. Not out here, not with Dave gone.

Travis takes a rotting board in both hands and tugs at it urgently, disregarding the pain as splinters dig deep into the palms of his hands. If he doesn't hurry it's possible that Corbin could suffocate under there. Reaching in again, he pulls out seemingly endless clumps of sodden Styrofoam and tattered bubble wrap.

"Please man, help me!" The sound of his voice is growing louder, and Travis figures he must be getting close.

"I'm almost there!" he assures him, redoubling his efforts.

But damnit to hell how his cheek itches! It's like there are live creatures crawling around in there, trying to get free. He knows that's impossible, of course, but he swears he can feel them twisting and squirming, their bodies pressed tightly against one another, their legs tap dancing with a frantic, pent-up energy. He stops what he's doing for a second, lets his right hand wander to his cheek. Tentatively he brushes his fingers against the skin and at once it bristles, flaring up painfully. Jesus God he would love to tear the damn thing open and have it over with! But that would be giving in, and what would Dave think of that? He pictures his friend, imagines him looking at him disappointedly, a scowl creasing his face.

'*Don't do it dude, just stay focused on what yer doin*', the Dave in his mind's eye tells him and he nods, as if the other is right there with him.

"I'll do my best buddy," he says aloud. "I'll do my fuckin' best."

And how is Dave fairing against the giant snail? he wonders. That was a brave thing he did, leading it away; he definitely took one for the team. He hopes with all his heart he's okay, that they'll meet up again soon and have a good laugh over this. I mean, giant snails? Come on man, if that ain't a gasser he doesn't know what is. And hell, knowing the other as he does, he figures if anyone can evade capture from man or beast, it's certainly Dave.

With renewed hope he digs faster and, at last, he sees a hand, then an arm. Knocking the debris aside, he finally uncovers Corbin's face. The crewman takes in great gulps of air, his eyes shining with relief.

"Holy shit!" Corbin gasps. "Thank God!" The crewman peels saturated pieces of cardboard from his face and chest, then pushes a splintered table off of his legs.

Travis grasps the other by his wrists and hauls him into an upright position. Corbin is covered in a thin film of slime and the odor that comes off him makes his stomach lurch sickeningly. Trying not to breath through his nose, he helps extract the crewman from his would be tomb.

"Thanks man, really. You don't know what it was like under there."

"Bad?"

"Beyond bad," he answers, shuddering. "Way beyond bad."

With Corbin on his feet Travis falls back a step, gulping great lungfuls of air. For some reason his exertions have made him extremely tired, and his cheek, which he momentarily forgot about, resumes it's infernal itching, intensified considerably from the last onset.

"Fuck!" He's trying to leave it alone but he is no longer in control. Upon their own accord his hands seek it out, digging into the tender skin. His nails (which he has always kept moderately short) find enough purchase to burrow into the inflamed lesion, and as he scratches he experiences a sensation that is nearly orgasmic.

"Hey man, don't do that," Corbin says, but his voice comes from far away. Travis can barely hear him, like the volume has been turned down on everything around him. Instead, all he can ear is a loud buzzing that seems to be coming from inside his head. A loud, angry buzzing...

This discomfort, man, it's worse than the time he had poison ivy, and he'd had it all over his body. He'd been screwing around with his girlfriend in a state park, having wandered off the path with nothing more than a six pack and a hard-on, and little did he know that the ground they were rolling around on was covered with the stuff. His ass, balls and dick erupted with large, red welts and, in his stupidity, he'd managed to spread it all over by scratching it and then touching himself. That had been bad, really bad, but this is a hundred times worse, if that's possible.

"Come on man, what are you doing?" Corbin says, watching Travis disgustedly. The guy is digging into his cheek with both hands, freshets of thick blood (co-mingled with dark green pus) flowing over his fingers, but the other pays him no mind, like he can't even hear him.

All of Travis' attention and energy are focused on bringing himself respite from the damned itching. He scrapes his cheek with his nails, moaning loudly.

"Jesus dude, you have to stop that!" he hears Corbin cry, a note of alarm in his voice now, but it's faint, distant. Travis feels as if he is floating up and away from everything, like his head has become detached from his body. The pleasure of scratching is so good he has a boner; he swears if it gets any better he's going to shoot a load in his pants.

Digging in deeper, his hands hooked into claws, everything takes a backseat as chills of ecstasy drive him to heights of bliss he's never known...

Corbin watches with horrified fascination as Travis attacks his cheek with the demented zeal of a man possessed. All reason has left the Naval seaman's eyes.

"Stop!" he urges, cringing as Travis burrows deeper into the wound, pulling it apart. His fingers are drenched in blood, his open mouth making a sound that is somewhere between a moan of pleasure and a groan of a pain. "You gotta stop doing that now dude!"

And that's when he sees something poke its head out of the crater Travis has created in his face, a creature about half the size of a triple A battery. Its body is thick and hairy, it's legs segmented and spiny. In fact it looks like a cross between a spider and a mosquito; its head is similar to a mosquito's, but as the body emerges it more resembles that of a tarantula.

Just like those bugs that attacked us when we came in on the lifeboats, only this one is smaller, like it just hatched. . .

Corbin suddenly becomes aware of a raucous buzzing, the sound low at first and then building in intensity. It seems to emanate from everywhere, bouncing off the stacks of trash and echoing back at him, but he quickly realizes that it's centralized to the thing coming out of Travis's cheek. Stunned, he retreats a step, then another.

Wriggling its disgusting body through the blood, pus and shredded skin, the insect is halfway out when its wings are released. They are opaque and Corbin can see clearly the veins that line them, greenish/bluish fluid pumping within as the insect flaps them experimentally, misting a fine spray of blood that showers Travis' cheek, well, what remains of it.

"No way…" he mutters, taking another shambling step backward. "No fucking way…"

The insect tugs itself free, flying into the air and circling Travis's head. He can see the pendulous stinger fidgeting back and forth, cloudy liquid dripping from the tip. Corbin watches Travis carefully; his eyelids are now closed, a dazed smile on his face. His head is tilted to one side as the blood flows freely, soaking his shirt.

The buzzing increases in volume and Corbin looks about him anxiously, expecting to see an approaching swarm, but there is just the lone bug hovering around Travis's head, flying aimlessly, alighting on his face momentarily and then taking to the air again.

"Ahhh man…" Travis burbles. "Better…so much better…"

Corbin runs a shaky hand over his face, his stomach in knots. He's vaguely aware that he should run, but he is stuck in this spot, unable to tear his eyes away.

And then there arises a sound like a balloon being stretched to the limits of its capacity, and Corbin notices that Travis's cheek is swelling, larger and larger. The laceration is dripping a thick, milky substance, pooling around his feet. Corbin stares wide-eyed as the other's cheek begins to undulate, the skin rippling as if undergoing the pressure of heavy G-forces.

"You gotta be kidding me…"

Travis' eyes flutter open briefly, the look of pleasure replaced by one of absolute agony. He locks his gaze on Corbin's for only a second before his cheek bursts open with a rending, repulsive *splat.* Chunks of skin explode in a spew of blood, followed by thousands of insects that enshroud his body like a living, squirming cloud. Corbin can no longer see Travis at all; where he once stood is now a bevy of flapping wings and fat, hirsute bodies that, if looked at closely, almost resemble the shape of a man. Then the horde expands and he can't discern anything; Travis simply disappears, as if he'd never been there at all. The buzzing amplifies, becoming deafening, painful. Corbin puts his hands over his ears, trying to block out the God-awful noise when at last the screaming starts and thick, hot drops of blood spatter outward like a torrential rain…

"I think I recognize somethin'," Kenny says, pointing at a familiar landmark. "We must be gettin' close."

"About damn time," Cole complains. "I'm hungry."

Kenny shoots the other a look, but bites his tongue. What good would it do to tell him that getting back to the shore where they came on this contemptible shit heap won't do a goddamn thing for putting food in their bellies in the near future? It would probably make him more upset, just hearing it said. He'll figure it out on his own.

Dr. Taylor recognizes certain items of debris as well. Even though they passed by in a state of raw panic, some things stood out from the rest, striking him as peculiar. Like the six-foot, carved oak cuckoo clock; the spring hung out like a flaccid phallus, the bird at the end looking mournful, it's painted eyes weeping mold. Or the life-size cutout of the popular TV body builder, his torqued pecs and washboard abs covered in bird crap... He simply can't believe the odd assortment of crap this floating toxic dump holds. If he didn't know better he'd swear he's standing in a land fill in Jersey. North Jersey to be exact.

Climbing over a mound that appears to be mostly melted plastic injected with rotting styrofoam french fry containers and cigarette packs, the shore suddenly looms before them.

"Thank God!" Cole cries jubilantly and Kenny flinches.

"Keep it down, will ya? We don't wanna send a invitation ta those damn birds!"

"Sorry," Cole mumbles, looking sheepish, but then something catches his eye and he's excited all over again. "Guys! Over there!"

Kenny and Dr. Taylor direct their attention to where he is pointing and Kenny lets out a low whistle.

"Well I'll be damned," he says, smiling. "It's our lucky day boys."

But Dr. Taylor doesn't share his sanguinity as he surveys the flat stretch of water beyond. With the sun shining down hot and mercilessly, the glare making his head hurt, he can see there is no call for any hasty merriment.

Kenny observes the gloomy look on the other's face and, squinting his eyes, peers in the direction the other is gazing.

"Ah shit," he grumbles and Dr. Taylor heaves a sigh.

"What? What 'ah shit'?" Cole asks, bouncing from one foot to the other like a little boy who has to use the potty but doesn't want to stop playing long enough to do so. "We found the lifeboats! We're safe!"

"Not if we don't have anyplace to go," Dr. Taylor says tiredly.

"What do you mean? We'll row out to the ship..."

And that's when Cole notices the empty space on the horizon; all there is to see is water. Endless miles of nothing but water.

"They left us here? Those bastards left us here?"

Kenny turns to the doctor, his good mood severely dampened. "Whatta ya think Doc? They dump us off here an split?"

Dr. Taylor weighs it out in his mind, finds that a complete evacuation doesn't make much sense.

"Captain Harvey and members of the crew are probably still here," he says calmly, trying to keep everything in perspective. "I can't imagine they would have abandoned them."

Kenny looks at him expectantly. "So maybe they just moved it?"

"That's the most likely scenario."

"Why would they do that?" Cole whines.

"The captain probably wants to hide the ship."

"From us?" Kenny cocks his head curiously. "Or…I mean, can't the government track it by satellite if they wanna?"

"They can," Dr. Taylor replies, "and there must be a tracking device on the ship as well…" He trails off, realizing that the captain or any member of the crew will most likely sabotage it.

"I wonder what they're tellin' Scripts," Kenny says, swiping at the beads of sweat that cover his brow. "Ya think they made up a story bout a accident?"

"Most likely," the doctor agrees, his convictions about the fate of the first ship confirmed.

It's like I thought. The first crew was lured (or taken against their will) onto the trash heap, just as we've been. If it wasn't by Captain Harvey than it was someone else who is sick, like him.

"Hey!" Cole says in a hushed whisper. "I see something moving over there!"

Kenny jerks his head toward the water, waiting to hear the telltale squawking of the mutant birds. His muscles tighten, his jaw clenching.

"Well what do you know?" Dr. Taylor says, the slightest trace of a smile on his face. "We've found somebody."

TEN

Jake is sitting down, taking five, when he realizes with dawning repugnance that he is perched atop a large pile of dung. It has hardened enough to support his weight, but the longer he sits the more it gives way, progressively sucking him into its festering sponginess.

"Goddamnit!" he gripes, getting to his feet. He knows it's useless to wipe the seat of his pants; his entire uniform is caked with a plethora of crap he's picked up along the way. The stench of the pile wafts toward him on a light breeze and he gags helplessly, feeling bile curdle in the back of his throat. "Son of a bitch..."

And that's bad, yeah, this stomach-churning odor, but what's worse is imagining what sort of beast on this lousy shit heap is large enough to produce such a load. The thought alone is enough to give him a bonafide case of the heebie-jeebies, and right now he needs to keep his cool. He's been wandering aimlessly for Christ knows how long; his watch stopped working after his plunge into the Pacific and he's become so confused that he can't pin point exactly when it was he lost his two traveling companions. An hour, maybe two? He has no idea.

Stupid bastards couldn't keep up. Let 'em find their own way out of this mess.

Although the truth of the matter (not that he wants to admit it) is that right now he would feel a whole lot better if he had some company. Being alone out here is unnerving, especially with the very real threat of those birds lurking about, not to mention whatever made this ginormous dump. Having to do this by himself isn't exactly boding well with him at this point.

How did it come to this? How could the captain have duped us all?

Although upon further consideration that's a stupid question, really, because all along he'd had a gut feeling that something wasn't right, yet he ignored it. Now that he actually thinks about it, he can recall instances when the captain behaved oddly but, being loyal to a fault, he'd dismissed it. For example, since when did they, the crew of a research vessel commissioned by the United States Government, search the passenger's cabins and then proceed to interrogate them? Sure, they found some guns, but they were in the possession of the security team. No surprise there. And the rest of the things they found (the booze, drugs, porn and sex toys) weren't any of their business, right? And how about knowingly sailing them into a storm without alerting the crew? When Corbin finally told him he'd just about had a heart attack. He could have gotten them all killed! And then there was his apparent health problems, the coughing and spitting and jaundiced looking eyes, not to mention the other odd little ticks and quirks that (in hind sight) were a signal of his unraveling sanity. God help him, Jake Anderson just wasn't a very perceptive fellow, never had been.

He looks up at the blue haze of sky, sees that the sun is well past the halfway point and is starting its descent to the west. To his credit he's been heading mostly east, but who knows (in his panic) which way he was going before he noticed. He could be far north of the cove, or far south, depending. And when he gets there what is he going to do? Will he confront the captain, demand he tell him what's going on? At present he's not sure he has it in him. He simply wants to return to the ship and get as far away from this place as he can, everything else be damned.

He ponders the fate of the others, hoping the crewmen are fairing better than he is, and vows that if he runs into that dickwad Tyler and his slut girlfriend he's going to have a few choice words with them. Words that involve his fists more than any actual conversation. Fucking go and leave him out here on his own will they. We'll just see who's left standing...

A rustling sound comes from off to his left, a noise that very well could be feet (*paws*) crunching over mangled plastic, and he freezes, holding his breath. He twists his head around slowly, trying to catch a glimpse of whoever (*whatever*) is approaching but sees nothing amongst the endless debris. Clutching his gun with hands that are slick with sweat and slime, his feet shifting restlessly, he considers making a break for it when someone says his name.

"What?" he calls nervously. "Who said that?"

"Jake," the voice says again, from where he doesn't know. It's disembodied, ethereal, like an odious phantasm floating unfettered on the stinking breeze.

"Who's there?" he cries out in a tone that betrays his bewildered fear. "Show yourself!"

An unearthly, low chuckle rumbles through the air like thunder, followed by the scraping sound of footsteps. Sweat stands out on Jake's forehead in large beads that drip into his eyes. At once a stinging pain blinds him, and he swipes at them gingerly, trying to clear his vision.

"Who's there?" he says again, his voice cracking in terror, his knuckles white from gripping the gun so tightly.

"Relax Jake," the other says and then, to his amazement, Captain Harvey steps into the clearing before him. He offers a warm, amiable smile, his empty hands held out innocently before him. "I'm here to help you buddy, it's all right."

He blinks with stunned alacrity, and his heart jumps a little in his chest. Damned if he isn't almost glad to see him, even if he's gone batshit crazy. That said he still doesn't think its safe to lower the gun.

"Stay where you are," Jake says, training the gun on the captain's chest. "You just keep your distance."

"What's the matter Jake? Don't you trust me?" The captain's stare is commanding, overpowering. "I told you, I'm here to help."

"Yeah, some help, bringing us all here," Jake replies, trying to avoid the other's eyes (*so dark... so cold...*) but finds he can't. It's as if his gaze has been captured, taken hostage. He can't tear himself away...

"I'm only looking out for your best interests Jake. You should know that."

"My…best interests?" he says, this time without much force. A warm stupor overtakes him; it's as if his hands are no longer a part of his body. He glances down at his rifle and sees it slipping from his grasp, like it's suddenly become very heavy. It's now pointing at the floor of the heap.

"That's right Jake, just put the gun down," Captain Harvey says soothingly. "You know you don't need it, not anymore."

Jake becomes aware of an encroaching dizziness, the world spinning around and around in a crazy, unending loop, but it's not bad, it's more like a mild intoxication.

"You…you tricked us…" he manages to say, hardly noticing as the M-16 falls from his numb fingers and clatters to the ground before him.

"I tricked no one," Captain Harvey says, his smile growing wider. "I brought you all here so you could share this paradise with me." He takes another step closer.

"Paradise?" Jake's vision is swimming, his knees shaking. "This…this is nothing near paradise."

"Oh, but it is my dear boy, it is. This is the Promised Land, the place where we shall start the world over. You just have to let yourself go. Just give in."

"Give in?"

"Give in," the captain nods, then coughs ferociously into a closed fist, wiping his hand on his pants. "You have to leave your fear behind and understand that who you are, *what* you are, is a transient shell capable of transforming. Capable of so many bigger, better things."

"But…this is awful…this place is, is…simply…awful…"

"Oh no my friend," Captain Harvey whispers gruffly as he comes ever closer. "Beauty is only skin deep, and what you are seeing may at first seem terrifying and ugly, but once you get past the surface and really look inside, you'll see it is magnificent. Utterly marvelous."

"Marvelous?"

"Yesssss," the captain hisses, close enough now to rest his hand on the other's shoulder. "You just need to be enlightened and then you will see. A simple process, really. A little painful at first but then you won't feel anything but the greatest joy, a rapture that will envelop your soul…"

"Painful?"

"All metamorphosis is a little painful. Do you think the caterpillar doesn't experience any discomfort before it becomes a butterfly?" The captain caresses Jake's neck, softly, lovingly, causing Jake's hair to stand on end. Revulsion arises inside him, making his stomach clench, but a potent, overriding feeling of contentment takes over, and he detects a certain sensuality in the captain's touch.

"There are several ways to transform you," Captain Harvey says, but his voice recedes as a sound grows in volume within Jake's head, a high-pitched drone that shoves aside logical thought and replaces it with a craven need he doesn't understand, can't even begin to explain, something so evil, so dark, that to look at it directly would dissolve all rationality like a sugar cube immersed in water. Jake's eyelids are rapidly becoming very heavy, his breathing more protracted.

"Some act quicker than others, while some are a drawn out process that can take hours to complete." The captain grins a shark's grin, thick phlegm and saliva dripping from his yawning mouth. "I need you to be my right hand man, my successor if you will." Captain Harvey continues to stroke Jake's neck, his rough, calloused fingers feathery, tender. "You will enjoy a status the other's don't, in that you'll be able to mimic humanity much better than they, at least, for a while…but let's not worry about that, shall we? We need to make you complete so we can move on to other things."

Gently, with reverential care, Captain Harvey eases his first mate to the ground, straddling his chest, then places his hands on each side of his face, holding him firmly.

"You will thank me for this Jake, trust me," he murmurs, then rears his head back, his throat working spasmodically as he begins to make wet, gasping, gurgling noises. His chest heaves violently, his body shuddering as he urges something to ascend from within him. Forcing open Jake's mouth and placing his own only inches away as if preparing to kiss him, he expels a copious stream of vomit, the thick, pasty substance jettisoning from him in a vile gush. Whitish, ropy worms writhe madly in the noxious fluid, spilling over the sides of his lips.

"Drink," Captain Harvey commands. "Drink and all will be well…"

Jake struggles to breath, choking miserably on the obstruction lodged in his throat. He gulps frantically so he can clear a passage for air, and feels the worms wriggling down his esophagus. He coughs and sputters, but when it hits his stomach there is a detonation behind his closed eyes, of color and light and wonder. Images unreel in a crazy kaleidoscope, visions of demented, rotting, laughing faces…of reptilian monstrosities, enormous in proportion…and endless piles of decomposing garbage, blowing through the air and creating a funnel cloud of roiling waste that swirls around him and sucks him up, taking him into it's infinite maw, devouring him with teeth of plastic and aluminum and steel…and then…nothing.

Leaning back, the captain sighs and smiles. His facial expression is one of complete serenity. It will only be a matter of minutes and Jake will now be one of them. One of *him*. His successor, should Lt. Ronson prove worthless. Only time will tell which man has what it takes to bring the plan to fruition, and then he shall make his choice. As far as the others, well, they'll be rounded up and chosen for conversion or sacrifice, depending.

"Depending on what they have to offer Garbage Island," Captain Harvey whispers cruelly, licking lips that look like two nightcrawlers squirming on rapidly drying pavement.

And when all of those aboard Garbage Island have been taken care of, they can move forward with the next phase, the final solution that will save them all. It will be so beautiful.

A few minutes later Jake opens his eyes. He feels wonderful beyond all human capacity for understanding. He feels…reborn. He looks at the captain standing before him, knows at once what they must do. He gets to his feet.

"We have work to do Jake."

"Yes," Jake agrees. "Yes we do."

The sun hangs suspended in the air like an image from a Dali painting, surreal, seamlessly tattooed into the blue fabric of the sky. Although it still has a ways to go before it disappears behind the towering piles of trash, Perry is getting worried that night will fall before they can find the cove. It's all the damn twists and turns; there is no such thing as traveling in a straight line here, not unless they are willing to crawl through waste in a state of putrefaction so rank it makes a septic tank seem appealing in comparison. To put it bluntly, they simply aren't that desperate yet.

Steven hasn't said anything for quite some time but this doesn't bother Perry, who is enjoying the silence or, more so, not having to entertain conversation. At this point he is far too weary, focusing instead on his own internal melancholic diatribe, a running litany of grievances he can't correct, things that are out of his hands. Incredibly, it makes him feel better.

They are both extremely thirsty, rapidly losing fluid due to the heat and humidity; it's draped over them like a blanket, this water saturated air, and as the minutes tick by they are progressively walking slower and slower.

"Enough," Perry gasps at last. "I have to rest."

Steven nods and the two plop down where they are, caring very little what they are sitting upon. After all they've been through they aren't the least bit concerned about getting dirtier.

"We shouldn't stay here too long though," Steven says, waving away the ever-present flies. "We don't want them to find us."

Perry nods. "After dark we'll be sitting ducks."

"If we still haven't found the shore by the time the sun sets we should probably find a place to hide for the night."

"We're getting close, I can feel it."

"Yeah? I don't recognize anything."

"You don't recognize anything," Perry says, "because we were running for our lives. I mean, I wasn't exactly paying attention."

"Yeah, I wasn't either."

A moment of silence elapses, nothing to be heard but the faraway cries of whatever life has adapted to this place and calls it home. That and their own ragged breathing.

"Man, I'm thirsty."

"You and me both."

"You know, there is something one can do if faced with this situation," Perry says and Steven looks at him sharply.

"How can anybody know what to do in the face of *this* situation?" he asks and Perry shakes his head.

"I don't mean this specifically, I mean if one is stranded and doesn't have any water. There is a way to replenish ones fluids…"

"Don't even say it dude."

"I know it's filled with bacteria, but your own won't hurt you."

"I can't believe you're even thinking about that."

"I've been thinking about it for the last two hours," Perry replies candidly, offering a bitter smile. The afternoon heat has been baking them like potatoes and they've been sweating profusely, becoming increasingly dehydrated. So, he's been holding it...just in case. He almost lost it when they heard the voices of those unimaginable inhabitants, but if fear had made him waste it, he would have been very sorry.

"I don't care what you think," he says, standing up and reaching for his zipper. "I'm going to have a drink."

"Jesus! Don't do it here! You think I want to watch you drink your own piss?"

"So turn around," Perry says, extracting his penis from his pants. "This is about survival."

He aims his cock at his mouth, shooting a jet of urine that misses and hits him on the chin. "Shit," he mumbles and tries again. Steven looks away.

Minutes go by, and the more Steven thinks about it, the more he has to take a piss. He hasn't gone the entire time they've been here. Eventually he turns around, sees Perry wiping his mouth with one hand and zipping his pants with the other.

"I can't believe you did that."

"I actually feel a little better," Perry admits. "Tastes like shit though."

Steven smiles. "You mean, 'tastes like piss'?"

"You know what I mean."

Astonishingly enough, Steven begins to contemplate doing the same thing. He is so thirsty, and right now he has to take the rager of all pisses. Maybe he will wait and see if Perry gets sick...

All of a sudden Perry's head swivels, his eyes going wide. He ducks down.

"I just saw somebody dude," he whispers, his face noticeably paler. "And...and I think they saw me."

Cold tentacles of fear race through Steven's already agitated nervous system, and simultaneously he feels a spreading warmth in his pants. Any thoughts of consuming his urine are out of the question, as it is now a mute point.

"It wasn't somebody from the ship?"

"I don't think so. No one from the ship walks like that."

'Walks like what?' Steven is about to ask when articles of trash nearby are disturbed, clattering and crunching together. Scurrying backward, they scan the area for a glimpse of the intruder and what they see flabbergasts them.

She is still a good distance away, but there is no mistaking who it is.

"It...it's Kim," Perry gasps.

She shuffles toward them on legs that appear to be barely holding her weight, her balance akin to that of a drunkard. Where her eyes once were are two ravaged craters, weeping crimson jelly. Her mouth looks like a clown's, smeared red all around and gaping. Inside, they see, is the blackened stump of her tongue, wriggling back and forth, and she is making a sound that is half gargling, half whimpering.

Perry slowly gets to his feet, an expression of guilt embossed on his face like a passport stamp.

"We have to help her dude," he says resolutely and, before the other can answer calls: "Kim! Stay where you are!"

Kim's head twists toward the sound of his voice and she screams, a strangled, wretched sounding resonance that's more animal than human. Clumsily spinning around, she stumbles away, reeling from side to side.

Perry dashes after her, wanting very badly to help her after they so thoughtlessly left her to die at the cove.

"Kim! Wait! It's me, Perry!"

Steven follows, albeit hesitantly. Unease fills him, a disquiet that steadfastly steals through him and won't let go.

"Wait!" he calls after Perry. "Be careful!"

But Perry pays him no mind. He crashes recklessly after her, kicking and shoving anything that gets in his way, moving with a deftness that's stunning. Yet just as he seems to be getting close she disappears, only to reappear somewhere else (further away) seconds later.

"Kim!" he cries. "Please, wait!"

She vanishes again and this time he stops, taking huge gulps of air. He can hear Steven blundering toward him from some ways off, but there is no time to wait for him. With all of them making this much noise they are bound to attract unwanted attention. He has to catch her quickly.

And then she rematerializes, some twenty yards away, only now she isn't running. She is standing still, her arms outstretched, a tranquil yet crooked smile adorning her horridly mangled face. Perry breathes a sigh of relief. She must have finally recognized him.

"Stay right there," he says, starting forward. "I'm coming to get you."

Between them is a large open area littered with waist-high mounds of opaque, melted plastic particles, covered with tattered pieces of paper and other unidentifiable mush. A potent, chemical-like smell emanates from them, one that Perry can't immediately place, but whatever it is, it's making his eyes water. However, going around isn't an option, not if he wants to hastily retrieve the poor, suffering girl before she takes it into her mind to run off again.

"I'll be right there," he tells her, making his way bit by bit through the piles, trying to keep from touching them, but they are spaced too close together to avoid completely. "Just stay where you are." The texture of the mounds is extremely sticky, and he notices that pieces are accumulating on his skin and clothes. He tries brushing them away but they are stuck fast. As he proceeds more and more pieces accrue yet he presses on, determined to save her.

He nears the end, coming upon two piles only scant inches apart. Just on the other side is Kim, standing motionless, staring sightlessly. He wedges himself between them and at once his forward progress halts; in an instant he realizes he is caught. He tries to kick his legs free but he can't move them, can't move anything but his head. He looks at Kim, observing grimly that her smile has taken a sinister turn. Glancing at her outstretched hands he now sees she is giving him the finger.

"Steven! Go back! It's a trap!"

But it's too late. His shipmate lunges heedlessly into the field, slipping and falling face-first onto the ground. He too is trapped, unable to move.

That's what the smell is: it's rubber cement...rubber fucking cement...

And then he hears lumbering footfalls, and soon there are several others gathered around Kim. Unlike her they still have their eyes (dark black, empty) and tongues but they are a disturbing lot. They are skinny, for one thing, emaciated well beyond what one would consider healthy, and their skin color is way off. Living tissue certainly doesn't look like that. And Perry doesn't know if it's a trick of the light but he'd swear one of the men is equipped with a set of gills. *Gills.* The peculiar illusion not ending there, they also appear to be made of…*plastic.* But that can't be right, can it? Must be something he's wearing, a decorative addition to his tattered clothing.

They move nimbly through the mounds, surrounding him, and the thought flitters away as rough hands take hold of his arms and legs, tearing him out of the trap (his skin peeling away painfully in places) and then his vision blurs as something is placed over his mouth and nose. The last thing he recalls is the terrible buzz saw sound of their laughter, that and his own muffled, terrified screaming…

ELEVEN

"We're gonna lose daylight pertty soon," Kenny says and Dr. Taylor grunts absently.

The five of them are sitting near the shore, trying to ignore the rumbling in their bellies and their aching, parched throats but it isn't easy to do, even with the view of the toxic sludge-laced sea lapping at their feet.

Tyler tells the others how Jake Anderson abandoned them and this is met with no real surprise. Did they really expect any camaraderie from a member of Captain Harvey's crew? Might as well expect special favors from the big man himself.

"I hope that asshole gets what's coming to him," Tyler complains futilely, swatting at and missing a bug that circles his head.

"We're all gettin' what's comin' ta us," Kenny says. "Like it or not."

"Do you honestly think they moved the ship or are you just trying to give us hope?" Melissa asks the doctor, and he slowly takes in her drawn, dirty face, the dark, bruised looking patches beneath her emerald green eyes. Even under duress the woman is incredibly beautiful, her long, sinewy limbs appearing somehow fragile yet strong, her eyes glimmering with a fierce intelligence that belies her ostensibly barbaric occupation. What she sees in Tyler he doesn't understand (although currently it appears there is a rift between them and he assumes they must have had a fight; they are sitting well away from one another, hardly exchanging glances, much less speaking) but he's never understood the fairer sex all too well. What little knowledge he'd had died with his fiancé.

"I can't see why they'd leave," he says tiredly, exhaustion only a stone's throw away. "The captain has a vested interest in this place and I doubt he's going to depart until he gets what he wants."

"I want to know what the point is," Tyler says, watching as the sun streaks across the sky, soon to disappear from sight behind the walls of garbage. "This doesn't make any sense."

"Dr. Taylor has a idea-a theory-bout what's goin' on," Kenny says, looking expectantly at the doctor. "Tell 'em."

"Sure," Dr. Taylor says, figuring what the hell. Now is as good a time as any. So he tells them about the pit trap and the blood, the evidence of other people.

"So the people from the other ship are alive?" Melissa asks and he nods gravely.

"Either them or someone else."

He then shares with them the rest, expounding on his supposition that propagating their species is one of the most critical components.

"Really?" Melissa asks when he is finished. "Is that possible?"

"Look around you," Dr. Taylor gestures to the trash surrounding them. "If ever there was a spawning ground for a new virus or a super strain of bacteria this would surely be the place."

"Do ya think the rest a the crew is like him?" Kenny says and the doctor reluctantly looks away from Melissa to answer him.

"I don't think so, not yet."

"If your presumption is true, I agree. I think some of them are still normal," Melissa asserts. "The men guarding us seemed as if they had no idea what was going on."

"Did Anderson say anything to you two?"

"I wouldn't know. I was barely conscious."

"He didn't say a thing either way," Tyler supplies, making an effort not to look at Melissa. "Not that he really had a chance."

"But did it seem as if he knew anything at all about what was going on?"

"Not really." Tyler shakes his head. "He was just as afraid as we were. Maybe even more so because he couldn't find it in his infinite kindness to wait for us."

"Interesting."

"Ya think he's the only one a them that's fucked up?" Kenny asks, picking up a rusted soda can and tossing it into the water. It lands in the thick, black goo and sticks there.

"I don't think so, I mean, he's got to have someone helping him. But maybe there are a few men aboard the ship who are still in their right mind."

"How does that help if we don't know where the ship is?"

"It doesn't, unless they decide to come looking for us. Or," he glances at the faces around him, "if we try and find them."

"How do we do that?"

Dr. Taylor points at the lifeboats. "We use those."

"Yeah, the lifeboats," Tyler says, sneaking a sly glance at Melissa. "Good idea. Wish I had come up with that."

She looks at him balefully, not saying a word.

"I mean, what better way to get off this dump," he persists, "than to use those boats. What do you think Melissa?"

"The doctor is probably right," she says quietly, looking away.

"Oh, so if it's my idea it's stupid and everything's hopeless, but if it's the doctor's idea than its swell and dandy. That right darlin'?"

"Let it go Tyler."

"The hell with that. Answer my question. If its somebody else's idea than it's all right, is that what you're saying?"

"I said let it go!"

"You can bet your sweet ass I won't, not after the hissy fit you threw-"

"Back off man," Kenny says, standing up. "Just leave her alone."

"This is none of your damn business chief, so butt out. This is between the lady and I, and I do use the term very loosely."

"Yeah? Well I'm makin' it my business. Just shut up."

"Fuck you, *man*," Tyler says when suddenly he gets a face full of Kenny, the large black man towering over him.

"First of all, don't ya ever call me chief, don't call me nothin' but Kenny, or sir, either'll work just fine. Second, yer wastin' our time. Shut up or I'll shut you up, got it?"

Tyler sizes Kenny up, taking in the muscled arms, the meaty fists. In a fight this guy could probably take him, unless he sucker punched him in the nuts... Shit, ain't that a B? This dumb ass has to go sticking his nose into his business when he has no clue what's going on. Screw him. And that stupid cunt...now that the lifeboats are someone else's idea she's all 'sounds great!' when before she was ready to throw in the towel, hating him for even suggesting it. Well fuck her, fuck all of them...and to think he'd saved her life back there.

"Fine," Tyler mutters, looking at the ground. Let these bastards have they're way, thinking he's the one who's wrong. They weren't here, they don't know what happened. But, still, fine. He'll let it go, for now.

"Okay then," Kenny says, sitting back down. "You were sayin' Doc?"

Doctor Taylor forces himself to look away from Tyler, struggling to keep a neutral expression on his face. For a second there he was actually hoping Kenny would haul off and smack him a good one. He doesn't know why but there is something about Tyler he simply doesn't like.

"If we don't come up with a plan we are going to die," Dr. Taylor resumes, his words cutting to the quick even though his voice is soft. "We have no drinking water and eating the creatures here isn't an option. From the trash heap or the ocean."

"So let's make a plan," Melissa says. She doesn't look at anyone when she speaks, much less Tyler. She sees no reason to explain to him that what the doctor is suggesting and what he was thinking are two different things entirely. What Tyler was proposing was suicide, an irrational 'let's-just-get-the-fuck-out-of-here' scheme, whereas the doctor's idea is meant to try and save them. Besides, she's on edge, and who wouldn't be after all they've just been through? All she wants to do is go home. "What do you suggest?"

"We need to split up. We have two lifeboats; one group of us will start around the trash heap to the south, the other to the north-"

"Great, just great," Tyler scoffs, unable to contain himself. "With no way to communicate with each other we have a fifty-fifty chance of survival."

"Yes, that's the long and short of it."

"I spose we ain't got no other choice," Kenny says. "But how do we decide who goes with who?"

Everyone looks at him solemnly, realizing exactly what he is driving at. Kenny is the biggest of the bunch, with Cole running a close second. And then there is the doctor, who is obviously the most intelligent. Which group gets the benefit of the brawn and which the brains?

"I'll go with Cole," Dr. Taylor says, "and you two go with Kenny. If either of our groups finds the ship than it will be their job to rescue the others."

Cole tosses his head from side to side, pursing his lips. "I ain't going nowhere without Kenny."

"Ya ain't got a choice. Yer a grown man. Ya can handle yoursef."

"Out here it don't matter if I'm *grown* or not," he replies and Kenny has to admit, although silently, that Cole has a point. Regardless, the decision has been made.

"Ya heard the doctor, that's the arrangement." He turns to Dr. Taylor. "Ya think we should go now?"

"I don't think traveling in the dark is a good idea," he says, nodding toward the vanishing sun. In minutes it will be on the other side of the heap and shortly thereafter twilight will be upon them. "We should get some rest and leave at daybreak."

"I don't know if I can sleep," Cole grouses. "I'm so thirsty I think I could drink my own piss."

"I wouldn't suggest it unless it were absolutely necessary," Dr. Taylor frowns. "Although it's safe to drink your own it has dehydrating properties and would do more harm than good at this point. It should only be done as a last resort."

"Would you do it?" Melissa asks, smiling slightly, and once again her beauty enchants the doctor. What would make a woman choose such an occupation? "I mean, if you had to?"

"If I absolutely had no other choice, yes," he confesses, wondering if he could really go through with it.

If I have to go another day without water, you bet. In a heartbeat.

Silence ensues as they consider this and, in the distance, some inhuman, indistinct shriek erupts, breaking the stillness. The group instinctively huddles closer together.

"I'll keep watch if ya guys wanna try an git some sleep," Kenny offers, then looks at Cole. "I'll wake ya up in a few hours ta relieve me."

"Don't say the word 'relieve'," Cole grins. "You'll make me seriously think about going through with it."

"Don't say 'goin'" Kenny counters, grinning in return, and this makes everyone (except Tyler) chuckle, breaking the tension slightly, even as the faraway cries of some inexplicable horror warbles unseen in the night.

"My mom always said I had a potty mouth. She'll never know how right she was."

"You guys are sick," Melissa says, giggling. She has a headache from where she bumped her head, and the argument she had with Tyler sure isn't going to increase her chances for sleep, but as she lies back against the remnants of a shipping crate she feels a shred of drowsiness overcome her. It's been a long, harrowing day. Maybe it would be nice to tune out for a little while. With that thought bouncing around in her head, she drifts off into a light slumber.

All is blackness and Dave is growing very tired. Although time is passing awfully slowly he's certain he's been down here for a few hours now, and while clinging doggedly to the idea that he can escape, he's gradually becoming pessimistic about finding a way through. At turns he rests his legs when he finds handholds to hang on to, but he can only do this for so long before his arms grow weary. Eventually he may lose the battle and succumb to drowning, but he tries to keep the thought at bay as long as he can. The idea of ending this life greets him with a bleakness he's never known, and when his mind turns in that direction he resolves to fight all that much harder, though it is growing increasingly difficult the more fatigued he becomes.

To pass the time he thinks of people he's known in his life, friends he's had, girls he's slept with, and wonders where some of them are now. He remembers a girl he dated in high school, a pretty blonde named Danielle. She was a gymnast and, man, was she nimble. She could stretch her legs straight up in the air and touch her toes to her forehead. He can only imagine the kinky sex they would have enjoyed if they'd stayed together longer than the year and a half they'd gone out. Sure, they'd had sex, but teenage sex has got to be the most boring, unimaginative sex one can have. For a young man, simply putting your dick in a willing participant is thrill enough.

What happened to her? Did she go to college to pursue her dream or did she stay in town and get married, have some kids? Does it matter? Would she care if she knew he was potentially breathing his last breaths? No, she probably wouldn't. It wasn't like they'd parted on amicable terms; she'd caught him with another girl, a slutty brunette whose name he can't even remember, and that had been the end of it.

His gang of deviant friends comes to mind, all those guys who spent most of their time working on old Camero's or Nova's, smoking dope and drinking cheap beer. That is, when they weren't breaking into houses and getting into fights with kids from other schools. He figures a lot of those guys are still living in town, having knocked up some girl and then forced to take a job at a slaughterhouse or a factory or something else unbefitting young men of such criminal design. Maybe some of them even traded in the muscle cars for SUV's, and now spend the weekends chauffeuring their children around instead of cruising the strip.

But that's no big surprise, is it? They certainly weren't as dedicated as he was. No, these guys weren't hardwired for crime like him. He was the only one who was truly committed to such illicit activities, well, until he got busted and had to make the choice he did.

Here in the stinking darkness he at last finds himself regretting his poor decisions, because if he hadn't been such a conniving, lazy son of a bitch than maybe he wouldn't have wound up in the Navy, which would mean he wouldn't have ended up here, alone, about to drown beneath the largest pile of floating garbage on earth.

An incredible sorrow overcomes him, and he feels sick enough to cry, but knows it won't do any good. He will take his regrets to the grave, but the last thing he'll do is mourn for himself. To him, that would be the ultimate sign of weakness. In a life beset with bad ideas, plagued by mistakes, a whole existence of having to 'learn things the hard way', he's not going out blubbering like a fucking crybaby. Not while he's still breathing.

Because there has to be a way out of here; after all, there'd been a way in. It's just taking him forever to find it. He has to acknowledge, though, that luck is on his side. The water is oddly warm, so he isn't cold. And at least the smell of the trash heap isn't so bad down here, although every now and then the water gets in his mouth and it tastes worse than rancid baby shit (not that he's ever tried it). Barring the taste of the water, he has a couple things going for him. And what the hell, it helps to look on the bright side…

He speculates whether or not Travis and Corbin escaped from the giant snails, decides that it will probably remain a mystery to him if he can't get out of here. But if he *was* able to help them make a getaway, he's glad. Maybe that will be the last act of his life and, in a way, it's very fitting. He'd lived very selfishly; it would be nice to think he went out helping someone else instead of himself for a change.

Yeah, that's not so bad. He sacrificed himself so that the other two could live. Maybe he's not as bad a person as he's come to think.

Something splashes in the water nearby and an icy fear settles over him. He twists and turns, squinting into the gloom, but down here there is no light, nothing but the impenetrable dark. Something brushes against his legs, and he can't help but lose the calm he fought so hard to keep. He cries out, a yell of unmitigated terror because now, more than ever, he's certain this is it, his last few moments.

Groping madly at the surface above him, his fingers seeking any nook or cranny that he can hoist himself up into, he finds there is nothing but mere handholds, in some places not even that. He kicks his legs as hard as he can, trying to keep his head above the water, and when it passes him again its skin feels scaly and gritty, like sandpaper. A strong current follows in its wake and he loses his grip; whatever is lurking down here with him is big, really big. It will have no trouble removing him from this earthly coil.

This is it. Guess I did all I could. . .

A stream of images comes to him, memories so faded as to be almost lost within the folds of time itself. His step-mom's cheerful face pops into his mind, and he recalls how he used to help her with the laundry when he was just a little kid, back when he was still her sweet little boy, before he grew up to be her 'secret embarrassment'. He pictures his step-dad, remembering how they used to toss a baseball around in the backyard when he needed to practice for Little League tryouts. His step-dad's smile was always slightly askew, the smell of warm gin on his breath, but he loved the man fiercely because he was his DAD. Nobody could fuck with that, could take it away from him, even if he wasn't his *real* dad.

He recollects the scent of a million delicious dinners (BBQ chicken and steaks on the grill, homemade lasagna, beef strogenov, fast food burgers brought home in greasy waxed paper bags) and remembers eating these meals while watching Monday Night Football and WWE wrestling, yelling and cheering and spilling his soda on the rug. . .man those were some good times, some really good times. He suddenly appreciates how much he loves his parents, beyond a doubt dearly loves them, and hopes they'll find it in their hearts to miss him when they learn he's gone. . .

A sob escapes him, tears trickling down his cheeks, and he realizes that it doesn't matter; he can cry for himself if he wants to. It's his life (death), after all.

Clawing urgently at the ceiling above him, trying to avoid the inevitable, he understands there is nothing he can do, nowhere he can go. He is trapped, a sitting duck just waiting for the hammer to fall.

And then he feels a sharp pain in his right leg as teeth sink into his flesh; teeth as sharp as a hundred hypodermic syringes, sinking in so deep he imagines they'll only stop when they hit bone.

"Ahhhhh!" He flails despairingly, in the wildest extremes of panic, and the last thing he's aware of is being pulled briskly under the water.

TWELVE

Shivering fitfully, Corbin cowers in a small recess of trash, tears cutting streaks through the grime on his face. He wipes his eyes with the back of his arm, wishing he wasn't such a goddamn sissy, but he can't help it. Not after what happened to Travis. That poor bastard. Of course, he doesn't feel half as bad for the other as he does for himself, all alone, the darkness barely penetrated by the meager light of the stars above. If only he had a flashlight, maybe he could try and find his way back to the shore, but good old Captain Harvey made sure that none of them was outfitted with anything more than the clothes on their backs, the heartless prick. If he were here right now he'd enjoy killing him with his bare hands, would relish the splintering crunch as his larynx collapsed, his eyes pleading for mercy.

He'll never forgive himself for his stupidity, knowing there was something wrong with the captain yet following him onto this floating landfill, especially after the dummied weather report and the bizarre accusations regarding the passengers. Because this place…this utterly sickening place…it shouldn't exist, not in a sane world, no sir…

There is no way he'll ever get the image of Travis out of his head, how those mutant bugs burst from his skin, swarming so thick the man literally disappeared within them. And then all that blood and the God-awful screaming…those things probably ate him alive. Not that he knows for sure as he didn't stick around long enough to find out. And who could blame him? It was less a cowardly gesture than an act of self-preservation.

When the horror of the situation finally broke his fear-induced paralysis he'd run until his legs felt like two rubber bands and his lungs burned excruciatingly. And when he couldn't run anymore he crawled, dragging himself along the ground, breaking his fingernails, whimpering softly all the way. He didn't know until later that he'd ripped his pants (and knees, hands and elbows) on broken glass; his mind simply wasn't registering pain while making his getaway. All he could think of was putting as much distance between him and those terrible insects as he could, everything else be damned.

And damned he most surely was, for now as he trembles in the dark, his body stinging in a dozen different places from the cuts he's accrued, he couldn't feel more wretched.

I'm screwed. I'm all alone and there is nothing that can save me now. Nothing.

What became of Dave? When Travis dug him out from the landslide Dave was no longer there, and because of the circumstances he'd never had a chance to ask as to his whereabouts.

Was he dead too? What about the others? For all he knows he's the last one alive, everyone else having been dispatched of by mutant birds, giant insects and God knows what else.

Something howls in the distance, a cursed, dejected sound that reeks of pity and self-loathing, and he almost cries out. Goddamnit he wishes he were still on the boat, lying in his bunk and reading the toilet humor in Hustler magazine, those funny cartoons in between the photos of airbrushed models, jokes about douches and chicks sneezing while wearing a tampon...hilarious. Hell, as long as he's going there, he wouldn't even mind if he was at his mother in law's house, bored off his ass while she and his wife watched brainless soap operas or Celebrity Blackjack and ate stale microwave popcorn. When all is said and done, anywhere on earth would be better than here.

If I survive, I'll take a vacation in North Korea.

The thought makes him giggle, an anxious, fearful twitter yet a giggle just the same, but his moment of bemusement is cut short by a scraping, clattering noise close by, the sound of trash being disrupted. He sits very still, instinctively clamping his eyes shut and holding his breath. Could it be one of those birds? Maybe some other walking horror that, on sight, will send him into screaming gales of hysterics before it pulverizes him into so much useless goo? Through his mind races a panicked whirl of thoughts, his heart thudding so painfully in his chest he is afraid that, in this silence, it's beating will give his position away. The sound occurs again, this time closer, and he curses that he lost his rifle while he was fleeing. In his mad scrabble to get away from the swarm it had simply slipped from his hands and he'd never noticed.

I wish I had a weapon! Anything!

But he has nothing and there is no time to scrounge around. Not that he can see well enough anyway. If he is found, he is going to have to fight with his bare hands.

Okay, come on then, if you think you can take me.

Then he hears someone clear their throat, followed by, incredibly, the unmistakable sound of humming.

You gotta be kidding me. . .

It takes a moment before he recognizes the song, a catchy rock anthem by an Australian band (Toxic Overload, if he remembers correctly) that was played over and over on the FM rock stations during the summer of 2013. It had been one of those 'one hit wonder' songs, the group enjoying brief popularity before disappearing altogether, probably succumbing to their wanton desires and overdosing on drugs, much like the band's name suggested.

Pushing himself up slowly, he shifts into a squatting position, his muscles tensed, ready to fight or flee, but a flicker of optimism steadies him. Could it be Dave? He cocks his head to one side, straining to hear better, and now he can make out not only humming but actual words to the song. The singing is low and slightly off-key, but it's clear enough:

"**Blackened skies and the storm clouds comin', apocalypse is on its way. Don't you know that the world is burnin' down again . . .?**"

Corbin smiles, nostalgia erasing his fear momentarily. He remembers listening to that song in his car, singing along with the chorus while he and his buddies worked their way through a case of cheap beer:

"Lay me down and don't say a word, close my eyes and fill them with dirt. I can't wait to meet you there. Bluest eyes shimmer and cry. Holding hands we commit suicide. Bury us in an unmarked grave..."

He gets up (ignoring the pins and needles from his sleeping limbs) and takes a couple of shambling steps.

"Hello?" he calls. "Is that you Dave?"

Suddenly it gets very quiet, as if all other life on the trash heap has decided to call it a night. In the silence he can hear the harsh intake and exhale of his breathing and nothing more.

"Dave?" he says, softer now. "Anyone?"

But there is no reply, and for a brief moment Corbin is afraid he's losing it, cracking up. Maybe there was no sound, no humming...it was all in his head, a hallucination brought on by fear and exhaustion. Apprehension fills him, a bitter dread that he is on the verge of a nervous breakdown.

Abruptly the stillness is broken by a dry, raspy laugh and Corbin recoils, startled.

"Dave?" he queries again, struggling to keep his voice from quavering nervously. "That you?"

A figure emerges out of the gloom, nothing but a silhouette against the backdrop of the midnight blue sky.

"Corbin?"

"Is...is that you Dave?"

"No, it's me, Jake. Are you all by yourself?"

"Ah thank God!" Corbin exhales loudly, stepping forward. "Man am I glad to see you!"

"Are you alone?" Jake asks again, and Corbin isn't sure why, but something about the first mate strikes him as odd.

"Yeah man, it's just me," he says uneasily. "I was with the two Navy guys but we, uh, ran into some trouble-"

A hand shoots out of the shadows, striking him soundly on the bridge of his nose. A riotous pain bursts in his head as he falls to his knees.

"I need you to come with me," Jake says, grabbing his right arm, his grip like a vice. "The captain wants to see you."

"The...the captain?"

Jake nods. "It's time to get back to work." And, forcefully, he pulls the other to his feet and drags him through the bruised darkness to where their leader waits.

The ship sways gently as night washes over it like a fine mist. All the lights have been extinguished except for one burning in the pilothouse. Lieutenant Michael Ronson sits at his desk, awaiting word from the captain.

He'll be happy to know that everything is taken care of, he thinks, staring out into the inky blackness. All of the men have been converted, there is no one left to cause any trouble, to get in the way of the mission. Now all they need is further instructions and they can proceed with the captain's plan.

As per order, he has contacted the White House to let them know all is well; data is being collected and they've found signs of life aboard the trash heap indicating the scientists from the other ship may be alive. He also passed along Intel stating that if all goes smoothly they'll be leaving within a few days, having sewn up all loose ends, preparing to demonstrate how they'll go about eradicating the problem swiftly and efficiently, proving the superiority of the United States over all other nations. He has to admit he laid it on pretty thick, but he was simply following orders. The captain also instructed he make some mention of the governor, to let them know he was a definite asset to the operation, an inside joke no doubt. Since that transmission the radio has been left unguarded, as there is no one aboard who will use it in an inappropriate manner.

The last of the men were taken care of before the sun set, and now it is only a matter of time before all of the passengers are found and dealt with. Ronson is very proud of his expediency. It is his hope that the captain will reward him for a job well done.

His mind and body in synch with a new frequency, he sits still and listens to the sounds of Garbage Island, to the shrieking of the creatures that were once the island's only occupants, it's only hosts. But then the Master was created, and he in turn began to recruit new souls, ready for service.

Eyes glazed over, breathing even, Ronson ceases all thought and simply becomes one with the environment. He knows that below deck, in the crewmen's bunkroom, the others are doing the same thing, for sleep is no longer necessary, not for them. They are either active or in a state of repose that resembles sleep, except that their eyes are open and they are ready at a moment's notice to do the Master's bidding. Of course he (unlike them because of his manner of conversion) is able to take his mental state to a higher level, one in which he can close his eyes and enjoy a vast array of vivid images, magnificent visions of dreadful wonder, although he chooses not to do so at present because it can be very distracting, and right now he needs to remain focused on the task at hand. The underlings enjoy no such benefits; in fact their remuneration is their lives, in that they can continue living them in order to serve the greater good. And it's with great joy and mindless servitude that they perform their duties. No more questions, no more insubordination. No free will, no random thoughts.

A fresh wind strikes up, blowing through the open window, and he inhales deeply, savoring the sour smell. He can't wait until he can leave the ship and join the others on Garbage Island, can start the life that awaits him there.

But that can't be done until the proper arrangements are made, the next stage that will ensure nothing in this world can stop them. Soon enough, he understands patiently. Soon enough.

Kenny paces back and forth, watching the sea for any tell tale source of light, something to indicate the ship is out there, or any other vessel for that matter, but there is nothing. Stars illuminate the night dimly, their pale light offering little more than glimmering pinpoints in the sky. He sees a shooting star, and the flickering red and green hues of a satellite.

The others are restless, and it doesn't appear they're getting any sleep. And how could they? With the night's arrival the trash heap has been active, alive with sounds so terrifying as to render slumber nearly impossible.

Everybody is huddled together, holding a makeshift weapon. Kenny has a steel rod that he holds over his shoulder like a baseball bat. Cole and the doctor are clutching identical wooden table legs, presumably from the same table. Melissa (who had somehow dozed briefly) has a power cord wrapped around one hand, the plug (the business end) lying in wait to be used should any-thing foolishly try and mess with her. And last and definitely least, good ole numbfuck Tyler has a large, Teflon coated frying pan sitting next to him at the ready.

Every so often raucous cries arise from sources unknown and everyone tenses, waiting for an attack that has yet to come. Faces are strained, anxious, and when the sounds eventually fade a collective sigh of relief arises amongst them.

Jesus, this night is gonna last forever.

Inside, Kenny feels a morose sense of doom that at turns convinces him this charade of defending themselves is useless. If something wants to get them, chances are it will, end of story. Sure, they can fight, and they will, tooth and nail, but whatever has taken over this place is stronger than they are. Stronger and a lot more determined. And, let's face it, with the ship gone they're sunk. He doesn't even fool himself that their expedition is going to turn up anything, at least not in time to save them from certain death. Soon enough the elements will prevail, the lack of food and water weakening them, and they'll be unable to fight off the creatures lurking just out of sight.

He remembers a program he watched while in the hospital, on the Discovery channel. The hospital was nice like that, offering premium cable to the more privileged patients. He was a celebrity, after all, and that had certainly been taken into consideration when he'd been assigned a room.

The show was about a group of people who got lost in the Sahara Desert while on safari. They'd been traveling in a humvee and it broke down out in the middle of nowhere. They lost radio contact, their cell phones didn't work, the whole nine yards. They had food and water, but only enough to last a couple of days. They had weapons but there wasn't much in the way of game to hunt. After their food ran out (rationing it, they were able to stretch it out for four days) it was up to them to find whatever they could. They hunted jackrabbits, snakes, lizards-anything they could find. And they set up sheets and blankets at night to collect dew, which they used as drinking water.

Via these tactics they were able to survive for three weeks before they were found, emaciated, malnourished, and dehydrated. Kenny remembers thinking how absolutely horrible that must have been, to be trapped out in the middle of nowhere, not knowing if the next day was going to be your last.

Looking about him now, he realizes they had it made, those people stranded in the desert. At least there was dew they could collect; at least there were animals they could hunt. Such resources are entirely lost on them, not unless they want to risk a serious viral or bacterial infection, according to the doctor, if his theory is correct. Kenny wonders how long it will take before contamination isn't a concern, before they are desperate enough to hunt and eat the creatures living here.

Of course, it must be taken into consideration that there is the very real possibility the creatures will hunt and eat them first, can't forget about that. Did those assholes in the desert have that to worry about? He honestly can't remember. Thinking has become a chore because of his ravenous hunger, his incessant thirst. It seems that food and water are, at times, all he can think about. That and a good, anesthetizing belt of booze.

He glances over at the others, sees that Melissa now appears to be sleeping again and Tyler *(stupid prick better keep his cool; he doesn't want to hand him his ass but he will if necessary)* looks to be breathing deeply and evenly. But Dr. Taylor and Cole remain ever vigilant, their weapons at the ready should anything approach that is less than friendly.

"Git some sleep guys," he whispers to them. "I got it covered."

Dr. Taylor offers a wan smile and Cole grips his table leg even tighter.

"I would if I could, cavrone," Cole whispers in return. "I would if I could."

No more than a few miles away, Captain Harvey strides purposefully, his feet knowing exactly which way to go. In his head is a radar system that easily guides him through the random hubris; there is no reason for him to even watch his step, to think about where he is going.

He knows where the last of the passengers are, and he has commanded the creatures of Garbage Island to leave them be. They are not for them, no, they are resources that the higher forms of life here will need to utilize. He will let them suffer through the long night, will wait until they are exhausted before taking them into his custody. If he and his minions are lucky maybe they will even find them asleep, however he doubts that. Before conversion it's very difficult to sleep on Garbage Island, and after conversion there is no need.

But not all of them are going to be converted right away. There are important jobs that require an unenlightened mind, and when these functions are fulfilled they will then be transformed, if Garbage Island hasn't gotten inside them already. They aren't going to like it, but that's none of his concern. His place isn't to be worried for anyone's well being, his job is to ensure the survival of his species. In the end, if it brings about his own demise, so be it. It is all for the greater good. He understands that his physical self is molting, mutating. His body is merely a shell that harbors the spirit of Garbage Island, and in the end it very well may break down to make way for…something else.

His belly rumbles and he swipes at the thick saliva that drips off his chin in dual runners, the fluid sticky and cool. Coughing harshly, a thick, splattering hack, his mouth fills with squirming, rice-sized worms and, relishing the taste, he forces them back down his throat. Since reaching the island he is constantly hungry, a deep, insatiable food lust that lingers within him at all times. It is the life that grows within him that demands sustenance, and he feeds it readily and willingly whenever it so desires. He has to, for to starve it is to starve all that he holds pure; he has no desire to stunt the growth of progress.

He knows the passengers must be getting very hungry by now, in fact must be contemplating eating whatever they can find, but his Intel has informed him it is the doctor who keeps them from feeding, telling them tales of bacterial infections and contamination. And he is right, of course, make no mistake about that. They will find out all too soon how correct he is about such things. Eating the creatures of Garbage Island causes...*changes*. He ought to know.

Reaching his destination, the captain seats himself atop a mound of trash and shuts his eyes for a while. Every so often he needs to do this to bask in the rapture of the visions, to re-enlighten himself as well as to recharge his physical being. It has been a long, eventful day, and tomorrow should prove to be even more so. He has so many fantastic things to share with the passengers, so many marvels to astound them with. He can hardly wait.

Kenny lifts his head in surprise, startled out of a light doze by a disturbance in the near distance. Beneath the din of the faraway, shrieking animals there is the crunching of what can only be footsteps.

"What was that?" Cole asks, too loudly, and Kenny shushes him. Dr. Taylor stirs from where he sits, getting to his feet.

"Stay there," Kenny says, taking a tentative step in the direction of the sound. "I'll handle this."

"I'm coming with you," Cole says with forced bravado and Kenny smiles.

"Atta boy."

The two move stealthily in the direction of the noise, their makeshift weapons raised above their heads. About a hundred yards in they reach a fork in the path, and Kenny points for Cole to go one way while he goes the other. If he could make out Cole's face in the dimness he would notice the conflicting emotions playing tug of war there, but instead all he sees is Cole nod his head reluctantly. They separate, each of them disappearing into the shadows.

Kenny hasn't gone more than a few feet when he hears Cole take in a sharp breath. He is certain the man is about to blow it by screaming his fool head off when he hears a quiet voice say: "Hey man, it's all right. It's just us."

Reunited with the others, Leeann momentarily feels better than she has in quite some time, since they came aboard the heap to be exact. Not that it's putting food in her belly, and not that she didn't trust the navigating and survival skills of one Mr. Dante Kellerman, but being within the supposed inviolability of a group has put her slightly at ease.

As dusk steadily approached with no sign of finding their way out, the more panicked she'd become. At one point she'd felt as if she were going to hyperventilate, and it was all Dante could do to keep her calm. She'd never been prone to panic attacks, but she'd also never been in such a terrifying situation as this. Living the sheltered existence she has, the most frightening thing she'd ever experienced was a minor auto accident caused by her brother six months after he'd gotten his driver's license. That had been scary, but it was nothing compared to this.

Dante hadn't felt much better, in fact considered himself a fool because he was the one leading the way. Even though it seemed simple enough to walk in the opposite direction of the sun, it wasn't as easy once you were actually doing it, and he'd gotten confused more than once. To make matters worse the pathways would abruptly end, leaving them to decide whether they should climb over the obstacle or retrace their steps to find a way around. Because neither of them wanted to touch anything more than they had to they generally sought alternate routes, and for these reasons he managed to get them lost several times over. As the sun sank ever closer to the far horizon he could sense Leeann's fear and frustration, but it wasn't until the night consumed them that her terror became unbearably evident. He'd stop walking and hold her tightly to his chest, assuaging her fears, calming her down as best he could before continuing on.

By the time the Big Dipper made it's twinkling appearance in the sky Dante had almost lost all hope when, faintly, he made out the sound of the sea. It was far away, but he could hear it just the same.

"We're almost there," he'd assured her and she'd brightened considerably.

But when the two finally arrived at what Dante thought to be the cove he found they were due north, standing atop one of the cliff walls surrounding it. Yet there it lay before them, the large indentation looking 'unnatural' from this vantage point, as if someone (a bunch of someone's) had excavated the trash in that area, allowing clear access to the heap.

Finding their way down was another harrowing adventure, fraught with perilous twists and turns and a too close for comfort escape from an avalanche caused by their blundering footsteps. It took them over an hour but eventually they'd made their way to the bottom.

And now, at long last here they are. Dante searches the faces, carefully noting who is missing.

"Is this everyone who made it out of there?" he asks Kenny but it's Dr. Taylor who answers.

"So far," he replies, taking Dante's hand and shaking it amiably, offering a warm smile. "Glad to see you two made it."

"I didn't think we were going to find it-this spot I mean," Dante says lamely, and the Doctor shrugs.

"Well, you did, and here we are." He gestures to the place where he was previously sitting. "Why don't you have a seat and we'll compare notes."

"So, no sign of the Navy guys?"

"Like I said, this is all of us. Now come on, take a load off. I'm sure you're tired after all you've been through."

Leann has already chosen to sit by Melissa, and the other woman receives her kindly. Wrapping an arm around the fretful girl, she offers what comfort she can. Leeann gives Melissa a tiny smile, whispers her thanks.

A momentary flash of jealousy gives Dante pause, an irrational animosity toward the strikingly beautiful woman. Here it was he who led Leeann back to the relative safety of the group and she abandons him to sit with the prostitute. How do you like that?

"Dante?" Dr. Taylor prods, and he dismisses the feeling, knowing she's just seeking reassurance from a member of the feminine persuasion. Why is he always so afraid that a woman is going to leave him?

Yes Dante, whatever would give you that idea?

"Fuck you," he mutters to his inner voice.

"What?" Dr. Taylor says.

"Nothing." And he follows the doctor and takes a seat beside him.

THIRTEEN

The President of the United States sits behind his desk sipping a tumbler of single malt scotch. It's very late (or early, depending on how you look at it), but he isn't tired. An hour ago he received word that the research vessel sent another communication, one that was a little puzzling, to say the least.

The communiqué stated that they'd found evidence of the other ship and their initial research has been successful. If all continues to go as planned they should be ready to return in as little as four days with a definitive proposal as to how to properly dispose (no pun intended, of course) of the island of trash for good. But that wasn't the peculiar part.

He figured that Governor Hallsly would be doing nothing but getting in the way, yet according to the message the governor has been a tremendous help and the crew insists his presence has been invaluable. He would have thought that an hour at the trash heap would be an eternity for the sleazy bastard, but the news states otherwise. Odd. He'd then wondered if the governor had delivered this message himself (trying to make himself look good after the news of his incarceration), but he hadn't. The acting man in charge, Lieutenant Michael Ronson, had sent all transmissions.

"Why didn't the captain send the message?" the president had asked his aide.

"Apparently he went aboard the trash heap with Dr. Taylor and his interns."

"And they're still out there?" He'd consulted his watch. It was 3:30 a.m. eastern standard time so that would make it roughly 9:30 p.m. out in the gyre. *"After dark?"*

"Yes sir."

What strikes the president as the most unusual is, in light of the fact that the North Pacific Garbage Patch is nothing more than a floating landfill, why they had decided to camp out there for the night like a bunch of Boy Scouts. That made absolutely no sense at all.

"Try getting Dr. Taylor on his cell phone."

"Already did that sir. It went right to voice mail."

"Did you leave a message?"

"Yes sir."

"Okay, that will be all. Goodnight."

At the moment the president ponders this, and figures it certainly merits further consideration but he has more important matters to attend to, items on his agenda that are more pressing.

He supposes that if the captain of the research vessel wants to investigate the garbage pile and join Dr. Taylor in sleeping under the stars surrounded by waste, so be it. He still thinks it's weird that Hallsly joined them (and isn't making a nuisance of himself), but it could be he's making more of it than it warrants. He trusts the doctor knows what he is doing.

The President drains his glass and clicks off the lamp on his desk. Standing, he decides to see if the First Lady is up for a little early morning rendezvous. And, if not, there is always the porn channel on the plasma screen TV in the Oval Office. Either one will be fine.

Hazy, nightmarish images haunt the governor's feverish brain, and at this juncture he can't tell what's real and what isn't. He isn't sure whether or not the ship actually sank and he's in the vast labyrinth of Hell, having earned this dubious honor from the life of sin and sordidness he lived so fearlessly.

He finds he is lying face down, and with a concentrated effort he works himself into a sitting position. He is in a cage made of molded plastic (what appears to be plastic milk cartons covering thick plastic milk crates), and in the dim, orange light he notices the walls are opaque (not allowing him a view of his surroundings), but the design looks crude and flimsy enough to kick his way out of. Pressing against a wall with both hands he discovers, disappointingly, that it is indeed solid. It feels real enough, of that he is certain, and at once he is aware of a hollow sensation in his stomach, a nauseating cramp that doubles him over in pain.

Clutching his moderately sized gut and taking short breaths, he suddenly recalls the people he'd come into contact with, if indeed one could call them 'people'. They were ridiculously emaciated, skeletal, their eyes like a great white shark's, pitch black and glassy. And, Christ help him, some of them had appendages no human should have, like gills and flippers. No, it is easier (possibly more comforting) to believe they must be the twisted concoction of Hades or, as he'd previously thought, nothing but a panic induced delusion, wrought by stress and fear. The only problem with this fantasy is the certainty that it's untrue; there is no mistaking the pain in his belly, or the hard feel of the cage bottom under his butt.

He recollects falling into a pit of syringes and being rescued by these creatures, only to be taken into their custody (forcefully) and then, he supposes, brought here. Where 'here' is, well, of that he has no clue. He doesn't remember much after they grabbed him because in the extremity of his terror he'd fought them, and it wasn't long before one of them cold cocked him on the noggin. Which brings him up to now, where he is currently cowering in this ridiculous, plastic cage.

A racket of squawking and screeching arises, animal sounds from close by, and for a second it feels as if his heart stops beating before it abruptly starts hammering wildly. He cries out, startled, then instantly feels foolish. They can't get him, not in here, and it's possible they are locked up, the same as he is. Either that or perched on top of his cage like vultures, waiting for him to die. He slaps the plastic ceiling but it doesn't elicit any movement. The animals may be confined after all.

This is no hallucination Hallsly old boy. Wherever this is, it makes Euro-Disney seem like paradise.

Gradually gathering his senses, he feels his old friend rage coming back good and strong. He doesn't care that these assholes look like a bunch of walking corpses, rejects from the fucking circus, no one but no one messes with Governor Theodore Hallsly Jr. Esquire the third.

Sons a bitches! Cage me will you! I'll see that all of you are brought up on kidnapping charges!

Naked fury helps to clear away some of the cobwebs, and he finds a small opening (an air hole?) and presses his face against it, trying to get a glimpse of the world without. All he can see are bare light bulbs strung up on plastic poles, casting the sickly orange glow that illuminates the environment around him. He doesn't see anyone, but that doesn't stop him from giving them a piece of his mind:

"You bastards will have a lot to answer for!" he shouts, his voice rough, scratchy but sincere. "Let me out of here and maybe I'll let it go, but if you don't I'll see to it that all of you face some serious charges!"

He is answered by the shrieks of the animals, terrified and angry voices like his own, possibly beseeching of their captors the very same thing. Let us go now and maybe we'll just melt back into the night. No hard feelings.

"Goddamnit!" No one treats him this way! No one! Not unless he's paid them good money to do so. "Ahhh!" He loses control of his propriety, which, quite frankly, isn't hard for him to do. "I'll kill you all, you hear me? I'll see to it that every last one of you hangs from the highest tree-"

"Jesus Christ! Get a grip will ya?"

He turns toward the sound of the voice, one that sounds vaguely familiar.

"Who said that?"

"I did," the other says. "Me, Perry."

"Perry?"

"I'm one of the interns from the ship. You know, the research vessel?"

"I know goddamn well about the ship!" Hallsly retorts. "You're one of the science dweebs?"

"Aye aye," the kid says sarcastically, although his heart isn't really in it.

"Where the hell are we?"

"Last time I checked we were on the Great Pacific Trash Heap," Perry replies, and it is all the governor can do not to fire back an acidic rejoinder. Instead he retains his composure (what little of it there is left) and rephrases the question:

"They knocked me out when they caught me and I didn't see where they brought me. What can you tell me about this place?"

"We're in some kind of village," another says, joining the first.

"Who is that?"

"It's Steven, another one of the science dweebs." His tone carries a hint of reproach, and in the governor's grand wisdom he sees fit to humble himself, if only slightly.

"I'm sorry I called you that," he says, anything but sorry, but if it will help… "Tell me more."

"We got captured, just like you," Steven elucidates. "They brought us here, to this, this village I guess you would call it."

"Who are these people?"

"We think they're the crew from the last ship, well, most of them anyway."

"They can't be. The people who caught me are monstrous, hideous-totally deformed. If they were from the missing ship they wouldn't be mutants and they would be glad to see us. Certainly they'd want to be rescued."

"Oh, they're glad to see us all right," Perry says mordantly and Steven tells him to shut up.

"They're the crew from the last ship but…in a way they aren't…"

"What does that mean?"

"He means that something changed them. They don't want to be rescued. This is their home."

"I don't think they're completely human anymore," Steven adds, and there is something in his tone that instantly defuses Hallsly. His anger and outrage are quickly replaced by his old acquaintance fear, and suddenly the cage becomes that much smaller.

"What," he asks in a deliberately calm voice, "do you think they intend to do with us?"

He waits as the two mull over the question, a period of time that seems to stretch on and on. When he can't take it anymore he blurts: "Well?"

"We don't know," Steven answers at last. "But whatever it is, it can't be good."

"So that's your plan?" Dante asks, looking at the solemn faces assembled around him.

"That's the best we have, like it or not."

"I didn't say I don't like it, I just…" His voice trails off as he gazes out to sea, which is nothing but a black outline under shimmering stars. "What are our chances of finding the ship?"

"Pretty slim," Dr. Taylor says, "but we have to at least give it a shot or we'll certainly die. We'll go at daybreak, not a moment later; we're sitting ducks here." He takes off his glasses, considers polishing them on his shirt before quickly changing his mind, and then continues: "The longest anyone can go without water in this climate is about seven days. Scientific fact, there is no beating that. We cannot drink the ocean water, as I am sure you all know-"

"Why not?" Tyler interjects and Dr. Taylor squints at him with mild annoyance.

"Because it's salt water," he says, wanting to add 'you *dumb-ass*' but refrains. "It will give you diarrhea and dehydrate you. Eventually you'll succumb to hallucinations and a horrible, painful death-"

"Okay, okay I got it. I didn't ask for your life story, Jesus!"

"And we cannot at all costs drink any water that we should find here, it wouldn't be sanitary. If it rains we can chance drinking the rainwater, but we shouldn't store it in anything. We have to assume that everything on this heap is contaminated and the consequences of such an indiscretion will be a condition similar to the captain's. That or you'll get terribly, most likely deathly, ill."

"I agree with you there," Dante says in a low voice. "We saw something that, well, I don't think I can explain." He eyes the doctor somberly. "It certainly lends credence to your contamination theory."

"What was it?"

Dante casts a sidelong glance at Leeann and sees she is looking at him apprehensively. He raises an eyebrow and she offers a small nod. "Something," he begins, not knowing exactly how to put it into words, "something…happened to the crewman we were with."

"Go on."

"It was horrible," Leeann says, her voice wavering slightly, her lower lip trembling. "I never, ever want to see something like that again in my life."

Dante proceeds to tell them what happened, keeping the details to a minimum in order to spare Leeann the ordeal of going through it again. When he finishes all eyes on him are filled with a terror he senses comes close to what the two of them felt at the time.

"You're certain of this? He transformed right in front of you?"

"No mistake. All of a sudden he wasn't human anymore. Fortunately I managed to grab his weapon and I shot him. Then we got the hell out of there."

"It seems you two were very lucky."

"Yeah…"

"Where's the rifle?" Cole asks.

"It was empty so we ditched it," Dante says uncomfortably, realizing how stupid he must sound. "We kept getting lost, and we were so tired…I just got sick of holding on to it."

"We really coulda used it," Kenny grumbles and Dante shrugs.

"Never mind that now," Dr. Taylor says. "What's done is done."

"I suppose that confirms you're theory," Melissa admits grudgingly, and Dr. Taylor can understand her reluctance to embrace his assumption. It is, after all, not very good news.

"We thought it might have had something to do with the birds," Dante offers. "You know, because they bit him."

"It could be that, yes, or possibly he infected the wound with his dirty hands."

"Speakin' a them birds," Kenny says, "anyone else wonder how come we ain't seen any since we been here on the shore?"

"The thought has crossed my mind," Dr. Taylor replies, glancing at the sky, noticing it's turned from black to a lighter blackish/gray. "As for food," he says, picking up where he left off, "until we find the ship we'll have to go without."

"How long can a person go without eating?"

"Tough to answer based on our situation, but technically about three weeks."

"What's different for us?"

"The lack of water will speed up the process, I suppose, but I guess that will be a mute point if we don't find any in three or four days."

A hush falls over the group, one that is indeed very dismal. Facing your own imminent demise is never an easy thing to do, and the conditions they find themselves in don't offer any quick-fix solutions.

"So we're goners in three or four days if we don't find water," Cole says in a mechanical voice. It's very hard for him to process this bit of information. "What are we going to do?"

"I suppose we could pray for rain," Dante says.

"Are you a religious man?" Dr. Taylor asks him sincerely, genuinely curious, and the missing link looks to the sky, thinks about his crazy mother, his dead sister, his brother who hasn't spoken to him in almost fifteen years…and shakes his head.

"No. If there was a God, certainly he or she wouldn't be this cruel, would they?"

No one replies and, because he was the one who inquired, Dr. Taylor offers a kernel of his own wisdom: "Within the vastness of the universe it is debatable whether or not we as a species are as important as we deem ourselves to be." He strokes his chin, considering. "With that said, if there truly is a grand designer of the infinite cosmos we may be, simply put, a mere afterthought. After all, it was our own recklessness that caused such a place as this to exist in the first place. Calling our presence here 'cruelty' is quite contentious, is it not? In the context of a supposed 'Maker'?"

"Well, when you put it like that, I guess so."

"I didn't understand a thing you just said," Tyler mumbles bitterly, still incapable of containing his resentment at Melissa, and consequently the others. Hell, he was here first; he should be the one who has dibs on the lifeboats, but no. These assholes come along and claim 'em for themselves, like he has absolutely no say in the matter and he should just be happy to accompany them. Fuck all these pricks…

"I think this place is proof there's a devil," Cole says. "If there's anyplace that's Hell on earth, this has gotta be it."

"Yer outta yer mind," Kenny objects, hitting the Mexican on the back of the head. "There ain't no God, no devil, no nothin'. Nothin' cept this big pile a shit we need ta find a way off a." He looks at the doctor. "I think it's high time we took a look at them lifeboats. The second I see the sun I wanna be ready ta go."

"No better time than the present." The two get to their feet. "Let's see what we have to work with."

FOURTEEN

The night is fading now, giving way to the coming dawn. The sun has yet to make an appearance, but within the hour it will be peaking it's fiery head over the horizon. Dr. Taylor accompanies Kenny to the edge of the heap, their feet making crinkling noises on the pliant plastic floor. The two men walk in silence, one watching the water, the other looking about them warily, a length of pipe clutched in his hands.

The others stay behind, gathered in a circle, regarding one another in the growing light. Everyone looks haggard, tired, their faces smudged with grime.

"Man, I wish I had a cup of coffee," Cole says wistfully. "You never know how much you take things for granted until you can't have them, you know?"

Dante places his hands on the small of his back, feeling exhaustion pour over him in dizzying waves. Jesus, he is so tired. Maybe a little action is just what he needs to breath some life into him.

Kenny suddenly returns, appearing slightly winded.

"We caught a lucky break," he says, grinning. "Come on."

It will soon be time to gather the rest of the passengers, Captain Harvey notes, lifting his eyes to the heavens. He has sent out a summons to the others and they should be here soon to help take the remaining few into custody. There is no need to rush things; they certainly aren't going anywhere. Might as well let them have a few more moments of 'freedom' before he ushers them into the next chapter of their lives.

His stomach growls ravenously, the pain acute, startling. He has to eat. If he's going to be at his best he needs to refuel. No waiting.

He raises a hand into the air, his mouth forming syllables unknown in any human tongue. The sound he emits is low, breathy, yet it carries for miles. Expending his air, he inhales sharply and with his exhale carries out the note again.

Presently a flutter of wings beats from above, and a Rancor bird settles on his outstretched arm. It's soulless eyes stare unblinkingly, it's reptilian tongue flicking in and out under the jagged, discolored beak.

"Thank you my warrior of the sky. Your sacrifice is most helpful."

With his other hand Captain Harvey grips the bird around the neck and squeezes. The bird produces a brief, piercing squawk before it's neck is broken, and then collapses limply in his hand. He rips the head off, tipping it to his open mouth and drinking the greenish blood that drizzles out. Casting it aside, he proceeds to consume the rest, feathers, scales and all. When he is done he issues a satisfied belch, wiping his mouth with the back of his arm.

Much better. He is now ready to confront the remaining survivors, to welcome them to his home in style. Time to get this show on the road.

Gathered around the lifeboats, the passengers jostle one another for a look.

"We've been thrown a bone," Dr. Taylor says cheerfully, showing them what turned up in one of the boats.

When Kenny and he had flipped over the first boat they discovered the corpse of one of the crewmen.

"Depending on how you look at it, he's better off," Kenny had said.

"I guess so," the doctor agreed.

Kenny dragged the body away so the other's wouldn't have to see him, and when he'd returned the doctor had righted the other lifeboat, only to discover with some surprise that their was a small cache of supplies aboard.

"Nothing to write home about, but this will definitely come in handy," Dr. Taylor says. "One of the lifeboats is equipped with a travel kit, a little lock box that's welded to the side. Kenny was able to pry this sucker open and voila! We now have some things that may give us a decided edge."

There is a first aid kit, which he hands to Kenny. "Everyone should use the antiseptic on any open wounds or bug bites; it will help prevent the spread of bacteria." He figures (based on what they are dealing with) that this is akin to putting a Band-Aid on a severed limb, but it's something anyway. If it can at least slow down the progression of the bacteria, than it has done its job.

He looks at Cole. "Well, it isn't coffee, but it's a little something to wet our whistles." He holds up a bottle of water. "There are four in here, and we have to make them last. Everyone can have a drink now and then another before we go. There's two bottles for each boat."

A general cheer rises up amongst them. Never in their lives have they been so grateful for a simple sip of water. Passing the bottle around, Kenny watches them to make sure no one gets greedy.

Tyler takes it from Melissa with shaking hands, upending the bottle and letting the water cascade down his throat. God is that good!

"Hey, enough!" Kenny wrenches the bottle away from him. "The doctor said a small drink."

"But I'm dying of thirst!"

"So's everyone else! Get yer head outta yer ass!"

Tyler submits gracefully, but the anger he'd dialed down to a low simmer is once again ignited to a raging boil. Stupid bastard, picking on him. He saw that beaner Cole take an even bigger drink yet Kenny had no problem with that. Probably 'cuz he likes spics better than whites.

Ain't that just like a nigger? But he'll let it pass, for now.

"Is there another kit in the other boat?" Dante inquires and the doctor shakes his head.

"Unfortunately no. But I think we should be happy with what we've got, right?"

"Better something than nothing."

Dr. Taylor shows them the rest of the contents, presenting a small knife, a flare gun, a pocket-size notebook and the stub of a pencil, a large bar of chocolate (which brings about another cheer) and the piece de résistance: a pair of walkie-talkies.

"Do they work?" Cole asks excitedly. "Maybe we can call the ship!"

"They work," Kenny confirms.

"Did you try to contact them?"

"Well," Dr. Taylor answers slowly, "here's the thing..." His tone brings about a measure of sobriety to their reveling spirit. The others eye him silently. "Since they've done nothing to rescue us, we have to assume they're not looking out for our best interests."

"Than what are we going to do if we find them?"

"This is a covert operation," Kenny expounds. "If we find the ship we hafta sneak aboard."

"What do we do then?"

"We hafta take it over by any means possible."

"Are you even listening to yourself?" Tyler sneers. "You sound like a character in a spy movie! 'This is a covert operation, blah blah blah blah blah'," he imitates mockingly. "Are you for real dude?"

"The first group that finds the ship will notify the other and wait until they get there," Dr. Taylor says, ignoring him. "With all of us we can certainly overtake them."

"But they have guns," Tyler points out, and Kenny wants to slug him in the kisser but grudgingly refrains.

"Look ya asshole, we don't even know if we're gonna find the goddamn ship! Unless ya got a better idea why don't ya shut the hell up?"

Everyone is looking at Tyler, who unconsciously takes a step back. A hot flush spreads across his cheeks.

"Okay man, okay." He holds up his hands in a decided show of surrender. "I'm just sayin'."

"We'll do whatever we have to." Dr. Taylor catches Tyler's gaze and offers a rigid smile. "We'll simply do our best."

"Sure, no problem," Tyler replies, but there is a trace of derision in his voice.

Fucking coon didn't have to call me out like that in front of everyone. Made me look like a chump.

"Okay everyone, we can all have a piece of chocolate and then we have to decide who is going with whom." Dr. Taylor holds out the candy bar and Melissa takes it, carefully peeling back the wrapper. "But before you touch the chocolate I suggest you all rinse your fingers with a little antiseptic. Not too much though, we need all we can get. And while you're at it take care of any wounds or bites."

Everyone presses in closer and the bottle of antiseptic makes the rounds.

"Weird thing bout those bug bites," Kenny marvels, looking at the fading red welts on his forearms, "is they ain't botherin' me."

"Me either," Melissa says, gingerly breaking off small pieces of chocolate and handing them out. "I only got bit in a couple of places but they don't itch, like a mosquito bite would."

"I think the water, or, rather, the oily coat on the surface has something to do with it," Dr. Taylor says, accepting his portion of chocolate. "I could be wrong, but I believe it's acting as a salve."

"Gross," Melissa says, making a face. She finishes the rounds, ending with Tyler. He accepts his piece silently, but inside he's simmering, feeling less than civil.

Who died and made that shit head boss?

He places the piece of chocolate on his tongue, but for some reason the sweet candy tastes bitter to him.

Picking his teeth with a shard of plastic, Captain Harvey lounges on the remains of an old mattress as he waits for the others to arrive. They should turn up in a few minutes, give or take. Pressing the sliver of plastic hard against his teeth, he feels movement in his mouth. Reaching in, he uses his thumb and forefinger to twist out another tooth. He studies it for a moment. It's one of his molars, and it's slightly rotten. Obviously, dental care on Garbage Island isn't exactly a priority.

That's two teeth in one day, he muses. *That ought to be some kind of record.* But it doesn't matter; as his physical being changes he in turn will adapt, of that he is certain. He puts it in one of his pockets and continues picking at his teeth.

The sound of footsteps announces his crew, and in a matter of seconds they step into the clearing.

"We'll be moving in soon," he says and the largest of the men, the former captain of the previous ship, nods.

"Aye...uhnnnggg...aye...sir." His right eye is gone, nothing left but a grisly, ragged hole where it used to be. Inside, maggots squirm where a fly has laid fresh eggs. His face is a mottled gray color, and when he raises a hand in a semi-salute Captain Harvey sees he's lost another finger.

"Got to be careful," he says, flicking away the makeshift toothpick. "We can make do without eyes but it's hard to get by with no fingers.".

"Aye...captain."

"The passengers are gathered at the cove, probably sulking and scared shitless. They're a pretty pitiful lot but," he smirks at the group assembled around him, "so were you when we first met."

They stare at him impassively, nothing registering on their emaciated, unsightly faces, but he knows they're savvy; he doesn't require verbal confirmation. Besides, as the lowest-rung-of-the-ladder subordinates they know it's best to hold their tongues, unless they want them ripped out of their mouths and fed to the Rancor birds. Jake Anderson and Lt. Ronson are allowed to offer their two cents because of the status they've been awarded, but he doubts those two will ever grow too big for their britches because they don't possess his finely honed skills, are merely carbon copies, second generation knock-offs. They may harbor obvious traits of superiority, but they'll always come in second to numero uno.

"Now remember, I want them all alive, is that clear?" No one speaks, no one nods; he knows this bit of info is now locked into their subservient brains. "They'll put up a fight, and when they do I want you to subdue them but don't break the skin." Captain Harvey returns his attention to the ex-captain. "Did you bring the nets?"

"Aye...*uhnnnggg*...aye...sir," he says, waving a hand at two others behind him. Corbin and Jake Anderson step forward, showing the captain their net, a contraption made of plastic beer and soda pop holders. Jake smiles broadly at the captain, who nods in return, while Corbin in turn stares blankly, drool running from one corner of his mouth.

"Perfect, and we'll have the advantage because we've got the element of surprise on our side." Captain Harvey gets to his feet. "Okay gentlemen, let's be quick and quiet about this."

"I don't like it, uh-uh." Cole crosses his arms, a sullen expression on his ugly mug. "I'm going with Kenny."

"The decision's been made," Kenny says, but not too unkindly. He understands how the other feels. Over the course of the last few days the Mexican has really bonded with him. God knows why, as Kenny has been his usual charming self, which means just a step above being a total prick.

"Yeah, but I don't like it."

"Don't matter man, let it go."

Dr. Taylor picked the groups by divvying up the largest men and the weapons. He figures that Kenny and Tyler should be in the same boat with Leeann and himself. They'll take the pocketknife. The other boat will contain Dante, Cole, Melissa and the flare gun. His reasoning is that when it comes to body strength, he and Leeann will count as one person. Cole may be short but he's built like a brick shithouse, and Dante towers above the rest. And then there's Melissa. He wouldn't want to fight her on his best day; she could probably whip his ass without even breaking a sweat.

"Does anybody else have a problem with the arrangements?"

Dante wants desperately to say something; letting Leeann out of his sight makes him feel vulnerable, alone. He looks at her, searching her eyes, but sees there is nothing there that appears vaguely reciprocal and holds his tongue. He shrugs.

"I guess it's all right," he says.

"I don't like it," Tyler declares. "I want to be in the same boat with Melissa and," he turns, gives Kenny a withering look, "I don't want to be anywhere near that guy."

"I've chosen as I have for logical reasons," Dr. Taylor says, a hint of exasperation in his voice. "We don't have time to sit and argue about this. We need to get going."

"Well, you asked us what we thought," Tyler says, looking at the others to see if he has any support. One look in Kenny's direction shows nothing but animosity, but he can see that the Missing Link is having some doubts. "What about you Sasquatch? You want to be with your little honey, don't you?"

Dante blushes (not that anyone can see it beneath his beard) but nods. "I would like to be in the same boat as Leeann, for her protection, but I understand what the doctor is getting at. I'm afraid his decision is for the best."

"Jesus! Since when is this guy our leader?" He turns to Melissa, looks at her imploringly. "First we got this numb nuts football player telling us what to do, like he knows shit about anything except throwin' a freakin' ball around, and now some dorkwad from D.C. is leading us into battle? Fuck it man, I don't need this!"

"Yer right," Kenny says, his voice even, composed. "Ya don't hafta put up with any a this if ya don't wanta. You can just stay right here for all I care."

"You'd like that wouldn't you?"

"Actually I wouldn't cuz, like it or not, we need yer help. How does that make ya feel Tyler? We actually need ya."

"I thought you just said you didn't care if I stayed here!"

"Enough!" Dr. Taylor explodes, startling everyone. "Kenny, thank you for backing me up on this and, yes Tyler, we need you. Now both of you shut up so we can get going! The sun is on the horizon."

All eyes turn to the east, witnessing the miracle that is the sun coming up over the tranquil sea. There is an infinitesimal scudding of clouds far off in the distance, unfortunately nothing but puny wisps.

"Fine. We'll do it your way."

"Thank you. Now we come to the hard part." Dr. Taylor fishes around in his pants pocket, finding a quarter. "We're going to flip to see who goes first."

"We're not going together?" Leeann asks, anxiety evident in her voice.

"I don't think there's any need for all of us to go in the water at once. We'll flip to see which group goes in and the other will wait and see if the first boat stirs up anything in the water that may...interfere with our progress."

"What do you mean?" Dante asks.

"You know what I mean," Dr. Taylor says quietly, and the others look around uneasily. They all remember the giant cockroaches, the mosquitoes crossed with tarantulas.

"It's the best way, trust me. Kenny, call it in the air."

And he flips the coin.

"Have your weapons at the ready men," Captain Harvey instructs, extracting a knife from a sheathe under his shirt. "But be careful. If any of them are ruined I will see to it that you suffer. Understand?"

The men shift their feet in the growing light, their faces as wooden as cigar store Indians, but they comprehend what he means all right: The Master has spoken; get it right or pay the consequences.

"Okay, let's round them up."

FIFTEEN

"Oh that's just great! Good call dick weed!"

"We're in the same boat ya jack-ass."

"Literally and figuratively," Dante says and Tyler casts his molten glare on him.

"You shut the hell up! You get to sit here and watch while we put our necks on the chopping block!"

"I don't give a crap about you, but I have to watch my…" Dante stops himself short, glancing at Leeann briefly before looking away, mildly discomfited. "I have to watch… her… go in the water first. You think I like that?"

"Why don't we swap then?"

Dr. Taylor sighs, turns around and places his hands on the boat. "Give me a hand Kenny, will you?"

"So that's it? Decision made?"

Kenny has had about all he can stand. His hands shoot out, taking the other by the lapels of his trashed designer shirt. "Ya'cn either help us or ya'cn stay here," he growls, his face inches from the others. "In fact, I take back what I said. We don't need ya."

"I'll go in the other boat," Tyler says sullenly, his eyes daring the other to do his worst.

"No ya won't. Either ya come with us in this boat or ya don't go at all." He looks around at the others. "Does anyone got a problem with leavin' this dipshit here?"

"Come on Tyler, just do it. It was the luck of the toss," Melissa says, her eyes beseeching him to suck it up. Even though they'd argued she doesn't wish him ill will, despite the fact that he's been nothing but a pain in the ass ever since.

"Yeah, the luck of the toss," he spits. "That's easy for you to say because you don't have to go in the water first."

Melissa shrugs exaggeratedly, her mouth twisting into a grimace.

"Fine," she says, her resolve at the breaking point. "You stay here then. If we find the ship maybe we'll come back for you."

"I save your life back there and this is how you show your appreciation? By siding against me with these guys?" He turns away from her. "There's something you all should know," he announces dramatically, and the others look at him warily. "I suggested we use the lifeboats and she didn't want to, in fact she got mad at me for even bringing it up. How about that, huh? You all think I'm the bad guy and she's the one who started it!" He turns back toward her. "How do you like that?"

"I was wrong, okay?" She chooses, very wisely no doubt, not to elaborate upon the fact that Tyler's idea was moronic compared to the doctor's plan, which actually has a chance of succeeding. "Now can we just go? You're holding up progress."

"Time is wasting," Dante says. "Make up your mind."

"Have it your way," Tyler finally relents. "But I still think you all suck."

"Duly noted," Kenny says. "Now let's get goin'." He walks over to the boat and helps Dr. Taylor push it into the water. "Hop in an I'll push us out."

"I don't see why we can't both get in the boat and use an…" Dr. Taylor pauses, glancing around, then claps himself on the head. He looks at the others, a self-deprecating smile on his face. "Looks like we forgot something."

"What?"

"The oars." He searches along the shore for a moment, looking first one way, then the other. "We don't have any oars."

"Shit." Kenny pulls the boat back up onto the heap. "Okay people, we gotta find somethin' to paddle the boats with. Everyone split up an start lookin'."

There are nods all around and they disperse, Dante trailing after Leeann.

"Are you all right with this?" he asks, noticing that (underneath her sunburn) she's grown several shades paler since the coin toss.

"I don't have a choice, do I?" she says bravely, although he's certain she's terrified. She looks at the water with trepidation, her hands shaking at her sides.

"Can you swim well?"

"Despite what you saw when we first got here, yes, I can. I had five years of swimming lessons at the city pool."

"Just stay with the boat if it overturns, and try not to get any of that sludge in your mouth or eyes."

"I know Dante. It's not like this is the first time." She uses the tip of her shoe to prod at something, making a face when she sees large, black, beetle-like bugs boil up from beneath a mound of sodden newspaper.

"Leeann," Dante says, reaching out a hand and gripping her shoulder.

"What?" She tilts her head up, meeting his gaze. Her eyes are the most brilliant shade of blue, especially in the early morning light. He feels his chest tighten and he compulsively swallows, his spit nearly the consistency of paste.

"Please," he gulps, "be careful."

"I will." She offers him a weak smile, but a smile just the same.

"Okay." He lets go of her, feeling a moment pass between them that is almost poignant, profound.

"I found one of the oars!" Cole calls out, dispelling the mood, and they look in his direction.

"I found somethin' too!" Kenny waves a large two by four over his head.

"Great. We just need to find two more candidates and we can successfully launch ourselves the hell out of here," Dr. Taylor says, nodding agreeably.

"How about another oar?" Melissa asks, displaying her find.

"That'll do."

After a few more minutes of blundering around Kenny finds another piece of wood that looks as if it will serve their purpose and the search is called off, the passengers reassembled at the shore.

"Okay," Dr. Taylor warns, "I know this is painfully obvious but everyone try and stay out of the water."

"No shit Sherlock," Tyler says and the others scowl at him. He shrugs, rolls his eyes. "Whatever."

"Good luck," Dante tells Leeann, wanting to hug her but refraining, and she smiles nervously. "Thanks."

"No words of encouragement for me?" Tyler asks Melissa, who simply looks away.

"Get going Sir Galahad, your steed awaits you."

"Yeah," he mutters. "I love you too."

Captain Harvey and his cohorts reach the edge of the cove and he raises a hand for them to stop.

"Silent and quick," he commands. "Get in and get out."

He waves them forward, stepping carefully around the last barrier before the cove. As they set foot on the beach he abruptly realizes he made a mistake, and a costly one at that. Somehow in all the commotion he completely forgot about the lifeboats. How could he be that stupid?

Disregarding his own instructions he bellows angrily: "Stop right where you are!"

Captain Harvey's booming voice echoes loudly across the clearing. All heads swivel toward the sound, stomach's sinking simultaneously when they see he's brought along some friends. The passengers gape in horror at the captain's grotesque menagerie, fear freezing them in place. At once it's as if all sound ceases: the water lapping and squelching at the edge of the heap, the squawking of the birds, the rustle of trash blowing in the offshore breeze. Time even stands still; the sun pauses in its skyward climb, clouds hanging in suspended animation, their shapes fixed in whatever image one can imagine: a ducky, a horsy, a decapitated human body...A paralysis so strong as to be almost indissoluble grips them in a bony, putrefying fist.

"Put the oars down and back away from the boats!" Captain Harvey's voice kick starts the clock, swinging everything back into motion.

"Grab the other boat!" Dr. Taylor hollers at the second group. "Everyone into the water now!"

Dante is the first to jump into action, followed quickly by Melissa and Cole.

"Get in and I'll push us out!" he orders and there is no argument from the other two. Melissa climbs in with Cole right at her heels. Dante (against his better judgment but knowing there isn't much time) shoves the boat into the black slime and plunges in after it, trying to keep his head above the water. Kicking frantically he propels them forward, his movements initially feeling clumsy, sluggish.

Kenny would later like to claim that he had the same idea, of ushering the others into the boat and using his brute strength to push them away from the edge, but the only reason he finds himself in this position is because he tripped. One second he's running for the boat, the next he's tumbling headlong after his left foot connects with some unseen piece of debris. Putting his arms out before him like he's about to execute a block tackle, he's able to grab onto the edge of the boat and heave it into the water as he drives forward, thrusting them from the shore.

"After them!" Captain Harvey shouts, and his minions bolt to the shoreline, their movement's jerky but their footing sure. They jump into the water without hesitation, sinking beneath the surface only to pop up seconds later like demented fishing bobbers. With erratic, awkward strokes they swim toward the retreating boats, thrashing through the contaminated water.

"Help me inta the boat!" In a short amount of time they've traveled a significant distance, and Kenny has had about all he can take of being in the ocean. Dr. Taylor and Leeann reach over the side, grabbing for his arms, while Tyler sits passively at the far end with his legs crossed.

"For Christ's sake, help us!" Dr. Taylor implores but the other doesn't budge, just stares at him impertinently.

Kenny makes it halfway up, his hands clutching the rim of the boat. Leeann gets an arm around him but he is too oily and she loses her grip. He falls back into the water with a despairing cry, the boat rocking dangerously back and forth, and a jet of black goo splashes her, getting in her mouth.

"Ug!" she sputters, spitting it out and gagging. For a second she's afraid she's going to toss her cookies (what little there is) into Kenny's frightened, upturned face, but she wins the battle within her, taking deep, calming breaths.

Over in the other boat Dante isn't fairing any better; Cole and Melissa are attempting to haul him in but he continues to slip out of their grasp. And as they persist in trying to aid him the gyres slow moving but unremitting current begins pulling them toward the trash heap.

Dr. Taylor looks up from Kenny's panicked face and notices the boat's stalled forward momentum, realizing instantly that if they don't start paddling they'll wind up back at the shore where the captain and his foot soldiers are waiting…well, not all of them. Several mutants are hot on their trail, fighting obdurately through the slick ooze, getting closer with each passing second. He turns to Tyler, blind fury overloading his circuits, burying the needle in the redzone.

"Get off your ass and start paddling you idiot!" His upper lip is curled, teeth showing. A flash of resentment registers in Tyler's eyes, but one glance over the doctor's shoulder gives him all the reason he needs to get in on the act of escape. Snatching hold of one of the oars and attacking the water with it, he watches with sick fascination as he pulls the lifeboat just out of reach of one of the approaching creatures.

"Hold on!" Dr. Taylor tells Kenny. "Those things are getting too close!" He grabs the other oar (the two by four) and desperately assails the water, using all his might to help drive them forward. "Make sure he stays with us," he instructs Leeann, and the girl reaches down and secures one of Kenny's hands in her own, doing her best to pacify him as he clings to her.

Melissa looks over at the other boat, noticing that Dr. Taylor and Tyler are rowing furiously, their efforts having given them a substantial lead on their would be hijackers; another fifty yards or so and they'll reach the slime barrier, entering the clear, untainted sea. She realizes that if they don't do the same thing they'll never get away.

"We have to paddle! If we don't the current is going to take us in!"

Dante and Cole look behind them and see that the creatures are closing in fast, despite the fact that their movements are anything but fluid; in fact they resemble monsters in those old claymation horror movies as they jerk and shudder onward, but they are advancing steadily. Soon enough they'll be able to reach out and grab the boat.

"Forget about me!" Dante urges. "Just get us out of here!"

Melissa and Cole make a mad dash for the oars, stabbing at the water with fretful, hurried strokes. At the onset they fight each other, rowing in opposite directions, but at last they coordinate their efforts and the boat pulls ahead, Captain Harvey's cohorts gradually falling behind.

"Fucking hell!" Dual pulsing jugular veins bulge hideously on either side of the captain's neck. His rage over the forgotten lifeboats blots everything else out, his vision narrowing down to a pinpoint. Through a scarlet haze all he can see are the fleeing boats, his chest hitching spasmodically as the life within him squirms, awakened. "Fucking goddamn hell!"

Where is my omniscience when I need it? How could the bacteria have failed to show me this?

Quaking with an unquenchable anger, he watches helplessly as his underlings thrash about in the bubbling sea.

"Try harder damn you!" His wrath ignites an incredible outpouring of emotion that burrows into his minion's infected brains, motivating them to push the very limits of their considerable strength. Their efforts are immediately doubled, tripled, and they shoot ahead as if pulled by invisible wires.

"Row faster!" Dante kicks his legs in tandem, figuring that between the three of them they should be able to keep a sufficient distance between themselves and the captain's men, but they're breathing right down their necks. If they pause for even a second they'll be on top of them.

Melissa throws herself at the water aggressively, the oar piercing the surface like a knife while Cole in turn flails away recklessly, whimpering and muttering to himself:

"Jesus, please let us get away from these cabrone bendeco's and I promise on the Holy Mother of God that I will do thy bidding as you see fit, amen and hallelujah and all that shit, huh? Please? Praise be the word of the Lord and, um, the father and, uh, Jesus, um, H, um, Christ…"

Because of their frenzied efforts no one notices that Melissa is leaning much too far over the edge, her feet sloshing around in the slimy water that's pooling on the boat's floor. Plunging the oar downward, her weight unbalanced, she loses her footing and tumbles overboard, the oar slipping from her grasp. Dante reaches for her as she sails over his head but misses, the fabric of her shirt snagging on his fingernails before she plunges in and sinks like a stone.

"Holy shit!" She disappears beneath the murky water, and just beyond the splash she makes is one of those things, floundering ever closer...

Melissa closes her eyes before she hits the water, and once immersed fights to keep her cool, not wanting fear to get the best of her. She twists herself around, sensing the surface right above her and, struggling courageously, pops up above the layer of greasy muck, gasping and spitting. But something catches her eye, movement close by.

"Ahhhhh!" She thrashes wildly but is too slow to get away as the humanoid wraps its arms around her torso, dragging her toward it. In a lightening quick moment that sears itself into her brain like a cattle brand, she gets a close look at him *(it)* and what she sees mortifies her beyond words. His gaunt face is a constellation of scars, bearing a wax-like, rubbery appearance; his *(it's)* ostensibly pliable features have a certain *melted* quality to them. His nose is like putty, running to one side of his face and his lips are lopsided and considerably discolored. He extends a greenish/blackish tongue, flicking it back and forth over his misshapen lips like a serpent. But the worst part is his eyes; there is no white to them, just an inexpressive black. His mouth opens and closes repeatedly, like a fish, his skeletal hands holding her fast; try as she may she can't break free.

"Let go of me!" She hammers him with her fists but when they connect it's like striking a cement wall. He clutches her tighter, fingers sinking into her tender flesh.

She registers with revulsion that his skin feels reptilian, scaly; it's extremely coarse, but also slick from the film on the water. For this reason it's hard for her to get a hold of him, to try and shove him away or push his head under. She realizes futilely that she is losing the battle; little by little he is dragging her toward the shore.

Dante releases his hold of the boat, considers swimming after her when another creature bobs out of the water only inches before him, it's withered, claw-like hands raking across his chest. Yelling hoarsely he flails backwards, keeping his eyes fixed upon its grisly face, when something bumps against him again, this time from behind. He twists around, ready to face another of these deformed bastards only to find it's the dropped oar. Reaching out with his right hand, he deftly snags it while kicking his legs forcefully to keep his head aloft. He grasps the shaft firmly and swings it as hard as he can, the flat end connecting solidly with its head, producing a bone-jarring thud before it drops below the surface. Without further adieu he turns away and performs a panicked, ungainly overhand crawl, returning to the lifeboat in record time, his lungs laboring for air, his energy exhausted. He clutches the rim and leans heavily upon it, causing the boat to tip abruptly and Cole stumbles, his feet skidding in opposite directions. He whirls his arms to keep his balance, slogging gracelessly in the slushy water lapping at his ankles, and the two by four drops from his hands, falling onto the floor of the boat.

"Son of a bitch!" He steadies himself against the lip, and for the first time notices the absence of the other passenger. "Where the hell is Melissa?"

Dante doesn't answer, just swivels his head and squints against the glare of the early morning sun on the water, dismayed to see her being towed farther and farther away as she beats feebly against him.

Watching expectantly, Captain Harvey licks his lips hungrily, eyeing what is no doubt a most treasured prize. If he can salvage this by getting her than at least not all is lost. Besides, where do the passengers think they're going to go? Surely they have no choice but to stay at Garbage Island as opposed to taking their chances on the open water. The probability of making it to the mainland in the lifeboats is next to zero. And the likelihood of them running into a garbage towing vessel is slim; the storm resourcefully took care of that. No one should be traveling this way for the next twenty-four to forty-eight hours, give or take.

"Bring her to me," he summons his minion. "Bring her to me and you shall be rewarded."

Knowing only what the bacteria tells him, the man creature of Garbage Island pulls her along, his sinewy muscles hardly taxed. Melissa lashes out violently but simply cannot tear herself free. She batters at him with her fists but he pays no mind, her blows going unheeded. She kicks her legs but they do nothing but churn the mucky sludge. To subdue her the minion pushes her head under the water and her world is reduced to an airless void. She clamps her eyes and mouth shut, the thought of taking this foul substance into her mouth and lungs enough to knock the fight out of her. She goes slack, ceasing her kicking and thrashing. He (*it*) eases up, allowing her above the surface and hauling her swiftly to the shore.

The minion drags her upon the heap and casts her aside, looking to the captain for approval. As she lay there, choking and gagging, Captain Harvey smiles favorably.

"Good work. You will get choice pickings at the feast tonight."

The minion makes a whining, grating noise that signifies its pleasure, a sound that's very unpleasant to the ears…

Having made it to a relatively clear patch of sea, past the thickest blanket of oily residue, Dante scans the shore and sees that Melissa is now in the custody of the captain. He experiences a deep-seated dread, co-mingled with an inextinguishable feeling of responsibility. How could he let this happen? One minute she was here, the next gone, and he'd done nothing. Looking about him, he sees that the other minions are far behind them now, still splashing about in the inky water.

"Okay!" Dante calls out to Cole, who's resumed his mad paddling. "You can stop rowing and help me over the side now."

Passing the ring of slime that surrounds the trash heap like a filthy halo, Dr. Taylor and Leeann help Kenny into the boat as Tyler continues to row. With their help he slides over the rim, taking great, rasping breaths, and he lies on the bottom shivering and wiping the sludge from his face, absentmindedly flicking his hand over the side. His enormous chest rises and falls as he gets his wind back, his exertions making him dizzy. He feels as if he just spent the last two hours doing wind sprints; his lungs are on fire, the muscles in his legs rubbery. He realizes how badly out of shape he's become since his football career, a point in time that seems like eons ago, in another life he can barely claim as his own.

"Are you okay?" Dr. Taylor asks him and he nods, grinning foolishly.

"I guess so," he coughs, trying to even out his breathing. "Feels like I just ran a marathon."

"For all practical purposes you just did." Dr Taylor nods toward the shore. "We lost our pursuers."

"Good." Kenny wraps his arms about himself, relishing the warming rays of the early morning sun. "Mission accomplished."

All heads turn toward the shore and they see the captain's men climbing back aboard the trash heap, the second lifeboat closing the distance between them.

"Where's Melissa?" Dr. Taylor says, and the others look askance at the approaching boat, straining to see.

"Maybe she's in the bottom of the boat and we can't see her?" Leeann says/asks tentatively, goose bumps rising on her arms, why, she doesn't know.

"Maybe…"

Several minutes later Dante and Cole paddle along side them, and it's clear by the hangdog looks on their faces that Melissa is no longer with them. The two groups stare at one another for a long moment, a shared silence between them that is heavy with malaise.

"Melissa…" Dr. Taylor starts and Dante shakes his head.

"They got her," he says quietly. "Those bastards got her."

"We have to go back for her!" Leeann says, looking from face to face expectantly. When no one responds she says again: "We're going back for her, right?"

Dr. Taylor's expression is one of insipid resignation. He looks at Kenny, then at Dante.

"What do you think?" he asks, but he knows that whatever they say he will veto. They can't risk going back, can't chance another of them getting captured, even though it was Melissa.

"I should go back for her," Dante says. "It's my fault."

"Its no ones fault. Don't blame yourself."

"But she was in my boat…I should have been looking out for her!" A sob issues from deep within his chest like the growl of machinery and hot tears fill his eyes, spilling down his cheeks and disappearing into his mangy beard. He feels horrible, as if he's betrayed her himself, yet there is another sentiment beneath that, one he doesn't want to recognize but can't be avoided: he is grateful that it was Melissa and not Leeann. If it were Leeann there would be nothing the others could say, he would definitely go back for her.

"If anyone should go back for her it should be him," Cole says, jerking a thumb at Tyler. "It's his woman."

"She's not my woman. I came along on this trip to be her bodyguard." He glares at the others, as if daring them to say anything more, but inside he is filled with conflicted emotions. A part of him is stunned and saddened that Melissa is no longer with them but he, like Dante, has another nagging feeling. His is purely selfish, of course. He is glad it was she and not he. "I agree with the doctor. There's no sense in anyone else getting caught. We need all the people we can, right?" He scrutinizes the others expectantly and they in turn look away. When his gaze rests on Leeann she spits over the side of the boat.

"You coward. You ought to be ashamed of yourself."

"The hell with you bitch! You go and get her if you want but I'm staying right here!"

"No one is going back there," Dr. Taylor says with an air of finality. "She was definitely an asset to us but we have to press on. Daylight's a wasting." He looks toward the shore one last time before returning his gaze to the others. "We'll all be dead soon enough unless we can find the ship."

The thought of their own mortality brings the conversation to a direct halt, closing the door on Melissa and her imminent fate.

"So who should go in their boat?" Kenny says at last.

Dr. Taylor thinks a moment, then his eyes settle on Leeann.

"Why don't you go with them? That should balance it out."

"Gladly," she says, tossing one last contemptuous look at Tyler. "I don't want to be in the same boat as that asshole."

Dante extends a hand, only too glad to do so. He is sorry for the loss of Melissa but this turn of events makes him very happy. He'll feel a lot better with Leeann close by where he can keep an eye on her. She reaches out and takes his hand, Kenny helping her over from their side while Cole takes over the job of holding the two boats together. When she is safely aboard the other boat he lets go and they slowly drift apart.

Dante glances upward, sees clouds moving in from the south. Even from far away they look dense and moisture laden.

"Looks like we might get a little rain."

"Let's just hope we don't get more than we bargain for. A storm will bring rough waters and these lifeboats may not be able to handle that. If it gets too heavy just head in and wait it out. That would be the safest thing to do. And if its manageable try and collect some but only use the water bottle, don't use any receptacle from the trash heap."

"Do you really think we stand a chance, that we'll find the ship and get rescued?" Leeann asks abruptly, her voice soft, her eyes studying the shore of the heap. The captain and his cohorts have disappeared back into the trash, Melissa's fate sealed in a manner no one wants to ponder too deeply.

"I don't know. All we can do is try."

"Do you think they're going to turn Melissa into one of them?" Cole says and Dr. Taylor sighs.

"Maybe," he replies wearily and Kenny gets the hint.

"Alright, let's get on with this. Let's test the walkie talkies one more time." He flicks the on switch up, presses the button with his thumb. "Testing, one two. Do you read me?"

Cole clicks on the other, hears Kenny's voice coming through. "Loud and clear good buddy," he says, smiling. "I hope we see you guys soon." His tone is pensive, and Kenny knows the little bastard is going to miss him. What the hell, Cole isn't all that bad. A little slow maybe, but he's a stand up guy. Not like Tyler, who he's going to have to watch like a hawk.

"I hope we see you guys soon too. Over and out."

He clicks off the walkie-talkie and the two separate groups set out. Eventually they are out of sight from one another, with nothing else to see but the enormity of the open water between them.

SIXTEEN

Lying prone on the rank surface of the trash heap and catching her breath, Melissa is in no hurry to get reacquainted with the illustrious Captain Harvey, a man who wore a chameleon's mask and doffed it in time for the party.

"Ah my dear, at last we meet again." He grins, stepping forward, his boots adjacent with her forehead. "I have so much to show you."

She feels the bile curdle within her, a hopeless, morose hatred, and with great effort she pushes herself to her knees and spits at him. The loogy lands with a wet splatter on his cheek.

"That's the spirit!" he cries, his voice tweaked to a near frenzied pitch as he absently wipes it away. "I'm glad to see you too!" Reaching down, he grabs one of her arms and hoists her to her feet. He examines her oil-covered face, her matted, filthy hair. "You are looking beautiful as ever."

"Yeah, and you're looking wretched as ever," she tosses back to no effect; his mirth is merely amplified. She tries to tug away from his grasp but it's too strong. He increases the pressure and at once she feels dizzying waves of pain shoot through her arm. "All right, enough! Let go!"

"I'm never letting go of you little girl," he whispers hoarsely, leaning forward. This close the smell emanating from him is absolutely repellent and her stomach summersaults dangerously. His breath reeks of dead things, *long* dead things, and he breaths it into her face with a nasty smile, taking great pleasure in her discomfort. "I have already selected a bride but I think I've found a successor to her throne." His smile is like watching live worms crawl through the eye sockets of decaying animals. "Yes indeedy, I do believe I've found a worthy successor."

Although her guts are churning and her head is pounding, the physical pain means very little compared to her dread at being caught. She wonders despondently if anyone is going to come back for her; surely Tyler wouldn't just leave her here without doing something about it, would he? But…no. Not after their fight. She knows he doesn't care about her anymore; he's not looking out for anyone but himself.

"You know," the captain says pleasantly, drawling out his words, "I do believe your friends have abandoned you, hmm? What do you think? Where is that boyfriend…oops! I mean *bodyguard* of yours when you need him, huh?"

"Do whatever the hell you want to me," she says, trying to project a fearlessness she doesn't truly possess. "I'm not afraid of you and your scrawny little butt-buddies."

The captain laughs, blowing his foul breath in her face with a force that nearly cripples her sense of smell permanently. "My butt-buddies! Oh my, that is a good one!" His laughter turns into a dry hack that soon becomes a coughing spasm, producing greenish/whitish mucus that dribbles over his bottom lip and runs off his chin, staining his shirt. Inside the mucus there are writhing, living things but he takes no notice of this, no, because nothing bothers the good captain. Not now, not ever. "They are much more than that, trust me. But you'll see…everyone will see soon enough."

Disgusted, Melissa turns away, but Captain Harvey takes her by the jaw and twists her head so she has no choice but to face him. The smile is gone now, replaced by a look so degenerate that for the moment she can't even pretend she is unafraid. His eyes take on a different hue, a singular shade of black so dark as to be fathomless, and his mouth curls into a grimace that makes his countenance even more nightmarish, if that is possible.

"You will soon see I have astonishing things in store for you, things you never dreamed existed, not in a million lifetimes."

Looking into his face, his eyes, Melissa has no reason to doubt him. Whatever it is he intends to do, there is no question about it, it will be horrible beyond anything she has ever imagined.

"Let's move out, shall we? Preparations are in order for the arrival of our other guests." He motions to a couple of his minions with a quick wave of his hand and they shamble over, taking her by the arms. She notices with no surprise that it is two of the crewmen from their voyage. One of them is Jake, the second mate; she doesn't know the other's name, doesn't really care. "And there is someone who is just dying to see you. He'll be so surprised."

Their hands clamped roughly on her biceps, they drag her back into the fetid stank of Garbage Island.

Melissa's head hangs limply, her steps those of one condemned to die. The walk is long and her feet are aching; hiking boots would have been a good choice for a trek this arduous, but she hadn't really been given that choice, had she?

"We have a nice little spread." Captain Harvey's voice is insanely jolly, as if every little thing amuses him immensely. "Think you're going to like it."

"Oh, I very much doubt that," she says softly and Captain Harvey's booming laughter is like the rumble of thunder: loud, startling and over in seconds. When it passes a great silence ensues until, gradually, the other sounds return, seeming distant in comparison.

Melissa closes her eyes momentarily, seeking within her a sense of tranquility that will vanquish her creeping anxiety, but to no avail. Her muscles are tensed, her jaw clamped tightly. Her nerves feel like frayed, exposed wires. With each passing minute, each torturous step, she's becoming more and more convinced that no one is coming after her. They've left her to whatever fate Captain Harvey intends for her.

Can I blame them, really? Would I have volunteered to go after that chick from Texas if she'd been taken? I'd probably vote to move on, to just keep going and to hell with everything else. Because, in the end, no one really knows me, no one really cares. If it would be anyone it should be Tyler, and that sorry asshole just wants to save himself.

A sigh escapes her, fraught with resignation.

It's over for her, all over...

Besides Captain Harvey's occasional observations there is no chatter. His underlings are silent unless he speaks to them, and only then do they offer the sparsest reply, monosyllabic grunts mostly. And as they walk deeper into the trash heap she becomes aware that the light is growing dim, diluted somehow. She glances upward and is amazed to discover she no longer sees the sky. The captain follows her gaze, nodding his head like a sage old Wiseman.

"Pretty clever, huh? It's how we keep the world from seeing us with satellite camera's."

"What is it?"

"We made a tarp out of plastic grocery store bags. The United States outlawed their use in 2014 but what do you know? Thanks to their overwhelming proliferation the world over they keep popping up in the refuse that gets dumped here. It took some doing, but we managed to cover all of it."

Hating herself for asking, Melissa says: "All of what?"

"Welcome to the capitol of Garbage Island!"

Stepping out of the maze and into a clearing, Melissa becomes aware of the sounds of other life, the hum of voices, the din of their toiling. And when they venture in a little further what she sees surprises her but, given all she's seen in the last day, it shouldn't.

"It's not much but we call it home."

Melissa is still, taking it all in as best as she can, as best as her senses will allow under the circumstances, until her captors continue to haul her forward.

The captain and his band of miserable cohorts have fashioned a community of sorts out of the various debris from the trash heap. There are actual structures representing crude homes. Some of them are extremely rudimentary, more like lean-tos than actual dwellings, while others are more advanced. She notices that the larger 'buildings' are constructed out of pieces of ships and *(is that what I think it is?)* airplanes.

The village itself vaguely reminds her of a place she once visited in Mexico, a dilapidated little speck on the map along the Rio Grande, outside of a national park. The semblance of one to the other is the single street running down the middle, lined with the crumbling, makeshift edifices, but this is where the similarities end. There is probably no place on earth that can boast such an architectural nightmare as this.

She looks on, mesmerized, at the humanoids carrying out tasks that only the damned can find any reason for. She sees two women constructing something out of soda or beer six-pack holders, while several men work on what she figures to be weapons. Glazed eyes glance up from what they are doing as she is brought by, eyes that contain very little curiosity. More so, they seem to hold a gleam of hunger in them, a look that is akin to a child peering into a candy shop window. The movements they make are stiff, forced, as if their bodies are working on autopilot; animated corpses that otherwise would be dead were it not for some uncanny force that kept them alive.

Walking deeper into the village, she witnesses creatures enclosed within primitive cages, lively things that cry and squawk their disapproval at being captured. Some of them are the birds they'd encountered upon their arrival, but there are other beasts as well, outrageous looking things that, like the birds, appear to be combinations of species.

Whatever evolution has done here, it certainly wasn't intended to make the world a better place.

There's an animal that looks like a cross between a seagull and an octopus, and another that appears to be part lizard, part centipede.

"I see you are admiring our petting zoo," Captain Harvey says. "Well, don't get too attached. That's actually our food pantry." His eyes sparkle with mischief. "Hungry?"

"God, no." The last of her appetite disappeared the second she was brought back aboard this foul place.

"You will be soon, make no mistake about that."

"I doubt it," she says, then starts when she sees what lies at the end of the main passage. The atmosphere seems to close in around her, the air tight in her papery lungs. "Jesus, is that…"

"Why yes. Do you like what we did with it?"

The building at the end of the road stuns her, convinces her there truly is no hope. Whatever she thought, whatever plans she and the others had for escape, those thoughts are dashed away in a single moment, a single glimpse.

"I like to think of it as the town hall slash Imperial Palace." He bats his eyes at her modestly. "And we'll be adding on to it soon enough-renovating if you will."

It's wreckage from the first research vessel, specifically panels stripped from the hull. On one broad, towering steel plate is embossed the name 'Script's Exploration Vessel'.

"As soon as we have some spare time we'll spruce it up a bit, but first we have our guests to attend to."

"How," she asks, mystified, "is any of this possible?"

Captain Harvey laughs yet again, an unnerving dissonance that shouldn't even be associated with human happiness.

"Where there is a will there is always a way my dear," he says, licking his malformed, overly moist lips. "Now, I need you out of my hair for a while." He nods to the two men holding her. "We have so much to prepare."

"What are you going to do with me?"

"You and I are going to have a little chat later," he proceeds, ignoring her. "I trust you'll be a good girl and tell me everything I need to know."

"If you want me to tell you what the others are planning I can't help you; I have no idea."

"And, like I said, a reunion is in order, but that can wait. I have some business to attend to presently." He nods to Jake and Corbin. "These two will show you to your quarters."

"Wait!" she cries as she is taken away, but she isn't really sure what it is she intends to say. What *can* be said, really? 'Stop'? As it turns out it doesn't matter; in a moment he is out of her sight. With no fanfare the ex-crewmen march her through the village, leading her behind a series of lean-to's where there are several diminutive plastic enclosures she has no doubt are cages. They stop in front of one and with a free hand Jake opens a small door, a piece of opaque plastic hinged with thin strips of plastic. It looks to be made out of milk crates and then covered with flattened milk cartons.

"You be...*uhnnnggg*...a...good girl...and...*uhnnnggg*...get in," one of them, the crewman she doesn't know, rasps gravelly.

"We'll come for you when you're needed," Jake Anderson says, his voice considerably more 'normal'. He places a hand on her head and forces her inside, and she scooches to the far wall, turning away from them. After they've closed the door and left, she places both feet against it and pushes as hard as she can. The plastic door bulges outward but doesn't open.

Left alone at last the terror of her situation catches up with her, and she places her face in her hands and weeps, deep sobs of utter shock and anguish.

I'm going to fucking die here. Tears spill from her eyes and into her cupped hands, pooling in the creases, forging swaths through the filth. *Goddamn I've never felt so completely alone...*

Several long minutes later she struggles for and retains some semblance of control. She swipes at her nose and eyes with the back of her hand, smearing the tears, snot and dirt on her face. Sickened, she wipes her hand on the side of the cage, leaving a trail of goo.

He'll want to know what the others are doing, what they are planning. That's what he wants to talk about.

She systematically searches along the furrowed, uneven bottom of the cage, looking for a seam between the floor and the sides, something she can peel away so as to see outside, but finds nothing. Frustrated, she gives up, slouching even further into herself.

Does it matter if I cover for them? They deserted me. They deserve to get caught too.

Her energy spent, she lies on her side, curls into a little ball and closes her eyes. She doesn't expect to sleep, in fact figures it to be impossible, but a few minutes later her breathing is calm and even and she is lightly snoring.

Lurid faces peer inside the air hole of their cage, disgusting caricatures of what any sane mind would consider to be *human* faces. They are twisted, distorted, resembling the outlandish, mutated animals. And they seem (*How can this be? There is no way it's even possible!* Perry's mind insists as he looks forth with rapt, horrified fascination that borders on psychosis) as if they are melding with the trash heap, are actually becoming a *part* of it.

These things move in an erratic manner, as if their joints have turned into...into...(*go ahead, say it*) plastic. And not only their insides, but apparently their outsides as well. Like the birds they saw, some of their body parts appear to be made of *plastic*. It's as if their DNA coding has been altered and they are gradually metamorphosing from organic tissue into a synthetic substance. How this is possible is, well, completely mind boggling to say the very least...

When he and Steven were captured they were knocked out with chloroform, or something of that nature. The last thing Perry remembers was seeing Kim's hideous visage leaning over him, the stump of her tongue wagging back and forth over broken teeth, her ruined eyes peering sightlessly upon his frightened face as if judging him, a strange noise emanating from her throat that may or may not have been laughter...

When they'd come to they were in the cage, and now, bathed in the glow of the burnt orange light, they are able to study them closely, more closely than they'd like.

Steven shies away, withdrawing to the back of the cage while Perry remains steadfastly up front, watching them avidly. Nearby, Hallsly is ranting and raving like a fool but no one pays any mind. For the time being they aren't interested in him.

"What do you want?" Perry demands fearfully. "What the fuck do you want from us?"

Lips that look like molded rubber stretch lewdly as their mouths spew dissonant, unintelligible sounds that seem almost sexual in nature. Hands that have transformed into misshapen claws reach into the air hole of the cage, trying to stroke the untarnished flesh within.

"You touch me and I'll kill you!" Perry threatens, but his tone carries no real menace, just betrays his outright mortification.

"Yah!" someone roars gruffly over the ruckus of muttering, hissing, growling and lip smacking. "Get your asses back!"

The creatures begin to whimper, shrinking away, uttering a word in unison that makes no sense to Perry at first, until it is repeated several times, ad nauseaum:

"Master...Master...Master..."

"It's the Master! The Master!"

"Get back!" this unseen intruder bellows again. "These two aren't for you!"

The mutants evacuate the area quickly, continuing to chant the word 'master' over and over. Perry and Steven at once feel an even greater fear than they've experienced thus far, for it is with great disdain that they should have to meet something that frightens these things.

And then Hallsly's voice, strident and angry, arises above the din.

"You?" he cries. "I should have fucking known!"

An ominous chuckle escapes the newcomer, a sound akin to breaking bones, analogous with the screams of the wasted and dying.

"Yes Hallsly, you should have known."

Steven recognizes the voice and suddenly everything makes complete sense: the accusations, the violence aboard the ship, their abrupt arrival on the trash heap...only one man could have made all this possible.

"Hello boys," Captain Harvey greets, dismissing the governor. "Comfy I trust?"

"They...they call you 'master'," Steven says dazedly. "Does that mean you created this?"

Again a sinister chuckle, something called up from the belly that has to pass through a bile filled throat. Bile and...other things.

"I suppose you could say that." He takes hold of a square of opaque plastic and wrenches it free, making it easier to see each other through the skeletal frame. What Steven witnesses makes his mouth suddenly very dry, his palms sweaty. The captain's smile is an outright leer, his eyes dancing merrily in sockets that are loose, red-rimmed and shimmering with a clear, slimy substance framing them like crude eyeliner. His face is yellow tinged, his clothing torn and filthy, the bib of his shirt crusted with green, white and red colored substances. "Yes, I suppose you could say that this is my grand creation."

"Hu-hu-how?" Steven sputters, trying to suppress a shiver that rips through him like an electric shock.

"Condensed version or you want to hear all the gritty details?" Captain Harvey grunts, his mouth awash with a thick, viscous fluid that spills over his plump lips. Then he waves his hands, a flippant gesture. "No time for that now, and you really don't need to know. If you are around when the good doctor gets here than I will share it with all of you, but we have more pressing matters to attend to."

"What do you mean 'if we're still around'?" Perry demands, trying to sound brave in the face of this unnamable evil but failing miserably. "What are you planning to do with us?"

"Do?" the captain says mockingly. "To you?" He closes his eyes for a second, running a hand through his short, bristly hair. When he opens them Perry feels a ripple of vertigo, as if the ground is swaying beneath him. The captain's eyes are now drained of color and they stare back at him fiercely, coal-black and shiny. "For starters I am going to feed you. Would you boys like that?"

"I asked you what you were going to do with us," Perry persists despite his terror, his voice a tremulous quaver that produces more laughter from the captain.

"Oh, we are the strong one, are we? While your little buddy cowers in the corner you snarl at me like a rabid dog, teeth bared, hackles raised. But we both know there is nothing you can do to me if I were to let you out, is there? Do you really want to have a go at me, see if you can take me you little fuckstick?"

Captain Harvey leans close to the cage, his sneering face inches away from the others. Perry can smell breath as rank as the trash heap itself, can see things twisting and swirling in the captain's mouth, down his throat. Living things that reside in his guts that, if so compelled, would love to come out and make sure Perry never asked another stupid question again.

"No sir," Perry acknowledges frankly, his stomach fluttering, alternating between nausea and terror.

"That's a good boy. You don't want any part of this." He runs his tongue over his lips and for the first time Perry notices it's forked, like that of a snake.

"I'm not hungry," Steven moans, the only other words he is willing to offer to this conversation. And this is the truth; even though he's dangerously dehydrated and starving his appetite has long escaped him in the face of this monstrous man and his grisly followers. His *creation*. Even if he was handed a rare roast beef sandwich on wheat bread with pickles and Swiss cheese he doesn't think he could eat it.

"Oh," Captain Harvey whispers, hot beads of saliva and mucous dripping like venom from his hideous tongue. "But you will be my boy, oh yes. You will be."

He snaps his fingers and two of his minions appear. Between them they carry a large, flattened piece of plastic that is no doubt intended to be a serving tray. Piled atop it are thick portions of rare (*raw*) meat. Perry can't help it, his stomach growls keenly.

"Your friend is hungry." Captain Harvey takes the tray from his subordinates and waves them away. He holds it up to the cage. "I have just what the doctor ordered."

"What about me?" Hallsly butts in. "I'm hungry!"

Ignoring him, the captain's eyes stay focused on Perry's.

"I'm not going to give him any. Know why? No? Because he doesn't deserve it. Not like you two do."

"What is it?" Perry asks. God help him he is suddenly ravenous, and what the captain is offering is driving him to a state of semi-delirium. Maybe if he knows what it is *(those bird creatures maybe, or something else equally revolting)* he will be able to resist.

"It's fresh meat, just like you two boys, and right now I am going to share something with you. A little secret just between us." His eyes glitter madly as he leans in closer, ablaze with humor only the sickest, most depraved soul can find amusing. "If you don't eat this than I am going to feed you to my friends out here. How does that sound? Eat or be eaten. Door number one, or door number two. Your choice."

Perry's fingers are twitching, desperately wanting to reach through the narrow slot and take some of the meat. His salivary glands have a mind of their own and he has to swallow hard several times to keep from drooling.

Steven is silent, considering, but really, what is there to mull over? It is apparent the captain doesn't make empty threats. Pushing the idea of free will aside, knowing he's been issued a command, he scoots forward, puts his hand through the hole.

The corner's of the captain's mouth curve sharply upward, grinning a grin that makes any other expression he's registered thus far seem like the blissful smile of a clown. Steven takes a chunk of the meat and, bringing it to his nose, sniffs experimentally. It has a putrid odor to it that is at first unpleasant, a scent that conjures up images of week old road kill left decaying in a hot August sun on black tarmac, but in his food-deprived state it in turn smells surprisingly good. And not only that, it smells fucking *delicious*. He stuffs a large wad in his mouth, chewing noisily.

Perry watches in amazement, appalled, yet he reaches over and helps himself as well, the captain looking on with debauched amusement.

"That's right boys," he murmurs, his tongue flicking in and out of his mouth. "Dig in."

"Don't let the boat drift too far beyond the oil slick," Dr. Taylor tells Kenny. "If we get out of eye shot of the shore it will be easy for us to get turned around."

Despite his lack of experience in the field, Dr. Taylor's extensive reading has prepared him somewhat for this adventure, if that's what you could call it. He's read a vast amount of literature containing survival tips, given that it's always been a fascination of his. Mountain climbers experiencing disaster, hikers lost in the wilderness, ATVers breaking down in the desert, ship passengers stranded at sea, you name it. For some reason it's a subject that's always been a guilty pleasure. He's never had any use for this info, of course, so he isn't exactly sure of the validity of said claims, but he supposes he and the others will find out soon enough.

Kenny is struggling with the makeshift oar as Tyler does his best to keep up with the proper one. They've been taking turns, swapping every fifteen minutes so that no one gets too tired. So far their progress has been slow, the heat of the day slowly cranking up, but the respite from being on the heap makes up for that, even though their escape cost them another life.

Tyler watches the water, his mind drifting as much as he'll allow under the circumstances. He thinks vaguely of Melissa, but doesn't linger on it too long; she's gone, and there is nothing they can do about it now. Best just to move on. He's still pissed off about how Kenny talked to him back there, but he supposes he can let it go for the time being. The big, dumb, bastard will get his, he'll make sure of it. He's also sore at Dr. Taylor, taking over like he has. Who says they need a leader? If an opportunity presents itself Tyler will take it and the others can screw themselves. Just see if he doesn't.

As Kenny battles with the improvised oar he thinks of his buddy Hank, wonders if he is on his third Jack and Coke of the morning.

This is probly what Hank'd see if he gave up drinkin' cold turkey.

The thought brings a smile to his face, albeit a small one. On the heels of it follows an impulsive craving for a drink, a little scotch, neat if you please, maybe with a couple of ice cubes he can rattle around in the glass. At once his mouth feels Sahara Desert dry, his heart chugging like an ailing locomotive, a light sweat popping up on his forehead. But, as he continues to row he finds, comfortingly, its allure is beginning to fade. It's no longer a raging necessity, but more like a wistful yearning. Something he can take or leave. Jesus, it's been a long time since he's felt like he could just walk away from it and not look back, and the relief he feels bolsters him, makes him stronger.

Suddenly there is movement in the water, creating a large ripple a few feet from the boat. Tyler cries out in surprise and Kenny stops rowing momentarily.

"Did ya see that?" Kenny says and Dr. Taylor peers over the edge of the boat, eyes flicking back and forth.

"Keep your hands in the boat fellahs and be on the look-out." Christ, he is so tired, and that sip of water and piece of chocolate have done nothing to ease his rampant hunger. His nerves feel tattered, raw and bleeding like open wounds.

The three watch the water, waiting for another sighting, but after a few minutes and nothing appears they exhale a collective sigh and continue rowing.

"Ya think we got lucky when we brung the boats out?" Kenny asks. "Ya know, that we dint run inta anythin'?"

"Yes, luck could have had something to do with it, or…something."

"Something?" Tyler taunts. "Like what? Devine providence?"

"Let's not assume that." Dr. Taylor's eyes are still on the water, watching the surface warily. "Kenny's right, we just got lucky."

"Are you suggesting someone was looking out for us?"

"*Never* assume that," Dr. Taylor replies ominously and this silences Tyler momentarily, but not for long. He's bored, agitated and restless. For this reason he feels the need to antagonize someone, anyone.

"So what do you think?" he says, looking at Kenny. "You think Jesus had a hand in this?"

"What?"

"Well," Tyler continues, as if he is explaining something to a child, "you're black. Don't all black people believe in Jesus and all that shi-"

Kenny drops his oar and grabs Tyler around the throat, the abrupt movement causing the boat to tip precariously.

"Ya wanna watch what ya say ta me buddy," he snarls through gritted teeth. "I just might get a hankerin' ta toss yer ass over th' side."

"Kenny," Dr. Taylor says tiredly, "let him go. And you," he looks at Tyler with eyes that have long passed weary and have taken the leap toward exhaustion ages ago, "keep your mouth shut. Just keep rowing."

Giving Tyler's neck one last squeeze, Kenny releases him, picking up the crude oar and resuming his duties.

"Watch yerself," he advises menacingly and, after he turns his back, Tyler sticks his tongue out at him. Dr. Taylor sees this and rolls his eyes.

Jesus, this is all I need, he thinks, his eyelids heavy as the sun maintains it's climb into the ever-brightening sky.

SEVENTEEN

"Are you getting tired?" Cole asks Leeann and she nods. Actually she's totally pooped but knows best not to complain. Thinking of Melissa, she figures things could be a whole lot worse.

We left her there to die. If that had been me, they would have done the same thing.

She relinquishes the oar to Cole, who takes it and her place on the side of the boat. She crumples in a heap on the bottom, shielding herself as best she can from the sweltering sun.

"Are you all right?" Dante says, his eyes searching hers thoughtfully as he dexterously maneuvers the two-by-four, keeping the boat heading in more or less a straight line.

"I'm fine," she replies, but her tone convinces him that she is anything but.

"Look," he says, returning his gaze to the water. "If it had been you back there I would have done whatever I could, you know that right?"

"Forget about it."

"Seriously, if it was you I would have done something, no matter what anyone said."

"I told you to forget about it!"

Dante realizes there is nothing he can say right now that is going to make her feel any better so he lets it go. If she doesn't want to talk about it that's fine, he just wanted her to know how he felt.

The walkie-talkie squawks and Cole scoops it up, pressing the button.

"This is Cole, go ahead, over."

"How are you holding up?" Dr. Taylor's voice, tinny and nasal, asks.

"Can't complain. We're still here. Over."

"Anything to report?"

"Nothing, just getting sunburned. Over."

"If you see anything, anything at all, give us a holler."

"You got it. What about you guys. Seen anything? Over."

"We saw some movement in the water about thirty minutes ago but we didn't see what it was. You guys should stay alert."

"Will do. Over."

"And hey, Cole?"

"Yeah? Over."

"You don't have to say 'over' every time you finish talking."

"Roger that," Cole says. "Over…um…"

"We'll check with you in an hour. We should save the batteries."

"Right," Cole agrees, and waits to see if there is anything else.

"Now would be a good time to say it," Dr. Taylor prompts.

"Say what?"

"Over," the other replies and clicks off.

Having filled their bellies, Steven and Perry settle back in their cage feeling (for the first time) a little bit of their apprehension slip away.

"I don't know if we should have eaten that," Steven says, belching into a closed fist, "but I feel tons better."

"I do too," Perry concurs, the strange aftertaste lingering on his tongue. He can't honestly admit that the meat tasted good, no; it had a strong, tangy flavor with an undertone of earthy muskiness, something that now reminds him of gristle and fluid drenched fat. The consistency was tough, stringy, the meat entirely uncooked, and there were bites in which he could swear he detected tiny organisms squirming within it, but in the extremity of his hunger he paid no mind. He finds that thinking about it makes him slightly ill, even though his whole body is recharged, a sensation of life surging within him again.

Nearby, Hallsly isn't quite so content.

"Enjoy your meal boys?" he says with more than a trace of contempt. He had to sit and listen as those two ass munchers chewed loudly and smacked their lips, all the while his stomach was growling like a pissed off timber wolf. "I hope you two choke on it."

Perry opens his mouth to say something but Steven shakes his head, silencing him. There is no use in egging him on, and there is nothing they can say that will make the man feel any better. None of this is in their hands. They are better off just leaving it alone.

"What, you giving me the silent treatment? Is that what this is?" he demands, when one of their 'guards' hits his cage with the back of one gnarly hand.

"Shut…up," it croaks, but this only serves to make Hallsly angry.

"Ah, go blow yourself you freakin' half-wit!"

"Shut…the…*uhnnnggg*…fuck…up."

"And if I don't what are you going to do, huh? Tell the captain on me?"

The guard turns away, getting down on one knee and punching a hole in the floor of the trash heap. Perry watches as he fishes around below the surface, rooting around until he finds something and then extracts his hand. In it is a little creature that looks roughly like a scorpion. But it isn't quite a scorpion, no, not out here on the trash heap. Mother Nature's taken a wrong turn at Albuquerque and it's something else entirely, with furry legs and round eyes protruding from stalks on the top of it's head. Holding it by the tail, the guard swings it in front of Hallsly's air hole, a warped smile canted on his otherwise expressionless face.

"Care...for...*uhnnnggg*...company?"

"Jesus Christ, get that thing away from me!"

"You...can...*uhnnnggg*...eat...it..."

"I'll shut up, I promise!" Hallsly pleads. "Just get it away from me!"

Tossing it over his shoulder, the guard makes a sound like two pieces of flint rubbing together, and Perry realizes he is laughing. He has to admit it is comical, seeing a loud-mouthed braggart like Hallsly being threatened with something so trivial as a little bug. A sudden urge to laugh overtakes him and he can't stifle it. A large grin spreads across his face.

Steven bursts into giggles, a weird giddiness washing over him like soiled bath water. Perry's grin widens and he issues a low chortle, and Steven finds this even funnier and issues a loud guffaw. One driving the other, they are soon overcome by gales of raucous hilarity.

"What's so goddamn funny?" Hallsly barks, but the two don't stop; in fact his outburst makes them cackle even more.

Steven feels lightheaded, spacey, like his brain has been replaced with helium, and he slaps the floor of the cage as he continues to bray laughter like the town idiot, Perry frolicking along with him. They certainly can't explain why they are doing it, but neither wants to quit either. As their merriment increases their terror and anxiety slips away, and for the first time since they've arrived the cage and their terrible situation doesn't seem so bad anymore. More like a minor inconvenience.

"They...*uhnnnggg*...gone...now."

"What are you talking about?" Hallsly's fear is displaced for a moment, curiosity getting the better of him.

But the guard doesn't reply; instead he makes that strange sound again, his own way of expressing amusement, and then he turns away, resuming his silent vigil.

"I've come for some answers and I expect you'll be a good girl and tell me."

Melissa glances up at the smiling, jaundiced looking captain as he kneels before her cage. The grin he wears is crooked, and at this angle she notices he's missing a couple of teeth, the gums around them looking raw, savaged.

"I don't know anything," she mumbles, turning away from him.

"Oh, but I think you do, I think you know plenty." He lowers his large frame and takes a seat, crossing his legs. In one hand he holds something that he waves in front of her like a magic talisman. "I have something for you. A peace offering."

"Go away."

"Don't you even want to know what it is? Why don't you sit up and talk with me."

She hears a sound that is at once familiar, something entirely commonplace in her life as she once knew it…but not here, not now. She'd recognize it anywhere, and it conjures an image of pleasurable relief. She swivels her head and sees it is what she thought it to be: the exquisite crackling of a plastic cap being twisted off a bottle of water.

"Now, you and I both know you're thirsty. I thought you might like this." He holds it up to the air hole, waggles it back and forth. "A little present, if you indulge me."

"I'm not taking any bribes from you."

"A bribe? No, no. Consider it a gift, in exchange for a little info." He tips the bottle to his mouth and takes a drink, letting the water trickle down his chin. The sight is simultaneously appealing and revolting.

"I don't want it now, not after you put your mouth on it." But she sits up, her overwhelming thirst commanding her to do so, as much as she'd like to appear indifferent. The problem with something like thirst or hunger is they simply cannot be denied. They are physical needs that have to be attended to. She stares at the bottle as he brings it to his lips again, making vulgar sucking sounds as he does so.

"I brought one for you." He produces another and shakes it enticingly.

"How do I know it isn't filled with something else?"

"The seal isn't cracked," he says, showing her. "Come on, take it. You'll feel better, and I want you to feel better."

"Go to hell." But even as the words are leaving her mouth she's reaching through the air hole, taking it from him. She lightly twists the cap, testing it, and she finds he isn't lying: it is unopened. She looks at him cautiously.

"And what if I don't want to tell you anything?"

"You will." He takes another drink. "You may not know it, but you will."

She turns the cap and the sound it makes when the seal breaks is beautiful, tantalizing. That which she took for granted in the real world is like buried treasure here, and she feels a sick pleasure, one akin to a junkie cooking up her morning shot. She sniffs it, but there is no odor, then puts it to her lips and tilts it, letting a little roll over her bottom lip. She is flooded with a feeling of peace, the chilled water kissing her parched tongue like a gift from heaven. Tilting the bottle further, she takes a long, luxurious drink.

"Careful," he says. "Don't want to go too fast or you might get sick."

Taking his advice she eases off, sipping at it slowly. He watches her pleasantly, occasionally licking his lips with a serpentine tongue. Minutes pass by, how many she doesn't know, she simply doesn't care. Right now it's just her and this bottle of water making sweet, sweet love…

"I don't know why you'd want to cover for a bunch of people you barely know, hell, folks who practically left you here to die. Do you think any of them would protect you if they were in your shoes? I doubt it. If I was you, I'd tell me what I want to know."

"I'm not you, and there's no way I'm telling you anything." The water feels good going down her throat, so cold, so fine. She almost feels vaguely human again, if only for these few moments.

"Why would everyone return to the cove, hmm? What could they possibly have to gain?"

"I don't know, it was the only thing anyone knew to do."

"Yes, being in an unfamiliar place that would be sensible." He takes a sip of water and then sets the bottle down beside him. "So are you telling me you *weren't* searching for the ship?" he asks and she shrugs nonchalantly. "Because if you *were* in search of the ship you should know there is no one aboard who can help you. They all work for me now."

"Didn't they work for you… um…before?"

"Yes, but now I *own* them. There's a difference you see. They have been stripped of their free will."

"How do you 'own' them? I don't see any difference between them and you."

"Than you aren't paying attention my dear," he says, leaning toward her, his smile now merely a contrivance, his posture that of a man whose limits have been tested. "So…why did you want to find the ship?"

"It's the only place to go," she says numbly, trying to look away but finding she can't. Her insides feel rubbery, her limbs sodden and heavy. "You…you put something in this water…" she accuses mildly and he shakes his head.

"No, I didn't. Whatever you feel is coming from within you. For the time being I need you just as you are."

"Just as I am?" Her mind seems cluttered, her senses dulled.

"Just as you are," he echoes. "So they're looking for the ship, taking the lifeboats around the island to find it." He regards her sternly. "Do they have any weapons, any communications devices?"

"We found some walkie-talkies and a flare gun," she says in a deadened monotone, dropping the uncapped bottle beside her, the contents spilling onto the floor of the cage.

"Did you?"

"Yes. And some bottles of water and chocolate bars. And a pocket knife."

"What's the plan?" he prods, his eyes gleaming ecstatically.

"To take over the ship." She slouches against the back wall of the cage helplessly. "To kill anyone who gets in the way."

He nods, his suspicions confirmed. "You've been a very good girl so I guess I'll make a confession: the water *was* drugged." He grins insidiously. "My bad."

"I would never sell them out…" she says weakly as consciousness slowly drifts away.

"Oh, but my dear, you just did."

Listening to the two interns carrying on, Hallsly is in turn furious, then puzzled. He at first thought it was directed toward him but, as they continue to cackle wildly, he's beginning to believe something is wrong with them. Not more than thirty minutes ago they were terrified, he could hear it in their voices. And damn straight they should be. He can't exactly say he is having the time of his life.

But after eating the meat their demeanor changed. They sound slaphappy, as if they've been sipping the funny juice.

Maybe there's something in the meat that intoxicated them, you know, like those toads people lick to get high. Maybe they've been poisoned.

But what would be the purpose? They weren't making any trouble; their fear was keeping them subdued.

Unless it's something else…but what? It doesn't make any sense. And why the hell are they starving *him*?

You know the answer to that one. Captain Harvey wants to make things difficult for me. He isn't happy unless I'm suffering.

And that seems right, but it also doesn't, like there should be more to it than that. But damned if he knows what it is.

"Are you boys all right in there?" he asks tentatively and the two burst into fresh gales of laughter.

"Are we alright he asks," Steven says, pounding his thigh. "Are we alright?"

"Better than you are!" Perry cries. "We got to eat!"

Hallsly broods over this, striving to make a connection that his feeble, starving mind simply can't muster. Even on the best of days (with a full stomach as well) he'd probably have trouble finding a correlation between their eating and subsequent laugh attack. He's never been an idea kind of guy. He likes action; that is what he's good at.

Well, whatever is going on in there, he's glad it's happening to them and not him.

Captain Harvey strolls through the front door of the 'town hall', swinging aside a large steel panel that represents the door. It's hot and steamy inside, the air still, but he doesn't mind. Temperature is no longer a factor to him or his creations.

Using scraps salvaged from various car, plane and boat parts, the immediate interior is furnished with a large table accompanied by several crude chairs. Beyond that is an expansive open space and, past that, two unwieldy, oversized eyesores decorated with human skulls that represents his throne and his Queen's. These two chairs are elevated by a makeshift platform so that he may look over his congregation while he is seated. This is where they have their important meetings, where he makes his vital decisions.

As he moves forward through the roomy enclosure he feels tiny prickles, like needles, swirling through his brain, pinpricks of irritation he can't shake. Try as he may he cannot mentally infiltrate those who aren't converted to life on Garbage Island and this blank spot, this dead place in his mind, fills him with unnerving rage. Surely he should be able to oversee all aspects of the island, shouldn't he? Why does it matter that they haven't yet been enlightened? After all, he is the Master and Lord; all things inhabiting his space should be subject to his bidding, regardless of their condition. He struggles to remember how it was with the first group, the original research vessel, and to his bafflement finds only the ghost of a memory, flitting through his head in shards, like mismatched puzzle pieces...

(He recalls voices speaking in tones reeking of conspiracy, and when he confronted them the scheming bastards relinquished nothing, even when brutally tortured. In the end he'd simply had to make them see things his way so he could know what they were planning, but when he did they were no longer of any use to him, their minds frizzle-fried like so much worthless clay, and that which he'd sought them out for was now hopelessly lost, gone, ruined...except for the pair he'd chosen for special transformation. Those two, well...let's just say their death's paved the way for his imminent voyage back to the mainland, a trip in which he'd thought he could make everything right on his own, without any help from his creations...)

Yes, yes, this much he knows, as he knows the whole story of how this all came to be, but it appears as if parts are gradually dropping out, slipping away. Are his neural transmitters breaking down in conjunction with his fleshly decay, affecting his memories and judgment? According to these mental lapses it would seem to be so, and he's beginning to think it's onset is rapidly increasing, more so than he'd first anticipated. He recognizes plainly that time is running out, the most valued of prizes on which everything is balanced. The fate of Garbage Island depends on his expediency, his ability to get things done before it is too late. It's for this reason that he's created not one but two successors (this time using men whose minds could be molded to his every whim, not intellectuals capable of sabotage); in the event that one should fail him, the other can carry out their ultimate task. And if they both succeed they can then fight it out for supremacy, he doesn't care. At such a point in time surely his presence will no longer be a factor.

At the moment, however, he's disgusted that he'd been forced to drug the captured girl just so he could find out exactly what the passengers were up to (nothing he hadn't figured, of course, but something he hadn't *known* for certain) and this lack of understanding makes him feel impotent, as if his role has been diminished in some way, even though he recently found out his capacities have always been somewhat limited. It makes him want to do something dreadful, wants to hurt someone to make himself feel that much better...

He sees his Queen is waiting for him, perched upon her throne. In the dim light she sits, silent, her back erect, unmoving.

"Ah, my Queen," he whispers, kneeling before her. She doesn't offer her hand so he reaches out and takes it, bringing it to his lips. As he kisses it he looks upon her ravaged face, taking in her blank, expressionless stare. "My beautiful, sightless Queen."

Where her eyes used to be, of course, are now dark, gore-smeared holes (dried blood framing her sockets like mascara), and there is no possibility that she will speak (now or ever after) because of her amputated tongue.

He stands, returning her hand to her lap. Leaning over, he places his lips upon hers, kissing her gently. When he is finished he straightens up.

"I feel it is only fair to tell you that there is another suitor who believes she is destined for your throne." Kim stirs, cocking her head to one side. "Yes my love, a woman who feels she is far more deserving than thou."

Kim stands, making harsh, gargling sounds, her mouth opening and closing, claw-like hands twitching at her sides.

"Yes," he continues, "she wishes to challenge you. Do you feel you are up to it?"

She whips her arms about violently, grasping at the empty air in front of her. Her dirty clump of hair rises and falls with her movements as she hisses and spits, the noises sounding feral, deranged.

"I knew you would be lover, I knew you would," he says soothingly. "Not now, but soon."

"Angnnngnn!" she fumes riotously. *"ANGGNNNGN!"*

"There is other work to be done first; rest assured I shall take care of all the preparations. For the time being I want you to sit back and relax."

As if she is a marionette suspended by invisible strings her body goes limp and she falls back into the chair. Her face immediately retains the serene expression she wore when he first entered.

"Good," he says. "Wonderful," he coos. "I will let you know when it is time."

He backs away and, turning, almost runs into another that has been waiting for him in the shadows.

"You summoned me, captain?" his minion asks and Captain Harvey smiles.

"Yes Jake, I have. Please," he gestures toward the table, "have a seat."

Jake Anderson shambles over, pulls out an approximation of a chair and sits down. Captain Harvey approaches slowly, taking out another and easing himself down.

"I have an assignment for you Jake."

"Aye, captain." Jake's eyes are no longer the pale blue they used to be; they are now a muddy brown, and when in full bloom a shade as black as night. His movements are slightly jerky, but nothing that anyone would suspect as being unusual. His body is taking to his conversion quite well, better than he'd expected; so far he's hardly showing any signs of change at all. Once the bacteria grows and multiplies within the host they begin to metamorphous, their genetic encoding becoming altered, which in turn disrupts their cognitive and motor functions. From past experience he knows Jake and Lt. Ronson will appear 'normal' longer than those who've ingested the bacteria via other sources, but they'll succumb to mutation nonetheless. No one is immune, not even he. As it stands, great changes have been going on within him, changes he has no way of understanding. What is evident, however, is that those he converts directly are superior to the rest; he figures they'll be around much longer than all the others, but by that time it won't matter, nothing will.

Like the scientists I converted directly. . .they were absolute replicas of me. But once they realized the potential of their power it went to their heads, allowed them to think they could commandeer my position, take control of the drones. No, no one of advanced intelligence should be privy to such supremacy, not while I'm around. If I hadn't killed them who knows what fate would have become of Garbage Island? But at least I learned. . .at least I know. And now I have Jake and Lt Ronson. Between them there aren't enough eggs to make an omelet, and that's how it should be. The bacteria will tell them what to do and they shall follow. . .

"I'm willing to dismiss the fact that you and the other minions let the passengers escape with the lifeboats." He regards the other disappointedly. "As long as you make amends by being more useful."

Jake looks at him blankly, saying nothing. His hands rest before him on the table, his fingers trembling ever so slightly.

"They are trying to find the ship so they can escape. Do you understand?"

"Aye, captain."

"Master," Captain Harvey corrects.

"Aye, Master."

Captain Harvey nods. "We're going to set a trap for them, using the ship as bait."

For the first time since they've sat down Jake looks at the captain frankly.

"But we hid it in a cave so it wouldn't be spotted by planes or satellite photos."

"Yes we did, but now I want you to contact Lt. Ronson and have him move it so it is visible." He wags a finger before the other's face. "Not *too* visible, not out in the open. Have him position it just inside the mouth of the cave so they can see it from about a hundred yards out."

"Aye, Master."

"Instruct him to have several crewmen standing on deck to lure them in with the promise of food and safety. They can tell them they've contacted the Coast Guard." Captain Harvey looks inquisitively upon his second mate, a man who very well may be the future of Garbage Island. "I want them all taken alive. Can you relay this information for me?"

"Aye, Master."

Jake begins to stand but the captain's hand reaches out quickly, grasping his forearm. "No Jake, I want you to relay the information from here."

"From...here?"

"Yes." Captain Harvey's eyes bore into the others. "From here." He taps Jake's head. "Can you do that?"

"I...I don't know." He appears confused for a moment. "I can try."

"Do it."

Jake closes his eyes, his face scrunching in concentration. He sits very still for several minutes, both hands against the sides of his head. The captain waits patiently, watching.

"Visualize it," he whispers. "Imagine Lt. Ronson receiving your transmission."

Jake's body begins to tremble with the force he's expending, his legs jerking and jittering, causing the table to shake.

"That's right, go on."

Jake's body goes rigid, his head arched back, his mouth a snarl of agony. He issues a tormented scream as blood simultaneously erupts from his ears and nose and he collapses facedown onto the table. But...yet...there is nothing...nothing at all.

"I...I can't Master," he says weakly, raising his head slowly.

Captain Harvey conceals his displeasure, smiling coldly. "You just need time Jake. Soon it will come to you." *Could he be of limited potency? Nothing but a mere copy? Is this what I get for choosing an imbecile?*

"Aye, Master."

"Use the radio instead and alert them of the news," Captain Harvey says briskly, standing up. "I'm going out there to oversee the operation myself so I'm putting you in charge of the village until I get back. That's a lot of responsibility. Do you think you can handle it?"

"Aye, Master." He knows it's not his fault, yet he feels as if he's failed.

"Very good," Harvey says, reading Jake's thoughts as easily as one would a street sign. "Don't let me down."

EIGHTEEN

The sun is well past the halfway point and is starting it's descent into the west when Dr. Taylor takes over for Tyler, who's been flailing away at the water for the past ten minutes like a drunken Mexican at a piñata. He sets down the little notebook he's been scribbling his observations in, tucking the stub of pencil inside.

"You're tired," he says, taking the makeshift oar from him. "Let me take over."

"Man, it's about damn time." Tyler flops down on the floor of the boat with an exaggerated air of fatigue. "And I don't know about you but I could sure use a drink of water and a piece of chocolate right about now. I'm dying over here."

Kenny glares at Tyler, wanting to say something, but a quick glance from the doctor silences him. For the last three hours it's been nothing but bitch bitch bitch from the arrogant little pansy and he'd like nothing more than to put a fist through his teeth, but if the doctor tells him to let it be, he'll let it be. What the hell, at least he's been helping with the rowing, even though he's doing a half-assed job.

"What do you think Kenny?" Dr. Taylor says. "Could you use a little break?"

He could have used a break an hour ago, but he keeps it to himself. Yeah, a little breather would be nice.

"Sure Doc, that sounds good."

Dr. Taylor puts the oar down and reaches into the metal box, extracting the chocolate and a bottle of water.

"When's the last time we checked in with the others?"

"I think it's been over an hour."

"Tyler, why don't you get them on the talkie and see how they're doing?"

Tyler looks up at him, sighs, then struggles into a sitting position. He takes the walkie-talkie from the bench next to the doctor, flips the toggle in the on position.

"Breaker breaker one nine," he says in an awful southern drawl, "I think we got ourselves a convoy."

"What?" Cole squawks through the tiny speaker. "You guys okay? Over."

"We got ourselves a convooooy and we're truckin' all night!" Tyler half yells, half sings, a cocky grin on his face, and Dr. Taylor scowls.

"Cut the shit Tyler," Kenny says and Tyler salutes him.

393

"Sir, yes sir."

"Are you guys all right? Over."

"Yeah, we're fine, fine. We just wanted to see how y'all are doing."

"So far, so good. Haven't sighted anything, good or bad. How about you guys?"

"Nothing yet, but it's not for lack of trying."

"We got a question for the doctor though."

"Go ahead Cole," Dr. Taylor says, breaking the candy bar into pieces and handing them around.

"What are we going to do if it gets dark and we still haven't found anything?"

There's an uncomfortable silence as Dr. Taylor takes a bite of his chocolate, glancing at his companions before he speaks. He's been wondering the exact same thing since they got in the boats this morning and has held off on addressing it with the others, not wishing to discourage them. In all honesty he's been dreading such an outcome, that they should come up empty handed by nightfall. Even with finding the bottles of water they've really only extended their time by merely a day or so, much less the ridiculous notion of three or four. He wants to impress upon them the severity of the situation while also comforting them, making them feel as if they have a fighting chance. If any of them felt there was no hope than what would their motivation be?

"Well," he says, wiping his mouth with the back of one hand, "if neither of us finds anything than we have to go back ashore for the night. It's the only way we can get properly rested for tomorrow."

His statement is greeted by a ponderous hush, on his boat as well as the other. The reality of returning and spending another harrowing night on the trash heap doesn't sit very well with anyone, and he can't say that he blames them. He doesn't like the idea either.

"We can't sleep in the boats?" Cole asks. "We have to go back?"

"It's the only thing we can do. If we sleep in the boats we face the possibility of drifting out too far and losing sight of the trash heap. If that happens we'll have much bigger problems to contend with."

"Couldn't we take our chances at sea? Maybe a garbage dumping vessel will find us."

"I wouldn't advise it. Without adequate supplies none of us would last very long. Our best bet is to find the ship."

After a long pause Cole finally says "Okay. Over and out."

"We have to go back?" Leeann says, her voice cracking on the word 'back'.

"Only if we don't find anything."

"We can't go back there, we'll get caught."

"Doctor's orders, not mine," Cole says, trying not to sound like a dick but failing.

Leeann makes a vocalization that sounds like "humph," glaring at Dante questioningly, but he says nothing. Instead he inspects the shore, hoping desperately that something, anything, will come into view. Something to give them hope, some reassurance that they are going to be all right. He sneaks a peek at her and sees clearly the strain imprinted on her face, a torturous despondency that creates worry wrinkles on her forehead and around her mouth. He wishes she didn't have to go through this, the poor girl. Given the life she's had, she isn't equipped to deal with a situation like this. Now he, on the other hand, feels like this is just another day in the life. Go figure.

"We'll find the ship," he says, trying to cheer her up, but her eyes don't meet his own. "They couldn't have gone too far."

Leeann ignores him, watching the shore gloomily, her mouth curved in a deep frown.

"When's the last time we had a water break?" Cole says, taking a brief recess from rowing and wiping sweat from his brow.

"Half an hour ago," she replies tonelessly.

"Man, I thought you were going to say two hours ago."

"Feels like it, doesn't it?" Dante says and the other nods.

"It feels like a freakin' lifetime even though it hasn't even been two days."

"Tell me about it."

"You want me to relieve either of you?" Leeann asks, and the two men regard her sun-reddened complexion, the exhaustion evident in the bags under her eyes. They shake their heads.

"We're fine," Dante says. "You just keep your face shielded from the sun and rest up."

"Okay." The more tired she becomes the easier it is to get lost in her thoughts, daydreaming about her home in Corpus Christi, her college days in San Diego. Like Cole said, it feels as if an eternity has passed, and everything she once knew seems so far away. As she reflects upon her life it seems to be progressively fading into the past, becoming nothing but a distant memory. All she's known and ever will know is this lousy trash heap, trapped in the middle of nowhere, fighting for her life. She sighs miserably and culls Stacy's image in her mind, her smiling face, her cheery laugh. She wonders what she is doing right now, her dear friend who found the ad for this job posted on the bulletin board in the commons, the ad that started this whole chain of events in motion. If Stacy had been an oceanography or marine biology major maybe she would have answered it herself, but since she studied computer sciences she'd passed along the information to her. Of course she had no idea it would turn out like this (how could she?) but Leeann can't help but curse her for it, for interfering with her life. If Stacy hadn't seen the damn ad Leeann would be sitting in a lecture hall right now, preparing for her finals instead of stuck in a lifeboat with a man she was trying to avoid and a stranger who's probably been picked out of a police line-up more than once in his illustrious life.

She looks over at Dante, noticing the muscles standing out on his arms as he strains against the water, sweat pouring down his face making tracks through the grime and disappearing into the shaggy growth of his beard. Her drug trial buddy. The guy who made her time at the clinic pass by quicker. She supposes she's glad he is here; he's a familiar face, and that's something isn't it? It's not much of a consolation but it's all she's got. What the hell, she should be grateful.

His anger long dissipated, replaced by unease, Hallsly watches as another villager approaches the guard, handing him a 'tray' of meat. This he takes to the science dweeb's cage.

"Hun-gry?" he asks and they commence a clamor that reminds him of monkeys at the zoo. He passes the tray through the air hole and Hallsly listens as they begin to feed. The sounds they make are appalling. Since their initial feeding and subsequent laugh-attack they've been mostly silent. He has no idea how long ago that was, but he's sure it couldn't have been more than a couple of hours. There is definitely something in the food they are being given but what (or why) is completely lost on him. Hallsly is an unimaginative guy and foresight has never been his forte. Since his capture and ensuing imprisonment he's been concerned about one thing and one thing only: his own ass. For the better part of his captivity he has carried himself through in a smoldering rage, one of the defense mechanisms he's employed his entire life to help him during tough times. But as the rage subsides and fear steps up to take its place, he finds himself growing increasingly discomfited. Hallsly isn't one to be afraid, it isn't a part of his general state of mind. When you come from such wealth and luxury as he is accustomed to there is nothing to be afraid of. He'd learned throughout his silver spoon fed life that money *can* buy anything, can make all kinds of bad things go away as if they never existed. Like when he got arrested for cocaine possession his junior year of college and thought he was going to get expelled, his father offered to add a new wing to the school library and all was forgotten. And when the newspapers caught wind of a scandal involving he and a transsexual prostitute (he could have sworn that asshole was a woman, and he'd let 'her' blow him for Christ's sake) his public profile manager and team of lawyers made sure it was reduced to a small paragraph in section B of the newspaper instead of gaudily splashed across the front page. Simply put, he's lived a life of throwing money at problems and watching them disappear, so what do you do when those who are holding your life in their hands aren't interested in cash? What will save you then? He finds it hard to believe that in this day and age there's a place in the modern world where commerce isn't king, where money doesn't talk and bullshit walk. He is so out of his element that he's simply frozen, shell-shocked, reduced to a vestige of the man he used to be.

And so he waits, listening to the science dweebs tear into the food they've been given, some butchered animal spawned from the trash heap that's doing weird things to their heads.

Hungry is bad, sure. It's something he's never known in the whole of his existence. But that's nothing compared to whatever is being done to these two. Even if they sound like they're having the time of their lives, he knows that what goes up must come down.

Wrapping his arms around himself to keep the chill of panic at bay, he sits and he watches, waiting, ever waiting.

"This is Lieutenant Ronson…go ahead."

He listens carefully as Jake Anderson gives him new instructions, asking no questions, making no small talk. When the other is through he tells him 'affirmative' and signs off. He then gets on the ship intercom and conveys the orders to the men.

Over the course of the last day and a half his movements have been getting stiffer, and it's becoming increasingly difficult to speak. It feels as if his joints are filling up with sand, or, more accurately, are turning from bone, muscle, cartilage and flesh into...plastic. Not that he is giving it any serious thought, for it isn't a concern of his, it's merely a vague observation he makes from time to time, a sensation that will dissipate shortly, as his transformation becomes complete. The rest of the men on the ship are experiencing the same thing, except that their conversion is more akin to a full frontal lobotomy; their free will has been completely taken away and replaced by the gift the captain (*Master*) has given them, along with their identity (something the Lt. is allowed to hold onto, along with the ability to make his own decisions). They are at long last liberated of everything except that which the captain (*Master*) and the bacteria of Garbage Island bids them to do, and it is this one singular purpose that they now serve willingly, unquestioningly, with no hesitation. For all practical intentions it is their true north and there is no reason they should think otherwise.

Opening her eyes, Melissa realizes she must have fallen asleep. How she could have done so under the circumstances is puzzling, but it shouldn't come as any surprise; she's completely wiped out, exhausted. She tries to stretch but the cage is much too confining to allow her to do so satisfactorily. She shifts restlessly, trying to get comfortable, but there's an unyielding pressure in her lower abdomen, of the floating teeth variety. How long has it been since her last pee? She has no idea, but her bladder is now achingly full and the need to empty it is overwhelming. Rising to her knees, she peers through the air hole, locating one of the captain's minions standing nearby, eyes closed, swaying gently back and forth in a light breeze.

"Hey!" she calls. "I have to pee!"

He opens his eyes, swivels his head slowly in her direction.

"You go...*uhnnnggg*...in...the...cage," he says, then turns away.

"I'm not going to pee in the cage!"

"You...*uhnnnggg*...hold it...then."

"You can't let me out to go to the bathroom?"

He doesn't reply; he simply stares straight ahead.

"Hello?"

Her bladder feels full to the point of bursting, and she wonders how this can be, given that she hasn't had much to drink in the last twenty-four hours.

Son of a bitch...

She recalls her visit from the captain, the bottle of water he gave her. Looking around, she sees it lying on its side, the cap off, empty. And then she remembers the conversation she had with him, how she let it slip that the others have weapons and communication devices, how they are looking for the ship.

Did he drug me? Is that how he got the information out of me?

Taking stock, tallying her various ailments, she notes with no surprise that she feels light headed, spacey, and her mouth is exceptionally dry, a bitter aftertaste lingering on her tongue. She'd been roofied once by an unscrupulous client who'd wanted much more than a sound beating, and when she'd awakened she'd felt a lot like this only with a pounding headache and vaginal bleeding. And she dimly recollects (now that she thinks about it) the captain telling her he'd done as such. That rotten bastard. He'd gotten what he'd come for after all.

And now what? Is he planning to capture the rest of them and place them in cages as well? To what end?

He's going to kill us all, that's what. He'll poison us and then we'll become like him, and if that isn't death than I don't know what is.

Of course, he did say that he wanted to 'keep her as she was', whatever the hell that means. Maybe he isn't going to kill her right away; possibly he has something else in mind, something worse. Because, when you truly consider it, there are things in life that are much worse than death, of this she is certain, and she is in no hurry to find out what they are.

She shifts awkwardly again, the need to piss annoyingly excruciating.

"Oh fuck it," she mutters, letting go. Urine runs down her thigh, it's ammonia smell at once heady in the confined space. Even though it appalls her, the act brings immediate relief, and despite feeling like shit at least she doesn't have to pee anymore.

Settling back, she leans against one side of the cage and closes her eyes, wishing that sleep would take her away once more.

The bright expanse of sky is an almost unbroken blue, stretching as far as the eye can see. The dense bank of clouds decorating the morning horizon never arrived, just lingered briefly before dissipating entirely. The sun beats down unmercifully, the stagnant air heavy and rank. High above them, so far away as to be nothing but a tiny speck, a jet flies over, leaving behind it a straight, uninterrupted contrail that gradually begins to disperse and widen as it moves across the sky. Kenny watches it, wishing he were on that jet instead of in this lousy lifeboat off the shore of this lousy floating pile of shit. He knows that wishing gets you nothing, that only action gets anything done, but he wishes just the same. There's no harm in the simple act, it's merely a flight of fancy.

Dr. Taylor and Tyler are taking care of the rowing (he'd nearly had to smack Tyler over the head with the oar just to get him off his lazy ass) and he is supposed to be watching the shore but his attention has been drifting.

We ain't gonna find nothing, ya might as well face it. We all gonna die, and probly sooner than any a us expects.

This depressing thought has been echoing over and over in his mind during the last couple of hours, after the doctor announced they would have to return to the heap by sundown if they didn't find the ship. They certainly won't survive another night, not with Captain Harvey and his mutant buddies out there somewhere, waiting for them. For all they know he's been tracking their position since they set out, keeping pace with their boat, just passing the time until they get within range and he can make his move.

Trying to dismiss these thoughts he returns his gaze to the shore, marveling at this abomination of nature, all this waste that has either been dumped or has found it's way over thousands of miles of ocean to collect in this spot. As his eyes take it in he leans back on the bench, feeling tiredness creep over him. All his muscles are sore from rowing with the two by four, and he can't remember the last time he got a good night's sleep.

Probly the last time I got drunk. Unexpectedly, the thought of a drink almost makes him salivate. Before, when he thought there was hope, he'd been arrogant enough to believe he had his demons under control, but now...now that their deaths are nearly certain, well, all bets are off...

Christ, yes, a drink would be perfectly wonderful, just a little something to wet his whistle. *Fuck me, I'd sell my soul for a bottle a Jim Beam right about now.* He licks his parched lips, the image of a large tumbler of whiskey with a few ice cubes becoming clearer in his mind's eye. Shit, he'd kill these two assholes next to him just for the promise of a taste...

And then, out of the corner of his eye, he catches a glimpse of something on the shore, what looks to be a large indentation in the heap. With the exception of the cove where they came on, so far all they've passed is one continuous cliff wall, varying in size. Sometimes it looms over them like a skyscraper, other times it appears to be scalable, as if a man possessing reasonable strength could climb to the top without too much effort. In most places it seems to be densely packed, in some it looks loose and easily collapsible.

This monotonous view is all they've seen for hours; on one side a wall of trash, on the other a carpet of water. Above them a blazing orb charring them to a crisp. But finally, for the love of freakin' God at long last they've actually stumbled upon something.

"Look over there," he says, pointing. Dr. Taylor looks up from the water, squinting his eyes against the sun's brilliance, wrinkles creasing his weary face. Tyler looks up absently, scowling.

"What the hell is that?"

"It appears to be a serration in the trash heap," Dr. Taylor says, pausing from his rowing duties for a moment as he surveys it.

"Huh?"

"In dipshit terms he means a cave," Kenny explains and Tyler glares at him in return. Smiling inside, he turns back to the doctor.

"Looks purty big," he says, rubbing his chin. "How high'd ya say that is?"

"Forty, maybe fifty feet." Dr. Taylor tries to suppress a feeling of hope that rises within him. No sense in jumping the gun, but if there was anywhere-*anywhere*-that the ship could be, this may very well be the spot.

They are getting closer now, close enough to look into the mouth of the great depression.

"I think I see somethin'! See that? Just inside?"

"You're hallucinating," Tyler remarks flatly but Dr. Taylor places his hands over his eyes, shielding them from the sun, peering into the contrasting darkness.

"By God, I think you're right." There's something tucked away in the recesses of the 'cave', something that stands out against the light filling the opening. Whatever it is, it's huge, big enough to be a ship.

As they draw nearer a sound can be heard over the squelching of the water and the creaking of the lifeboat, a resonance that's unmistakable: the hum of machinery. And, as they scrutinize it more thoroughly, they see that the surface of the water is churning beneath it.

Dr. Taylor turns to Kenny, an expression on his face that is one of relief mingled with disbelief, a faint skepticism that it shouldn't be this easy.

"It is, ain't it? What else it could be?"

Dr. Taylor senses something amiss about the situation, a nagging feeling that makes him wary; surely they shouldn't be able to find the ship this easily, if indeed it was the captain's intention to hide it. But maybe they merely moved it so that it couldn't be viewed via satellite or plane? It doesn't make any sense…either way there's something clandestine about the operation, yet why it would be moored in the mouth of the indentation when they could have anchored further in escapes him. Unless…

Kenny studies the other's face, the doctor's expression giving him away.

"Ya think it's a trap, don't ya?"

Dr. Taylor nods his head slowly. "I think it's possible."

"So whadda we do? Should we call the others?"

"No," the doctor says, albeit hesitantly. "Let's check it out, *carefully*, and if it's safe we'll radio them. No sense in all of us getting caught."

"If you think it's a trap than why are we going in there?" Tyler's brow is furrowed. "Like, do we want to get killed?"

"Ya got any better ideas hot shot?"

"Hot shot? How eighties dude."

"Better'n a throwback from the grunge-era nineties."

"In yer fuckin' dreams man-"

"Shut up!" Dr. Taylor snaps. "For Christ's sakes Tyler we've been listening to your bullshit all day and it isn't getting any easier to swallow! And you Kenny, Jesus, don't encourage him…" He places his hands on his head, runs them through his thinning hair, taking a deep breath. A minute goes by, then another. The other two are silent, watching him with mutual looks of surprise. Who knew he had it in him?

"Look," he says eventually, calmer, "I'm sick of hearing you two go back and forth. Yes, Tyler, it could be a trap, but we have to take our chances because we are out of options, got it? You know the saying 'do or die'? Well this is it. And Kenny," he looks at him exasperatedly. "Quit egging him on, all right? Let's try and work together, huh?"

Kenny looks at the doctor somberly, shoots a glare at Tyler, and then glances away. What he'd like to do is put a size twelve boot up the fucker's ass but begrudgingly he realizes the doctor is right. They have to work as a team.

"Okay, Doc, right. No problem."

"And you?" Dr. Taylor stares hard at Tyler, his eyes the color of flint.

"Yeah, sure," Tyler says, shrugging indifferently. "Whatever."

"Okay then, let's get a little closer and see what we find."

Slowly, cautiously, they begin to paddle toward the mouth of the cave.

NINETEEN

Lieutenant Ronson holds the wheel steady, backing the vessel toward the opening of the cave. He's followed the captain's instructions to the letter; crewmen are waiting on deck to spring into action as soon as the passengers arrive. This could be minutes, it could be hours; it makes no difference to them.

He eases back on the throttle when the ship is about thirty feet from his intended destination, slowing to a crawl.

Their orders are to take the passengers alive; none of them are to be harmed. Of course, if any of them should put up a fight than the men are cleared to do whatever it takes to subdue them. This much is understood.

"They are going to be on our side soon enough," Jake Anderson told him over the radio. *"Keep excessive force to a minimum but don't let them get away."*

When he decides he is far enough he shuts off the engine, the ship gliding gently into place. He calls down to the men on deck and, using large harpoon guns, they fire at the surrounding walls to secure the ship in place, tying off the ropes on the rails. Now all they have to do is wait. The hook is baited, all they need are the fish. ,

"Purty hard to sneak in there without bein' seen." Kenny takes over the rowing duties for the doctor; they are re-entering the oil slick that surrounds the island, and they need his brute strength to maneuver them through the morass.

"Row toward the side closest to us, but not too close," Dr. Taylor says, stowing the walkie-talkie, first aid kit, notebook and water bottle in the metal compartment. "Easy goes it and keep your voices down."

"Gotcha."

"You think the guys on board are like the captain?" Tyler asks and Dr. Taylor shrugs.

"That's what we're going to find out."

"We gotta take them bastards by surprise."

"How do we know they aren't waiting to ambush *us*?"

"We don't, and unless we take this chance we're going to die anyway." He glares at the other, irritation getting the best of him once again. "You've got a choice Tyler, how would you like to die?"

"What? What did you say to me?"

"He ast ya a simple question shithead," Kenny snarls. "Or maybe this question'd better suit ya: 'Where do ya see yerself in, oh, I don't know, ten minutes?'"

"All I'm saying is that they are probably waiting for us-"

"We know what yer sayin' an we don't care. If we don't take a chance-any chance-than we might as well slit our own throats an be done with it."

"Well what's the plan then? We need a plan."

Kenny looks at Dr. Taylor and he nods.

"This is good right here. Do your best to hold the boat in place while I scope it out."

Dr. Taylor peers into the shadows, letting his eyes adjust. Where they are currently positioned they shouldn't be easily visible to anyone on the ship who might be looking out to sea because of the sun's glare off of the water, but as soon as they get closer all bets are off. How can they get to the ship without being seen? The most logical answer is to wait until dark, but then they'll be fumbling around like a bunch of fools, hoping for enough natural light to guide the way. And how are they going to gain access?

"Whaddaya think Doc-"

"Shh." Eyes finally accustomed to the gloom, Dr. Taylor can see an indeterminate distance beyond the ship, and what he beholds is amazing. The cave is vast, simply enormous. The ship could easily be moored deeper within the recesses of such a large space, indicating that his suspicions were dead-on. Studying the water around the hull of the ship, he at last locates something that might be useful.

"Take a look over there Kenny." He points to a spot near the ship's stern, close to the water's surface. "What does that look like to you?"

Kenny stares where the doctor is gesturing, squinting. He shrugs.

"Don't know."

"Doesn't it appear to be ladder rungs leading up from a diving platform?"

He squints harder, at last nodding his head.

"Yeah Doc, I think so."

"So if we can make it to the ship without detection we can probably climb aboard there, right?"

"Yeah!" Kenny replies, nodding. "So what're thinkin', wait til dark?"

"I think that's our best bet."

"So what are we going to do until then?" Tyler interrupts impatiently. "The current is pulling us in."

"Let it."

"What?"

Dr. Taylor scans the trash heap, the sheer walls surrounding the cave.

"We'll drift in a little closer and then steer toward the right side of the cave. When we're near enough we'll find a place to hold onto until the sun goes down, that way we don't have to stay out here and tire ourselves out. It'll probably only take one of us to keep the boat in place while the other two rests. We'll take turns. That way we'll conserve our energy."

"I like it," Kenny says, smiling at the doctor. He looks at Tyler. "Ya gotta problem with it?"

"There's no way we can take all of them. I think the idea is stupid man, plain old fuckin' stupid-"

"Here we go again! Ya wanted a plan, so we got a plan. Now it ain't good enough for ya. What the hell ya want from us Tyler?"

"How about coming up with a good idea?"

"Jesus Christ! I'm tired of yer shit man, got it? Sick and fuckin' tired!"

"Hey, easy now…" the doctor warns.

"I should have gone in the other boat," Tyler says, slumping onto the bench. He doesn't like this, any of it. He wishes he were at a strip club right now, stuffing someone else's money in a hot bitch's g-string and chugging a beer, preferably something imported.

Kenny grunts and rolls his eyes disgustedly.

"Pussy."

"What?" Tyler says, getting back to his feet. "What did you call me?"

"Ya heard me ya spineless maggot! Yer a freakin' pussy. Deal with it!"

"Screw you!"

"Yeah, you'd like that."

The two edge closer, dropping the oars, squaring off in the middle of the lifeboat. Dr. Taylor looks from one to the other like a spectator at a tennis match.

"Quiet you two! For Christ's sakes we aren't that far away-"

"I don't like you," Tyler sneers. "Know why?"

"I don't give a shit."

Dr. Taylor looks toward the cave, sees they have drifted much too close, are actually beginning to enter the mouth, the current pulling them slowly toward the ship.

"Knock it off! You guys need to start paddling-"

"Cause you're a nigger-"

Kenny's fist catches him under the chin, sending him over the side of the boat and into the oily water. Tyler goes down like a rock but surfaces moments later, thrashing about wildly.

"You nigger bastard! You sucker punched me!"

"Ya ever call me that again and I'll carve ya up like a Halloween jac-o-lantern!"

"Guys, guys! Shut the hell up!" Dr. Taylor looks at the ship, sees movement on the deck. Crewmen are approaching the railing, alerted by the commotion. "You're going to get us caught!"

Suddenly a voice booms through a loudspeaker, the shape of the cave funneling the sound toward the entrance, creating a bullhorn effect.

"Gentlemen, welcome!" the voice says, the lack of emotion in it unsettling, and Dr. Taylor shakes his head in consternation.

"You jack-asses! So much for the element of surprise."

"Ah shit Doc, I'm sorry. I lost it when he called me a nigger..."

"Nigger nigger nigger!" Tyler screams at the top of his lungs, treading water next to the boat.

Ignoring him, Kenny says: "What are we going to do?" but Dr. Taylor doesn't reply, just looks ahead.

The ship looms closer as the current draws them deeper into the cave, and he follows the doctor's gaze up to the deck. The crewmen are lining the railing, holding automatic weapons. He also sees a man standing in the wheelhouse, his eyes boring into his own.

"What can we do?" Dr. Taylor sighs. "They've seen us."

Ronson stares into the eyes of one of the men in the boat, the black man. He doesn't appear to be frightened, which is good. Fear can make a man do crazy things. A levelheaded man will want to talk, and talking is just what he has in mind. Keep them talking until the Master arrives and tells them what to do next.

The door abruptly swings open and Captain Harvey steps into the wheelhouse.

"Good work Ronson," he says, a twisted grin on his face. "They fell for it hook, line and sinker."

"Thank you, sir," Ronson answers, his head swiveling clumsily on his neck, drool dripping from his slack jaw. The captain regards these symptoms distastefully before turning toward the window.

"Inform the crew not to fire unless I say so."

Ronson sticks his head out the door. "Safety's on men!" He calls and they nod imperceptibly, standing stock still against the rail.

"Now let's reel those bastards in."

The three men watch helplessly as a rope ladder is tossed over the side of the ship and one of the crewmen climbs down, his movements sluggish, erratic. Dr. Taylor realizes his hypothesis is correct; the bacterium (if that is what it truly is) has infected the crewmen. No doubt Captain Harvey had something to do with it.

The crewman reaches the bottom of the ladder, beckoning them toward him.

"Please come aboard," the voice thunders through the speakers. "We have food and...ah... beverages waiting."

"Why are you pointing guns at us?" Dr. Taylor yells through cupped hands, his words echoing throughout the chamber.

After a brief interval the crewmen drop their weapons, kicking them away.

"Is that better?" the voice asks. "We mean you no…ah…harm."

"Yeah right," Kenny says.

"What do we do?" Tyler says, his teeth chattering with cold and fear. He's got one arm hooked over the side of the boat, hanging on for dear life as he considers his options. No way out now unless, well, unless he is willing to do whatever it takes to save himself…

"Should we make a break for it?" Kenny asks, and the doctor shakes his head.

"They'll shoot us if we do."

The goddamned plan is ruined because these two had to whip 'em out and lay 'em on the table. As if things aren't already bad enough, these two buttholes had to engage in a pissing contest…

He wants to be angry with Kenny but a quick glance at the other erases his hostility; the large black man looks wholly remorseful, wringing his beefy paws to beat the band. Instead he finds his fury is directed solely at Tyler, the insolent dumb ass. He's the one who had to go and play the race card. It probably would have been better if they'd left him at the cove like Kenny had wanted, what with all the trouble he's caused.

"So you're saying we should give up and climb the ladder?" Tyler asks nervously, his gaze shifting from them to the ship and back. The thought of surrendering, of simply giving in, does not sit well with him. Because there's no way they can fight; they are out manned three to one. It would be suicide.

And then an idea comes to him, a way out, yet it does nothing to ease his fear. There is no sureness in his plan, nothing but a vague hope that he can somehow gain their favor if he gives them what they want.

"Son of a bitch!" Kenny curses impotently. "Looks like our only damn choice. Just be ready to fight like ya gotta pair." He turns to Dr. Taylor, observing the tight-lipped grimace on his face. "Ya okay Doc?"

"I'm fine. Really pissed off, but fine."

"I'm sorry Doc, I shouldn't a let my temper get the best a me-"

"What's done is done. Just be ready to take advantage of any opportunity."

"I will, ya'cn count on it."

They watch silently as the lifeboat drifts ever closer. The crewman stands perched on the last rung of the ladder, waiting with an outstretched hand and a vacant look on his face.

"Grab the flare gun for me Doc," Kenny says quietly, holding out his hand.

"Can't, it's in the other boat."

"Shit! That little pocketknife won't do squat. Hand me the oar than, huh?"

Dr. Taylor nods, leaning over and reaching for it when Tyler grasps the side of the boat with both hands and launches himself over the lip. The boat tips precipitously and Dr. Taylor cries out as he loses his balance and falls into Kenny, the two of them crashing to the floor. Tyler quickly snatches the paddle and cocks it over his left shoulder.

"You make a move for the other one and I'll knock yer block off."

"What the hell are ya doin' Tyler?" Kenny groans but the other pays him no mind. He looks up at the crewman, a wicked smile playing on his face.

"I got 'em!" he hollers. "Come and get 'em!"

Walking as fast as his newly transformed legs can take him, Lieutenant Ronson descends from the wheelhouse, his .38 clutched tightly in his right hand. Captain Harvey stays behind, watching from a distance.

The crewman on the ladder reaches out and grabs the bow of the lifeboat, swinging it toward him. Tyler steps gingerly to the front, holding the oar before him like a peace offering.

"Take it. They were going to use it as a weapon."

Ronson approaches the ship's railing, looking down at the lifeboat and it's passengers. He raises his gun and aims it at Kenny and Dr. Taylor.

"I'm sure you are hungry and...ah...thirsty," he says. "Come aboard and we'll get you...ah... something to eat."

"I'll give them something to eat all right," Kenny mumbles.

"What does he think he's doing?" Dr. Taylor balks, watching as Tyler performs his little song and dance routine, making a show of cooperation.

"I'm not sure, but I think its called 'turning coat'."

Tyler scurries quickly up the ladder (*'If I get my hands on the other oar while yer still in range yer gonna be sorry'* Kenny had promised him, and Tyler's eyes sought out the two by four, seeing it on the floor of the boat behind Kenny, and quickly made for the ladder). Dr. Taylor follows wordlessly while Kenny scoops up the improvised paddle and turns to face the crewman, brandishing it menacingly.

"Ahem," Lt. Ronson says from above, indicating the gun he's holding. "Don't force me to... ah...fire upon you."

"I ain't droppin' it."

"Bring it with you if you...ah...must, then."

After Kenny passes (ably climbing the ladder one handed) the crewman attaches the lifeboat to the ladder and ascends behind him.

"Welcome...gentlemen," Ronson greets as they tumble over the side.

Dr. Taylor gets to his feet quickly, examining the other suspiciously. He can't remember meeting this fellow, but he supposes it doesn't really matter, not anymore. He's a part of the machine now, his life interchangeable with any of the others.

Kenny raises the two by four over his shoulder like a baseball bat, his gaze shifting from one crewman to another, his eyes daring them to do their worst. They in turn look upon him idly; their guns are lying on the deck behind them, yet they seem unconcerned.

"Y'all better stay as far away from me as ya can, less ya want yer heads knocked into next week."

"There's no need for that, I…ah…assure you." Ronson attempts a smile that doesn't seem at home on his face. "We are here to…ah…help you."

"Help us what? Become like you?" Dr. Taylor asks, keeping a wide berth from the crewmen who stalk them in predatory circles.

"I'm not sure what you…ah…mean." He nods toward his men. "These gentlemen want to… ah…assist you. Come to the galley and we'll serve you some lunch. I'm sure you must be…ah… starving."

"Thanks, but we're fine."

"You better keep an eye on the dude with the two by four," Tyler says, sidling up to Ronson. "He'll use it."

"What're ya doin'?" Kenny barks and Tyler regards him dourly.

"What does it look like?"

"Whatever you're thinking Tyler, it won't work. You can't reason with these people-"

"That's where you are wrong my friend," a familiar voice says and Dr. Taylor looks up, startled, to see Captain Harvey making his way down the ladder from the wheelhouse. "We are very civil people, and we do listen to reason. Don't we Lieutenant Ronson?"

"Yes…sir."

"I should have known you'd be close by," Dr. Taylor says resignedly. "Where there's smoke…"

"Ah yes, certainly there will be fire. Good to see you again Dr. Taylor. I trust your stay on Garbage Island has been pleasant?"

"Oh yeah…this is a regular paradise."

"Glad you think so! That's how I plan to advertise it in our travel brochure." Captain Harvey turns to Kenny, tips him a wink. "And the football player. Always up for sport, eh?"

"Anyone gets near me they goin' to wish they'd kept they hands to themselves."

"Right! Good show!" Captain Harvey applauds appreciatively. "But that won't be necessary, no, we don't wish to harm anyone."

"What have you done with Melissa?" Dr. Taylor asks, shooting a look at Tyler who, to his credit, flinches slightly at the mention of her name.

"She is safe and in good company at our village. She's resting now, having been given some refreshments."

"Refreshments?"

"Well," Harvey says, sobering, his brows knitting together. "To tell the truth she hasn't been fed, not yet. We've been waiting for the rest of you so that we may have a grand feast upon your arrival to our humble community."

"I think I know what happens when people eat the food from the trash heap." Dr. Taylor watches the other keenly, hoping to gauge his reaction. "They…they, change."

"Do they now?" Captain Harvey laughs, unruffled. "And what do you think of this Tyler? Do you believe that's true?"

Tyler summons his courage and looks at the captain, studying the black, soulless eyes, the dead yellow/gray skin of his face, his gore streaked bosom. He knows he's walking dangerous ground and that this charade may very well end badly for him, but he wants desperately to try and win his favor anyway. What the hell, nothing ventured, nothing gained…

"I don't know about any of that," he says, his eyes darting back and forth nervously, "but I can help you get what you want." He licks his lips compulsively, holding the other's gaze as best he can, "If you give me what I want."

Captain Harvey howls delightedly, a boisterous, penetrating resonance that makes the hair on Tyler's arms stand up. As his chest shudders with his folly he coughs powerfully and regurgitates a thin stream of fluid that puddles on the deck at his feet. Long spaghetti strand sized worms wriggle madly in the milky fluid, and Captain Harvey uses the tip of one boot to grind them into the deck as he takes a step toward Tyler.

"We have a man here who wants to strike a bargain!" he announces to his crew, who look on with dead eyes. "Pray tell, my good sir, what it is that you have to offer?"

"I can get the others for you."

"We got you," Harvey frowns. "What makes you think we can't round up the others in due time?"

"I'm sure you can, but I can get them for you right now. I can call them and have them meet us here."

"Ah, I see." Harvey nods his approval. "You have to admire a man who will do anything to assure his own safety, even if it means compromising the safety of others."

"I think ya mean despise," Kenny says, keeping the crewmen at bay with the two by four.

"And what is it you want in return for this favor? Certainly you know I can't let you leave."

"I want to be treated special. Whatever you do to the others, I don't want that to happen to me."

"Don't make deals with this man!" Dr. Taylor blurts, looking at Tyler as if he has lost his mind, which, very possibly, he has. "He won't honor anything he promises!"

"Ignore him," Harvey says, stepping closer, placing an arm around Tyler's shoulder. Up close, the man's stench is dizzying, the smell making Tyler's stomach twist and turn uproariously. He places a hand over his mouth in an attempt to suppress his gag reflex and it works, just barely. Fortunately his stomach is mostly empty, otherwise it's entirely possible that he'd be decorating the other's boots with puke right about now.

"You appear to be a lusty man, am I right?"

"What do you mean?"

"Women…they enjoy your company, am I right?"

"Of course they do." He offers a strained smile. "Never had a problem in that department."

"I'm looking for someone to spearhead a special research project I'm launching, something that requires an extremely virile young man-"

"I think ya mean 'viral'," Kenny opines and Tyler scowls at him.

"I'm your guy," Tyler says and the captain guffaws again, blowing rotten breath in his face with enough force that Tyler's mouth fills with warm bile, his cheeks bulging comically. With a great effort he manages to force it back down.

"This, uh, this job." He swallows thickly, placing a hand over his nose. "It doesn't require that I, um, change in any way…does it?"

"Change?"

Tyler nods at the crewmen, indicating their empty eyes and staggering gait. "Yeah, you know... *change.*"

Captain Harvey shakes his head vigorously, small gnats flying out of his hair as he does so, clouding around his head. He waves them away.

"No my friend, what I need, I need from a healthy, *normal* man." He grins. "A man just like you, just as you are."

Dr. Taylor and Kenny watch this interplay with escalating unease, knowing full well the nefarious nature of the captain's intentions and wondering why this moron doesn't see it.

"Don't be a idiot Tyler, he's lyin' to ya. What's happened to these guys, it's gonna happen ta all a us."

"No," Captain Harvey disagrees. "Not all of you, and that's the truth." He looks at Dr. Taylor, disregarding Kenny. "You see, I have certain positions that need to be filled, positions that require complete humanity."

"Yeah?" Kenny says. "Like what?"

"In due time my friend, in due time." He returns his attention to Tyler. "So, is it agreed then?"

Tyler looks at the captain dumbly. "What?"

"You deliver me the others and I'll give you the job you were born to do. Deal?"

Tyler shifts restlessly, wondering for a moment if he's making a mistake. He looks at Kenny, sees the big man glaring at him furiously. He glances at Dr. Taylor, reading what might be concern in his eyes, maybe, or dismal, resigned dread, he can't tell for sure. The question is, is he stupid enough to think these guys give a crap what happens to him? All along they've been riding him like a burro in a Tijuana donkey show. They don't care about him, they just don't want him to give up the others. What-fucking-ever.

To hell with 'em'. Let 'em figure their own way out of this.

"There's a walkie-talkie in the metal box on the lifeboat," he says, raising his voice to be heard over the groan of disapproval Kenny makes. "I'll call the others, let them know we've found the ship and everything's fine."

"Excellent!" Captain Harvey says gleefully. "Go get it!"

Dante takes over for Leeann, who they've allowed to help out under the condition that she wear Cole's shirt over her head like a turban. She agreed, and did her best to keep the boat parallel with the shore while Cole struggled to keep them moving forward. He's been paddling almost nonstop, and his face is covered in a film of sweat and grime.

Suddenly the walkie-talkie starts beeping and they all jump.

"Jesus, that scared the hell our of me!" Cole says.

"It's about damn time." Dante scoops it up from where it lies on the bench. "Maybe they found something." He flips the switch and presses the button. "Dante here."

"Hey, you guys all right out there?"

"We're fine Tyler. Any news?"

"Great news. We found the ship."

"They found the ship?" Cole says breathlessly, almost dropping his oar. "Is everything okay?"

"Is the crew present?" Dante inquires, holding a finger to his lips to shush Cole, trying to hear over the growling static.

"Yeah, a couple of the men who escaped. They let us use the radio and we called for help."

Dante can't believe his ears. He looks at Leeann, who has a rapturous look on her sun-beaten face. He turns and glances at Cole, who is practically jumping up and down in his excitement.

"You called for help?" he repeats, trying to keep calm.

"The Coast Guard," Tyler confirms. "Best thing for you guys to do is turn around and head in our direction. There's food and water and everything!"

"Is Dr. Taylor there?" Leeann asks and there is a pause, not a long one, granted, but an interval just the same. "Tyler?"

"He's here," Tyler says, his voice hitching slightly. "He's below deck, taking a shower."

"And Kenny?" Dante presses, a smile flitting upon his lips. "He's all right as well?"

"He's eating just about everything in sight. Better get here before he eats us out of house and home."

"Goddamn!" Cole whoops. "About time we were tossed a bone!"

"We're on our way." Dante feels relief flood his addled nervous system. The nightmare is almost over. "Are you guys clearly visible?"

"Oh yeah, no worries," Tyler chuckles. "You can't miss us."

TWENTY

"It will take them hours to get here," Dr. Taylor says after Tyler has completed his task. "What do you plan to do with us in the meantime?"

Captain Harvey's face stretches into a contorted rictus of joy. "No sense wasting the daylight. I guess it's time you went to the village."

"I ain't goin' nowhere," Kenny says. "Not without a fight."

"Than a fight it shall be my good man." He turns his gaze on Lieutenant Ronson. "Subdue him and the doctor. Tyler is going to stay here with me."

"Is there anything I can do?" Tyler asks eagerly, wanting to show Captain Harvey just how useful he can be.

"Nothing for you to do until the others get here, then I just need you to lure them aboard the ship."

"Can do."

"When the others find out ya turned on 'em their gonna be pretty goddamn pissed off," Kenny says, clenching the two by four so tightly his knuckles are bone white.

"Doesn't matter," Tyler smirks, forcing a laugh. "Nothing matters anymore. Not for any of you, that is."

Dr. Taylor shakes his head sadly. "Are you really that stupid Tyler? You know how this is going to end, don't you?"

"I know how it's going to end for you, so spare me, huh?"

"That's my boy." Captain Harvey places an arm around Tyler's shoulder. "You deserve something to drink. All this deceit must have you parched." He waves a hand and one of the crewmen steps forward. "Take him down to the galley and let him have something cold to drink, maybe a little snack, but that's all." He turns back to Tyler. "Sorry, but we're having a great feast once all of you are gathered. I want everyone to save their appetites."

"But..." Tyler falters, looking at the captain uncertainly. "I thought that wasn't going to happen to me..."

"Tole ya so," Kenny jeers.

"Actually, what I told you is true," Captain Harvey says, ignoring Kenny once more and fixing his eyes on Dr. Taylor. "I need you for specified tasks. For this I will require you as you are."

He returns his attention to his new friend. "For the time being anyway. And I have a special treat, a delicacy that's come a long way to be here. It should be most succulent."

He releases Tyler and claps his hands, signaling the crewmen to move in. They surround Dr. Taylor and Kenny, inching ever closer. Kenny doesn't hesitate; he advances several steps and swings the two by four at the first crewman who gets near. His aim is dead-on, the board connecting with the other's head, and suddenly the crewman's neck is bent at an odd angle, his mouth cocked open ludicrously, black eyes wide, unblinking. But the blow fails to stop him, it only slows him down. He presses forward and Kenny swings again, this time at his belly, and it doubles the crewman over, laying him out on the deck. The others continue to close in, stepping over his body.

"That's right, come an git it. I know ya fuckers ain't unbreakable."

But, incredibly, the fallen crewman gets up, his body looking crimped at the middle, yet back on his feet nonetheless, rejoining the others. Slowly but surely they are reducing the space between them, driving the two toward the railing of the ship. Dr. Taylor looks over his shoulder, quickly calculating the drop.

Twenty-five feet, maybe thirty? Hallsly and Tyler fell from that height at sea and they were fine...

Sensing what the doctor has in mind, Captain Harvey signals to Ronson, who raises his gun.

"Halt, or this man will shoot both of you dead!"

"Ya said ya need us," Kenny says, his hands sweaty, swinging the board wildly. "Ya won't shoot us."

"Lieutenant Ronson," Captain Harvey replies calmly, "please prove this man wrong."

Ronson pulls back the hammer, aiming the weapon at Kenny's right knee. A loud blast echoes throughout the cave, the sound deafening in the enclosed space. Kenny cries out, clutching his knee and dropping to the hard steel deck. The two by four falls from his grasp and one of the crewmen quickly snatches it up.

"Ya son of a bitch!" He snarls, his lips curled in agony. Where his kneecap once was is a mass of blood and shredded tissue. "Jesus!"

"That's right, call upon your savior," Captain Harvey laughs in his crazy, worm-spraying manner. "If ever there was such a man I don't think he'd waste his time coming back from the dead for such a sorry lot as you, trust me."

"Are you all right?" Dr. Taylor asks, when two crewmen step forward and grab hold of his arms.

"I'll be fine," Kenny reassures him, but they both know he is lying. Blood is pouring down his leg, pooling on the deck around him, and his face has lost some of its color.

Captain Harvey snaps his fingers and another two crewmen seize Kenny, hauling him to his feet. He bites his lip to keep from crying out but involuntarily a groan escapes him.

"What are you going to do about his wound?" Dr. Taylor demands.

"One of my men will clean it and dress it. I still need him, even if he won't be able to walk so well anymore." He nods to his men. "Take them to the infirmary and patch him up, but be quick about it. I want them on their way before the sun sets."

"We don't have to cooperate with you!" Dr. Taylor shouts over his shoulder as he is dragged away. "You can't make us do that!"

"Oh my good man," Captain Harvey chortles. "When you see the alternative you will be more than happy to do as I say." He waves as they disappear below deck. "See you soon."

"That cold drink you mentioned?" Tyler butts in, his voice needling, whiny. "You think it could be a beer maybe? That would really hit the spot."

"Oh my beautiful little worm," Captain Harvey says softly, reaching out a hand and caressing the other's cheek. "You can have whatever your heart desires." He smiles, his grin like that of a coiled snake. "The women will be so pleased to see you, to, to…love you."

One of the crewmen comes forward, taking Tyler gently by the elbow and leading him toward the galley.

"Do make sure our guest is comfortable. I will send for you when we are in need of your services again."

As Tyler descends the ladder to the deck below, the captain's coarse laughter follows him down.

An hour passes, then another. The sun is leaning far to the west now, casting long shadows that make the occupants of the boat appear much taller than they really are. As the day begins slipping away hordes of insects come out, roughly the size of horse flies but, like the bugs on the trash heap, they are lumbering and mostly innocuous. Dante waves one away as he continues to row, his eyes focused on the sea.

"First thing I'm gonna do when we get there is have me a shot from the bottle they took away from me," Cole declares, switching from one side of the boat to the other, the two by four held loosely in his hands. A fly alights on his neck and he slaps it away. "In fact, I'm gonna have two."

"Before I do anything I'm going to take a shower and get all this crap off of me," Leeann says, looking at herself distastefully. In the whole of her life she has never been this dirty and it absolutely disgusts her. She's always been a very cleanly sort; she had a roommate during her freshmen year of college who was a 'hippy', a girl who wore loose, brightly colored skirts and headbands, listened to Janis Joplin, held liberal political ideals and smoked pot. Leeann had nothing against her lifestyle choice except for the fact that she rarely bathed, preferring to mask her body odor with patchouli oil. The musky scent was simply more than she could take, that and looking at the bottoms of her feet, which were most often black with grime. Fortunately she'd only had to endure her for a semester before the girl dropped out to join an all female acid-rock band named Tit's and Giggles. Apparently she and her hippy friends weren't big on women's rights.

"Both of those sound good to me," Dante says, "in no particular order."

The three share a laugh, a *real* laugh, for the first time in as long as any of them can remember, and it feels good, purifying. The fear that had followed them through the quagmire of the heap and into the long dreadful night, only to be there as they'd made their hasty escape from the captain and his men, well…it feels so good to finally shrug it off, to bid it a fond adieu, c'est la vie, goodbye.

But even better (a thought amongst them that goes unspoken, for truly there is no place for it now, not here, not while they are still enroute to the ship) will be imagining the look on Captain Harvey's face when he realizes he has lost. Of all the things they have to look forward to, surely that will be the most pleasant.

"If I find my tequila I don't care when I take a shower," Cole jokes as he deftly handles the two by four, keeping the boat straight as Dante leans into the oar, pulling them ever closer to their eventual freedom.

"Eww!" Dante and Leeann say in unison and once again the three of them laugh, the sound reverberating off the wall of trash to their right. Ahead of them the blue sky is streaked with splashes of crimson, orange and purple, arcing toward them brilliantly, the sun nestled amidst the colors like an egg in a nest.

"As long as you stay on one side of the ship and I'm on the other," Leeann says, "that's fine with me."

"No problem my lady, no problem at all.",

Walking is pure agony, his shattered kneecap shrieking bloody murder with every step. The bastard had to go and shoot him in his injured knee. All that time and money he'd spent trying to rehabilitate it, all the pain, his subsequent pill addiction...all up in smoke. Captain Harvey's men have made him a crude splint using materials from the ship and found it in their *(heart's? infinite passion?)* to allow him to use the two by four as a crutch, but still the journey is long, arduous. Dr. Taylor has his arm around him, offering whatever assistance he can, but it takes every last ounce of his strength not to scream each time he puts his full weight on it. And to make matters worse darkness is falling; even with the illumination provided by the crewmen's flashlights Kenny still manages to stumble and trip over unseen obstructions that find their way in front of every other step.

"Not...*uhnnnggg*...far now," one of the crewmen says. "Almost...there."

This thing, what used to be a man, has tiny slits on each side of his neck that don't appear to be cuts; it's as if he is developing gills. Dr. Taylor twists his head to see, to examine this phenomenon more closely, and the creature pokes him with a sharpened plastic rod.

"Keep...walking."

"Can you breath underwater through those?" Dr. Taylor inquires and gets another poke in the back for his troubles.

"No...talking."

The sudden movement causes Kenny's knee to twist and he takes in a sharp intake of breath as a bolt of pain shoots through it.

"Save the questions fer later, huh Doc? My knee can't take it."

"Sorry," he says, tightening his grip on the other. "My curiosity got the best of me."

"I'm sure the captain'll be glad to enlighten us shortly," Kenny grunts, unaware of how true his words will prove to be. "Whadaya think?"

"I suppose we'll find out."

"That fuckin' asshole Tyler." It doesn't come as any surprise that he'd managed to get them caught, but to offer information in trade for preferential treatment, well, that just about takes the cake. "If we get outta this I'm gonna make sure he gets what's comin' to him," he vows, his words coming out in short bursts, interrupted by the disjointed rhythm of his breathing.

"Don't worry," Dr. Taylor says, keeping his eyes on the path, doing his best to steer Kenny around anything that may trip him up, "he'll get it, one way or the other."

"Whadaya think the captain means, havin' jobs fer us?"

"I don't know," he replies, but the question is one that's been circling his thoughts like a persistent fly, the answer eluding him at every turn. So far they're every consideration has been of survival, leaving very little time to ponder the captain's underlying intentions. One thing for sure, it's all tied in to this abysmal anomaly of genetic engineering, this cesspool of human waste that has taken evolution by the tail, consumed it, and vomited forth all they've witnessed thus far.

A ghastly radiance appears in the distance, the orangish haze casting a hideous glow on the debris around them, at once creating the ominous impression that the trash heap is a sub-level of Hell itself.

I don't believe in Hell, Dr. Taylor thinks bleakly, sweat running down his temples as he struggles to keep Kenny upright. But what was it the priest at his parent's church always said to the non-believers, way back when, when he was just a child and the foolish imagery of leering devils and demons still had the power to frighten him? *'Don't worry,'* these old men with their beer bellies and red, vein-lined faces said. *'It believes in you.'*

TWENTY-ONE

Darkness is descending as Cole, Dante and Leeann paddle in silence. The sun has slipped out of sight, the last of the light fading from the sky.

"Going to be full dark soon," Cole observes unnecessarily. "Remember what the doctor said."

"We all remember." Leeann leans heavily on the oar a moment, brushing damp hair from her face. "But it's different now."

"You want me to spell you?" Dante asks, reaching for the oar, and Leeann shakes her head.

"I'm fine, you stay right where you are."

Maybe it's because it has cooled off, or maybe it's because she knows that rescue is imminent, whatever the case, Leeann is doing her best to pitch in with the rowing, is actually on her third turn. Dante doesn't mind, in fact he finds it touching, and he covers his mouth with one large hand to hide a grin that spreads across his face, feeling a warm flush suffuse his cheeks.

I think I'm in love with her. How freakin' corny is that?

Even though this has been the worst two days of his life (which is saying a lot, given the horrible existence Dante has had the distinct displeasure of living) he wouldn't want to be anywhere else in the world right now because, when all is said and done, he is with Leeann, the woman he knows with all his heart he truly loves. When lovers attest their faith by saying they will go to the end of the world and back for one another, very few have to go to these lengths to prove it.

"Should we call the ship?" Cole says, wiping his clammy hands on his filthy shirt. "Let them know we're still on our way?"

"They know," Leeann says, toiling relentlessly even though she is at the very end of her endurance. "But if it would make you feel better to know they are still there..."

In fact, it would make them all feel better. It's been over four hours since they received the message and soon enough it will be difficult to see, making their travel increasingly dangerous. But paddling back to shore and waiting until morning to find the ship isn't a viable option by any of their standards; another night on the trash heap simply isn't in the cards. Also, the clear day has given way to a murky early evening. Thick banks of clouds are looming ever closer on the darkening horizon.

"I'll give them a holler," Dante says, retrieving the walkie-talkie from the floor of the boat, "and tell them we're still enroute."

"Okay."

He twists the dial to turn it on, wiping water from the back of the unit. At first there is no sound, no hissing or crackling, and for a second he's afraid the batteries may have gotten wet. He shakes it and wipes it off again, and his efforts are rewarded by a brief burst of feedback. Sighing gratefully, he presses the button and says: "This is Dante, is anyone there?" but he hears nothing but static. He presses it again. "This is Dante, Leeann and Cole calling from the lifeboat. I repeat, is anyone there?"

Again, nothing but static buzzes from the tiny speaker, a weak, muted resonance that seems insignificant against the enormity of all the nothingness surrounding them. Dante looks up from the walkie-talkie, his eyes first meeting Leeann's, then Cole's. He takes a deep breath and lets it out in a prolonged exhale, his gesture saying more than words can.

"Maybe they're resting," Cole suggests, trying (nonetheless failing) to keep the sour note of disappointment out of his voice. "Or maybe no one is near it-"

"Hey guys," someone says over the other end and the gloom is dispelled from the lifeboat in a nanosecond. Dante smiles at Leeann through his disheveled, mangy beard and she pantomimes wiping sweat from her brow.

"Hey yourself," Dante says, then to his companions mouths 'Tyler'.

"You coming or what?" The timbre of his voice gamely indicates his utter contentment, and why wouldn't it? He is safe and secure aboard the ship, enjoying food and water and comforts that only three days ago were subpar but are now the equivalent of heaven on earth.

"We've been making pretty good time but I think we may still have a ways to go."

"We're going to turn on the running lights," Tyler says, either not hearing or simply ignoring Dante's comment. "You should be able to see us from the fucking moon."

"Good deal," Dante says, then adds: "Kenny didn't eat all of the food, did he?" He is trying to be jocular, showing that he can make light of a bad situation.

"What?" Tyler asks uncertainly. "What do you know about Kenny?" There is a hint of confusion in his voice, something that sparks a feeling of alarm in Dante.

"You told us to hurry," he says, looking away from his shipmates and staring at the water, "because Kenny was going to eat everything in sight."

"Oh," Tyler replies, sounding relieved. "Yeah, that's right. That big ox has had his head in the trough for, like, *ever*." His voice rises in pitch on the last word, and he utters a laugh that sounds forced, unnatural.

"I'm sure he wouldn't like to hear you calling him a 'big ox'," Leeann mutters and Dante puts a finger to his lips.

"Is everything okay there?" He doesn't know why, but all of a sudden he has a nagging suspicion that something isn't right. "Do me a favor," he says, scratching a bug bite on his neck. "Put Dr. Taylor on for me, huh?"

There is a pause on the other end, a moment of silence that carries on longer than it should. The three look at one another worriedly, their faces creased by frowns.

"Tyler?"

"Look, I drew the short straw so for the time being I'm all you got," he says finally, sounding annoyed. "Let me do my job, huh?"

Dante says nothing in return; he can't put his finger on it but, if pressed, he would say that Tyler's voice sounds phony, almost rehearsed.

"Jesus guys," Tyler continues, "just get your sorry asses here so we can arrange a search party for Melissa. The sooner we find her the sooner we can get out of here. Besides, we just heard from the Coast Guard and they're only a few hours away. Soon enough," he says, his voice a sign of solidarity for all of them and their struggles, "this is going to be all over."

"Okay," Dante says at last, deciding to dismiss the feeling as paranoia. He's jumpy, hell, they all are. And Tyler isn't exactly the most tactful person to begin with. He's probably pissed that he has to man the radio. "We'll be there as quickly as we can." He clicks off and puts the walkie-talkie down.

"He sounded funny." Leeann is looking at Dante worriedly, her brow furrowed. Personally, he thinks this makes her look cute.

"I thought so too for a moment but, then again, it is Tyler."

"He sounds like he found my stash," Cole contends, hawking and spitting over the side of the boat. "His speech was slurred."

"Do you think something's going on?" Leeann persists, the look on her face turning to something resembling panic. "Do you think he's one of them?"

"Christ, I hope not."

"Anything could have happened since we talked to them last," Leeann says dolefully. "Since we talked to Dr. Taylor last," she amends.

"If he was one of them wouldn't his voice be all robotic and shit?" Cole says. "He sounded like a sailor on shore leave." He shakes his head and spits again. "He better save some for me."

"I don't know guys, I'm as new to this as you are."

They resume paddling, idle chatter at a standstill, thinking their own thoughts. The approaching night comes alive with piercing shrieks and squawks of the various animal life, interrupted every so often by an eerie calm that makes them even more uncomfortable. An hour slips by, then another.

Once night falls the dark becomes almost total because of the overcast sky; currently there are very few stars and no visible moon to help guide their way. Their progress has become more plodding, deliberate. Dante peers fretfully into the gathering dusk, figuring they'll have to steer toward shore if they don't find the ship soon, and the thought makes him slightly ill. He is about to share this depressing news with the others when an enormous wall of trash appears before them, looming out of the shadows like a ghostly apparition. As they get closer they see that it curves sharply.

"Slow up," Dante says to Cole, who has taken over the rowing with the standard paddle. "Easy does it."

The water squelches and burbles against the side of the lifeboat and, peering closely at the makeshift oar, Dante sees they've reentered the oil slick that surrounds the heap.

"We're pretty close to shore," Cole says. "Probably closer than we should be."

"Just keep going, it looks like we're almost around the bend."

Navigating their way carefully to the other side, they see the glow of lights just ahead in the near distance.

"We're almost there," Dante whispers, why, he doesn't know.

They continue forward another hundred yards and the wall opens up, revealing a large indentation, and the light grows brighter.

"Holy shit…"

The three of them look upon it in awe, ceasing their rowing, the sound of the ocean loud in the momentary stillness. Under the canopy of the night sky the ship's lights take on an ethereal hue; their reflection on the water makes it appear as if there are two ships moored within the deep recession.

"Looks kinda creepy, don't it?" Cole says, breaking the silence, but no one answers him.

Dante doesn't know why but he feels as if freezing fingers are pressing against his heart, and at once his arms break out in goose bumps. He glances over at Leeann and sees she has her arms folded across her chest, clutching herself as if she's unexpectedly caught a chill.

She feels it too.

"What do you think?" he asks Leeann, and for a moment she doesn't answer, just stares ahead with a look of growing trepidation on her face. "If you think it's a trap-"

"We don't have any choice," she interjects sharply, the pitch of her voice two octaves too high. "We could sit here and do nothing or we can sneak up and see what's waiting for us."

"Is that what you want?"

Not averting her gaze from the ship she nods, her head moving slowly up and down.

"And you?" He turns to Cole. "What do you think?"

"Yeah, okay. But let's keep a low profile until we know what's up."

"Okay." Dante can't shake the feeling that something is amiss, but he's hoping they are all just nervous, jumping at shadows after everything they've been through. "With any luck we'll all be laughing about this in, oh, thirty minutes."

"I hope it's sooner than that," Leeann comments dryly. "I have to pee."

As the last of the sun retreats over the far side of Garbage Island and darkness begins to gain a foothold, the village gradually brightens thanks to lights mounted on large plastic poles, lashed in place with pieces of twine. They glow a sickly orange shade, their power coming from multiple gasoline powered generators taken from various ships, the crude wiring violating all kinds of federal safety protocols that none of the island's 'engineers' could give a tin shit about. The gasoline running the generators comes from ships that came to Garbage Island to illegally dump trash and then found (much to their everlasting dismay) that they couldn't leave.

Hallsly, of course, is unaware of the logistics of the light source; that surely isn't his degree of expertise, nor has it even remotely come to mind. For the last hour he's been watching curiously as the inhabitants of the village comb through the endless piles of debris, extracting materials for-what? He doesn't know. Staring with obsessive fascination through the cage's air hole, he watched them unearth large plastic drain tubes, two by fours, and huge flat sheets of particleboard. For all practical intents and purposes it looks as if they are fixing to build something. Whatever it is, however, is beyond him.

The patience he's shown over the last hour is very unlike him; usually the only thing he can masterfully concentrate upon is pornography, and that generally only lasts him about ten minutes tops, unless he's snorting cocaine. In that case it could last up to forty-five minutes.

After watching the creatures offer Perry and Steven food for a third time he'd decided to shut his mouth and keep his eyes open, something he isn't accustomed to doing. In his old life there was no point; nothing anyone said or did was of any interest to him unless it pertained to him. In this, his new existence, he feels it best to pay attention because, frankly, he has no idea what is going to happen next.

One thing he'd noticed since he started observing them was how they craftily utilized the plastic waste. What he wouldn't have discerned otherwise (had he not been a captive audience) was how many thousands and thousands of plastic grocery sacks there were blowing all over the place. The villagers collected and used them for all sorts of different things-from storage to cloth-ing to animal snares-it seemed there wasn't a single function they weren't perfect for.

And to think the United States passed a law making those damn things illegal. If they knew all the different uses for them surely they'd change they're minds.

Presently he's watching as they heap the items they've gathered into a large pile, and others come forth to sort it, arranging it by size, while still others begin the task of assembly. For some reason, it gives him a very bad feeling.

A crewman he recognizes from the ship (he forgets his name but, what the hell, he never remembers *anyone's* name) directs them, pointing this way and that, and they scurry about under his tutelage.

He glances over at Steven and Perry's cage, but the two have grown quiet over the passing hours. The very last sounds they'd made were nauseating chewing and slurping noises as they devoured the meat. In between they didn't make a peep, no more laughter, snide comments, noth-ing. To Hallsly that's even more unnerving. He returns his attention to the villagers, sees their structure is beginning to take shape.

What in God's green earth are they doing?

They are setting up a crude platform with the sheets of particleboard, erecting the plastic poles on top of them in the form of a large X.

Looks like they're constructing some kind of torture device...

The thought instantly sends a shiver down his spine.

Terror replaces all other emotions an hour later when several villagers appear at his cage holding handmade weapons, muttering crudely amongst themselves, words he doesn't recognize.

Behind them is the crewman who'd been supervising, but he stands away from them, a grin cocked on his decidedly 'normal' looking face, arms hanging limply at his sides.

"You," one of them says. "You get…*uhnnnggg*…out and…*uhnnnggg*…come with… us."

"What?" he cries, his voice cracking. "What do you want?"

"We getting…*uhnnnggg*…ready to…prepare…*uhnnnggg*…food," another says. Thick, black drool dribbles from the corners of his mouth, and in his hands he clutches a sharpened plastic rod. "You come…*uhnnnggg*…and help."

"You need *my* help preparing dinner?"

"You guest…of…*uhnnnggg*…honor," it says, stepping forward, opening the door and offering a hand. "Please…come."

Instinctively he shrinks against the back of the cage, shying away from his *(it's)* hands.

"No, I'm fine, really. I'll just stay in here. Quite cozy actually…"

Tossing his weapon aside, the villager gets down on his knees and crawls in the cage, taking Hallsly by the lapels of his torn and soiled shirt. He fights him but the strength the other possesses is astonishing. To the governor's credit he hasn't had much to eat or drink in the last two days, ultimately reducing his vigor to a shadow of it's former self (not that his usual vigor is anything worth writing home about), but it's still incredible how this wan, gaunt creature can wield power over him that he has no might to resist. In a matter of seconds Hallsly is out of the cage and in their custody.

"Okay, okay!" he wails. "I'll be glad to help with dinner, all right? Now would you please let go? That hurts!"

Ignoring him, they drag him toward the platform.

Warm wind blows through her hair and she can smell the pleasing fragrance of lilacs. How she knows they are lilacs isn't clear, but somehow she just does. Their perfumed aroma is so sweet, so incredibly delightful that a feeling of serenity enshrouds her like a gossamer veil. She takes a deep breath, savoring the heady scent as if this pedestrian gesture is a restricted pleasure she doesn't often encounter, exhaling slowly, contentedly. Warm light glows tenderly on her face, and when she opens her eyes she sees the beautiful expanse of a field stretching before her. Rich hues of purple, lavender and magenta assail her ocular senses and at this moment she feels more than just alive, she feels reborn. It's true she can't recall how she got here but it doesn't matter, nothing does. She simply wants to pick some flowers and take them home, maybe place them in a vase on her kitchen table so they may beautify her otherwise dreary existence.

She walks forward, the stems brushing against her bare legs. She is wearing a billowing skirt, one imprinted with a colorful interweaving floral pattern, and she marvels at the texture of the fabric *(so soft)* and wonders where she found it *(must have been in the back of the closet behind the denim, wool, lycra and cottons)*. But this revelation, like the first, is unimportant. All that matters is that she is joyous, at ease, the miraculous essence of life awake and blooming within her…

Without warning a nagging thought snags within the gears of her tranquil reflections, the ghost of a memory that insists that prior to this moment (this single event in time) life as she knew it was slavery…bondage…torture…yet she shrugs it aside because all of that is insignificant, faraway-whatever it was it's behind her, over, at long last finished. Right now she's in this beautiful field, smelling these wonderful bouquets, taking in the splendor with eyes that were once blind but are now graced with the amazing ability to see.

Reaching out carefully she takes a flower by its stem, attempting to detach it from the restraining vine when something sharp pricks her fingers. Glancing at her hand she sees blood flowing from an impossibly large, jagged wound. Fat crimson drops fall from her fingertips, splashing brightly onto the petals. Upon contact the flowers blacken and wilt, and abruptly the sun, which was so radiant only a second ago, is shadowed by dark clouds that boil up like malevolent sentinels.

'You're spoiling it, don't you realize?' a husky voice croaks, from where, she doesn't know. 'Everything you do brings about their demise.' The voice is unsettlingly familiar, and instantly icy tendrils of fear blossom within her, her heart beating like an over-wound cuckoo clock, thudding dreadfully against her ribcage. She looks about her desperately, trying to locate its origin but there is no one present, no one but the clouds and the wind and…

The field of flowers is gone, replaced by mounds and mounds of rotting trash. She stumbles backward, feels something scrape against her legs and, looking down, sees it's a demented facsimile of a flower, a sculpture made of used syringes and broken glass. She gasps as another, and then another, pops out of the ground, row upon row of these appalling figurines bursting forth from steaming piles of plastic feces, glittering evilly with a ghastly greenish glow, swaying in a scorching breeze that blows in from nowhere. Instantaneously she understands she is not where she thought she was, that the glorious field of flowers was only a mirage covering up something far more treacherous, a place considerably more sinister.

Bringing her hand to her mouth to staunch the flow of blood, she sees she is no longer wearing a dress but is clad in her leather bondage suit, only it is much too tight, so constricting she's having trouble breathing.

'A uniform befitting a woman as devious as you are,' the voice speaks again, and she becomes aware of it's owner's presence in the air around her, this foul entity apparently inhabiting multiple spiritual realms and dimensions, filling her soul with a glacial chill so bitter she's convinced it has the power to leach through her skin from the inside and leave her frostbitten, her skin blackened and useless.

"You have no business being here!" she shrieks and her voice is whisked away by a wind so rank she gags, a stench so fetid it conjures up images of moldering corpses, rotting away under a hot, unforgiving sun. "This is my field! Give it back to me!"

But there is no going back, this she knows as surely as she does the owner of the voice.

'I can't do that, but I can give you this…'

Shimmering before her, rolling slowly forward on squealing, corroded wheels is a gigantic grime-encrusted dumpster, it's metallic paint chipped and rusted, it's façade heavily worn by years of use. She squints her teary eyes against the tainted breeze as the lid pops open with a jarring clang. "Oh God…" she mutters as trash-strewn bodies tumble out one after the other, the carcasses of people with no faces, the skin stripped away to reveal the musculature and bone beneath, eye sockets empty yet staring at her nonetheless.

'God has no place here,' the voice laughs. 'I've killed it and become my own God, one of hate, lust, envy… and trash.'

Sinking to her knees, she buries her head in her hands, tears spilling from her eyes as the horrible smell threatens to choke her, closing in until she feels as if she can breath no more. Her chest heaves violently, her mouth open and gasping, dizziness overwhelming her…

'God…has…no…place…here…'

With a start she awakens, sitting up so quickly that she bumps her head on the ceiling of the cage.

"Goddamnit!" Melissa sobs, the images dissipating swiftly except for the very last wisp of the dream that clings tenaciously, the image of the corpse-choked dumpster. "Goddamnit I want to go home!"

TWENTY-TWO

"You do your best to act natural now," Captain Harvey instructs Tyler as they lounge in his quarters. Tyler is sipping (more like chugging) from a can of Pabst, reclined cozily in a chair. He is more than sufficiently buzzed and, all things considered, feels pretty damn good. "They'll be here any time. You should go up top."

"Relax man," Tyler says, a sloppy grin on his face. "Let me finish my brew."

Captain Harvey nods, a smile adorning his face that would make the Devil leery. If Tyler weren't so intoxicated he would realize that the captain's tolerance of him is based simply upon his need for assistance, but his perceptions are marred, his thinking muddled-well, more so than usual.

"Okay then," Captain Harvey says curtly, "chug a lug. We have an agenda to keep to."

Maybe Tyler catches on, or perhaps he is just in an agreeable mood.

"Alright." He slams the beer and sets the empty can on the captain's desk. "I'm out."

"Take that with you." Captain Harvey points at a black bundle sitting on the edge of his desk. "It's going to the village with us."

Tyler stares at it, a look of discomfiture spreading across his face.

"What's the matter son? You look like you've seen a ghost."

"Nothing…it's just…ah, nothing." He scoops it up and tucks it under his arm, trying to ignore the memories the item conjures in his booze-addled brain.

"Good boy. I know someone who is going to be awfully happy to see that when the time comes. Don't disappoint me and forget it."

"I won't." He staggers slightly to the door, hoping the captain doesn't notice. Man, but those beers went right to his head. How many did he have, four or five? He doesn't remember, and he can't recall being such a lightweight but hell, he hasn't eaten anything in a couple days except for the small bag of potato chips and two Slim Jims the crewman offered. Once they showed him their cache of beer, well, it was off to the races. And damned if he didn't need something to take the edge off. It isn't every day you sell everyone out for some munchies and as many beers as you can pound in one sitting. Not to mention preferential treatment, can't forget that, oh no no no. That was surely the most important part, wasn't it? But those bastards deserved it, treating him like they did. What did they think he was, an idiot? Like he didn't understand every nasty remark, every put down? They can go screw themselves for all he cares. And the captain can go to hell too if he thinks he can make him feel bad by making him carry this to the village. He's beyond guilt at this point and no one can touch him.

He makes a quick stop at the galley for more refreshments, nodding to the crewman who stands guard at the door, and then heads down the hallway to the ladder that leads topside. Is the ship rocking back and forth or is it him?

The ladder to the upper deck is more of a problem to navigate than he would have imagined one-handed. He should have waited to open his beer until he got to the top. Holding the bundle tucked under his arm doesn't help any either. He sways left and right, gripping the rungs in one sweaty hand while his other struggles to keep the can upright. Pausing, he takes five to emit a deep, satisfying belch that echoes loudly off the steel walls. Shit, how the hell do these guys do this every day? Must get used to it after a while.

The deck is mostly empty, save for a couple of crewmen who are keeping watch.

"See anything boys?" he asks and they look at him briefly before turning away. "Not talking? That's cool." He takes a sip of his beer and lets it roll around on his tongue. He'd better nurse this biotch. Not going to be much else to do while he waits.

What was it the captain said? Pretend like he was a natural? Act like he was natural? Something like that. No problem. Shouldn't be a big deal luring those suckers onto the ship. Hell, the freakin' thing practically sells itself! Who wouldn't want to get out of a lousy lifeboat and hop onto a nice, big, warm ship with food and beverages and what have you? Only a dumb ass, that's who.

"Might as well take a seat," he mutters to himself. "This might take a while." Slumping to the deck, he tosses the object aside and sits cross-legged, looking up at the ceiling of the cave, awestruck by how compacted all this shit is, how its all pressed together to form something so solid. He inspects it curiously, individually sorting through the potato chip wrappers, dog shit bags, newspapers, plastic bottles, disposable diapers, CD jewel cases, vinyl handbags and what have you. He spots an outcropping of what appears to be rubber humps and, after some study, realizes it's three or four condoms filled with fluid, hanging from the ceiling like malformed stalactites. Jesus Christ. This place is a total trip. The next time he's ashore he'll have to find himself a skin mag. Got to be one around here someplace, what with all the other crap. Been a while since he busted a nut, well, since…

Since Melissa. He looks at the item laying on the steel floor next to him and a feeling of remorse summarily follows. He fights it, and it only takes a couple of minutes before he conquers it with a decisive thought that pardons him of any responsibility: *Fuck it, it doesn't matter anymore. What's done is done.*

Like Governor Hallsly, Tyler lacks imagination. Not the scheming type of imagination, the lying-make-excuses kind, but the sort that has the ability to realize what his actions have wrought, of seeing things for what they truly are, instead of solely how they work out for him. Selfishness is like that, a special gift for understanding only how things are going to affect you, the rest of the world be damned. If asked, he'd honestly admit he has no idea where Melissa is or what's happening to her. Does he care? Possibly, but it's hard to say, given the circumstances. If he still had a vested interest maybe things would be different, but now, seeing as there is no financial gain, that's about as much thought as he's given it. Does he think he may see her again? He doesn't know (hasn't thought about it). Would he help her if he could? Only if it doesn't hinder his status quo with good ole Captain Harvey, who has now become his benefactor. Can't piss on the hand that feeds ya, or however the saying goes…

One of the crewmen grunts a few words at Tyler, his way of saying it's time to get to work, no doubt, and he gets to his feet, peers out into the darkness. Against the jet-black hue of the night sky he can see the outline of a boat on the water, just outside the perimeter of the ship's lights.

"Ah," he says. "Showtime."

The ship is lit up like a department store, as if every light on the damn thing is ablaze.

"What do you think?" Leeann asks Dante as he peers up at the deck.

"I don't know, seems to be all right."

"What are you basing that on? The lack of dead bodies?"

"Maybe…"

Truth be told, Dante doesn't see anything that either arouses his suspicion or assures him that all is copasetic. He can see some crewmen standing along the railing (probably keeping a lookout for them) but from the distance it is impossible to tell if they are a threat or not. They aren't carrying weapons, for whatever that's worth. What he wishes would happen is one of two things: either Dr. Taylor comes out and offers them a nice, cheery greeting or the Coast Guard appears out of nowhere and whisks them all to safety.

"Maybe what?" Cole asks impatiently. "We have to do something, we're drifting closer. If we're going to abort we need to put her in reverse, like, pronto."

He's right, of course, and Dante knows this, but he also hates the fact that they are relying on him for a decision. What if he's wrong and they get captured? Will they hold it against him? And what if he's wrong and they spend another night on the shore of the heap, risking attack when they could be sleeping in warm beds, filling their stomachs with food and drink. Only a few minutes ago they'd all agreed it was in their best interest to board, but now these two are waffling and, stoic as he is, it annoys him.

"We need to make a group decision," he says at last. "I don't want to be the one responsible for getting us all captured or…or worse." He looks from one to the other. "Are we clear on that?"

The question hangs in the air before them. Minutes pass, heads are scratched, considerations made.

"What the hell," Cole says at last, "I say we take our chances. What do we have to lose, right?"

"What do you think Leeann?"

She is quiet, looking gravely from the ship to Dante and back. She opens her mouth to speak but reconsiders and closes it again. And then, just like that, her mind is made up for her:

"Hey guys!" Tyler calls down from the deck, waving a beer can. "Good timing! I'm working my way through the crew's beer right now!"

Cole smiles, then laughs. "Shit, you bastard," he says, "you better save a couple for me!"

"What the hell are you doing? Let go of me!"

But they are too strong, overwhelming him. There is no way he can get free. He resists fiercely anyway, throwing ineffectual punches that land on bodies solid as concrete. It's useless; they drag him ever closer to the structure he watched them build over the course of the last few hours.

"No!" Terror and indignation ignites his over-privileged, coddled brain. "You can't do this to me! I'm the governor of California!"

But they can do it, and they do.

The screaming brings Melissa out of a state of tortured delirium. Half awake, half asleep, she recognizes the voice even before he declares who he is and why he can't be touched. Well, fancy that. She wondered what had become of him.

"Stupid bastard," she mutters, "probably getting what he deserves."

But the next cry he utters, one of agonizing horror, is intensely disturbing to say the very least, and a chill runs through her. She didn't know it was possible for people to make sounds like that, and she's inflicted a *lot* of pain in her lifetime. She can't help but feel a small amount of pity for the man, even if he is an asshole. Whatever it is they are doing, it doesn't sound good.

Kenny and Dr. Taylor are standing before their intended cages when they hear the scream, more of a guttural, anguished cry, and Kenny lifts his head, looking in the direction the sound came from.

"Get in...*uhnnnggg*...cage!" his captor says gruffly but he ignores him.

"Ya recognize that voice?" Kenny asks Dr. Taylor, who nods.

"Sounds like Governor Hallsly."

"Well I'll be damned. The gang's all here."

"Get…in…*uhnnnggg*…cage!" his captor says again, this time striking Kenny's wounded knee with his sharpened plastic rod.

"Ah, shit! Why the hell did'ya do that?" He falls, fortunately landing on his good knee, his hands out before him.

"Get in…*uhnnnggg*…cage!"

"I'm goin', I'm goin'. Christ, relax will'ya?" And Kenny crawls through the small opening of the plastic box, leaning against the back wall, his knee throbbing terrifically. Dizziness courses through him, his head swimming.

"You all right?"

For the moment Kenny can't answer; he just takes deep breaths, trying not to focus on it as it beats in tandem with his heart. After a while the pain subsides to a dull ache, but he knows every movement will be excruciating.

"Kenny?"

"Yeah," he says eventually. "I'm okay." He listens to the tormented shrieks of the governor, noting the pitch and frequency. "But it don't sound like Hallsly's havin' a very good time."

Judging by the nature of his screams, the governor has reached a state of hysteria, his yells volleying out at a nerve racking pace, one after the other with no let up.

"Must be torturin' him," Kenny says, shifting his weight delicately. "Wonder what they want."

"I don't want to know-"

"Shut-up!" their captor says, striking the doctor's cage with the plastic rod. "No more… *uhnnnggg*…talk!"

"What're ya gonna do, shoot me?" Kenny jokes but Dr. Taylor grows silent. Hallsly's hoarse cries are getting to him, their anguished desperation, their escalating intensity. Whatever is happening it must be truly awful.

So they sit quietly, listening to the governor's distressed wails, wondering what fate awaits them.

Dante steers the boat next to the other, looking inside for any clues but sees nothing amiss, except that one of the paddles is gone, the two by four. This he easily shrugs off as unimportant. He detaches the lifeboat and Cole finds a small cord to fasten the two together while Dante grasps the rope ladder so Leeann can climb up first. He then allows Cole access, then himself. They clamber over the side and onto the deck, a communal sigh of relief rising amongst them. Tyler stands there, weaving slightly, a can of beer clutched in one hand, the other scratching his crotch.

"Well all right, Dante, my main man! How' it hanging dude?"

Dante grins. "Pretty good Tyler. Glad to see you."

"I wish I could say the same," Tyler replies coolly, draining the beer and tossing it over his shoulder. The can clanks hollowly on the ship's floor.

"What?"

Leeann looks at him suspiciously, comprehension dawning upon her. In the periphery of her vision she spots the crewmen inching forward, hands outstretched, their Halloween mask faces devoid of emotion.

"Oh no Tyler, tell me you didn't do what I'm thinking you did," she says, watching as they creep nearer, employing a shambling gait that causes them to lurch from side to side absurdly. "You couldn't have…you, you wouldn't…"

"If you were black, right here is where I'd expect you to snap your fingers and say 'oh no you di-in't'," an all too memorable voice says and, stepping out of the shadows, they see it is none other than the infamous Captain Harvey himself. "But since you're white I guess you're not going to, huh?"

"Fuck!" Cole eyes the captain with a look of repugnance. "Should have known," he mutters, "should have known." He glances to the closest side of the ship, searching for an escape route, but the crewmen have blocked all obvious paths.

"Yes, you should have but you di-in't," Captain Harvey laughs gaily. He is looking even more pallid than he did before, his complexion blotchy, dark rings around his eyes, foamy drool issuing from his mouth and nose. "Glad you could make it. We have much to do before the night is over."

Leeann shrinks against Dante, who puts an arm around her protectively. He wants to tell her it will be all right, that he will do everything in his power to protect her, but there is no time. Rough hands grab them, tear them apart and hold them while Harvey makes his inspection. Dante resists but their grip is like steel. His eyes find Leeann's and she shoots him a look of bitter reproach before she turns to the captain.

"You sick bastard." Her upper lip is curled in a snarl. "Why are you doing this?"

"Why does anyone do anything?" he chuckles. "To get it done." He looks from her to Dante to Cole, nodding to himself as if he is conducting a general inventory. "We have a little journey ahead of us before the festivities can begin and then, and only then, will I let you in on the ground floor of my little operation here. I'm sure you'll all get a kick out of it. It really is a hoot."

Cole struggles fearlessly against the men holding him, thrashing and swearing, but he can't get loose. They stagger from side to side to contain him but progressively he comes to realize his efforts are in vain; he isn't going anywhere.

"You can't break their grip little man," Captain Harvey says, fingering a loose piece of skin hanging from his forehead. He tweezes it between his forefinger and thumb and pulls it downward, yanking it off when it reaches his chin. "The strength they possess is, well, beyond anything you have…for now. But don't worry. Soon you'll understand. You'll love it, it's so…liberating."

"Fuck you, you freak!" Cole sputters, his face red with exertion.

"Yes," Captain Harvey continues, "in good time you will understand, will come to love it I suspect."

He turns away, looking toward the mouth of the cave and into the night sky. The clouds have dissipated and stars are just beginning to peek out, accompanied by a pale sliver of moon. It peers down at them like an eerie smile, framed by glittering jewels. He turns back, his eyes wide, deep black yet crawling and pulsing with squirming things just below the surface.

"We better get going, we have a party to attend. Are you hungry?" He smiles a mischievous, devious smile. "Oh, but I know the answer to that one. And I have a feast waiting for you. You'll just love it, simply love it." He licks his lips, a lascivious gesture that makes Leeann shudder with revulsion. "Bind their hands and let's move out."

TWENTY-THREE

All of them are gathered, the remaining survivors. They are lined up in a neat row, two creatures per each of them standing guard, their wrists bound behind their backs. Their reunion is a strained event, hampered by a helpless foreboding pertaining their fate. Kenny, Dr. Taylor, Dante, Leeann and Cole shoot venomous glares at Tyler, who stands separately from them, hands unbound, eyes bloodshot, his legs unsteady. Melissa glances at him inquisitively, wondering why he is getting special treatment, and he looks away indifferently.

Hallsly's tireless screaming is at last reduced to a throaty whimpering, yet nonetheless can still be heard throughout the village. As his cries dwindle in volume it in turn tweaks the degree of the survivors unease.

"What are they doing to him?" Leeann entreats of Captain Harvey as he paces before them, his greedy eyes alight with a fury that readily indicates his sinister intentions, and the look he affixes her with makes her lower her head.

"Soon you will see little girl, soon. And simultaneously you will have some answers to the questions that no doubt burn so fiercely in your overworked, underfed minds."

"Is this all of us that are left?" Dr. Taylor asks, looking at the tired, dirty remainder of the group that set out from San Diego for the trash heap less than a week ago.

"Yes and no." Captain Harvey fiddles with one of his ears, which has become partially detached from his head. "Yes, some of them are dead, nothing I could do about that. Bugs or animals got to them first. But there are others still with us, just not as you remember them to be."

"And is that what you intend for us?"

"Dr. Taylor I am disappointed in you." Captain Harvey scowls, his unearthly, decaying face creasing grotesquely. "You are a smart man but you lack the ability to listen."

"I listen," Dr. Taylor says. "I lack the ability to believe the source."

The captain nods. "Very well, can't say I blame you." His frown deepens as he continues exploring his ear, and as they stare in disbelief he tears it off of his head with a savage yank, blackish/greenish blood spewing forth, then waning to a subdued dribble. He smells the ear and then puts it in his mouth, chewing it like one would a piece of gum.

"Like I've already told you," he says, his words garbled by his chewing, "I have a plan for each and every one of you, one that requires you stay (for the time being) in your natural state. Now, there is something I must share with you, something you aren't going to like very much. Are you sitting down? No? Well here goes anyway: whether you like it or not Garbage Island is infecting you as you stand here, has been since the moment you came ashore."

"Infecting us?" Dr. Taylor says. "How?"

"Dude, you ass too many damn questions," Tyler interjects drunkenly, staggering back a step, then forward another.

"Why the hell aren't his hands bound?" Melissa says sharply. "What's going on Tyler? You one of them now?"

"No." He smiles crookedly. "I'm still one of me. I just got the fast track to an inside angle." He looks at the captain, tipping him a wink, and Captain Harvey sighs, annoyed at the interruption.

"Yes Tyler, about that…" He snaps his fingers and two minions come forth, taking him by the arms.

"Hey dude, what up? I thought we had a deal!"

"Unfortunately for you the good doctor was right: never make a deal with the Devil, he'll most surely break it and make you look like a fool."

Binding his hands, they rudely shove him into line with the others.

"Welcome back dickhead," Kenny growls.

"What about the job you said you had for me? The stud position?"

"Oh, I still need you for that, rest assured. I have no doubt that you are the most virile man of the bunch." He laughs, a low rumbling sound. "But I can't let you prance about like you own the place, can I? Makes me look stupid."

"Uncool man, uncool," Tyler says, a hitch in his voice. "We had a deal, dude."

"Consider it broken."

"You never answered my question," Dr. Taylor interrupts. "How are we being infected?"

"How do you think?" The captain grins, displaying several more missing teeth. "Certainly you don't believe yourself to be immune from the oily muck that surrounds the island? The second you went swimming it was all over for you."

Somehow that had never occurred to him. "But how is that possible if we didn't ingest any of it?"

"The bug bites, my dear friend, through the bug bites."

"Good Christ…" But is that really true, or is Harvey simply toying with them, hoping they'll comply if they think they don't stand a chance against it?

This place is a scientific anomaly on so many levels that anything could be possible. But how would he know that? How does Captain Harvey come by his information?

"If that's so, how long do we have until it takes effect?"

"I don't know," Captain Harvey shrugs. "No one has ever gone more than a few days without being converted in some other manner."

"Than you don't really know for sure…"

"My good doctor," the captain says most convivially, "I know *everything* about this place."

The two regard each other silently, one looking perplexed, the other grandly amused.

"So what is all this," Dr. Taylor asks at last, "and how have you come to be a part of it?"

"All questions will be answered in good time, like I've said but, for now, I have a feast prepared for you, this being, of course, our inaugural dinner together. Our first and last supper, if you will."

He claps his hands and the minions take hold of them, forcing them to walk further into the village, in the direction where Hallsly can be heard weeping and moaning.

A few of them struggle against their captors but their resistance is futile; they are too strong, these humanoids of Garbage Island, and there is no chance of escape. The passengers are weak with hunger, tired and dehydrated. Any fight left within them is a product of their fear, the last of their adrenaline amping their depleted systems.

They are brought through the center of town and, as they're forced march progresses, an increasing number of creatures emerge from their crude dwellings, watching with silent, impassive eyes.

"Jesus, look how many of them there are," Cole says to Dante, who pays him no mind. Right now Dante's only concern is Leeann, but a distance of more than six feet separates them. If one of these things tries to hurt her he is afraid he will have to simply stand by and watch, unable to help. This frightens him more than anything.

"Are they the people from the other ship?" Kenny asks Dr. Taylor, whose wrists have been unbound so as to assist the other because of his injured knee.

"Perhaps," he says, studying their faces for one he recognizes. "Others probably wound up here by accident and then found they couldn't leave."

"Quiet!" Captain Harvey commands, his voice strident and authorative. "I want silence as we pay tribute to the man who is gladly giving his life for us this night. A man who needs no introduction!"

The group pauses before the bits of wreckage from the previous research vessel that serves as the town hall, their shocked surprise at this use of resources cut short when their guards direct them toward an enormous platform that has been erected just for this occasion.

"Oh my God!" Leeann gasps, the true horror of their situation slamming home with the velocity of a freight train. Instantaneously she realizes they are here to stay; leaving is clearly not an option.

"Ladies and gentlemen I present to you a man whose humble servility goes unsurpassed in any state, of any nation! I give you Theodore Hallsly Jr., Governor of California!"

He wishes they would stop, would just let him die already. The pain is beyond anything he's ever withstood in his whole life, but that's not saying much. The worst pain he's ever endured (with the exception of the beatings and spankings and whippings administered by professionals)

was a sprained ankle he got when he totaled a Corvette driving shit-faced, crashing his candy apple red '69 Stingray into a highway guard rail and rolling it three times. He killed his passenger (a prostitute named Laquisha who was missing her front teeth because of a bad meth habit but as a result gave head like a demon) but he came out with only a few scrapes, bruises and the afore-mentioned sprained ankle. It took a lot of his daddy's money to cover that one up but in the end it weren't no thang but a chicken wing, as Laquisha would have eloquently put it, had she lived to tell the tale. Throw enough money at any problem and it goes away, guaranteed.

This extended agony is beyond excruciating, well beyond the limits of his dubious fortitude. He's finally stopped screaming simply because his throat is raw, blistered. The only sounds he can make anymore are muffled grunts, which are most undignified. God, he wishes he were dead, which is saying a lot for such a pompous jerk as he. Living the pampered life he's had the distinct pleasure of enjoying, he's never had a reason to crave his own demise. Thanks to Captain Harvey and his merry band of pranksters he now has a reason. A very good reason.

"What are you doing to him?" Melissa blanches. She doesn't like Hallsly any more than the rest of them (in fact probably dislikes him even more than they) but she certainly can't stand to see him treated this way; she wouldn't want to see *anyone* treated in this manner. She may have been a professional pain dealer in her old life (a life that seems so far away now, so long gone as to be almost the memory of a memory of a memory) but she would never go to these lengths to torture someone; she can't even imagine it.

"Go on, you're a smart girl," Captain Harvey says, chewing his ear noisily. "You make your-self an educated guess."

All eyes are glued to the contraption Governor Hallsly is strapped to, the torture device made especially for him. They are trying not to look at him directly or, more importantly, in his eyes, which are wide with pain and fear, imploring them for mercy. They are also trying to ignore the spatter of gore that coats him from the waist down.

Melissa takes in the rudimentary design; the large plastic tubes are crossed in the shape of an 'X', his wrists and ankles bound by the same material that is binding their wrists. It's obvious that being fastened to the apparatus isn't what's causing his pain, no, that would be due to the work of the captain's minions, who've peeled the skin from his legs like one would a banana, exposing the fat and muscle beneath. Lying on the platform in long strips before him are the pieces of flesh, moist and glistening under the muted haze of the orange colored lights.

"You're…you're skinning him alive?" she asks when at once Dr. Taylor gasps involuntarily, emitting a garbled, choking noise.

"Oh lord no…" he grimaces, looking away.

"What?" Kenny says, watching the doctor's face grow pale. "What is it?"

Everyone is looking at him, their expressions betraying their bafflement. The captain's face, however, illustrates how proud he is at this moment.

"He told us that we were invited to a feast," Dr. Taylor croaks, his head and neck twitching from an itch that is more imagined than real. "That," he says, nodding toward the governor, "is what's for dinner."

Captain Harvey spits out his ear and wipes his mouth with the back of one hand.

"Do you like the design? Came up with it myself."

Jake Anderson, who stands near the edge of the platform, utters an indignant moan.

"Oh all right," Harvey concedes. "He helped."

"Why on earth are you doing this?"

"I'll explain Dr. Taylor, and you will understand, even with your limited intelligence. I'm sure that all of you will understand. In fact, I'm going to go one further and tell you all a story after we eat, the story of how all this began, since you are so curious."

"You...you expect us to eat him?" Melissa says incredulously, and the others realize that the doctor wasn't merely speculating, his observation was right on the money.

"Surely you must be hungry. All of you must be starving."

It has been almost two days and none of them (except for Tyler) has had more than a little water and a few scraps of chocolate, but at the thought of dining on a human being (raw, no less), whatever appetite any of them has vanishes quickly.

"What is this, some kind of sick joke?"

"I do love the occasional prank Dr. Taylor, that I must confess but, no, I am doing this for practical reasons, in fact, let me show you." He spins around and waves to someone (*something*) beyond the glow of the lights. Two figures shamble forward and, as they step closer, the shadows slipping away, everyone catches their breath.

"I'm sure you remember these two, Tweedle Dee and Tweedle Dum?"

Steven and Perry stand before them, their faces slack, eyes dilated, arms hanging uselessly at their sides. Leeann winces', uttering a small moan. Seeing her fellow interns reminds her of Kim. What became of her? The last time she saw her was yesterday, shortly after they first arrived...

"I've been feeding these two a steady diet of Rancor birds over the last few hours. The birds I fed them were dead. Uncooked, but dead." He glances around at the group, pointing at the two ex-interns as if they are an item up for auction. "What is happening to them is they are becoming one of us, one of *me* if you will."

So it's true. If you eat the creatures you become like them. But what is he talking about? Of course they'd be dead...

"Why did you point out that the creatures were dead? As humans we're not exactly in the habit of eating food that's alive."

"That's the beauty of the whole scheme! Thank you for asking doctor. The bacterium infecting this lovely wonderland I call home is a tenacious beast, to say the very least. It works fast. It takes over immediately, the moment any creature dies, if it hasn't already, of course. Don't ask me how, the details escape me, but that's what it does. Therefore, eating anything dead will cause," he gestures to Perry and Steven, "this."

Dr. Taylor is silent, considering. The captain's knowledge of science is surely dubious at best, yet this place's existence is without a doubt an incongruity of evolution as they know it. But still, the theory he is postulating is ridiculous...

Captain Harvey grins sadistically. "Pretty wild, huh?"

"So," Dr. Taylor says, humoring him, "if we want to stay as we are, at least for the time being, given the fact that we've been infected by the *water*, we have to eat something that is...alive?"

"Precisely! My but you are a sharp one!"

"But he was in the water too. If we're slowly being infected than so is he."

"Yes, but he isn't infected *right now*."

"How do we know that for sure?"

"Look at him," Captain Harvey points. "See him wriggle and cry? After the bacteria gets a hold of you that is no longer a part of the program."

"This doesn't make any sense," Dr. Taylor argues, tired of playing games. "You're insulting my intelligence. The Rancor birds are already infected with the bacteria so alive, dead, it doesn't matter how you serve them the results will be the same."

"I'm not serving you Rancor birds, I'm serving you *him*."

It appears there is no reasoning with the captain and his flawed logic yet Dr. Taylor simply can't help himself. As a man of science he's unable to accept such a wonky, cock-eyed theory of bacterial transmission.

"So what you are saying is that since there isn't anything on this heap that isn't already infected we have to eat the governor? That's a little hard to swallow."

"That's what she said!" Harvey cries, slapping his knee. "Man, I kill myself, I tell ya...but, seriously, things aren't what they seem here. What you knew in the old world is nothing like what we know here, forward progress and all that...but I'm getting ahead of myself. I told you I had a story for you and I intend to tell it. But first," he waves a hand and three humanoids step forward, carrying tools scavenged from the ship. One holds a saw, another a large butcher knife, the third a sledgehammer. "These gentlemen will carve the bird, so to speak."

A clamor arises amongst the group, an act of insubordination that is eventually quelled by the guards. Captain Harvey watches silently as the survivors are beaten into submission, smiling. He casts a quick glance at the governor before returning his attention to the group, addressing them in a strong, clear voice.

"Do any of you really care what happens to this man? Do you really? I chose him because of all of you he is the most vain, the most self-centered. He is impossible to love, much less *like*, so I thought it fitting that he be my candidate. I figured he would serve you much better, so to speak, in this manner than he ever would have in the 'real' world." He looks around, gauging their reaction. "Am I wrong?"

No one answers, they don't need to. It is obvious that a man such as Governor Hallsly is nothing but a human parasite, a worthless, posturing son of a bitch. But, still...

"I ask you," he repeats, "am I wrong?"

The minions creep closer, clutching their carving tools. Hallsly's eyes beseech the passengers for pity yet somehow, amazingly, continue to radiate his hatred, his vanity, his outright contempt for his fellow man.

"Can't you see?" Captain Harvey wipes thick, foamy drool from his lips that drips off the back of his hand. "His eyes betray the belief that he's better than you, that you should help him because that is what you are *supposed* to do, what people of your class were meant to do."

Aghast, they simply stare, the shock and outright atrociousness of the situation rendering them speechless.

"Gentlemen," Captain Harvey waves to his 'butchers', "carve us up some governor."

"Wait!" Dr. Taylor says, looking from the governor to the captain to the creatures brandishing their weapons. "Let's forget about you're fucked up explanation regarding the bacteria for a moment and concentrate on the tangible facts. Technically, once you chop off one of his body parts, you cut off the blood supply hence killing the limb. The flesh will be dead."

"But *he* isn't dead," the captain says. "That's all that matters."

"That's bullshit."

"As I just said, things aren't quite what they seem here my good doctor." He turns toward his minions. "Carve him up!"

They step up onto the platform, surrounding him. The weapons gleam dully beneath the lights.

"No!" Hallsly screams hoarsely. "No no no!"

The creature holding the saw places it against the governor's thigh, just below his groin, and sinks the blade into his skin.

"Aaaahhh!"

He works the saw with mechanical determination and blood spurts from the wound. Hallsly jerks and thrashes wildly but to no effect; despite his efforts these things have a job to do and, moving target or not, they will get what they're after. The second minion joins in, sinking the butcher knife into the soft flesh and cutting deeply.

"The trick to it," Captain Harvey explains, as if he is the host of his very own exotic cuisine program, "is that we have to make sure he doesn't die right away. It's the only way to keep the bacterium at bay. You have to eat the tissue quickly, while it is still fresh."

Dr. Taylor watches, transfixed, his rational, scientific mind in a state of upheaval. Everything the man says is a contradiction to the laws of science; anyone with half a brain would know that. Yet he has witnessed things on this heap that he cannot explain, abnormalities that wouldn't exist in the outside world. Right, wrong-they clearly don't matter here. The undisputable facts he learned in his many years at university and through his extensive research are turned upside down, made to seem insignificant in the shadow of all this overblown twaddle. So, that said, barring the impossibilities of the captain's half-assed interpretation regarding the gestation of bacterial organisms, he is certain he will do no such thing; there is no reason that he, a sane man, will resort to cannibalism, no reason at all.

Sure there's a reason, his feverish mind sings out, the voice like that of the captain's: dark, ominous, overriding. *You are starving and this is meat. If you want to keep being who you are a little while longer than you'll have some. Certainly the governor won't mind.*

But who's to say he will go on being himself? Contaminated, uncontaminated, all of this is making his head hurt. And he's hungry, so goddamned hungry...

Tyler grins broadly, his eyes fastidiously following the butchers every movement. Even though he's been played like a chump and is now back in the position he was before (worse, actually, because now everyone *really* hates him) he doesn't care. They can go fuck themselves. Involuntarily imitating the captain, he licks his lips hungrily. The chips and jerky did little to alleviate his hunger and the beer has made him ravenous. He doesn't know about anyone else but he's ready for a little Hallsly tartar...

Jesus, what kind of life have I lived that it all comes down to this? Dante wonders, looking over at Leeann for strength. She has her eyes closed, her head bowed and he sees that tears are coursing down her cheeks. The poor, poor girl...

And then, interrupting these tender thoughts, his stomach issues a growl so fierce it's painful. Man he's hungry, simply starving. He wants to resist, more than anything, but the thought of eating is intoxicating, making his head swim.

The minion with the knife finally strikes bone, so he steps aside so his partner with the sledgehammer can take over. Raising it high above his head, he strikes Hallsly's leg once, twice, and the splintering sound of breaking bone causes several of the survivors to cry out in harmony with the governor. He sets it down, takes the leg in both hands and with a brutal tug wrenches it free. Tendons and veins tear and burst, blood droplets splattering his emotionless face.

"Goddamn!" Hallsly howls, his head rolling back and forth, his body shuddering. "Jesus Christ in fucking Heaven you mother fucking sons a bitches! Oh God oh God oh God oh God..."

Another minion rushes forward, carrying something that seems so out of place in this setting that at first glance Dr. Taylor can't make the connection. It's an ordinary item, something found in just about every home, except maybe a single man's. The creature takes hold of the governor's thigh (stub) and presses it hard against the shredded flesh.

"AAAAAAAHHHHHHH!"

It's an iron, a clothes iron, Dr. Taylor realizes, although it isn't exactly rocket science. *If they don't cauterize the wound he'll bleed out and die before we can eat him.*

"Oh yes," Captain Harvey purrs. "Music to my ears...well, ear anyway." He looks about him, recognizing that something (or someone) is missing. "Where is my Queen?" he demands. "Bring me my Queen!"

Two villagers scurry off toward the 'town hall', their departure vaguely reminiscent of the Wicked Witch of the East's flying monkey's, minus any flying, of course.

"We can't have a feast without my Queen by my side." He turns to gaze longingly at Melissa, who is watching the proceedings unblinkingly, her face a mask of consternation. She catches him staring and glares viciously before averting her eyes.

The two humanoid villagers return quickly with someone between them, each holding an arm. They approach the captain and place her before him.

"Ah, my chosen one. Come here, take my hand."

Kim steps blindly forward, holding out her hand. Even draped in darkness she is horrifying, her eye sockets deep black holes, her vermilion mouth sitting lopsidedly on her severely lacerated face.

"Holy shit," Kenny whispers.

Her clothing is in tatters, her small breasts protruding from the front of her ripped shirt, one of her nipples peeled back and hanging by a thin thread of flesh. The captain turns her to face the others, his arm around her shoulders.

"Behold my Queen!" he cries, his tone accentuating the dreadfulness of their situation, bringing everything into sharp, living, breathing color, establishing clarity in the group that the witnessing of Hallsly's butchering has muddied. Achingly lucid, they look upon the ravaged girl, their expressions frozen with astonishment.

"Bow to her!"

The villagers drop quickly to their knees while the survivors continue to gawp in fixated repugnance.

"I said get on your knees!" The captain snaps his fingers and their guards get up and rush forward, shoving the passengers roughly to the ground. Heads bowed, accepting that all hope is gone, they crouch subserviently in the diffuse light, recognizing that free will is long a thing of the past, their lives now in the hands of a maniac whose intentions are far worse than any of them ever would have suspected.

This just keeps getting worse. Dante's head is cluttered with conflicting emotions. She looks truly horrid, vile even, but her condition almost breaks his heart. She is a devastated ruin of her former self. *If there is a Hell, surely this is it.*

"Are you hungry my dear?"

Kim makes a groaning, snuffling sound, her mouth flapping wildly, trying to make words without the luxury of a tongue.

"I thought so." He fixes his eyes on the kneeling survivors. "On your feet! It's chow time!"

TWENTY-FOUR

"We're not going to eat him." Dr. Taylor tries to sound confident but his face gives him away; worry lines crinkle his brow and anxiety shows in his eyes. "You can't make us."

"Oh but I can. Surely you don't want a demonstration."

Kim slithers up to him, hands outstretched before her. She continues to make those horrible, gurgling noises deep in her throat, her mouth working furiously as the nub of her blackened tongue wriggles inside. She takes his face into her gnarled hands, her nails digging into his skin, and he flinches, trying to twist away but her grip (like that of all the humanoids) is too physically powerful, and she easily restrains him. She leans in closer, and Dr. Taylor can see worms wriggling in her empty eye sockets, disgustingly plump little suckers that ooze down her face like demented tears. Pressing her lips together (pursed almost sensuously) she kisses him, the stench of her breath bringing tears to his eyes. He chokes frantically on bile that rises swiftly, acrid and foul and, unable to control himself, he vomits. She slurps at it greedily, rolling her head back and forth, smearing it all over his face and hers.

Gasping, sickened, the others turn away. With the lapse in conversation the sounds of Hallsly's sobbing and the intermittent yowling of some far away beast seem overly loud, punctuated by the groans the doctor is making as he struggles ineffectually against the despoiled girl.

"That's right." Captain Harvey rubs his crotch. "Slip him some tongue...well, you know what I mean." He beams merrily at the doctor. "It's okay if you fuck my girl, but you're going to need all your strength to take on *this* bitch, let me tell ya. Care for a snack?"

One of his minion's brings him Hallsly's leg and, taking it, he offers it to Dr. Taylor. "Go ahead, you can have the first bite if you'd like."

Kim releases him and slinks away, barf dribbling from her face. She smacks her lips, savoring the tasty treat, returning to the captain's side.

"I'll...I'll pass..." Dr. Taylor gags, trying to wipe his mouth on his shoulder.

"Well, don't mind if I do," Captain Harvey says, appraising the governor's leg a moment before sinking his remaining teeth into it and tearing out a large, bloody hunk. He chews noisily, spittle and pieces of flesh spraying from his mouth. "Ah, Hallsly, the other white meat! Whose next?" He turns to his minions. "We need some plates over here."

Two of them lurch off and return a few minutes later with flattened pieces of plastic that might have once been two-liter size water bottles. The survivors watch dumbly, mouths agape.

"Keep cutting!" he instructs his butchers, who begin work on the other leg.

"We're not going to eat him," Dr. Taylor says again, unable to look the captain in the eyes, his voice wavering.

"Yes you will," Captain Harvey replies. "I'll show you."

He snaps his fingers (the last time he'll ever perform this gesture as his middle finger detaches in the process, becoming airborne and disappearing amongst the detritus) and two of the humanoids take Leeann by the arms, thrusting her forward. Captain Harvey towers over her, holding Hallsly's leg inches from her clamped mouth.

"Come on, have some. It's delicious!"

"You leave her alone!" Dante warns, starting forward, but two minions seize him and hold him in place. "She isn't going to eat that!"

"No, that's where you're wrong." His voice is somber but his eyes glitter madly. "She will be the one to get this party started."

One of the minions seizes her chin, forcing her mouth open. She squirms, whining pitifully as he forces a piece of meat between her lips. The minion then closes her mouth, manually moving her jaws up and down.

"That's right, chew on it honey. You got it."

The expression on Leeann's face is one of utter abhorrence. She struggles, trying to spit it out, but it lodges in the back of her throat and she starts coughing, a nasty, wretched hack.

"Leave her alone!"

Captain Harvey scowls, ignoring Dante. Grasping Leeann's throat, he gently massages it with his rough, scarred fingers. "Come on now, relax. Just let it slide down."

Leeann is turning a dark purple color, her eyes wide, bulging from their sockets, and Dante instantly realizes what is happening but is powerless to intervene. The chunk of meat is blocking her airway, asphyxiating her. Foamy drool runs from the corners of her mouth, and she shakes her head violently from side to side.

"Stop!" Dante is near tears, his voice nothing short of pleading. "She's going to choke to death!" He takes in a sharp, wheezing breath. "Give me some, I'll eat it!"

Captain Harvey turns toward him, the leer on his face growing. "So we have a volunteer?"

"Yes, anything if you just leave her alone!"

"Alright, for the moment she can go hungry." He lets her go and, looking absurdly like a chicken (though no one laughs), she bobs her head back and forth as she urgently works her throat and jaws to extricate the offending substance. After a brief struggle she's able to dislodge it and spit it on the ground. She takes huge, tearing breaths, coughing pathetically, but to Dante's relief the crisis is over, if only for the moment. The captain spins on his heel and faces him. He holds up the leg. "Go on then," he urges. "Take a bite."

Dante closes his eyes and tries to imagine that it is what football fans would lovingly call a 'cannibal sandwich', even though the name could use a little revising. *Rare hamburger meat, that's all. It's rare hamburger meat.* But his brain is clamoring like an errant fire bell, shrieking out a warning that this isn't hamburger but a chunk of the man who once governed the state of California. A piece of human meat…raw. He can smell the sharp, coppery tang of blood, can hear the owner of this offering whispering gravelly prayers that fall on deaf ears. His stomach churns miserably and he can taste acid in the back of his throat, but he knows that if he refuses the captain will continue torturing poor Leeann, and he can't let that happen. He's already let her down in so many ways; firstly by stowing away aboard the ship, secondly by getting them ridiculously lost during their fist day on the heap and, thirdly, by leading them to the ship when it was clearly a trap. If there is anything, *anything* he can do for her it is this, to make her tormentor stop. He leans forward and tentatively sinks his teeth into the severed leg, shuddering. Taking a small bite (suppressing the urge to retch) he masticates it quickly and swallows. And then something unexpected occurs: the second the meat hits his stomach a rush of pleasure detonates within him, coupled by an uncontrollable hunger.

"Good Christ…" he mutters, his salivary glands taking over despite the horrendous nature of the entrée. He knows beyond a doubt this is disgusting, absolutely appalling, but he simply can't help it. The scent of sizzling flesh from Governor Hallsly's cauterized stumps is making him feverish. He takes another bite, then another, chewing and swallowing rapidly. It is so good to be eating that he involuntarily sobs. He leans in again and again, the saltiness of his tears mingling with the congealed blood that stains his face and beard.

The others watch with unbelieving eyes, astonished at his brazen animalism. They'd always figured Dante to be more beast than man, the 'missing link' if you will, and this surely proves it. No one entirely human would do something like that, would they? Because, no matter how hungry they are they won't give in, as what he's doing is horrible, utterly repulsive. No way in hell are they going to shrug off thousands of years of genetic conditioning to regress to that of a common brute, absolutely no fucking way…and then Leeann speaks in a soft voice, barely above a whisper:

"It…it didn't taste that bad…" she says, a blush riding high on her cheeks, her head lowered in shame. "It really didn't taste all that bad…"

The others regard her curiously, their stomach's betraying them. Kenny's growls loudly, a sound as jarring as approaching thunder. He glances around at the group, shakes his head and says:

"Goddamnit I'll take some."

The captain smiles.

"Unbind his hands and give this man a plate."

One of the minions steps forward and releases him. Taking the proffered piece of flattened plastic, Kenny holds it up before him. The captain tears off a large chunk and slaps it down, the meat making a wet, plopping sound, like a cadaver hitting pavement, but Kenny doesn't care. He rips into it with his fingers, stuffing the meat into his mouth greedily, chewing loudly.

"She's right," he says between bites. "It ain't that bad." He crams more into his mouth, wolfing it down hungrily.

"Anyone who wants to partake of this feast," Captain Harvey announces, "speak now or forever hold your peace!"

Gradually several others nod, murmuring softly to themselves. Hands are at once unbound and 'plates' are handed out.

"Enjoy!"

The meal lasts all of about fifteen minutes, give or take. The group chows through Governor Hallsly's first leg and then moves on to the second. Eventually his movements on the platform cease, his cries abating.

"He's dead," the captain says. "The meat isn't safe anymore."

"If we're already infected than why does any of this matter?" Dr. Taylor asks, having to admit (if only to himself) that he feels worlds better now that he has something in his stomach. The gnawing desperation of hunger is a maddening one, leaving one to think and act in ways you otherwise wouldn't. His mind is clearer now, his thoughts resuming their orderly fashion instead of bellowing in his head like a symphony of schizophrenic voices. He feels an underlying shame at what he's done, yet he expected that, didn't he? After all, it isn't every day you consume someone you've recently had a conversation with. But what does it matter? According to the captain they're all as good as dead anyway.

"It is time that I told you the tale of the Origin of the Garbage Island Species," Captain Harvey decides, ignoring the doctor's question. "Now that you've eaten I'm sure you'll find it a lot easier to concentrate on what I'm saying. It really is quite fascinating."

"You know how all of this began?"

"Not all of it, not from its inception Dr. Taylor. But what I do know is how we came to be, and that really is the best part." Tossing his plate down, he walks slowly before them, looking into each face as he passes. "Please," he says, "take a seat and I will regale you with the story of our grand creation. Maybe then you will understand, will come to appreciate the roles you'll all be playing in the very near future."

'Once upon a time I was a highly decorated Naval Captain; a brave man if ever there was one. Before all of the accolades I did five tours of duty in Vietnam, my first in 1969 when I was only seventeen years old. During my first tour I received the Medal of Honor for my combat efforts, and in my third the Legion of Merit for going above and beyond the call of duty, all for my country and fellow man. In my fifth and final tour I received the Purple Heart when I was critically wounded saving twenty sailors during a three-day siege that left 123 Americans dead. The Vietcong were obstinate little peckerwoods, fought tooth and nail for every square inch of that God-forsaken country. Can't help but admire that.

After Vietnam I stayed on as a career Naval man, doing my part for Democracy by taking part in other skirmishes conducted by the US of A. I was very good at what I did; tough, skilled, ruthless. . .ultimately unstoppable. I was shot seven times, stabbed four times, took shrapnel from IUD's, strangled with piano wire-you name it. It seemed I was very nearly immortal, and as the years passed I collected enough medals to decorate the breast of my uniform from top to bottom. As I mentioned I rose through the ranks until I became a Captain, ordering other men to rush to their imminent deaths instead of tearing headlong into such disaster myself. To say the very least my job became boring, but I held on so I could receive my pension when it came time for my retirement, which I did at the age of fifty-five. At that point I wasn't sure what I was going to do, thought maybe I would take it easy for a while. Didn't last long though, boredom was an intolerable bitch. Sitting around my house with the wife didn't suit me and, after she died (which wasn't long after I retired; I must have drove her to an early grave with my unrepentant surliness), I sold the house and bought me a sloop with the intention of sailing around the world. I made some legendary trips, I'll tell you, had some experiences that would make land lubbers like you piss your pants and cry for your mommy's, but by the age of sixty-four I'd never successfully circumnavigated the globe.

So I decided to give it one more shot, considering it could possibly be my last solo voyage, what with arthritis setting in, and set sail from San Francisco, intending to re-supply in Hawaii, and then the Marshall Islands, eventually stopping over in the Philippines. But the first leg of the trip was so harrowing I nearly lost my life in a storm that overturned my boat, left me hanging onto the rudder for dear life until I was rescued by a fishing boat off the coast of the Solomon Islands. How I strayed so far off course is beyond me; all I can recall of those tortured days is fragments, bits and pieces of memories that seemed like someone else's, not mine.

I stayed there for three weeks, mending the ship and myself, before deciding to move along, to continue my journey. Was I crazy? Probably, but what else did I have to do with my time? It was either that or rot away in front of a television, cheering for game show contestants who by all rights should be shot in the head rather than awarded prizes, or withering away on a pier on the San Francisco bay, casting my line for brown sharks and catching jellyfish instead. Fuck all that hooey! I was pressing on!

I made it to the Philippine islands without a hitch, nothing but clear skies and tranquil water, and stayed abroad for two weeks drinking myself silly and fooling around with the whores. You may not know it to look at me, but I like a nice piece of pussy every now and then. Well, I got my fill. If I'd spent any more time I probably would have wound up with herpes and cirrhosis of the liver; as it was I'd just about outstayed my welcome. It was time to decide what my next move was. Did I continue westward or did I go home?

I gave it some thought, considering my options, and realized that such an endeavor would most likely kill me. Did I care, you may ask, if I died on the open sea? No, surely not, as that would be a fitting death for a man such as myself, but I'd left my financial matters unsettled and, as I failed to mention, I sired two children, a son and a daughter. These two children were full-grown, of course, living lives I could honestly be proud of and doing quite well for themselves, but I'd invested some money in the early 2000's that had grown into quite a nest egg and I wanted to make sure that upon my demise they were entitled to all of it. If I were to expire on this voyage it would be unavailable to them, scooped up by the unscrupulous hands of the government because I'd made no formal will. No, I had to go home and sort these things out, at which time I could while away the rest of my days sailing the San Francisco Bay and daydreaming about my past travails.

I set sail on a warm, cloudless day, spirits high for another adventure, but little did I know that fate had other plans for me, that things are never really quite what they seem no matter what your intentions are.

Not wanting to carry too much weight, I took only enough supplies to last me about two weeks, intending to make a stop along the way at North Marcus Island. As it would turn out the wind was blowing in from out of the south, so if I wanted to sail uninterrupted I had to take what I could get and follow her. Didn't have an outboard motor on that sloop; never saw the need for one. Had to go wherever the wind took me. I also deliberately failed to equip the ship with Doppler equipment, and not once did I check radio transmissions for weather updates. The sailor's of centuries past didn't have luxuries as such, so why should I? It made the adventure all the more interesting, not knowing what to expect from day to day. Also, I employed a system known as 'celestial navigating', an antiquated manner of navigation but one that suited my needs just fine. None of those fancy navigational gizmo's for me, thank you very much! Well, I missed Marcus Island (passing well to the north) but I was doing just fine, my supplies holding steady. I figured I could probably make it to Hawaii and restock there.

Things were going smoothly for the most part, good weather, calm seas, then in the second week a storm hit in the middle of the night, just like the one we sailed through during our journey here. Oh, and by the way, I knew that storm (our storm) was coming, but you probably figured that out by now, intuitive devils that you are.

So the storm hit, but it didn't scare me, no, even though it should have, seeing what I'd just been through, but that is my nature, reckless and headstrong in the face of danger. Only this time my boat hit something and I was taking in water fast, was pretty sure I was going to sink and wind up in Davey Jones's locker, if you catch my drift. I sent out an SOS, which I felt was pretty much useless given my estimated coordinates, and shortly thereafter lost my footing when the sloop pitched steeply to one side and I conked my head, knocking me out cold while I drifted off course in the black of night. When I awoke just after sunup I was surprised to find I was alive and the ship was still intact, upright even. I was lodged on something, something solid the boat had run aground on.

Well, turns out I was here. The Rancor birds made my first introduction to Garbage Island, and I would be lying if I told you I didn't nearly crap my pants seeing those foul little bastards skittering through the air like Hell's sentinels. Scared me enough that I shot at them with my .45 while working to repair my boat. Took almost a whole clip to take just one of those suckers down; wasn't much left but a pile of feathers and scales. Kept the others at bay though, and I considered myself lucky. At the time I didn't know how long I was going to be stuck here, didn't know what this place had in store for me. The radio was busted, you see, and I couldn't call for help. And I'm old fashioned, never carried a cell phone, most likely never will, heh-heh. Probably wouldn't have been able to get a signal out here anyway. As you've probably gathered, walking the tightrope without a net is the only way I chose to live, even if it meant I was going to die.

Anyway, the ship was damaged pretty badly and I wasn't going anyplace soon. Eventually I ran out of food and, well, I had to eat something so I started eating the Rancor birds. Pretty tasty I might add, just like chicken. Okay, I'm lying. They're nothing like chicken.

I won't kid you; my first explorations of Garbage Island appalled me. I couldn't believe that something of this magnitude existed, that humankind's waste had become a problem of this significance. I've never been one of those Mother Earth types, but when recycling became the thing to do I did my part. Didn't see any reason in trashing the earth just because I was too lazy to separate my paper, glass and cans from the rest of the trash. So this floating heap of garbage had me sick to my stomach, I'll tell you, but after a steady diet of Rancor bird's things began to change. I began to see things, well, differently you might say. At first I thought I was losing my mind, going around the bend you know, until I realized I was undergoing physiological changes as well. After a couple of meals my body was suddenly more capable than it had been even when I was a young man. I was stronger, more virile. My movements became somewhat stiff, forced, like sand had been poured into my joints, but the strength I felt was twice my old self's, and eventually the stiffness passed. Almost like how rigor mortis sets in and then goes away after a while.

The best part was my newfound vision; Garbage Island became a place of beauty to me and I wandered its vast landscape in awe, discovering all of the wonderful creatures that called this place home. Did you know there are snails here larger than elephants? With brightly colored shells straight out of a Technicolor dream? Well, you will, in time you will.

I became a part of this place and it became a part of me. We were one... happy. But I could tell she wasn't satisfied; she wanted more people to share her paradise. She needed me to become a one man recruiting team, and so it was that I undertook the mission. With my rejuvenated mind I was able to fix my radio, and I sent out phony SOS signals in hopes of snagging any sea faring vessels in the vicinity. Well, luck was with me, and I quickly lured a Japanese garbage barge in, taking all hands.

Now she (the bacterium) was very specific about how I had to go about creating the others, if I wanted to be King. I couldn't allow the new recruits to have the capacities I have, otherwise who would be in charge? In a delirium filled dream she showed me, describing to me the process in which I would generate my army of loyal compatriots, those who would follow my every order, would seek nothing in return for serving me, serving Garbage Island.

As you've seen, the transformation takes place through the eating of the flesh, but in order for me to produce the first batch I had to do it myself, to literally carve them out of stone. Give them a little bit of what was inside of me personally, but not too personally, if you know what I mean. I later found out that a direct transfer would act in forming equals, and one thing I did not desire was someone identical to me.

If I am going too fast for you I apologize, but there is so much we have to do, so much you have to see that I simply can't do more than give you the condensed version of a tale that could fill pages and pages. Suffice it to say I am hitting on all the major points, trust me.

So, with my workforce aiding me, we set out to find more human resources to augment our ever-growing numbers. We then began the construction of this village, as well as safety measures to insure prying eyes such as satellite cameras wouldn't detect us. And as we progressed we became increasingly adept at luring in the garbage dumping vessels. Of course there was the occasional providential finding of small crafts that had gotten lost or were driven here by foul weather...we welcomed them all with open arms.

As these pilgrims came to us and our colony expanded I eventually found I could simply feed the newcomers Rancor bird meat and the outcome would be just the same as if I was the one who'd converted them personally. Of course, I now know that it doesn't matter how anyone is altered, as I am the undisputed King of Garbage Island and there is no changing that, unless I should choose to create a successor, but that's privileged information-none of your never mind. Anyhow...there are other conversion methods as well, techniques I have no hand in, such as the muck surrounding the island, but that's just the beginning. There is a particular genus of fly that's bite injects you with the bacteria, while other insects use you, the host, as an incubation chamber. That's something to see! You can also get it by allowing mold to grow on open wounds, and like I told you it's fast. I think that may be the quickest way, but feeding the newcomers is the easiest, after they get hungry enough. I suppose it is also the most humane. I may seem like a monster to you but I assure you I am a very benevolent ruler. I don't endeavor to make you suffer any more than I or Garbage Island sees fit. We need you, and we welcome your servitude.

But our greatest find was the research vessel that came here just over a month ago. What a Godsend! Not only for the laborers but the materials. As you can see we used pieces of the ship's hull to construct our town hall. It was with that generous gift that Garbage Island spoke to me again, told me what I needed to do in order for us to expand, to take this to a whole new level. For, you see, this is just the start, the very tip of the iceberg. But everything has to begin somewhere, right? Rome wasn't built in a day and all that happy crap. I realized we needed to take this worldwide if we were going to make a difference.

Knowing they would send another ship to search for the one gone missing, I journeyed back to the states and infiltrated the Scripts Oceanic Research Facility. With my excellent military record I figured it wouldn't be too difficult to get a job captaining one of their ships, and it wasn't. You'd be surprised how unpopular the position was! I soon found myself in charge of overseeing this operation. Now there was no way anyone could muck up our plan, and this ship we could use for the next phase: that of bringing the bacterium to the rest of the world, starting with the United States. Expansion is the key, friends! Expansion is the key.

Now, it wasn't only the ship I wanted, as we could have used any of the various trash dumping vessels for such a purpose, it was also the need for assistance from one of science's top minds. Surely if they'd sent the very best and brightest on the first trip, the second would yield someone superior, someone without a doubt more intelligent than all of them combined. At least, that's what I was hoping. Enter one Dr. Corey Taylor. I risked it all for this, and am happy to be rewarded so handsomely. Why, you ask yourself, is Dr. Taylor's role so important? Didn't I already have enough inspired minds? In a word: no. The scientists from the first ship simply did not work out; because of their stubbornness I eventually had the majority of them converted (those I chose not to banish entirely from the island), and in that capacity they were no longer of any use to me. With the exception of Dr. Connelly, that is, who has been instrumental in helping with our breeding program. Some of you will be meeting him very soon.

Oh, Doctor Taylor, don't look at me like that. You know I have your best interests in mind. Okay, you got me... I don't. But you are here, and with your help we can bring this amazing discovery to the rest of the world, this brilliant plan to fruition! And, yes, you will help me, whether you like it or not.

And so here we are, you and I and my minions, soon to be one big happy family, at least, those of you I choose to keep involved. Some of you I have other plans for, but rest assured that your sacrifice is necessary and it will not go unnoticed or unappreciated.

Tomorrow we begin, ushering in a new era. I am proud, excited, nothing short of abso-fucking-lutely tickled pink. And I know that all of you will be as well, once we get everything underway. Whatever your position should be, you are all contributing to history, the history we shall all be creating very soon...

Story time is over. You shall all be taken to your quarters. Tomorrow is a big day, the biggest day we've seen so far, with the exception of my investiture of course. For tomorrow heralds a new epoch for Garbage Island, and humanity itself. This planet has been dying for some time because of the waste and sloth brought upon by the human race. Why not skip to the chase? Who needs plants and trees and clean water and soil when we can fill it with humanity's greatest gift: trash. And why not? That is one thing we are so good at...creating waste. We might as well make it our full time occupation, if it isn't already, mind you.

So sleep, rest and dream. Dream of a new tomorrow, one that is bountiful with the idea of a new world, one that will never need to be worried about again. One that can't be destroyed but rebuilt with the abundant materials we already have at hand, all of those items we've so thoughtlessly thrown away.

Surrender to me my children, and you will find solace in the fact that you are taking part in a wonderful venture, one that will determine the course of your destiny, as well as the rest of the world's. What could be better than that, more important? If you find that the answer on the tip of your tongue is nothing, than you are right. Nothing is more important than that.

TWENTY-FIVE

"That motherfucker's crazy as a shithouse rat," Kenny mutters as Dr. Taylor helps him along. There is a guard in front of them and one a few steps behind, escorting them to their cages. They stumble through the muted light, entering an area of the village as of yet unexplored by the two weary men. "Where the hell we goin'?"

"Keep...walking."

"They moved the cages," Dr. Taylor says. "Probably didn't want us all grouped together, we might plot amongst ourselves." Licking his lips, he can still taste the salty tang of the governor's flesh, and he tries to push the thought of what he did (what they all did) out of his mind. He knows the sustenance helped, but that doesn't make it any better. "And he's not so much crazy as he is infected," he adds, grunting with exertion as he helps steer the other along. "He has no control over what he does, none of them do. We shouldn't take their actions personally."

"Are ya sayin' he ain't to blame?"

"As wrong as it seems, yes. None of them are doing this on purpose, it's the bacterium controlling them."

"Can a bacteria really do that?"

"Apparently." He looks at the other, considering. "If it is a bacteria. For all I know it might be a virus. But one thing's for sure: he ain't right."

They reach their cages and Dr. Taylor eases Kenny down. Their guards open the door and Kenny obliges them by crawling in.

"So this is it," he says after the doctor is situated in his own cage and the minions fade into the dark. "Our last night as ourself's."

"Maybe, maybe not," Dr. Taylor replies, pushing against the door with both hands. It doesn't budge. "We might have a few more days, depending on what 'jobs' the captain has in mind for us, or how long it takes for the infection from the water to take effect, if what he told us is true. His science regarding the bacteria is screwy to say the very least."

"Sound like he gots somethin' extra special planned for you, that somehow yer gonna be the one to put this whole thing over the top."

"That's what he said, but I'm not so sure about that."

"Whadaya mean?"

"Something about his story didn't add up," Dr. Taylor says, scratching his chin thoughtfully. "I think he was lying. I don't know what the real deal is, but risking his ass like that for one scientist? Nah, I'm not buying it."

"Are ya sayin' ya ain't all that and bag a chips?"

"No one man is, unless he kidnapped Stephen Hawking."

"Who?"

"Never mind. All I'm saying is that I think he had a different motive for visiting the states and, whatever it was, it didn't go as he planned."

"Like what?"

"I don't know, and it might not be important. Right now we have to figure out a way to save ourselves."

Kenny shifts in his cage, trying to get comfortable, but the pain in his knee is a constant reminder that it isn't going to happen. He tries one side, then the other.

"Whadaya think about his plan, ya know, to take over the world?" he says eventually, giving up on the idea of 'comfort' and settling for whatever he can get. "Sounds pretty goddamn egomaniacal."

"Well, I'm not surprised, if that's what you mean."

"Ya don't think he'll succeed, do ya?"

"Not if we stop him."

"Stop him? How the hell we gonna do that?"

Good question. Dr. Taylor lies on his back, the hard plastic bottom of the cage fantastically uncomfortable, but his energy is spent. He figures he could probably sleep on a bed of nails right now.

"I don't know," he answers, closing his eyes. "Get some sleep. Sounds like tomorrow is going to be a big day."

"Kinda hard to sleep with the pain in my knee," Kenny replies. "But I spose I'll give it a shot."

"That's the spirit."

And, the creatures of the heap crooning a funhouse lullaby, they both drift off into an agitated slumber.

"You're a piece of shit, you know that? Of all the things you could do you go and sell everyone out. Nice work. Real classy."

"Whatever, bitch," Tyler retorts, wondering why they had to put him in a cage next to Melissa. He's probably going to hear about it all night, about how he didn't try to rescue her, about how he was only looking out for himself, how he sent everybody up the river-the works.

"'Whatever bitch?' Is that the best you got? You've got to be kidding me!"

"Look, they drove me to it, okay? Everyone was like 'Tyler you're a dumb ass this and Tyler you're a dumb ass that'. I figured fuck 'em. Let 'em rot." There's a lot more to it than that, like how that arrogant doctor took over without anyone asking him to, or that nigger cocksucker pushing him around, but Melissa doesn't need to know all the details; his belly is full and he's tired. Man, but Hallsly made a mighty fine meal. At least that asshole was good for something.

"You sold them out because you couldn't take a couple of insults?"

"I did what I did for my own reasons. I don't need a lecture from you about it."

"Yeah, well plan on it."

"Duly noted."

Melissa continues to stew over what he said as Tyler lies down and closes his eyes. Thanks to the miracle of alcohol he supposes he'll sleep like a baby, unless Melissa keeps nagging him, trying to piss him off. He could tell her to shut her pie hole or he'll fill her corn hole but that would probably only serve to anger her further. Besides, he doesn't want to talk anymore because he's starting to get a headache.

For her part she isn't exactly shocked by his behavior, but it is disappointing to say the least. Although they'd argued at the cove she hadn't entirely given up on him, even when he'd done his best to behave like a petulant child in front of the others, questioning every aspect of the plan and being a general pain in the ass. No, she was still willing to push boldly forward, damn the torpedoes and all that jazz. But then he proved what a truly worthless bastard he was by leaving her to die. That was unforgivable, even if it's true that she's unwilling to sleep with him anymore.

No one tried to help, they all abandoned me.

Yeah, but it wasn't their job. If it was anyone's it was Tyler's, and he showed you how much he thought of *your* sorry ass.

Didn't we share something out there while we were running for our lives? He saved me, made sure I wasn't left behind. Doesn't that mean anything at all? Did our fight irrevocably change everything?

"So you weren't even going to try and come looking for me?"

Tyler opens his eyes and blows a loud raspberry.

"Jesus Christ, tell me what you want to hear already so I can get some sleep! If you want me to lie and tell you I had a plan in mind for your rescue I'll tell you that, but if you want the truth I'll simply say 'no'. No, I decided you were a cunt and it was everyone for themselves, end of story."

"You selfish son of a bitch." She lies on her side, turning away from him. "I knew all along you couldn't change, yet I lied to myself that I thought you would. It just goes to show how easily we can delude ourselves."

"Look, you're the one who told me off on the ship, told me you didn't need me. If anything, this is your fault."

"My fault? Jesus, there's no getting through to you!"

"If it wasn't for me you'd still be lost out there, probably would have gotten eaten by those birds or something! I helped you and this is the thanks I get?"

"All right Tyler," she says quietly. "I give. Thanks. Thanks for nothing."

"No problem."

Abruptly her urge to argue subsides. Does he have a point? On the ship she'd told him she didn't want to have anything to do with him anymore, but that was before the captain went crazy and they were scrambling for their lives.

Oh fuck it, seriously, fuck it. It's not important who's right or wrong. We're all going to die anyway.

She feels used up, empty inside. Throughout her adult life she's always been the strong one, the one who dealt the cards that others played, not the rube who got played, but it doesn't matter, not anymore. It won't add up to a hill of beans once the captain has his way and transforms them into freakin' zombies like the rest of the people here. After that their lives and how they lived them will become inconsequential, so much fodder for the funny pages.

And what will it be like? Mind erased of all traces of one's former self, a blank page ready to serve the captain's nefarious intentions? God, she doesn't want to think about it but there is nothing she can do; it haunts her, possesses her, all these terrible things adding up, growing, like what they did tonight, eating Governor Hallsly. She certainly didn't wake up this morning and foresee that on her agenda. She supposes the only good thing about being 'converted' (as the captain calls it) will be that she won't have to live with that on her conscience. Nope, she suspects it will all be wiped clean and left bare. Will she make new memories, have new feelings, or will her mind exist on another level devoid of such things? She shudders at the prospect, wrapping her arms around herself and shutting her eyes, but when she does she can see Hallsly's face, the impassioned look of terror etched on his features like a tattoo, can hear his strangled, petrified screams as the minions cut off his legs...

Opening her eyes, she decides she probably isn't going to get a whole lot of sleep tonight. From Tyler's cage comes the sound of sawing logs, and she curses him for being able to shut down like that. What a wingnut. Despite the fact that she may be wrong, that he may indeed have a point, she hopes the captain has something nasty in mind for him, she really does.

"We're monsters, aren't we?"

"I wouldn't say that, no, we just did what we had to do. Anybody would have."

"It's not like we've been without food for very long, it was only a couple of days."

"None of us were thinking straight, probably because we were so dehydrated as well. Don't make yourself feel bad-"

"The thing is I *don't* feel bad!" Leeann interrupts harshly. "And I think that's why I feel guilty."

"What?" Dante asks, not sure if he understands.

"I would think I'd feel suicidal over something like eating a person but I don't feel that way at all. I don't think I feel *anything* at all!"

"You're in shock. We all are."

"Do you feel bad?"

Dante opens his mouth to tell her yes, of course he feels like a total degenerate, despicable beyond words, but he realizes he would be lying. Truth be told, he doesn't feel bad, in fact feels better for having eaten. Maybe it's because of their situation, or maybe it's because Dante is the kind of person who (with the life he's lead) isn't surprised he would wind up having to resort to cannibalism. Hell, he should be surprised it hasn't happened sooner. But then, all that aside, why doesn't she feel bad? 'Little Miss Sheltered' came from a normal family, a normal life. If anyone should feel awful it would certainly be her. And, hey, wasn't she a vegetarian?

"I don't," he replies. "But that's because I'm a weirdo and the governor wasn't exactly the nicest person…"

"So you can eat someone if they aren't quote unquote 'nice'?"

He sighs, takes a deep breath and lets it out. "I don't know Leeann, maybe, maybe not."

"I think we're already changing," she says with an unsettling certainty. "I think we've been changing since we got here, like the captain said, after we went in the water. I don't think I would have done that otherwise."

"You tried to refuse, the captain made you."

"I could have tried harder, but I gave in. I… I… I guess I just got sick of fighting." Her voice breaks and Dante sits up, her sorrow *his* sorrow, and this makes him angry.

"We can't give up Leeann-"

"Face it Dante, we're fucked."

"Hey, it looks bad, I know, but I'll think of something, all right? We're going to get out of here. I don't know how, but we're going to. Trust me."

"Oh Dante," she sighs in a breathy voice that makes him feel tingly inside. Oh, how he yearns to be by her side, to hold her and comfort her against the chill of the night and the horror of these walking apparitions, these terrifying things that used to be people but are now something immoral, tainted. "If you can get me out of here I'll be very grateful," she says in a suggestive tone of voice, and damned if he doesn't feel a stirring in his pants. "I could be very…generous…"

"I'm going to get us out of here," he says with a conviction he's not sure he truly believes but, then again, wars have been mounted, advanced weaponry created and countries conquered when there was the promise of nookie on the table. Man's ever-ready encouragement from the fairer sex. With the thought of Leeann's naked body in mind he suddenly feels as if he can move mountains and walk through walls. "Trust me, nothing is going to happen to us."

"Oh Dante, " she coos again, sounding as if she is slipping off into sleep. "If anyone can do it, I think you can."

His heart skips a beat, a flush creeping over his face. *For you,* he thinks, *I can do anything.*

Cole occupies the cage that once housed the former governor. His is the furthest away from the others (the *normal* others). Steven and Perry are in a cage next to him and they aren't talking. He tried asking them a couple of questions but they'd already shut down, were conveniently on their way to la la land. Why they are in a cage at all is anyone's best guess, but he supposes it's because there might still be some small vestige of their former selves hiding inside.

He wishes he had someone to talk to, wishes he could have been placed near Kenny. Hell, he'd be happy to be with Dante or Leeann right now, anyone for Christ's sake. He's never been fond of being alone, but under these conditions it's intolerable.

Occasionally he hears strange noises coming from the intern's cage, and he closes his eyes, holds his hands over his ears and does his best to ignore it. The sounds are…unsettling.

This is going to be long night…

Suddenly his stomach clenches and he feels a tightening in his bowels.

Great. On top of everything else I have to take a shit.

Pinching his cheeks together, he grits his teeth, trying to wait it out. It is going to be a very long time until morning.

"You are beautiful, the most beautiful woman in the world." Captain Harvey clutches Kim's naked body, his penis still buried inside her as small insects swarm around them, attracted by the smell of sex. He doesn't notice or, more so, doesn't care. Kim, well, she doesn't notice anything anymore.

She gurgles a response, inarticulate sounds that would have an African with a dialect of clicks and whistles scratching their head. But Captain Harvey understands, he understands all.

"What can I say? She issued a challenge. You have to defend your honor."

Kim issues an uproarious clamor that is apparently a protest. Her hands seek the soft flesh of his throat, grasping him and squeezing, but not too tight.

"I'm not lying. She probably wants to win my favor to save herself from the chore I have in mind for her."

But the truth is that he *is* lying. He simply wants her, has since the first time he spoke to her alone aboard the ship. He may be a product of Garbage Island but he still has urges, still has needs. Kim has been a most useful plaything but he wants a woman he can converse with, and Melissa, he's found, is actually quite intelligent. She will be the one to undertake the revolution with him, the one who will help him see this through.

And, for the time being, Kim can be his sex slave, his sperm bank, his dick cushion. She is, after all, well qualified for the job.

"Tomorrow you two shall battle for my love. The winner will be my Queen and the loser, if still alive, will be placed into forced servitude. You know, my love, that I'll be rooting for you."

Kim squirms beneath him, trying to break free, but his full weight is upon her, lying there like a dead man. She growls thickly and lunges with bared teeth, nipping viciously at his throat. He feels a sharp prick of pain and blood oozes down his neck, dripping onto her face.

"You bitch!" he thunders, appalled at such a violent overture. He rolls off of her and clasps a hand over the wound, feeling the pulse of his jugular beneath his fingers. A few centimeters to the left and he would be bleeding like a stuck pig. He sits up, glaring down at her. "That wasn't necessary." He rises quickly to his feet, the urge to kick her in the ribs foremost on his mind, but he hesitates, smiles.

"I know you are concerned honey, but don't worry. She is no match compared to you."

Kim utters a volley of unintelligible babbling, her mouth working frantically, spittle flying from her wounded, awful mouth, and Captain Harvey watches her in rapt fascination, noting how her breasts jiggle in accord with her disjointed speech patterns. He kneels down, places a finger on her lips.

"Shhh," he says calmly and at once she is quiet. "Don't worry my love. You know where my heart lies." He stands again. "I must go now, I have work to do. I will see you soon."

Turning away from her he visualizes Melissa's face, her long black hair, her smooth white skin. She is the one that he and Garbage Island genuinely want, more than anyone else. And she will be the one they shall have.

TWENTY-SIX

Legs twitching, the pain in his knee a steady, continuous ache, Kenny at last manages to fall into a fitful slumber, exhaustion getting the better of him. His last wakeful thoughts before conscious-ness deserts him are gloomy and hopeless, the knowledge that he's trapped in a situation he has no way of escaping making him feel deflated, defeated, and these reflections gradually segue into an onrush of surrealistic images-scenes and settings that only make sense in the nocturnal fantasy world, where anything can happen. They start out innocuously at first, simply random images of places and people stored within his subconscious mind, progressively morphing to fit the dream-scape's own disjointed reality.

He's with Sheila, a girl he dated many, many years ago, but her hair is longer, colored a vibrant red instead of the shade of black he knew it to be, and she's taller, towering over him. They are walking along a busy sidewalk, people jostling past them impatiently as if they are standing still, and in the dream he knows he's in Green Bay but this city looks more like Chicago. His rational mind knows there are no bustling sidewalks in Green Bay, no parts of the city congested by so much human traffic, nevertheless as they continue along they pass block after block of shoulder to shoulder pedestrians and endless rows of buildings, the names of the business' indecipherable yet he knows they are convenience stores and dry-cleaners and accounting firms and taverns. Glancing into the immediate distance he sees a motley conglomeration of skyscrapers, dilapidated, warped looking structures that appear to be covered in a thick film of forest green moss. He turns to Sheila to ask her where they are and she answers by pointing to something ahead. Following her finger, he sees Lambeau Field materialize in front of them as if it has just sprouted out of the ground, floating before them like shimmering heat waves hovering over sun-scorched blacktop. At once he understands why there are so many people in the street, and when he looks down at himself he notices he's in his football uniform.

'Are you going to play?' Sheila asks him, and when he tries to answer 'yes' he feels a stabbing pain shoot through his leg and he stumbles, almost collapsing to the ground but she catches him, her large hands cradling him to her bosom.

'Coach!' she calls as she clutches him in her powerful arms. 'We need help coach!'

The crowd parts, the spectators whispering ominously amongst themselves, words Kenny can't make out. Whoever (*whatever*) is heading toward Sheila and he has them frightened, confused.

Rough hands take hold of Kenny and wrench him away from Sheila, unmindful of his injury. He hears her calling his name but her voice gradually recedes, growing dimmer and dimmer until it's gone. Complete silence fills the void, no sound whatsoever, not even the murmuring of the wind. And then he's in a dark tunnel, the insistent hands dragging him along, hands belonging to someone he can't even see, just a shadowy figure whose every exhalation is a choppy grunt of either discomfort or displeasure, Kenny can't tell which. He wants to ask this person what they want of him, where they are taking him, but a light appears at the end of the tunnel and before he can form the words he's thrust out into blinding brightness and the figure behind him is gone, vanished...

And...then...

He's on the sidelines with the other players, snow whirling around them chaotically, his breath steaming from his mouth in large plumes as he watches his team battling valiantly against the Kansas City Chiefs. He wonders why he isn't out there with them but then remembers he's sidelined because of his wounded knee. He looks down at his leg, sees it's wrapped in lumpy, forest green colored gauze. He tries to flex it but it screams in misery, dizzying pain making him reel, and he grasps the shoulder of another player to hold himself steady.

"Sack the damn quarterback!" his teammate yells but his voice is lost in the din of the crowd. Kenny glances up at the scoreboard and sees they are down six points and there is only six minutes left in the sixth quarter. Man he wishes he could help, they need him for Christ's sake, but his knee is killing him. He can't even put his full weight on it.

The crowd is chanting something he can't understand, the words blending together and swirling around his head like pesky flies. He cranes his neck, looking into the stands, and observes grimly that the spectators are gaunt, pale, their eyes black holes in their faces. Many of them are missing body parts, and they clutch the severed appendages in bony fists, waving them in the air like banners. Adults, children, all of them ashen and disfigured, their cries becoming increasingly frantic over the eerie, kaleidoscopic music that warbles from the speakers, the volume getting steadily louder, drowning them out.

He suddenly becomes aware of an unpleasant odor, one that permeates his nostrils with an urgency that makes him nauseous, and cold sweat breaks out on his face despite the frigid air. He wipes his forehead with his right arm and discovers with rising alarm that he has lesions covering the back of his hand and wrist, red, inflamed looking sores that appear right in front of his eyes, blistering up from the skin like bubbles in a pot of thick tomato sauce. He wants to cry out in disgust but his vocal cords are paralyzed; try as he may he can utter nothing but hoarse, guttural grunts.

Panic explodes within him then, a hysterical fit of full-tilt terror and, returning his gaze to the field, he sees enormous piles of putrid trash strewn about, blowing randomly in the wind. The players have stopped momentarily and are swaying unsteadily on their feet, their eyes dazed under the harsh glare of the sodium arc lights. The announcer's voice over the booming public address system is a high pitched drone, like the whine of insects, and it breaks into wild cackling every few sentences, the words running together in a mish mash of logic defying syllables. He glances sidelong at the player standing next to him but the man is gone, replaced by something so hideous Kenny gasps and stumbles backward, almost losing his already unstable footing.

"Uhnnnggg…" it snarls at him. *"Uhnnnggggggg!"*

He raises his hands to ward it off and sees they are pulsating with a network of bulging veins running with blackish/greenish fluid. He examines the undulating squiggles, following them up his arm where they intertwine amidst the inflamed lesions. With this revelation his skin at once feels clammy, dirty, his whole being saturated with something foul that seems to be working it's way through him from the inside out.

"No," he tries to say yet can't. *"Oh my God no…"*

Bloodcurdling shrieks and moans abruptly fill the air, a painful, grating racket that overtakes the din of the crowd, the music, the announcer, and when he glances back at the field he stares wide eyed at the opposing quarterback who, going back to pass, launches his own severed head high into the air for the waiting receivers. When it comes down the players attack it with ravenous zeal, fighting over it as if it's a sacred prize, like coyotes tearing into a kitten and, finally, Kenny can stand no more. He takes a step forward, his knee aching terrifically, and lurches onto the field. The grass beneath his shoes feels spongy *(that's impossible, the field is frozen)* and it is all he can do to stay on his feet as he sinks into the ground, which has suddenly become a quagmire of brownish, blackish sludge. Each time he lifts a foot his footprint fills up with the stuff, boiling up from the earth like tar, the effluvium thick and heady.

"Game over!" he tries to holler but no real words come out of his mouth, only rasping, non-sensical grunts.

His heart beating madly, his mouth dry, he witnesses the players from both teams assault one another viciously, literally tearing each other limb from limb. The Chief's quarterback runs around in an ever-widening circle, his body refusing to believe he can't participate simply because he no longer has a head.

The fans show their anger and discontentment by showering the field in an atrocious rain of body parts; hands, legs, arms, heads, entrails pour down as the lights suddenly flicker and grow dim.

As darkness settles upon the stadium, Kenny feels his blood freeze within him, his joints becoming stiff, a bone-jarring ache detonating inside him which will be the very last physical sensation he ever experiences before everything goes numb, including the throbbing in his knee, which disappears like the last lone star at the end of a long, feverish night. His anxious mind becomes calm; the transformation is complete, everything will be okay. Ripping off one of his own arms (feeling nothing but the slightest twinge), he runs back and forth on the field, waving it high over his head, issuing inarticulate groans and screams that blend in with the others as he at last joins his teammates in a celebration that will undoubtedly go on forever…

(In the early gray light of dawn Kenny's eyes pop open, deep black, unblinking. There is no more pain in his knee and his mind is free of worry; he is at last absolved of any lingering doubts or apprehension to bind him to his old life. Only one urge eddies in his newly transformed mind: to serve the Master, to serve Garbage Island.)

Guilt is what brings Dr. Taylor to wakefulness. He licks his lips, the rancid aftertaste of human flesh evoking in him the memory of the night before in all its vivid glory, and his stomach roils nauseously. Last night he'd been able to justify his actions with the rationale that they were all going to die anyway, but today is different. Now he realizes it was simply a defense mechanism, something to validate the events that transpired so as to shift the responsibility. To think it had only been two days that he'd been without food. Two days! What would he have done if it were three, start eating himself? Jesus!

But on the tail of this reaction he experiences a surge of anger, an instantaneous response that helps to dissolve some of his culpability. Surely neither he nor the others can be blamed for what they did, as they did it out of self-preservation. It wasn't a malicious act; it was simply done to ensure their survival. Yet, still, he feels remorse, and this infuriates him because the captain holds all the cards, has every advantage and they have none.

He sits up, stretches as best he can in the confines of the cage and peers out the rectangular slot to see if Kenny is awake. He can see the outline of his slouched figure through the cloudy plastic; he is sitting hunched over, his chin resting on his chest.

"Kenny," he says softly. "Hey, are you awake?"

The other groans, a thick, syrupy resonance that barely resembles a human voice, and when Kenny leans forward and puts his face up to the air hole a sickening realization blossoms in the doctor's guts.

"Oh shit," he murmurs, noting the dark, vacant eyes, the slack mouth. "Kenny?"

The thing that used to be Kenny smiles a crooked smile, one that is empty of humor and humanity. He moves his lips to speak but at first nothing issues from his mouth but indistinct grunts. After several attempts he finally gets it right, but what he mutters is unintelligible, words with no discernable meaning.

One of the creatures hears this utterance and steps forward, opening Kenny's cage and letting him out. The ex-football player moves with a stiff gait, but he no longer appears to be suffering from his knee injury. Looking at his leg, Dr. Taylor sees the bandage is gone and that a sickly, forest green moss has grown over the wound.

The bacteria got to him through the wound in his knee. He watches in amazement as Kenny takes his place amongst the other creatures. *None of us have very long at this rate. If we don't do something, and do it quick, we're all done for.*

He runs a shaky hand through his short hair, feels the sweat that is rapidly evacuating his pores starting to soak through his shirt. He's not sure what time it is exactly but he knows its early, not quite six o' clock. The day is going to warm up considerably once the sun makes it's way into the sky and his throat already feels rough and sticky from thirst. The heat will only make it worse if he doesn't get something, anything, to drink.

"Good morning Dr. Taylor," Captain Harvey addresses him, appearing as if from nowhere as per usual. "I trust you slept well?"

"You know I didn't," Dr. Taylor replies with distaste, his hopes of escape abandoning him as he regards the other. With Kenny's departure from the land of the living he can feel his patience and motivation slipping away.

"You've seen that Kenny is now one of us."

"Yes."

Captain Harvey issues a deep chuckle, one that segues into an extended coughing spell. Dr. Taylor looks at him sharply and notices upon closer scrutiny that the captain is looking even more ragged than the previous day, more telltale signs of decay disfiguring him, as well as a fresh wound on his neck speckled with congealed blood.

"Going to miss him, are you?"

Dr. Taylor doesn't reply, doesn't feel there is any need. Kenny's conversion is proof that all of them will shortly follow, and it is something that is taking him a moment to process.

"He isn't in any pain any more."

"He wouldn't have been in pain if your man hadn't shot him."

"A necessary action," Captain Harvey says glibly, picking at the wound under his jaw. "He had to be stopped."

"You need to be stopped."

Captain Harvey grins. "Maybe so, but I don't think that's going to happen, do you?" He posits it as a question but Dr. Taylor takes it more as a declaration. And the thing is, the awful thing, is that he's progressively realizing that the captain is probably right. Despite anything they do, Captain Harvey and his cohorts are in control, have been since the beginning. And that god-damn bacteria is unstoppable. Look at how fast it worked on Kim, Steven, Perry, and now Kenny.

One of the captain's minions approaches his cage door, releases the lock and swings it open.

"Hop on out doctor," Captain Harvey commands. "We have a very busy day ahead of us."

"I'm not feeling in any mood to cooperate."

"Really? I wonder why that is? Could it be you regret satiating yourself on the entrée at our midnight feast?"

Dr. Taylor says nothing, looking away.

Captain Harvey licks his lips. "He was very...tasty. He served us better as dinner than he ever did as the governor of California."

Dr. Taylor finds he can't dispute this claim; the governor was an awful man, one of very low moral fiber. A sniper's bullet would have been too good for him...

"You should be thanking me, but no, you sit there acting as if I forced you to eat him."

"You did!" Dr. Taylor replies. "You forced all of us!"

"I did no such thing. You did what you did of your own volition."

"Only because you starved us into it."

"I'm in no mood to argue with you this morning Dr. Taylor, I came here because we have work to do. But since you are being so obstinate maybe it's time for a little refresher course regarding what is truly at stake here." He gestures for Kenny to step forward and the large man does so, albeit robotically. "This man is now free of everything that ever bothered him in his old life. His obsessions, his addictions, his worry—all gone without a trace. Can you imagine how liberating that must be? Can you?"

"As humans we thrive on our misery," the doctor argues futilely. "It's what makes us who we are, whether we like it or not."

"Wouldn't you like an end to that?"

"No." Dr. Taylor shakes his head adamantly. "No I wouldn't."

"Well," the captain says, snapping his fingers (on the hand still possessing all of them) at two minions who lean in and pull the doctor out of his cage, "pretty soon you won't have a choice."

A loud, shrill animal cry awakens Tyler. He sits up quickly, startled, looking around him fearfully. As the last of the cobwebs slip away he realizes he is in a cage, and this situation, accompanied by his hangover, makes for a lousy way to greet the day. Not to mention his bladder is so full it feels like any second now its going to burst like a freakin' balloon.

"Fuck," he mutters, the details of his confinement coming back, hazy, but mostly intact. He remembers helping the captain capture the others for the promise of immunity, a promise that had been nothing but a lie. Impotent rage swells within him, knowing he's been deceived, but it is a hollow, empty feeling. He knows he never should have trusted him but what else was he going to do? Take the other passengers abuse with good humor? It was the only thing he could think of at the time. Besides, they are all going to die anyway, at least he had the pleasure of getting drunk once more, something he wouldn't have been allowed had he not cooperated. Looking at it from that angle, he decides he has no regrets. If faced with the same decision he would do it all over again.

Rubbing his temples, he remembers he's housed next to Melissa, and he gazes through the air hole to see if she is awake. Through the opaque plastic he can make out her silhouette.

"You alive in there?" he asks, a note of acrimony in his voice, and his question goes unanswered. "Come on, don't tell me you're sleeping in today."

"Don't talk to me Tyler," Melissa says at last. "You are dead to me, got it? You don't exist any more." Overnight she's decided that everything Tyler has ever done (back in Sacramento, on the ship, on the trash heap) is just plain fucked and he is the worst person she's ever known. She no longer blames herself for anything, and focusing her hatred on him rejuvenates her, makes her feel more assured, more centered.

"The problem," he says, "is that I'm not. I'm right here, living and breathing."

"Thanks to you none of us will be for long."

"This isn't all my fault!"

"No, it isn't, but as far as I am concerned it is. I'm blaming all of this on you, not just getting captured but the gyre's water currents, the formation of this trash heap, the captain's insipient craziness, eating Governor Hallsly—all of this is *your* fault. As illogical as it sounds those are my belief's and I'm sticking to them."

"You're out of your mind."

"That's right, and this is all your fault," she says with an air of finality. "Now shut the hell up. The sound of your voice makes me want to rip my own ears off."

"And what pretty ears they are!" Captain Harvey says. "They would look great on a piece of string, hanging around your neck."

Melissa looks out the air hole, sees the captain approaching with Dr. Taylor in tow. The doctor wears a look of resignation on his face, a sign that all is not well in camp, and his expression produces within her a dark apprehension that chills her even though it is already quite warm. But she isn't going to show her fear, not to that bastard Harvey. Since the arrival of the others last night she feels her strength resurging, finding the charged inner vigor that has carried her throughout her life when nothing else could. Of course, it is with the help of her anger that this is made possible, for she has always thrived when her ire is raised.

"Well well well, look what the cat dragged in. Good morning Dr. Taylor. It's always good to see *you* but did you have to bring Captain Ugly along? Not exactly the first thing I want to see in the morning if you get my drift."

Dr. Taylor nods to her, wishing he could offer some words of consolation but knowing it is useless. Unfortunately for her he's utterly spent.

"The doctor isn't feeling so well this morning," Captain Harvey says. "His buddy Kenny didn't make it through the night."

"He...he's dead?" This takes her by surprise, almost dismantles her facade of bravery, but she forces it aside and regains her composure.

"No, not dead," Captain Harvey counters. "But he certainly is in a better place."

She looks to Dr. Taylor, her eyes searching his, and he sighs, nodding in affirmation.

"Well son of a bitch," she says. "Why don't you throw a party?"

"I believe I already did," Captain Harvey replies tersely. "I put out a generous spread and the lot of you made pigs of yourselves."

"Not much for side dishes but the main course was a hoot. Can't say I'll ever order it at my favorite restaurant though."

"Hey man, are you going to let me out of here?" Tyler interrupts. "I gotta race like a piss horse."

The captain looks distractedly at Tyler, scowling. "In time you'll be summoned, when you are needed."

"Yeah, uh, that's cool. But I really gotta piss *now*."

The captain turns away from him, returning his attention to Melissa. "It seems you have made an enemy," he starts, eyeing her threateningly, finding her insolent behavior irritating. If he didn't want her for his own he would probably serve her to his minions for lunch. "My Queen believes that you wish to usurp her throne."

"What, Kim?" Melissa says skeptically. "You're nuts."

"Oh, that very well may be the case." He smiles, hearing (though it is very well hidden) the trepidation in her voice. "I'm certain I'm somewhere around the bend but, in no uncertain terms, my Queen wishes to challenge you to a duel."

"Say what?" She tries to keep her voice steady, self-assured, but feels her reserve slipping. Kim Leung presently looks like something out of a George Romero horror film. The idea of physically engaging her in the quest for supremacy not only frightens her, it makes her sick to her stomach.

"That's right," Captain Harvey smirks, not only hearing the fear in her voice now but also smelling it dripping from her pores like so much sweat. "She has made her terms clear. You and she shall have it out today. The winner will be my Queen and the loser will die a horrible death."

"Great," Melissa says. "It's a lose/lose situation. I couldn't be happier."

Fury wells up within the captain, a rage founded in rejection. This woman is practically laughing in his face! His hands twist at his sides, longing to take her by the neck and squeeze until she is begging for mercy, beseeching him for the chance to serve beside him. He steps forward, staring down at her, his eyes ablaze with an electrified ferocity.

"I feel it only fair to warn you that fighting Kim with your bare hands will surely be a lost cause. Of course, if I were persuaded nicely, I might see to it that you are given a weapon, something that will make the task much easier. The choice is yours, all you have to do is ask me politely." His thick, moist, monstrous lips curl back in a sneer, which he attempts in vain to masquerade as a smile.

Dr. Taylor looks on in horror, wondering what in God's name she is doing, provoking the captain like this. Surely it can't end well. Tyler, in turn, watches the exchange with a look of impertinent curiosity, his eyes volleying back and forth obnoxiously.

Melissa can feel the intensity of the captain's anger, can sense she is getting very close to the danger zone the more she presses his buttons, but she couldn't care less. With all that she's been through (what they've all been through) there is no way in hell she is going to kiss his ass to save her own. It's evident that none of them are going to get off of this floating garbage dump alive, so why should she beg for mercy, plead for any kind of compassion or assistance? If she doesn't die she is most certainly going to become one of them, a blank-faced automaton without freewill. Given a choice, she'd opt for death. Judging by the captain's progressively decaying visage it would have to be world's better than the alternative.

"Fuck that whore," she says at last, spitting out the words with an inspired vehemence that takes them all by surprise. "And fuck you." She glares at him defiantly. "I'm not going to grovel to you." She shoots a pitying look over at the doctor, then a contemptuous one at Tyler. "As far as I'm concerned I would rather die."

"Very well," Captain Harvey concedes, his mottled, ashen gray face bearing a startled look that betrays his discouragement. "I hope your death isn't too…painful." He turns to Dr. Taylor. "We have things to attend to." He glances back at Melissa. "If you will excuse us."

"As *if*."

Captain Harvey spins around quickly, reaching through the air hole of her cage in one deft movement and wrapping a hairy, scarred hand around her throat. At once her expression changes to one of shocked astonishment.

"In a few hours time you are going to regret this little song and dance you've performed for me this morning. You may not know it at this very second, but you will. Maybe you feel the need to show off for Dr. Taylor or your boyfriend over there, but trust me when I tell you it won't mean a thing when Kim Leung is ripping you limb from limb and my beautiful creations are standing by, ready to eat the pieces."

"Better bring the barbeque sauce then," she croaks, forcing what she hopes to be a reckless, wicked smile, and the captain releases her, hurling her to the back of the cage.

"Mark my words," he whispers ominously, turning away.

"Good bye Melissa," Dr. Taylor murmurs as Captain Harvey takes him roughly by the arm and leads him away.

"Y'all take care now, ya hear?" she calls after them, then shifts her attention to Tyler one last time. "What the hell are *you* looking at?"

"Nothing," he mutters. "Nothing at all."

TWENTY-SEVEN

Dr. Taylor stumbles along behind the captain feeling weak, absolutely exhausted. He is so parched that his tongue easily sticks to the roof of his mouth and he fantasizes briefly about how nice it would be to brush his teeth. He's never been one to brush less than twice a day, and presently it's been over two days since he's last had the pleasure.

"I'm very thirsty."

"I'll get you something to drink, in time."

"I could really use some water now."

"In time."

Along the way Dr. Taylor watches the creatures carrying out their duties, making fishing nets and weapons, fashioning clothes from the scraps they find amongst the heaps of trash.

It truly is a cornucopia of crap. All this shit that society has found no use for; these life forms should be honored for their recycling efforts.

They reach the structure that represents the town hall and continue past it to the edge of the village. The torture rack and Governor Hallsly are gone, disassembled sometime during the night no doubt. The humanoids probably ate what was left of him.

Passing through an opening in a wall of garbage that towers above their heads- running, it seems, the width of the village like a barrier between their encampment and the untamed dump beyond-Dr. Taylor sees there are more structures back here and, faintly, he can hear unsettling sounds coming from within the crude construction the captain is leading him to. Cocking his ear, listening carefully, he can't tell if they are human (*non-human*) or animal sounds.

"As you are a learned man of science," Captain Harvey says, pausing outside the dwelling, "I'm very eager to get your opinion, your insights on how to ensure their proper development."

The captain sweeps aside a plastic shower curtain that represents the front door and the foul stench of fresh feces slaps Dr. Taylor in the face like an open hand. Ushering him inside, the doctor squints in the dim light, his eyes taking a few minutes to adjust but, before they do, he already knows that what he is about to witness is undoubtedly an abomination of nature.

"Oh…my…God," he murmurs in a broken voice once he is able to see. He turns to the captain, noting the look of satisfaction on the other's face. "What is this?"

Smiling iniquitously, the captain swings his arm around the room with a flourish. "This," he says, "is how I'm creating a new race."

One of the captain's minions appears at the door of Cole's cage, carrying a flat piece of plastic piled generously with glistening heaps of raw flesh.

"Food for…*uhnnnggg*…you," he says, offering it through the air hole. "You…eat."

Cole looks at it suspiciously, making no move to take it. The captain told them himself what happens when you eat the animals. He'd have to be a fool to eat it willingly, even though his stomach is rumbling. Last night's feast is now a festering mound of shit in the farthest corner of the cage; he'd held out as long as he could but eventually nature had to take its course.

"I ain't hungry," he says.

"You…take," the minion repeats. "You…*uhnnnggg*…eat."

Cole shakes his head. "Uh-uh, no thanks guy. I'm good the way I am."

The minion regards him silently, his glazed, dead eyes unblinking. Cole tries to hold his gaze but it unnerves him, those cold, lifeless eyes. He looks away, shuddering. "You heard me. Thanks but no thanks."

The minion retracts the tray, turns and plods away. Cole watches him go, wondering if he's really giving up that easily, when he returns with another in tow, someone much bigger, his movements uneven and off-balance. The first thing that enters Cole's line of sight is a familiar pair of boots, and he follows them up to an even more familiar face.

"Ah shit man, no," he moans, observing the slack expression, the vacant eyes. Kenny now holds the tray before him like a peace offering. "How did they get you?"

Kenny offers no reply; he simply extends his arms forward with the tray, placing it at the lip of the air hole.

"You…take," Kenny says. "You…*uhnnnggg*…eat."

"What the hell *is* this?" Dr. Taylor asks in a choked voice, covering his mouth with one hand. What he is seeing, it defies the existence of a humane God, it defies the humility of the human race…but what it does not challenge is the unquestionably relentless nature of the bacterium that has infected Captain Harvey's brain. This, this is truly horrible. Beyond anything he ever could have imagined, could ever have dreamed.

Two female creatures are in attendance, and Captain Harvey claps his hands and motions to the door, sending them away. They scurry out through the plastic tarp without a sound, their eyes downcast.

"You are witnessing the birth of my new race, my legions of followers who are going to help take over this ignorant planet. All those you see out there? They are just the beginning."

And to think I figured I'd seen the worst this place had to offer. How wrong I was. This is much, much worse.

"What," he asks, barely aware he is speaking, "do you want from me?"

"Your help of course," Captain Harvey says genially, placing an arm around his shoulder. "I want you to oversee production, make sure everything is working up to snuff."

"I'm a marine biologist," Dr. Taylor balks. "Not a genetic engineer."

"This is one of the reasons I brought you here, to do for me what the other scientists refused. The man I mentioned last night, Dr. Connelly? He's been doing a piss-poor job, too many fatalities. It's my belief that he's been deliberately sabotaging this project. In fact, as of this morning he's been relieved of his duties. You'll be taking over for him, continuing the research. Surely you aren't going to disappoint me?" There is a deliberate finality in his words, one that insinuates it can't be argued with. "I'll take your silence as affirmation that you're onboard."

Dr. Taylor stares at the rows of crudely designed and built cribs. Each one contains an infant, well, creatures that vaguely resemble human children at any rate. To say they are deformed is being generous; some of them are missing limbs, some missing eyes (on faces that have no room for the extra sense), while others don't look to be completely human at all. Like the old ads intended to scare kids from smoking marijuana (the ones that contended reefer abuse would lead to children born with misshapen heads and flippers) some of these living abortions *have* flippers. Some gills. Others scaly, translucent skin that show the network of veins flowing with dark green blood.

"Are these...were these...created by...the transformed humans?" He's not sure how to say it delicately, not that delicacy is necessary for the captain, but Dr. Taylor can't easily ridicule nor treat callously these young lives, even if they are truly horrific.

"Unfortunately, no. I haven't had much luck with my minion's sperm," Captain Harvey says, shaking his head. As he does so Dr. Taylor notices his remaining ear is hanging by a thin flap of skin, swinging back and forth and slapping against the side of his head, but the captain appears unconcerned. He reaches up and fiddles with it absently, detaching it further from it's mooring. This close, in this light, Dr. Taylor becomes aware of how rapidly his skin is peeling away, can see that it's only a matter of time before the mask he wears which he calls a face will eventually be nothing but a memory. "These children are the product of uninfected sperm and someone who is newly converted."

"So you have someone new to the island supply the uninfected sperm?" the doctor asks, aghast. "How do you get them to comply?"

The captain smiles sagaciously. "Your good buddy Tyler is soon going to find out."

It can't be, it simply can't be. Kenny was his rock, the only thing that kept him from going batshit crazy. His was the strength of many, the stamina that he couldn't muster himself, the only one he really trusted besides the doctor. And now he is gone.

"How did they get you buddy?" he asks forlornly, staring at the drooping face, the empty, seemingly sightless eyes. "What did they do?"

Kenny doesn't answer because that's beyond him now. Thoughts, feelings, pain, right, wrong- they are all gone with no memory of what they once were. All he knows now is what his infected mind tells him to be his objective, his modus opperandis, his new way of life.

"You...take," he repeats tonelessly. "You...*uhnnnggg*...eat."

A reeling sense of loss fills him, a crushing dread that comes unbidden and inexorable. Like the finality of a grave filled with dirt that was once hard packed earth, it is all over. Apparently there is no escape, no way off this fucked up island. If they could get to Kenny, well, there isn't much hope left for him. Besides, according to the captain they've all been infected already, it's just a matter of time. Might as well skip to the chase...

Slowly, with hands that tremble slightly, he reaches for the tray. Grasping it tightly he pulls it through the air hole.

"So it all comes down to this," he says, his heart fluttering in his chest. The meat looks gristly, unappetizing, but if he was able to eat the governor than this should be a snap. "If they got you I suppose I don't stand a snowballs chance in hell."

Kenny takes a step back, his arms at his sides. He waits, watches.

Cole takes a piece of the meat between his finger and thumb, holds it under his nose and sniffs. It has the distinct reek of carrion, and it drips blood down his arm, feeling sticky, somehow obscene. His stomach clenches painfully and his eyes water but he knows that he has to do it, he must. And then the infection will follow and he will no longer be a person, he will be just like Kenny, just like the rest of them. This thought frightens him badly, but the thought of trying to live through this without Kenny's aide scares him even more. There is nothing left to be done, no way that help is going to arrive at the eleventh hour and save them from this insanity.

"I guess this is it," he sighs, and takes a bite of the meat.

Their voices awaken one of the 'infants' and it begins to howl, issuing a screech like jagged metal on a blackboard. The noise is deafening in the small enclosure, but more so than the auditory displeasure it creates, it hurts the doctor because he feels pity for these little things, these creations that by all rights should not exist, an experiment dreamed up by an infected man who is being eaten alive.

The squalling thing awakens others, and soon the lot of them are shrieking dissonantly. Dr. Taylor feels nausea roll thick and strong through him and, involuntarily, he gags. The odor in the closed quarters suddenly becomes unbearably overwhelming. He turns, staggering toward the exit but Captain Harvey clutches his shoulder, holds him fast in his grip.

"Uh-uh," he says, his grin gone, replaced by a look of severe foreboding. "You're not going anywhere, you have work to do."

Taking deep breaths, trying to will away the unflagging need to dry heave, Dr. Taylor struggles to compose himself. This contagion is well beyond anything humankind has ever known, something so tenacious it would be ludicrous to think it could be stopped by anyone, much less himself. Suddenly, with a rapidity that shocks him, he wishes he could just end it all, could simply slit his wrists and cease to be. Over, done, gone. Death would be a relief from this lunacy, a swift death that would take him from one plain of existence to another and, if not that, into a cold, black void. Lights out. Game over.

"What," he asks, his voice husky with undisguised repugnance, "do you want me to do?"

"I want you to examine them, study them as a scientist would. I want to know if they are healthy." The captain gazes at the creatures affectionately, like a proud new father. They are gradually quieting, their cries winding down to soft whimpers as their tiny hands (*flippers*) search the air in front of them, perhaps seeking the absent maternal figure they so desperately long for.

Rage quickly dispels the doctor's apathy, wrought by a deep pity for these poor, doomed infants. Looking at these fragile, cursed things is like staring into an abyss that yields laughing demons with crazed eyes, their intentions nothing but pain, terror, destruction…eventual madness. "Healthy?" he says harshly. "How can you even use that word? Look at yourself for Christ's sake! You're falling apart as we stand here! It's twisted your mind into something sick…sick and utterly foul. The term healthy cannot be applied to any living organism on this island! This is beyond science, this is something that has no right being alive at all!"

Captain Harvey is silent, his gaze blackening, the reek of anger spilling from his pores like locker room sweat. His eyes bore into the doctor's, his mouth twisting into a snarl of derision.

"And here I thought you were a scientist, a man who could look at things analytically and probe them for deeper meaning, leaving emotion behind because it's a hindrance to progress."

"This," Dr. Taylor says, his fury growing, engorging his whole being, "is nothing short of atrocious, an affront to everything I stand for." He glares into the captain's ever-darkening eyes, fighting the temptation to look away. "I will have no part of it."

Captain Harvey shakes his head sadly, as if the doctor's words hurt him profoundly. "You disappoint me Dr. Taylor, truly you do." He claps his hands and two of his minions' enter the room, taking him forcefully by the arms. "If you can't help than you are of no use to me, just like Dr. Connelly. And to think I got rid of him for *you*. Maybe you will serve me better once you've been enlightened, but I doubt it." He addresses his minions: "Take him back to his cage and prepare him for a force feeding." He returns his gaze to the other. "I am so very, very saddened that it should come to this doctor, but you leave me no other choice. You are just like all the others, and to think for you I made a special trip. What a grand waste of my time and, as you've so thoughtfully pointed out, time is one thing that's running against me." He motions to his decaying body, the crumbling remnants of his outer shell. "I suppose you need to see things through a fresh pair of eyes. A new perspective, as it were. Maybe then you will understand the importance of all this and choose to help us carry on with our work…if you are able, that is."

"That's the only way you'll get my cooperation," Dr. Taylor retorts. "I'll never assist you willingly."

"Willingly, unwillingly, it's all the same to me." Captain Harvey turns away. "With or without your cooperation my plan will be carried out, make no mistake about that. There is nothing that can stop me now and," he casts a glance over his shoulder, "no one that can save you. Soon we'll see eye to eye. I shall speak with you then." With a wave of his hand the minions haul Dr. Taylor through the plastic curtain, his feet dragging behind him.

Her stomach twisted in knots, Melissa sits fidgeting in her cage, trying to control the surmounting fear that rises within her. The idea of fighting Kim Leung is preposterous, nothing short of suicide. She's witnessed the strength of these things and knows she doesn't stand a chance, weapon or not. Like a prisoner sentenced to face the executioner, she wallows in hopeless misery, awaiting her fate.

Scenes from her life flicker through her head and, try as she may, she can't escape the memories that surfaced during the storm. Terry's horrible, pockmarked face leers in her mind's eye, her evil stepfather with the wandering hands and, lingering in the periphery, is her mother, her mouth scowling in denial, abound with accusations that it had somehow been her fault, that she'd invited his touch. Oh how she hated them then, and God knows she hates them now, the fact that they could do something so despicable to a little girl, a child goddamnit! Are some people really so stupid that they can't imagine what their actions will elicit, or is it intrinsically a callous insensitivity that rebuffs culpability, allowing them to commit any sort of atrocity without fear of consequence? No wonder she turned out as she did, becoming a hired sex-worker…yes, even though she doesn't 'turn tricks' she can honestly call it for what it is. When all is said and done, she is employed to administer sexual gratification in the form of punishment so, in some sense she can be considered a whore, although she's never taken money for fucking. Not that *she* would classify herself a prostitute and, all self-loathing aside, she isn't ashamed of what she does, but is this how she would have turned out had she not been raped as a child, or would there perhaps have been some other future in store for her, some other ending that didn't involve whips and chains and leather, leading to her meeting the sleazy governor, in turn bringing her here? She can't answer that, but somehow feels certain her life would have taken a much different turn if she'd had a normal upbringing. The transformation from an innocent girl into a bloodthirsty pain-monger certainly didn't happen overnight, it evolved slowly, all the ingredients simmering together and congealing into the stew that was her damaged psyche…

She recalls her first forays into cutting herself, the sharp pinch of the blade as her skin split open and warm blood trickled from the wound like an accessory to a crime, watching it flow thickly down her forearm, decorating her wrist like an obscene bracelet. She got a rush from doing it, her endorphins exploding in her head like a nebula of stars, but why, *why* would pain induce pleasure within her? Why did she feel she needed it? Did she think she deserved to hurt, or did the physical pain overwhelm her mental anguish in a manner that stifled it, held it at bay? Yes, yes, that was it. By cutting herself she exchanged her emotional problems for something corporeal, something tangible she could see and touch in order to distance herself from the abuse that so ashamed her, made her feel worthless, suicidal… and eventually the pain helped her drive those memories deep underground, buried in the subterranean depths of her mind where they'd never be excavated. It was her way of coping, of getting on with her life.

Because the bloodletting was only the beginning…the cutting, the bruising, the self-asphyxiation. Next came the thrill she got when she could dominate someone, both physically and mentally, taking away their free will as easily as one breathed the air-maybe this was her way of taking back her inner power. Instead of only hurting herself she found pleasure in bringing others pain, but not in an exploitive manner, only in such a way as to assert her control. As her teens gave way to her early twenties she'd found an authority inside her she never knew to exist, and it's unbridled immediacy unleashed within her a positive sense of her own self-worth, something she'd been lacking for quite some time.

Becoming a dominatrix brought her world into a sharper focus than she'd ever known, and at last happiness wasn't simply an elusive feeling that hid around every corner no matter how hard she tried to rein it in, it became a palpable reality.

Yet even though she'd 'found' herself, she could still thank Terry for creating doubt within her in the first place; his lecherous advances may have disappeared within the folds of her subconscious mind but a lasting impression had been made. Why else did she fall for guys like Tyler? Simple, because she still felt insignificant, no matter how she tried to sugarcoat it. It was a self-destructive tendency she followed blindly, unknowingly, no matter how hard she tried to break the cycle. And a scumbag like him could easily read it in her eyes, knowing he could take advantage of her because she felt she deserved it, the stupid, filthy sack of shit…

She glares over at his cage, seeing through the almost translucent plastic that he has fallen back to sleep, having urinated through the small space in the front. She'd heard the splattering sound it made as it struck the compressed garbage of the heap's floor, and simultaneously realized she'd had to pee herself. She's been holding it ever since because the thought of pissing her pants again infuriates her. Once was bad enough.

Like a fire that smolders down to the last remaining coal, producing the hottest flame, her anger burns within her, seething in a manner which suddenly makes her feel very much alive. Captain Harvey can blow himself if he thinks she is simply going to lie down and die. She'll take that cunt Kim Leung by the hair and give her the thrashing of a lifetime, but she needs to plan her strategy, needs to gather her strength if she has any chance at all.

How can I beat her? And what will become of me if I do?

Her thoughts spin frantically, trying to work this problem in her mind like a mathematician would an extremely difficult set of numbers. There has to be some way she can gain the upper hand; she is, after all, an extremely intelligent woman. These zombified fuckholes shouldn't be able to outsmart her. Harvey's body is falling apart faster than a counterfeit Mona Lisa so it only stands to reason his mind must certainly be crumbling as well. Surely she should be able to outfox him...

And just like that an answer comes to her, one that brings about a smile, makes her feel human for the first time since she's come to this rotten place. At last she has an idea, something to give her a leg to stand on anyway. It may or may not help her win, but it will at least offer her some protection and, for the time being, she expects that's about as good as it's going to get.

Staring thoughtfully at his beautiful creations, Captain Harvey feels something move within his chest, a powerful sensation that grasps him solidly in an iron grip, making his eyes water. At first he believes this stirring to be of an emotional nature, given his attachment to his 'children', and he smiles, wiping a tear away with one stained, scarred finger.

"Oh, my lovelies..."

Suddenly it intensifies, becoming constricting, and a sharp twinge explodes inside him.

Uhnnnggg...Pain? What the hell is this?

It increases drastically and he involuntarily cries out, clutching himself and gulping for air. His heart and lungs feel as if they are drowning in fluid, and he shoves two fingers down his throat, fighting frantically to clear his airway.

"Oh...fuck..." he gasps, hiccupping, then expels a mouthful of foamy green and black liquid laced with long, thin, white worms that squirm blindly on the floor before him. He struggles to gain another breath and, his lungs and heart burning excruciatingly, he expectorates another steaming pile of the oversized larva, eyeing it curiously. "Holy fucking *(aaaahhhccckkk!)* shit!" he pants, prodding at the mass experimentally with the toe of one of his boots as he considers his health's escalating decline.

My deterioration is advancing more rapidly than I would have thought, goddamnit. I have to act quickly before it gets the better of me.

Wiping his mouth with the back of one hand he turns away from his creations, his mind whirling. He'd planned another experiment before the duel this afternoon, one to determine how fit his successor was, so to speak, but he wonders if there is still time. Should he cut short this procedure (assuming it to be superfluous) in favor of an earlier battle royal ala Kim and Melissa? Does it really matter?

This is all your fault, you know. We wouldn't be at this point if you hadn't been so pigheaded.

The thought comes to him unexpectedly, but nonetheless he knows it to be true. The story he'd told last night, the origin of Garbage Island, was mostly factual with the exception of his reason for traveling to the states. He'd no more gone there to procure a brilliant scientist and the job of overseeing the mission than he'd gone to buy himself a new suit at the Men's Warehouse. He'd gone because...because...

Because I thought I could do it alone.

Yes, that was it in a nutshell. Because in his infinite vanity he'd thought that he and he alone could spread the contagion. He didn't need his creations, he didn't need anything. All he needed was his own wonderful self and ashes ashes they would all fall down...

But something happened and my plan went to hell; fuck if I know what it was.

The scientists had driven him to it, of that he is certain. When they wouldn't help him he'd tortured them within an inch of their lives and, when that failed he'd converted them and found they were useless, except the two scientists he'd transformed personally. They'd retained their intelligence only too well; those sons a bitches tried to usurp his position, thinking they were superior to he but, in the end, he'd found them out without even trying very hard, without breaking a sweat. It had simply come to him, their covert intentions, their imminent plans. It was this intervention that made him believe he was invincible, a demigod in his very own right, one who could take over the world without so much as batting an eye...

He'd been less than a hundred miles off the California coast, south of San Diego, skimming carelessly through a late night drizzle with the running lights off. One second he was gloating at his insurmountable power and the next he was registering a grinding, rending screech of tearing metal and was sent tumbling through the air, ass over teakettle. His head connected with the hard steel of the ship and then...nothing.

He'd come to (how many days later he had no idea) on a beach in Rosarita, Mexico, wearing ill-fitting clothes that weren't his own and sporting a golf ball sized lump on his forehead. He had no clue how he'd gotten there or what had become of his own clothes; try as he may he could only come up with brief snatches of memories, splintered recollections that seemed more like dreams than reality. He'd crashed the ship, that much was obvious, but what had happened in the interval between then and now? His fractured imaginings seemed to indicate he'd been held captive somewhere and he'd escaped, but where or what it was he had no idea. Jail possibly, but perhaps it had been a psyche ward or hospital. Searching his inner data banks he could find nothing concrete, nothing that yielded any answers.

Anger had clouded his judgment then, and when a woman and her child stooped over his prone body to ask if he needed assistance, speaking in broken but passable English, he'd grabbed her by the hair and tried to rip out her throat with his teeth, but he was impossibly weak, drained. After a brief struggle she easily broke free and, casting a reproachful look over her shoulder, she and her boy had fled. Of course he had enough sense to know she'd probably alert the authorities so with great effort he got to his feet and staggered away, making his way further up the beach and successfully blending into a throng of beachgoers.

How much time passed he wasn't sure. A week? Maybe two? During that period he disappeared into the chaotic sprawl of Tijuana, slowly nursing himself back to health. Whatever had happened to him during his fugue state had stripped him of his powers, had actually left him weaker than he'd been before his transformation. As an experiment he'd tried to convert a prostitute by vomiting into her mouth but found he'd had nothing within him, barely a trace of the bacterium to share.

What the hell had happened? He found himself asking this question over and over, and all he could come up with was that it must be his proximity from Garbage Island; somehow, this far away, his powers were dampened. To have done this successfully he most likely needed strength in numbers; in retrospect he should have brought along his creations to help him but his egotism had commanded he do it alone.

But was that correct or merely speculation? It gnawed at him like a rat feasting on a steaming pile of entrails…what am I missing? Yet the more he tried to figure it out the more the answer evaded him, and in the end he realized there was no sense dwelling on it, at least not at the moment. The plan had to be continued, fulfilled so as to appease the bacterium. There was no time to waste. The only thing to do was to find a way back to Garbage island and, having no other options because of his weakened state, he decided to seek out a man he knew at the Point Loma Naval Base. He hadn't seen him in many years but that was of no matter. Their bond went all the way back to Vietnam, and that in itself was ironclad. With his help he could procure a sailboat, if not outright than possibly by allowing him easy access to a marina on the San Diego Bay where he could steal one.

Getting across the border had been another affair altogether, but he'd found himself a ride with a coyote, paying for it with money he'd stolen from the prostitute he'd fruitlessly tried to convert. Riding in the back of an old Chevy pick-up with a dozen others, they'd stealthily crept across a barren stretch of the border just before sunup on a clear, windy day, crossing from Baja into Imperial County. From there it had been a matter of getting to San Diego, as well as finding some suitable clothes for his reintroduction. None of that had been a problem, thanks to the fine young man and his wife who'd picked him up on highway 8. He almost regretted having to deceive them, and he took very little pleasure in taking their lives. Unfortunately it was unavoidable. The man was uncannily the same height as he (good fortune was certainly smiling down on him that day), dressed in a suit that had seen very little wear. When he bashed their skulls in with the tire iron he'd made sure they didn't suffer.

After that locating the man in question was a breeze. Fortunately Admiral Craig 'Stony' Hatchet was still affiliated with the Navy, and after a brief chat over the phone Harvey arranged to meet him for drinks at an officer's lounge on base. Over large tumblers of single malt scotch they got reacquainted, and during this reunion he casually inquired about the other's knowledge of a scientific mission to the North Pacific Gyre. As luck would have it, he did. He'd always been in the know about such operations; he made it his business to keep abreast of all things nautical in San Diego. After a brief summary about the mission's apparent failure (the ship's disappearance, taking all hands), nodding respectfully at Harvey's feigned concern, he told him about the preparations being made for a second journey. By nothing short of divine providence there just happened to be an opening for the captaining position, one in which Harvey's Naval accolades easily made him eligible for. That, and the fact no one else wanted the job, with the exception of a man dangerously unqualified. Aided by his colleague's referral he interviewed for the position and, in one fell swoop, had command of the second expedition as well as a free ride home.

And over the course of the journey he'd begun to feel like his old self again, could sense the bacterium growing inside him, getting stronger the closer they got. This in itself reinforced his theory, that his power had been diminished by distance, so he knew not to make the same mistake again. The next time he had to bring his entire army, his newborns and samples from the island. The Rancor birds would probably suffice, as well as buckets of the slime that surrounded the heap as extra insurance.

Yet even though this made sense to him he still couldn't shake the feeling that he was missing something, what, he had no clue. Occasionally a vague idea would come to mind, a word or an image he couldn't quite grasp, formless and elusive no matter how hard he tried to rein it in…something he desperately needed to know…

Upon his arrival to Garbage Island his strength returned to him twice fold, but he found within him a new problem: his powers of reasoning were slipping, as if he'd subjected his brain to heavy bouts of repeated binge drinking and it was finally catching up with him. He found he couldn't make simple connections at times and, with his *second coming, his exterior was rapidly wearing away; perhaps the bacteria was exacting a toll for what it had given him. Like Icarus, he'd flown too close to the sun and ultimately he had to pay the price.*

And here at last it was, the realization that he was fallible, and with this revelation he knew his time was short. He'd been in a state of denial all along but now it was time to face the music and accept the facts: soon enough he wouldn't be able to think straight and, shortly thereafter, he'd probably be reduced to a moldering, maggot-infested corpse...

But that didn't mean it was all over, no, not by a long shot. The bacterium would undeniably have its way, even if he didn't live long enough to see it happen.

He caresses his chest tentatively, seeking out any tenderness, any pain, but there is none forthcoming. He takes in a large, hitching breath, expecting it to be greeted by agony but, again, nothing. The feeling has passed but something inevitably terrible is happening within him, he'll just have to wait and see what it is.

The hell with it. We'll continue as planned.

After his Queen is secured (be it Kim or, hopefully, Melissa) he will convert anyone who's left and pack the ship for their return trip to California. If he is lucky maybe he'll get to enjoy Melissa for a little while before he turns over the reins to Jake. Either Jake or Ronson...

Which brings us back to the experiment. Let's just see what kind of man Jake has become.

There is a rustling of footsteps and Melissa looks up, sees Dr. Taylor approaching, escorted by two of the captain's minions. One of them moves toward Tyler's cage and kicks the door, awakening the bastard within.

"What the hell dudes?" he says in a sleepy voice, sitting up. "What's happening?"

"You...*uhnnnggg*...get out. Captain...need you," the creature grunts, opening the door. Tyler looks at them with a wry smile, a smug gesture that is out of place under the circumstances.

"Bought damn time." He crawls out and gets to his feet. "What's up Doc?" he says to Dr. Taylor, who eyes him distastefully. "Think I'm about to go to work."

"That's a first," Dr. Taylor replies indifferently. The doctor looks like a man who is lost, adrift on a sea of despair, searching for an elusive horizon to a better tomorrow that simply doesn't exist.

"You...*get in...uhnnnggg*...cage," the minion orders and he does so without a word, the door closing behind him.

Grabbing Tyler by his arms, the creatures bustle him off to some appointed place where his talents can truly shine, no doubt, and he protests loudly the fact that they are holding on to him.

"I'm going willingly ya dickheads, let go huh?"

His voice trails off into the distance, the doctor and his ex-lover not knowing this will be the last they shall ever see of him.

"How are you holding up?"

"Not so well," Dr. Taylor answers tonelessly, and it doesn't take a genius to know he is feeling crushed under the weight of all of this, beaten into submission. He turns to her, and through the opaque cage she can't see his features clearly, but she can sense the look of distress etched into a face that's aged ten years over night.

"We're in way over our heads," he says softly, his voice almost too low to hear.

"I know, but we have to keep it together."

"Seriously, piss on it all. You heard what the captain said last night: we're infected anyway. Face it, we're going to die here."

Melissa is surprised to hear him talk like this since he's been so strong throughout this whole ordeal. Something must have happened to extinguish his spirit, something that's taken the life right out of him.

"Don't talk like that. It isn't over until it's over. Besides, he was probably lying about that just to scare us into thinking there was nothing we could do."

"I wish I shared your perspective Melissa, I really do, but I think we're screwed. We might as well accept the facts."

"You can't give up on me now Doc. Until we know for sure we're done for there is always hope."

"Yeah," he says, uttering a crazy, high-pitched laugh. "And it's always darkest before the dawn..."

She can't bear to hear him talk like this; this defeatist attitude won't help them at all, not if they truly expect to find a way out.

"Look man, snap out of it. We have to stay positive or otherwise they've beaten us already. We have to find any advantage and use it to our benefit. I'm not giving up yet, and I have to fight Kim today. How does that sound for an afternoon of entertainment?"

"Daunting."

"To say the least."

"So the captain has taken a shine to you, I guess. Aren't you afraid?"

"Terrified," she admits. "But I have an idea."

"Enlighten me," he says, than shudders at his choice of words.

So she tells him her plan, an inspired scheme that may help her gain a slight advantage over her competitor, and he listens intently, nodding. When she is finished he shrugs, a gesture she senses more than she sees.

"I suppose it could work."

"Well, it's all I got."

"And if you win, then what?"

"I...I don't know," she says haltingly, "but that's not going to stop me from trying." She sits up and peers through the air hole, trying to look him in the eyes. His voice is still far away; she can tell he is in need of more convincing.

"You know we can beat him." She cranes her neck and in her peripheral vision she can see him but his head is down. "Look at me," she says, and when he doesn't respond she repeats more forcefully: "Look at me, goddamnit!"

Slowly his head comes up, his eyes morose, the bags underneath discolored, dark brown smudges.

"We have to keep fighting, you understand? He wants you to give up."

"He wants me to help propagate the species."

"Fuck him! Fuck what he wants! I need you to get your head out of your ass and listen to me. There has to be some way to beat him. Think!"

He looks at her mutely, his mouth working but nothing coming out. Staring into her eyes and witnessing the fury burning within her, the absolute rage she radiates like a nuclear sunrise, something finally ignites inside of him; he can almost hear it fall into place like the tumblers on the lock of a safe. She's right, of course. This is no time to simply lie down and die...

"Okay," he says, looking at her with the slightest of smiles. "It's just that for a moment there everything seemed so hopeless..."

His tone denotes an improvement in his demeanor, a return of his strength of mind as he, no doubt, is encouraged to come up with an initiative of his own.

"That's how he wants us to feel, like we're powerless to stop him. But if we don't at least try he'll certainly kill us, and we're the last line of defense between him and the rest of the world. Can you imagine the chaos if he spreads the infection?"

"The outcome will be nasty, to say the very least."

"We have to give it a shot, if only for our own self satisfaction. The thought of that asshole succeeding makes me want to hit something." She smiles insidiously. "So I'll channel those feelings directly at Kim, for better or worse."

"My fate isn't much better. Captain Harvey is going to have me force fed if I don't help him in his 'lab'."

"His what?"

"You don't want to know, not now anyway. Shit, maybe never." He frowns, chin in his hands, eyes screwed shut in concentration. "I need to come up with a way to win back his favor before they hold me down and shove some of that awful bird meat down my throat."

"Well get thinking Doc," she says glumly, pointing. "Because here they come."

TWENTY-EIGHT

The coarse voices of the humanoids are the first thing Dante hears when he wakes up. It's already quite light outside and getting warm, although the daylight is muted, as if there is something filtering out the sun. He tries to stretch his legs but the cage is much too small for him to do so. Sitting up, he looks out the air hole, trying to get a glimpse of what is going on. He looks over toward Leeann's cage, sees a lock of her dirty auburn hair.

"You awake?" he whispers, and then hears a rustling of movement from within.

"I can't believe I was able to sleep," she says in a dreary voice. "This isn't exactly the Taj Mahal."

"Not even close." He looks in the direction of the voices, wondering what the illustrious captain and his crew have in mind for them today. If it's anything like the hoe down he sponsored last night than they are in for one hell of a treat. "How are you holding up?"

"I've been better."

"Me too." He's silent a moment, taking into consideration how he will sound saying this out loud, but ultimately decides he doesn't care. Their situation is going to get a whole lot worse before it gets any better so he might as well spit it out. "Leeann?" he says tentatively.

"Yeah?" she replies listlessly and his heart flutters sympathetically. The poor girl is so lost, so scared...

"I don't know what is going to happen next, but I want you to know how I feel about you-"

"I know Dante."

"Please," he begs, "just let me say it."

She doesn't reply, as if what he wants to share is something she doesn't want to hear, yet at last she sighs and says: "Go ahead...if you want to."

"I..." He swallows, wondering why this should be so hard. What he has to say, it's the truth isn't it? Honesty shouldn't have to be so difficult. "I...I love you."

476

"I'm glad," she says, and her words destroy something inside of him, a barrier comprised of spite and hate and rejection, tearing it down and obliterating the pieces. He feels free, liberated.

"Thank you," he whispers, very near to tears. "Thank you Leeann…"

"Oh Dante," she says, her voice wavering slightly. "You are more than welcome."

He brushes a stray tear from one large, hard-boiled egg eye, then swipes at another.

"There's something I want *you* to know Mr. Dante Kellerman," she continues, rising to her knees and peering at him through the air hole, looking at him earnestly.

"What's that?"

"If I was ever going to be stranded on an island of garbage with anyone in the world, I'm so happy it's you."

Dante feels warmth spread through his whole body, starting in his cheeks and working its way into his chest and stomach. He would be a liar if he said he didn't feel a little tug in his groin as well. He is, after all, a man.

"I'm glad that I can be here for you," he says, his voice breaking with emotion. He wants so badly to take her hand, to hold her tightly against him, to kiss her and assuage her fears. "I'm going to do everything I can to get us out of this, I promise."

"Don't go making promises you can't keep Dante."

"No, I swear. I'm going to do whatever it takes to beat these bastards. We just need a plan-"

"A plan you say?" Captain Harvey interrupts, appearing at the front of his cage, bending over to look inside. "I like plans. In fact, I *(aaaahhhccckkk!)* have a few of my own." His eyes blink rapidly, his mouth twitching spasmodically. He tilts his head to one side as if he is listening for something, and then dismisses it as if the tick never happened. "Would you like to hear it?"

Dante takes note of this sudden paroxysm, realizing it can only mean that the captain's mind is deteriorating along with his body, hopefully on the same downhill schedule if they are lucky. The ever-tenacious bacterium is hard at work and doing its part, mowing through him like a Lawn-Boy, shredding him from the inside out.

"No, but I suppose you're going to tell us any way."

"Of course! Can't keep my good old buddy Dante in the dark now, *(aaaahhhccckkk!)* can I? I think not!"

He gets to his knees so that he and Dante are face to face. This close, Dante can see phosphorescent shadows swimming behind the captain's corneas, thin white wisps that swirl around in the liquid blackness of his eyes.

Those are worms. He tries not to shudder. *The man is full of worms.*

"What I'm about to do may upset you a little bit, Dah-Dah-Dante, but rest assured it is for the good of Garbage Island."

"Everything you do is for the good of Garbage Island no doubt."

"What a sharp lad! You win a prize!" He claps his hands, urging his minions to do the same. They bring their hands together but the effort is forced, nowhere near the sound of the enthusiastic standing ovation Captain Harvey is trying to conjure. Their hearts just don't seem to be in it. "Now, I have to warn you: you aren't going to like it."

"I don't like anything you do."

"Oh, I'm quite aware of that," the captain says in a husky, menacing tone, leaning even closer, and Dante can see slender green veins writhing just beneath his skin, veins that resemble the strands in his eyes. As he looks on, he sees they are moving, making irregular patterns that twist and twirl. And the scent that comes off him is appalling; it emanates thickly from his mouth, his nose and pores. If asked his opinion, Dante would say the bacterium is probably starting to get the better of Captain Harvey. Soon enough it will be time to pass on the torch. "But you're really not going to like this." He smiles, his lips twitching and contracting, his eyes wide (the left wider than the right) and he stands. "Take the girl," he commands of his minions. "It is time to put her to work."

Three of them move toward her cage, opening the door.

"What the hell are you doing?" Dante cries.

"No!" Leeann screams. "Get your hands off of me!" She tries to brace her feet against the sides of the cage but they are too strong. It only takes a few seconds before she is hauled out, thrashing and kicking.

"Don't do this!" Dante pleads, struggling to get an arm out of the air hole so he can grab the captain, make him listen. "No! Take me instead! You don't need her!"

The captain leans down again, looking peevishly at the other. There is a thick, dark green substance oozing from between his lips, and in it Dante can see filament-sized worms wriggling blindly in the hot sun.

"This isn't a job for *(aaaahhhccckkk!)* you Dah-Dah-Dante. Only females need apply."

Dante stares hard at the captain, comprehension surrendering the last of his calm. "No! You son of a bitch, no!" He batters the inside of his cage, pounding at the plastic walls. Using his legs, his hands, his arms, his head…anything to try and wrest himself from its horrible confines. "You goddamn prick! You do anything to hurt her and I'll kill you!"

"Science is a road paved with casualties my boy," Captain Harvey smirks, straightening up. He swipes at his mouth with his left hand, looking at the collection of ooze briefly before flicking it onto the ground. "To proceed into the future we must first accept that things may not always be to our liking, that there are certain things in life that are beyond our *(aaaahhhccckkk!)* control. You understand, don't you?"

"You sick bastard!"

"Dante!" Leeann bawls as she is dragged away. "Help me! Please!"

"Leeann!" he calls after her. "I'll come and get you!" He pummels the inside of his cage, punching and kicking. The captain backs away, grinning.

"That's right boy, you try and *(aaaahhhccckkk!)* break free so you can save your girl. You waste that strength and get yourself good and tuckered out, maybe work yourself up an appetite." He utters an abrasive, brutal laugh. "That's it! Getting hungry in there big boy? Huh? Perhaps one of my minions can prepare you a snack, yes?"

Dante's efforts soon become feeble, his fists bruised, a knot rising on his forehead. He begins to sob as a terrible certainty fills him, the conviction that he is never going to see Leeann again. At least, not the way he knew her.

"You awful man," he moans, scrubbing his eyes with the heels of his hands. "You awful, awful man."

"Yeah," Captain Harvey nods. "I know." He snaps his fingers and another two minions step forward. "This man is famished. It's about *(aaaahhhccckkk!)* time he's had something to eat. Whip him up something special, will you?" He runs his blackish, serpentine tongue over his lips in a seedy manner that makes Dante's skin crawl. "Now if you will excuse me I have another matter to see to."

The minions bring Tyler into one of the small, decrepit dwellings on the outskirts of 'town', just beyond the wall. Within the confines of the structure the smell of decay is overpowering.

"Jesus dudes! Ever think of putting an air freshener in this place?" He squints, his eyes adjusting to the darkness inside. He can make out what appears to be a row of cots on the far side. Holding his hand to his nose, he walks slowly forward. "What the hell is this?"

Without a reply, two of the minions take his shirt in their knotted hands and rip it from his body, baring his lean torso.

"Hey dudes, what gives? That was a hundred and seventy-five dollar shirt!"

They then reach for his pants and he tries batting their hands away but another joins them, pinning his arms against his sides. Holding him tightly, they lower his dirty dungarees until they are pooled around his ankles, leaving him clothed in only his filthy underwear, a pair of boxers decorated with bright yellow bananas.

"You...*uhnnnggg*...get...hard," one of them says. "You...fuck."

"What?" He swings his head back toward the cots, aware for the first time that a motley assortment of women occupies them. There is a white woman, a black woman, an Asian woman—all in various states of repose. "These are the bitches you want me to screw?" Even in the subdued light he can see they are infected, can tell by their rigid movements, the dull look in their eyes, their lesion covered bodies in varied stages of putrefaction. "No way dudes."

One of the minions takes hold of his boxers, wrenching them down to his knees. Never one to be shy, Tyler stands immodestly before them, a look of disbelief on his face.

"Really?" he asks, an eyebrow arched. "Seriously?"

"Seriously," Captain Harvey says, stepping into the room. "I've chosen you for my reproductive testing, as we agreed."

Tyler looks at him skeptically, then returns his gaze to the women. Some of them aren't half bad; good bodies, minimal deterioration... "Wait dude, hold on now. I can't imagine touching them, much less...You're pulling my leg, right?"

"I need healthy human *(aaaahhhccckkkk!)* seed for this experiment. You told me you were the man for the job. Is there a problem?"

"Yeah dude, there is." He gestures to the *(creatures)* women. "These chicks are like...I'm not into narcolepsy dude!"

The captain's eyes twinkle, or maybe it's the writhing of the worms within. In any case he smiles broadly, his bottom lip tearing away as he does so, creating a flap that dangles over his chin.

"I think you mean necrophilia, but rest assured, these women aren't dead. They are in a recently modified *(aaaahhhcccckkk!)* state. They are fresh, so to speak."

"They don't smell too fresh."

"You want me to have them douche for you?"

"That might be a start-"

"Look you cocksucker," Captain Harvey affixes a hand around Tyler's throat, applies enough pressure to make the other's eyes bug out of his head. "You're lucky I didn't have you killed on the ship after your *(aaaahhhcccckkk!)* insubordinance. You want to know something? I don't like you, never have. You make me sick to my *(aaaahhhcccckkk!)* stomach you slimy little toad." He twists Tyler's head so that it is facing the *(creatures)* women on the rickety, handmade cots. "You either start fucking or I'm going to give you a send off like the governor. How does that sound? And after what you did to your *(aaaahhhcccckkk!)* buddies from the ship I think they just might enjoy it. In fact, I know a few who definitely will."

Tyler feels the weight of an unimaginable reality tugging at him, experiences terror deep in the pit of his stomach that is like a physical ache. All of his good-natured kidding is gone, as well as any delusions he might have had about his invulnerability. At long last he is aware that he is nothing special in the grand scheme of things and he's just like the others: dead meat whether he likes it or not.

"So…I screw these chicks and…then what?"

Captain Harvey lets go and claps him on the shoulder. "You bust a few nuts, have a good time, what else?"

Tyler shakes his head, trying to look the captain in the eyes but failing. "No, I mean…what then? Is what you said last night true? Are we already infected?"

The captain puts his arm around Tyler's shoulder, drawing him close. The smell of the man is harsh, like breathing in the fumes of an open sewer grate. His skin feels slimy, and beneath it (as crazy as it sounds) he can feel things wriggling and squirming, like his veins are worms and they are pumping more than blood through his body. It's almost as if *(and this is absolutely fucking out there dude, totally over the rainbow and gone, call the men in the white coats and tell them to have a straight jacket ready for me)* the captain is made entirely of worms, his bones, his muscles, his skin…everything has become a mass of worms. If you cut him open he wouldn't bleed so much as he would seep creepy crawly things.

"I made that up Tyler," he says, his breath the stench of a million dead bodies; the corpses of the war ravaged Afghanistan villagers, the dead gangbangers laying on the sidewalks of Chicago, L.A., New York, Miami, Detroit, Milwaukee, the bullet-ridden bodies of children on school playgrounds across America everywhere… "I just wanted all of you to do what you are told." He frowns, and then belches a mouthful of dark green bile that dribbles down his chin, covering his bottom lip, which sways back and forth like a light bulb on the end of a string. "Can you *(aaaah-hhcccckkk!)* do that for me?" He eyes him somberly. "Can you?"

Tyler swallows, his Adam's apple bobbing up and down furiously to try and keep last night's supper down. Looking at the putrefying captain is like watching time elapsed films about nature in science class. The death, the flies, the maggots, the ants and so on until the carcass is nothing but a pile of sun bleached bones…This guy is crumbling, the bacterium slicing him up like cheese through a grater, and it seems as if he isn't even aware of it…

And suddenly, in the dim recesses of a brain he's mostly allowed to be on holiday for the better part of his life, Tyler makes a connection, one that fills him with hope.

He's dying, he must be. Why else would he be making those weird sounds and spitting out mouthfuls of green crap? Soon enough the bacteria will reduce him to nothing but a lump of rotten flesh and then I'll be free! We'll all be free. Because wasn't it he who controlled the others? Without someone to lead them wouldn't they become directionless? Probably walk around in circles bumping into one another like a bunch of undead three stooges.

All he has to do is play his game, bide his time and in short order it will all be over. The captain will eventually succumb to the worms that are eating him alive and they'll be able to escape, those who haven't been converted, those who haven't already died.

"I can," Tyler gulps, managing a weak smile. "You bet."

"That's the spirit boy," he says, patting him on the cheek. "Now *(aaaahhhccckkk!)* get to work."

"What are you going to do?"

"I think I have an idea."

"It better be a damn good one."

"We're about to find out."

Four minions approach Dr. Taylor's cage. One of them carries a dead Rancor bird, plucked of all its feathers, stripped of its scales. Another reaches for the door of the cage, swings it open.

"You," he rasps. "Get…*uhnnnggg*…out!"

"Okay, okay," Dr. Taylor says calmly. "Let's all be sensible now." He climbs out of the cage and gets to his feet, his hands in the air before him.

Two of the minions grab him, wrenching his arms behind his back while another grasps his jaw, forcing his mouth open. The fourth member of the group begins ripping the bird carcass apart, tearing it into small, bite size pieces.

"Wait!" Dr. Taylor cries. "I need to talk to the captain! I want to help him after all! Please!"

Ignoring him, the minion with the bird twists the head off, stuffs it in his own mouth and chews vociferously. Melissa and Dr. Taylor can hear the sickening sound of the beak and skull crunching between its teeth. He then extends his arm, a piece of the bird held in between thumb and forefinger.

"Aren't you listening to me? I told you I need to speak to the captain!"

"Listen to him you dummies!" Melissa hollers. "You got shit in your ears?"

The minion holding the bird thrusts a piece of the meat in his mouth, and Dr. Taylor quickly spits it out. It bounces off of the others chest and lands on the ground. The feel of it in his mouth makes the doctor think of tapeworms, leeches, round worms…

Ripping off another piece, the minion again tries to stuff it in Dr. Taylor's mouth but this time he turns his head away just in time and the other misses.

"You… hold…*uhnnnggg*…still!" one of the minions snarls. "You…eat!"

"I need to speak to the captain! He needs my help with his breeding experiments and I want to assist him in any way I can!"

Here I am at the crossroads of too little and too late, he thinks dismally as they bear down on him harder, the strength of their collective grip agonizing. It feels as if their fingers are going to break right through his skin and crush the bone. *I should have thought of this sooner but, like they say, hindsight is 20/20. It might not have been the best idea anyway, but it's the only one I could come up with on short notice…*

"Let him go!" Melissa's voice is amazingly loud. "You heard the man! He needs to speak to the captain!"

"Don't you understand me?" Dr. Taylor says, attempting a last ditch effort before they can successfully stuff the meat in his mouth and make him swallow. "The captain needs my help! He needs me!"

The minion holding his jaw squeezes hard (harder) and he finds he can no longer speak. The one with the bird rips off a large piece and, now that the other two have him effectively pinned, he carefully places the piece of meat on his tongue, as if he is administering *(un)* Holy Communion.

This is the body of the Rancor Bird. Eat it and be damned…

"Hold it!" a voice thunders, and the minions halt what they are doing. His jaw released, the doctor spits the piece of meat onto the ground. "You say you want to help the captain?"

It's Jake Anderson, well, the man who used to be Jake Anderson anyway. Not that he appears to be in the exact condition the other creatures are, no, he seems to have more control of his movements, like the captain.

Maybe it has to do with the conversion process. Dr. Taylor smiles gratefully, knowing his sudden emergence has saved him (at least temporarily) from the fate of the others. *Harvey mentioned something about how it was done last night, a method he could employ if he wished to create an equal…*

"Yes," he says. "I want to help the captain with his children. He needs my scientific mind to ensure that his creations are healthy." He smiles wider, trying to sound as sincere as he can. "I want to do everything within my powers to assist him."

"You, let him go," Jake commands and the humanoids do so, releasing the doctor's arms. "Come with me."

Dr. Taylor turns to Melissa, catches her eye through the air hole. He tips her a wink. "See you soon," he whispers and she nods.

"I hope so."

Following Jake, Dr. Taylor sees he is heading back in the direction of the atrocity that Captain Harvey calls his breeding laboratory, but this time he has an idea, a proposal the captain may or may not accept.

Don't know if it will work or not. Maybe I just bought myself a few more minutes. Who knows? But I'll tell ya what: another few minutes of being me is worth it, whatever happens next…

TWENTY-NINE

Dante leans against the back of the cage sobbing, the sorrow within him total, all encompassing. A desperate feeling of impotence courses through him, and he kicks at the walls, crying aloud in his anger and frustration. Leeann is gone and there is nothing he can do about it, zilch, unless he can break out of here. He rages against the formidable walls and wishes there was some way he could help her. Anything, anything at all…he'd sacrifice himself just to save her.

"You fucking bastards!" he bellows in a gravelly voice, his throat aggravated by the yelling and crying. How can he carry on without her? How? She was the only reason he'd been so strong, had been motivated to press on even when it was apparent the odds were so terribly stacked against them. Without her, well, there just doesn't seem to be any point in continuing this charade of bravado. He's lost, drifting, a balloon cut from the string that kept it tethered to the earth.

And, beneath his fury and grief, an overpowering hunger rises within him, a ravenous force that swells and grows, screaming to be satiated. It's as if he hadn't partaken of the feast the previous night at all; his appetite clamors inside him maddeningly, chewing at his guts like a school of piranhas. As a kid he'd seen some pretty lean years, especially while he still lived with his mother, before his stepfamily, but for obvious reasons the old pain is trivial, nothing compared to this. This starvation has him feeling restless and hostile, frantic to end it by any means necessary. He's so rattled by the loss of Leeann that at once he considers it as a form of suicide. He could eat, consume the meat of Garbage Island and simply let go, let it do to him what it has done to countless others. And why not? What else does he have to live for? They are going to get him anyway, one way or another, so why not give in, just let it happen? The captain told them last night that they were already infected; why not speed up the process?

But what about Leeann? He can't let them violate her, which he knows full well is what the captain intends.

He wants to use her for breeding. The thought comes to him unbidden, foreboding and dark. *My poor, sweet, innocent Leeann...*

No, he can't give up, he has to help her, but he is utterly despondent, and so very, very hungry. What can he do? How can he get out of here so that he can go to her aid?

He hears someone approaching his cage, shambling, dragging footsteps that stop once they are directly outside.

"Captain...*uhnnnggg*...say he...don't...*uhnnnggg*...need you," the creature says, and Dante leans to the front of the cage, peering out the air hole at the atrocious thing that was once like him, a human being with thoughts, feelings, likes, dislikes. "He say...you...*uhnnnggg*...eat or... die."

"About one in the same, don't you think?" he replies, staring up at the other, but the creature makes no gesture that he understands, simply stands his ground, his blank eyes looking somewhere over Dante's left shoulder.

"What do you think?" Dante persists, knowing it's pointless, that he won't get an answer, but what the hell. "Is it worth it? Are you happy as you are?"

"Captain...says," the minion repeats tonelessly, "you eat...or...*uhnnnggg*...you die."

"Okay," Dante says resolutely. He's been given his choice and what he wants to do-needs to do-is acquiesce. "You got it buddy. Serve it up. I'm so hungry I could eat just about anything right now. I guess a little Garbage Island Special ought to hit the spot."

The minion turns away.

You sure you know what you're doing, Dante old buddy? You do this and you can say goodbye to all you ever knew. Adios mother fuckers. I guess I've had a pretty good run, huh? I even found love, though it was probably never meant to be I suppose. Nothing was ever meant to be for me, all the niceties this planet had to offer. No love for you Dante, no happiness for you. You'll never become the man you want to be, never get anything in this world because deep down you know you simply don't deserve it. Not you. The other guys, sure, those pretty boys like Tyler who get all the girls and have all the fun. They are far more deserving than a piece of shit like you, a worthless, waste of life if ever there was one. Can't even think of a way out of this you fucking coward. Taking the easy way out. I hope you're proud of yourself, hope this makes you happy you pathetic loser...

The humanoid returns, clutching the bloody remains of a plucked and scaled Rancor Bird.

"Mm Mm looks delicious."

"You...eat." It holds the bird up to the air hole.

Dante takes the bird from him, rips off a wing. His stomach rumbles ominously. "I don't suppose you have any A-I sauce, huh?" he jokes but the other doesn't reply, just looks at him with that signature blank stare, his slack jaw hanging like the local yokel selling home made jerky by the side of the road. Road kill jerky he and his stepbrother Michael used to call it, back in the bad old days after his sister had died and his mother had been locked up for involuntary manslaughter. Good old road kill jerky. "Here's to your health," he says, and stuffs a piece in his mouth.

"So you've come to your senses and decided to help me? To what do I *(aaahhhcccckkk!)* deserve the honor?"

Captain Harvey sits atop his throne, his Queen Kim Leung by his side. She is so wretched that it is almost impossible to look upon her countenance without involuntarily gagging. And the erstwhile captain cum 'King of Garbage Island' has added a new wrinkle to his ever-growing bag of tricks: a tick that must mean his deterioration is quickening, his decomposition on the fast track to the next level, whatever that is.

"Well," Dr. Taylor starts, knowing that this is his moment to shine, to do or die. What he says now will either get him killed or will offer him a chance at redemption. "I've long been fascinated by many facets of science-"

"You told me you specialized in marine biology," the captain interrupts, glancing over Dr. Taylor's shoulder and waving his hand impatiently. "Thank you for *(aaaahhhcccckkk!)* bringing him to me Jake, that will be all. You have your orders, now *(aaaahhhcccckkk!)* go."

"Aye Master," Jake says and quickly takes his leave.

"Yes," Dr. Taylor resumes, "specifically I studied oceanography and marine biology but, as a man of science, I am naturally inclined to be interested in all aspects of scientific data collection."

"Let's cut to the *(aaahhhcccckkk!)* chase, shall we? I know why you are doing this. You can't fool me."

Doctor Taylor eyes the other with what he hopes resembles surprise and not the miserable surge of dread he feels burrowing it's way into his belly like a rabid gopher. "Oh?" he asks. "And why is that?"

"Don't be coy Doc, we both know you just want to *(aaaahhhcccckkk!)* hang in there as long as you can." Captain Harvey smiles and Dr. Taylor sees that two of his front teeth are missing, one top, one bottom. Between them the green fluid leaks over his lips and, when he swipes at it with his hand, he catches his loose bottom lip between two fingers and pulls it most of the way off. He frowns, extending it so he can take a look, then, as if he is handling a Band-Aid, tugs it free. "I didn't need that anyway." He dangles it above Kim's head and she bares her teeth, chomping at it like a dog would after a biscuit. "Here girl!" he encourages, swinging it from side to side. "Who wants a treat?" And he drops it into her mouth where it disappears quickly in the black void of her throat. "That's a good girl!"

"You are correct captain," Dr. Taylor says, eyes averted from the bizarre display, taking deep, even breaths. Just when he thinks he's seen it all, well, he realizes it can *always* get worse. Much worse. "I'm not quite ready to, to...change."

"So you'll *(aaahhhcccckkk!)* help me?" the captain asks, focusing his attention back on the doctor. "I need to ensure that my lovely children will be safe to travel."

"How soon?"

"By tomorrow at the very latest, but tonight would be *(aaaahhhcccckkk!)* ideal."

"To do that I'm going to need some instruments, if I am to go about it properly."

"Instruments?"

"Yes sir, medical equipment I can use to run some tests."

The captain looks at him suspiciously. "And just what are these 'instruments'?"

"Nothing unusual I assure you. I would like to run blood work, and for that I'll need syringes and test tubes, and a microscope if you have one. Certainly you have some of these items on the ship?"

Captain Harvey strokes his chin, greenish/blackish blood coagulating where his lip used to be. "What are you looking for?"

"Anything out of the ordinary," Dr. Taylor ventures, knowing that everything related to this place is what one could consider 'out of the ordinary'. "Deviations of the white and red blood cells to start (*like they aren't already massively deviated*), and it wouldn't be a bad idea to study the bacterial organism-"

"What for?"

"To make sure it's thriving within them, of course," Dr. Taylor replies hastily. "They are the future of not only Garbage Island but of Garbage World, right?"

"You know they are," the captain nods, grinning. He reaches out and absently strokes Kim's head, kneading her hair with his fingers. "I like that," he says. "'Garbage World'" has a nice (*aaaah-hhccckkk!*) ring to it."

"I thought you'd think so."

"So you want to study the bacteria?"

"Don't you want to know how it's progressing within your offspring?"

Captain Harvey studies him, his eyes shifting from side to side. What Dr. Taylor is hoping (counting on to be absolutely honest) is that the captain's thinking capacity is weakening at the same rate as his outer tissue. Since this bacteria overtakes its host from the inside (stomach, colon, intestines, bloodstream, whatever) he calculates that it must be destroying the normal, healthy cells as it works its way outward, brain cells included. His fingers figuratively crossed he is anticipating that, what with the advanced state of disintegration his body is exhibiting, the good captain's thought processing abilities are becoming jumbled as his brain is gradually being pummeled into so much useless pudding, hence making it easier to sway him toward something that would otherwise strike him as unwise, possibly an act that could be utilized as an escape attempt.

Dr. Taylor sees the distrust in the other's eyes, watches the black orbs in his head roll aimlessly as he tries to figure out what his angle is, but it appears to be eluding him.

(*I'm missing something. . .what the fuck am I missing?*)

"And what do you (*aaaahhhccckkk!*) get out of this?"

"You already said it yourself. I get to remain as I am as long as possible and also investigate what is surely a marvel of modern scientific study."

Captain Harvey smiles again, an awful thing to behold because of his missing lower lip.

"So you agree that what we have here is (*aaaahhhccckkk!*) a 'marvel'?"

"Very much so," the doctor answers without hesitation but, not wanting to seem suspicious, adds: "Albeit a mostly inhuman, disgusting one."

"Oh doctor, you do have a way with words, I'll grant you that, but certainly you don't think I'm stupid enough to (*aaaahhhccckkk!*) allow you access to the ship. Who knows what mischief you plan to perpetrate?"

(*He knows something I am missing. . .what does he know? I can't see inside him, can hardly see inside anyone anymore. . .*)

"I'm not asking you to let me go alone. Send some of your men with me or, better yet, come with me yourself."

He hopes like hell the captain doesn't personally take the bait; because as sure as the sun is hot and the night is dark he does not want Captain Harvey to escort him. If he did there certainly wouldn't be any opportunity to look around, not that there is any guarantee he could if accompanied by the creatures, but he feels with them he stands a better chance.

The captain is quiet, rubbing the spot where his lip used to be. He looks at the doctor keenly, wracking his brain in an attempt to ascertain what the doctor is hiding but, plainly, he is coming up empty handed.

"You want to do blood tests," he says, smearing the viscous fluid on his chin with his fingers.

"Among other things. The tests I can perform all depend on the type of equipment I have."

"Yes…" The captain looks at Kim. "What do you think dear? You think we should *(aaaah-hhccckkk!)* trust him?"

Kim rolls her head back and forth, issuing god-awful gurgling noises that sound eerily similar to a clogged bathtub drain after getting pipe-snaked. She waves her hands around, and he can see the nub of her frayed and blackened tongue waggling up and down. The captain listens to her as if she is offering sane, rational advice, nodding every so often at each valid point. After several minutes of watching this painful display, the captain raises a hand in the air and she ceases at once.

"She has made an excellent suggestion, one that *(aaahhccckkk!)* makes me feel much better about the whole thing."

"Yes?"

"You can go, but you will be accompanied by your old buddies Kenny and Cole." The captain beams, something sinister *(more sinister)* in his grinning rictus. "Do you know why I choose to *(aaaahhccckkk!)* send them with you?"

"No," he relents, hiding the unexpected sentiment he feels regarding Cole's departure. It must have happened sometime this morning, shortly after Kenny passed over to the other side. "I do not."

"If you try anything, *anything*, I'll have them commit atrocities upon you and *(aaaahhccckkk!)* the rest of your pals such as you've never imagined." His smile turns into a leer, his upper lip curving in a manner that is utterly hideous. "If you even so much as think of deceiving me I'll have those two pop out your eyeballs and skull fuck you, both at the same time, a dick in *(aaaahhccckkk!)* each eye socket. Is that understood?"

"Yes sir," Dr. Taylor replies, his voice quavering ever so slightly.

"Good," Captain Harvey says decisively. "Just keep that in mind." His gaze is powerful, his scrutiny intensely focused and Dr. Taylor fights to retain his composure, to keep his expression as neutral as possible. He stares back at the captain with a bland look of disinterest on his face, as if the whole thing makes no difference to him. At last, after several nerve-wracking seconds tick by very slowly, the captain looks away. He claps his hands and two of his minions step forward. "Go and fetch the new guys. Tell them I *(aaaahhccckkk!)* have a job for them."

Wordlessly they turn and exit. The captain's eyes find Dr. Taylor again. "We are going to have a tournament today," he says, switching topics. "Maybe you've heard?"

"A tournament?"

"Yes. It appears that slut Melissa has challenged my beautiful Queen Kim. They are to fight to the *(aaaahhhcccckkk!)* death this afternoon."

"The purpose being?"

"Why certainly that's obvious. They are fighting over who gets to be *(aaaahhhcccckkk!)* the Queen Of Garbage Island, ultimately the world."

"And why would Melissa want this dubious honor?"

"For the same reason you want to run tests on my offspring: she wants to remain herself as long as she can. You do remember what I told you *(aaaahhhcccckkk!)* last night, do you not? Whether you like it or not the bacteria is slowly changing you. You can put it off by *(aaaahhhcccckkk!)* avoiding its infection directly, but in the long run it is futile. It always wins. The house always *(aaaahhhcccckkk!)* wins."

Dr. Taylor swallows uneasily. Has he felt any changes within himself yet? Hard to tell, he decides. How he feels is physically and emotionally drained, coupled with an unquenchable hunger and thirst. Dealing with all of that, not to mention his incessant anxiety, it's hard to sense if anything else is developing within him.

"So soon enough we'll be like you anyway?"

"You'll never be like me," the captain laughs, a grating, unnerving liquid sound that proceeds into a hacking cough. Dr. Taylor winces as the captain expectorates a large mass of writhing, whitish worms into his own lap, followed by a large amount of greenish/black-tinged blood. He stares at the mess, his face blank for a moment, but when he looks up again his eyes are rimmed with a sheen of unspeakable lunacy, bearing an expression that contends he's never been human at all... He scoops up the pile with both hands, holding it high over his head, fat drops of gelatinous fluid spattering down upon him.

"Does my beautiful Queen want a treat? Yes? Do you *(aaaahhhcccckkk!)* want a treat?"

Dr. Taylor turns away, sickened, holding a dirty hand to his mouth. Of all the things he's had to deal with over the last few days (landing aboard Garbage Island amidst the chaos of the insects and the sludgy, creature infested sea, the foul stench of this place, the fear and uncertainty, the hunger and thirst, the horror of being captured, the utter dreadfulness of eating Governor Hallsly alive and witnessing the captain's monstrous maternity ward) this surely takes the cake, watching Kim Leung snap and grovel for a handful of grisly worms coated in a slimy layer of the captain's inner fluids. He can taste pungent bile creeping up the back of his throat.

And then, like two ghostly apparitions, Kenny and Cole appear before him, their arms dangling flaccidly at their sides, their eyes as blank and sightless as two mannequins.

"You...come," Kenny intones hollowly. "We...*uhnnnggg*...go."

One of the captain's minions appears at the door holding a handful of Slim Jims and a bottle of water. Tyler lifts himself off of the woman (*creature*) he's just had his way with and walks on unsteady legs to take the provisions.

"Bought damn time dude," he says, tearing off a wrapper with his teeth. "Can't fuck on an empty stomach."

He's lying, of course. Tyler could fuck after going a week without food, in sub-zero temperatures, missing both of his legs. All he really needs is his cock and balls and possibly his torso, to get a good pumping motion going. Hell, he doesn't even need arms.

The Slim Jim hits the spot, the water cold and refreshing. Screwing these mutant broads, he finds, ain't too bad, once you get over the smell. He's worked his way through three of them and all he needs is, like, ten minutes and he'll be ready for number four. That's one thing about him that chicks always dug: his ability to get hard again and again and again. Hell, he'll never need anything as ridiculous as Viagra when he's got a constant supply of blood heading to his penis and strong capillaries to make sure it stays put.

He takes another swig of the water when at once he feels lightheaded, almost giddy. It's as if he's just snorted a good blast of mostly pure cocaine (okay, the best he *ever* got was maybe 40% pure) or about 10 milligrams of MDPV. A euphoric rush ripples through his brain like a tsunami, and a sense of contentment follows. He feels good, really good, and he smiles dazedly, lifting his arms, which seem as if they could just float away.

"Whoa baby, whoa now."

Back in the day when he couldn't find cocaine he used to get this shit at the head shops called 'bath salts', until it was declared illegal in 2012 because people were, well, dropping like flies. It was powerful stuff, especially the blends that contained MDPV (methylenedioxypyrovalerone, a chemical compound synthesized in the 60's intended for use as a weight loss drug or to combat chronic fatigue but was never approved for human consumption because of it's highly addictive nature) and it only took a tiny bit to get yer motor runnin'. It made you feel euphoric like cocaine, and in some people it acted as an aphrodisiac, similar to MDMA (ecstasy). Tyler found he could fuck forever on it, and he loved secretly spiking his date's drinks with about 5 milligram's (what he considered a 'safe' amount) and waiting to see if they became aroused, eventually helping them to slip into something more comfortable, like his bed, if they did. Yeah, he'd had a great time with the stuff, but there was a downside.

The thing was you had to be very careful, not only because it was extremely addictive, but also because it was easy to get in over your head with. When you thought you were coming down and you took another bump, the amount that was already in your system re-activated, over-stimulating you. Your heart would race and it was hard to catch your breath, the room spinning, sounds you never noticed becoming loud, almost painful. It could be pretty damn scary. Also, it didn't take long for the drug to produce genuine psychosis, which in turn lead to vivid hallucinations. He'd once stayed up for six days snorting and smoking it and by the end the apartment was full of shadowy figures, otherworldly (yet very real) specters that he conversed with, laughing and screaming and crying until he'd finally decided it was time to go to the emergency room and get something to help him come down. After that he'd stopped using it, sticking to the blow instead just to be on the safe side.

His heart rate continues to rise and then it skips a beat, then another, and another.

Oh shit. . .

The perception of impending tachycardia is enough to sober him instantly. His heart beats several beats then misses one, chugging along irregularly. Taking a deep breath, he rubs his chest in a circular motion, backing up until he reaches the far wall. He closes his eyes in an attempt to center himself but dizziness suddenly overcomes him, the feeling quickly taking an awful turn, making him nauseous. He massages his stomach, wondering if the Slim Jim isn't sitting right.

"How old is this shit dude?" he says to the creature guarding the door but, of course, he doesn't look, doesn't answer, just stares into space. "You hear me man? Is this shit, like, expired?"

And then, with the unexpectedness of a hard rain falling from a cloudless sky, he feels the floor drop beneath him, as if he were perched atop a trapdoor that has opened without warning. He presses himself flat against the wall as the sensation washes over him, his pulse soaring, his mouth agape, taking large, frightened breaths.

"Fuckin' A!" he gasps, his left arm going numb, his vision tunneling down to a fine point of light that seems so very far away. He hears the sound of chimes, tinkling madly like the soundtrack to a nightmare, and everything goes dark, his world reduced to blackness (*Holy shit, I think I'm having a heart attack. I must have over exerted myself or those Slim Jims are poisoned. . .*). Clutching his chest with both hands, pressed hard over his heart as he physically tries to cease it's runaway-train thumping, he leans forward too far and trips over his own feet, crashing onto the floor.

A moment passes, silent, nothing but the background murmur of the villagers as they go about their chores. He realizes gradually that his heart rate is slowing down and, blinking hard several times, his vision slowly returns. The din in his head recedes, echoing faintly as it dissipates, the air about him undulating, reverberating, until the dissonance disappears altogether.

"What the hell. . ." He takes stock of himself, naked, laying on the floor of the room, his cock lolling uselessly on his thigh, these slathered with the juices of sex, from him, from the women (*creatures*). He sits up, puts a hand to his head and tentatively explores the spot where he hit it on the floor. There is a small lump there, nothing serious.

"Whoa man," he says to the creature guarding the door, who doesn't appear to have noticed. "Those Slim Jims are bad dude. You gotta look at the expiration dates."

He gets slowly to his feet, knees wobbling, hands shaking. Damned if that wasn't reminiscent of an MDPV overdose, but where did it come from? Can food poisoning do that to you? He rubs his stomach, noting pleasantly that the queasiness has passed. He puts a finger on the inside of his wrist, finding his pulse, and confirms that it's more or less back to normal.

"Fuckin' weird man. . ."

Senses regained, his recovery complete, he looks over at the woman (*creature*) who is next on his list and sees it's the Asian lady. His cock stirs to life, the thing an automaton, just doing its job.

Total fluke dude, nothing to worry about. No more Slim Jim's if I can help it. Those shitheels are trying to poison me.

He returns his attention to the task at hand.

"Okay baby," he says, climbing on top of her. "Get ready to have yer world rocked."

Sightlessly the woman (*creature*) stares at the ceiling. She offers no response, as if she hasn't even heard him. Her legs are slightly parted and he grabs one in each hand, spreading them wide. Does Tyler care that it's like screwing chicks under the influence of roofies? Nope. Not at all. Been there before baby, been there, done that, got the t-shirt…all in a day's work honey, all in a day's work…

Dante shoves the carcass of the Rancor Bird out the air hole, nothing left but a skeleton with fragments of gnawed flesh sticking to the bones. He manages a belch.

"Thanks guys," he says, wiping his mouth. "Much better."

A creature standing guard picks up the remains of the bird and, with the efficiency of a vulture, strips the last of the flesh with the nubs of his rotting teeth.

"That's right," Dante nods approvingly, "don't want any to go to waste."

Then the thing turns away, tossing the bird aside. Dante watches him go, caressing his belly thoughtfully. Only a matter of time now and things will change. Let's see how the progression goes…

"Hey you! Yeah, ya dumb ass! That's right. Get over here!"

The humanoid approaches Melissa's cage, stands silently before her.

"I need to speak to the captain, like, pronto."

It stares at her mutely, mouth slightly open, drool forming in the corners.

"Did you hear me? I need to speak to the captain. Tell him I have some demands before I fight Kim today, okay? Tell him I'm ready to whip that bitch's scrawny little ass but I have a couple of requirements first. Can you do that? Can you relay the message for me?"

He continues to stare, appearing as if he's heard nothing, understands not a word she's spoken, but then turns around and heads in the direction of the town hall. She smiles to herself.

"That's right you bastard," she mutters. "You tell him I still have some fight left in me and let's see if this works."

She feels anxious, but she is no longer terrified. The dominatrix inside of her relishes a good fight, an opportunity to get her hands bloody. We'll just see who's helpless or not, you cadaverous motherfuckers.

And if the captain denies her request, what then?

Then I'll just have to fight with my bare hands, God help me.

She's had it with this craphole, had it with the confinement of the cage and, most of all, has had enough of being scared, wondering what's going to happen next. If anything she's simply looking for something final, something to end this travesty before it can rip what's left of her sensitive ego apart. These three days have felt like three years, and it seems like forever since she was on the research vessel, lounging on the bunk in her cabin, whiling the time away. She thinks of the sex she had with Tyler, wonders how he is using his tool right now.

"I hope it rots off you asshole," she mumbles spitefully. "I hope the damn thing falls right off."

THIRTY

Cole leads the way, Dr. Taylor in the middle, Kenny bringing up the rear. Morning has given way to early afternoon and the sun is beating down mercilessly. Any hopes of rain are futile, as the clear blue sky confirms.

The doctor's observations of the creatures have yielded very little but the obvious (vacant stare, monotone speech pattern accompanied by panting and grunting, stiff, lumbering gait, possibly limited intelligence but hard to know for sure because of their awkward communication technique), but right now he adds another characteristic to the list: they don't sweat. He is losing what little fluid he has left in his body at an alarming pace and they don't appear to be affected at all. Wiping perspiration from his brow, he casts a glance at Kenny but there is no 'Kenny' left. He is just a shell of his former self, nothing left inside but the bacteria directing his movements, controlling his thoughts. Like all the others, Kenny's eyes are empty, but he knows that if he should try anything suspicious he will see him all right, and dire consequences will follow.

Captain Harvey's words were clear (despite the lisp because of his missing lower lip) as they left the town hall: "If the doctor tries anything stupid, anything at all, torture him and then rip his head off."

"Rip his…*uhnnnggg*…head…off," Kenny had repeated, his droning voice lacking any compassion, making his words all the more menacing.

They come upon the sign that announces the village, the crudely drawn and constructed marker that he couldn't read his first time through because of the dark. He reads it now, figuring it sums up the captain's idea of humor: *'Welcome to the End of the Road'*. It's the end of the road all right, the end of the line, the end of the night, the end of everything sacred and pure. If Captain Harvey's plan to spread the bacteria to the rest of the world does come to fruition it will be a bad day for humankind, to say the very least. Something like this will spread like wildfire, jumping borders with the speed and efficiency of a Mexican coyote. Within a month the whole world will be infected.

But there has to be something that can fight it, if it isn't too twisted a strain. We have medicines to fight off all kinds of bacteria. For all I know some strong antiseptic soap might be all these guys need…

That is, of course, if the captain is correct about it being caused by bacteria. How can he be certain? Everything he knows is probably wrought from hallucinations brought upon by his sickness. What if it is a virus, born of the bacteria? What if the two are acting concurrently, the first one created by the filth and germs from the garbage, the other evolved from the former? Without being able to test it there is no way he will ever know.

Dr. Taylor feels frustration mounting within him at a puzzle he will most likely never solve. For the moment, all he is looking to do is extend his life a little longer and, if he can do that, possibly make some kind of escape attempt. The only way that's possible, he knows, will involve a great deal of luck, something that's been in short supply as of late. As far as he knows he'll be dead or mutated as soon as the captain realizes he isn't really running any tests, or Kenny and Cole catch him trying to remove an item from the ship that can be used as a weapon. Because-even though he's scared, for Christ's sake he's literally shitting bricks-he knows in his heart that if such an opportunity should arise he is going to take it. And why not? He has absolutely nothing to lose. He'll feel bad about Melissa having to fend for herself against Kim Leung, but soon enough they'll all be dead anyway. Whatever effort he makes will be with her in mind at any rate, so all for one and one for all. Either they both live, or they both die.

He stumbles, the lack of fluids catching up with him in this hot, pounding sun. At least the covering over the village kept its powerful rays at bay. Currently he can feel the life slipping out of him with every drop of sweat, and he figures if he doesn't get a drink of water soon that it won't matter what happens, he'll die of dehydration.

Wouldn't that make everything nice and easy? Just collapse and fall into a sunstroke induced coma. That way I won't have to worry about being turned into one of those things, or getting torn to pieces by my old ship mates.

But as much as the thought appeals to him, a seemingly simple way to make everything just go away, he doesn't want it, no, for it would do nothing to alleviate the anger burning inside him. Because in the end he would love to see good old Captain Harvey's diseased world blown to smithereens, would love to see the look on his face if his plans went up in smoke…

"You think you guys might see it in your hearts to let me have something to drink when we get to the ship? I'm almost ready to tap out here."

"Captain say…you…*uhnnnggg*…allowed…water when…get…to…*uhnnnggg*…ship," what used to be Kenny says, and the doctor feels a mild surge of relief. He figures he's earned it, now that he's willing to cooperate.

"That's the best news I've heard all day fellah's," he says with a smile. "Let's shake a leg."

Struggling to sit up, Leeann finds she is bound to a makeshift bed, her arms and legs held fast by thin strips of plastic, much like the apparatus' the police sometimes use instead of hand-cuffs. Her head aches dully, resulting from her resistance; it was the only way they could get her to calm down. She'd fought like a wildcat even though she knew she was powerless to stop them because the knowledge of their intentions was too much to bear. She'd heard what the captain said to Dante, heard the insinuation in his voice and Dante's resulting horror. To get her to stop her incessant kicking and squirming one of them had cold cocked her a good one and it was lights out after that.

They're going to rape me. One of those things is going to. . .oh God. . .

She opens her mouth to scream but there's an object wedged inside, something that tastes soiled, nasty. Whatever it is, it effectively keeps the sounds she emits to a minimum. She tosses her head back and forth, moaning, fighting against her restraints.

"Relax," someone says, and for a moment hope rises within her. It sounds like a normal, sane, *human* voice. Can it be possible?

She rolls her eyes, trying to see where it came from but she can't lift her head up high enough. A hand looms above her and rests on her forehead, pushing her down gently. It feels calloused, rough, anything but tender, but it caresses her slowly, almost lovingly. Could it belong to someone who means her no harm, someone who is maybe here to help? Anticipation flickers within her, a brief boost of optimism piercing the blackness of her trepidation, and for a second she is comforted.

A face appears above hers, one she recognizes, and the small amount of hope that had arisen within her dies, the last of her resolve withering away piteously, and a profound coldness clutches and embraces her heart.

"Hello sunshine," he says, smiling, and Leeann tries but can't quite remember his name. He is one of the crewmen, one of the men whom the captain referred to quite often.

"Remember me?" he asks, then answers his own question: "I can see you do. It's Jake, Jake Anderson, the Master's second in command."

His voice is like the captain's, almost 'normal', no long pauses followed by an unearthly grunt or a monotone drone like the others. And his eyes, they aren't dull and empty, no; they hold the vestige of the man he used to be, even though his pupils have dilated to the extent that there is very little white showing.

As if reading her mind he nods, his smile growing ever wider.

"I'm not like the other's, am I? That's what you're thinking. I'm almost like. . .yep! You guessed it! Like the Master! How can that be, you wonder? Well, I'm no science geek like you but I think it's because of the method he used to convert me, as I'm to be his successor in the event that something happens to him." He trails his hand down her face, caressing her cheek. "Now, don't get all excited because nothing has happened to him, he is 'right as rain' I believe the saying goes. I'm the back-up plan is all, because every good plan needs a fail-safe, don't you think?"

She shakes her head, eyes wide. Her muffled words make no sense but he nods and smiles, nods and smiles as if they are having a pleasant conversation, like any two reasonably well-mannered people would.

"That's right, I knew you'd see things my way," he says, his hand on her shoulder now, moving slowly downward. "This is a test, an experiment the Master asked me to conduct in the name of science. You understand, don't you? Being a wannabe scientist and all?" His hand is just at the top of her breasts now, and he runs a tongue thick with spit over his lips as he makes the final descent into the holy land. "It may take us a few times until we get it right, but we'll just keep trying until we're successful. . ."

Leeann issues hoarse, muffled shrieks, her eyes clenched tight, and this makes him laugh, although in gesture only; his 'mirth' sounds forced, humorless.

"Oh, I know it's going to take some getting used to, trust me," he says somberly, yet she can detect the delight in his voice. "That's why I have you tied up like this, so we can make the final transition without…difficulty, hmmm? Just want to make it easy for everyone. What do you think? You ready to have some fun?"

He stands up, his awful hands off of her at last, but when she takes a peek she watches with dismay as he reaches for his belt buckle, undoing it and then unzipping his pants.

"This might feel a little…awkward… at first but after a little while it will go away and everything will be just fine, okay? Nothing to worry about."

He slides out of his slacks and then slips his t-shirt over his head. He isn't a bad looking man, no, and his torso is lean and muscled, his chest lightly covered with thick, black hair, but this is no ordinary circumstance, and once he gives her his 'gift' she knows it's all over for her, knows it as if he's told her as much. Because, when all is said and done, he has, hasn't he? Once you go bacterial, you never go back…

He rips off her shirt, tearing it down the middle, exposing her tan 'Cross Your Heart' bra. He smiles lasciviously and snakes a hand beneath her, finding the clasp and unfastening it with a quick flick of his fingers.

"My, my," he approves, taking in her C-cup sized breasts. "Daddy likee. Now let's see what you got downstairs."

He unbuttons her jeans, sliding them down until they catch where her legs are bound. He gazes longingly at her midnight blue panties as if he has never seen anything more beautiful in all his life.

"Don't mind if I do," he whispers, his voice husky, aroused.

Leeann attempts a mournful cry, her head reared back, eyes shut tight once again, but the gag contains it. All he can hear are sounds that, to him, are words of encouragement.

"Oh baby, that looks so nice." He leans down, places his nose in her crotch and takes a prolonged sniff. "Smells nice too," he says appreciatively. "We're going to have ourselves a real fine time."

Captain Harvey stands in front of Dante's cage, peering happily at his newest convert to Garbage Island. Kim stands beside him, mouth open and panting, thick drool cascading over her chin and dripping onto the frayed remnants of her shirt.

"Your transformation has only just begun," he says, his arm draped over his Queen's shoulders. "Soon you shall see the wonders that we (*aaaahhhccckkk!*) see, will begin to understand the beauty and enchantment that is Garbage Island."

Dante's chin rests on his chest, his legs splayed out before him, his arms like two wilted flower stems at his sides. He looks like a man who has just taken a bullet to the chest, minus the blood and entry wound.

"In an hour I'll have some more yummy Rancor Bird sent your *(aaaahhhccckkk!)* way and, after that, I might be able to let you out." He turns to his Queen, gooses her with his thumb. "We're almost a big, happy *(aaaahhhccckkk!)* family, aren't we?"

Kim gurgles and spits, her head bobbing up and down.

"Okay, let's go check on your *(aaaahhhccckkk!)* competition."

Forty minutes of uninterrupted walking at last brings them to the ship, looming before them like an oasis in the desert. Dr. Taylor's thirst has reached near panic levels. His heart thumps distressingly in his chest, his mouth and throat feeling as if there is no fluid left within him except for the blood which pumps in his veins. He gazes at it through a haze of near delirium, his legs ready to give out.

The walkway (the one he and the other passengers used to board the ship all those long days ago) is extended and the three of them make their way up it's narrow steps.

It is deathly quiet, no sound except for the gentle slap of the water against the hull. Kenny and Cole look around, their faces giving away nothing, but Dr. Taylor knows they are looking for others, the crewmen that should very well be in attendance.

"Can I," he croaks in a voice that is paper-thin, "get something to drink now? I'm really hurting here guys."

Kenny turns toward the ladder leading to the lower deck and Dr. Taylor follows, Cole close behind. In the hollow of the garbage cave the silence is enormous, the faint squawking of the Rancor birds off in the distance emphasizing the stillness. To the doctor the desolation is unexpected, spooky, but also encouraging. Surely the others must be around here someplace, yet it appears no one is guarding the ship, as if it's been abandoned. Descending the ladder, they step into the fetid heat of the lower deck. Maybe there is no one here in the flesh, but their smell lingers like a bad memory.

"The Galley," Dr. Taylor gasps. "Please, can we go to the Galley?"

Kenny leads the way down the hall, peeking his head into each door they pass. Nothing but empty rooms, no one here but us chickens...

The Galley is a mess of dirty dishes and rotting food, the stench almost unbearable. Even so, Dr. Taylor stumbles past Kenny and lurches to the fridge, throwing it open and seizing a bottle of water. His hands are almost too weak to break the seal on the cap, but after several tries he at last wrenches it open and pours half the contents down his throat in a swallow. Good Christ he has never enjoyed a drink of water so much in his entire life! It's as if Heaven's Gates have been opened before him and he is signing the register at the front desk. Pausing, allowing his stomach to settle, he pours the remainder over his head, savoring the feel as it trickles inside the collar of his shirt, sluicing down his sides. Man, a shower would be great right now, the water cranked up so high it's almost scalding, a fresh bar of soap clasped in one hand, a luffa sponge in the other. He imagines the grime would probably stain the stall floor black, would need to be bleached and scoured immediately after, but there would be joy in such a task, knowing he was at long last clean...wouldn't that be wonderful?

Tossing the empty aside, he reaches in and grabs another, but Kenny's hand shoots out and takes him by the wrist, applying steady pressure until he drops the bottle to the floor.

"No...more," Kenny grunts, pointing down the hall. "We get...*uhnnnggg*...supplies."

"Okay, okay," Dr. Taylor says, his face twisted in pain. "But can you let go? I'm going to need that hand."

Kenny releases him and steps back into the hallway. Cole prods Dr. Taylor from behind and he follows, wishing he could get just one more bottle of water. The drink he took barely scratched the surface; it feels as if he has merely awakened his thirst from an extended slumber. What he wouldn't give for just another taste...but for now he'll do what he's told, maintaining his charade of assisting the captain while keeping his eyes open for something he can use to defend himself. Perhaps there will be something in the medical center that will come in handy, although he knows well enough not to count on it, not to count on anything. If an opportunity should arise it will probably come from out of the blue, something he least suspects. All he can do is stay alert and carefully bide his time.

Dr. Taylor had visited the infirmary once during his stay on the ship, when he was given the grand tour. The first mate had adeptly conducted the majority of their sightseeing excursion (Skip Wagner he thinks his name was) but had stepped aside once they'd reached the sickbay, allowing that sector's personnel to take over while he attended to another matter. The doctor recalls that the laboratory was small but the equipment was contemporary, some of it cutting edge. The onboard 'physician' (the man in charge of their physical well-being was no more than a trained technician, someone who could wrap bandages and administer medications; if a passenger had gotten seriously hurt or sick he would have had no choice but to contact the Coast Guard) took great pleasure in showing him around, and Dr. Taylor suspected it was because it made him feel important, somehow more valuable to the mission than the other crewmen. Whatever the case, Dr. Taylor presently cannot remember (tour or no tour) if the infirmary contains anything of use to him, any items that can be utilized as weapons. His 'plan' very well might end right here, with nothing to show for it, and what is he going to do then?

Good question...

They reach their destination and Kenny pauses at the door, blocking the way. He turns to Cole.

"You check...ship...*uhnnnggg*...for...others. I...*uhnnnggg*...watch...him."

Without a word Cole passes them and continues down the hallway.

"Go...in," Kenny motions, and Dr. Taylor eases around him, the touch of the others skin cold and clammy.

Probably why these guys don't sweat. His body temperature can't be more than sixty, sixty-five tops.

Stepping into the small, cramped room, he looks about him quickly, scanning it for anything useful, something resembling a weapon he can pick up quickly and swing even faster, but nothing grabs his eye. No fire extinguisher, no broom, no axe under glass, nothing but the cold steel surface of the examination table and rows upon rows of hardwood cabinets and drawers. Inside these cabinets and drawers, he knows, will be the syringes and test tubes and assorted other miscellany, but is there anything else-a scalpel perhaps? Maybe some razors? Inspecting the cabinets carefully, he spies one with a polished steel lock and knows instantly that this must be where the controlled drugs are kept.

"I need to check inside this one but it's locked. Can you help me?"

The thing that used to be Kenny regards him impersonally, looking from the doctor to the cabinet and back. His eyes reveal nothing, but Dr. Taylor senses he is trying to determine what it is he wants. He tilts his head slightly, like a dog that hears his name or the word 'walk' or 'treat', and after a long, tense moment he at last steps forward, grabbing the cabinet handle and yanking the door off its hinges, the rending sound of metal screeching against wood deafening in the tiny room.

"Wow," Dr. Taylor smiles. "Impressive."

Inside are rows of glass vials, the names visible as he turns them in his hand. You have your standard issue morphine in case of physical injury, Diazepam (liquid and tablets) for mental injuries, Lorazepam in case of anxiety attacks and, what do we have here? Off to the side, minding their own business, are vials of unconstituted antibiotics, garden-variety penicillin. The vials contain powder that requires they be mixed with water in order to be drawn up in a syringe for injection. His mind spins, theories crashing around in his head like stock cars at a demolition derby.

Maybe a good dose of penicillin would fight off the bacteria, possibly weaken it if not out and out destroy it if used properly. But how do I reconstitute it without arousing suspicion? Does this thing know what any of this stuff is? Even if I could mix it up and get it in a syringe, how the hell am I going to stick him?

These questions racing through his mind he stalls, shifting bottles back and forth, taking a few out and placing them on the counter. He opens a drawer, sees plastic packets of sterile needles. Removing several packs, he turns casually toward the other, observing him silently. Kenny is watching him, his hands at his sides, fingers twitching mildly.

"Hurry..."

"You got it, I just need to find a few more things-"

And then Cole's voice rings out from down the hall, his robotic tone sounding almost human in its panic and anger:

"*Uhnnnggg*! Here! Come...here!"

Kenny's eyes widen, his nostrils flare.

It senses danger and they aren't used to that, no, they're used to having the upper hand.

"Wait...here," Kenny orders gruffly, his blank eyes grave, serious as a heart attack. "You try...*uhnnnggg*...anything and...*uhnnnggg*...you...die."

"I'll be right here," the doctor assures him and, what the hell? He actually means it. "I'll get the supplies I need."

And Kenny dashes out the door, his clumsy (yet sure) feet clambering down the echoing chamber of the hallway, in search of his good buddy Cole and whatever has crawled up his zombified ass.

"Take your time," Dr. Taylor mutters, tearing open a package of syringes with his teeth and grabbing several vials of antibiotics, as well as a couple containing Diazepam. "Take your goddamn time."

"Ah, my good woman, you are *(aaaahhhccckkk!)* looking well."

Captain Harvey and his wench (*Kim Leung*, Melissa chastises herself mentally. *Her name is Kim*) stand before her cage looking remarkably similar to a couple of rejects from Michael Jackson's extras casting call for the 'Thriller' video.

"And you look like shit, you know that? You're falling apart."

As if in demonstration of her flippant comment, one of Captain Harvey's eyebrows peels away and flutters to the ground like a caterpillar, floating on a mote of muted sunlight, disappearing amidst the clumps of hardened, flattened trash.

"All part of the grand design, trust me." He leans closer, his sneering face a mask of insincerity. "For all you know I am molting, the ugly *(aaaahhhccckkk!)* worm turning into a beautiful butterfly."

"God, I hope not," she says flatly. "I want to see you die, watch that smile get wiped right off your disgusting face."

He frowns, his eyes darkening.

"That is no way to talk to me." His voice is gruff, throaty and dangerous. "I am the King of this island and I have *(aaaahhhccckkk!)* the power over life and death. Dissenters are treated most unkindly."

"Yeah, like I'm sick of getting the red carpet treatment over here." She yawns expansively, her expression bored, unamused. "I'd hate to see what the four star rooms look like compared to the five."

His glare turns molten, and for a moment she is afraid he's going to burst into a raging tirade, maybe manhandle her like he'd done previously, but he composes himself, his features softening.

"Are you ready to fight for my hand?" he asks, eyeing her judiciously, and she leans back nonchalantly, flicking her hand absently as if she is swatting at a bug. Funny thing about the real bugs: for some reason they are mysteriously absent in the village, save for the tiny gnats that encircle the captain's head like a halo. Could it be this place is so foul that the vast majority of the insect population steers clear?

"I suppose, but I think I should be compensated for my condition, you know, like maybe you should cut me a little slack."

"Cut you some *(aaaahhhccckkk!)* slack?"

"I'm only human," Melissa says, nodding at Kim. "She, on the other hand, is all 'night of the living dead' over there. I deserve some special consideration."

"Special *(aaaahhhccckkk!)* consideration?"

"Yeah, you know, something to give me an edge."

"I should've guessed you'd expect special *(aaaahhhccckkk!)* treatment, judging by the kind of woman you are."

"Oh yeah? And what kind of woman am I?"

"One of questionable moral fiber." Captain Harvey grins, wiping away the ever-present greenish/blackish fluid that's continually oozing from within him. It's as if he's brimming with the stuff, simply overflowing with it. Any time now he'll run dry, and what will become of him then? She sincerely hopes she's around to find out.

"Yeah? Sorry you feel that way. And coming from a such a Boy Scout as yourself, I gotta tell ya, that really hurts."

"So you want something to give you an advantage, hmmm? Is that to be your *(aaaahhhccckkk!)* final request before we commence?" Captain Harvey's eyes dance joyously, the blackened orbs alight with a sickly glow that rings the outer edges neon green. "As you can see, my current Queen is just dying to get her hands on you."

Kim Leung reacts as if stung, jumping manically to life. She throws herself at the cage, her outstretched hands clawing through the air hole. Melissa scoots back, startled, amazed at how quick Kim is despite her outward physical appearance. She may look ready for the grave but she moves faster than a hyperactive monkey on PCP.

"Jesus!" she cries involuntarily. "Back that ho the fuck up!" She struggles to retain her cool but her heart is beating so hard she can feel it pounding in her skull, high-octane terror explod-ing dangerously within her. Staring into the slavering jaws of lunacy that was once a pretty, petite Asian girl, she finds, is like staring into a crypt and seeing that the dead are still alive although their flesh is rotted and their brains have long ago dried up into hard little balls resembling peach pits. It's like peeking into the gaping mouth of Hell and watching snarling demons cavorting about, using Hitler's head as a basketball and Sadam Hussein's balls as craps dice...

And then, surprising her with it's immediacy, she feels the onset of rage, brutal and raw, welling up inside her like a fresh-water spring that only needed to be drilled a little deeper before it released it's cool, tantalizing payload. The pounding in her temples, she realizes with no small amount of relief, becomes unadulterated fury; at Captain Harvey, at this floating heap of shit, at what has happened to all the innocent people from the ship...the fighter inside of her awakens fully at last, giving birth to the absolute need (an almost unholy desire) to rip someone a new asshole. To kick ass and take names. To tear someone's fucking head off and shit down their god-damn neck. She feels this in her like an electrical current, her hands clenching and unclenching, her mouth twisting into a smirk of pure hatred.

"Bring it," she grunts, leaning forward, batting away Kim's claw-like hands. "But you heard me. I have a request."

"You are in no position to *(aaaahhhccckkk!)* barter."

"Whatever," she says, finding the strength to look into his beady, black eyes with undisguised hostility. "I want something, and you damn well better give it to me or after I take care of her sorry ass I'm coming after you."

"Ooo, salty!" Captain Harvey replies enthusiastically. "I love a woman who *(aaaahhhccckkk!)* takes charge!" He pulls Kim back and squats down next to the cage, eyeing his treasure inside. "And what," he rasps, "does my little flower want?"

Melissa grins mischievously, telling him what she is going to need. The captain scratches his chin (skin peeling away in little flakes that sprinkle to the ground like snow) and then smiles in return.

"Fine. I think it might be lying around here somewhere." He glances once more at Kim, leering madly before returning his smutty gaze upon her. "But I hope you understand it will *(aaaahh-hccckkk!)* take a lot more than that."

"You better fucking hope so."

THIRTY-ONE

His hands trembling, Dr. Taylor draws up most of a fifteen-milliliter vial of twenty-five milligram Diazepam into a twelve-milliliter syringe and, after peeling away the foil top, he fills a vial of the antibiotic. His heart races as he shakes the vial to reconstitute the drug, looking over his shoulder nervously. When it is mixed he sets it down and does the same with another, and another, until he has repeated the process several times. The vials of antibiotics hold no more than about two milliliters, and he wants to make sure Kenny gets as much of both drugs as possible. If Kenny isn't incapacitated the antibiotics won't have a chance to work, if this little experiment of his is a success. Of course it could have no effect at all; he is trusting that the captain is right and that it *is* a bacterial infection. If it's viral than the penicillin will have no effect on it whatsoever, and there are no antiviral drugs in the cabinet.

Maybe it is a virus, I mean, wouldn't the captain have known to remove the antibiotics if it was a bacteria? It would be something that could stop it (or slow it down), so why leave these lying around? It doesn't make sense, but what the fuck. Nothing ventured, nothing gained. . .

He stops what he is doing and listens carefully, hearing nothing but the creaks and moans of the ship. Whatever Cole *(the thing that used to be Cole)* found is keeping them occupied. They've been gone for several minutes but it feels like two seconds. He's certain he'll hear the thumping of their boots when they return, but he wishes one of them would make a noise so he can determine how close they are.

Returning his attention to the task at hand, he sticks the needle into a vial and draws it up, then repeats the process with the others, filling the syringe. He then caps it and delicately places it into the right front pocket of his trousers so as not to accidentally press the plunger and waste any. Then he continues digging in the drawers and cupboards for more syringes, test tubes, etc. He finds a plastic bag and stuffs the packages of syringes, test tubes, glass slides (for microscopic use), Q-tips, morphine, Diazepam and sterile tissues inside. The vials of antibiotics he tucks into his underwear, shifting them so they rest snugly under his balls. Good thing he wears whitey-tighties; a pair of boxers wouldn't hold them in place and he'd be forced to shove them someplace only airline security and DEA agents dare go. Unless, of course, these two are so inclined to give him the rubber glove treatment when they return (sans gloves, no doubt) but that's a chance he simply has to take. He can sit here and second-guess himself all he wants, but in the end it will get him nowhere. Action is what is necessary right now, for that is the only thing that can save him.

Another question that tugs at his mind is one of simple human physiology: antibiotics are generally administered in a muscle whereas Diazepam can be given intravenously. When and if he gets a chance, where is he going to stick the needle? And how long will he have before it takes effect, if indeed it does?

His thoughts are interrupted by the sound of clomping boots coming down the hallway. Picking up the bag, he holds it in his left hand so that his right rests over his front pants pocket, his fingertips touching the plunger of the syringe, ready to draw it out like a gunslinger would his six-gun: as fast as humanly possible with his finger on the trigger.

Kenny lurches into the room bearing what almost looks to be an expression of confusion, although it's hard to tell because these things have such a limited range of emotions. Something is bothering him, that much is sure.

"You..." he says, his dark eyes boring into the doctor's. "Come..."

"I need to find a microscope," Dr. Taylor says, clutching the bag tightly, the fingers of his other hand quivering ever so slightly. "I can't run blood tests without a microscope."

"You..." he repeats, "come..."

"Okay," Dr. Taylor complies, taking a step forward and, as if fate has decided to give him a hand after all, Kenny turns toward the door, his back to him momentarily.

This is it man, do or die.

Pulling the syringe from his pocket and uncapping it in one smooth motion, Dr. Taylor swings it overhand into the back of Kenny's neck, pressing the plunger. Kenny reacts violently, groping at the back of his neck and issuing a wounded cry. He turns, his dilated eyes wide, his mouth curled in a sneer, and the hand he thrusts forward is like steel on the doctor's throat. Fingers tightening, the Kenny-creature squeezes with paralyzing strength, and at once the world goes gray and fuzzy.

I knew that's where the problem lie: where to inject him. I'll be dead before either of the drugs takes effect, if there was a possibility that either of them would have worked anyway...

Dr. Taylor senses that his feet are no longer on the floor, and they kick and jerk spasmodically upon their own accord as he fights to hold on to the thin membrane of life that keeps him tethered to this earth. His lungs are on fire, his chest heaving. A few moments more and he will see nothing but black, will know nothing but the infinite depths of darkness that is death itself. But it can't end like this. It mustn't...

Struggling valiantly, the doctor gets a hand on Kenny's face and, grappling the other desperately, he locates an open eye. With his last bit of strength he thrusts a finger into the gooey moistness of the other's eyeball, forcing it in to the second joint. Kenny utters a groan that sounds more angered than pained, but his grip loosens (if only for a brief moment) and Dr. Taylor is able to gasp a painful, tearing breath before his grip tightens again.

Jesus, this mother is strong! What is he doing with his other hand? Scratching his balls?

He finds out soon enough when Kenny uses it to twist Dr. Taylor's wrist backward, extracting the finger from his eye and applying steady, bone crunching pressure.

"Ahhh!" The pain is enormous, intense. Any second now and his wrist is going to snap like a wishbone.

The last of the light fades into grayish blackness and a sound like waves' crashing against the shore is all the doctor can hear. He is aware that he is slipping away, knows this is, indeed, the final act for him as the curtain slides inevitably to the stage floor. The throbbing in his arm grows dim as a white light appears above him, a light that is too bright to look into directly but is inviting, comforting.

Maybe I'll just float on up there and see what's happening. Could be a lot easier than all this...

Weightless, he feels himself soaring upward, the floating sensation changing into a burst of rapid ascension.

So this is what it feels like to die. It's not so bad...

And then, like a bucket of cold water splashing over him, he crashes to the ground and twists his right ankle, the pain shooting up his leg like a lightening bolt, causing him to cry out. As he grasps his aching leg he suddenly realizes he is breathing and that everything that was once faint is coming back to him, the bright light dissipating, the rushing, hissing sound of waves receding. Gradually he becomes aware of his tender right wrist, his raw, burning throat, and the back of his head throbs dully from hitting the floor. His eyes flicker open and closed as he takes breath after breath, savoring the taste of the air even though it is stale and flavored with the odor of a hundred sweating men. He is conscious of Kenny standing over him, and a quick look reveals the other swaying back and forth, bracing an arm against the doorframe to steady himself. Using his good hand, the doctor pushes himself into a sitting position and watches the other like a lumberjack would an old oak tree he's sawed just about all the way through, studying it in anticipation of which direction it's going to fall.

Kenny shakes his head, trying to clear it, but the Diazepam is working like a charm. He staggers from side to side, issuing guttural grumbling noises that emanate thickly from deep within his chest. He sounds wounded, confused.

Dr. Taylor hurries to his feet, watching the other with feverish fascination. Will it put him out or merely slow him down? And, more importantly, will the antibiotics do anything? And if they do, will it bring him back or simply diminish the bacterial infection? Jesus Christ, all these questions he has no answers for...

Scrambling for the plastic bag he's dropped in the melee (meanwhile sneaking a glance down the hallway to see if Cole has heard the commotion and is on his way to investigate) he keeps an eye on the other as he prepares another syringe, this one intended for Kenny's little buddy. He doesn't know if he is up to another fight, as the skirmish with Kenny almost killed him, but he needs to have a weapon and this is all he's got, like it or not.

"Kenny?" Cole's voice calls from somewhere down the hall, his boot-clad feet galumphing on the steel floor. "We go...*uhnnnggg*...now?"

Kenny turns his head, looking in the direction of the voice, and Dr. Taylor can swear there is something almost human registering in his eyes, well, in his good eye, that is. The other one looks like a broken egg yolk, the fluid dribbling profusely down his face.

Sorry about that Kenny, but you were trying to kill me.

He can't tell for sure, but his cornea appears to have receded, allowing some of the white to show.

Might be a trick of the light, or a side effect of the Diazepam.

Kenny swivels his head and faces Dr. Taylor, swallowing thickly, clearing his throat and blinking rapidly several times. His remaining eye is clearing with each blink and, increasingly, the doctor is aware that he is looking at a human again.

"Doc?" Kenny asks in a husky voice that no longer rings hollow with an alien drone. "We back on the ship?"

"Yes Kenny," Dr. Taylor replies with relief. "Yes we are."

"I ain't feelin' so hot."

"Yeah, I know. I regret having to do that."

"Am I gonna be all right?"

Dr. Taylor nods, smiles, wants to assure him that he will be when Cole bursts into the room, his black eyes burning with loathing, his gnarled hands clutching a metal pipe.

"Hold...him," he growls, knuckles white as he twists the pipe, his mouth screwed up in a snarl of fury. "We...*uhnnnggg*...finish him."

Breathing evenly, his sexual appetite satiated, Jake Anderson allows himself to shut down, closing his eyes and letting his mind wander to another level of consciousness. Once the bacteria takes hold the need for sleep is all but nonexistent, but permitting your brain to decelerate every now and then is refreshing, almost intoxicating. It opens up a picture show world of bright lights and colors, hallucinations filled with unimaginable delights. He's found he enjoys this very much, like how he used to take pleasure in alcohol in his old life. Besides, the girl isn't going anywhere, is she? There are guards at the door. If she tries to leave they'll catch her, if he doesn't notice and seize her himself. No, there's nothing to be concerned about. Excuse me while I kiss the sky...

Is he sleeping? Leeann wonders, glancing sidelong at him, trying to ignore the slick wetness that coats the inside of her thighs, her stomach twisting unpleasantly as she thinks about what just transpired. *Bastard raped me, shot his infected sperm in me. I suppose it's only a matter of time...*

Much to her surprise he'd removed her gag and untied her after he'd taken her the first time, unbinding her hands and legs so he could have her from behind on the second go-round, her face pressed flat against the grubby mattress to muffle her screams. Afterward, in his sex-induced haze (or maybe because he simply didn't care), he'd left her unbound and appeared to drift off to sleep. She contemplates getting up, making a break for it, but her nerves are worn thin and she's tired, used up.

At least he didn't hurt me; I mean...I don't think he did.

She reaches down and runs her fingers along the inside of one thigh then brings her hand to her face to inspect it in the soft light. Her fear is that she will see crimson, will know she is bleeding and that the surest, quickest way to an infection is the transference of his seminal fluid into her blood. But does she really know that, or is it just a fear she harbors? It isn't as if this is HIV they are dealing with, this is something else entirely. A bacterial infection gone south of the border like a gangster in a stolen El Camino with a loaded shotgun and two bodies in the trunk.

Looking at her hand, she exhales with relief when she sees the liquid is clear, his and her sweat mixed with semen and vaginal fluid. It stinks to high heaven, but that's no surprise, is it? She's been immersed in this trash heap for three days without showering, without so much as the smallest hint of soap. Wrinkling her nose in distaste, she wipes her hand on the canvas bedding.

If she did try to escape, would he hear her right away, grab her before she could even make it off the cot? Or would he come to as she made it to the door and fling one of his boots at her with homicidal accuracy, knocking her down and then pummeling her with a flurry of blows for her troubles? Maybe (for the sake of speculation) there are others waiting outside, just in case such a situation should arise. Even if she got out of here would she be caught within a few steps of the door?

She sighs futilely, the awareness that her life is no longer in her own control (hasn't been for several days now) bringing about a feeling of sheer insignificance, a helplessness that knows no release. She thinks of Dante, his face entering her mind vividly, his bushy beard, his hard-boiled egg eyes behind the thick Buddy Holly glasses, his mouth pursing and smiling, pursing and smiling as he looks at her nervously, shifting his legs like a little boy who has to go potty but is afraid to ask. She wonders how he is handling this, if he can indeed come up with a plan to save them. She won't blame him if he can't as, after all, what *can* he do? They are greatly outnumbered and the bacterium has probably taken hold of her anyway, either from the water or pumped into her system by this terrible man who forcibly had his way with her.

Dante's probably worried sick wondering what happened, because that big, dumb oaf is in love with me.

It is this thought that finally brings tears to her eyes, her soul chilled with a penetrating sorrow, and she is somewhat surprised it exists within her at all. Could it be she's found it in her heart to love him back? Could it really, truly be? Or is she at last so empty that the acceptance and return of Dante's love is the lesser of evils? Tears trickle down her face, bathing her pale, freckled countenance. Her chest heaves in a shaky rhythm, hitching every so often as her breath catches in her throat. Somehow everything has come down to this, this dilapidated shack and soiled bed, caught in a world where nothing should survive amongst all this contaminated detritus...

She turns over onto her side, feeling the cot shift slightly beneath her, making a slight creaking noise. She glances at Jake quickly, afraid it will awaken him, but he doesn't move, his deep breathing continuing unabated.

For Christ's sake you should at least try! Her mind screams, making her arms and legs itch. *You don't have anything to lose by at least making an effort!*

It makes sense, this internal dare, and suddenly she feels bravado flow within her, a bold certainty that she can overcome her terror and make one last ditch attempt. Slowly, tensely, she eases one foot to the ground, the tip of her toes touching the floor of compressed garbage. Bit by bit she slides away from him, closer to the edge, her foot gently flattening out until her instep is touching, and then her heel. As smoothly as she can muster she follows with the rest of her body until half of her is hanging over the side, her left arm outstretched, reaching to balance herself. Another couple of inches and her palm should be able to touch the floor...

Jake coughs, expelling a thick wad of black mucous from between his bluish lips, the offending substance sailing a few inches into the air and landing on his torso. Leeann freezes, her heart pounding so hard she is afraid he will hear it, that it will awaken him from his *(slumber?)* and he will hurt her, will use those large, brawny hands to beat her mercilessly, possibly strangle the life out of her. He coughs violently again, and uses his right hand to swipe at his face, then turns, smacks his lips, and settles down once more. Leeann doesn't make a sound, realizing she's been holding her breath. Trying to be as still as possible, she quietly fills her lungs and releases the air softly, repeating the process several times. While she does this she waits, listening to his low inhalations and deep exhalations, at last hearing distinctly that they've leveled off, becoming even. It appears he is back within the recesses of *(sleep?)*. If ever there was a time to make a break for it, this is surely it.

Carefully, gently, she rests her weight entirely on her left hand and scoots sideways, easing herself onto the floor. It feels spongy and damp, but even this fails to bother her, just like the ripe scent of her own body. Currently such things are intangible, nothing to worry about in the grand scheme of things. If she can make it to the door without waking him and exit this shack without anyone seeing her maybe she has a chance.

She sits up and gets her feet beneath her, rising slowly, and her joints pop so loud it's like a champagne bottle being uncorked. She pauses halfway, crouched, immobile, her eyes sliding over to look at Jake, and observes gratefully that his state of repose is undisturbed. Standing, she takes a tentative step, than another toward the door. The 'door' is nothing but an opaque piece of plastic, it might have been an oil tarp in its last life, or maybe something intended to collect drips of paint from a sloppy worker. Three steps. Four. Hardly breathing she crosses the last of the distance, glances back once more, then snakes a hand out and peels the tarpaulin back an inch. As delicately as she can she peers out, looking for any immediate obstacles, any imminent threat.

The coast is clear, none of those things loitering around to make this even more difficult than it's already been.

Go, scat, get! Her mind urges and, before she can give it another thought, she tugs back the tarp and dashes from the shack, running in the opposite direction of the village and into the desolate wasteland beyond.

His dick aching like it's taken a spin in a food processor, Tyler leans heavily against one wall of the shack, his heart beating too fast, his head feeling as if it's been pumped full of nitrous oxide.

"Shit, ladies," he tells the 'women' (all of whom have made no sound except for the occasional miscellaneous groan). "I gotta take five. I'm starting to feel a little chafed."

His cock itches and burns and his balls are sore, feeling heavy, laden with something other than his diminishing seminal fluid.

Christ, you'd think I'd be all emptied out. I must've tossed off at least eight or nine loads.

There are four women and he's done the rounds twice and then once more for good measure. He's honestly not sure if he ejaculated the last time, as his head had begun to swim and his nuts throbbed painfully, but by-God he tried.

He cups his testicles in his hands gently, his torso glistening with sewer-scented sweat. The odor in the room is thick, the air sodden with spent sexual energy, and suddenly he finds it difficult to catch his breath. He isn't sure if it's because of the closed quarters or if it's simply because he's tired, but it feels like he's just run a marathon. Worse still, his stomach abruptly complains as dizziness overcomes him; for a moment he's certain he's going to blow chunks but when he leans over the sensation passes, although the lightheadedness remains. He straightens up and inhales deeply, sucking in air for all he's worth and then letting it out slowly, trying to calm down, but nonetheless a blinding rush of panic creeps through his dim-witted brain, an unwanted note of fear that plays along the edges of his mind.

I don't feel so hot, but when was the last time I fucked this much in such a short time? I'm exhausted, that's all. Just cool it.

But its more than that and he knows it, he can tell by his ragged breathing, the sudden sharp, stabbing pain in his groin, the lead ball that sits in his stomach rapidly becoming a living thing, twisting and squirming.

"Holy hell," he gasps, clutching his belly with both hands, bending over. Beads of sweat pop up on his forehead as cramps rumble through him like earthquake tremors. "I definitely don't feel right."

He slides down the wall and into a crouch, hyperventilating, the pains growing in severity. His bowels cramp, his sphincter contracting. He swipes a hand over his face, licking his lips with a tongue as rough as sandpaper. This reminds him of how he felt after swimming through the thick sludge when they arrived here, except this time is worse, much worse. He tries to relax, allowing his body to do what it needs to, but nothing comes out.

I don't care if I shit all over the place. The way it smells in here it would probably be an improvement.

He strains, trying to force out what he thinks to be a diarrheic bowel movement but the aching intensifies and, involuntarily, his sphincter clenches shut, a thick wave of nausea rolling through him with the force of a Mack truck, toppling him off of his feet and onto his ass.

"Jesus Christ!" he gripes to the recumbent women but they, of course, offer no reply. They stare silently at the ceiling, their lesion covered legs parted, their arms lying limply at their sides. "Feels like I got the screamin' demons!"

Rising to his knees, he presses hard against his belly with both hands, trying to push the pain away. Whenever he's got the runs this is what he does, hoping this act will help to expel it and relieve the pressure. But this time is different, he notices with escalating unease. At first his stomach felt taut, unyielding, similar to being full from eating too much in one short sitting, but now it distinctly feels like there is something moving around in there, as if his belly contains a writhing coil of snakes. And not only that but his balls feel tender as well, unbearably engorged.

The light in the shack is diffuse, but when he takes his hands away and looks *(Jesus Christ you have got to be fucking kidding me)* he swears he sees the skin rippling up and down, back and forth, akin to a raging sea roiling just beneath his muscled abs. His gaze continuing downward, he sees something that literally takes his breath away, and his heartbeat amps up radically as he resumes taking large, panicked gulps of air.

"Fuck!"

His testicles are swollen to the size of grapefruit, his once wrinkled sac almost smooth, and it appears to be growing as he watches, becoming progressively more distended.

Abruptly a monstrous, disabling pain shoots through him and his whole world becomes a fiery agony, like a million hot needles are poking him from the inside.

"Goddamn!" he groans, falling onto his back, rolling from side to side, seizing his scrotum with both hands and pressing against it as hard as he can, as if he can stop it's erratic growth spurt by sheer force. The pressure within is beyond belief, becoming so severe that everything else is entirely blotted out. It feels like something (*fuck that, a million something's*) is pushing from the inside trying to fight it's way out…

"No no no no no!" he pleads, watching incredulously as his balls continue to swell, expanding steadily. Pinpoints of skin pop up (hundreds of them) at varied intervals, like there is an angry swarm of wasps inside trying to break free, and the sensation moves to his abdomen, his stomach bloating to the size of a beach ball.

"AAAHHHH!" At last the pain takes him over the threshold of intolerable and into the land of 'Just kill me' and, with a rending, wet, tearing sound, his stomach splits open, blood, entrails and viscous fluid splattering outward and splashing everything in it's path. This is closely followed by a sound hideously similar to that of two balloons popping as his balls explode in another terrific spray of gore.

Before Tyler loses consciousness (the last consciousness he will ever know) he watches as thousands of pale, fat slugs slither out of him, their bodies sticky with his blood, gastric juices and semen as they evacuate their incubation chamber. There is a high-pitched ringing in his ears, and he wonders vaguely if they are making this sound. And, below this noise, faintly, he can hear the voices of several women laughing…

THIRTY-TWO

Dr. Taylor's eyes dart from Cole's to Kenny's, one set cold, black, homicidal, the other's single orb filling with dawning clarity. But Kenny's lucidity is short lived; he abruptly shuffles backward, losing his balance, eye rolling up to the white, and Dr. Taylor realizes miserably that he probably used too much Diazepam. He just saved and killed him in one swift move.

Great, I used him as a guinea pig and I didn't know what I was doing...

But it's too late for regrets, what's done is done.

Cole stares at Kenny, watching as the others knees buckle and he drops to the floor.

"Kenny?" he says uncertainly, and in his tone Dr. Taylor can hear a trace of the old him, the man who looked up to Kenny and was happiest when they worked together. "Get...up!"

But Kenny remains where he is, slouched against the wall, his head hanging slackly. From where he stands Dr. Taylor can no longer tell if he is breathing.

Cole is still, scrutinizing the other, and to the doctor it seems as if time stops, this single moment encased in amber, trapped for all eternity. In amazingly slow motion he watches Cole lean over, reach out a hand and rest it on his friend's shoulder. His grip on the pipe is loose, the weapon all but forgotten as he studies the man he trusted above and beyond anyone else.

"Kenny," he says again, his voice hollow, and he shifts his glance to Dr. Taylor, his black eyes twin vortexes of unadulterated rage. "...*Uhnnnggg*...Kenny..." he utters a third time, a flat statement of finality, the hand holding the pipe tightening around it. He straightens up, taking a step forward and raising it when suddenly Kenny grabs his nearest ankle and tugs him backwards. Taken completely by surprise, Cole falls on top of the other, the pipe flying from his grasp and clanging against the far wall.

"Ya got another one ready?" Kenny cries and Dr. Taylor, who's looking on as if in a trance, motionless, eyes wide and far away, appears not to hear him. "Doc!" Kenny hollers as he wrestles with the other. "Hit 'im with what ya used on me!"

Dr. Taylor shakes his head, dispelling the ruminations that held him in a grip of near paralysis. Maybe it was the look in Cole's eyes, or maybe it was the dreaded certainty that he'd just murdered someone when he was merely trying to save him. He uncaps the syringe, wondering how he is going to accurately hit a moving target.

"Poke him!" Kenny urges desperately but he and Cole are a mass of writhing limbs, their bodies twisting this way and that as they compete for control.

"I can't! You have to hold him still!"

"Ya gotta do better'n that Doc!" Kenny hammers Cole in the face repeatedly with his elbow, the blows seemingly having no effect as the other's teeth snap and click like a wolf's just inches from Kenny's throat. The two battle for leverage, fighting for any advantage.

"Do it fer Christ's sake! He's stronger'n I am!" Kenny shifts to one side, trying to roll over, and swiftly Cole gains the advantage and gets on top, pinning the other on his back. "Come on man!"

Cole's ass is in the air, looking for all the world like a target. All it needs is a bull's eye painted on it to give it the final touch. Should he try it? One quick, straight jab through his pants and maybe the needle won't bow, successfully releasing it's payload. But if the needle breaks than they are screwed, and is that a chance worth taking?

"Goddamnit Doc, fore he fuckin' kills me!"

Cole has both hands around Kenny's throat, squeezing as hard as he can. He is making gruff, animalistic noises, foam lathering his mouth as he thrashes from side to side.

Okay, here goes nothing.

Dr. Taylor dashes forward, holding the syringe like one would a butcher knife (if imitating a Hollywood serial killer) and in one determined motion thrusts it into Cole's left cheek. The needle pops through the denim, jamming in to the hilt, and the doctor presses the plunger quickly as Cole bucks, letting go of Kenny and turning toward him.

"Oh shit," he mutters, backing up.

"Run!" Kenny bawls as Cole climbs off of him, enraged by this unwanted distraction. His black eyes are infinitely blacker, and he issues a furious growl that readily bespeaks his indignation.

Dr. Taylor bolts past them, his left shoulder connecting with the doorframe and knocking him off balance, but he makes it out of the lab and into the hall. He can hear Cole's footsteps close behind him, and without thinking he takes a right, running in the opposite direction of the ladder leading topside, making his way further into the ship. For the moment the ship's floor plan escapes him, and he can't remember if there is another exit in this direction or if it's a dead-end.

Good going chump. This is just what you need, your back against the proverbial wall.

His legs pumping, adrenaline propelling him, he doesn't dare look over his shoulder for fear that he'll find the other right on his heels. Cole is issuing awful noises, and he can almost feel his hot breath blowing upon the nape of his neck.

The end of the hallway looms in sight, and with it the last room.

Yep, dead-end. Smooth move man, real smooth move. . .

The door is slightly ajar, beckoning to him promisingly. His chest hitches frantically, his lungs burning. If he can beat him there than maybe he has a chance, slim, but a chance just the same.

At least the needle didn't break; I don't know what we'd have done otherwise.

He is scant inches away when he feels fingers in his thinning hair, Cole's nails raking across the back of his scalp, but somehow he makes it across the threshold. Spinning around quickly, hands sweaty on the door, he slams it just as Cole is reaching inside and the heavy steel pins his groping hand against the frame. Cole bellows furiously, struggling to get free, and Dr. Taylor opens the door just enough for him to pull his arm back then closes it again, twisting the bolt with trembling fingers. Cole rages helplessly on the other side, his fists making dents in the thick metal, yet Dr. Taylor is certain there is no way he is getting in. The mutants might be strong, but the ship is stronger. Now all he has to do is ride it out, wait for Cole to succumb to the drugs. Shouldn't be long. In the meantime he backs away, exhaling a shaky breath, and his foot slips in something wet yet slightly tacky. He turns around and at once realizes why the two men were gone so long, why they were so obviously upset.

The room is the scene of a grisly bloodbath, the remains of several crewmen littering the floor. Greenish/blackish blood is splattered across the walls, the ceiling, the floor, the corpse's sightless eyes staring blindly. "Well I'll be damned."

The door to Dante's cage is opened about an hour after his second feeding. He crawls out and gets to his feet, swaying slightly. His head hangs slackly on his bull-sized neck, and he follows the minion who released him, his steps slow and clumsy, his bearing awkward. The creature leads him to the center of the village, and as they draw closer he can hear voices chanting in unison.

Other creatures emerge from their hovels (those that aren't already gathered) and they fall in behind Dante and his new pal. Like a great big convoy they keep on truckin' until they reach the commotion, and what lies before them is no less than a bona fide event.

Captain Harvey is presiding, of course, his Queen at his side. Melissa stands nearby with her hands bound behind her back, two minions guarding her. Her facial expression reveals nothing; in fact she appears bored, indifferent to the proceedings transpiring before her.

The humanoids form a large circle, much like children on a school playground, and in the middle are Perry and Steven. The two stumble and lurch around each other, one clutching a long plastic tube with a sharpened end, the other a stubby, crude knife that resembles a prison shank. Steven has blood running down the side of his face and Perry is favoring his left leg.

"Come on!" Captain Harvey yells, his voice rising above the din of the crowd. "Cut that (*aaaahhhccckkk!*) fucker!"

Dante finds a place next to the others within the circle but he doesn't join them in their cheering and cajoling, he merely stands there lifelessly, his head down. And when Steven slashes wildly at Perry, the tip of the blade slicing jaggedly through the other's throat and producing an explosion of blackish/greenish droplets that speckle Dante's face, he doesn't even lift a hand to wipe them away.

Her long, black hair swept back over her shoulders, Melissa stands rigid, her eyes tracking the fight in progress. The warm up act. Can't have the main event without the opening number, and in this case Captain Harvey has deemed Perry and Steven worthy of the honor. And why not? What else were they going to do? Might as well finish each other off, as it's better than spending the rest of their days as his slaves. Of course, judging by Captain Harvey's steadily deteriorating condition it doesn't seem all too likely that he is going to be around for very long. For all practical purposes it appears his shelf life is nearing expiration.

She surveys the crowd, studying the faces of the mutants. Although they have an extremely restricted array of emotions the one they do employ with great aplomb is anger. They either look like they're bored stupid or deliriously unhinged in a maniacal rage.

Sounds like a real blast, where do I sign up?

Glancing back at Tweedle Dee and Tweedle Dumb, she can't help but pity them; the hapless bastards are just two more pawns in Captain Harvey's game. Two more corpses to toss onto the pile. But, then again, if she's to be totally honest (which can't hurt, not at this point) she feels worse for herself than she does for them. The sooner they kill one another the sooner she is in the ring, battling it out with the hideous wreckage of a girl who used to be an aspiring marine biologist but now resembles something dug up from the grave.

In this corner we have Kim Leung, weighing in at ninety pounds, missing her tongue and her eyes, possessed by a flesh-eating bacteria that turns humans into drooling idiot slaves with inconceivable strength. In the other corner we have Melissa Grant, weighing in at one hundred and fifteen pounds, a dominatrix by trade who has had very little to eat and drink over the last three days (if you don't count the governor and a drugged bottle of water) and besides being tormented by these walking pusbags has been confined to a cage where she has urinated on herself repeatedly. The house favorite is Kim Leung, so place your bets one and all, place your bets!

Fear prickles within her and at once she feels lightheaded, making everything seem surreal, dreamlike. But she doubts very much that she has the imagination to conjure up something so incredibly detailed, this utterly convoluted mess that is her waking reality. It is much too involved to be one of her dreams…

(Suddenly she remembers the nightmare she had the night before last, the field of flowers that rotted and turned into gruesome plastic and glass statues, swaying in a hot breeze of squalid trash. In it she was wearing her bondage suit, as she is now, only in her nocturnal fantasy the leather felt too tight, constricting…she suppresses a quiver, realizing that the dream and her reality have merged into one and are now forever more intertwined…eternally interchangeable…)

She rotates her shoulders, savoring the sound the cowhide makes as it crinkles, enjoying its snugness as if it is a second skin. And it truly is a second skin, is it not? In what other aspect of her life does she feel more comfortable, more in control? If she is going to die today at the hands of Kim Leung, than she is glad that she'll go out in fine style, in what she considers to be the height of fashion.

Instead of watching the fight she resumes observing the crowd, her eyes alighting on face after face after face, realizing with something almost akin to sympathy that these were once normal people just like her, people with hopes and ambitions who (if asked before their infection) would have given an entirely different answer to the question 'where do you see yourself in five years?' These poor sons a bitches, reduced to this because of a bacterial infection fostered and spread by the iniquitous Captain Harvey. But, all things considered, it's not entirely his fault either; it isn't as if he is doing this willingly as he is, after all, a slave to the bacterium as well. But if she embraces this knowledge and accepts it as truth than her hatred for him will falter; it will make him out to be a victim, just like the rest of these unfortunate souls. And thinking of him as a victim won't help in her fight against Kim, no, she needs to hate them because that's her only chance at survival. Although they are innocent like her she needs to pretend that what they are doing is personal, that they are acting this way because they simply want to hurt her, will in fact take great pleasure in seeing her suffer, these cold-hearted, mutant bastards…

The crowd grows, more and more of the infected coming out of the woodwork to enjoy the festivities. They straggle up alone and in pairs, their seemingly sightless eyes unblinking, occasional insects flying in and out of their open mouths, their hair, skin and clothing beyond atrocious, beyond repair. Sizing them up, she glances across the circle and is startled by a familiar face.

"No freakin' way," she mutters, unable to suppress her exclamation.

They got Dante, the Missing Link. I thought for sure he'd be one of the last of us standing.

His head lolls on his massive shoulders, his gaze downcast. She can't see his eyes but is certain that if she could they would resemble the others: black, soulless, dull, empty. She wonders when they converted him and figures it must not have been too long ago, judging by his appearance. *Well, bon voyage dude. Maybe I'll join you, maybe I won't.*

She returns her attention to the brawl, sees that Steven has gotten the better of Perry. The latter is crawling around on the ground, bleeding profusely from his throat and groping blindly for his lost weapon as the other dishes out brutal punches and kicks, delivered with bone-crunching accuracy. The crowd is having the time of their *(lives?)*, their fists clenched over their heads, their voices a rising crescendo, and Melissa knows that soon enough their bloodlust will turn on her. Yes, it is easy to hate them because they no longer resemble normal humans in any way; these things are simply skin-covered skeletons acting on autopilot. If she had her way she'd kill every last one of them and not feel a hint of remorse. She'd be doing them a favor.

You just watch, I'm going to gut that bitch like a deer and play jump rope with her entrails. And, if not, I'll see you fuckers in hell.

Jake Anderson bolts upright, sensing that something is wrong. Seeing the empty cot he throws his head back and lets out a loud wail. *The bitch got away! Captain Harvey won't be happy about this, won't be happy about this at all!* He scrambles to his feet, looking about him anxiously as if he will find her crouched beneath the bed or hiding in the shadows. But she isn't here; he is alone in the small enclosure, rank with the smell of rot, dank with the accumulation of rancid mold. He paces back and forth, thinking things through.

For one thing, where would she go? How far does the bitch honestly think she is going to get? Even if she does make it out of the village and to the ocean, what then? Unless she plans on swimming across the Pacific than she is stuck here, like it or not.

Then another thought occurs to him, one that jars him considerably: What if she walks off into the place where they dare not go? The part of the island that Captain Harvey has warned them against, where the other creatures are bigger and more powerful, where even he in his enlightened state wouldn't venture unless his life depended on it. The captain regaled them with anecdotes of snails the size of elephants, caterpillars bigger than anaconda's, spiders larger than cows-all of them with an insatiable appetite for human flesh. And, besides that, (as if that wasn't enough) not all of the island is stable. There are large patches just outside of the village that aren't solid; they are comprised of loose particles that appear firm but are actually similar to quicksand. If one were unlucky enough to stumble into such a trap they would sink into the quagmire of Garbage Island, most likely never to be seen again. Should she have wandered out there than the girl (*my Queen, soon enough, my Queen*) will be lost forever.

Lurching out of the shack and into the scorching heat he hears chanting coming from the center of the village, the voices crazed, fever-pitched. He turns toward the sound, for the moment forgetting about Leeann as the tantalizing thought of the afternoon's festivities distracts him. Jake would love to see Kim Leung tear that whore Melissa apart, watch her twist off her head and prop it on a plastic pole. That would serve her right, the stupid cunt. He'd been so nice to her, so polite, and she was rude in return, acting like he was an idiot, some ship-jockey who didn't know the difference between sincerity and sarcasm. Watching her die would be satisfactory indeed.

He looks to the west, toward the outskirts of the village, his eyes scanning the landscape for any sign of the wayward girl, but the voices from the village beckon him, begging him to join in the celebration. He takes an indecisive step back toward the shack then changes his (*mind?*) and heads in the direction of the fight. Fuck it, it won't last long. Melissa doesn't stand a chance. After Kim is done with her she won't be much more than a fly infested puddle for the Rancor Birds to suck up through their beaks. And then he can go and find his soon-to-be bride (possibly the mother of his child) and when he does he will chastise her most harshly for leaving him, of that he is certain.

Dizzy and disoriented, Leeann peers over her shoulder and sees the village rapidly receding behind her. She's not sure where she is going, in fact knows the ship is the other way, but she doesn't care. All she wants to do is get away from those filthy things, wants to get as far away from the madness as she can…

Her heel slips in something slimy and she loses her footing. Putting her hands out, she breaks her fall but lands in a puddle of something that instantly makes her queasy. A rotten, gassy smell arises from it (much like the odor of sulfur but more cloying) making her gag. Is there anything on this heap of crap that doesn't reek to high heaven? Holding her hand away from her she glances around, looking for something to wipe the offending substance on but there is nothing except for her skin. In her blind dash for freedom she'd forgotten (well, hard to say she forgot; overlooked would be a better word) she was naked. The floor of the heap is cutting into her feet, blood trickling from several small cuts, but that's the least of her worries. She pushes herself up, absently wiping her hand on her leg, continuing forward.

I don't care where I'm going as long as I get away from them, from, from...him. For all I know he impregnated me with some horrible, mutant atrocity...

This thought makes her nauseous and the world swims before her bleary eyes, filtered through the lens of her own terror. Her legs become unsteady and she knows that at any moment she is going to overbalance and hit the ground again but this time she just may choose not to get up. Because, after all friends and neighbors, what is the point? There is no rescue, no escape. Just a taste of freedom before she is found naked and half dead...at which time they'll drag her back to the shack where she will be violated again and again until something takes, spawning a creature that only Satan himself could love, well, he and Captain Harvey. And Jake, of course; can't forget about him, he of the stiff penis and wandering hands.

Faintness takes a swift hold of her, her world turning a dreadful shade of gray, and she loses her balance and falls forward, tumbling toward the floor of the heap where she will hopefully be knocked out cold and never wake up...

A pair of arms wraps around her and catches her before she can execute a face dive into the trash. She cries out and a voice (*a human voice!*) shushes her calmly, soothingly. Her fear eddies away and her breathing slows, the little dots that were dancing before her partially open eyes fading, allowing the light to trickle back in.

"Hey," the voice says. "Are ya okay?"

She relaxes, lulled into a state of security. The arms feel so good around her, almost awakening a sexual desire despite what she's just been through. She blinks tears away, focusing on her savior and is surprised to see who it is.

"Aren't you...weren't you..."

"Yep," Dave smiles easily, caressing her face with his free hand. Even though he's been to hell and back he can almost forget all about it for the moment, just looking into this pretty girl's eyes. "I was one a the Naval seamen aboard the ship."

Leeann leans her head back so she can get a better look at him. His uniform is ripped and dirty and his face is bloody and battered, coated with a thin layer of slime, but he appears as if he has a few rounds of fight left in him. There is a cocky gleam in his eyes that bears witness to the fact that he's done battle and will gladly do it again. Suddenly she becomes self-conscious of her nakedness and pulls away from him, placing one hand over her breasts and the other over her crotch.

"I'm, uh, you'll have to excuse me..." she says falteringly, flustered.

"Hey, it's okay, I ain't lookin'. I'm just glad ta see someone else is alive." He clears his throat and asks hesitantly: "Is there anyone else that's still like us?"

She nods, albeit slowly, with some deliberation.

"At the, um, the village there are a few more...well, maybe a couple more." She struggles to think of who else is still *them*, but only a couple of faces come to mind. "Dr. Taylor I think, maybe Melissa...and Dante." At the mention of this last name she begins to cry, and Dave takes her into his arms once more, holding her tightly against his chest and comforting her.

"Shhh, it's gonna be all right."

"How can you say that? Have you seen what they're doing? Nothing is all right and I can't see how it ever will be again!"

"Not if I can help it," he says, and something in his voice dries up her tears, her breath catching in her throat. She wipes her eyes and studies him somberly.

"Where have you been?" she asks, scanning the cuts and bruises that line his face like road map markings. "What happened?"

"It's kinda a long story and I'd love to tell ya all about it, but I think we better get goin'."

"Going? Going where?"

"We're gonna rescue anyone left alive in the village."

"You know about the village?"

He smiles calmly. "I bypassed it to set up shop out here, to take stock a the situation so to speak."

"Set up shop?"

"You wanna see what I found? I think ya'll be impressed."

"Sure," she says, then becomes aware of her nakedness again. "But I'd really like to cover up. I feel a little...exposed."

"We'll find ya somethin' to wear before we make our move. In the meantime let me show ya my arsenal. I know yer gonna dig this..."

THIRTY-THREE

Dr. Taylor prods experimentally at the first body with the tip of his shoe and, satisfied that it's dead and not in a somnambulistic state (despite the fact that it's riddled with bullet holes and by all means *should* be dead), moves on to the second. Kenny and Cole stand just inside the door, looking fatigued but otherwise back to their old selves.

"So this is what you called Kenny to see?" he asks and Cole nods.

"Yeah, man this feels so weird, so, so schizoid...but I remember being concerned that these guys were dead, that something was threatening us, was threatening the island."

"That's how I felt too, Doc, that there was danger and we hadda kill anythin' that got in our way, got in the way a carryin' out our plan I guess."

"Interesting." He moves on to the third. "You were gone a long time Cole, long enough for me to inject Kenny, somehow hold him off and then make another shot for you. What were you doing?"

Cole shakes his head, looks at the bodies and then at the doctor. "I was searching all the other rooms on the way back to the sickbay...looking for whoever did it I guess."

"Makes sense."

Finished examining the corpses, Dr. Taylor turns and studies the two before him.

"How do you guys feel?"

"Tired," Kenny says. "Must be all the Valium ya pumped into us. But I feel like myself again, minus a eye a course."

"Yeah, sorry about that," Dr. Taylor frowns. "We'll clean that up when we hit the medical station. So, what did it feel like to be, um...altered?"

Cole answers the question without hesitation: "It was like watching yourself through a fish-eyed lens. Some part of your brain is aware of what you are doing but you have no control over it. You simply have to do what it tells you, there is no other way."

Dr. Taylor nods, stepping away from the carcasses.

"I wonder who we should be thanking for this."

Everyone's gaze returns to the bodies of the crewmen, five in all. One of them is Lieutenant Ronson, his eyes wide and unseeing, greenish/black blood spilling from his mouth. It's apparent it took a lot of bullets to put these men down for good.

"Whoever it was they deserve a freakin' medal," Kenny says, bending his leg and grimacing. Now that he is back to himself the pain has returned in his knee but, thanks to the Valium, it is a distant throb. His eye, on the other hand, feels as if it was scooped out with a melon baller. "Ya think maybe the Coast Guard arrived?"

"I don't know, but we can't count on it. We have to get moving. I have no idea how long the penicillin is going to keep the bacteria at bay. For all we know you could turn back at any time."

"What are we going to do?" Cole asks, a note of unease in his voice.

"We need supplies, more penicillin, food, water-"

"Guns," Kenny interjects. "We need some firepower."

"Yes, we should arm ourselves." Dr. Taylor rubs his chin thoughtfully, weighing out all of their options. He briefly mulls over what he's going to do about Kenny and Cole, wondering if regular doses of penicillin will completely eradicate the bacteria, allowing them to return to their regular lives once this is all over. And not only them, but himself and anyone who took a dip in the ocean. It's definitely too late for Captain Harvey, who looks like he is now suffering from a parasite infestation, but there might be hope for some of the others, if they aren't too far gone. The penicillin will probably work on those recently converted but once it gets a good foothold all bets are off. He returns his attention to his friends, having made a decision in between his musings.

"We have to destroy the ship."

"What?" Kenny looks at him dubiously. "How we gonna git outta here?"

"We'll use the radio and call for help, send out an S.O.S. to anyone within range. If we're lucky either the Navy or the Coast Guard will get it and come to our aid."

"So ya don't think this *is* the work a the Coast Guard?"

"Like I said I don't know, but if we assume it is and it isn't than we aren't going anywhere. Can't hurt-"

"We should just get out of here now," Cole says. "Let's fire this bitch up and get gone."

"There are others still alive in the village. What kind of people would we be if we didn't try and rescue them, not to mention whomever did this?"

"Yeah...guess I never thought of that."

"Well git yer head outa yer ass," Kenny says, slugging him on the shoulder. Then to Dr. Taylor: "Ya really think we needa trash the boat though?"

"If we don't Captain Harvey or his cohorts could sail it to a populated area and spread the contagion. We can't take the chance of letting this out."

"Couldn't they just kill it with antibiotics like you did?"

"As much as I don't want to burst your bubble, I'm not sure if we *have* killed it or not. That remains to be seen. Until then we can only hope for the best."

"Okay," Kenny replies, the look on his face revealing without question that the aforementioned bubble was indeed popped. "What's your idea?"

"Let's get what we need." Dr. Taylor starts for the door. "We'll head to the pharmacy and gather the medical supplies. This might be a long shot, but maybe I can scare up some amphetamines. You guys look like you could use a boost. While we're there I'll see what I can do about your eye. After that I'll hit the galley and you two go find the weapons and stock up. Once we're set we'll send out a distress signal then get some gasoline from the engine room and set this thing ablaze. If we're lucky we'll blow it to bits before anybody comes looking for us." He smiles, feeling, at last, as if things might be swinging their way. "We should probably start with a round of penicillin injections, just to be on the safe side."

"You're the boss," Kenny says, and they follow him back down the hall to the medical bay.

Steven stands before the crowd triumphant, holding Perry's severed head in his hands and grinning idiotically. Melissa's fear increases twofold, despite the reassuring pep talk she'd given herself.

This is it, now it's my turn.

Captain Harvey strides into the middle of the circle and takes one of Steven's hands, hoisting it into the air.

"And the winner, by technical decapitation, is *(aaaahhhccckkk!)* the science dweeb!"

The crowd cheers and, if you close your eyes, you can almost imagine them as spectators at a pro wrestling match, albeit an exceptionally disturbing bunch; besides the clapping there is a reverberation that sounds disquietingly as if they are collectively gargling marbles.

"What does he win Kim?"

Kim Leung lunges forward and leaps on Steven, knocking Perry's head from his grasp and sending him sprawling to the ground. In one savage move she rips open his throat with her teeth before he can so much as make a startled squawk of protest. Dark green blood spurts from the wound and she bathes her face in it, making a mewling sound that sets Melissa's hair on end.

Oh shit, I am so fucked.

Captain Harvey roars his approval, clapping his hands together extravagantly. As he does so the pinky finger on his left hand bends backward and snaps off. He doesn't even notice. He's now down to six fingers, one ear (barely), one lip and God knows how many teeth.

"Good show! Good show!" he cries jubilantly. "Now the moment you have all been *(aaaahh-hccckkk!)* waiting for, the main event!" He swivels on his heels, locking eyes with Melissa. "Are you ready my dear?"

Melissa's heart thuds heavily in her chest and she swallows compulsively, looking from the captain to the twitching body on the ground.

Well, this is it. Maybe I should think of an epitaph for my tombstone, huh? Here lies Melissa Grant, one tough bitch who could take a licking and keep on ticking. . .but enough about my sex life...

She steps forward into the circle, a smile flitting upon her otherwise somber face. "What about my other request?" she asks in a voice she can hardly believe is her own. It possesses confidence and strength that she doesn't truly embody. Her knees are trembling ever so slightly, and if she were to hold her hands out in front of her she's sure they would shake like dead leaves in a strong wind.

"Yes," Captain Harvey says, "your other request, of course. Love the bondage suit yer rockin' by the way, it really makes this contest *(aaaahhhccckkk!)* official."

"Glad you like it."

"Oh, you know I do," he leers suggestively, his attempt at flirtation all but ignored by her. He shrugs. "Well, I suppose we can *(aaaahhhccckkk!)* accommodate you."

Captain Harvey signals to one of his minions and the creature staggers away to fetch the item. The captain smiles at her again, winking, and in that moment a startled realization hits her, something she should have known all along.

He wants me to win! He wants me to vanquish poor mutilated Kim because then he can have me for his own!

The minion returns, clutching the second article she'd called for. Seeing it at once slaps Melissa with an astonishing state of clarity, a lucidity so pure she feels momentarily as if she's watching the proceedings from someone else's eyes, from another vantage point all together, maybe through the scope of a high powered rifle. The sensation is eerie, disturbing. She shakes her head slowly, focusing on the object before her.

Clumsily clutching the whip in the hand that is now missing its pinky and middle finger, Captain Harvey holds it before him like a treasured prize.

"Come my dear, take it and *(aaaahhhccckkk!)* let the games begin."

"Holy cow!" Leeann exclaims, peering into the duffle bag. "You got these from the ship?" She is wearing a thick, plastic oilcloth Dave found along the way. He used a rusty steak knife to cut holes for her head and arms.

"There was more but I only grabbed what I could carry. This one," he says, reaching in and taking out an M-16A4 automatic rifle, "is the one I brung with me. When I saw it I almost got a chub." He blushes. "I know that sounds kinda weird, but I know this weapon inside and out. They taught us ta treat our rifle's like they was our girlfriends. Ya hafta know every inch of her very well."

Leeann smiles, becoming aware for the first time that he is just a kid, probably a couple of years younger than she is. The lack of food and water (and probably the events of the last few days) have taken their toll, but his youthful, unlined face is still that of boy, one who has been forced through adversity to become a man.

"I know I already asked you," she says, color suffusing her cheeks to match his own, "but what happened to you? How did you avoid getting caught and get back to the ship?"

"We ain't got time for that right now," he replies, but she senses a swell of pride. "Let's just say I was the recipient of some mighty good luck. Bad luck first, but then good."

"I'd like to hear the story."

"And I wanna tell ya, but we hafta get goin'. We got work to do."

"So we're going to save them, just the two of us?"

"That's the idea."

"Dante will be kind of put out, you know, me saving him instead of him saving me." She laughs. "You know Dante right? The big guy with the beard and bushy hair?"

"Sure," Dave says, and he dimly recalls someone matching that description but the name means nothing to him. He wasn't a part of the crew like she was. He was just the hired (if you can call unpaid 'hired') help. "I'll bet he'll be glad ta see us."

"What happened to the other guys with you, the other Naval men?" Saying the word 'men' seems almost silly to her because of his obvious youthfulness, but wouldn't saying 'Naval boys' sound even sillier?

"They met a bad end," he replies simply and the conclusiveness of his statement hangs in the air like a rotten smell. "So," he says, brightening considerably. "Do ya know how ta shoot a gun?"

"I've never fired one before."

"Ain't you from Texas?"

"How did you know?"

"Yer accent gave ya away. I thought everyone from Texas knew how to shoot a gun."

"I suppose I'm the exception."

"Well, I guess it's time for a crash course in automatic weapons 101," he says, smiling, and she smiles back.

"Cool."

Dave's story, if he were able to just sit down, open a beer and tell it in his amiable drawl, would duly impress the other survivors. The statement he'd made to Leeann about being lucky certainly holds true, he can't discount that, but what he humbly failed to mention was his own dogged resistance; he wasn't going down without a fight. Maybe it was the naval training, or perhaps something ingrained inside of him, something that wouldn't back down no matter how bad the odds were stacked against him. It was his perseverance and guile that brought him here, to this point, yes, coupled with that good old buddy 'luck'.

While running from the giant snails he'd fallen into a soft spot in the heap, submerged in an oddly warm sea. Searching along the ceiling of trash above him he discovered that he couldn't find his way out because the current had pulled him away from the opening. Panic had stolen over him then but he'd fought it off and kept his cool. Fortunately there was a small space between the bottom of the heap and the ocean, allowing him to breath, but as he drifted he found that was not always the case. There were times when he'd had to go under the water and swim blindly (the toxin-ridden sea stinging his eyes madly) probing along the ceiling above him. Sometimes he was lucky and he found another pocket of air quickly, sometimes he wasn't. On those unlucky times he simply kept searching until he found one, several times reaching the very last of his strength, his lungs feeling as if they were going to burst, head reeling from lack of oxygen. He traveled quite a distance like this, pulling himself forward until an obstacle forced him under. His biggest fear as he crept along regarded what he might encounter in the water, some mutant fish that would catch him completely defenseless, hopelessly out of his own element. And soon enough, in the darkness and putrid stench of the underwater world beneath the heap he did, several times over in fact. Large, unseen creatures brushed past his legs, and in one terrifying instance something locked its mouth onto his leg, it's teeth digging into his skin and clamping on. In that brief, terrible moment he knew it was over, his life, everything he'd known, gone. There'd be nothing left but his bones, and then, after a while of soaking in *this* water, nothing but dust…and no one would ever know what happened to him, what all he'd endured…

But somehow (Christ only knows; Dave does not) all his kicking and thrashing scared it off and it let him go, receding into the murk. Perhaps it would be appropriate for him to say that something (or someone) must have been looking out for him, but he wasn't a person to say such things. He got lucky and that was all.

So through the thick, foul, disquietingly tepid sea he towed himself along the bottom of the heap, groping urgently for anything he could use to propel himself forward. The direction he chose to travel was simply a guess, based on the current and the overwhelming dread that it had to be the correct way *or else*. Of course, was there really a 'correct way'? What he needed was to a find another hole like the one he fell in; he didn't think it at all possible that he could haul himself along the bottom like this until he reached an end to the trash heap, based on its size. He had to find another patch that wasn't solid or he would eventually succumb to the elements or drown or worse. One thing he didn't spend much time doing was thinking about possible worst-case scenarios involving the unseen beasts in the water. It was easier to think about drowning because that was something he understood, was a tangible fact of life for someone trained to work at sea. But the things he'd seen here, creatures beyond his wildest imagination, these were truly horrific, nightmarish, and in the darkness under the heap it was all too easy to picture these ghastly things swimming out of the shadows and taking hold of him as easily as he would pick an apple off a tree.

So he dragged himself along, sometimes the gentle current working with him, sometimes against. And he lost all track of time, for down there a minute was an hour, an hour a day, a day a lifetime. He would be lying if he said he didn't have moments of manic anxiety, and that these moments sometimes came with an alarming frequency. He'd swear that something just brushed past him, could feel the water churning as if something big (something REALLY BIG) had just swum by and was swinging around to take a second look. He'd freeze, paralyzed with fear, waiting for it to yank him away from the relative safety of the air pocket and into the deep where it's sharp teeth would snap him in half, feasting on his flesh and bones and organs. Or maybe it would drown him first, pulling him under and waiting until he could hold his breath no more, until he involuntarily opened his mouth to take an urgent, much-needed breath, only instead of air his lungs would fill painfully with seawater, burning and screaming. The Lieutenant junior grade who'd trained him couldn't emphasize enough the downside of drowning, assuring he and the others that it was probably one of the most painful ways to die, this side of being burned alive. Dave had made a mental note all those months back, staring at the older man with the thick, black eyebrows and bushy nose hairs: Don't drown at all costs! And so this terror would overwhelm him and he'd stop, not moving, not making a sound, taking shallow, rapid breaths, waiting until he was certain it passed or until he convinced himself there was nothing there. Then, and only then, would he begin moving again.

He had no idea how long he was down there, truly none at all. After what felt like an eternity he'd finally come upon an opening similar to the one he'd fallen into and, following a terrific struggle to pull himself topside (he'd been in the water so long he was, understandably, exhausted) he lay there, shivering and twitching. He rested for a while and in the heat of the sun his uniform dried out a little, helping to restore in him a semblance of humanity. But again apprehension got the better of him and, feeling exposed, he got to his feet and wandered until he found an indentation in the trash that served as a cave. Crawling within the tiny alcove, he fell into a heavy slumber. Like his time spent beneath the heap, he had no clue as to how long he slept, only that when he awoke he was more aware of his hunger than ever and could sense dehydration settling into him like hooks into tender flesh. He knew he needed sustenance soon if he was to continue on. Utilizing a compass he'd found in one of his many pockets (water had gotten in the casing but somehow it still worked) he headed east and, following a sunset and well after a sunrise, he came upon the ocean. Having no resources and not knowing what else to do he decided to follow the coastline, picking his direction by mentally tossing a coin. He randomly decided to take a right. It was this decision that was his biggest saving grace: eventually it brought him to another, larger cave and, lo and behold, the ship. He wept with relief seeing it tucked away in the recesses of the grotto and, after brushing away his tears, he slipped back into the water and swam to where a rope ladder hung over the side, attached to the lifeboats. These he inspected quickly, but he knew they weren't of any use to him. What he needed was on the ship.

Using the naval training he was mostly unaware he possessed, he crept stealthily aboard, successfully attracting no attention. His first mission was to find and retrieve his weapon, his second to kill anything that got in his way. He almost failed at both tasks when two crewmen spotted him crossing the top deck and a too-close-for-comfort pursuit led him deep within the ship to his shared cabin on the third deck (near the engine room) where he beat them by mere inches, shutting and bolting the door behind him. He'd been stripped of his rifle the day they'd been taken prisoner but the crew didn't know about the .9 MM he'd kept in his duffle bag. He located and loaded it, his hands shaky but sure. Subsequent to a brief moment spent psyching himself up, he flung open the door and fired, his weapon spitting out bullets as the empty shell casings fell to the floor around him. It took a lot of lead but eventually they succumbed, their bodies twitching frenziedly while he changed the clip and emptied it into their jellied remains. He then relieved them of their automatic rifles.

The uproar alerted the others and they came running, but when they saw the carnage their roles were reversed: they attempted to flee as he proceeded to hunt them down. He cornered them on the second deck, not allowing them topside access, driving them into the last room at the end of the ship's long passageway. Once inside he fired upon them mercilessly, their bodies jittering and jiving under the rain of fire as he grinned and hooted like a redneck after a jug of moonshine and a lie down with his sister. When the smoke cleared there was nothing left but a flyblown pile of corpses, their blackish/greenish blood washing over the floor in a tidal wave of gore.

He sat down then, setting the rifle aside and putting his head in his hands. For several minutes he didn't move, just sat there listening to all the nothingness around him. It was very still, only the creaks and groans of the ship audible as she rocked gently in the subtle current. He sat like this for some time, tears coursing down his cheeks yet again, for what, he wasn't sure.

When he at last felt himself growing restless he knew it was time to go, but Jesus H. Christ what a mess! Even though he'd gained the upper hand he couldn't help but be somewhat humbled by these creatures ability to absorb so many hits before finally lying down for good. For fuck's sake he'd pumped countless rounds into their bacteria infested bodies and they still struggled, managing to get to their hands and knees, attempting to crawl away. He'd had to use two full magazines on them. He was utterly vexed at how difficult it was to kill these bastards; they were like monsters in a video game that just kept coming and coming even after you'd shot them dozens of times. There was no way he could wipe them all out, simply no way.

After careful deliberation he decided he'd grab as many guns as he could carry (finding his rifle amongst theirs) and see if there was anyone left alive in need of saving. What the hell, what else was he gonna do? Maybe the old him would have cut the moorings that held the ship fast, fired it up and sailed away without looking back, but that person was gone, left treading water below the heap. He'd been given a second chance at life so he was going to extend the favor, no matter what eventually became of him. Later it would occur to him that he could have gotten on the radio and sent out a distress signal, but these thoughts never crossed his mind at the time, possibly because he knew it would do nothing to help anyone in the immediate future, but most likely because of the state he was in. In the here and now he was alive, healthy, and armed to the teeth.

Following a meal of canned goods and bottled water (eaten methodically, deriving very little pleasure except for driving away the hollow sensation in his gut) he left the ship, his duffle bag full of guns and ammo over his shoulder. Although he felt rather glum in regards to his future prospects he did have to admit that killing the creatures perked him up some, had actually put a little zip in his step, even though in the grand scheme of things it was a somewhat empty victory. Dave=1, crewmen creatures=0, but how many of them were there all told? All he could really hope for was maybe putting a small dent in their numbers, possibly rescuing some of the passengers from the ship, if any of them were alive to be rescued, that is.

So, guided by the well-marked path, he headed to the village, abandoning the trail as he grew near so as not to draw anyone's (anything's) attention. His ears attuned to the sounds of life that thrived within, he picked his way through the fields of garbage until he came out on the other side, near a wall that divided one part of the community from the other. It was from this vantage point that he figured he could best scope out the area before he made his move, giving him an idea of what he was up against.

And it was shortly thereafter that he stumbled upon a young girl in need of assistance (not to mention something to wear) and the relief of finding another normal person bolstered his strength, assuring him that he'd done the right thing in coming here in search of others; his actions had not been in vain.

Presently he is ready to blast these mutant sons a bitches into smithereens, starting with Captain Harvey and working his way down.

Oh, and there was something else that made it all worthwhile: it'd been quite some time since he'd seen a real, live, in-the-flesh naked chick. Oh yeah...that definitely made his day.

"Hold it like that, with yer left arm there, and you wanna gently squeeze the trigger, not tug at it, just ease it back."

"Alright."

"And there's a switch next to the trigger, it changes it from safety to semi-automatic to fully automatic. Just keep it in the fully automatic mode so you don't accidentally put the safety on."

"Should I fire it?"

"This one ain't loaded, I just want ya ta get a feel for it."

"Okay." She does like he says, gently squeezing the trigger, and when she does it comes alive in her hands, a short burst of fire exiting the muzzle, startling her. "Whoa!"

"Crap! There musta been a round in the chamber."

The bullet whizzes off the floor of the heap and produces a spark. A small puff of smoke arises from it, followed by the trace of a flame. It burns for a moment and then appears to snuff itself out. Dave and Leeann look at it curiously, waiting a few seconds to see if anything else is going to happen. When nothing does they return their attention to the rifle.

"Sorry bout that," Dave says, taking the weapon from her. "I thought it was unloaded."

"So that's how guns kill people," Leeann says and giggles. "That's the story everyone tells in court: 'I thought it was unloaded.'"

He smiles, pulls the lever back and peers into the chamber. "I shoulda checked. My bad."

"It's okay, no harm no foul."

"How was the kick on yer shoulder? Do ya think ya can handle it?"

"No sweat," she replies in a soft and innocent voice that instantly arouses him. There is something so hot about a cute chick with a gun...

"We better get goin' then," he says, removing several weapons from the bag and carefully loading them. "Are ya sure yer up ta this?"

"Are you kidding? I have someone in mind I'd like to start with."

"The captain?"

"You can take him out. I'm thinking about someone else."

THIRTY-FOUR

"Come on, take it. I don't bite…well, not that hard." The captain grins, revealing yet another missing tooth. Most of his front teeth are gone, his gums raw, inflamed. "We'll see if it gets your *(aaaahhhccckkk!)* pretty ass out of this jam or not."

"We'll see." His creepy, lascivious candor suddenly evokes in her a strong sense of futility; even if she wins she loses. The outcome of this battle determines very little except that her life may be prolonged a few days. In the end only her dignity is on the line, the one thing she truly has left. Well, what the hell, if that's all she's got she'll take it.

She approaches slowly, her eyes on his, reaching out carefully and taking the whip. The handle feels good in her hand and she flicks her wrist, giving it a test run. The sharp crack it makes pleases her, and at once she feels better than she has since this shitstorm began. She sneers at him.

"So where's the hood? The suit isn't complete without it."

"Perhaps I forgot, perhaps I *(aaaahhhccckkk!)* didn't." His eyes sparkle wickedly, his expression so lecherous it would make a child molester run for their life. "Maybe I just didn't want your *(aaaahhhccckkk!)* face covered. I like a chick with a few scars." His gaze shifts to something over her shoulder, a quick look and then back at her. "What do you think, shall we *(aaaahhhccckkk!)* get underway?"

A dreadful scream erupts from behind her, the noise mounting, becoming shriller the closer it gets. Turning swiftly, Melissa sees Kim lunging at her without warning and, instinctively, she falls flat to the ground just as the girl reaches her, the other missing the mark and sailing over her, tumbling end over end.

What, no bell, no 'let's have a fair fight'? Should have expected that.

The crowd resumes its disquieting roar, the sound grating and obstreperous, the creatures spitting and hissing and waving their misshapen limbs about. Their bloodlust drives them closer, the circle tightening around her. Melissa gets up quickly, trying her best to ignore them, her knees slightly bent in her best fight stance. She dances about limberly, scrutinizing the other carefully, trying to guess her next move.

Kim is on her feet in a millisecond and coming at her again. God but the bitch is fast, and she's clearly operating on some kind of radar, as she knows exactly where Melissa is even though her eyes are nothing but a memory. As she gets close Melissa draws back her arm and squats into a crouch. She cracks the whip and, just as Kim is almost on top of her, it wraps around her legs, taking them out from under her. She sprawls onto the ground again, issuing choppy grunts that don't even sound vaguely human.

She isn't human, remember that, she is nothing but tissue and bacteria now. Tissue and bacteria that is trying to kill you.

Kim rises and flings herself forward yet again, her teeth gnashing, her hands hooked into claws. If this thing gets a hold of her than she is done for, of that Melissa is certain, judging by how quickly she took out Steven. One second he was the gloating winner and the next he was nothing but a carcass drawing flies. Above everything else she can't let her get within a few feet or it's all over.

"Come on, I want to *(aaaahhhccckkk!)* see blood!" Captain Harvey thunders, his voice reedy, petulant.

Melissa pivots on her left heel, keeping her right arm forward. As Kim gets within range again she flicks her wrist, the whip lashing out with deadly accuracy. This time the tip cracks against Kim's forehead, knocking her back for a second *(Jesus, only a fraction of a second)* before she regains her wits and continues her forward momentum. Before Melissa can draw her arm back again Kim is on her, taking her to the ground. The air whooshes out of her as she lands on her back with a spine-jarring thud, Kim crashing down on top of her.

Twisting and wriggling, struggling for dominance, Kim manages to straddle Melissa, becoming a whirling dervish of limbs and teeth, and it is all the dominatrix can do to keep her at an arm's length as the nightmarish girl grapples her roughly, teeth clicking the air just inches from her face. Planting her right foot flat on the ground, Melissa uses the leverage of her leg and body to squirm sideways, bending so that she can place her left hand palm down and propel herself upward, forcing the other off of her. Not that Kim is deterred for long, but it gives her just enough time to scramble to her feet and lash out with the whip, tripping Kim once again.

I can't keep up like this. She's going to wear me down and then move in for the kill.

She glances over at Captain Harvey and wonders: *If he wants me for his Queen so badly, what is he going to do to save me?* Surely he doesn't think she can take on Kim with her whip and cunning alone. He'd have to be…

Crazy? Is that what you were going to say? Just look at him! He's falling to pieces one body part at a time and he's been making that weird sound and retching worms for days! Crazy? He's the fucking poster child for out and out lost his goddamn marbles!

Then it dawns on her, another revelation that eclipses the first, dismantling her original theory: he intends for this to play itself out. However the chips may fall is how they lie. If she should win, *if*, then he will take her as his Queen. But if she should lose? Well, then she is dead, and dead is dead, nothing more. What she thought she read in his eyes was unquestionably a whimsical fantasy; she saw what she wanted to see, and what she desired very badly was assurance that this was a fight she could win.

Anger swells within her, the anger she'd felt in the cage when everything seemed hopeless, when it appeared that all was lost. She glares at Captain Harvey, her eyes drilling into his, the fire flashing inside clearly conveying the message '**First her and then you motherfucker, just you watch me**' and damned if the captain doesn't catch her drift, a startled expression crossing his moldering features. She lashes out with the whip yet again and strikes Kim on the cheek, tearing open a gash that gushes a rancid looking substance, but the thing is undaunted, in fact the blow hardly breaks her stride. Kim streaks toward her with a momentum that is frightening and Melissa wallops her over and over, the loud snap of the whip overriding the taunts of the crowd. Where the cat o' nine tails connects it lacerates flesh, creating large welts all over Kim's putrefying body, grisly fluid seeping thickly from the wounds, yet she keeps coming, this insatiably homicidal beast, and eventually Melissa recognizes that all the whip lashes in the world aren't going to stop Kim from having her way. In fact, her arm is growing tired and she's breathing heavily while the other doesn't appear to be winded whatsoever. Just the opposite, she's recharged, ready to finish the battle.

As quickly as the anger arose within her it recedes, replaced by an awful certainty that it's all over, this thing is going to rip her to pieces and Captain Harvey is going to watch with indifferent eyes. He isn't going to do anything, isn't going to lift a finger (*hah! Good one!*) to save her. And in the split second between Kim's lunge and the inevitable impact Melissa stands bravely, the whip dangling at her side, her eyes set, solemn. She surveys the crowd around her, her thoughts going out to all those who have passed: Kenny, Cole, Governor Hallsly, the two science dweebs, Leeann, and last but not least Dante (who is staring dumbly from the far side of the circle, his long curly hair in his eyes, his hands twitching at his sides…).

And then she notices something extraordinary: Dante is dashing toward her, attempting to get in between Kim and herself. His movements are fluid, his footing sure, and when he hastily glances up at her she sees his eyes are clear, filled with a purposeful intention.

As Kim is almost upon her Dante fills the gap between them, reaching out and shoving the girl/thing just as she would have collided with Melissa at full speed.

"What are you (*aaaahhhccckkk!*) doing in the circle?" Captain Harvey cries, outraged. "This fight has nothing (*aaaahhhccckkk!*) to do with you!"

Kim bounces back up, knocking Dante to the ground, and they roll end over end as Melissa watches, stunned. The crowd begins to make a different noise, a disgruntled racket that grows increasingly louder. She looks from face to face, sees they are inching forward, their hands out before them, opening and closing. The job that Kim was supposed to do has now been passed onto them, and instead of being ripped apart by one bacteria infested creature she is now going to be drawn and quartered by the lot of them. She spins crazily, looking for any way out but there is none, nowhere to go. Their bodies are pressed closely together, allowing no room to push past. Even if she tried to shove her way through them they would simply force her back, overtaking her as easily as a wolf would a cornered rabbit. Her fear spiking within her, she can taste her own imminent death, the flavor on her tongue metallic, like the coppery smell of blood. This is it, the end of the proverbial line. This is the end, my beautiful friend…

The machinelike sound of gunfire tears apart the air like tissue paper, and before her startled eyes she watches as the creatures turn away from her and toward their new source of irritation. Greenish/blackish blood sprays in torrents as bullets rain from some unknown source, and she automatically dives for the ground, covering her head with her hands.

We're saved! She thinks triumphantly. *The Coast Guard or the Marines or the Navy are here to save the day! Fuck you Harvey; fuck you and the dead horse you rode in on!*

Bullets whine and ricochet around her and, without thought, acting purely on impulse, she gets up and crouch walks away as fast as her legs will allow, putting as much distance between her and the creatures as she can. Glancing back, she observes that they've broken the circle and are stumbling forward en masse to protect the King, who in the melee is slinking away…

"Do you hear that?" Cole says, cocking his head in the direction of the village. "Is that what I think it is?"

Dr. Taylor and Kenny stop walking, their arms laden with the items they've liberated from the ship, listening. The doctor shifts the bag he is carrying from one hand to the other, the sun gleaming on the rifle barrel that pokes out the top. If this had been a regular scientific mission there is no way in hell there would have been so much firepower on board, of that Dr. Taylor is certain. Only because Captain Harvey had perpetrated this charade was there an arsenal large enough to sustain a small army, and at this point it's a good freakin' thing. Poetic justice is what it's called. Dr. Taylor is sure the irony will aggravate the captain to no end.

Miles behind them the ship is in flames, black smoke smudging the sky as the fire eats its way through anything combustible. They'd started the blaze in the engine room using gasoline, splashing it upon wooden chairs, pillows, bedding, books, clothing…anything flammable they could get their hands on. This was after they'd taken everything they needed, of course, and sent out a distress signal that would repeat itself on an endless loop until the radio was no more. They'd tried to make contact with someone, anyone, but the radio had issued nothing but erratic bursts of static.

"Sounds like automatic gunfire!" Kenny exclaims, looking to Dr. Taylor for confirmation.

"It does."

"We're saved!" Cole cries joyously. He looks at the other two inquisitively. "We are, aren't we? Saved I mean."

"Whatta ya think Doc?"

"I'll wager that whomever dispatched of the crewmen on the ship is now taking care of the villagers," he says, eyeing his companions speculatively, noting with satisfaction that the two of them are perspiring, large drops of black sweat dripping off their grimy faces. "How are you guys feeling?" Before collecting their cache of weapons and starting the fire he'd given them both another injection of penicillin (as well as one for himself), spiking it with an amphetamine chaser to counteract the Valium.

"Like I can jump a tall building in a single bound," Kenny answers with a grin. Cole nods his agreement.

"Then let's shag a little ass and go help them."

It was a trick he'd developed as a child, a little slight of hand so he wouldn't have to eat his Brussels' sprouts or lima beans or whatever food it was he despised. Being as poor as they were, his stepparents fed them whatever was the cheapest to procure, which were always the least popular vegetables at the market it seemed. Dante would shovel the offending item into the side of his cheek and, when the coast was clear, he'd spit it back into his hand and make it disappear up his sleeve for later disposal in the deepest recesses of the trash or down the toilet. If it was a meat item, like liver, it was easier because he could use his hands instead of a fork and that way it wouldn't have to spend any time in his mouth; he would 'eat' with his hands, pretending to stuff the pieces in when they were actually being stowed in various parts of his clothing. If it was something greasy and therefore likely to leave a stain he would use pieces of his napkin to wrap it in so there would be no evidence on his shirt or pants. He'd gotten so good at this trick that he was never caught, and his stepmother always commented on what a good eater he was, using him as an example for his stepbrother Michael, who knew what Dante was doing but didn't have the guts to rat him out. Michael would look at him jealously, knowing that he'd have to eat his squash/beets/gizzards etc. or accept the consequences simply because he lacked the skills that Dante had perfected.

And so this was what Dante did when the Rancor bird was served: he'd cheeked the nasty meat and made as if to chew and swallow and when the creature guarding him looked away he stowed it up his sleeve. Since his clothes were so dirty there was no need to be concerned about staining them; who would notice? When he was eventually left alone he tossed the pieces out of the cage as far as he could, hoping they weren't found. And the trick worked, just like it always had when he was a boy, and after his second serving he'd been allowed to exit the cage upon his own (well, the bacteria's) reconnaissance. He'd merely kept his head down so his eyes weren't visible and walked in a shuffling, awkward gate, mimicking the other creatures. Fortunately no one studied him too closely; the captain's growing arrogance/negligence was probably to thank for that. If he wasn't deteriorating at such a steady rate he might have checked Dante more carefully, but as luck would have it, he didn't.

While he stood in the circle (standing well away from Captain Harvey) he watched through hooded lids as Steven and Perry's fight came to a shocking, brutal end, his stomach turning queasily at the sound of shredding flesh and snapping bones. And after the winner received his grand prize (an all expenses paid trip down the River Styx to Hell) Melissa walked up to the captain on what appeared to be steady legs, her eyes radiating courage, trading remarks with the son of a bitch and taking the whip from his rotting hands. Before she could properly prepare herself the other charged, and she successfully avoided Kim's first attack and launched a counterattack that seemed promising until Dante recognized how unevenly matched they were. No matter how hard or accurate Melissa's blows were, Kim rebounded in seconds as if she hadn't been struck at all. It was obvious that even with the whip and the bondage suit protecting her she hardly stood a chance.

Bearing witness to this spectacle made him feel accountable, knowing he couldn't live with himself if he just stood there and watched her die, but the problem was that he didn't want to give his secret away, as he was doing this to save Leeann. If he tried to help Melissa than they would know he was faking. His only chance to rescue Leeann rested on his ability to slip throughout their ranks undetected.

So he watched as the battle went back and forth, Melissa doling out punishment that didn't seem to faze Kim at all, the wrecked, deplorable girl getting to her feet again and again with no loss of impetus, making it clear that Melissa, in her weakened state, was simply not up to the challenge of defeating her. When it appeared that Kim was going to overtake Melissa and dish out a fatal blow he at last ditched his pretense and dove in, momentarily oblivious to the outcome of such an action. He simply couldn't stand idly by while another human being needed aid, and he'd be damned if he wasn't going to give it. Of course he'd had no foresight as to how it would play itself out, this chivalrous deed, and as he now struggles with the mangled, psychotically strong girl he begins to think he's made a mistake, that now he AND Melissa are going to die, either by Kim's hands or those of the oncoming masses. Not only that he's also given himself away; Leeann is certainly doomed as well.

Another foolish move by one Mr. Dante Kellerman larva's and germs, but should that come as a surprise? It shouldn't, seeing as he condoned his mother's murder of his youngest sibling, contributing to her depraved indifference by keeping her alive all those years, and then found a career in selling his blood, piss, shit and semen to a pharmaceutical company who gave him drugs that would eventually render him blind, impotent or sterile because he never, ever read the damn contracts, much less the fucking fine print. He was, incontrovertibly, a very stupid, stupid man, and by all accounts probably didn't deserve to live anyway. . .

Suddenly the sound of gunfire overtakes the din of the creatures and he feels a burst of optimism buoy him, giving him renewed strength. Kim leaps off of him and scurries away, and he gets quickly to his feet, looking about him alertly. Somebody has finally come to the rescue and they have a chance after all. After three grim days there is at last a light at the end of the tunnel, and it feels good baby, it feels really freakin' good.

"When we get there just fire at everythin' that moves. When the magazine is empty replace it as quick as ya can and keep firin', but take care and make sure the clip locks snugly inta place or the gun might jam. These things are hard to fuckin' kill so ya hafta act fast."

"What about the survivors?"

"You'll know who they are; they'll be the ones crouched down or runnin' in the other direction."

"Okay."

"Ya ready?"

"I. . .I guess so."

"Then let's kill us some mutants."

The gun jerks and kicks in Leeann's hands as fire spits out of the barrel, and she grips it tightly, trying to keep the muzzle level. She's astonished by the power she feels, giving her a flush of pleasure to see the creatures twitch and stagger as the bullets strike home.

Dave plunges ahead, screaming like a charging Apache, sweeping the gun back and forth. He too feels a rush of satisfaction watching the creatures' movements become even more ungainly, their bodies growing heavy with lead. What he really wants is to find Captain Harvey and empty a full mag into the bastard's head, but throughout their ranks he is nowhere to be seen.

Course he ain't, whatta ya expect? He's like any other figurehead: he lets the lowly peons fight while he runs for cover.

Continuing forward, Dave sees out of the corner of his eye a big guy, a *really* big guy, creeping toward them on his belly. He has a tangled, shaggy beard and a thick, bushy head of hair and at the speed he's crawling toward them he'll be upon them any second. He swings the rifle in his direction, ready to blast him into the next century when he hears Leeann's voice, high-pitched and piercing even over the roar of the guns. He turns toward her, fearing that she is in trouble, but she is pointing at the approaching man and shaking her head.

"No! Not him! That's Dante!"

"I don't care who he used to be, he's nothing but a carcass now!" He trains his weapon on the other, his finger tensing against the trigger.

He stands quickly, his hands raised before him, and Dave can see his eyes behind his crooked glasses, big, hardboiled egg eyes, the whites a clearly defined backdrop to his brown iris's.

"Are you still human?"

"As much as I've ever been," he says in a shaky voice, managing a grin. "Where can I get one of those?"

Dave relaxes his finger, points the gun away. "In the duffle bag. Hurry."

Dante scrambles for the bag, produces one of the M-16A4's. Dave looks on approvingly, nodding.

"Magazines are in the side pocket. Grab as many as you can."

"With pleasure."

At the first sound of gunfire Jake abandons the fight (upon which he'd just arrived), fear stealing over him as he sprints away.

Can't be, there's no way, he thinks, bolting for the edge of the village. He briefly considers searching for the captain but dismisses it quickly. *No sense in going back. Someone has to survive to keep the bacteria alive.*

He pauses a moment, listening. He can hear shouting (human) and groaning (his cohorts). It doesn't sound good, in fact it sounds like a goddamn blood bath. He has to get to the ship at once, has to leave the island before anyone can stop him from making a beeline for the California coast. It is the necessary next phase and at all costs he cannot be stopped.

It can't end here, no; we've only just begun.

Sticking to the outskirts of the village, he slowly makes his way around, his eyes and ears open for any sign of trouble. Either he or the captain has to sail the ship back to the mainland, and Captain Harvey isn't looking so hot. Jake doubts the other can make the voyage, will probably expire en-route and the ship will be lost at sea. If that happens than all of this will have been for nothing, all of their hard work flushed right down the crapper. And that isn't part of the plan, not if he can help it. He may have to fight Ronson over who is ultimately going to take control, but that doesn't bother him in the slightest. In fact, he is looking forward to it.

Keeping low to the ground, Melissa crawls away from the creatures until it is safe to stand up. Looking over her shoulder, she clears the line of fire and slowly doubles back, staying well away from the mutants so as not to get clipped by a stray bullet. She wants very badly to know who is behind this rescue, wants to find out if they have a spare gun and, if so, would love to pump a few rounds into these shitheads herself. She'd thought that escape was impossible, her death unavoidable, but now there is hope. Hope and a second chance.

As she gets closer she sees one of the shooters in profile, and recognition makes her smile. "No fucking way," she mutters. She steps closer, cups her hands around her mouth. "Leeann!" she calls. "Don't shoot! It's me, Melissa!"

Leeann swings around, gun aimed at her, a look of alarm creasing her dirt seamed face.

"Jesus!" she exhales noisily, lifting the gun so it's pointing at the sky. "I almost shot you! Get over here!"

Melissa dashes over, putting her arms around the girl and giving her a hug.

"You don't know how glad I am to see you!"

"Me too!" Leeann says, patting the others back with her free hand.

"Can I help?"

"Grab a gun!" She gestures with her head to the large green duffle bag, metal gleaming from inside.

"I thought you'd never ask."

Fetching what looks to be a rather formidable firestick, she hefts it experimentally, wondering what to do next.

"Clips are in the side pocket!" Leeann shouts over the tumult. "Just stick it in the opening in the bottom until it clicks securely, cock the lever right here and then point and shoot!" She shows Melissa her own gun. "Like this, okay?"

"Sure."

Hands trembling from exhaustion and nervous energy, Melissa fumbles a couple of magazines from the bag, eyeing them carefully before trying to insert one. To her surprise it clicks into place with ease and, after pulling back and returning the lever, she raises it to her shoulder and squints through the sight just in time to see four of the creatures bearing down on her. She squeezes the trigger and the gun jumps to life in her hands, the bullets spraying wildly over their heads.

Not going to do any good like that. Try harder!

Setting her feet solidly, she tucks the gun tightly into her armpit and aims it at their torso's, firing again. This time the bullets hit their intended target, and the creatures shudder and scuttle as she fires round after round into their contaminated bodies. Yet they keep coming, these sick, demented things, even as their limbs are blasted off and chunks of their skulls disappear in spouting geysers of putrid blood.

"Die you mother fuckers!" she screams, unaware that she is running forward, actively engaging them. The closest one finally drops face first to the ground, its legs twitching, body wracked with spasms. But it stays down, she notices with approval, and that's a start, a damn good one. She points the weapon at the next closest and hits it with a continuous volley of fire, trying to aim between it's eyes but the weapon is hard to direct, jerking and bucking uncontrollably. Using all her strength she manages to get the muzzle up and, in a fantastic splatter of blood, brains and bone, its head explodes, the fragments flying every which way. But still it continues forward until, at last, its body realizes that its main control center is gone and it falls to its knees, collapsing in a heap.

"This is fun!" she cries, uttering a laugh that is just this side of unhinged, and she aims at the next, anxious to see what kind of damage she can inflict upon this one. It's like a video game, only it's all too real; she can smell the sharp tang of blood in the air, intermingled with the acrid odor of gunpowder.

Without warning the gun runs empty, simply making a dry clicking sound as she continues to tug at the trigger.

"Get back here!" she hears Dante yell, and at once becomes aware that she has strayed too far from the group. She is much too close for comfort, especially now that she is essentially disarmed. She turns tail and flees, rejoining her comrades where they are huddled together, standing shoulder-to-shoulder, creating a veritable wall of gunfire. "Grab another clip from the bag!" Dante tells her without taking his eyes away from his intended target. "Grab a bunch!"

"Right!" An onrush of heat explodes within her, her bloodlust strong, unquenchable, and instantly she feels more alive than ever before in her life. Maybe it's because of the horror she's been through, the bleak circumstances that she'd felt were most surely going to result in her death, or maybe it's the sound of the machineguns and watching the creatures getting a taste of their own medicine; whatever the reason she recognizes it for what it truly is:

This is the ultimate pain, she thinks with wonder as she jams another clip into the gun. *But its more than just pain, this is wholesale slaughter and it feels so good to be on the side that's finally winning. . .*

"They're starting to back off!" Dave hollers triumphantly as the nearest creatures at last shy away from the gunfire, taking to their heels, stumbling into the others crowded behind them. "Everybody move forward!"

Like an inexorable force of encroaching death, the four of them advance upon their prey, driving them away from the center of the village, scattering them into smaller groups.

"We've got them on the run!" Dante brays, a large, dopey grin on his face that Leeann, who is pausing to reload, notices and returns. A sudden burst of emotion hits her and it is in this exact moment she realizes that she could love this man simply for who he is. She can see beyond the bushy beard, the shaggy hair, the Coke bottle bottom glasses that make his eyes look gigantic. She understands in this fraction of a second that beauty is only skin deep and that one's inner splendor is worth so much more than the mask we wear that we call our face. It is our actions that truly define us, and Dante has stayed with the program the entire way, just as he'd promised, doing everything he can to make sure they get out of this alive. For this she is proud of him because, when it really came down to it, did she really believe anything he'd said? Did she really? She doesn't know, in fact, doesn't care, because that was then and this is now. Presently they have each other and they have these damn things on the run. After three days of sweating it out they are at last getting some much-needed payback and, hopefully soon, they'll be able to go home. That thought alone causes a giddy spin in her stomach...

"Leeann!" Dante screams, the terror in his voice palpable, and as she takes in his horrified expression and frantic gestures the muscular grip of a cold hand grasps her throat, exquisite pain drowning everything else out as the fingers punch through her skin, digging and clawing at the juicy meat inside. She turns and sees the horrible visage of Kim Leung, half of her head blasted to smithereens, her brain leaking out one side, the stump of her tongue wagging back and forth like a dog's tail on amphetamines. She has only a moment to register the lightheadedness that overtakes her before she feels wet, flowing warmth coursing down her neck, trickling onto the tarp she's wearing and splashing on her toes. And then, an instant later, she senses nothing more.

THIRTY-
FIVE

"We must be gettin' close. Anytime now we'll see that damn sign," Kenny says, and Dr. Taylor notices his color is better, more robust. It means the penicillin is working better than he'd planned. Good news, it seems, travels in packs.

"I don't hear gunshots anymore," Cole says. "You think they're alright?"

Dr. Taylor stops and listens, Cole's statement abruptly bringing to light the silence that seems terrifically loud in the wake of all the racket. Could it be they were overtaken, possibly after running out of ammo? Or maybe (and this is what he would like to think, what they would all like to think) that whoever was doing the shooting has the creatures on the run. That would be the version of the story he'd like to believe.

"I don't know. I guess we'll find out soon enough."

"I'll tell ya one thing," Kenny says through gritted teeth, "I can't wait ta see that bastard Harvey an give him a piece a my mind."

"If there's anything left of him," Dr. Taylor says, shifting the bag he's carrying from one shoulder to the other. Damned if he isn't running on fumes; exhaustion is just a stones throw away. The fact that he is still on his feet is a miracle in and of itself. "I know it might be just wishful thinking, but maybe he isn't a threat to us anymore."

"We could only be so lucky," Cole says, and Kenny is about to comment when he hears something, a scraping, crunching noise to their left, unseen and off the path.

"I think we got company," he says in a low voice. "I heard somethin' come from over there." He points in the direction he heard the sound. "Could be a animal but..."

Dr. Taylor sets down the bag and takes out a handgun. "This isn't a good time to take any chances. Best to be safe and have a weapon handy."

"Ya know what yer doin' with that thing Doc?" Kenny asks, arching an eyebrow. "Ya ever use one before?"

"No, have you?"

"A pro football player who don't know how ta fire a gun? Ya jokin'?"

Dr. Taylor smiles and holds it out to the other. "Well then by all means enlighten us-"

Suddenly two arms shoot out from around a blind corner, grabbing the doctor and pulling him backward. He disappears behind a wall of trash, out of sight. The gun clatters to the ground as he simultaneously utters a high-pitched scream, one that is cut short, closely followed by a low chortle that Kenny and Cole recognize all too well.

"If you don't want me to kill him than I *(aaaahhhcccckkk!)* suggest you two toss those bags toward me and step back."

"Son of a bitch." Kenny angrily drops the knapsack containing the weapons and drugs.

"I told you to toss it over here. What about my *(aaaahhhcccckkk!)* request did you not understand?"

Kenny stoops, picks it up, and then tosses it over to where Captain Harvey is hiding.

"There, ya happy?"

"Cole, you too. Hurry now. I don't want to *(aaaahhhcccckkk!)* ask again."

"Do as he says!" Dr. Taylor cries and Cole follows suit.

"Good, now back off."

Kenny and Cole retreat several paces, cautiously watching the spot where the voice emanates from. Captain Harvey emerges from his hiding place, the doctor in tow.

"I don't know how you *(aaaahhhcccckkk!)* did it," he whispers into Dr. Taylor's ear, a smile on his decaying face, although it is a horrible sight, what with his missing teeth, ears and bottom lip, "but I can't say that I'm surprised. I never should have trusted to let them *(aaaahhhcccckkk!)* take you to the ship but, if truth be told, I haven't been thinking all too *(aaaahhhcccckkk!)* clearly lately."

"Lately?" Kenny scoffs and Captain Harvey's trademark leer turns on him.

"You two are going to make like porn stars and fuck off, got it? The doctor and I have an *(aaaahhhcccckkk!)* appointment we need to keep."

"If ya plan on takin' the ship, think again," Kenny says, matching the other's smile with a wily one of his own. "Any time now an that mother is gonna blow."

"What?"

"We set it on fire," Dr. Taylor says. "We couldn't let you take the contagion off the heap so… no ship, no exit."

"No…you couldn't have! You didn't!" Captain Harvey looks from one to the other, the grin melting from his face as an expression of terror replaces it. It isn't that he can't procure another ship; trash barges will be arriving any day, now that the storm cell has passed. This is a major impedance simply because he's run out of time, his deterioration far too advanced. In three or four days he may not even exist anymore.

"We did," Cole confirms. "That baby is toast."

"You fools! You have no idea what you've *(aaaahhhcccckkk!)* done!"

"Yes, we do," Dr. Taylor says as the captain's grip goes slack, his coarse fingers resting lightly on the nape of his neck. "We knew that we had to stop you-"

The captain's hands tighten around his throat, and in one quick move he picks him up as if he weighs no more than a rag doll and tosses him aside. Dr. Taylor experiences a momentary flying sensation that ends abruptly when his head strikes something, hard. And then, nothing.

Captain Harvey stalks forward, his eyes alight with a rapacious fury, and when he opens his mouth to speak a violent flood of ropy worms spurts out, spilling down the front of his shirt. He coughs and sputters but this does nothing to slow him down. Unaware they are doing so, Kenny and Cole are backing away.

"Do you know how hard I've *(aaaahhhccckkk!)* worked to see this plan to fruition? Do you? You stupid assholes!" He takes another step forward, the others another step back. "And I would have shared it with you, my *(aaaahhhccckkk!)* victory. You would have been high up in my army, could have been *(aaaahhhccckkk!)* generals, enjoying all the spoils of war."

"Ya dint give us a choice bout our participation," Kenny says, trying to sound tough although noodles of fear slop through his guts. "We wasn't willin' accomplices."

"No one is. Do you think I was when I first *(aaaahhhccckkk!)* came here, huh? I was just as afraid as you two, maybe even more so because I was *(aaaahhhccckkk!)* the first." He stops within a few feet of them and his body begins to shudder, his throat working spasmodically, his eyes never leaving theirs. They can sense something rising within him, not just rage but something actually growing inside, trying to work its way out. His chest bulges outward grotesquely, his shirt rippling, yet still his gaze stays trained on them. They take another step back. The captain's eyes are so wide they can see green hued blood rimming the blackness. His throat undulates, stretches, and abruptly his head jerks back and forth convulsively, his mouth yawning open, wider than any human mouth should.

"Holy shit…"

Two black, skinny rods emerge from his mouth, bristling with short, prickly hairs. Kenny stares disbelievingly. It's impossible, yet to him they look a lot like…like…

Antenna. Those are fuckin' antennas!

A head materializes, something that bears a strong resemblance to a carpenter ant crossed with a centipede. The thing is twice as wide as a fire hose, God knows how long. It pours outward like a hairy, slimy gush of water, it's multiple legs wriggling madly, its segmented body heaving from side to side. Kenny casts a horrified glance at the captain's face and witnesses a look of triumphant victory there, a glee that is fanatical, obscenely swollen with pride.

The creature flops onto the ground with a disgusting plop, it's many legs scratching at the floor of the heap, scurrying in their direction.

"Jesus Kenny! What the hell is that?"

"Fuck if I know, fuck if I want to find out!" he bellows, fear and repulsion getting the better of him. "Run!" And the two scamper off, the hirsute, scraggly mutant nipping at their heels as the captain roars demonic laughter behind them.

"Leeann!" Dante kneels before the stricken girl, her head cradled in his large hands. Blood pumps profusely from her severed carotid artery and her mouth opens and closes, making a sickening, sticky sound. "Jesus Christ! No!"

As he looks upon her, her eyes glaze over, the spark of life slipping away in one swift moment. One minute she was here, the next she is gone.

Oh my poor sweet Leeann. I loved you more than you will ever know...

A terrible wrath sweeps through him, almost bowling him over with the devastating force of its power. Gently resting her head on the ground he gets up, hands trembling uncontrollably. Kim Leung is crab-walking away, burbling and babbling her crazy gibberish, her hands making crinkling noises over the floor of crushed, compressed trash. Dave and Melissa are frozen, watching the scene play out before them.

"Dante..." Dave says but his words falter. What bit of wisdom is he going to impart upon the stricken man anyhow? Is there really anything he *can* say at this point?

Dante ignores him anyway, stalking toward Kim, an intent ferocity gleaming in his deep brown eyes. Her head is a runny mess of brains, blood and goo; it is a wonder she is even moving. She hisses at him viciously as he gets close (through the half of her mouth that remains) but he knows it's meaningless, ineffectual. Even though she managed to kill Leeann it's obvious she's on her last legs.

"You fucking whore!" With deadly accuracy he swings his right foot forward, kicking her as hard as he can, the toe of his boot connecting solidly with her chin. Her head snaps backward and the appalling sound of fracturing bone is loud in the relative stillness. She screeches deafeningly, but her head (what's left of it) is leaning at an impossible angle and she collapses to the ground, convulsing. Dante lifts his leg again, bringing his heel down on her face, leaning into it with all his weight. Her head caves in with another atrocious crunch, his foot sinking in to his ankle. She utters one last groan of misery, her legs kicking and twitching, but after a moment she lies still.

"Oh my God," Melissa whimpers, turning away.

Dante continues to grind his heel in, rotating his foot back and forth as if he is putting out a rather tenacious cigarette butt, grunting with pleasure.

"You fucking whore!" he repeats as he does so, repeats it over and over. He's unaware that tears are streaming down his face, great, big, fat droplets that run into his beard, soaking through and wetting his shirt. He grinds his foot into the mess that was once a pretty Asian girl's face, pulverizing it until it's unrecognizable, nothing but thick, syrupy goop he'll later have to wipe off the bottom of his boot.

Dave approaches cautiously, puts an arm around Dante's shoulder.

"Hey buddy, relax. She's dead, okay? Come on now."

"Th-th-the fucking whore!" Dante bawls, his face a mess of blood, snot and tears.

Could be the name of a band, Dave finds himself thinking for no apparent reason. *'Blood, Snot and Tears, comin' to a local venue near you. Get yer tickets today.'* A giggle rises up in his throat that he struggles to contain, knows he must if he doesn't want this large man to misconstrue it and belt him with a beefy fist. It's irrational, he knows, but it's probably trying to force its way out because everything he's dealt with in the last three days has been absolutely horrific. A little comic relief right about now would be just what the doctor ordered, but the timing couldn't be worse. He swallows, hard, his mouth so dry it's like there's no spit left in him.

"It's okay buddy," he says, winning the battle within him. "She's finished."

Dante turns toward him, shrugging off his grip, his eyes blazing intensely. Dave instinctively recoils, almost certain the behemoth is going to turn on him, when Dante crumbles forward, folding Dave in his giant arms, sobbing piteously. The noises he makes are *(again with the sick humor you fuck)* almost comical but neither he nor Melissa laughs. Dante's chest heaves and his shoulders quake, sobs wracking his body with tidal force. No, they don't laugh, for it is not an amusing spectacle, not in the slightest.

"She's dead!" he weeps, burying his face in Dave's neck. Dante towers over the other by several inches, so he has to lean over to do this. "One minute she wa-wa-was here and now she's gone."

Mounting emotion overcomes Dave as the tears wet his neck, hot and sticky with despair. After all, he was the one who found the girl at the outskirts of the village, naked, afraid. He was the one who'd helped find her something to cover herself with, taught her how to fire a gun. Unexpectedly he feels the unwanted sting of tears in his own eyes, and against his will he issues a low moan, bringing up his arms and clutching Dante around his broad back, patting him rhythmically as men tend to do in an attempt to retain their masculinity in these types of situations.

Melissa watches them, feeling sapped, empty inside. She tries not to look at the shattered visage of the Asian girl, but finds her eyes straying in that direction against her will, taking in the crumpled body, the squashed, liquid remains of the girl's face before she can compel herself to look away. Her eyes roam over the abandoned structures of the village, the dilapidated shacks now empty, the mutants having fled to who-the-fuck-knows-where. Besides the sound of the two men comforting one another there is nothing but a disquieting silence, only broken every so often by the squawk of a Rancor bird, and gradually this alerts her, sobers her into realizing where the captain and his minions have gone and what they intend to do.

"Guys," she says softly, gently placing her hands upon them. "We have to go. Captain Harvey is fleeing to the ship." She strokes the backs of their heads tenderly. "We have to stop him."

The two men part, looking at one another momentarily with what appears to be shame, then shaking it off just as quickly.

"You're right," Dante says thickly, clearing his throat. "That son of a bitch is going to try and escape."

"I'll grab the guns," Dave says, turning away. He swipes a hand across his face, surprised he would show such emotion; after all he didn't really know the girl, hell he doesn't truly know any of them. But he wasn't crying for them, was he? No, he was crying for the loss of Travis maybe, or the relentless fear that almost crushed his spirit while he was trapped beneath the heap, the premonitions of his own death blinding him, choking him with their intensity. And maybe, just maybe, he was crying for their lost innocence, all of theirs, in the wake of this horrible place, where once you saw something so terrible, so breathtakingly evil, only the hot, salty tears could scrub your eyes clean...Grabbing the duffle bag, he slings it over his shoulder, his M-16A4 in his free hand.

"Let's go make that bastard sorry he was ever born-" he is saying when a concussive blast they can feel both within their ears as well as under their feet cuts him off. The trash heap vibrates and rumbles.

"What the hell was that?" Melissa gasps, holding her arms out to steady herself.

A smile appears on Dante's face, a twisted, wicked looking expression that very nearly rivals that of the captain. "The ship," he says, the smile stretching wide, his eyes tinged with a touch of lunacy. "Someone blew up the ship."

I have to get to the ship, I have to get to the ship! Jake thinks, an ongoing litany in his head that revolves around and around and around like a merry-go-round, when suddenly the sound of an explosion stops him *(dead?)* in his tracks. He looks up into the distance, sees thick black smoke splotching the cloudless sky and at once knows what it is.

"Fuck!" Without the ship there is no mission, without the mission there is nothing. It can't be, it simply can't be. Who could have done such a thing? Who? Who was left *to* do it? That god-damned doctor?

He begins to run down the path, muttering and grumbling to himself, hurrying toward the billowing smoke so dark against the light blue of the clear, sun drenched sky.

Captain Harvey cringes when the explosion goes off, the ear-splitting noise bringing Dr. Taylor out of his stupor. His head aches fiercely and little blue pinpoints of light dance before his eyes but he ignores them and gets to his feet. Dizziness creeps over him *(I must have a concussion)* but there is no time to nurse his wounds, he has to escape before the captain does something perma-nent to him. Shuffling away, he gains several feet before the captain notices and takes after him.

"Come back here!" Captain Harvey growls. "There's no escaping the *(aaaahhhccckkk!)* inevi-table!"

Dr. Taylor doesn't reply, in fact is physically unable, he's breathing so hard. He continues to sprint away when wooziness overtakes him and he falters, gasping urgently for air. He collapses onto the ground, clutching his chest, and Captain Harvey almost falls right on top of him. Instead he drops to his knees and leans over him, resting his elbows on the other's chest.

"Gotcha!" he croaks, worm-laced spittle spilling over what remains of his missing lower lip. "You didn't *(aaaahhhccckkk!)* think you were going to get away that easily, did you?"

Doctor Taylor squirms beneath him, twisting and turning, but the captain is dead weight. "Guh…get off of me!" The pressure on his chest is immense; he can feel his lungs being com-pressed, drawing another breath becoming harder and harder.

"Not so *(aaaahhhccckkk!)* full of yourself now that your buddies can't help you, hmm?"

"Can't…breath…"

"Oh, is the doctor in *(aaaahhhccckkk!)* pain? Your poor, poor boy!"

"Puh-puh-please…"

"Oh, all right." The captain eases up, lifting his weight off of the other. "But only because I want some answers."

Dr. Taylor draws in large mouthfuls of air, the lightheadedness retreating. For the second time today he's had the distinct displeasure of being suffocated. Must be some kind of record.

"Wha-what is it you want?"

"What do you *(aaaahhhccckkk!)* think? I want to know how you did it."

"Did what?"

"All along something has been eluding me, some piece of knowledge that's been slipping through my grasp like water through a sieve." The captain's gaze is hungry, displaying a deplorable frankness. "How did you bring them back?"

"Bring them back?"

The blow the captain dishes out detonates an avalanche of pain in his head and his vision doubles, triples.

"Yes doctor, and I won't ask nicely again. How did you bring those two dipshits back? What kind of medical miracle did you perpetrate?"

He really doesn't know…it's why there were antibiotics on the ship. The bacterium directs what he does but it doesn't know dick about the real world. And, apparently, neither does he.

"Come on now doctor. I'll torture you if *(aaaahhhccckkk!)* necessary."

Does it matter if I tell him? Will it change anything?

"Time's up." The captain wraps his hands around Dr. Taylor's throat, exerting gradual yet continuous pressure. The doctor gags, struggling feebly, then tries to cough out the word.

"What? I can't *(aaaahhhccckkk!)* hear you."

"Penicillin," he whispers hoarsely.

"Come again?" Harvey releases him, eyeing the other thoughtfully.

"Penicillin!" Dr. Taylor blurts. "I gave them penicillin!"

"You gave them…" he trail off, his face blank for a moment. How come he never thought of that? How was it that the bacterium never warned him? "All you did was *(aaaahhhccckkk!)* give them a fucking antibiotic?"

"Yes. Penicillin I found on the ship."

"You found these drugs to *(aaaahhhccckkk!)* sabotage me on the *ship*? Goddamnit!" Anger and confusion combined make his blood pressure accelerate dangerously, and at once his vision retreats to a pinpoint. He can sense the world receding around him, slipping away, everything turning a shade of dishwater gray. He feels weightless, unencumbered by all the misery that has so beset him over the course of the last few days. The doctor fades before him, disappearing, and instantly he's enshrouded in darkness, the world he knew nothing more than a black stain on the porthole of time…

He's been transported to another place, another realm of being...It's quiet here except for a faint hiss of white noise, like static emitted from a radio. Is this. . .could this be. . .death?

"You're not dead," a voice he immediately recognizes says to him. It's a voice he hasn't heard in some time but it is as familiar to him as. . .as. . .

"As your own voice?"

Images slowly begin to penetrate the fog that engulfs him, his eyesight clearing, and he finds himself standing face to face with a man he knows, has, in fact, known all his life. But this man, he looks-

"Healthy? Is that what you want to say?"

His tanned face is seamed with wrinkles yet he appears fit, his large arms bulging out of a thin cotton t-shirt, white/blonde hair spilling over a broad forehead. His hands are knotted with arthritis and his bandy legs seem unsteady but the man carries himself with an air of confidence that can't be denied. It glows within his eyes like a white, hot light, so piercing it's like looking directly into the sun.

The sound of the ocean becomes louder, more distinct. Gulls shriek and flutter about in a light breeze, the slap of the water against the hull beyond a doubt indicating he is...he must be. . .

"Welcome back aboard the Sea Wolf. We've been waiting for you."

It's incredible-impossible actually-but standing before him at the helm of his sailboat (entirely restored, it seems) is. . .himself. Captain Oswald Harvey before the bacterium got a hold of him, before Garbage Island became his every waking thought, his life's foremost preoccupation.

"Been a while stranger. What took you so long?"

Harvey can't find the words to answer. A terrific outpouring of emotion rises from deep within him, closing his throat and making his eyes water.

"Now now, don't feel so bad. None of this was your fault. Like you told the other two, no one was a willing accomplice in any of this. You played along because you had to."

Harvey's mouth works but nothing comes out but a low moan.

"In fact you were played like a fiddle at a hillbilly hoe down. That bacteria, it doesn't care who you are, who you were, it indiscriminately rips through anyone it can sink its teeth into."

Tears trickle down Harvey's ruined face and, across from him, his picture perfect pre-infected self has the decency to shed a few with him.

"It used you, making you do whatever it wanted. You had no control against it, that's not the way it works. When you were rescued in Mexico after the boat crash those doctors tried to save you by pumping your body full of antibiotics. You were virtually unharmed physically but they could tell you had a nasty infection of some kind. They almost killed it, but unfortunately it had the strength for a last ditch escape attempt. And when it succeeded it took it out on you, made you what you are now."

"Why. . .after this happened. . .why. . ." Harvey gasps, "didn't it warn me about antibiotics?"

His self looks at him with an expression so compassionate it's almost heartbreaking, radiating an undying love that will never be relinquished no matter what happens.

"It's a bacteria buddy," he says softly. "It doesn't have a brain, it can't think. It only acts and reacts. The power you thought it was giving you? Omniscience? It was merely able to communicate with itself. That's why you thought you were clairvoyant. And because you weren't completely treated at the hospital it warped inside you somehow, caused you to start coming apart, inside and out."

"But. . .I thought it, it needed me. . ."

"No more than anyone else. You said it yourself at one point: no one is immune. It always wins, the house always wins."

"It. . .it used me. . ."

"Like a bitch in a puppy mill-used you up until there was nothing left but sagging tits."

Harvey looks about him, at his old sloop bobbing up and down on the calm sea surrounding them. There is nothing else to see but water, miles and miles and miles of water. *"So. . .what do I do?"*

"Nothing you can do. It's going to play itself out, drain you until there's nothing left."

"Do I. . .can I. . .fight it?" Looking at the man he once was he feels a crushing sense of loss flood his veins like ice. What he's turned into is unacceptably wretched, loathsome. Seeing the magnificent, handsome man he used to be and comparing it to this thing he's become fills him with an overwhelming desire to stave it off.

"No," is the single word reply. *"Right now, this limbo you're in is just a split second of time. As soon as I'm gone you'll forget I was here, and everything you've been working so hard for will once again be your top priority. I simply wanted to see you one more time. Wanted to tell you none of this is your fault and that I forgive you for everything."*

"I'll fight it. . ."

"You can't. No one is immune." The world slides drastically to one side-colors smearing and blending into one another, swirling around and around-then slides drastically to the other, like a photo being changed on a single frame projector. One second his sane, lucid, healthy self is standing before him and then the next. . .*"It always wins. The house always wins."*

"Nuh-no. . .no!"

"We have to bring the contagion to the rest of the world." His old self is gone, replaced by the spitting image of his current self: his bottom lip is missing, as well as several fingers, teeth, an eyebrow, and both ears. His eyes are coal black, rimmed neon green, his mouth lathered with foamy slobber, and his shirt is soaked through with an off-white pasty substance, speckled with dark green and black material. Wriggling within this goop are long, ropy worms. He smiles at himself, a leer befitting a madman. *"You have work to do."*

For a fraction of a second Harvey is still, looking stunned at the admission that the penicillin had been on the ship all along. His face goes momentarily slack, his eyes rolling back in his head, and Dr. Taylor watches him, wondering what sort of transformation he is undergoing when, just as quickly, it is over. The captain's eyes revolve back and they focus on the doctor's.

"I must (aaaahhhccckkk!) say that is very clever. Can't put anything past you."

"Maybe I can help you too. I have antibiotics in that bag. We can start your treatment right now-"

"Oh no, I don't think so. Thanks but no thanks. I think it's long (aaaahhhccckkk!) overdue that you see exactly what it is you've been fighting. Long overdue."

"No. . .wait. . .please!"

Captain Harvey straightens up and swings one leg over the doctor's chest, straddling him, bringing his knees up alongside Dr. Taylor's head, his groin just below his chin. He rests his weight upon his chest, smothering him, and leans closer.

"You'll see it's not so bad." A sickly smile dances on his lips, and he grasps Dr. Taylor's face in both hands, his fingers clawing at the others lips, which are pressed tightly together. The doctor's arms are pinned at his sides, useless, and he huffs and grunts as he resists but his attempts are weak, ineffectual.

"No escaping the Piper when he *(aaaahhhccckkk!)* comes to call Dr. Taylor, not when he's Hell-Bent on retribution."

Wrenching his mouth open, the captain leans in closer, opening his own maw. The doctor can see down the captain's throat, can see the mass of white, round, wriggling worms just past his epiglottis, and in an instant he knows the battle is over, the captain has beat him. But he also knows the captain has lost as well; he won't survive long enough to spread the contagion to the rest of the world. In no time he'll be just another piece of detritus aboard this floating shit pile.

Tossing his head from side to side, he feels the first of the worms dropping onto his face, feels their plump, warm bodies' writhing on his skin.

Of course, it isn't all in the captain's hands; he has his successor, Jake. If the captain expires before another ship comes along than Jake will take up the cause in his stead. Unless someone stops him that just very well might happen...

"Open wide," Captain Harvey hisses, tugging Dr. Taylor's mouth open even wider and holding his head still at last. "Say 'ah'!"

Kenny trips over something, almost losing his balance but regaining it before Cole crashes into him from behind, knocking them both over. The two lay in a pile of twisted limbs, trying to get free of one another and recover their footing but their movements are slow, clumsy.

"C'mon, git up!" Kenny tries to shove Cole aside but the other's foot is somehow wedged beneath him.

"I'm trying!"

Kenny struggles to lift his upper body off the ground, hoping to free Cole's foot, when he catches a glimpse of the insect bearing down upon them. The creature is enormous, hideous. That the captain was harboring such a thing in his body is inconceivable, but it does explain why he'd been continuously vomiting worms.

"Try harder!" Kenny urges, when the bug spans the distance between them in a heartbeat, lunging at and attaching itself to Cole's rump.

"Ahhh!" Cole jerks backward, trying to reach behind him and get a hold of it but the insect crawls quickly up his back to his neck, wrapping around and sinking long teeth into the soft flesh beneath his chin. Kenny watches from a disturbingly close vantage point as the creature gnaws at Cole's throat, whipping its head around brutally. Cole looks at him with pleading eyes, trying to beg for help but there is nothing the other can do. The thing swiftly tears his throat out and bright red blood sprays from his severed jugular, drenching Kenny in a warm spray.

The blood is red though, not green. The doctor was really on to somethin'...

Disgust being an amazing catalyst, Kenny easily pushes Cole off of him, sending him sprawling. Using a hand to steady himself he gets to his feet, swiping at his face and backing away.

Nothing I could do, that fuckin' thing was too quick. Sorry buddy, I'm really sorry...

He stumbles on legs that feel wooden, on feet that seem attached to someone other than himself and, not watching where he is going, he trips and falls.

"Son of a bitch!"

Rising quickly, he turns in time to see the creature launching itself at him and, lifting his hands just in time, he catches it in mid air.

Goddamned thing looks like a caterpillar but it took lessons from Rocky the flyin' Squirrel. Course the damn thing can fly. What'd ya expect?

Holding it at arms length before him it is all he can do to keep the head (and it's terrible gnashing teeth) from getting at the meat of his gullet. He tries to fling it away but its spindly legs wrap around his fingers, holding on tight. It's making a grating, chittering sound that assaults Kenny's ears, hell, his whole head. And the thing is heavy, goddamnit, *really* heavy. It takes everything he's got to keep it from dragging him to the ground with it. And if it did, then what? Why death, of course, what else? A nice little neck nuzzling that results in massive blood loss. Might feel a little weird at first but hey, Cole got used to it didn't he? Just a brief flash of pain and then its goodnight Irene. Couldn't have taken more than a few seconds.

He staggers backward, terrified his legs will betray him at any moment, his bad knee throbbing terrifically, when he backs into something solid.

Back's up against the wall man, here it is.

The insect thrashes vigorously as it tries to get at him, Kenny's arms bending at the elbows as it works its way closer, so close he can smell it's fusty breath as it's teeth chomp and click, a thick drizzle of saliva spattering Kenny's face. He's steadily weakening, his stamina all but gone. Soon enough the bug will rip out his throat and he will be dead and he won't have to worry about anything any more, not this lousy garbage patch in the middle of the Pacific, not the fate of the world, nothing. He won't even be bothered by the fact that his carcass will be eaten by parasites, nor will he be troubled that no one will ever know what became of him, the ex-football legend, the man who indorsed all those health food and exercise products, the guy who smiled into the camera and told people as honestly as he could that the 'Quicker Zipper Upper' was one of the best products on the market, and for only $39.95 they too could take care of all their zipper needs...

Leaning heavily against the compacted trash and using the last of the ebbing strength in his muscle-laden arms, he swings the creature back and forth just to keep it away from him. He inches along the wall as he does this, his mind awhirl but finding nothing concrete that can save him, when he feels something sharp scrape against his face, gashing his cheek. Stifling a cry, he rolls his eye *(man I'm lucky that thing wasn't on my blind side)* as far to the right as he can, seeing a jagged pole sticking about twelve inches out of the wall. Sensing an opportunity, he edges back toward the left, then spins on his right heel, swinging the bug around in one fluid motion, hoping against hope he'll be right on the money.

"Shit!" Searing pain rips through him; the good news is that is aim was true. The bad news is that his aim was *too* true. He's managed to impale the creature on the shaft (right through its head, damnit, right through its head) but in the meanwhile he's also speared one of his own hands as well. As it writhes in its death throes he is forced to suffer through its repulsive quivering, his right hand pinned beneath it. After what feels like an eternity the insect finally stops moving, lying limply, although its multitudinous legs continue to shudder and kick.

"Little bastard," he breathes, using his other hand to tug it free. It isn't easy, and the texture of the creature's scaly, bristly thorax is totally revolting, but little by little he works it loose and it tumbles end over end to the ground. "One down, one to go."

Sucking in a deep breath he closes his eye, counts to three and jerks his hand forward. Luckily the rod isn't barbed and he is able to extract it smoothly albeit very painfully. Blood pours copiously from the wound, and he tears away part of his shirt and ties it tightly around it, trying to staunch the flow.

"Little bastard," he says again, kicking at the insect's lifeless body. With regret he glances over at Cole, sees the flies swarming around his face, the pooling blood fanning out beneath him like a grisly corona. "Sorry man," he mutters. "I am so sorry."

Because he knows his work is not done (*far from it*) he lurches forward, his leaden feet somehow connecting with the ground, gripping and allowing him to move ahead with a steady, encompassing purpose. Somewhere back in the maze of trash the captain is trying to hurt the doctor, and Kenny has to do everything in his power to stop him, if he isn't already too late.

But Kenny tries not to think about that, about being too late. Instead he simply stumbles along, tasting bile deep in the back of his throat as he hums an old classic by Tupac, from back in the day when niggas was straight up trippin' and the world wasn't such a bad place as long as you had a knife in yer sock and a Glock in yer waistband.

"I'm comin' Doc," he breathes in between verses. "I'm comin'."

THIRTY-SIX

"Ya think that was the ship?" Dave says, looking at Melissa before reluctantly turning his gaze on Dante, who is once more kneeling down next to the dead girl. He glances at him quickly before looking away, staring off in the direction the villagers fled. The large man's grief hangs heavy in the air, an exquisite sorrow so profound it's unsettling, and Dave finds within him an immeasurable empathy like he's never known, feelings that are entirely new to him. Yet he's not ashamed that he cried, in fact has never been the type to think it unmanly, but if he gets going again he wonders if he'll be able to stop, and that's not what these people need from him right now. Currently they need someone to take charge, to help them end this farce before anyone else gets hurt.

"What else could it be?" Dante says absently, caressing Leeann's face one last time before he steels himself and accepts that he can walk away from her. There is no time (at least not at the present) for a proper burial. As much as it hurts to think of her lying here, exposed to any and all the horrible things that call this place home, he knows this is what he must do. He has no choice.

"Are you going to be all right?" Melissa asks, watching Dante with a troubled heart. She knows he loved her very much, could tell by the way he communicated with her, every word, every gesture. She's not sure if the girl loved him in return, but she's certain it didn't diminish his feelings any.

"I'll be fine," Dante says, standing and shouldering his weapon. "We should find Dr. Taylor; I'll bet he's the one who blew up the ship and, besides," he looks at the others coldly, "that's the direction Captain Harvey was heading, I guarantee it. We have to get to the doctor before he does."

"Let's go," Dave says abruptly, wanting to get moving, but also wanting to get away from this mess-the scene of the crime. After all that has happened he'd like nothing more than to put it behind them. He grabs the duffle bag and takes a deep breath, bracing himself, storing his emotions for another time. "Everyone got enough ammo?"

"I only have two clips," Melissa says and Dave reaches in the bag, producing another three magazines.

"Make the shots count. We're running out."

"Can do."

"Dante?"

"I'm good," he says, patting his pockets. "Let's get that son of a bitch."

He walks in the direction of the sound, a gagging, gurgling resonance that fills him with dread. The images it produces in his mind are bad, real bad, but there is nothing he can do to shut them out. He wants very much to believe that Dr. Taylor is still alive but, well, things haven't exactly been going according to plan.

He's closer, almost on top of them...

"Ah Kenny, welcome back! I see your good buddy Cole is no longer *(aaaahhhcccckkk!)* trailing you like a shadow. How do you feel? Good? Bad? Indifferent?"

Kenny regards the captain momentarily before his attention is drawn to the heap lying on the ground at his feet. The gagging noises are dying down, the body reduced to the last of its quaking spasms. Dr. Taylor's face is frozen in a rictus of agony, his cheeks and lips covered with plump, squirming worms. Kenny swallows hard several times, trying to grasp exactly what he is seeing but he simply can't comprehend it, it is so horrific. At last he has to look away, and when he does his remaining eye alights on the captain.

"Ya kilt him," he says flatly.

"Oh no Kenny, not at all. You'll be so excited! He'll be up and around in *(aaaahhhcccckkk!)* no time, no time at all. In fact I gave him the Royal Treatment and made him *(aaaahhhcccckkk!)* just like me! Just you wait and see-"

Kenny dives headlong at the captain, executing a tackle that would have made his old coach proud. Captain Harvey is taken completely by surprise, in fact is only able to utter a short grunt before he is airborne. The two crash headlong into a wall of trash, the captain's head kissing it with concussive velocity, and for a moment is still. Kenny lies on top of him, breathing hard and wondering if he's knocked him out cold when the other whispers gruffly:

"Ah, so you want to *(aaaahhhcccckkk!)* fight, huh?"

His arms come up, his hands like steel clamps. He shreds Kenny's shirt with razor sharp nails, excising large chunks of flesh. Kenny has to bite his lip to hold back from screaming, and reacting on instinct alone drives his right elbow into the captain's throat. Harvey sputters and chokes, eyes popping open wide in surprise and pain, and a gusher of parasite-laden fluid erupts from his mouth like he is Vesuvius in human form. The warm, wriggling spray hits Kenny in the face but he takes little notice, shaking his head to clear it away. He digs his elbow in deeper, trying to punch it through the other's neck but Captain Harvey is able to twist his body, squirming lithely, and Kenny loses his balance and topples over onto his side. Captain Harvey scrambles to his feet, a mad grin locked in place, made even crazier now that his top lip is hanging by a thread.

"You didn't want to do that," he says, swaying from side to side, his words muffled. "You really *(aaaahhhcccckkk!)* didn't."

He retracts his leg and swiftly brings it forward, a cheap shot, but no one ever said the captain played fair. An unbearable, nauseous throbbing shoots from Kenny's balls to his stomach to his head and back. Clutching himself, he stifles a groan, trying to roll away.

"Where do you think you're *(aaaahhhcccckkk!)* going?" Captain Harvey dishes out another kick, then another. Kenny takes the blows (one to his ribs, one to his kidney) without so much as a grumble but the pain is enormous, overwhelming. If he doesn't turn this shit around quick he's going to wind up like Dr. Taylor, like Cole. "You wanted to fight me now come on, get up and *(aaaahhhcccckkk!)* be a man about it!"

Kenny turns over onto his back, trying to regain his breath, watching Harvey warily. The captain's black eyes glimmer with impish delight, his tongue flicking back and forth, licking at the empty space where his bottom lip used to be. His top lip is hanging on by a thin piece of skin and, as Kenny looks on in amazement, the tip of his forked tongue opens like a mouth and vacuums the flap of flesh in, making a repulsive sucking sound.

"Tasty," he mutters, offering what might be a smile but it's hard to tell. "Time to rearrange that *(aaaahhhcccckkk!)* sambo face of yours..."

Captain Harvey raises his leg yet again and swings it forward, but just as his boot is about to connect with Kenny's chin the ex-football player catches it in his large mitts, gripping it tightly.

"I don't fuckin' think so man," Kenny says, twisting his ankle cruelly, the loud snap of breaking bone punctuating Kenny's grunting exertions.

"What the hell?!" Captain Harvey gasps before losing his footing and pitching backward, falling into a pile of soggy cigarette butts. Kenny takes advantage of the moment, hastily getting to his feet and dropping all his weight (knees first) on the captain's chest. His injured leg protests mightily but Kenny ignores it, batting aside the captain's flailing arms. The air whooshes out of him (as well as the expected liquefied discharge) and Kenny leans forward, letting gravity do the work, his intention to keep the other from drawing another breath. The captain wheezes and thrashes but Kenny has him pinned; in his deteriorating state he simply can't shake him loose. His mouth works but no air comes, his serpentine tongue lolling hideously, turning different colors as it flops against his cheek.

"Didn't think I had it in me, did ya? Come on, do somethin'! I dare ya!"

Captain Harvey's eyes are wide, staring into Kenny's, beseeching him for mercy that will not be extended. His mouth opens and closes dramatically as he tries to speak but nothing comes out, nothing but the last of the air stored in his rotten, diseased lungs. The large black man smiles, raising a battered, dirty middle finger and holding it below the captain's nose.

"Fuck you, ya prick. Ya'cn go ta hell-"

With amazing dexterity and lightening quickness that Kenny should have foreseen the captain lunges forward, taking Kenny's middle finger in his mouth. Kenny has only a second to comprehend what is about to happen when Harvey's jaws click together, chomping off the finger at the second knuckle.

Goddamn!" he bawls, retracting his hand, clutching it in his other.

Captain Harvey uses this diversion to toss the other aside as if he weighs no more than a pillow sack full of feathers. Rising instantly to his feet, impervious to his no doubt shattered ankle, he swipes away thick fluid from his mouth, the sick, malevolent (grin?) ever present, black eyes fairly twinkling.

"This just keeps getting better and *(aaaahhhcccckkk!)* better, doesn't it?" he laughs, making a sound similar to two pieces of styrofoam being rubbed together, and the hair on Kenny's arms stands up. "Thought you had me, didn't you?" He stalks back and forth, eyeing the other like a lion hunting his prey. "Lucky for me I had just enough teeth left for that to work. Another day or so and I would have had to gum your finger off."

Kenny holds his wounded hand to his chest, knowing he's failed.

This is it. I had him an I blew it. Good fuckin' goin'. . .

And then he sees something that gives him one last, desperate surge of hope. Lying on the ground just behind the captain is a large, jagged piece of metal that looks like half of a car's bumper. Most of it is corroded with rust but portions of it gleam in the late afternoon sunshine invitingly. If he can get past the captain and retrieve it he might have a chance. Slim, but a chance just the same.

"I gave you the opportunity to see the miracle of life in a *(aaaahhhccckkk!)* whole new way and what did you do? You rejected it." The captain shakes his head disappointedly. "Well I now revoke that *(aaaahhhccckkk!)* privilege, you understand? In a few minutes you will be *(aaaahhhccckkk!)* nothing more than another piece of meat for the insects to feast upon."

"An what's ta become a you?" Kenny says, scrambling to buy time, to create an opening. "The ship is gone and yer fallin' apart. Yer plan is *so* over man."

"Oh no, that is where you are wrong my *(aaaahhhccckkk!)* good sir, dead wrong." He sniggers, an insidious, unnerving sound. "I'll still be able to leave the island and bring this *(aaaahhhccckkk!)* gift to the rest of the world."

"How?" Kenny gets slowly to his feet, still cradling his injured hand. The blood pours freely from the stump, and Kenny realizes bleakly that it's the same hand that was impaled by the pole; the damn thing is becoming numb from blood loss, in fact it feels like a dead weight at the end of his arm. But there *is* one piece of good news: it isn't his predominant hand, the one he uses to throw, to write, to jerk-off with. And the captain doesn't know that, at least, he doesn't think he does.

"I know that Dr. Taylor wasn't *(isn't)* stupid," the captain says. "He wouldn't have blown up the ship without first *(aaaahhhccckkk!)* creating a contingency plan." His eyes bore into Kenny's, the blackness almost hypnotizing. "You called for help, didn't you? Before you blew up the ship you used the radio to send out an *(aaaahhhccckkk!)* S.O.S. signal. Anytime now a ship will come along and I will *(aaaahhhccckkk!)* be the one they find, ready to be rescued. That or a trash barge, either will suffice."

"What about the...the others?"

"They're in hiding until I tell them to come out. Don't need all that hard work to go to *(aaaahhhccckkk!)* waste. Besides, there aren't many of you left. I think I can dispatch of *(aaaahhhccckkk!)* the rest of you without too much trouble."

The captain paces as he talks, his eyes leaving Kenny every so often to look off into the distance where clouds of black smoke progressively erase the horizon. Kenny shuffles a step forward, than another.

"So ya'll jus leave 'em here alone?"

"I didn't *(aaaahhhccckkk!)* say that. Some of them will be joining me. The others will be *(aaaahhhccckkk!)* fine."

"Unless someone is firin' at 'em with machine guns."

The captain looks at him angrily. "That will never happen again, trust *(aaaahhhccckkk!)* me."

"No," Kenny says, taking yet another step forward. With one good sprawling dive he can have the piece of metal in his hand. With any luck he can also get to his feet before the captain has time to react. "It certainly won't." Without giving it any more thought he leaps forward. Captain Harvey starts at the sudden movement, recoiling as if shot. Kenny scoops up his intended weapon and, executing a perfect summersault, returns to his feet in one fluid motion. He clutches it firmly in his left hand, swinging it back and forth to get an idea of its weight.

"Well I'll be damned. You still have some *(aaaahhhcccckkk!)* fight in you."

"I got a lot more'an that ya asshole," Kenny snarls, drawing it back over his shoulder, bracing it with his bleeding hand but maintaining his grip with the good one. "A hell of a lot more'an that."

"Let's see what you got-" Captain Harvey starts when Kenny swings, tilting the jagged metal so that it catches the other under his chin with the sharp edge. Kenny's arms shudder as it sinks into the captain's throat, a flash of pain flaring up from his injured hand but he ignores it, driving the polished chrome in deeper.

"Aaaahhhcccckkk!" Captain Harvey bellows for what will be the very last time. Worms and thick green fluid spurts from his mouth as he tries to twist away, but Kenny is too quick. Extracting the piece of metal (not without some difficulty), he retracts his arms and swings again, this time slicing cleanly through the others neck. His head spirals up into the air, turning end over end as a geyser of thick, parasite-laden blood gushes forth from the stump, his mouth yawning open in an expression of bewilderment. The captain drops to his knees, balancing precariously before he collapses onto the ground, legs twitching.

And then silence, nothing but the sound of Kenny's labored breathing. In the distance an animal cries, and only seconds pass before the buzzing drone of insects fills the air. A swarm settles around the captain, tasting him tentatively before deciding they have a full-fledged feast on their hands.

"Tell Hitler an Jeffery Dahmer I said 'hi'," he says thickly, wiping sweat from his brow.

Now, one would think this to be sufficient for Kenny; on the surface it certainly should be. Kill the head and the body will die. But it isn't, not by a longshot. Kenny raises the weapon and brings it down again and again and again, shooing the bugs away, bathing himself in the other's blood as he flails away at the body, chopping off his arms, his legs, all the while issuing a growling/whimpering sound he's completely unaware of. He hacks and slashes, slashes and hacks, bits of slimy tissue and viscous fluid flying, taking pleasure in the sound the other's flesh makes as it rips and tears. He punches the metal bar through the captain's stomach and a mass of tiny caterpillar-like creatures crawl out of the hole, writhing in the white-hot sun.

"Whatta we got here?" he says and, whistling a cheery little tune, dances an Irish jig on them, crushing them out of existence.

All this he does with a smile on his face, one of vast merriment. For he couldn't be happier, no, he certainly couldn't. All the interceptions in the world couldn't top this high, nor all the booze or Vicodin or Oxy-Contin. After all of this he'll never need another drink again as long as he lives, guaranteed.

"They're getting closer."

"Just keep movin'. If any a them gets too close blast 'em back to the stone age." Dave surveys the contents of the bag, seeing they have less ammo than he originally thought. Well, with any luck, this will all be over soon.

Ahead of them a large, greasy black cloud is slowly blotting out the sun.

"Do you think the explosion set the heap on fire?" Melissa asks no one in particular as they trudge along. She spots mutants creeping ever closer in the periphery of her vision, but so far they are keeping their distance.

"I certainly hope so," Dante says, the acrid smell of smoke thick in his nostrils. The thought of this place burning itself out of existence is a heady one, one that makes each step a little easier. Also, the thought of killing Captain Harvey motivates him, keeps his fatigue at bay. Seeing Lee-ann's face mottled with blood, her short life extinguished so unfairly in one, quick moment has him thinking of one thing and one thing only: revenge.

"When we find the doctor how are we going to get our of here?"

Dave studies Melissa's face a moment, sees the strain and exhaustion etched into the lines around her eyes, on her forehead. He wants to give her an answer that sounds assured, confident, something to keep her moral up, but he's not sure if he wants to lie. They very well might have to go down with this ship, like it or not.

Fuckin' A man, she don't need to know that. Tell her what she wants to hear.

He shrugs. "We gotta construct a raft an hope we ain't floatin' out there too long before someone finds us." He looks at Dante. "Right?"

Dante doesn't reply, just grunts. He isn't really listening, in fact isn't even thinking about their escape so much as he is thinking about killing everything that steps in his path. It's so unfair. She made it through all of this only to have her life snuffed out just as they were picking up momentum. If there was a God would He/She be that cruel, that infinitely heartless? It's a question he's been asking himself his whole life, and he really, truly wonders. This place is an aberration to all that is sane, all that is logical, something that proves that a mythical Deity is either asleep at the switch or has little to no power over a species that is hell bent on their own self-destruction. Wouldn't a kind God, a just God step in and intervene? Or are our thoughts about a caring 'holy being' nothing but smoke and mirrors, and in the end God is inside of us, not an omnipotent presence, the fall Guy/Gal that we make It out to be? Something to blame when things don't go right, something to thank when we feel our prayers have been answered. Do we fault God for this place's existence or hold Him/Her responsible for creating *us* in the first place? No, in the end we have to admit our own culpability, have to realize that in the grand scheme of things we have no more foresight than the other creatures that inhabit this world, despite how highly we regard ourselves.

Because, the theological ramifications aside, what this place truly proves is how humankind has systematically fucked up this planet, ignoring hundreds of thousands of years of development and destroying it literally overnight. Nothing like this ever could have happened before the dawn of the Industrial Age, that much is certain. Oh, we all know that science has been a boon to our modern society, with the invention of medicines that have the ability to prolong human and animal life, advanced surgical procedures to eradicate our crippling pain, our failing organs, our crumbling minds. Not to mention all of the conveniences we enjoy from controlled environments to state of the art travel, communication and entertainment, but the by-product of this modernization has been a wasteful, disposable society, one in which ease and comfort have replaced clear, rational thinking. When one thinks about all the things we throw away everyday, from fast food wrappers and cigarette butts to the packaging that covers every single product we buy, it boggles the mind. Pieces of plastic that encase everyday objects, from entertainment devices to food utensils to the food itself, all these seemingly minute bits of chemical compounds that add up over time. Non-reusable containers made of non-biodegradable material that no one gives much thought to at all, dumping it into their household trash and forgetting about it. And who cares, right? In whose lifetime is it going to become a problem when there is so much space on this enormous planet, so many places to dump this crap and simply walk away? Before the twentieth century people made products that were reusable, the bulk of their trash consisting of food scraps and materials crafted from non-chemically derived sources. Items with the ability to break down and return to their original components over time. With the advent of our contemporary world that is long a thing of the past, leaving us with ever-increasing toxic chemicals that seep into the groundwater and oceans to be fed on by the organisms therein. And who would guess that these chemicals in conjunction with corrupted organic matter have the ability to produce ever-stronger bacteria, bacteria that in turn can control minds, poisoning and altering human and animal life?

This atrocity, the garbage heap and it's inhabitants, has to burn, but the only shame in it's destruction is that maybe no one will ever be aware of how bad it became so as to learn from it, to know that changes have to be made in order to avoid making this mistake again. But that, unfortunately, will be a fairy tale, a story in which there is a moral and the possibility of a happy ending. Reality in itself is a bitch, where anything can happen, mostly with depressing results. Where there is no patent, Disney-happy outcome, where the guy gets the girl and everyone lives happily ever after as the birds sing in the trees. This utopia (where the happy couple has children and they get good jobs and become affluent members of society and pay their taxes and take a three-week vacation every year, and the children grow up to be excellent students and go to fancy East Coast colleges where they study to be doctors and lawyers and engineers) doesn't exist. Instead life comes at you like a freight train, and the chances of your marriage lasting more than five years is slim, and the children you sire will probably become addicted to prescription drugs they steal from your medicine cabinet and sell them to their peers on the playground. And your son whom you hoped was going to excel at football comes home one day and tells you he's gay and wants to study drama at a state college, and your daughter gets knocked up in her junior year of high school and informs you she wants to keep the baby but she's afraid it's going to be addicted to methamphetamines. Then your wife lets you know she's been sleeping with the gardener and they are going to elope to Mexico where they can raise a household of bilingual children.

No, things never happen as we plan them, when young girls with their future ahead of them endure amazing odds and end up cold and dead just when the referee was about to blow the whistle and call time out-

"Look!" Melissa cries, interrupting his thoughts. "There's Kenny and Doctor Taylor!"

They look to where she is pointing, seeing that the two are engaged in battle, the bigger man clutching the smaller man's neck in his great, beefy paws while the other swipes viciously at his face with hands hooked into claws.

Melissa starts forward but Dave grabs her shoulder, stopping her. "Is either one a them infected?"

"Kenny is," she sighs. "He was transformed sometime last night."

Dave aims his rifle at the ex-pro ball player, his finger steady on the trigger. "I'll take care of this." Drawing a bead on Kenny's head, he flicks a lever and switches the rifle from fully automatic to semi. No sense further endangering the doctor's life with an errant spray of bullets. Taking a deep breath he fires, preparing to do so as many times as necessary.

The shot is dead on (no pun intended), and Kenny is thrown sideways, his body crumpling in a heap to the ground. One of his legs kicks but he gives no sign that he is going to try and get up.

"That was too easy..." Dave says, shaking his head.

"Hey, Dr. Taylor!" Melissa waves, a relieved grin on her face. "Bet you didn't think you were ever going to see us again!"

Dr. Taylor turns toward them and, as he does, Dante realizes something about him isn't right. "Oh shit."

After his confrontation with the captain, Kenny needed a few minutes to catch his breath. When he felt as if his heart rate was somewhere near 'normal' (what is normal to him now? A very good question indeed) he cautiously approached Dr. Taylor, dropping to one knee (his good knee) beside him. Reaching out, he'd searched for his pulse, feeling nothing. He plopped onto his butt, exhaling slowly, every so often gazing over at the captain to make sure the pieces weren't somehow knitting themselves back together, like something in a B-grade horror movie. No such luck for Harvey; his hacked up corpse wasn't reanimating, it was merely attracting bugs. He scratched his head, fingers nimbly probing the various bumps and contusions, and wondered how long he had until the penicillin wore off, wondered what could possibly be next...

And that was when the icy hand settled on his arm, startling him out of his reverie. He'd turned and stared into the inexplicable black eyes of the recently morphed, the claw like fingers digging into his skin causing him to cry out in surprise. He'd yanked his arm back, rising quickly to his feet.

"Hello Kenny," Dr. Taylor said hollowly. "Guess we got something in common now."

"Stay right where ya are Doc," Kenny said, retreating a step. "I'cn help ya, but yer gonna hafta trust me."

"What, you think I'm going to let you give me a shot of penicillin?" Dr. Taylor scoffed. "Ain't going to happen Kenny, not now, not ever."

Kenny involuntarily took another step back. "If ya don't allow me ta do it willinly I'm gonna hafta force it on ya."

"Oh, really?" Dr. Taylor stood up, swaying unsteadily a moment before getting the hang of gravity. "You'll have to mix up the medicine first, and I don't see how you are going to have time to do that before I stop you." He moved forward a step, and then another.

Apprehension arose within him then, a sudden realization that things were slipping beyond his reach. He was drained from his struggle with the creature, then doing battle with Captain Harvey; the last thing he wanted was another fight so soon, and with Dr. Taylor no less. Not only did he not have the strength for it, he didn't have the heart.

"Stay back! Just keep yer distance."

"Or what?" Dr. Taylor laughed. "Or you'll do what?"

"Just stay where ya are."

But the doctor advanced upon him and his only choice was to defend himself. They scrambled madly for control, attacking one another brutally. Kenny's hands had found the other's throat, were doing their best to render him unconscious when he felt something go off inside his head, a bright fireball of light before blackness descended. . . .

"I see the cavalry is here," Dr. Taylor smiles, and it is a sick thing to behold. Dried worms stick to his cheeks, his lips, but he cares not at all. His color is incredibly pale, and his eyes, which once displayed an astonishing clarity, are muddled and vacant. He opens his mouth wider and a large, fat worm wriggles out and falls onto the front of his shirt. He absently picks at it, poking it back into his mouth like a plug of tobacco. "I hate to piss on your parade but it appears you fuck-ups shot the wrong person."

"What?" Melissa tears her gaze from the doctor and stares at the man sprawled on the ground behind him. "But...but that's not right. You told me yourself what happened..."

"Yeah, well, things change rather quickly around here now don't they? I'd like to share with you the medical miracle that made it possible but far be it that I'll be the one to pass on said info, not when there is so much work to be done." He extends a finger toward a pile of something that lies on the ground several feet away, something that has drawn the attention of thousands of hungry insects. "Captain Harvey is no longer in any position to get the job done, as you can see. I suppose it's up to me."

All heads turn to where he is pointing, and once Melissa actually comprehends what she is seeing (*looks like a pile of green jelly*) she puts a hand to her mouth. There's nothing left but pieces. But on the tails of her nausea is a relief like none other than she has felt in a long time.

"That," she says, the joy evident in her voice, "is the captain?"

"Unfortunately so. Kenny got the best of him, probably would have done me in as well if you guys hadn't come along. Many thanks."

"I'm afraid yer enjoyment is gonna be short lived Doc," Dave says, lifting the rifle to his shoulder again. "This is where it ends."

"You would think so, wouldn't you? But that is where you are wrong." Dr. Taylor sounds confident, looking unflinchingly into the barrel of the gun.

"The hell we are-" Dante is saying when someone clears their throat behind him. Turning quickly, the hair on the back of his neck suddenly bristles and his heart thumps laboriously in his chest.

"Howdy-do all!" Jake Anderson greets them with a boisterous grin, an automatic weapon cradled in his hands. Behind him is a veritable army, the mutants decked out in all their gruesome glory, clutching weapons of all sorts. Their faces are slack, expressionless, but their hands clench and unclench on the various items they heft, from plastic rods to fistfuls of rusty syringes.

"Jesus Christ," Dave says, his mouth falling open.

"That's right," Jake agrees. "The captain is dead and it is now time for the Second Coming." He nods to the guns they hold in their hands. "I'm going to need to take those." He tips them a wink, much like his predecessor. "Nothing personal, you understand. It's simply time to get you meddlers out of the way." He looks over at Dr. Taylor. "I don't mean to commandeer your position but I do believe I was next in line for the job."

"As it should be."

"How are you holding up?"

"Never felt better."

"Wonderful. Welcome aboard."

THIRTY-SEVEN

Dave retreats several paces but makes no move to drop his gun.

"Git behind me," he says brusquely, his voice urgent but hardly louder than a whisper.

"What?" Dante gapes and Dave shoots him a quick, irritated look.

"Ya heard me. Do it!"

Dante shuffles quickly to his right, Melissa to her left.

Jake watches bemusedly as they perform this maneuver. "What do you think you're going to do sailor boy? Take us all on? Y'all be dead in a matter of seconds."

"Not if I shoot ya first," Dave says, matching Jake's smile with one of his own. "I bet if I take out you and Dr. Taylor tha rest a these numbfucks won't know if they should shit or turn sideways. Whatta ya think?"

Jake raises the weapon to his shoulder, tucking it into the hollow of his armpit.

"You want to try me? It's your funeral."

"It's my funeral anyways, no matter what happens," Dave replies, nodding toward the clouds of smoke on the horizon. "It's gonna be everyone's funeral. This shitheap's on fire, or ain't ya noticed?"

Jake glances briefly into the distance and a look of unease comes over his face. On the breeze you can smell the foul odor of burning garbage, of melting plastic. He appears to give this some thought before quickly returning his gaze to Dave.

"Doesn't matter," he says, shrugging. "This island is huge; there's no way it can all burn-"

As if in answer to his ignorant declaration the floor of the heap shudders as something detonates somewhere to the east. The sound it makes is muted, still far enough away so as not to be a concern, but soon that will change. Dave is counting on it. He stands patiently while the others study the outlying sky (all but Jake, whose eyes never leave his own) watching as ashes and pieces of singed trash rain down like diseased snowflakes. He smirks at the other, his lined and dirty face a mask of impenitent grit.

"What the hell was that Doc?" Jake calls to Dr. Taylor, who's staring into the smudged, blackened yonder.

"I think it's the sludge pools…" he says and his words trigger Dave's memory. He recalls Leeann firing the single shot while he was teaching her how to use the gun, and when it ricocheted off of the heap it produced a spark that turned into a small flame.

"That's right," he nods. "The shit is flammable. Whatever chemicals it's made of makes for a mighty nice explosive."

"That true Doc?" Jake looks more than just uneasy now, he looks downright panicked. Dr. Taylor appears to be mulling it over, his head tilted in thought. "Well? Yes or no?"

"I haven't had time to…to study it but…but it sounds like it could be right."

"It is right. I'd stake my life on it. This whole thing is gonna blow sky high." He grins. "Party's over motherfuckers."

"Shut up!" Jake's eyes dart back and forth between Dave and the doctor. "And drop your damn guns now!"

"Afraid I can't do that. Why don't you and yer buddies get outta here while ya still can? This place is sposed to be three times the size a freakin' Texas so y'all should have plenty a room ta spread out."

Jake's frown deepens, a look of indecision on his face. He glares at Melissa, then Dante, and at once his mood lightens.

"Had a real good time with your girl, bud," he purrs, grinning salaciously, and Dante's eyes snap toward his, a look of horrified surprise on his face. "Had me a *real* good time. I mean, you fucked her, right? Pretty damn tight."

"Shut up," Dante growls. "Don't you talk about her like that."

"Course what that tightness tells me," Jake persists, "is that you must have a pretty small dick, huh? She probably thought she was getting stung by a mosquito."

"I told you to shut up!" Dante lunges out from behind Dave, raising his weapon, and Dave grabs him by the arm, yanking him back.

"Stay put! Don't let him get to you!"

"What exactly do you have in mind?" Melissa asks in a husky murmur, looking from Jake to Dave and back.

"Yeah Dave," Jake says mockingly. "What ya got up your sleeve bro?"

On the surface Dave looks calm, but his nerves are as taut as an archer's bow. He's simply waiting for an opportunity. If he can keep Jake talking until the right moment arrives than he can take the bastard out and they might have a chance. Slim, but anything's worth fighting for. Even if they don't all make it out of here alive maybe he can at least stop this shit for brains dead in his tracks.

"You and me should be men about this," he says, relaxing his arms and letting the barrel of the rifle point downward. "How bout it, no weapons, just our fists."

Jake rolls his eyes. "I don't have time for this. Just drop the damn guns and get over here. I'll make it quick and painless, I swear-"

For the second time (this occurrence very possibly a response to Dante's allegations that there is no God they can rely upon in their moment of need) another terrific blast rips the air to shreds, this one so close the sound is deafening. Everyone cringes except for Dave, he alone standing tall.

This is it, this is my moment.

Dave raises his gun, draws a bead on his target and pulls the trigger. But the good luck that had gotten him this far (escaping from the giant snails, surviving beneath the heap, successfully managing to kill all the crewmen aboard the ship, stealing their weapons and effectively launching a counter strike) finally abandons him, a two-part harmony of disaster. First the ground tilts as a result of the explosion, diverting his aim, and second the muzzle flashes fire only three times. As it does, he realizes his mistake.

My rifle is still set on semi-automatic...

The first shot pierces Jake's left shoulder and the second two zip high over his head. The man doesn't even flinch, just looks at him incredulously, and before Dave can squeeze off another round the other open fires.

"Ah ha ha ha ha ha!" Jake laughs over the roar of the M-16. "Ah ha ha ha ha!"

Dante and Melissa instinctively dive for cover as Dave's body is riddled with bullets, the gun slipping from his lifeless hands as he dances and jitters. It happens so swiftly he never even so much as makes a peep, the only indication of his awareness the surprised look upon his blood soaked, shell torn face.

"Thought ya had me, huh?" Jake barks deliriously. "Well fuck you!"

Dante grips Melissa's arm in his left hand, clutching his rifle in his right. "Let's go!" he yells, spraying bullets in Jake's general direction as they scramble to their feet. Dante's shots go wild in the air, nowhere even close to his intended target in fact, but the other ducks just the same, offering them a few precious seconds to beat a hasty retreat.

"Oh no you don't!" Jake recovers his poise and returns fire, but they manage to scoot behind a towering mound of trash, the shells ricocheting off the rubble and debris.

"After them!" he yells, waving his arm like he's General Custer organizing the troops for one last stand. "Don't let them get away!"

Dante stumbles forward, clutching Melissa so tightly he's probably bruising her, but it doesn't matter, not now. After all they've been through they have to get away goddamnit, they have to. Captain Harvey is dead, everyone from the ship is either dead or mutated...it plainly isn't a matter of whether or not they are going to get caught. Pure and simple they *can't* get caught.

"What's your plan?" Melissa gasps as they dodge and weave through the seemingly endless maze of trash.

"We're gonna try and make it to the water," Dante says breathlessly. "After that, I don't know."

"Okay, but ease up. Running in a full body leather bondage suit ain't exactly a picnic."

"Just do your best to keep up with me."

The path twists and turns, inevitably leading them to a never-ending succession of dead ends, leaving them no choice but to retrace their steps as the cacophony of voices swells behind them, getting louder, closer. Melissa falters and almost trips, thankfully righting herself at the last second before she drags them both down, and Dante pauses to make a quick decision before choosing a trail leading to the right and hauling her onward. They're heading toward the worst of it but that, it seems, is the direct line to the ocean. They have no choice; if they want to escape this is the way. Regrettably, the heat is becoming oppressive, the choking clouds of smoke getting thicker. Soon enough they'll catch up with the flames and he has no idea what they'll do then, how they'll get through, but they'll have to cross that bridge when they come to it, won't they? Getting captured isn't an option. Hell, he'd rather burn to death than become one of them. He glances over his shoulder to see how Melissa is doing, and one look at her sweat-drenched, anxiety-ridden face tells him everything he needs to know.

"Come on," he urges. "Just a little farther."

Melissa wants to stop him, suggest that maybe they try a different direction. The heat and smoke are getting to her, making it difficult to breath. Maybe the creatures will shy away from it and turn around, at least, they can only hope, right? They probably don't like this anymore than she does.

"This sucks…" she wheezes pitifully when Dante comes to an abrupt halt and she bumps into him.

"What the hell?"

They've reached yet another blocked passage, she sees, and Dante stares speculatively at the wall before them, thinking things through. Melissa follows his gaze and, looking at him tiredly, shakes her head.

"I can't climb that thing," she says. "Forget it." She exhales loudly and plops down onto the ground. "I can't run anymore. I'm done."

"No you're not!" Dante reaches down and takes her by the arm. "We came this far, we're not going to let them get us now!"

"Can't you see it's over?" She pulls her arm away from him, tears forming in her sparkling, green eyes. "You know what's on the other side of this, don't you? Just look at all the smoke!"

"It's probably not as bad as it seems," he lies easily. "Come on, I'll give you a boost. It looks as if there are enough hand holds."

"I can't do it Dante, no way! If you want to try go for it, but just leave me here…"

He stares hard at her, an expression of barley controlled rage on his impossibly disheveled face. Below his eyes (just above his beard) she can see his cheeks are blazing red.

"You want to become one of them, huh? Cuz that's what you'll be looking forward to if they catch you." He leans over and grips her by the shoulders, shaking her from side to side. "They won't kill you darling, they'll turn you into one of them. How does that strike you?"

Melissa opens her mouth mutely, wanting to tell him that it's fine by her, she couldn't care less at this point because she's so damn tired…but then she thinks about Kenny and Dr. Taylor, and she wonders what it must feel like to be infected by such a relentless pathogen, one that makes you do and say things that go against all of your beliefs, controlling your every action, your every thought…and not only that but to physically mutate, to have creepy crawly things gestating in your body as the outer husk decays, falling apart piece by piece…

"Alright, I'm convinced," she says, getting up. "We'll probably burn to death anyway but fuck it, right? Give me a boost."

Jake leads the mob onward, convinced that at any moment they will come upon the two escapees and he can take them into his custody, moving on to bigger things. He has to hurry as time is running short, the heat becoming more intense, urging him on. In the back of his mind he questions whether or not it matters if the two get away, or if they really need them, but something inside him insists that this is what he *must* do; they are a threat and they must be stopped. It is this predominant voice that spurs him on, keeps him running through the network of trails, backtracking when they come upon passages that are impassable.

And behind him the minions follow, asking no questions, their minds pliable as clay, willing to do anything he summons. It's for this reason he ultimately knows he must succeed: he has tasted power and he likes it. Nothing can take this away from him now, nothing.

"Come on you bastards!" he coaxes as they fall behind. "Faster!"

On and on they go, the pungent reek of smoldering trash growing stronger in his nostrils, the sting of it at last reaching his eyes. He blinks rapidly, one of his eyelids twitching up and down like a broken window shade.

And then, as they round yet another corner, they find them.

"I have it!" Melissa calls triumphantly, pulling herself upward. "Come on!"

"Are you sure?"

"Yes, now start climbing!"

Dante takes hold of a table leg, hoisting himself up the nearly vertical wall. He is several feet off of the ground when he hears movement behind him.

"Hold it right there!" Jake rasps hoarsely. "Just step down."

Dante peeks over his shoulder, sees the gun aimed at his head. His own weapon he has abandoned at the foot of the wall; it is lying uselessly on the ground beneath him. He looks up, sees that Melissa has gained the top and is straddling it, one leg on each side. Black clouds billow in the air above her, blazing ashes swirling around her like fireflies.

"Go!" he calls to her. "Get moving!"

Her face contorts with conflicted emotions. She too has ditched her weapon and there is nothing she can do but look on in horror, helpless to save him.

"You too, missy. I can shoot that pretty smile right off your face from here, trust me."

The mutants gather behind Jake, Dr. Taylor amongst their ranks, pushing tightly up against him. They look hungry, greedy, their black tongues licking lips slathered with rancid saliva. Dante feels an aching hollowness in his stomach, a bottomless dread that spells calamity for him. He is reminded of every disaster movie he's ever seen, feels like he is the guy who almost makes it out of the burning building (sinking ship, crashing airplane etc.) and gets killed right before the end. Frustration boils up within him, but it is of a weary sort. He's tired of this chase, of everything, but he won't, *can't*, give up.

"I'm not coming down," he says with bitter finality, continuing to climb. "You'll just have to shoot me." Hand over hand he goes, sharp edges digging into his palms, warm blood trickling down his wrists. And the higher he gets the harder it is to breathe, the smoke progressively taking its toll.

Jake lifts the weapon, looks through the sight. "Gladly," he says, his finger tensed on the trigger. "See you in hell monkey boy."

His first shot misses, pings off of something metallic just over Dante's head. His second is so close Dante can hear it wiz by his left ear.

"Third times the charm." He's about to squeeze the trigger again when another explosion rocks the island, this one right on top of them, and a shower of flaming debris rains down on Jake and the others. The mutant's recoil, howling, their cries shocked, outraged, but beneath it Dante can sense fear, can hear it in their distorted, garbled voices. Jake raises a hand to protect his face, momentarily forgetting about the easy target lined up in his sights as he's peppered with large pieces of burning plastic.

"Aaaaahhh!" He swipes at his face and the gun drops from his hands, clattering uselessly to the ground.

Dante struggles higher up the wall when abruptly his foothold gives way. His heart thuds thickly as he claws desperately at the compacted trash, and he just barely manages to hang on as fiery chunks of garbage descend upon him. He briefly lets go with one hand to brush smoldering embers from his hair, and when he grabs hold again whatever he clutches is amazingly sharp, cutting him badly. Crying out, he's about to retract his hand when something pokes him in the face, just below his left eye. Looking up, he sees Melissa holding a long plastic pipe.

"Grab it! Hurry!"

Her leather bondage suit is charred and bubbling but it appears to be adequately keeping the fire at bay. This gives him cause to smile, if only at the ludicrousness of it all.

"Hold on tight!" he cries, grasping it firmly in his right hand. The blood from his palm makes the rod slick, so he lets go and wipes it on the seat of his pants before taking hold of it once more. Heaving mightily he hauls himself upward, but a moment later he's slipping again. He lets go of the pipe and fortunately finds a ready handhold.

"You can't lift my weight! Just get out of here!"

"Not without you! Climb!"

Utilizing muscles he never even knew he had until this moment, he lifts his left hand, finding another handhold, then lifts his right. Like a man swimming an immense stretch of water over unfathomable depths he keeps at it, hand over hand, until he sees the top nearing.

"That's it! Keep coming!"

A bullet whines off the wall three feet to his left, and then another punches through the fabric of his shirt, just missing him. He pulls himself upward frantically, scrambling for purchase, his fingernails cracked and bleeding. He's getting close, a few more feet and he'll be there, yet for some reason he has an urge to look over his shoulder once more. He knows he shouldn't, he should just keep going for Christ's sake, but the temptation is impossible to resist...

Jake looks like a capering comic book villain, some scoundrel who, in his quest for world supremacy, got nuked by his own chemicals. Surrounding him is an apocalyptic turmoil of flaming waste; it's apparent his insatiable wickedness has invited upon him Hell's wrath. In layman's terms, the dude is totally fucked.

"Gonna get you one of these time you son of a bitch!" he cackles wildly. His clothes are smoking rags that hang loosely from his charred limbs, half of his face a seared, blistered ruin. "We'll just see who has the last laugh buddy!"

Behind him the majority of the mutants are actively scattering, their fear getting the best of them. Mewling and gurgling they beat a hasty retreat, hoping to escape the scourge that has overtaken their island. Dr. Taylor, Dante sees, is thrashing wildly on the ground, his body engulfed in flames. He issues strangled, high-pitched screams that sound queerly like air being slowly let out of a balloon. This, it would seem, does it for him; at last he has to turn away.

"Come on, hurry!"

Dante makes the last couple of feet in two quick moves. When he arrives at the top he throws one leg over, reaching out a hand to balance himself before another bullet glances off the wall only inches away.

"Go go go!" he urges Melissa and, without hesitation, they dive headfirst into the vast conflagration that stretches as far as the eye can see.

"No!" Jake howls, watching as they disappear over the top, gone. He turns angrily to his few remaining minions, huddled together behind him. "What are you standing there for? Go get them!"

Mindlessly they rush forward as another explosion rips through the air, and the wall comes tumbling down upon them, enveloping them in smoldering debris.

"Nooooo!"

Jake is at once aware that his hair is ablaze, can smell the cloying aroma of cooking flesh as his shirt ignites. Lifting his hands before him, he watches as the skin liquefies, leaving nothing but blackened bones.

This is it, it's all over. No taking this back.

He gasps for air but smoke fills his lungs instead. His pants are now alight as well.

Chestnuts roasting over an open fire...

The screaming of the mutants burning along side him gradually fades as he realizes with a crushing, forbidding certainty that he has failed. Inexorably, utterly failed. Weeping tears of fire, he falls to his knees as the inferno consumes him.

EPILOGUE

"You think anyone is going to find us?"

Dante looks up from his toiling and regards Melissa's soot streaked face, honestly wondering the same thing. His opinion? Probably not. They'll float around the Pacific in the fire-ravaged lifeboat for several days until they die of exposure, their last moments grueling, tortuous. And that's if a storm doesn't turn the sea into a churning quagmire of foamy death, upending the boat and drowning them both. But it's either this or burning to death on the trash heap, it's not like they really had much of a choice.

"Maybe," he shrugs, offering a half smile that he hopes is sincere. The heap is slipping away behind them like the fragments of a nightmare, the air becoming cooler and clearer, the smoke thinning. They've passed the ring of sludge that surrounds it, the rowing becoming much easier now that the boat's no longer bogged down, the oars washed clean of the oily substance. And their exit from it's contaminated grip occurred just in the nick of time; as they were reaching its end it caught fire at the shore, the flames moving with impressive speed across the water's surface, racing toward them. For one crazy second Dante thought it was actually going to catch up with the boat, ironically burning the two alive after they'd made such a heroic getaway, but before it could reach them they paddled out into the open water, the last part of their evacuation complete prior to another calamity befalling them.

"Now there's a confident answer if I ever heard one," Melissa laughs, lounging in the bow of the boat, her legs over the side. She tilts a bottle of water to her mouth and takes a long, languid drink. "Man, this is like the nectar of the god's."

"We're lucky to have found this," he says.

As they'd made their way through the fire and smoke and raining debris they'd stumbled upon the remnants of the ship. How the lifeboat survived the blast is a mystery, unless Dr. Taylor had thought to remove it as an escape measure, should they need it. They'd found it at the water's edge, singed but unharmed, and fortunately for them the survival kit was still inside, largely intact. It contained one and a half bottles of water, some snacks, a first aid kit, a small notebook and stub of a pencil. The notebook was filled with observations made by Dr. Taylor, yet neither Dante nor Melissa cared to read it. The walkie-talkie was also in the boat but the battery was dead, having probably been left on.

When they shoved off from the heap they realized if they were to have any chance of rescue it would be from a ship they happened upon. Some boat on its way to dump garbage no less, those being the predominant vessels that traveled these coordinates.

Melissa stares off into the distance, her thoughts, like her mood, mellow. It will take a while to digest everything that's happened, and right now she is content to simply live in the moment. After all she's been through over the last several days this languorous passage is like a vacation.

"I can't believe it's come down to just us," she says, holding out the bottle. He glances at her briefly, making no comment, not wanting to think about Leeann's absence; it's simply too painful. He reaches out silently and takes it, drinking deeply, the lukewarm liquid cascading wonderfully down his parched throat, then passes it back. Removing his shirt, he reaches over the side, cupping his hands and splashing himself with handful after handful of sea water, washing away the accumulated grime of the last few days. It feels good, especially on his beard, which is matted and disgusting.

Watching him, Melissa sets the bottle on the seat beside her and unzips her bondage suit, peeling it down to her waist. Underneath she is wearing a white t-shirt, stained with sweat and blotchy with filth. She dips her hands into the ocean and bathes herself vigorously, enjoying the feel of the cold water trickling down her sides.

"The first thing I'm going to do when we get rescued is take a shower."

He stops what he is doing and looks at her, her words triggering within him a memory of Leeann saying the exact same thing after they thought rescue was imminent, after Tyler betrayed them. He is silent, sentimentally bidding farewell to the girl who'd so effortlessly stolen his heart, and Melissa senses something in his gaze.

"I'm really sorry," she says. "You did everything you could-"

"But it wasn't enough, was it?" he snaps before he can help himself, and he instantly feels remorse. "I...I didn't mean to bite your head off. It's not your fault."

"It's okay. Really. I'm thicker skinned than that."

I'm sure you are...

"So, you know where we're going?"

"East," he says, attempting a smile. "It's the only way to go."

"Then east it is," she replies, sweeping her hair off her face and gazing into the hot, brilliant sunshine.

The day passes and night falls. As it does Dante feels fear creeping into his belly again. Night time at sea in a lifeboat isn't exactly the most pleasant place in the world to be but, to ease his anxiety, all he has to do is think about where they've come from and all they've been through and it makes it a little better.

Melissa dozes for a while but wakes with a start, flailing at some imaginary terror, tipping the boat precariously.

"Hey, hey!" Dante cries, grabbing her, holding her in his arms. "It's all right, I got you."

Her eyes are blank, looking at him but not really seeing him, and for one horrific moment he imagines he is staring into the eyes of a mutant. But she doesn't struggle, and in the pale glow of the diffuse moonlight he sees her eyes hone in on his own. He breaths a sigh of relief and she buries her head in his chest, shivering.

"I'm cold," she says, her voice barely louder than a whisper.

"I know. Me too," he replies, and he holds her, needing the warmth of her body as much as she needs his, and they remain like this until the first rays of sun come up over the horizon. In the pastel light of dawn, the sun peeking its fiery head above the churning waves, Dante notices they are now bearing toward the south.

"I better get us headed in the right direction," he says, letting her go, and she nods, returning to the bow of the boat.

The sun beats down on them relentlessly as the day progresses, the two of them sweating profusely. They talk very little, only exchanging words when they are deemed necessary. The first bottle of water is gone and they are now working on the second. Dante finds he doesn't have much of an appetite but makes himself eat a small piece of chocolate anyway. Melissa does the same, and as the sun reaches the apex of the sky they are both feeling the ill effects of sunstroke and dehydration.

This is how it will go, he thinks, pausing to splash water on his face and body. *We'll run out of food and water, becoming weaker and weaker until neither one of us can row the boat. After that we'll drift along until we either start hallucinating or we break down and decide to drink the seawater. And then it's only a matter of time until the end. . .*

Melissa is thinking the same thoughts as the boat bounces up and down over the increasingly choppy sea. She is wondering how bad it will be to starve to death, or to die of exposure. Will it be more painful than burning or dying of smoke inhalation? She supposes they will soon find out, but the more fatigued she becomes, the less she cares. At night is when the terror is the worst; during the day it's easier to believe they have a chance, that someone will come along and rescue them before they turn into human jerky. During the night is when all hope is gone, when everything seems to be on the verge of collapse.

"How are you doing?" Dante asks as the sun begins its descent into the western portion of the sky.

"Good, I guess, all things considered. You?"

"I'm getting tired."

"You don't look so hot," she says matter of factly, observing his sallow complexion, speckled with scarlet splotches. "You want me to row for a while?"

"You think you can?" In all honesty he doesn't feel very well, has been feeling a bit peaked since early afternoon. She doesn't look that much better but there is no sense in telling her.

"Sure," she says, trading places with him. He lays down in the bow of the boat and closes his eyes, feeling the motion of the water beneath them, trying not to think about how deep it is, that they are only a few scant feet from being submerged in its icy depths. It is best to try and keep his mind clear of such thoughts, of any reflections that create unease. Maybe he'll try to get a little rest.

And the afternoon wears on, bringing them that much closer to sunset and the looming night.

Melissa is slipping in and out of sleep, her limbs heavy and her heart beating sluggishly. She runs her parched tongue over her lips and finds they are cracked and brittle, painful. Her entire face feels the same. Too much sun. Her stomach growls painfully but there is nothing left of the provisions, not even any water. One more day and they are surely done for.

At least we escaped the garbage heap. We didn't let those bastards get us and we stopped them from spreading the bacteria. At least we aren't going to die for nothing.

Settling back against the seat, it is this thought that helps rock her to sleep, Dante's warm body next to hers, his beefy, hairy arms covering her like a human blanket.

The weight on her is crushing, brutal. She opens her eyes and tries to squirm away but she is stuck fast beneath him.

"Dante," she says. "Get up, you're smothering me."

But he makes no sign that he has heard her; he doesn't move, doesn't react, doesn't make a sound. She prods at him with a free hand and it feels as if she is nudging a corpse. Fear settles within her then, cold and clammy.

"Dante?" she whispers, her heart suddenly beating very fast. The first rays of dawn are coming up over the horizon, and she sees that once again they are drifting southward.

Finally he stirs, just a little, and makes a sound, a gravely, incoherent resonance from deep within his throat.

"Dante?" she says again, twisting her head and looking into his face, the beard a tangled mass, shaggy and repulsive. And then he opens his eyes and she sees that she is now all alone in the boat.

How she manages to extract herself from him is nothing short of a miracle, something she could never explain if pressed. All she knows is that her survival instincts took over and, after thrashing this way and that she somehow finds herself free and in the center of the boat, watching as Dante gets slowly to his feet, his black eyes staring at her vacantly, his fingers twitching. He opens his mouth and vomits a thick, white, pasty substance that saturates his shirt, the sound he makes gruesome, terrifying.

How could it have happened? How could he have become one of them?

And then comprehension washes over her, something the captain told them the night they ate Hallsly. The bacterium had many ways of attacking healthy tissue, and one of them was via the contaminated water seeping into their wounds. Based on that, it only stands to reason that she will come down with it at any time as well, he simply succumbed to it first.

"Stay back," she warns. "Just stay where you are."

But Dante isn't listening; he starts toward her, his intentions, though not entirely unclear, undesired at best. She takes a step back *(no where to go dear)* and stumbles over something. Glancing down, she sees one of the oars at her feet and, snatching it up, takes a swing.

"I told you to stay back!" she cries, her voice tiny in the grand vastness of the empty sea. In two steps he'll be able to grab her and, after that, rip her apart like a stuffed doll. He takes another step, then another…

She swings the oar again and it connects with his head; she feels the force of the blow in her wrists, palms tingling, yet he continues forward. She strikes him with it again and again, screaming her misery into the lonely predawn sky, and he stops, standing stock-still, absorbing each wallop patiently, probably feeling nothing more than vague irritation.

"Die!" She is at the very end of the lifeboat, no place to go but into the water. "Fucking die already!"

He tilts his head to one side, as if he actually understands what she is saying, maybe wants to comply with her command, but then he breaches the space between them, his hands raising before him, a rumbling snarl emanating from his barrel chest.

"No!" She twists the oar sideways and slashes at his throat, the tapered end opening a yawning gash that spews greenish/blackish blood that soaks quickly through his shirt, and for a second he pauses, an enormous blood bubble swelling from his mouth as his knees give out. She swiftly retracts the oar and brings it forward again in a stabbing motion. It hits him squarely in the chest, knocking him backward and over the side of the lifeboat, into the sea. He sinks immediately, simply disappearing beneath the waves.

She stands motionless, the paddle clutched tightly in her hands. She gulps great, tearing breaths, heart beating frantically, her exertions having thoroughly exhausted her. The sound of the ocean slapping against the side of the boat seems overly loud, and she concentrates on it's lapping and squelching as she tries to get her breathing to return to normal. Her eyes scan the surface keenly, waiting, for what, she isn't sure.

Suddenly his head pops up above the surface and he is crawling hand over hand, swimming toward the boat. In seconds he is beside it, reaching toward her with one giant, scarred hand.

She shrieks deliriously, bringing the oar down on his head once, twice, three times, then loses count. She thinks she might have blacked out. The next thing she knows she is curled up in a ball in the bottom of the boat and it is night and the waves are battering the little vessel, tossing it around like a cork. She is cold and frightened and hungry and she knows death is imminent but she doesn't care; if she survives than she will bring the contagion with her and that can't happen, *won't* happen. Waves splash over the rim of the boat, the icy water drenching her, and the last lucid thought she has is about her dream of the beautiful field of flowers, but just the beginning, the good part... All that dazzling sunshine, all those pretty colors, the dust motes floating on the air as she eased herself down upon the ground, gazing up into the clear blue sky, making shapes out of the wisps of clouds that floated by...

"Where do you think they came from captain?"

The balding, rotund man shakes his head, an unlit pipe in his mouth. "No idea. There's no land around here for hundreds of miles."

"What the hell are they?"

Again he shakes his head. They're damn ugly, that's for sure, and they darken the sky above them as they flutter about, they're caterwauling deafening, grating.

"They're birds, you dipshit," the first mate says to the crewman, a note of derision in his voice. "You can tell because of they're ability to fly."

"I know they're birds," the other retorts, "but what kind? I've never seen anything like those before."

"What, and you're the expert?"

"Shut-up!" the captain barks, watching curiously as they descend upon the ship, and suddenly the man stationed in the crow's nest begins to scream.

www.ingramcontent.com/pod-product-compliance
Lightning Source LLC
Chambersburg PA
CBHW080816020726
47501CB00009B/2315